select
editions

Reader's
Digest

Reader's Digest

The condensations in this volume
are published with the consent of the authors
and the publishers © 2011 Reader's Digest, Inc.

www.readersdigest.co.uk

Published in the United Kingdom by Vivat Direct Limited
(t/a Reader's Digest), 157 Edgware Road,
London W2 2HR

For information as to ownership of
copyright in the material of this book,
and acknowledgments, see last page.

Printed in Germany
ISBN 978 1 78020 021 7

**select
editions**

contents

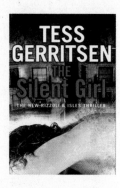

The Monkey King from Chinese legend is, bizarrely, central to Detective Jane Rizzoli's current murder case; one that involves an ancient sword, a martial arts expert and two silver hairs from a non-human source. Crime-writing at its best.

Warm, perceptive and full of wisdom gained from years of teaching children and inspecting schools, Gervase Phinn's fictional tale tells of the trials and tribulations that face the new head teacher of Barton-in-the-Dale primary school.

buried secrets
joseph finder

313

When his daughter is kidnapped,
hedge fund mogul Marshall Marcus turns
to private investigator Nick Heller to find
her. But this is no ordinary kidnapping,
and the case quickly becomes a matter of
life and death. An edge-of-the-seat thrlller.

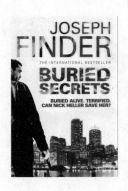

dark matter
michelle paver

463

A 1930s ghost story set in the cold, dark
wilderness of Norway's Arctic north. When
an expeditionary team arrive in a remote,
uninhabited bay to spend a year studying
ice geology and weather patterns, they
find far more than they bargained for.

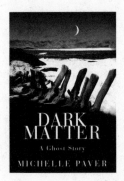

TESS GERRITSEN

THE
SILENT
GIRL

A murder in a shadowy alley in Boston's Chinatown, has

Detective Jane Rizzoli perplexed.

Forensic tests on two strands of silver hair, found on the

victim's body, have shown that the origin is non-human,

while other evidence appears to connect to a notorious

multiple murder case nineteen years earlier.

The only person who can help Rizzoli is Iris Fang, a gifted

martial arts teacher, but she is unwilling to reveal what she

knows about the mysterious killer who is terrorising

Chinatown with centuries-old cunning and a swift,

avenging blade.

ONE
San Francisco

All day, I have been watching the girl. She gives no indication that she's aware of me, although my rental car is within view of the street corner where she and the other teenagers have gathered this afternoon, doing whatever bored kids do to pass the time. She looks younger than the others, but perhaps it's because she's Asian and petite at seventeen, just a wisp of a girl. Her black hair is cropped as short as a boy's, and her blue jeans are ragged and torn. Not a fashion statement, but a result of hard use and life on the streets. She puffs on a cigarette and exhales a cloud of smoke with the nonchalance of a street thug, an attitude that doesn't match her pale face and delicate Chinese features. She is pretty enough to attract the hungry stares of two men who pass by. The girl notices their looks and glares straight back at them, unafraid, but it's easy to be fearless when danger is merely an abstract concept. Faced with a real threat, how would this girl react? I wonder. Would she put up a fight or would she crumble? I want to know what she's made of, but I have not seen her put to the test.

As evening falls, the teenagers on the corner begin to disband. First one and then another wanders away, leaving only the girl, who has nowhere to go. She lingers alone, as though waiting for someone. At last she leaves the corner and walks in my direction, her hands thrust in her pockets. As she passes my car, she looks straight ahead, her gaze fierce, as if she's mentally churning over some dilemma.

She's probably unaware that two men are following her.

Seconds after she walks past my car, I spot the men emerging from an alley; it's the same pair who had stared at her earlier. One of the men looks at me through the windshield, just a quick glance to assess whether I am a threat. What he sees does not concern him in the least. He and his companion move like the confident predators they are, stalking weaker prey.

I step out of my car and follow them. Just as they are following the girl.

She heads into a neighbourhood where buildings stand abandoned, where the sidewalk seems paved with broken bottles. The girl betrays no hesitation, as if this is familiar territory. Not once does she glance back, which tells me she is either foolhardy or clueless about the world and what it can do to girls like her. The men don't glance back, either. Even if they were to spot me, they would see nothing to be afraid of. No one ever does.

A block ahead, the girl turns right, vanishing through a doorway. I watch what happens next. The two men pause outside the building the girl has entered, conferring over strategy. Then they, too, step inside.

It is a vacant warehouse posted with a NO TRESPASSING notice. I slip inside, into gloom so thick that I pause to let my eyes adjust. I hear the floor creaking. I smell burning candle wax. I see the faint glow of the doorway to my left. I peer into the room beyond.

The girl kneels before a makeshift table, her face lit by one flickering candle. Around her are a sleeping-bag, tins of food and a small camping stove. She is struggling with a can opener, unaware of the men closing in from behind. Just as I draw in a breath to shout a warning, the girl whirls round. All she has in her hand is the can opener, a meagre weapon.

'This is my home,' she says. 'Get out.'

I had been prepared to intervene. Instead, I pause where I am to watch what happens next. To see what the girl is made of.

One of the men laughs. 'We're just visiting, honey. You look like you could use the company.'

'You look like you could use a brain.'

Not wise, I think. Now their lust is mingled with anger. Yet the girl stands perfectly calm, brandishing that pitiful kitchen utensil.

As the men lunge, I am ready to spring.

She springs first and her foot thuds straight into the first man's sternum. He staggers, gripping his chest. Before the second man can react, she slams the can opener against the side of his head. He howls and backs away.

This has become interesting.

The first man has recovered and rushes at her, slamming into her so hard that they both go sprawling onto the floor. Her fist cracks into his jaw. But with a roar he rolls on top of her, immobilising her with his weight.

Now the second man grabs her wrists, pinning them against the floor. As fierce as she is, the girl is green and untrained, and the inevitable is about to happen. The first man yanks her jeans down past her skinny hips. His arousal is evident. Never is a man more vulnerable to attack.

He doesn't hear me coming. One moment he's unzipping his fly. The next, he's on the floor, loose teeth spilling from his mouth.

The second man is not quick enough. I am a tiger and he is nothing more than a lumbering buffalo, helpless against my strike. With a shriek he drops to the ground and, judging by the grotesque angle of his arm, the bone has been snapped in two.

I grab the girl and yank her to her feet. She zips up her jeans. 'Who the hell are you?'

'That's for later. Now we go!' I bark.

'How did you do that? How did you bring them down so fast?'

'Do you want to learn?'

'Yes!'

I look at the two men groaning and writhing at our feet. 'Then here is the first lesson: Know when to run.' I shove her towards the door.

I WATCH HER EAT. For a small girl, she has the appetite of a wolf, and she devours three chicken tacos, a lake of refried beans and a large glass of Coca-Cola. Though the girl's features are Chinese, she is clearly American, from her cropped hair to her tattered jeans. A crude and feral creature who slurps the last of her Coke before gnawing on the ice cubes.

I begin to doubt the wisdom of this venture. She is already too old to be taught. I should release her and find another way. But then I remember how close she came to single-handedly taking down the two men. She has raw talent and is fearless—two things that cannot be taught.

'Do you remember me?' I ask.

The girl frowns. She shakes her head.

'It was a long time ago,' I say. 'Twelve years.' An eternity for a girl so young. 'You were small.'

She shrugs. 'No wonder I don't remember you.' She pulls out a cigarette.

'You're polluting your body.'

'It's my body,' she retorts.

'Not if you wish to train.' I snatch the cigarette from her lips. 'If you want to learn, your attitude must change. You must show respect.'

She snorts. 'You sound like my mother.'

'I knew your mother. In Boston.'

'Well, she's dead.'

'I know. She wrote to me last month. She told me she was ill and said she had very little time left. That's why I'm here.'

I'm surprised to see tears glisten in the girl's eyes, and she quickly turns away. But in that instant she brings to mind my own daughter, who was younger than this girl when I lost her. My eyes sting with tears, but I don't try to hide them. Sorrow has made me who I am.

I need this girl. Clearly, she also needs me.

'It's taken me weeks to find you,' I tell her.

'Foster home sucked. I'm better off on my own.'

'If your mother saw you now, her heart would break.'

'She never had time for me.'

'Maybe because she was working two jobs, trying to keep you fed?'

'She let the world walk all over her. She was spineless.'

I lean forward, enraged by this ungrateful brat. 'Your poor mother suffered in ways you can't possibly imagine. Everything she did was for you.' This is not the girl I'd hoped to find. She may be strong and fearless, but no sense of filial duty binds her to her dead mother and father, no sense of family honour. Without ties to our ancestors, we are specks of dust, adrift and floating. 'Someday, I hope you find the wisdom to understand what your mother sacrificed for you.' I pay the bill for her meal and stand. 'There's nothing I can teach you.'

'Why would you want to, anyway? Why did you come looking for me?'

'I thought I would find someone different. Someone I could teach. Someone who would help me.'

'To do what?'

I don't know how to answer her question. For a moment, the only sound is the tinny music spilling from the restaurant speakers.

'Do you remember what happened to your father?' I ask.

She stares at me. 'That's why you came looking for me. Because my mother wrote to you about him.'

'Your father was a good man. He loved you, and you dishonour him. You dishonour both your parents.' I place a bundle of cash in front of her. 'This is in their memory. Get off the street and go back to school.' I turn and walk out of the restaurant.

In seconds she runs after me. 'Wait!' she calls. 'Where are you going?'

'Back home to Boston.'

'I do remember you. I think I know what you want.'

I stop and face her. 'It's what you should want, too.'

'What do I need to do?'

I look her up and down. 'It's not what you need to do,' I reply. 'It's what you need to be.' Slowly I move towards her. Up till this point, she's seen no reason to fear me, and why should she? I am just a woman. But something she now sees in my eyes makes her take a step back.

'Are you afraid?' I ask her softly.

Her chin juts up, and she says with foolish bravado, 'No. I'm not.'

'You should be.'

TWO
Seven years later

My name is Dr Maura Isles. I'm a forensic pathologist, and I am employed by the medical examiner's office in the Commonwealth of Massachusetts.'

'Please describe for the court your background, Dr Isles,' said the Suffolk County assistant district attorney, Carmela Aguilar.

Maura kept her gaze on the assistant DA as she answered: far easier to focus on Aguilar than to see the glares coming from the defendant and his dozens of supporters in the courtroom. Maura was acutely aware that a large segment of her audience was law enforcement officers and they were not going to like what she had to say.

The defendant was Boston PD Officer Wayne Graff, the vision of a square-jawed, all-American hero. The room's sympathy was with Graff, not with the victim, a man who had ended up battered and broken on Maura's autopsy table six months ago. A man who, two hours before his death, committed the fatal sin of shooting and killing a police officer.

Maura recited her curriculum vitae.

'I am board-certified in both general and forensic pathology and before I worked here in Boston, I was a pathologist with the medical examiner's office in San Francisco for seven years.'

Formalities completed, Aguilar got down to specifics. 'Did you perform an autopsy on an individual named Fabian Dixon last October?'

'I did,' answered Maura.

'Tell us how Mr Dixon came to be a medical examiner's case.'

Maura felt the tension instantly ratchet up in the courtroom. 'Mr Dixon was a twenty-four-year-old man who was discovered unresponsive in the back seat of a Boston Police Department cruiser approximately twenty minutes after his arrest. He was transported by ambulance to Massachusetts General Hospital, where he was pronounced dead on arrival. He was subsequently transferred to our morgue.'

'Describe for the court Mr Dixon's appearance when you first saw him.'

'He was a well-nourished man, of average height and weight, who arrived at our facility clothed only in cotton briefs and socks. His other clothing had been removed during resuscitation attempts in the emergency room.' She paused. Here was where things got uncomfortable.

'Would you describe the condition of his body for us?' Aguilar prodded.

'There were multiple bruises over the chest, the left flank and the upper abdomen. Both eyes were swollen shut, and there were lacerations of the lip and scalp. Two of his teeth were missing.'

'Objection.' The defence attorney stood. 'There's no way of knowing when he lost those teeth. They could have been missing for years.'

'One tooth showed up on X-ray. In his stomach,' said Maura.

'The witness should refrain from commenting until I've ruled,' the judge cut in severely. 'Objection overruled. Ms Aguilar, proceed.'

Her lips twitching into a smile, the assistant DA refocused on Maura. 'So Mr Dixon was badly bruised, he had lacerations, and at least one of his teeth had recently been knocked out.'

'Yes,' said Maura. 'As you'll see from the morgue photographs.'

As the first slide went up, there were audible intakes of breath from all round the room. Maura had known the photos would tell the story better than she could. The truth staring from that image was obvious to all: Fabian

Dixon had been savagely battered before being placed in the police cruiser.

Other slides appeared as Maura described what she had found on autopsy. Multiple broken ribs. Aspirated blood in the lungs. And the cause of death: a splenic rupture, which had led to massive intraperitoneal haemorrhage.

'And what was the manner of Mr Dixon's death, Dr Isles?' Aguilar asked.

This was the key question, the one that she dreaded answering.

'Homicide,' said Maura. She restricted her answer to that one word, but she couldn't help glancing at Wayne Graff. The accused sat motionless, his face unreadable. For more than a decade, he had served the city of Boston with distinction. He was a hero, they said, and Maura believed it.

But on the night of October 31, the night that Fabian Dixon murdered a police officer, Wayne Graff and his partner had transformed into angels of vengeance. Dixon was in their custody when he died. Subject was agitated and violent, as if under the influence of PCP or crack, they wrote in their statement. They described Dixon's crazed resistance, his superhuman strength. It had taken both officers to wrestle the prisoner into the cruiser. During this struggle, he was making grunts and animal sounds and trying to take off his clothes, even though it was a cold night. They had described, almost too perfectly, the known medical condition of excited delirium, which had killed other cocaine-addled prisoners. But the toxicology report showed only alcohol in Dixon's system. It left no doubt in Maura's mind that the manner of his death was homicide. And one of his killer's now sat at the defence table staring at Maura.

Morris Whaley, the defence attorney, rose for the cross-examination, and Maura felt her muscles tense. Whaley, an attractive man in an expensive suit, approached the witness stand as if he intended to have a friendly chat. Maura stared at his smiling face, wondering from which direction the attack would come.

'I don't think anyone doubts that you've worked hard to get where you are today, Dr Isles,' Whaley said. 'Especially taking into account some of the challenges you've faced in your personal life in the past few months.'

'Objection.' Aguilar heaved an exasperated sigh. 'This is not relevant.'

'Your Honour. It goes to the witness's judgment,' said Whaley. 'Past experiences can affect how a witness interprets the evidence.'

'What experiences are you referring to?'

'If you'll allow me to explore that issue, it will become apparent.'

The judge stared hard at Whaley. 'I'll allow this line of questioning. But only for the moment.'

Whaley turned his attention back to Maura. 'Dr Isles, do you happen to recall the date that you examined the deceased?'

'The date of the post-mortem was November 1st of last year.'

'On that same date, did you also specify the manner of death?'

She hesitated. 'No. I wanted to wait for the results of the toxicology screen to see whether Mr Dixon was under the influence of cocaine or other pharmaceuticals. I wanted to be cautious.'

'As well you should when your decision could destroy the careers of two dedicated peace officers.'

'I only concern myself with the facts, Mr Whaley.'

He did not like that answer; she saw it in the twitch of his jaw muscle. All semblance of cordiality had vanished: this was now a battle.

'So you performed the autopsy on November 1st,' he said. 'What happened after that?'

'I'm not sure to what you're referring.'

'Did you take the weekend off? Did you spend the following week performing other autopsies?'

She stared at him, anxiety coiling like a serpent in her stomach. 'I attended a pathology conference in Wyoming.'

'Where you had something of a traumatic experience. You were assaulted by a rogue police officer.'

Aguilar shot to her feet. 'Objection! Not relevant!'

'Overruled,' the judge said.

Whaley smiled, his path now cleared to ask the questions that Maura dreaded. 'Is that correct, Dr Isles? Were you attacked by a police officer?'

'Yes,' she whispered.

'And how did you survive that attack?'

The room was silent, waiting for her story. She remembered the lonely hilltop in Wyoming. She remembered the thud of the deputy's vehicle door as it closed, trapping her in the back seat behind the prisoner grating. She remembered her panic as she'd futilely battered her hands against the window, trying to escape a man she knew was about to kill her.

'Dr Isles, how did you survive? Who came to your aid?'

She swallowed. 'A boy.'

'Julian Perkins, age sixteen, I believe. A young man who shot and killed that police officer.'

'He had no choice!'

Whaley cocked his head. 'You're defending a boy who killed a cop?'

'A bad cop!'

'And then you came back home to Boston and declared Mr Dixon's death a homicide.'

'Because it was.'

'Or was it merely a tragic accident? The unavoidable consequence after a violent prisoner fought back and had to be subdued?'

'The police used far more force than was necessary.'

'So did that boy in Wyoming. He shot and killed a sheriff's deputy. Do you consider that justifiable force?'

'Objection,' said Aguilar. 'Dr Isles isn't on trial here.'

Whaley barrelled ahead, his gaze fixed on Maura. 'What happened in Wyoming, Dr Isles? While you were fighting for your life, was there an epiphany? A sudden realisation that cops are the enemy?'

'Objection!'

'Or have cops always been the enemy? Members of your own family seem to think so.'

The gavel banged down. 'Mr Whaley, you will approach the bench now.'

Maura sat stunned. So it had come to this: the dredging up of her family. Every cop in Boston probably knew about her mother, now serving a life sentence in a women's prison in Framingham. She saw that the defendant, Officer Graff, was staring at her. Their gazes locked, and a smile curled his lips as she read in his eyes: *This is what happens when you betray the thin blue line.*

'The court will take a recess,' the judge announced. 'We'll resume at two this afternoon.'

As the jury filed out, Maura sagged back against her chair.

'That was dirty pool,' said Aguilar. 'It should never have been allowed.'

'He made it all about me,' said Maura.

'Well, that's all he has. Because the autopsy photos are pretty damn convincing.' Aguilar looked hard at her. 'We could lose this case if that jury thinks you're not on the level. Is there anything else I should know about you, Dr Isles?'

Maura considered the private embarrassments that she guarded. An illicit affair that she'd just ended. Her family's history of violence. 'Everyone has secrets,' she said. 'Mine aren't relevant.'

'Let's hope not,' said Aguilar.

WHEREVER YOU LOOKED in Boston's Chinatown, there were ghosts. That, at least, was tour guide Billy Foo's story. Whether he himself believed in ghosts hardly mattered: his job was to convince the tourists that these streets were haunted. People wanted to believe in ghosts; that's why so many of them were willing to pony up fifteen bucks apiece to listen to Billy's gory tales of murder. Tonight, thirteen of them had signed up for the late-night Chinatown Ghost Tour, including a pair of bratty ten-year-old twins who should have been in bed hours ago. But when you need the money, you don't turn away paying guests. Billy was a theatre major with no job prospects, and tonight's haul was a cool $195, plus tips. Not bad pay for two hours of telling tall tales, even if it came with the humiliation of wearing a satin mandarin robe and a fake pigtail.

Billy cleared his throat to get the group's attention. 'The year is 1907. August 2nd, a Friday evening.' He pointed across the street. 'There beats the heart of Boston's Chinese quarter. Walk with me now, as we step back into another era. Come back to a night when murder was in the air!'

'Mahhhh-mee!' one of the brats whined. 'He's kicking me!'

'Stop it, Michael,' the mother snapped. 'You stop it right this minute.'

Gritting his teeth, Billy continued. 'It was a steamy night in August. After a long day's work in their laundries and grocery stores, a crowd of Chinamen sat resting. Here in this square, a battle was about to erupt between two rival Chinese clans that would leave this square awash in blood. Suddenly the night explodes with gunfire! Scores of Chinamen flee in terror! But some do not run fast enough, and when the bullets fall silent, five men lie dead. They are just the latest casualties in the bloody and infamous tong wars . . .'

'Mommy, can we go now?'

'Shhh! Listen to the man's story.'

'But he's borrrring.'

'On foggy nights like this one,' Billy said through clenched teeth, 'you can sometimes see shadowy figures flit past in mortal terror, for ever desperate to escape the bullets that flew that night!' Billy turned, waving an arm. 'Now follow me to another place where ghosts dwell.'

Billy led the group across the street. He only had to maintain the energy for another hour. They headed to Knapp Street, scarcely more than an alley, poorly lit and little travelled. The temperature suddenly seemed to plummet. Shivering, Billy wrapped his mandarin robe tighter. His tour group seemed to notice as well. They fell silent. Even the two brats were quiet. Billy came to a halt outside an abandoned building, where a locked gate covered the door and steel bars secured the ground-floor windows. A rusting fire escape clambered up to the first and second floors, where every window was boarded up tight.

'Welcome to the setting of one of Chinatown's most grisly crimes,' said Billy. 'Nineteen years ago, behind these barred windows, was a little Chinese seafood restaurant called the Red Phoenix. It was late on March 30th, a damp and cold night like this one, when the normally bustling streets of Chinatown were strangely quiet. Inside the Red Phoenix, two employees were at work: the waiter, Jimmy Fang, and the cook, an illegal immigrant from China named Wu Weimin. Three customers came to eat that night—a night that would be their last. We'll never know what made the cook go berserk. Maybe it was the long, hard hours he worked. Or the heartbreak of living as a stranger in a strange land.' Billy paused. His voice dropped to a chilling whisper. 'Or maybe it was some evil that possessed him. An evil that made him pull out a gun. Made him storm into the dining room and . . .' Billy stopped.

'And what?' someone prompted anxiously.

But Billy's attention was fixed overhead, his gaze riveted to the roof, where he swore something had just moved: a flutter of black on black. He strained to catch another glimpse of it, but all he saw now was the skeletal outline of the fire escape.

'Then what happened?' one of the brats demanded.

Billy looked at the thirteen faces staring at him expectantly, but he was rattled. All at once, he was desperate to get out of that dark alley. He took a breath and blurted, 'The cook shot them all. And then he killed himself.'

With that, Billy quickly waved them on, leading them away from that blighted building. Ahead, the lights of Harrison Avenue beckoned. He was walking so quickly that his group fell behind.

A woman's loud shriek made him spin round. Then the group suddenly erupted in laughter. One of the men said, 'Hey, nice prop! Do you use it on all your tours? Looks pretty damn realistic.'

'I don't know what you're talking about,' said Billy.

The man pointed. 'Hey, kid, show him what you found.'

'I found it over there, by the trash bin,' said one of the brats, holding up his discovery. 'Ewww. It even feels real. Gross!'

Billy froze, staring at the object the boy was holding. He saw inky droplets trickle down and spatter the boy's jacket, but the boy didn't seem to notice it.

It was the boy's mother who started screaming first. Then the others joined in. The baffled boy just stood there holding up his prize as blood dripped onto his sleeve.

'HAD DINNER THERE just last Saturday,' said Detective Barry Frost as they drove towards Chinatown. 'I took Liz to see the ballet at the Wang Theatre. I fell asleep halfway through. Afterwards, we walked over to the Ocean City restaurant for dinner.'

It was 2 a.m., too early in the morning for anyone to be so damn chatty, but Detective Jane Rizzoli let her partner babble on about his latest date as she focused on driving. An hour ago, she'd been warmly cocooned in bed with her husband, Gabriel; now she was trying to shake herself awake as she navigated the traffic.

'Who's Liz?' she said. 'I thought you were seeing Muffy.'

'Maggie.' He shrugged. 'That didn't work out.'

'Neither did the one before her.'

'Hey, it's been for ever since I was on the market. I had no idea there were so many single girls around.'

'Women.'

He sighed. 'Yeah, yeah. Alice used to pound that into my head, too.'

Jane glanced at him. 'You and Alice talk much these days?'

'What's there to talk about?'

'Ten years of marriage, maybe?'

He looked out of the window. 'There's nothing to say. She's moved on.'

But Frost hasn't, thought Jane. Eight months ago, Alice had moved out of their home. Ever since, Jane had been subjected to a chronicle of Frost's frantic but joyless adventures with women. He related all the tales with a mingling of bewilderment and wonder, but it was sadness, more than anything else, that she saw in his eyes these days. By no means was he a bad catch. He was lean and fit and good-looking, so dating should be easier for him than it had been. *But he still misses Alice.*

They turned onto Beach Street, and were nearly blinded by the flashing lights of a Boston PD cruiser. She pulled up and they stepped out into the bone-chilling dampness. Despite the ungodly hour, there were several onlookers gathered on the sidewalk, and Jane heard murmurs in both Chinese and English.

She and Frost walked down Knapp Street and ducked under the strand of police tape, where a patrolman stood guard. 'Detectives Rizzoli and Frost, homicide,' she announced.

'It's over there,' was the cop's terse response. He pointed down the alley at a dumpster, where another cop stood guard.

As Jane approached, she realised something was lying on the pavement. She halted, staring down at a severed right hand.

'Whoa,' said Frost.

The cop laughed. 'That was my reaction exactly.'

'Who found it?'

'Folks on the Chinatown Ghost Tour. Some kid picked it up thinking it was fake. Soon as he realised it was real, he dropped it right where it is now. Guess they never expected that on the tour.'

'Where are these tourists now?'

'They all insisted on going back to their hotels, but I got names and contact info. No one saw anything except the hand. They called nine one one, and Dispatch thought it was a practical joke.'

Jane crouched down. It was a startlingly clean amputation. The hand appeared to be a woman's, with slender fingers and a disconcertingly elegant manicure. No ring, no watch. 'It was just lying here on the ground?'

'Yeah. Fresh meat like that, rats'd be at it pretty quick.'

'No nibbles that I can see. Hasn't been here long.'

'I spotted something else.' The cop aimed his flashlight on a dull grey object lying a few yards away.

Frost moved in for a closer inspection. 'This is a Heckler & Koch. Expensive,' he said. He glanced at Jane. 'It's got a silencer.'

'Did any of the tourists touch the gun?' asked Jane.

'No,' the cop said. 'They never saw it.'

'So we've got a silenced automatic and a freshly severed right hand,' said Jane. 'Who wants to bet they go together?'

'This is a really nice piece,' said Frost, still admiring the weapon.

Jane rose to her feet and looked at the dumpster. 'Have you checked in there for the rest of the body?'

'No, ma'am. Didn't want to contaminate anything before you got here.'

She pulled a pair of gloves out of her pocket. Together she and Frost lifted the lid, and the stench of rotting seafood smacked them in the face. She stared down at a bulging black garbage bag. She untied the bag and looked inside. Saw shrimp and crab shells.

They both backed away and Jane looked at the severed hand. 'So where's the rest of her?'

'We did a walk-around,' the patrolman said. 'Didn't find anything.'

'Still, I think we'll take a stroll round the block ourselves,' said Jane.

Together, she and Frost moved slowly along Knapp Street, their flashlights cutting through the shadows. She knew they would have to make this same inspection again by daylight, but she did not want to miss any time-sensitive clues. So she and Frost continued their painstaking circle round the block, from Harrison to Beach Street. By the time they were back at the dumpster, the crime scene unit had arrived.

Jane watched as the weapon and severed hand were bagged, wondering why a killer would dump a body part where someone was sure to spot it. Was it a rush job? Was it meant to be a message of some kind? Then her gaze lifted to a fire escape that snaked up the building facing the alley.

'We need to check the roof,' she said.

The bottom rung of the ladder was rusted, and they couldn't pull it down; they'd have to reach the roof from a stairwell. They returned to Beach Street, where they could access the front entrances to that block. Businesses occupied the first levels, all closed at that hour. Above were apartments.

Jane climbed the steps to the front entrance and pressed a button at random. No one answered. She tried another button and, this time, a voice crackled over the intercom.

'It's the police,' she said. 'Can you let us into the building, please?'

'Wei?'

'Please open the door!'

A few moments passed, then a child's voice answered: 'My grandma wants to know who you are.'

'Detective Jane Rizzoli, Boston PD,' said Jane. 'We need to go up on the roof. Can you let us in the building?'

At last the lock buzzed open. The building was at least a hundred years old, and the wooden steps groaned as Jane and Frost climbed to the second-floor landing and then up a narrow set of steps to the roof. The exit was unlocked, but the door gave a piercing squeal as they swung it open. They stepped out into the predawn gloom. Shining her flashlight, Jane saw a sagging clothesline and laundry dancing like ghosts in the wind. Through the sheets, she spotted something else near the roof's edge.

She and Frost automatically took paper shoe covers from their pockets and bent down to pull them on. Only then did they duck under the hanging sheets and cross towards what they had glimpsed.

For a moment neither spoke. They stood together, flashlights trained on a congealed lake of blood. On what was lying in that lake.

'I guess we found the rest of her,' said Frost.

CHINATOWN SAT in the very heart of Boston, but as Maura walked under the *paifang* gate, with its four carved lions, she felt as if she were entering a different world. She spotted a uniformed Boston PD cop towering over the mostly Asian crowd and worked her way towards him.

'Excuse me. I'm the medical examiner,' she announced.

The cold look he gave her left no doubt that the police officer knew exactly who she was: Dr Maura Isles, whose testimony might send one of their own to prison. He didn't say a word, just stared at her.

She returned the stare, just as coldly. 'Where is the deceased?'

'You'd have to ask Detective Rizzoli.'

He was not going to make this easy for her. 'And where is she?'

Before he could answer, she heard someone call out: 'Dr Isles?' A young Asian man in a suit and tie crossed the street towards her. 'They're waiting for you up on the roof. Come with me. I'll walk you up the stairs.'

'Are you new to homicide? I don't believe we've met.'

'Sorry, I should have introduced myself. I'm Detective Johnny Tam, with District A-1. Rizzoli needed someone from the neighbourhood to translate, and since I'm the generic Chinese guy, I got pulled onto her team.'

'Your first time working with homicide?'

'Yes, ma'am. Always been a dream of mine. I only made detective two months ago, so I'm really psyched.' He cleared a path for her through the crowd of mainly Chinese bystanders, asking people to move aside. He opened a door to a building that smelled of garlic and incense.

'I notice you speak Mandarin. Do you speak Cantonese, too?' she said.

'You can hear the difference?'

'I used to live in San Francisco. A number of my colleagues were Chinese.'

'I wish I could speak Cantonese, but it's like Greek to me,' he said as they climbed up the stairwell. 'I'm afraid my Mandarin's not very useful round here. Most of these old-timers speak Cantonese or the Toisan dialect. Half the time, I need an interpreter myself.'

'So you aren't from Boston.'

'No. I was born and raised in New York City. My parents came over from Fujian Province.'

They reached the roof and stepped out into the glare of the early morning sun. Maura saw crime scene personnel combing the rooftop and heard someone call out: 'Found another bullet casing over here.'

Suddenly the voices went silent and Maura realised they were all looking at her. The traitor had arrived.

'Hey, Doc,' Jane called out, crossing towards her. 'I see Tam found you.'

'What's this about bullet casings?' asked Maura. 'On the phone, you said it was an amputation.'

'It is. But we found a Heckler & Koch automatic down in the alley below. Looks like someone fired off a few rounds up here. At least five.'

'Were there reports of gunshots? Do we have an approximate time?'

'The gun had a silencer, so no one heard a thing.' Jane turned. 'Victim's over here.'

Maura followed Jane to the shrouded body lying near the roof's edge. She lifted the plastic sheet and stared, unable to speak for a moment.

'Yeah. It kind of took our breath away, too,' said Jane.

The woman was a Caucasian in her early thirties, slim and athletic, dressed in a black hoodie sweatshirt and leggings. She lay on her back, face staring up at the sky. Her skin was pale and flawless and she had a model's jutting cheekbones. But it was the wound that Maura focused on, a slash so deep that it divided skin and muscle and cartilage, severing the lumen of the trachea and exposing the pearly surface of the spine. The arterial gush that had resulted had been powerful enough to spray blood in a radius that left splatters across the curtain of sheets hanging on the nearby clothesline.

'The amputated hand fell in the alley right below,' said Jane. 'So did the Heckler & Koch. My guess is, her fingerprints are on the grip. And we're gonna find gunshot residue on that hand.'

Maura tore her gaze away from the neck and focused on the right wrist, which had been cleanly divided, and she tried to picture what sort of instrument could have so efficiently slashed through cartilage and bone. It had to be appallingly sharp. She imagined the slash of the blade and the hand tumbling over the roof's edge.

She stared down from the roof at the police officers standing at the far end of Knapp Street, holding back onlookers. The crowd looked twice as large as it had only moments before. The curious can always smell blood.

'Are you sure you really want to be here, Maura?' Jane asked quietly.

Maura turned to her. 'Why wouldn't I be?'

'I'm just wondering if it's too soon for you to be back in rotation. I know it's been a tough week for you, with the trial and all.' Jane paused. 'It's not looking too good for Graff.'

'It shouldn't look good. He killed a man.'

'And that man killed a cop who had a wife and kids.' Jane looked at Maura. 'I have to admit, I might've lost it, too.'

'Please, Jane. Don't tell me you're defending him.'

'I'm just saying, it's a sensitive time right now. We all respect Graff, and we can understand how he lost it that night. A cop killer's dead, and maybe that's a kind of justice.'

'It's not my job to deliver justice. I just deliver the facts.'

Jane's laugh was biting. 'Yeah, you're all about the facts, aren't you?'

Maura looked across the rooftop at the criminalists scouring the scene. *Let it roll off and focus on your job. You're here to speak for this dead woman, and no one else.* 'What was she doing on this roof?' she asked.

Jane looked down at the body. 'No idea.'

'Do we know how she gained access?'

'Could've been a fire escape or a stairwell. Once you're on one roof, you can access all the roofs on this block. No one we've spoken to remembers seeing her last night. And we know it happened last night. When we found her, rigor mortis was just starting to set in.'

Maura focused on the victim again.

'ID?'

'No. All we found in her pockets was three hundred bucks and a Honda car key. We're searching the area for the vehicle.'

'Strange, how she's dressed all in black.'

'Goes with everything, as they say.'

Maura replaced the sheet. 'Where is the hand?'

'It's already bagged.'

'Are you sure it belongs to this body?'

Jane gave a startled laugh. 'What are the odds it doesn't?'

'I never make assumptions. You know that.' She turned away.

'Maura?' Maura looked at Jane. They stood face to face in that blinding sunshine, where it felt as if all of Boston PD could see them, hear them. 'About the trial. I do understand where you're coming from.'

'And you don't approve.'

'But I understand. Just as I hope you understand that it's guys like Graff who have to deal with the real world. They're the ones on the front line. Justice isn't as clean as a science experiment. Sometimes it's pretty damn messy, and the facts just make things messier.'

'So I should have lied instead?'

'Just don't forget who the real bad guys are.'

'That's not in my job description,' said Maura. She retreated into the stairwell, relieved to escape the eyes of Boston PD personnel. But on the ground floor, she came face to face once again with Detective Tam.

'So when's the autopsy?'

'I'll do it tomorrow morning.'

'May I observe?'

'You're welcome to be there, if you have the stomach for it.'

'I've watched a few. Managed not to keel over.'

She paused to regard him for a moment. Saw humourless dark eyes and sharply handsome features, but no hostility. On a morning when all of Boston PD seemed to regard her as the enemy, Detective Johnny Tam was the only cop who didn't seem to stand in judgment of her.

'Eight sharp tomorrow morning,' she said. 'I'll see you there.'

MAURA DID NOT sleep well that night. After a heavy meal of lasagne, washed down with three glasses of wine, she had climbed into bed exhausted. The next morning, she arrived at work groggy. She saw that Jane was already standing by the table, waiting for her.

Yesterday, they had not parted on the most congenial of terms, and Maura still felt stung by Jane's sarcastic retort. Yes, facts mattered to her. They were immutable things that could not be denied, even when they threatened a friendship. The trial of Officer Graff had driven a wedge between her and Jane, reminding Maura how unlikely their friendship had been from the start. As she tied on her gown, it was not the corpse she dreaded confronting, but Jane. With a deep breath, she pushed through the door.

Her assistant, Yoshima, had already transferred the body bag onto the table. On a tray beside it was the severed hand, covered by a drape. Maura gave Jane a businesslike nod and said, 'Isn't Frost joining us?'

'He's going to miss this one, but Johnny Tam's on his way. In fact, I think he can't wait to watch you start slicing.'

'Detective Tam seems eager to prove himself.'

'I think he's got his eye on joining homicide. From what I've seen so far, he may have what it takes.' She glanced up. 'Speak of the devil.'

Through the viewing window, Maura saw that Tam had arrived and was tying on a surgical gown. A moment later he approached the table, his gaze impassive as he focused on the draped body.

'We'll start with the easy part,' said Maura, and she indicated the tray with the severed hand. It had already been swabbed and found positive for gunshot residue. Fingerprints from the hand had been found on the grip of the Heckler & Koch, leaving no doubt that the victim had fired the bullets, scattering five casings on the rooftop. Maura examined the severed wrist.

'Whatever made this cut divided a carpal bone. And these bones are very dense,' she said.

'So it had to be a sharp blade,' Jane said.

'Sharp enough to amputate with a single slice.' Maura looked up. 'I don't see any secondary cut marks.'

'Just tell me this hand matches that body.'

Maura turned to the table and unzipped the body bag. The cadaver inside was still fully clothed, the head tipped backwards, exposing the gaping wound in her neck. As Yoshima took photos, Maura's gaze was drawn to the woman's auburn hair. *Beautiful hair*, she thought, *and a beautiful woman.*

'Dr Isles, we've got some hair and fibre evidence staring at us,' said Yoshima. He was bending over the corpse's black sweatshirt, peering at a single pale strand that clung to the sleeve.

With a pair of tweezers, Maura examined it under the light. It was about two inches long, silvery grey and slightly curved. She glanced at the cadaver. 'This obviously is not her hair.'

'Look, there's another one,' said Jane, pointing to a second strand clinging to the victim's black leggings.

Maura slipped the strands into separate evidence envelopes and set them aside. 'OK, let's undress her.'

What emerged was a well-toned body, slim but muscular. Maura had once heard a pathology professor assert that he'd never come across an attractive corpse. This woman proved there could be exceptions to that rule.

Maura and the two detectives stepped out of the room so that Yoshima could take X-rays.

'A woman like that,' said Maura, 'is going to be missed by someone.'

'You saying that because she's good-looking?' Jane said.

'I'm saying it because she looks incredibly fit, she has perfect dentition, and those are Donna Karan leggings she was wearing. The point is,' said Maura, 'she's not some penniless stray off the street. She was carrying a lot of cash, and she was armed with a Heckler & Koch which, I understand, is not your usual street gun.' Through the viewing window, she saw Yoshima give a wave. 'He's done,' she said, and pushed through the door back into the lab.

Maura examined the incised neck first. Like the cut that had amputated the hand, this wound appeared to be a single slice, delivered without hesitation. 'It's almost eight centimetres deep,' Maura said. 'Transects the trachea and penetrates all the way to the cervical spine. Wider than it is deep. Not a stab but a slash.' She paused, studying the exposed incision. 'Odd how smooth it is. There's no bread-knifing, no secondary cuts. It was done so quickly, the victim never had a chance to struggle.' She shifted position a little. 'Can someone hold the cranium in position for me?'

Without hesitation, Tam stepped resolutely forward and cradled the head in his gloved hands. He stared straight into the dead woman's eyes, as though hoping they might provide answers to his many questions.

Maura slid the magnifier over the skin. 'This angle is strange,' she said. 'To penetrate this deep, all the way to vertebrae, you'd usually approach from behind. You'd grab the victim's hair, pull the head back, and slice across the front, from ear to ear. But this slash is angled upwards, right to left. It was delivered with the head in a neutral position, not tilted back.'

'Maybe the killer was standing in front of her,' said Jane.

'Then why would she just stand there while someone practically slices off her head?'

Yoshima said: 'I've put up the X-rays.'

They all turned to the viewing box where the radiographs were now displayed, bones glowing white on the backlit screen.

'It's definitely her hand,' Maura confirmed.

Next she focused on the neck X-rays. Her gaze fixed on a bright sliver in the cervical vertebra. 'Did you do a lateral on this C-spine?' she asked.

Yoshima clipped up a new radiograph, this one a side view. 'I saw that thing earlier. Thought you'd want to see more detail on it.'

Maura stared at the lateral view of the fifth cervical vertebra. The object, razor-thin, was visible on this X-ray as well.

'What is that?' asked Jane, moving close beside her.

'It's something metallic. I think part of the blade sheared off when the killer made his cut.'

'Which means we might be able to analyse the metal,' said Jane. 'Identify who manufactured the knife.'

'I don't think it was a knife,' said Maura.

'An axe?'

'An axe would leave a cleft, and we'd see crush changes on the soft tissues. This incision was made by a blade that's razor-sharp, and long enough to practically transect the neck with one sweep.'

'Like a machete?' asked Jane.

'Or a sword.'

Jane looked at Tam. 'We're looking for Zorro.' Her laugh was interrupted by the ring of her cellphone. 'Rizzoli.' She turned away to take the call.

'Dr Isles, would metal analysis tell you if this was a samurai sword?' Tam asked, still studying the X-ray.

'They're mass-produced these days, so it probably wouldn't help us unless we could find the weapon itself. Still, you never know when trace evidence like this ends up being just the piece needed to convict.'

'Tam,' said Jane. 'That was Frost. We found the victim's car.'

THE BLUE HONDA CIVIC sat in a remote corner of the Tyler Street garage. As Jane and Frost inspected the vehicle, their only audience was a lone garage employee and the two officers who'd spotted the car earlier that morning.

'The entry ticket on the dash has a time of eight fifteen on Wednesday evening,' said Frost. 'I checked the security tape, and it shows the Honda driving in at that time. Five minutes later, a woman walks out of the garage. Her hoodie's up, so you can't see her face. Car hasn't left the garage since.'

As Frost spoke, Jane walked slowly round the Honda. It was a three-year-old model with no major dings or scratches. The trunk was open, the hatch lifted for her to inspect the interior.

'Licence plates were reported stolen five days ago in Springfield,' said Frost. 'Vehicle was stolen a week ago, also in Springfield.'

Jane frowned into the empty trunk. 'Geez, it's a lot cleaner than mine.'

Frost laughed. 'Glove compartment's got the real owner's registration and insurance card. And you're gonna love what was left on the front seat. Handheld GPS. I'm guessing it's a brand-new unit, because she'd plugged in only two addresses. Both in Boston.'

'Where?'

'The first is in Roxbury Crossing, a Louis Ingersoll.'

Jane glanced at him in surprise. 'Would that be Detective Lou Ingersoll?'

'One and the same. It's the address Boston PD has listed for him.'

'He retired from homicide, what, sixteen, seventeen years ago?'

'Sixteen. Can't get hold of him right now. I called his daughter, and she says Lou took off up north to go fishing for the week.'

'What about the second address on the GPS?'

'The Dragon and Stars Martial Arts Academy here in Chinatown. They open at noon.' Frost glanced at his watch. 'Ten minutes ago.'

THE MARTIAL ARTS ACADEMY was located on the first floor of a tired brick building on Harrison Avenue. As Jane and Frost climbed the narrow stairway, they could hear chants and thumping feet. Inside the studio, a dozen students garbed in black, pyjama-like costumes moved with such total focus that not a single one seemed to notice the two detectives' entrance. For a moment Jane and Frost stood near the door, watching the class leap and kick.

Suddenly a young Asian woman stepped out of formation and ordered, 'Complete the exercise!' Then she crossed the room to meet the two visitors. She was slender as a dancer, her skin aglow, but despite her exertions she did not seem at all out of breath. 'May I help you?' she asked.

'We're from Boston PD. We'd like to speak to the owner of this studio.'

'May I see identification?' The request was brusque and not at all what Jane had expected from someone who looked like she was barely out of high school. As the girl studied Jane's ID, Jane studied the girl. Early twenties and American Chinese. With her short, spiky hair and her sullen gaze, she looked like an Asian version of a Goth girl, small but dangerous.

'May I ask your name?' said Jane, pulling out a notebook.

'Bella Li. I teach the beginning and intermediate classes.'

'Your students are amazing,' Frost marvelled, still watching the class as they leaped and whirled. 'It's like what you see in kung fu movies.'

His remark was met with an icy stare. 'The proper name for this art is *wushu*, and it was invented thousands of years ago. What you see in those movies is fake Hollywood crap.'

'May we speak to the owner?' asked Jane.

'*Sifu* Fang is in the back room.'

'How do you spell that name? You said it was She—'

'*Sifu* isn't a name,' Bella retorted. 'It's the Chinese word for "master" or "teacher". A term of respect.'

'Then may we speak to the *master*?' Jane snapped, irritated by the girl's attitude. 'This isn't a social call, Ms Li. It's official business.'

Bella weighed her request. 'A minute,' she said and walked across the room to knock at a door: '*Sifu*, there are two policemen here to see you.'

'Send them in,' said a voice.

Unlike lithe young Bella Li, the Chinese woman who rose from her chair to greet them moved slowly, as if struggling with aching joints, although she appeared to be only in her fifties. Middle age was barely etched in her face, however, and her long black hair was streaked with only a few strands of silver. She faced them with the confidence of an empress. Although she was Jane's height, her regal posture made her seem far taller.

'I am Iris Fang,' the woman said. 'How can I help you?' Both her formality and her accent told Jane the woman was foreign born.

'Detective Rizzoli and Detective Frost from the homicide unit,' said Jane. 'We need to ask a few questions about something that happened in Chinatown last night.'

'I assume this is about the dead woman on the roof?'

'Then you already know about it.'

'This is a small neighbourhood. They say her throat was cut, and her hand was thrown off the rooftop. And they say she had a gun. Are these stories true?' asked Iris.

Iris and Jane regarded each other for a moment, and Jane suddenly thought, *I'm not the only one seeking information here.* 'We have a photo we'd like to show you,' she said.

'This might be upsetting,' Frost said. 'Maybe you'd like to sit down first?'

His respectful tone seemed to melt some of the ice from the woman's eyes, and she nodded. 'I am feeling weary today. Perhaps I will sit down, thank you.'

Frost quickly scooted a chair closer, and Iris sank down with a sigh of relief. Only then did he reveal the digital image of the dead woman that Maura had emailed from the morgue.

Iris Fang stared at it, her expression unchanging.

'Do you recognise her, ma'am?' said Frost.

'She's beautiful, isn't she?' Iris said. 'But I don't know her.'

'You're sure?'

'I have lived in Chinatown for thirty-five years, ever since my husband and I emigrated from Taiwan. If this woman came from my neighbourhood, I would know.' She looked at Jane. 'Is this all you came to ask me?'

Jane didn't answer immediately, because she'd noticed the fire escape, which snaked right past the window. *From this room*, she thought, *you'd have access to all the rooftops on this block, including the building where the victim died.* She turned to Iris. 'How many employees work here?'

'I am the sole owner of this school and the primary instructor.'

'What about that young woman who just showed us in? Bella Li.'

'Bella has been with me for almost a year. She teaches some of the classes, and has her own students, too.'

'You mentioned your husband. Does Mr Fang also work here?'

The woman looked away. 'My husband is dead,' she said softly. 'James has been gone for nineteen years.'

'I'm sorry to hear that, Mrs Fang,' Frost said quietly, and it was apparent that he actually meant it.

Iris's gaze settled on Jane. 'Why did you think that I might know this dead woman?'

'We found the victim's car this morning. One of the addresses in the memory of a GPS unit in it was your studio. Do you know why?'

Iris frowned. 'Here? My studio?'

'This was the victim's destination. Do you know why?'

'No.' The answer was immediate.

'May I ask where you were on Wednesday night, Mrs Fang?'

'I taught an evening class. Then I walked home around ten. It is only a short walk. I live on Hudson Street, just at the edge of Chinatown.'

'Did anyone walk with you?'

'I was alone.'

'And do you live alone?'

'I have no family, Detective. My husband is gone, and my daughter . . .' She paused. 'Yes, I live alone.'

In the next room, the class had ended. Iris looked up at the clock on the wall. 'Are we finished?'

'One more question,' said Jane. 'Are you acquainted with a retired Boston PD detective named Louis Ingersoll?'

The woman sat frozen, her face as rigid as stone.

'Mrs Fang, are you all right?' said Frost.

Jane said, quietly, 'So you do know that name.'

'I met Detective Ingersoll nineteen years ago. When my husband died.'

Jane and Frost glanced at each other. Ingersoll worked homicide.

'Mrs Fang,' said Frost. 'What happened to your husband?'

Her answer was barely a whisper. 'He was shot to death. In the Red Phoenix restaurant.'

FROM MY WINDOW, I can see the two detectives pause on the street below. They glance up, and although every instinct tells me to back away, I remain in full view. I refuse to hide from either friends or enemies, so I face them through the glass, my gaze focused on the woman. *Detective Jane Rizzoli*, it says on the business card that she left me. At first glance, she seemed just another hard-working woman in a grey trouser suit and practical shoes. But her eyes reveal much more. They search and observe and assess. She has the eyes of a hunter, and she's trying to decide if I'm her prey.

I stand unafraid in open view. They may study me as long as they wish, but all they'll see is a quiet and unassuming woman, my hair streaked with the first light snow of the passing years. Old age is still years away but today I feel its relentless approach. I know that I am running out of time to finish what I've started. And with this visit by the two detectives, the journey has just taken a disturbing detour that I had not anticipated.

On the street below, the two detectives finally depart. Back to the hunt, wherever it takes them.

'*Sifu*, is there a problem?'

I turn to look at Bella. She stands unafraid and confident. Perhaps too confident: on the battlefield, arrogance can prove fatal.

'Why did they come here?' she asks.

'They're detectives. It's their job to ask questions.'

'Did you learn anything about the woman? Who she was, who sent her?'

'No. But whoever she was, she knew how to find me.'

'She won't be the last,' says Bella darkly.

She does not need to warn me; we both know the match has been struck and the fuse lit.

In my office, I sink into my chair and stare at the framed photo that sits on my desk. I know the exact date the picture was taken, because it was my daughter's birthday. Laura and I stand together in front of the Boston Symphony Hall: she is still aglow from watching a wonderful performance. My husband, James, does not appear in any of our photos because he was always the one holding the camera. How I wish I had thought, just once, to take that camera from his hands and snap a picture of his sweet face. But it never occurred to me that the opportunity would suddenly vanish. That his smile would survive only in my memory, his image frozen at the age of thirty-seven.

They are both gone now. First my daughter, then my husband. How do you go on living when your heart has been cut out not just once, but twice? Yet here I am, still alive, still breathing.

For the moment.

THREE

'I remember the Red Phoenix massacre. It was a classic case of amok.' Criminal psychologist Dr Lawrence Zucker looked across his desk at Jane and Frost with the penetrating stare that always made Jane feel uneasy.

She focused on the folder lying open on his desk. It contained his nineteen-year-old report on the Red Phoenix, including the psychological profile of Wu Weimin, the Chinese cook responsible for the shootings. She knew Zucker to be a painstakingly thorough clinician, so she was surprised by how thin the file appeared.

'This is your complete report?' she asked.

'It's everything I contributed to the investigation. It includes the psychological post-mortem of Mr Wu, as well as the four victim reports. Have you spoken to Detective Ingersoll?'

'He's on some fishing trip with no cellphone coverage,' said Frost.

Jane said, 'And Charlie Staines, the other detective, is deceased. We were hoping you could share your insight into the case.'

Zucker nodded. 'The basics of what happened were apparent from the crime scene. We know that the cook, a Chinese immigrant named Wu Weimin, walked into the dining room and shot four people. First to die was a man named Joey Gilmore, who'd dropped in to pick up a take-out order. Victim number two was the waiter, James Fang, reportedly the cook's close friend. Victims three and four were a married couple, the Mallorys, who were seated at a dining table. Finally the cook returned to the kitchen, put the gun to his own temple, and killed himself. It was a case of amok followed by suicide.'

'You make amok sound like a clinical term,' said Frost.

'It is. It's a Malaysian word for homicidal outbursts without apparent motive, where an individual goes into a killing frenzy. The phenomenon now goes by the name of SMASI—sudden mass assault by a single individual.'

'What do these killers have in common?' asked Frost.

'You can probably guess. They're often isolated from the community. They have problems with relationships. Some sort of crisis precipitates the attack—

loss of a job, collapse of a marriage. And they also have access to weapons.'

Jane flipped through her copy of the report. 'It was a Glock 17, with a threaded barrel, reported stolen a year earlier.' She looked up. 'Why would an immigrant on a cook's salary buy a Glock?'

'For protection, maybe? Because he felt threatened?'

'You're the psychologist, Dr Zucker. Don't you have an answer?'

Zucker's mouth tightened. 'No, I don't. I'm not psychic. And I had no chance to interview the one person closest to him—his wife. By the time Boston PD requested my consult, she had left town. My psychological profile of Mr Wu is based on interviews with other people who knew him. And that list wasn't long.'

'One of those people was Iris Fang,' said Jane.

Zucker nodded. 'The wife of the waiter. I remember her well. For one thing, she was a beautiful woman. Absolutely stunning.'

'We've just met her,' said Frost. 'She's still stunning.'

'What else do you remember about Mrs Fang?' Jane said.

'Quite a lot, actually. I spoke with her several times, since she was my primary source of information about Wu Weimin. That was my first year working with Boston PD, and that particular incident was so horrific, it's hard not to remember it: you go out for dinner in Chinatown, and instead of enjoying kung pao chicken, you end up getting slaughtered by the cook. It made the public feel vulnerable because anyone could have been a victim. Plus, there was the usual hysteria about dangerous illegal immigrants. How did Mr Wu get into the country, how did he get a gun, et cetera.'

'What did you conclude about the shooter?' asked Frost.

'He was a sad character, really. He came over from Fujian Province and slipped into the US when he was maybe twenty. It's impossible to be sure of the dates because there was no documentation. All the information came from Mrs Fang who said Mr Wu was close friends with her husband.'

'Who died in the shooting,' said Frost.

'Yes, but despite that, Mrs Fang refused to say anything negative about Wu. She didn't believe he did it. She called him gentle and hard-working. Said he had too much to live for. He was supporting his wife and daughter, as well as sending money to a seven-year-old son from a previous relationship.'

'So there was an ex-wife?'

'In another city. But Wu and his wife, Li Hua, had been settled in Boston for years. They lived right above the restaurant and pretty much kept to themselves. Probably afraid to attract attention, because they were illegal. Also, language may have made life difficult since they spoke Mandarin.'

'While most of Chinatown speaks Cantonese,' said Frost.

Zucker nodded. 'So the man's got multiple sources of stress. He's hiding his illegal status. He's isolated. And he's got a family to support.'

'But what made him snap?' asked Jane.

'Mrs Fang didn't know. The week of the shooting, she was out of the country visiting relatives. I interviewed her after she returned home. She insisted that Wu would never kill anyone and he certainly wouldn't have killed her husband because the two men were friends. She also claimed that Wu didn't even own a gun.'

'How would she know that? She wasn't married to the man.'

'Well, I couldn't ask Wu's wife. Within days of the shooting, she and her daughter vanished. Even Iris Fang had no idea where they went.'

'You're going entirely by Mrs Fang's word. How do you know she was telling the truth?' said Jane.

'Maybe I'm naive, but I never doubted her sincerity. There's just something about her.' Zucker shook his head. 'Such a tragic figure. I don't know how anyone survives as many losses as she's had.'

'Losses?'

'Iris and James had a fourteen-year-old daughter who'd vanished two years earlier. No trace of the girl was ever found. I didn't put that in my report, since it wasn't relevant to the Red Phoenix incident.'

This was pain that Jane could not imagine. She thought of her own daughter, Regina, only two and a half years old. Thought of not knowing if her child was dead or alive. *And then to lose a husband as well . . .*

'In the wake of any tragedy,' said Zucker, 'there are always aftershocks. But what happened after the Red Phoenix went beyond the devastation to the immediate families. It's as if the massacre had a curse attached to it. It just kept claiming more victims.'

The room suddenly felt colder. 'What do you mean, a curse?' Jane asked.

'Within a month, Detective Staines died of a heart attack. A technician working on the crime scene unit was killed in a car accident. Detective Ingersoll's wife had a stroke and later died. Finally, there was the other girl who disappeared.'

'What girl?'

'Charlotte Dion, the seventeen-year-old daughter of Dina Mallory, one of the restaurant victims. A few weeks after Dina was killed, Charlotte vanished during a school outing. She's never been found.'

Jane could suddenly hear her own heartbeat, loud as a drum in her ears. 'And Iris Fang's daughter vanished, too.'

Zucker nodded. 'They disappeared two years apart, but it's still an eerie coincidence, isn't it?'

'Was it a coincidence?'

'What else could it be? The two families didn't know each other. The Fangs were struggling immigrants. Charlotte's parents were well-to-do Bostonians. There was no other connection between them. You might as well blame it on the Red Phoenix curse. Or maybe it's that building. They say that when you step inside, evil attaches itself to you.' He looked at Jane. 'And follows you home.'

JANE DID NOT LIKE coincidences. They happened, of course, but she always felt compelled to examine whether there was some grander design at work. And so she sat at her desk trying to trace the disparate threads that had tragically intersected in a Chinatown restaurant nineteen years ago.

For homicide detectives, a murder-suicide is the kind of case that comes neatly wrapped up with a bow: justice conveniently dispensed by the perp himself in the form of a self-inflicted bullet. The police report by Staines and Ingersoll focused not on the *who* but the *why* of the shooting, and their analysis relied heavily on what Dr Zucker had already told Jane and Frost.

So Jane looked at the four victims.

Victim number one was Joey Gilmore, aged twenty-five, born and raised in South Boston. He had a police record of burglary, trespassing, assault and battery. His employer's name—Donohue Wholesale Meats—instantly caught Jane's attention. The owner, Kevin Donohue, was one of the three most powerful names in the local Irish mafia.

Jane flipped to the image of Joey Gilmore's body. He'd been felled with a single bullet to the back of his head. Dr Zucker might call this a case of amok, but to Jane it looked a hell of a lot like a gangland execution.

Victim number two was James Fang, aged thirty-seven, who worked as host, waiter and cashier. Sixteen years earlier, he had arrived in the United

States as a graduate student in Asian literature. During the day, he taught in the after-school enrichment programme at the Boston Chinatown neighbourhood centre.

Victims three and four were a married couple, Arthur and Dina Mallory of Brookline, Massachusetts. Arthur was forty-eight, president and CEO of an investment firm. For both Arthur and Dina, forty, this was a second marriage. Arthur's first wife had been Barbara Mallory, née Hart, and they had a son, Mark, then aged twenty. Dina's ex-husband was Patrick Dion, and they had a daughter, Charlotte, then aged seventeen.

The police report specifically addressed the issue that every good homicide investigator automatically explores—any and all conflicts that resulted from the victims' divorces and remarriages: Even after the divorce and remarriage, Dina Mallory and her ex-husband, Patrick, remained on friendly terms, and the families often shared holiday dinners.

Jane could not see it happening in her own family. She tried to imagine a Rizzoli reunion that included her father, her mother, her father's bimbo and her mother's boyfriend, Vince Korsak. Now, *there* was a massacre waiting to happen. But the information came from Mark Mallory, who would know.

Jane turned to the last page in the file and found a brief addendum to the report: Charlotte Dion, daughter of Dina Mallory, was reported missing April 24 while on a school field trip. According to Detective Hank Buckholz, evidence points to likely abduction. Investigation continuing.

Two missing girls, Laura Fang and Charlotte Dion. Both of them were daughters of victims killed in the Red Phoenix, but nothing in this report indicated that this was anything more than a sad coincidence, just as Dr Zucker had said.

'You know, Rizzoli, all you had to do was ask me.'

She looked up to see Johnny Tam. 'Ask you what?'

'About the Red Phoenix massacre. I just ran into Frost. He told me you two have been hunting down all the files. If you'd just talked to me, I could have told you all about the case.'

'How would you know about it? You were, what, eight years old?'

'I'm assigned to Chinatown so I have to know what goes on there. The Chinese still talk about the Red Phoenix, you know. It's like a wound that never healed. And probably never will, because it's all tied up in shame.'

'Shame? Why?'

'The killer was one of our own. And by our own, I mean all Chinese.' He pointed to the folders on her desk. 'I reviewed that case file two months ago. Didn't it occur to you to ask me? I thought I was part of the team.'

She didn't like the accusatory tone in his voice. 'Yes, you're part of the team,' she acknowledged. 'But things'll go easier if you get rid of that chip on your shoulder.'

'I just want to be right in front of the hunt. Not treated like the geeky back-up guy, which happens way too often round here.' He paused. 'Boston PD's supposed to be one big, happy melting pot, right?' He laughed. 'Bullshit.'

For a moment she studied him, trying to read his stony expression. Suddenly, she recognised herself at his age, hungry to prove herself and resentful that, too often, she was ignored. 'You think I have no idea what it's like to be a minority?'

'I don't know. Do you?'

'Look around. How many female homicide detectives do you see? I know what it's like having guys shut me out because I'm the girl and they think there's no way I'm good enough. You need to learn to deal with all the jerks and the bullshit, because there's an endless supply of both.'

'It doesn't mean we stop calling them on it.'

'For all the difference it makes.'

'You must have made a difference. Because now they accept you.'

She remembered what her life used to be like when she'd first joined the unit and had to put up with the snickers and the tampon jokes and the deliberate snubs. Things were better now, but the war had been hard-fought.

'It's all about doing the job better than anyone else.' She paused. 'I hear you aced the exam for detective on your first try.'

His nod was curt. 'Top score, as a matter of fact.'

'And you're what? Twenty-seven? That's working against you, you know.'

'What, the fact I'm seen as just another Asian geek?'

'No. The fact you're still a kid. The point is, there's a dozen different reasons to feel like you're at a disadvantage. Some are real, some are in your head. Just deal with it and do the job.'

Tam sighed. 'Why don't you let me do some legwork on the Red Phoenix, since I'm already up on it. I can make calls, talk to the victims' families.'

'Frost already plans to interview Mrs Fang again.'

'So I'll talk to the other families.'

She nodded. 'Fine. Now tell me where you've gone already.'

'I first checked it out back in February, when I heard some of the Chinatown locals talking about it. I remembered the case from when I was a kid in New York City.'

'You heard about it in New York?'

'The whole Chinese community gossips about it. I remember my grand-mother telling me how shameful it was that the killer was one of us. She said it reflected badly on everyone who was Chinese.'

'Geez. Talk about collective guilt.'

'We're really good at that. I grew up with the burden of representing an entire race every time I stepped out of the door. So, I already had an interest in the Red Phoenix. Then when that ad in the *Boston Globe* came out in March, I read through the case file a second time.'

'What ad?'

'On the anniversary of the shooting. It ran a photo of the cook, Wu Weimin, with the word "Innocent" in bold letters.' He stared across the desks in the homicide unit. 'When I saw that ad, I wanted it to be true, just so we could erase that black mark against us.'

'You don't really think he was innocent, do you?'

He looked at her. 'I don't know.'

'Staines and Ingersoll never once doubted he was the shooter. Neither does Dr Zucker.'

'But that ad got me thinking. It made me wonder if Boston PD got it wrong nineteen years ago.'

'Just because Wu was Chinese?'

'Because people in Chinatown never believed he did it.'

'Who paid for the ad? Did you find out?'

He nodded. 'I called the *Globe*. It was paid for by Iris Fang.'

Jane's cellphone rang. Even as she reached for it, she was wondering why, nineteen years after the event, Iris would buy an ad in defence of the man who had murdered her husband.

The incoming call was from the crime lab. 'I'm looking at those hairs,' said criminalist Erin Volchko. 'And I'll be damned if I can identify them.'

'You mean those hairs from the victim's clothing?'

'Yes. They have similar morphology and colour, so they're probably from the same source.'

Jane felt Tam watching her as she asked, 'Are they real or synthetic?'

'They're definitely organic.'

'So are they human?'

'I'm not sure.'

JANE SQUINTED into the microscope's eyepiece. What she saw looked scarcely different from all the other hairs that she'd seen over the years. 'So what does this hair come from?' she asked.

'It might be easier,' said Erin, 'to tell you what it doesn't come from. There are no coronal scales, which eliminates rodents and bats. It lacks spinous scales, which tells us it didn't come from a cat, a mink or a seal.'

'Are we going down the whole list of animal species?' asked Jane.

'To some extent, this is a process of elimination.'

'And so far you've eliminated rats, bats and cats.'

'Correct.'

'Great,' said Jane. 'We can cross Batman and Catwoman off our list of suspects.'

Sighing, Erin pulled off her glasses and massaged the bridge of her nose. 'I'm just explaining how difficult it is to identify an animal hair using light microscopy. This specimen isn't like anything I've encountered in this lab.'

'What else can you eliminate?' asked Tam.

'It's not in the deer family. The colour argues against raccoon or beaver, and it's too coarse for rabbit or chinchilla. I'm guessing it's some sort of non-human primate. A species I can't identify with microscopy. There's one more test I'm thinking about. I found a scientific article from India, about electrophoretic analysis of hair keratin. They have a huge problem with the illegal fur trade, and they use this test to identify the furs of exotic species.'

'Which labs can run that test?'

'There are several wildlife labs in the US I can contact. It may turn out to be the quickest way to identify the species.' Erin looked at the microscope. 'One way or another, I'm going to find out what this hairy creature is.'

JANE FOUND retired detective Hank Buckholz in his usual spot at the bar in J. P. Doyle's, staring into a glass of scotch. It was still early for the usual crowd at Doyle's, a favourite hangout for Boston PD cops.

With one wave, Buckholz was able to catch the bartender's attention.

'Her drink's on me,' he announced, pointing to Jane. 'What would you like, Detective Rizzoli?'

She nodded to the bartender. 'Sam Adams lager.'

'And a refill for me,' added Buckholz.

'You want to move to a table, Hank?' asked Jane.

'Naw, I like it right here. Besides,' he glanced round at the nearly empty room, 'who's here to listen in? This is such an old case, no one's paying attention any more. Except for maybe the family.'

'And you.'

'Yeah, well, it's hard to let go. The ones I never closed still keep me up at night. The Charlotte Dion case especially, because it ticked me off when her father hired a PI to follow up on it. All that money he wasted, just to prove that I didn't miss anything.'

'So the PI never got anywhere, either?'

'Nope. That girl just plain vanished. No witnesses, no evidence, except her backpack left in the alley. Whoever snatched her did it quick and clean. Had to be a spur-of-the-moment thing.'

'How do you figure that?'

'It was a school field trip. She went to this fancy boarding school, the Bolton Academy. Thirty kids came into the city to walk the Freedom Trail. Their stop at Faneuil Hall was a last-minute decision. I'm thinking the perp spotted Charlotte and just moved in.' He shook his head. 'Considering Patrick Dion's net worth, I expected there'd be a ransom demand. But it never came. Charlotte just dropped off the face of the earth.'

'Her mother was killed just a few weeks before that.'

'Rotten luck in that family. Money can't stop the Grim Reaper.'

'You think that's all it was? Rotten luck?'

'Lou Ingersoll and I talked and talked about it. We couldn't see a way to tie the two events together, and we looked at it every which way.'

'Nothing? Even though Arthur ran off with Patrick's wife?'

He laughed. 'Can you figure? They started off two happy families. Patrick, Dina and Charlotte. Arthur, Barbara and their son, Mark. Both kids attended that snooty Bolton Academy, which is how the families met. They started having dinners together. Then Arthur hooks up with Patrick's wife, and everyone gets divorced. Arthur marries Dina, Patrick gets custody of Charlotte, and they all go on being friends. It's unnatural, I tell ya.'

He set down his glass. 'The normal thing would've been to hate each other.'

'Are you sure they didn't?'

'I guess it's possible they hid it. It's possible that five years after their divorce, Patrick Dion stalked his ex-wife and her husband to that restaurant and shot them in a fit of rage. But Mark swore to me that everyone was friendly. And he lost his own father in that shooting.'

'What about Mark's mother?'

'I never got a chance to talk with Barbara Mallory. She had a stroke a year before the shooting. The day Charlotte vanished, Barbara was in a rehab hospital. She died a month later. Yet another bad-luck family.' He set down his glass. 'So that's the story in a nutshell. Charlotte Dion was seventeen, blonde and gorgeous. She had everything going for her, then—poof. She's snatched off a street. We just haven't found her remains yet.'

'You have any thoughts about the other girl who vanished? Laura Fang?'

'She was a different case. It happened right after school got out and she was walking home. One of her schoolmates saw Laura voluntarily climb into someone's car. But no one got a licence plate and the girl was never seen again. Does that help any?'

'I don't know. Right now, it's just one piece of a very confusing puzzle.' Her cellphone rang.

'I see you're a girl in demand. Lucky you.'

'Depends who's calling.' She answered her phone. 'Detective Rizzoli.'

It was a man's voice. 'I believe you're Detective Tam's supervisor?'

'Yes, we work together.'

'I'm calling on behalf of all the victims' families. Detective Tam has managed to upset everyone, especially Joey Gilmore's mother. After all these years, why are we being subjected to these questions again?'

'I'm sorry, sir,' she said. 'I didn't catch your name.'

'Patrick Dion.'

She straightened. 'Dina Mallory was your ex-wife?'

'Yes. And it's painful, being reminded of how she died.'

'I understand, Mr Dion. But Detective Tam needs to ask these questions.'

'Dina died nineteen years ago. There was never any doubt about who killed her. Why is this coming up again? Mark Mallory is livid and it's got both Mary Gilmore and her daughter upset. First we get those notes in the mail and then Detective Tam starts calling us.'

'Excuse me,' she cut in. 'What's this about getting notes?'

'It's been going on for six, seven years. Every March 30th they show up in our mailboxes, like some grim anniversary reminder.'

'What's in these notes?'

'I always get a copy of Dina's obituary. On the back, someone writes: "Don't you want to know the truth?"'

'Do you still have those notes?'

'Yes, and Mary has hers.'

'Who's sending these things? Do you know?'

'I have to assume they come from the same person who took out the ad in the *Globe*. Iris Fang.'

'Why would Mrs Fang be doing this?'

There was a long pause. 'I hate to speak badly of Mrs Fang. She lost her husband so I know she's suffered, too. But I think the woman is insane.'

MAURA HAD JUST set the kitchen table for dinner when her cellphone rang. 'Dr Isles,' she answered.

'This is Detective Tam. I wondered if I could ask your opinion on an old homicide. It happened nineteen years ago in a Chinatown restaurant. It could be connected to our Jane Doe on the rooftop.'

'What do you want me to do, exactly?'

'Review the autopsy. Tell us if you agree with the conclusions.'

'I'm busy this week,' she said. 'You might try asking Dr Bristol.'

'But I'd rather have your opinion. I know you always tell it like it is, no matter what. I trust your judgment.'

That startled her, because it was not an opinion shared among Boston PD's rank-and-file these days.

'I'll be home this evening,' she said. 'You can drop off the files anytime.'

'I'M SORRY about intruding,' Tam said, when he arrived just after 9 p.m. He handed her a bundle of photocopied pages. 'That's all five autopsy reports, plus the Boston PD report.'

'Wow. It looks like you put a lot of effort into this.'

'This is my first homicide case. Freshman effort, you know?' He pulled a flash drive out of his pocket. 'I scanned the photos and X-rays. I'm sorry about dumping this on you.'

She looked at the flash drive. 'Before you leave, let me make sure these files load up on my laptop,' she said. They went into her home office and she inserted the drive. After a moment, a series of thumbnail photos appeared on the monitor. She clicked on the first, revealing a view of a woman's nude body on the autopsy table. 'Looks like this loads up fine. I can't promise when I'll review them, but it probably won't be until next week.'

'I really appreciate this, Dr Isles.'

She looked at him. 'Doctors Bristol and Costas are very good pathologists. Is there a reason you didn't go to them?'

He said, reluctantly, 'I'm guessing you know what's being said about you. Because of the Wayne Graff trial and all.'

Her mouth tightened. 'I'm sure that none of it is flattering.'

'That's why I came to you. Because I know you tell the truth.' His eyes met hers, direct and unflinching.

'What are you hoping I'll find in these reports?' she asked.

'Contradictions, maybe. Things that don't add up or don't make sense.'

'Why do you think there'd be any?'

'From the moment Detectives Staines and Ingersoll walked onto the scene, it was called a murder-suicide. I read their report and they didn't explore alternative theories. It was too easy to sign it off as a crazy Chinese immigrant shooting up a restaurant. And then himself.'

'Do you think it wasn't a murder-suicide?'

'I don't know. But nineteen years later, it's giving off some strange echoes. Our Jane Doe on the roof had two addresses in her GPS. One for Ingersoll. The other for Iris Fang, the widow of one of the massacre victims. She was obviously interested in the Red Phoenix case. We don't know why.'

'OK. I'll review the files when I have the time. I assume there's no hurry.'

'It would be nice to make some progress on Jane Doe.'

'The Red Phoenix happened nineteen years ago,' she said and turned off her laptop. 'I'm sure this can wait a little longer.'

EVEN BEFORE I see him, I know that he has entered my studio, his arrival heralded by the whoosh of damp night air. I do not interrupt my exercise. In the mirror I can see Detective Frost watching in fascination as I enact the Chant of the Sabre. Today I feel strong, my arms and legs as limber as when I was young. All the moves are second nature to me, one blending into the next. My sabre slices and whirls, but my thoughts are on the policeman, and what I will say to him. Finally I stand at attention, my weapon at rest. Only then do I turn to face him.

'That was beautiful, Mrs Fang,' says Detective Frost, his eyes wide with admiration. 'Like a dance.'

'It brings a calming end to my day.'

'Is that a real sword?'

'Her name is Zheng Yi. She was passed down to me from my great-great-grandmother.'

'So it must be really old.'

'And battle tested.' I make two lightning slashes through the air and he flinches away. I extend the handle to him. 'Take it. Feel its weight.'

Cautiously he grasps the handle and gives the sword a clumsy swing through the air. 'The balance seems strange.'

'Because it is a true Chinese sabre. This design is called a willow leaf. It was the standard sidearm for soldiers during the Ming dynasty about six hundred years ago. Zheng Yi was crafted in Gansu Province during a time of war.'

'So this sword saw actual combat?'

'I know it did. I can feel old battles still singing in her blade.'

'If I'm ever attacked in a dark alley, Mrs Fang, I want you by my side.'

'You're the one with the gun. Shouldn't you protect me?'

I can see it makes him nervous, just being in proximity to that razor-sharp edge. With a bow, I take it back and look straight at him. He flushes at my directness, a reaction I don't expect from a policeman. But there is a vulnerability in him that reminds me of my husband. In this man's face I see James's abashed smile, his innate eagerness to please.

'You had more questions to ask me, Detective?'

'Yes.' He seems reluctant to say what is on his mind. 'It's about your daughter. Laura.'

The mention of Laura's name is like a blow and I sway from the impact.

'Are you all right, Mrs Fang?' he says, reaching out to steady me. 'Do you want to sit down?'

'It's just that . . .' I give a numb shake of my head. 'I have not eaten since this morning. Perhaps we should talk another day.'

'It would only be a few questions.' He pauses. Adds, quietly: 'I haven't had dinner, either.'

For a moment his words hang in the air. He is a policeman, but I see nothing about him to be wary of. And I want desperately to know why he is asking about Laura. I slide Zheng Yi into her scabbard.

'There is a dumpling house on Beach Street.'

He smiles. 'I know the place.'

'Let me get my raincoat, and we'll walk.'

Outside, we stroll through a fine spring drizzle. I have brought along Zheng Yi because the sword is too valuable to leave behind at the studio. Detective Frost is talkative.

'This is my favourite part of Boston,' he says, throwing his arms wide, as though to embrace Chinatown. 'Sometimes I feel like I belong here. Like it's an accident I wasn't born Chinese.'

'Ah. You think you're reincarnated.'

'Yeah. As the all-American kid from South Boston.' His face gleams in the dampness. 'You said you're from Taiwan.'

'Have you ever been there?'

He gives a regretful shake of the head. 'I haven't travelled as much as I'd like. But I did go to France on my honeymoon.'

'What does your wife do?'

'She's in law school,' he says quietly. It takes him a moment before he adds, 'We separated. Last summer.'

'I'm sorry.'

'It hasn't been a good year,' he says, then seems to remember he's talking to a woman who has lost both her husband and her daughter. 'I have nothing to complain about, really.'

'I'm certain you will find someone else.'

He looks at me. 'You never remarried, Mrs Fang.'

'How can you replace the love of your life?' I say simply. 'James is my husband. He will always be my husband.'

He takes a moment to absorb that. Then he says, 'That's the way I always thought love should be.'

The dining room of the dumpling house is packed, and we are lucky to claim the last table. At the next table chopsticks clack against bowls, and a family chatters in noisy Cantonese.

Frost looks bewildered as he scans the menu. 'Maybe I should let you order for both of us.'

'Are there any foods you won't eat?'

'I'll eat everything.'

'You may be sorry you said that,' I say. 'Because we Chinese really *do* eat everything.'

He cheerfully accepts the challenge. 'Surprise me.'

When the waitress brings out an appetiser platter with cold jellyfish and pickled pig's feet, his chopsticks hesitate over the unfamiliar selection. But when he bites into a translucent chunk of pork cartilage, I watch his eyes widen with a look of delight.

'Wonderful!'

The dumplings come, soft, warm little pillows plump with pork and shrimp. I watch in amusement as he struggles to pick up the slippery morsels.

'These were my husband's favourites. He offered to work here without pay for a month, if they would just give him their recipe.'

'Was he also in the restaurant business in Taiwan?'

'My husband was a scholar of Chinese literature. He worked as a waiter here only to survive.' I look straight at him. 'It's too easy to assume that the waiter you see is just a waiter. But in Chinatown, you can't assume anything. Those shabby old men you see playing chequers under the lion gate? Some of them are millionaires. People are not what they seem in Chinatown.'

He gives a chastened nod. 'I'm sorry, Mrs Fang, if I sounded disrespectful of your husband.' His apology sounds utterly sincere.

I set down my chopsticks. 'You came to ask about my daughter.'

He folds his napkin. 'Have you ever heard the name Charlotte Dion?'

'Detective Frost,' I sigh, touching my head, 'those events are embedded here, for ever. I know Mrs Mallory had a daughter named Charlotte who disappeared a few weeks after the shooting. I know about all the victims and their families, because I'm one of them. I've never met Mr Dion, but after his daughter vanished, I wrote him a condolence card. I told him how sorry I was. I told him I understood his pain. He never wrote back.' I look up at him. 'So. I know why you're asking about Charlotte. Our families are linked by both the Red Phoenix and the loss of our daughters. You wouldn't be the first policeman to ask me about it.'

'Detective Buckholz did, I assume.'

I nod. 'When Charlotte vanished, he came to ask if the two girls might have known each other. Charlotte's father is very wealthy, so of course she received a great deal of attention. Far more attention than my Laura ever received.'

'In his report, Buckholz wrote that both Laura and Charlotte studied classical music.'

'My daughter played the violin.'

'And Charlotte played the viola in her school orchestra. Is there any chance they met? At a music workshop, maybe?'

I shake my head. 'I've already gone over this with the police, again and again. Except for music, the girls had nothing in common. Charlotte went to a private school. And we lived here, in Chinatown.'

The waitress brings the bill to our table. I reach for it, but Frost snatches it up first. 'Please,' he says. 'Let me.' He sets cash on the table. 'Let me give you a ride home.'

'I live only a few blocks from here. It's easier to walk.'

'Then I'll walk with you. Just to be on the safe side.'

It is still drizzling when we step outside. Despite the chill, I feel unexpected warmth in my cheeks. He has paid for dinner and now he insists on walking me home. It's been a long time since a man has been so solicitous.

We walk south on Tyler Street, towards the old enclave of Tai Tung Village, in a part of Chinatown where there are no tourists. The lights fade and the shadows thicken. My hand moves to the pommel of my sword, where it rests in readiness. The darkness comes alive. Everywhere there is movement. A rat skittering in the alley. The drip of water trickling from a rain gutter. The man beside me is oblivious, believing that it is his presence that keeps me safe. Never imagining that perhaps it is the other way round.

We arrive at my modest row house. I pull out my keys and he lingers, waiting until I am safely inside. I insert my key into the lock and suddenly go very still. It's my sharp intake of breath that alerts him.

'What is it?'

'It isn't locked,' I whisper. Already Zheng Yi is out of the scabbard and in my hand. The door swings open and I see only darkness beyond. I step forward, but Detective Frost pulls me back. 'Wait here,' he orders.

Weapon drawn, he steps inside and flips on the light switch.

From the doorway I watch as he moves through my modest home. As Frost heads to the kitchen, I scan the living room. My gaze halts on the empty picture frame. Someone has been here.

From the kitchen, Frost says: 'Does it look OK to you?'

I don't answer but move towards the stairs.

'Iris, wait,' he says.

Already, I'm darting up the steps. I grip my sword with both hands as I step towards my bedroom door.

I know at once that the intruder has been in this room. The air is foul with the smell. I hear Detective Frost running up the stairs. He defends my back, but it's what waits ahead that terrifies me.

I step across the threshold just as Frost turns on the light. The room comes into sudden, shocking focus. The missing photograph is on my pillow, fixed there by a knife blade. Only when I hear Frost punching numbers into his cellphone do I look at him.

'What are you doing?' I ask.

'My partner needs to know.'

'Don't call her. Please. You don't know anything about this.'

He looks at me, his gaze suddenly focused with an intensity that makes me realise I have underestimated him. 'Do you?' he says.

JANE STOOD in Iris Fang's bedroom, staring at the photograph that had been stabbed through by a butcher's knife. It was a picture of a younger Iris, her face aglow as she held an infant in her arms.

'She says the knife is from her own kitchen,' said Frost. 'And the baby is her daughter, Laura. That photo is supposed to be in a frame downstairs.'

'Stabbing a knife in her pillow sure as hell isn't wishing her sweet dreams. What is this all about?'

'She doesn't know.' He dropped his voice. 'At least, that's what she says.'

'You think she's not being straight with us?'

'I don't know. She didn't want me to call you. In fact, she asked me to forget the whole thing. That doesn't make sense to me.'

Me neither, thought Jane, frowning at the knife, which had been plunged hilt-deep, crushing the picture against the linen. It was an act of sheer rage, meant to terrify. 'Anyone else would be screaming for police protection.'

'She insists she doesn't need it. Says she's not afraid.'

'Are we sure someone else was actually in here?'

'What are you implying?'

'She could have done this herself. Taken a knife from her own kitchen.'

'That's not how it happened. I was right here when she found it.'

Jane turned to him. 'You came up to her bedroom?'

'I walked her home, that's all. We noticed her front door was open, so I came in to check the place. That's all it was!'

Then why do you look so guilty? She stared at the mutilated photo. 'So why doesn't she want us to look into it?'

'It could be just a cultural thing about the police. Tam says that folks in Chinatown are leery of us.'

'I'd be a lot more leery of whoever did this.'

Downstairs, she found Iris seated on the faded brown sofa, looking calm for a woman whose home had just been violated. Tam was pacing nearby, cellphone pressed to his ear.

Jane studied Iris for a moment without saying a word. The woman stared straight back at her. It was not the gaze of a victim.

'What do you think is going on, Mrs Fang?' Jane said.

'I don't know.'

'Has your home been broken into before?'

'No.'

'Is there anyone you know who'd do this, Mrs Fang? Maybe some man you've been dating, someone who's angry that you rejected him?'

'There is no man. And there's no need for the police to be involved.'

'Someone breaks into your home, stabs a knife through your photo and pillow. Yet you don't want us to look into it.'

The woman stared back, revealing nothing. Jane let a moment pass. She saw Tam and Frost intently following their conversation. Three sets of eyes were focused on Iris, yet the woman's composure did not crack.

Time for a new approach.

'I had an interesting conversation today with Patrick Dion, the ex-husband of one of the Red Phoenix victims. He tells me that every year in March, you mail notes to him and the other families.'

'I've sent no one any notes.'

'For the past seven years, they've been getting them on the anniversary of the Red Phoenix massacre. The families believe you're doing it. Trying to bring back the bad memories.'

'Bring *back* the memories?' Iris stiffened. 'What kind of families are these, needing to be *reminded*?' Her voice shook. 'My memories never leave me.'

'Have you received any notes?'

'No. But then, no one needs to remind me.'

'If you aren't sending them, do you know who might be?'

'Maybe it's someone who believes the truth has been suppressed.'

'Like you. We know you placed the ad in the *Globe* last month.'

'If your husband were murdered, and you knew the killer was never punished, would you do any less? No matter how many years went by?'

Jane imagined herself waking up every morning in this shabby home, imagined living with unspeakable grief, obsessing over happiness lost.

'It's been nineteen years, Mrs Fang,' said Jane. 'I understand it's not easy to move on. But the other families want to. Patrick Dion, Mark Mallory— they have no doubt that Wu Weimin was the killer. Maybe it's time for you to accept what they accepted long ago.'

'I won't accept anything less than the truth.' Iris's eyes were as hard as flint. 'This is my final chance to make things right.'

Jane frowned at her. 'What do you mean, your final chance?'

The look Iris gave Jane was both dignified and calm. 'I am sick. I have a chronic form of leukaemia. One day, this illness will probably kill me, but I'm not afraid. I merely refuse to die without seeing justice done.' She paused. 'I feel time running through my fingers.'

Frost moved behind Iris and placed his hand on her shoulder. It was simply a gesture of sympathy, something anyone might do, but Jane was troubled by that touch.

'She can't stay here alone tonight,' Frost said. 'It's not safe.'

Tam said, 'I just got off the phone with Bella Li. Mrs Fang can spend the night with her while the CSU processes the scene.'

Frost said, 'I'll drive her there.'

'No,' Jane said. 'Tam will take her. Detective Frost, can you step outside with me?'

The instant the door swung shut, she said, 'What's going on?'

'Obviously someone's trying to scare her.'

'I'm talking about *you*. How come you went out to dinner with a suspect?'

'She's not a suspect.'

'We don't know that.'

'For God's sake, Rizzoli, she's a victim. She lost her husband in a shooting and now all she wants is justice.'

'We don't know what she really wants. Frankly, I can't figure out what you want, either.'

'I feel sorry for her,' he said. 'And I just wish . . . It's been nineteen years since her husband died, and she still loves him. Alice couldn't even make it ten years before she walked out on me. I think, Why the hell didn't I marry someone like her?'

'The woman's almost old enough to be your mother.'

'That's not what I'm saying. I'm not talking about going out with her. This is about loyalty. About loving someone your whole life, no matter what happens.' He turned away and said softly, 'I'm never going to know what that's like.'

They both turned as Tam escorted Iris out of the building. Iris gave a nod to Frost, then climbed into Tam's car. Even as the taillights faded into the mist, Frost was still staring after her.

'I have to admit,' said Jane thoughtfully, 'she's got me wondering now.'

Frost turned to her. 'About what?'

'She's obviously rattled someone. Someone who's angry enough or feels threatened enough to break into her house. To stab a knife in her pillow.'

'What if she's right about the massacre? And the cook didn't do it?'

Jane nodded. 'I think we're going to have to take a closer look at the Red Phoenix restaurant. But first we've got to do something else.'

PATRICK DION'S PROPERTY was a private Eden of woods and lawn. As Jane and Frost drove through the wrought-iron gate, they glimpsed the residence, a massive Colonial set on a knoll, commanding a view of Dion's expansive estate.

Jane pulled to a stop in the driveway, where two cars were parked. 'We've got to do some damage control in there. From what Mr Dion said, Tam didn't exactly charm them.'

Frost shook his head. 'That boy goes at everything full-throttle.'

'He says he wants to make homicide before he's thirty.' She pushed open her door.

They climbed granite steps and the front door swung open. A silver-haired man in his late sixties stood before them. Though he was still fit, there was a gauntness to his face.

'I saw your car coming up the driveway,' he said. 'I'm Patrick Dion.'

'Detective Rizzoli,' she said. 'And this is my partner, Detective Frost.' They shook hands and Patrick's grip was firm, his gaze steady.

'Come in, please. Mark Mallory's here and I invited Mary Gilmore to join us as well. A united front, because we're all upset about this.'

Patrick led them straight into the front parlour, where the other two visitors were already waiting. Mark Mallory rose with athletic grace from the sofa. He was fit and tan. His handshake was perfunctory, a clue that he was impatient to get on with the business at hand. The third person in the room would have been easy to overlook, had Jane not already been alerted. Mary Gilmore was so tiny and hunched over that she was almost invisible, swallowed up in a huge armchair. As the woman struggled to stand, Frost quickly moved to her side.

'You just sit right back down, Mrs Gilmore,' Frost urged.

'My daughter wanted to be here,' said Mrs Gilmore. 'But she couldn't get off work, so I brought the note she got.' She pointed an arthritic hand at the coffee table. 'It came in the mail the same day as mine. Every year they arrive on March 30th, the day my Joey died. It's emotional harassment. Can't the police do something to stop her?'

On the coffee table were three envelopes. Before touching them, Jane reached into her pocket and took out a pair of gloves.

'There's no point with gloves,' said Mark. 'There are never any fingerprints on the letters or the envelopes.'

'How do you know there aren't any prints?'

'Detective Ingersoll had them analysed in the crime lab.'

'He knows about these?'

'He gets them too. So does anyone connected with the victims: up to a dozen people that we know about. It's been going on for years. She must wear gloves when she sends them.'

'Mrs Fang denies sending any notes.'

Mark snorted. 'Who else would do it? She's the one who ran that ad in the *Globe*. She's obsessed by this.'

Jane picked up the envelope addressed to Mrs Mary Gilmore. It had a Boston postmark. She slid out the contents: a photocopied obituary of Joseph S. Gilmore, age twenty-five. 'Survived by his mother, Mary, and his sister, Phoebe Morrison.' Jane flipped over the mailing and saw a single sentence written in block letters: *I KNOW WHAT REALLY HAPPENED.*

'It's the same note I got,' said Mark. 'Except I get my father's obituary.'

'And I get Dina's,' said Patrick quietly.

Jane picked up the envelope addressed to Patrick Dion. Inside was the photocopied obituary of Dina Mallory. 'Survived by a daughter from a previous marriage, Charlotte Dion.' On the reverse side was written the same sentence: *I KNOW WHAT REALLY HAPPENED.*

'Detective Ingersoll told us the envelope's a standard brand,' said Mark. 'The ink's the same as you'd find in any Bic pen and the stamps and envelopes are self-adhesive, so there's no DNA. The handwriting is always the same block letters. The same black ink.'

'But the note's different this year,' said Mrs Gilmore. 'All the other years, the notes said, "Don't you want to know the truth?" This year it says, "I know what really happened."'

'It's basically the same bullshit,' said Mark.

'No, the meaning is different.' Mrs Gilmore looked at Jane. 'If she knows something, why doesn't she just tell us what the truth is?'

'We all know what the truth is, Mrs Gilmore,' Patrick said patiently. 'I have complete faith that Boston PD knew what it was doing when they closed the case.'

'But what if they were wrong?'

'Mrs Gilmore,' Mark said, 'these notes have only one purpose: to make us pay attention to that woman. Patrick, tell them what you found out about Mrs Fang.'

Patrick looked down at his hands. 'Detective Ingersoll told me that Mrs Fang suffers from, well, delusions of grandeur. She believes she's descended from an ancient line of warriors. That it's her sacred mission in life to track down her husband's killer and exact vengeance.'

'Can you believe it?' Mark laughed. 'It's like something out of a Chinese soap opera. The woman is completely nuts.'

'She is a martial arts master,' said Frost. 'Her students certainly believe in her, and you'd think they'd recognise a fraud.'

'We're not saying she's a fraud,' said Patrick, 'but her claims must strike you as being a little absurd. I think Mrs Fang was deeply traumatised by her husband's death. And her way of coping with grief is to search for something that gives his death significance. She needs to prove that something bigger killed her husband, and she'll never stop searching because it's the one thing that gives her life purpose.' Sadly, he looked round the room at Mark, at Mary Gilmore. 'But we know that it was just a senseless crime committed by an unstable man. We accept it, but she can't.'

'So we have to put up with that harassment,' said Mark, pointing to the mailings on the coffee table. 'And we can't get her to stop sending them.'

'But there's no proof she's sending them,' said Frost.

'Well, we know she's the one behind this,' said Mark, and he pulled from his pocket a clipping from the *Boston Globe*. Under the word 'INNOCENT' was a photo of Wu Weimin. Beneath the photo was the date of the massacre, and a single sentence: 'THE TRUTH HAS NEVER BEEN TOLD'.

'Now she's got the whole city paying attention to her delusions,' said Mark. 'Where does this stop?'

'Have any of you spoken to Mrs Fang about this?' Jane asked.

Mark snorted. 'I, for one, wouldn't waste my time.'

'Then you haven't tried to confront her?'

'Why are you asking me?'

'You seem the angriest about this, Mr Mallory,' she observed.

'Look, we're all upset,' said Patrick. 'But we know that it would be unwise to establish any contact with the woman. I called Detective Ingersoll thinking he might intervene. But he hasn't returned my call.'

'He's out of town this week,' said Jane. She slipped the mailings into evidence bags. 'We'll speak to him when he returns. In the meantime, please let me know if you receive anything else like this.'

Patrick walked them to the door, reluctant to see them go.

'Please call me anytime,' he said, as they shook hands. 'About this matter, or . . .' He paused, and a shadow seemed to pass over his eyes. 'Anything else.'

'We're sorry this had to come up again, Mr Dion,' said Jane. 'I can see it's hard for you.'

He shrugged. 'Especially since it's so closely connected to the . . . other event.' His shoulders drooped. 'I assume you know about my daughter.'

Jane nodded. 'I spoke to Detective Buckholz about Charlotte.'

Just the mention of his daughter's name made his face contract in pain. 'Dina's death was difficult. But nothing compares to losing a child. These mailings, and that ad in the paper, they bring it all back. That's what really hurts, Detective. That's why I want this stopped.'

'I'll do what I can, Mr Dion.'

Although they had already shaken hands, he grasped hers once again, a farewell that left her depressed and silent as she and Frost walked back to her car. She stared across the lawn. *He owns all this, yet he has nothing*, she thought. The ghost of his daughter still haunted him. Having a child meant your heart was always at the world's mercy.

'Detectives?'

Jane turned to see Mrs Gilmore coming down the porch steps. She walked towards them with grim determination.

'I know Patrick and Mark are convinced that there's no question about what happened in the restaurant. But what if they're wrong?'

'So you do have doubts,' said Jane.

The woman's mouth tightened into hard lines. 'I'll admit this. My son wasn't a saint. You probably know that Joey got into trouble.'

'I know he was working for Kevin Donohue.'

At the mention of that name, Mrs Gilmore spat out: 'Piece of crap! The whole Donohue clan is. But my Joey liked easy money. By the time he realised what was involved, he couldn't get out. Donohue wouldn't let him.'

'You think he had your son killed?'

'It's what I've wondered from the start.'

'There was no evidence for it, Mrs Gilmore.'

'You think Donohue couldn't buy off a few cops?'

'That's a serious charge.'

'I know what goes on in this town, and I know what money can buy.' Her eyes fixed on Jane. 'I'm sure you do, too, Detective.'

The implied charge made Jane stiffen. 'I'll give your concerns the attention they deserve, Mrs Gilmore,' she said evenly and slid into her car.

As she and Frost drove away, she saw the woman glaring after them.

'That,' muttered Jane, 'is not a nice old lady.'

Frost gave a disbelieving laugh. 'Did she just accuse us of taking bribes? And she looked so sweet.'

'To you, they're all sweet.'

Frost's cellphone rang. As he answered it, she thought about how easily Frost charmed the older ladies. He had certainly made inroads with Iris Fang. She remembered what Patrick had said about her. Iris might be delusional, but someone real had broken into her residence and stabbed a knife into her pillow. *Whose cage did you rattle, Iris?*

Frost sighed as he hung up the cellphone. 'Guess our day's not over yet.'

'Who was that?'

'The realtor for the Knapp Street building. He says if we want to see the place, he'll meet us in an hour.'

JANE AND FROST stood outside what had once been the Red Phoenix restaurant and tried to peer inside. Beyond the barred windows, Jane saw only thin curtains translucent with age.

Frost looked at his watch. 'Mr Kwan's now fifteen minutes late. I don't think he has a cell. I played phone tag with him all day through his office.'

'A realtor who doesn't have a cellphone?'

'I just hope we understood each other.'

'We could really use Tam. Where is he?'

'He said he'd be here.'

Jane peered at the rusting fire escape, gate and boarded-up windows. 'Looks like it's been abandoned a long time. Centre of town; you'd think it'd be prime real estate.'

'Except for the fact it's a crime scene. Tam says that in this neighbourhood, a haunted building's bad luck.' He paused, staring up the alley. 'I wonder if that's our man coming?'

The elderly Chinese man walked with a limp but moved with surprising alacrity as he negotiated his way along the uneven pavement.

'Hello, hello. You Detective Frost?'

'Yes, sir. And this is my partner, Detective Rizzoli.'

The man smiled, revealing two bright gold teeth. 'I tell you now, I always follow the law, OK? OK? Everything always legal.'

'Sir, that's not why I called you.'

'Very good location here, Knapp Street. Very good price.'

'Then why hasn't it sold?' asked Jane.

His wrinkles deepened into a scowl. 'Bad thing happen here,' he finally admitted. 'No one wants to rent or buy.'

Kwan pulled out an enormous set of keys and the gate swung open with a deafening screech. They all stepped into what had once been the Red Phoenix restaurant. Mr Kwan flipped the light switch, and a single bulb came on overhead.

Jane moved to the centre of the gloomy space and looked round the empty room. Only the built-in cashier counter offered any hint that this had once been a restaurant dining room.

Mr Kwan shook his head. 'Chinese people too superstitious. They don't even like to come inside.'

I don't blame them, thought Jane. Violence leaves a mark, a psychic stain that can never be scrubbed away. In a neighbourhood as insular as Chinatown, everyone would remember what had happened in this building.

Jane looked down at the linoleum, the same floor where blood had flowed. Although the walls were repainted and the bullet holes plastered over, in the seams of this floor, chemical traces of that blood still lingered. A crime scene photo suddenly clicked into her head: an image of a crumpled body lying amid fallen take-out cartons.

Here is the spot where Joey Gilmore died.

She looked across the cashier counter, and the memory of another photo superimposed itself on that patch of floor: the body of James Fang crumpled behind the register.

She stared at the corner where Dina and Arthur Mallory had sat, sipping tea. That image was replaced by the police photos of Arthur Mallory slumped forward over the spilled teacups. And, a few feet away, his wife lying face-down on the floor. Standing in this vacant room, Jane could hear the echo of gunshots.

She turned towards the kitchen, where the cook had died. She did not want to step through that doorway. Frost, who walked in first, flipped the light switch. Again, only a single bulb came on. She followed him, and in the dim glow she saw the blackened stove, a refrigerator and stainless-steel countertops. The concrete floor was pockmarked with wear.

She moved to the cellar door. Here, with his body blocking that door, was where Wu Weimin, the cook, had drawn his final breath. She remembered how eerily intact his face had been, except for the lone bullet hole punched into his temple. That bullet had not killed him immediately. They knew this because of how copiously he had bled during his final moments while his heart continued to pump, spilling a waterfall of blood down the cellar steps. She opened the door and peered down a wooden stairway that descended into darkness.

Frost crossed the kitchen and unbolted another door. 'The alley's here. Report said this is how the cook's wife walked in. She heard a gunshot, came down to check on her husband, and found him dead in the kitchen.'

'So, if that door was unlocked, any intruder could have come in that way,' said Jane.

Kwan seemed confused. 'What intruder? Cook, he kill himself.'

'We're re-examining the incident, Mr Kwan,' said Frost.

The realtor shook his head in dismay. 'That was very bad thing for Chinatown,' he muttered. 'Better to forget about it.'

Jane glanced up towards the first floor. 'Wu Weimin and his family lived on the first floor. Could you take us up to their apartment?'

Kwan sighed deeply, as though they were asking him for a favour beyond all human measure, and led them out of the kitchen exit, into the back alley. The door to the upstairs apartments was secured behind another steel gate.

Inside was blackness. The stairwell light had burned out, so Jane turned on her flashlight. The darkness seemed to magnify the sound of their shoes on the steps. At the top of the flight, she paused outside the door to the first-floor apartment. It was unlocked, yet she did not want to see what lurked beyond. Only when she heard Mr Kwan reach the top step, wheezing right behind her, did she finally push open the door.

She and Frost stepped into what had once been the home of Wu Weimin. The windows were boarded shut and her flashlight seemed a feeble weapon to cut through the darkness. Although the apartment had been vacant for years, she could still smell the scents left by those who had once lived there. The ghostly fragrance of incense and oranges still lingered, trapped in the darkness. She crossed to a doorway at the far end of the room, and when she walked through it, the scent of incense seemed stronger.

A face stared back at her. She jerked backwards, colliding with Frost.

'What?' he said.

All she could do was shine her light at the framed portrait hanging on the wall. Beneath was a low table where she saw the remains of joss sticks. On a porcelain plate were five oranges.

'It's a photo of the cook,' Frost murmured.

As she stared at the face, Jane realised the man in the photo was indeed Wu Weimin, but this was no homicidal maniac. He was laughing as he clutched a fishing pole. A happy man on a happy day.

'This looks like some kind of shrine to his memory,' said Frost.

Jane turned to Mr Kwan. 'Who else has a key to this building?'

'No one,' he said, rattling his jailer's ring. 'I have the only key.'

'But these oranges are fresh. Someone's been in here recently.'

'These keys always with me,' he insisted.

'The gate downstairs has a dead bolt,' said Frost.

'Then how could anyone . . .' She turned towards the doorway.

Footsteps were thumping up the stairs.

In an instant her weapon was drawn. Pushing aside Mr Kwan, she slipped out of the room, Frost behind her, and eased her way across the living room, her heart banging. She focused on the stairwell door, a black portal to something that suddenly took on the shape of a man.

'Freeze!' Frost commanded. 'Boston PD!'

'Whoa, Frost.' Johnny Tam gave a startled laugh. 'It's just me.'

'What the hell, Tam,' said Frost, as he and Jane holstered their weapons. 'I could have blown your head off.'

'I would've gotten here sooner, but I got stuck in traffic coming back from Springfield.'

'You talk to the owner of that Honda?'

'Yeah. Said it was stolen right out of his driveway. And that wasn't his GPS in the car. So what's going on in here?'

'This is Wu Weimin's apartment.'

'Someone's been visiting,' said Jane, turning back towards the room that contained the shrine. 'And they left behind . . .' She halted, her beam frozen on a blank wall.

I must be looking at the wrong spot, she thought. She swept the beam all round the room until she flashed on the little table with the joss sticks and oranges. Above it, the wall was empty.

'What the hell?' Frost whispered.

As she slid out her weapon again, she whispered: 'Tam, take Mr Kwan into the stairwell and stay with him. Frost, you're with me.'

'What's going on?' protested Mr Kwan.

'Doorway there,' she murmured, her light shining on a black rectangle.

Together she and Frost inched towards it. Her breath was a roar in her ears, every sense sharpened. The weight of the gun, heavy and reassuring. *On the rooftop, Jane Doe had a gun, too, and it didn't save her.* She thought of blades slicing through neck and windpipe, and dreaded stepping through that doorway and confronting what waited on the other side.

One, two, three. Do it. She was first through, dropping to a crouch as she swung the light round and glimpsed a porcelain toilet, a rust-stained bathtub. No bogeyman with a blade.

Another doorway.

Frost took the lead this time, slipping through into a bedroom where wallpaper hung peeling, like a room shedding its skin.

Through one more doorway, and they were back in the living room. Jane walked out into the stairwell, where Tam and Mr Kwan stood waiting.

'Nothing?' said Tam.

'That photo didn't walk off on its own.'

'We were right here in the stairwell the whole time. No one came by us.'

Jane reholstered her gun. 'Then how the hell . . .'

'Rizzoli!' called out Frost. 'Look at this!'

They found him by a boarded-over window in the room. When Frost nudged the board, it swivelled aside.

'Fire escape's here,' said Frost. He poked out his head and craned to look up towards the roof. 'Hey, something's moving up there!'

'Go, go!' said Jane.

Frost scrambled over the sill and clanged onto the landing. Tam exited right after him, moving with an acrobat's grace. Last out of the window was Jane and, as she dropped onto the metal grate of the landing, she caught a glimpse of the street below. A bad drop, any way you looked at it. She forced herself to focus on the ladder above, where Frost was clanging up the rungs. She scrambled up right behind Tam, the breeze chilling the sweat on her face. She heard Frost grunt, saw his silhouette against the night sky as he pulled himself onto the rooftop. The fire escape shuddered, and for a panic-stricken moment she thought the brackets might give way.

A shriek above her made every hair stand up on the back of her neck. Frost. She looked up, expecting to see his body hurtling towards her, but all she glimpsed was Tam as he vanished onto the rooftop. She clambered after him and crawled onto the roof. Spotted Tam crouched a few feet away. *Where is Frost?*

She jumped to her feet. Glimpsed a shadow flitting away. Under the night sky, Jane saw empty rooftops, jutting chimneys and ventilation shafts. But no Frost.

'Frost? Frost?' Tam yelled as he circled the roof.

Jane pulled out her cellphone. 'This is Detective Rizzoli. Beach and Knapp Street. Officer down—'

'He's here!' Tam yelled. 'Help me pull him up!'

She spun round and saw Tam kneeling at the roof's edge. She ran to his side. Saw Frost clinging with both hands to the rain gutter, his feet dangling above a three-storey plummet. Tam dropped to his belly and reached down to grab Frost's left wrist. The roof sloped and a misstep could send them both sliding off the edge. Jane grabbed Frost's right wrist. Together they pulled, straining to drag him up. With a loud grunt, Frost flopped onto the roof beside them, where he sprawled, gasping.

'Jesus,' he whispered. 'Thought I was dead!'

'What the hell? Did you trip and fall?' asked Jane.

'I was chasing it but, I swear, it flew over the roof like a bat out of hell.'

'What are you talking about?'

Frost sat up, and even in the darkness Jane could see he was pale and shaking. 'It was standing where you are now. Turned and looked straight at me. I jumped back and lost my footing.'

'It?' said Jane. 'Are we talking about a man or what?'

'I don't know.'

'How can you not know?'

Slowly, Frost rose to his feet and stood facing the direction that the thing had fled. 'It moved too fast to be a man. I know it sounds crazy, but there was something here. You've got to believe me!'

'OK,' Jane said, clapping him on the shoulder. 'I believe you.'

They saw Tam's shoulders lift in a shrug. 'Maybe there's more to that ghost tour than we thought.'

'It was no ghost,' said Frost. 'It was real.'

'No one saw it but you,' said Tam.

Frost stared down at the street below. 'That may not be entirely true.' He pointed towards the corner.

A surveillance camera.

EVEN AT 9.30 P.M., the employees of Dedham Security were on the job, monitoring properties all over the Greater Boston area.

'Bad guys usually get to work after dark,' said Gus Gilliam of Dedham Security as he walked the detectives past a bank of surveillance monitors.

'So we have to stay awake too. And *our* cameras are actually operational; some are just dummies.'

Tam surveyed the monitors. 'Wow. You have eyes all over the city.'

'We're lucky that camera on Knapp Street is real,' said Jane.

'Yeah.' He led them into a back room, where four chairs were set up round a monitor. 'That particular camera was installed about five years ago. You said you were interested in a first-floor fire escape landing?'

'I'm hoping it's in your camera's field of view,' said Jane.

'Let's take a look.'

Gilliam clicked the Play icon, and a live view of Knapp Street appeared.

'Look,' said Frost. 'You can just see a corner of the fire escape.'

'Unfortunately, not the window itself,' said Jane.

'It might be enough.' Frost leaned in closer to read the date and time on the recording. 'Go back around two hours. Seven thirty.'

Gilliam rewound to 7:30. At 7:50, Johnny Tam appeared outside the Red Phoenix. He vanished through the front door.

At 8:06, something jerked into view on the fire escape. It was Frost, having tumbled out of the window. He climbed out of view.

'What the hell?' Frost murmured. 'Nothing came out ahead of me. I know I chased something up that ladder.'

'It doesn't show up,' said Jane.

'And there's you, Rizzoli. How come Tam doesn't show up, either?'

Tam snorted. 'Maybe I'm a ghost.'

'Your problem is the field of view,' said Gilliam. 'We're catching just a corner of the fire escape, so the camera misses anyone who makes a more, er, graceful entry and exit.'

'In other words, Frost and I make lousy cat burglars,' said Jane. She sighed. 'So we caught nothing on this camera.'

'Assuming this was the only time the intruder entered.'

Jane knew someone was regularly visiting that apartment, leaving offerings in memory of Wu Weimin. 'Go back two nights ago and move forward.'

Gilliam nodded. 'Worth a look.'

On the monitor, time wound back to forty-eight hours earlier. As the video once again advanced to 10 p.m., then to midnight, pedestrians walked past. By 2 a.m., Knapp Street was deserted, and they watched an unchanging view of pavement.

At 3:02, Jane saw it: just the twitch of a shadow on the fire escape landing. 'Go back!' she snapped.

Gilliam reversed the video and froze the image.

'It could be a cat casting that shadow,' said Tam.

'Let's see what happens next,' said Gilliam, and advanced the video. Seconds later Jane gave a gasp. 'There.'

Gilliam froze on a crouching shadow on the fire escape and stared intently at the screen. 'What the hell is that?'

'I told you I saw something,' said Frost. 'That's it.'

'I don't even know what we're looking at,' said Tam. 'You can't see a face; you can't even be sure it's a man.'

'But it's bipedal,' said Frost. 'Look how it's down on its haunches.'

Jane's cellphone rang, the sound so startling she had to steady her voice before she answered. 'Detective Rizzoli.'

'I'm returning your call,' a man said. 'This is Lou Ingersoll.'

She sat up straight in her chair. 'Detective Ingersoll, we need to talk to you about a homicide in Chinatown. Happened last Wednesday night.'

'You do know that I've been retired from Boston PD for sixteen years?'

'We think this death could be connected to the Red Phoenix massacre.'

There was a long silence. 'I don't want to talk about this on the phone.'

'How about in person, sir?'

She heard his footsteps moving across the floor. Heard his laboured breaths. 'Okay, I think that vehicle's gone now. Wish I'd gotten the goddamn licence plate.'

'What vehicle?'

'The van that's been parked across the street ever since I got home. Probably the same son of a bitch who broke in while I was up north.'

'What, exactly, is going on?'

'Come over now, and I'll give you my theory.'

'We're in Dedham. It'll take us a half hour, maybe more. You sure we can't talk about it now?'

She heard his footsteps moving again. 'I don't want to say anything over the phone. I don't know who's listening, and I promised I'd keep her out of this. So I'll just wait till you get here.'

'What is this all about?'

'Girls, Detective,' he said. 'It's all about what happened to those girls.'

'AT LEAST NOW you believe me,' Frost said, as he and Jane drove towards Boston. 'Now that you've seen it for yourself.'

'We don't know what we saw on that video,' she said. 'What do you think it was?'

Frost stared out of the window. 'You know, Rizzoli, there's a lot of things in this world we don't understand.' He paused. 'I used to date a Chinese girl back in high school. She was really sweet.'

'Maybe you should've married her instead of Alice.'

'Wouldn't have worked: her family was dead-set against any white boy. But her great-grandmother was OK with me.'

'Geez, Frost, is there an old lady alive who doesn't like you?'

'I liked listening to her stories. She said that ghosts are everywhere in China. Old Mrs Chang told me stuff that sounded crazy, but she believed it. About holy men who walked on water. Fighting monks who could fly through the air and make themselves invisible.'

'Sounds like she watched too many kung fu movies.'

'But legends must be based on something, don't you think? Maybe our Western minds are too closed to accept what we can't understand. Don't you feel that in Chinatown? China's been a civilisation for five thousand years. They must know things. Secrets they'll never tell us.'

Jane could see Tam's car right behind theirs. She wondered whether he'd be offended by this talk of the exotic and mysterious Chinese.

'I wouldn't mention this to Tam.'

Frost shook his head. 'But I'm just trying to open my mind to what we're not seeing.'

'What I'm not seeing is how this all fits together. A dead woman on the roof. An old murder-suicide. And now Ingersoll, muttering about a van watching his house. And something about girls.'

'Why wouldn't he tell you over the phone?'

'He wouldn't say.'

'Whenever someone starts talking about their phone being bugged, those psycho warning bells go off for me. Did he sound paranoid?'

'He sounded worried. And he said he'd promised to keep "her" out of it.'

'Iris Fang?'

'I don't know.'

Frost looked ahead at the road. 'Old cop like him, he's probably gonna be armed. We'd better take this nice and slow. Don't spook him.'

Fifteen minutes later, Jane pulled up in front of Ingersoll's residence, and Tam parked behind them. Inside the triple-decker town house, the lights were on, but when Frost rang the bell no one answered.

'I'll call him,' said Jane, tapping in Ingersoll's number on her phone. They could hear his phone ringing, then the answering machine picked up.

Jane said to Frost, 'You keep trying the bell. Tam, let's go round to the back. Maybe he can't hear us.'

The narrow path between buildings was unlit and overgrown with shrubbery. Through a window, she glimpsed the blue glow of Ingersoll's TV set. On the coffee table was a cellphone and a half-eaten sandwich.

'This window isn't latched,' said Tam. 'I can climb in. You want me to?'

They looked at each other in the shadows, both of them considering the consequences of entering a house without permission or a warrant.

'He did invite us,' she said. 'Maybe he's just in the john.'

Tam slid open the window. In seconds he was up and over the sill, without a sound. The man really would make a superb cat burglar.

'Detective Ingersoll?' Tam called out as he walked into the next room. 'It's Boston PD. Are you here?'

Jane considered huffing and flailing her way through the window as well, then decided that by the time she could finally scale the sill, Tam would have the front door unlocked.

'Rizzoli, he's in here! He's down!'

Jane grasped the sill and was about to launch herself through the window when she heard bushes rustle and footsteps thud in the darkness.

Back of the house. Suspect in flight.

She took off in pursuit and reached the rear of the building just in time to see a dark figure scramble over the fence and drop to the other side.

'Frost! I need back-up!' she screamed, sprinting to the fence. Sheer adrenaline sent her up and over it. Her quarry was in view. A man.

She heard someone scrabble over the fence behind her but didn't glance back to see if it was Frost or Tam. She stayed focused on the figure. She was gaining on him, close enough to see that he was all in black. Definitely dressed for crime. But not fast enough to outrun this cop. Already she was within a few dozen yards of him.

'Police!' she yelled. 'Freeze!'

He darted right, slipping between buildings.

That pissed her off. She sprinted round the corner and found herself in a dark alley. Her footsteps echoed back as she pounded ahead, then stopped.

Where is he? Where did he go?

Weapon drawn, heart hammering, she scanned the shadows. Saw trash cans, heard broken glass clatter away.

The bullet slammed into her back. The impact sent her flying and her weapon flew out of her hands. Her Kevlar vest had saved her, but she lay stunned, her gun out of reach.

Footsteps slowly approached, and she struggled to her knees. The footsteps came to a halt right behind her.

She twisted round to see the man's silhouette towering above her. Shadows hid his face, but enough light spilled into the alley from a distant streetlamp that she saw him raise his arm. Saw the faint gleam of the gun he was pointing at her head. *Gabriel*, she thought. *Regina. I never got the chance to tell you how much I love you both.*

She heard Death hiss like the wind past her ear. Something splashed her face and she blinked. When she opened her eyes again, the silhouette looming over her was toppling forwards. It landed across her legs like a felled tree. She felt liquid warmth soaking into her clothes. Recognised all too well that coppery smell.

Something now loomed where the gunman had stood. She saw no face, just a black oval and a halo of silvery hair. It said not a word but as it turned away, something flashed in its hand: a bright arc of reflected light. Then she was alone, pinned against the pavement by a man who spilled his last blood onto her clothes.

'Rizzoli? Rizzoli!'

She struggled to free herself. 'I'm here! Frost!'

The beam of a flashlight moved closer, sweeping back and forth across the alley. With a grunt of effort, Jane finally managed to shove the body away. She scrabbled backwards, and stood, shakily. The light landed squarely in her eyes, and she raised a hand against its glare.

'Jesus,' Frost cried. 'Are you—'

'I'm OK. At least, I think so.'

'All this blood . . .'

'Not mine. It's his.'

Frost aimed his flashlight at the body, and she sucked in a shocked breath. The body was lying chest-down, and the decapitated head had rolled a few feet away. The eyes stared up at them, the mouth open as though in a last gasp of surprise. Jane gaped at the cleanly severed neck. The night began to spin and she sagged against a building.

'What happened?' said Frost.

'I saw it,' she whispered. 'The thing. Your creature on the roof. It just saved my life.'

I should be dead, she thought. *I should be lying here with a bullet in my brain. Instead I'm going to go home tonight. I'm going to hug my husband and kiss my baby. And I owe this miracle to whatever it was that swooped out of the night.*

She looked at Frost. 'You must have seen it. It would have run right past you when you came into the alley.'

He shook his head. 'It's like what happened on the roof. I was the only one who saw it, and you didn't believe me.'

She focused again on the body. On the gun that was still clutched in the headless corpse's hand. 'I believe you now.'

FOUR

As Maura climbed out of her car and walked towards the barrier, the three police officers turned their backs. Only when she formally announced herself did they deign to meet her gaze.

'Is Detective Rizzoli in the residence?' she asked.

'I don't know, ma'am,' one of the patrolmen answered. 'Why don't you check inside?'

Was he being intentionally unhelpful? As she ducked under the tape, she heard them laugh and wondered if it was directed at her. Wondered if this was what she'd face at every future death scene.

The front door opened and Detective Tam stood looking at her.

'Dr Isles. Sorry to drag you out at this time of night.'

'Are both victims in the house?'

'One is in the kitchen. The second's a few blocks away, in an alley.'

'How did number two end up so far away from number one?'

'He was trying to get away from Rizzoli. She's a hard gal to shake.'

She followed Tam into the kitchen and was surprised to see the commander of Boston PD's homicide unit standing next to Barry Frost. It was rare to encounter Lieutenant Marquette at a crime scene, and his appearance told her that something was different about this homicide.

The victim, a heavyset white man in his seventies, lay on his side on the tiled floor, his face in a congealing pool of blood. The bullet wound in his left temple left little doubt about the cause of death. Maura scanned the floor for a weapon. She saw no gun. Not a suicide.

'He was a cop,' said Jane quietly.

Maura had not heard her approach. She turned and stared at Jane's blood-splattered blouse. Instead of her usual dark trouser suit, Jane was wearing baggy sweatpants: obviously an emergency change of clothes.

'My God, Jane.'

'Things got a little rough out there.'

'Are you all right?'

Jane nodded and looked down. 'I can't say the same for him.'

'Who is he?'

Lieutenant Marquette answered: 'Detective Lou Ingersoll. He retired from homicide sixteen years ago. He deserves our very best effort, Dr Isles.'

Was he implying that she would give this victim any less? She crouched down. It took her a few seconds to register the name. Lou Ingersoll.

She glanced up at Tam. 'This man worked the Red Phoenix massacre.'

'You know about him?' asked Jane.

'Detective Tam and I discussed it.'

Jane turned to Tam, 'I didn't know you had consulted her.'

Tam shrugged. 'I just wanted Dr Isles's opinion.'

'Detective Rizzoli?' One of the criminalists stood in the kitchen doorway. 'We swept the room with a radio frequency scanner, and you're right. There's definitely a signal coming from his landline.'

'A signal?' Marquette looked at Jane.

'Ingersoll thought someone was monitoring his phone calls,' said Jane. 'It wouldn't be for the usual reason. He's been widowed for eighteen years, so there's no divorce war.' She stared down at the dead man. 'This just gets weirder and weirder. He complained about a van watching his house. He said someone broke in here while he was away. To me, it sounded like crazy talk.'

'Not so crazy after all.' Marquette looked at the criminalist. 'Let's get all his phone records: cell and landline. See who he's been talking to lately.'

Maura rose to her feet. 'I understand there's a second victim.'

'The shooter,' said Jane. 'At least, the man that we assume is the shooter. I chased him a few blocks away.'

'You brought him down yourself?'

Jane drew in a deep breath. 'It's not easy to explain. I'll show you.'

They walked outside, where a crowd was gathering. Jane led Maura round the corner to a quiet side street. Although Jane walked at her usual brisk pace, the swagger was gone, and her shoulders were slumped.

'Are you really all right?' Maura asked.

'Aside from having my good suit trashed? Yeah, I'm OK.'

'You don't look OK. Jane, talk to me.'

Jane stared down the street as if afraid to look at Maura. 'I should be dead right now,' she murmured. She frowned at her hands, as if they belonged to someone else. 'Look at this. I've got the goddamn shakes.'

'You said you chased down the perp.'

'I got cocky. Followed him into an alley. I'm the one who went down.' She hugged herself, as though suddenly chilled. 'Remember how Gabriel bought me a Kevlar vest for my birthday? How you and I laughed: so romantic, what every gal wants. Just to keep the peace, I put it on occasionally.' She swiped a sleeve across her face.

'Jane, you need to go home. Right now.'

'In the middle of this?'

'You're barely holding it together. Your team can process the scene.'

'With Marquette here? Seeing that I can't handle a little thing like being shot in the back? Fuck that.' Jane turned and walked away.

They came to a barrier of crime scene tape, where a patrolman guarded the entrance to an alley.

'And here's bachelor number two,' announced Jane, aiming her flashlight. The flippant remark left Maura unprepared for the horror at their feet.

The head, wearing a dark knit cap, had come to rest a few feet away from the torso—a white male, perhaps forty. The body, garbed entirely in black, lay chest-down; the hand still clutched a gun.

'Meet the asshole who ruined my favourite suit,' said Jane. 'I followed him from Ingersoll's back yard. He got off one round and hit me in the back. Still hurts like hell.'

'Then how did he end up . . .'

'A third party stepped in. I was here on the ground, and this guy was about to pump a bullet in my head. I thought I was dead. Then I heard a sound, this whoosh in the air. He just collapsed on top of me.'

'Did you see who did this?'

'Just a shadow. Silver hair.'

'That's all?'

Jane hesitated. 'A sword. I think he had a sword.'

Maura remembered the amputated wrist of Jane Doe: joints and tendons so cleanly divided. Her gaze sharpened on the gun in the dead man's grasp. 'This gun has a silencer.'

'Yeah. He's dressed in black and carrying a hit-man's special. Just like Jane Doe, the woman on the rooftop.'

'This is not any run-of-the-mill burglar.' Maura looked up. 'Why was Ingersoll's phone bugged?'

'He never got the chance to tell me, but he was worried and wanted to talk. Something about girls. "What happened to those girls", he said.'

'Which girls?'

'I think it's connected to the Red Phoenix. Did you know that two of the victims had their daughters go missing?'

Maura heard voices and the slam of vehicle doors. She looked up the alley and saw the approaching flashlights of the CSU team. 'I'll do the autopsies first thing in the morning. If you want to be there.'

'You're going to do both of them? Is that a good idea? Ingersoll was a cop.'

Maura heard the discomfort in Jane's voice and knew the reason for it. 'Am I no longer allowed to autopsy cops?'

'I'm not saying that.'

'Trust me, you don't have to. I'm fully aware of what's being said about me and the Graff trial. I'm aware of it every time a cop looks at me, or refuses to look at me. They consider me the enemy.'

'It'll pass, Maura. It just takes time.'

Until I testify against the next cop. 'I'll ask Dr Bristol to do the post-mortem on Ingersoll,' she said and walked away.

JANE STOOD before the viewing box, studying the dead man's X-rays. His cranium had been separated from his body, severed cleanly between the third and fourth cervical vertebrae. Although Tam and Frost were already standing at the autopsy table, waiting for the post-mortem to begin, Jane stayed rooted where she was, not yet ready to face what was lying beneath the drape. *If not for my nameless saviour*, she thought, *my X-rays would be hanging here.*

'It's hard to imagine a blade sharp enough to do this with one stroke,' she said, her gaze still on the X-ray.

'It's a matter of anatomy: the angle at which the blade hits the joint,' said Maura. 'In medieval times, a skilled executioner could behead a prisoner with one stroke.'

Maura whisked off the drape and Jane sucked in a sharp breath at the sight of the severed head. She knew nothing about this man. The only clues they had so far came from the items removed from his pockets: an ammunition clip, a roll of cash, and keys to a stolen Ford van, parked two blocks from Ingersoll's residence. He carried no ID.

His face was unremarkable; a man you'd forget the moment you'd passed him on the street. The hands had already been swabbed and his fingerprints collected the night before upon arrival. The body was stocky and well muscled. A scar ran diagonally across the right knee—a souvenir of old surgery. Jane thought, *Now I know why I was able to run him down so easily.*

Under the magnifier, Maura examined the incised soft tissues. 'The wound is uniform,' she said. 'This was a single slice delivered at an odd angle. Which hand was holding the sword, right or left?'

Jane hesitated. 'I didn't see the actual slash. I was lying on my back.' Abruptly she turned from the table. 'You guys finish up here. I'm going to check with the lab, find out if Ingersoll's cellphone turned up anything.'

The anteroom door suddenly swung open, and Jane was startled to see her husband walk in. Special Agent Gabriel Dean, FBI, was wearing a gown and shoe covers, and his face was grim as he approached the table.

'This is the man from the alley?' he asked bluntly. 'The one who almost killed you?'

'Hello to you, too, sweetheart,' said Jane. She looked at Tam. 'In case you're wondering, this is my husband, Gabriel. And I have absolutely no idea why he's here.'

Gabriel's attention remained fixed on the cadaver. 'What do we know about him so far?'

'We? Since when did you join the team?' asked Jane.

'Since this man took a shot at you.'

'Gabriel.' She sighed. 'What is this all about?'

'It's about fingerprints.'

'We got nothing back on him from the lab.'

'I'm talking about the woman on the rooftop.'

'We didn't get any match on hers, either,' said Maura.

'I sent a notice to Interpol,' Gabriel said. 'Because it's clear to me this is adding up to something bigger. Think of how Jane Doe was dressed. The weapon she was carrying. The fact that she had no ID and was driving a stolen vehicle. Like this man.'

'You've heard back from Interpol?' said Jane.

He nodded. 'An hour ago. She's in their database. Not her name, but her fingerprints turned up on components of a car bomb that exploded in London two years ago. It killed the driver, an American businessman.'

'Are we talking about *terrorism*?' asked Tam.

'Interpol believes the bomb was a hit by organised crime. A paid assassination. Your woman on the rooftop was clearly a professional, and this man, as well.' He looked at Jane. 'A Kevlar vest isn't going to save you against people like this. You have a daughter. *We* have a daughter. Think about this.'

'What's there to think about?'

'Whether Boston PD can handle this.'

'Hold it right there. Can we take this into the next room, please?' She pushed through the door. It wasn't until she and Gabriel were in the hallway that she blurted out: 'This is my turf, OK? I decide what happens here.'

'Do you have any idea what you're dealing with?'

'I'm going to figure it out.'

'In the meantime, you're taking bullets and collecting dead bodies. Including a cop. Ingersoll knew how to defend himself, and now he's in a body bag.'

'So you want me to run home and hide under the bed?'

'Who brings in professional killers, Jane? This has got to be organised crime. The Russian mob. Or Chinese—'

'Kevin Donohue,' she said.

Gabriel paused. 'Irish mafia?'

'We're already digging for dirt on him. One of his men died in the Chinatown massacre. Gilmore's mother believes it was really a paid hit on her son, ordered by Donohue. Ingersoll was the lead detective.'

'If it's Donohue, he has a very long reach. Maybe into Boston PD itself.' She stared at her husband. 'Can the Bureau back up that charge?'

'There's not enough evidence to make it stick. But if he has a channel into Boston PD, he already knows exactly what you're up to. He knows you're coming for him.'

She thought about the police officers who'd turned up at Ingersoll's residence last night. How many cops had been keeping tabs on her? How much had leaked to Donohue?

'Take a leave of absence,' said Gabriel. 'You need time to recover.'

'I don't need to hear this from you,' she said. 'Not now.'

'Then when am I going to say it? At your funeral?'

Her ringing cellphone cut into the silence between them. 'Rizzoli.'

'It's Erin in the crime lab. Remember those weird hairs I was having trouble identifying?'

'Yeah. The grey ones.'

'I can't wait to tell you what they are.'

THE CONVERSATION with Gabriel was still weighing on Jane's mind as she and Frost drove to Schroeder Plaza. He knew her moods well enough to stay silent for most of the drive but as she turned into the parking garage, he said wistfully: 'I miss that part about being married. The part about having someone worry about you.'

'That's supposed to be a good thing?'

'Well, isn't it? It means he loves you.'

She pulled into a parking space. 'He doesn't want me to work on this case.'

'I'm not sure I want to be working on it, either.'

She looked at him. 'Scares you?'

'I'm not afraid to admit it.'

They heard a door slam: Tam stepped out of his car a few spaces away. 'Bet it doesn't scare him,' Jane muttered.

By the time they reached the crime lab, Tam was already sitting at Erin's microscope, peering at a slide.

'Detective Tam and I were just looking at some sample primate hair strands,' said Erin.

'Any of them look like the hairs from our gal?' asked Jane.

'Yes, but as I said, microscopy can't pinpoint the precise species. For that, I went to a different technique.' Erin spread out a page printed with columns in varying shades of grey. 'These are keratin patterns. Hair has different protein components that you can separate by electrophoresis.'

Frost shrugged. 'Doesn't look all that exciting.'

'When I emailed this pattern to the Wildlife Forensics Lab in Oregon, they were able to match it against their database of keratin patterns.'

'So what is it?'

'It's an Old World monkey, genus Semnopithecus. This particular species is known as the grey langur.'

'Grey?' said Jane, glancing up.

Erin nodded. 'The same colour as those hair strands from your Jane Doe. These monkeys are quite large, with black faces and grey or blond hair. Their range is South Asia, from China into India, both terrestrial and arboreal.' She turned to her computer. 'Here's a photo.'

What Jane saw on the screen made her hands suddenly go cold. Black face. Grey hair. She felt the ache between her shoulder blades from the bullet slamming into her. 'How large are these monkeys?'

'The males are about two and a half feet long.'

'You're certain they don't grow taller?'

'They're not apes. They're just monkeys.'

Jane looked at Frost. 'It's what you saw on the roof, isn't it?'

Frost shook his head. 'It was way taller than two and a half feet.'

Jane nodded. 'I agree.'

'It had that face,' said Frost. 'And grey hair. But it couldn't have been a monkey. And what monkey carries a sword?'

'Now, that just sent a chill up my spine,' said Erin softly. 'In India, this monkey is also known as the Hanuman langur. Hanuman is the Hindu god known as the Monkey Warrior.'

'Is that the same character as the Monkey King?' said Tam. 'I know that legend. There's a Chinese version of it, too.'

'Who is the Monkey King?' asked Jane.

'In China, his name is Sun Wukong. He starts off as just a stone monkey then he transforms to flesh and blood and gets crowned king of the monkeys. He becomes a warrior and travels to Heaven to learn the wisdom of the gods. But he gets into all sorts of trouble.'

'So he's a bad character?' asked Frost.

'Not evil. Just impulsive and mischievous, like a real monkey. There's a whole book of stories about him. How he eats all the peaches in the heavenly orchard. Drinks too much and steals a magic elixir. So they kick him out of Heaven and temporarily lock him up inside a mountain prison.'

'So then what happens to him?' asked Jane.

'Sun Wukong has a series of adventures on Earth. Sometimes he causes trouble. Sometimes he performs good deeds. I can't remember them all.'

'Fairy tales don't shed real hair,' said Jane.

'I'm just telling you what the legends say. He's sometimes helpful, sometimes destructive. But when faced with a choice between good and evil, the Monkey King almost always chooses to do the right thing.'

Jane stared at the photo on Erin's computer screen. At a face that, only a moment ago, had so chilled her. 'So he's not evil at all,' she said.

'No,' said Tam. 'Despite his flaws, despite the chaos he sometimes causes, the Monkey King stands on the side of justice.'

THE SCENT OF roasting chicken and rosemary drifted from Angela Rizzoli's kitchen and, in the dining room, silverware clattered as retired detective Vince Korsak set the table. Outside in the yard, Jane's daughter, Regina, was laughing and squealing as Gabriel pushed her on a swing. But Jane was oblivious to it all as she sat reading on her mother's sofa, half a dozen library books spread out before her. Books about Asian primates, grey langurs and Sun Wukong, the Monkey King.

In a book of Chinese folk tales, Jane found an introduction to the legend:

And from one of the rocks of that earth popped out a stone egg. That egg became a stone monkey. It could run and jump and climb, a monkey with eyes that flashed shafts of light so brilliant that even the Jade Emperor in heaven was startled.

The stone monkey soon became king of all monkeys. They lived in perfect harmony until, one day, the Monkey King came to understand that Death awaited them all. So he set out to learn the secret of immortality, a journey that took him to Heaven and temptation, to

*mischief and imprisonment. While marching to his own execution, the
Monkey King sprang free, and his fight to survive turned Heaven
upside down until the gods were forced to seal him inside the
Mountain of the Five Elements.*

*There he waits in stony darkness through the centuries, until the
day when he is needed. A day when evil is in the world, and the
Monkey King must emerge once again to wage battle.*

'So, how's it going with the monkey books?'

Korsak's voice made her glance up with a start. After a heart attack a few
years earlier, he'd lost thirty pounds, but his weight was starting to creep
back up again, and his belt was straining against an ever-expanding belly.

'It's for a case,' said Jane.

'I heard. Got yourself another weird one. Started off with that dead lady
on the roof, didn't it?'

Korsak flopped down in the armchair—the same armchair that her father
used to sit in. But her dad had forfeited all rights to that chair the day he
walked out on Angela and moved in with the Bimbo. Because of the
Bimbo, Vince Korsak was now sitting in the armchair, fat and happy on
Angela's cooking.

'What do you remember about the Red Phoenix shooting?' she asked.

'That one was a shocker. Why would a guy with a cute little girl shoot
four people and blow out his own brains? Never made sense to me.' He
shook his head. 'Such a sweet kid, too. Real daddy's girl.'

That surprised her. 'You knew the cook's family?'

'I used to eat there. The place was always open. I was there once at ten on
a Sunday night, and that little girl brought out my fortune cookies. She
looked like she was happy to be hanging out with Daddy.'

'You sure it was the cook's daughter? She would've been pretty young.'

'She looked pretty young. Maybe five? Cute as a button.' He gave a sad
sigh. 'Can't believe a father would leave a wife and kid behind. Not to mention all the other families he screwed up. But that's not what I want to be
thinking about tonight. Time to talk about happy things, OK?'

Not about dead people, thought Jane. *Not about mass shootings and kidnapped girls.* But when Gabriel came into the house holding Regina by her
tiny hand, Jane couldn't help thinking about Charlotte Dion and Laura

Fang. Even as she tied the bib round Regina and cut her meat into child-sized morsels, Jane was thinking about missing girls and devastated parents. She wondered if Iris Fang had ever considered ending her own misery. *How much easier than living with grief, day in and day out, pining for loved ones whom you'll never see again.*

'Something wrong with your meal, Janie?' said Angela.

'It's great, Ma. You outdid yourself tonight.'

'Then why aren't you eating? I hope you're not on a diet, because you don't need to lose any weight, sweetie.'

'I'm not on a diet.'

'All these girls, they're always on diets. Starving on salads, and for what?' Angela shook her head.

'Sure ain't doing it for men.' Korsak winked at Angela, then straightened in his chair. 'You know, this is a good time to bring up you-know-what.'

Never had three words sounded so ominous. Jane's chin snapped up, and she looked at her mother. 'What's you-know-what?'

'Well, you know that Vince and I have been seeing each other for quite a while,' said Angela.

'It's been only, what? A year and a half?'

'That's plenty of time to get to know someone, Janie. To see that he has a good heart.' Angela beamed at Korsak, and they leaned in for a noisy, lip-smacking kiss.

'You dated Dad for three whole years,' Jane pointed out. 'Look where that ended up.'

'I was fifteen when I met your father. I married too young. It's only now that I know what I want.'

Jane looked at Korsak and thought, *You cannot be talking about him.*

'You and Gabriel are going to be the first to know. Your brothers, they just won't understand. But you're my daughter, so you know what we women have to put up with in this world.'

'Ma, there's no need to rush into anything.'

'Oh, we're not going to rush. We're going to have a nice, long engagement and do it the old-fashioned way. This time, I'm going to go slow and enjoy every minute of my wedding,' said Angela. 'And it'll give your brothers a chance to adjust to it all.'

'What about Dad? How's he going to adjust?'

'That's his problem.' Angela's gaze darkened. 'He'd just better not try to rush up the aisle first. Ooh, I can see him doing that, you know.' She looked at Korsak. 'Maybe we should move up our date.'

'No! Ma, look, forget I even mentioned Dad.'

'I wish I could forget him, but he's always gonna be there, like a splinter in my foot. I hope you never know what that's like, Janie.' She paused and glanced at Gabriel. 'Of course, you won't. You have such a good man here.'

A good man who's still annoyed I'm a cop.

Gabriel wisely stayed out of the conversation and focused instead on coaxing tiny cubes of potato into Regina's mouth.

'So now you've heard our big news,' said Korsak, and he lifted a glass of wine. 'Here's to family!'

'Come on, Jane! Gabriel!' urged Angela. 'Let's all toast!'

Stoically, Jane raised her glass and mumbled, 'To family.'

'Just think,' said Korsak, laughing, as he gave her a happy punch in the arm. 'Now you can call me Dad.'

'IT'S NOT AS IF you didn't see this coming,' said Gabriel as he and Jane drove home with Regina asleep in the back seat. 'They were two lonely people, and look how happy they are now. They're perfectly matched.'

'Yeah. She cooks. He eats.'

'They could do a lot worse. Life is short, Jane. You should know that better than anyone.'

Yes, she did know, because she saw life cut short far too often. Saw how every death cast ripples among the living.

'Frankie's going to throw a fit. He hates the idea of Mom and another man, you know . . .'

'Sleeping together?'

Jane winced. 'I like Korsak. He's a decent man and he'll treat her right. But geez, she's my mother.'

Gabriel laughed. 'And your mother still has sex. Accept it. Just call Frankie and get it over with.'

But when they got home, she avoided the phone. Instead she set the kettle on the stove and sat down at the kitchen table to look at her library books again.

The scream of the kettle wrenched Jane from the story. She looked up to see Gabriel pouring hot water into the teapot. She had not even heard him come into the kitchen.

'Fascinating reading?' he said.

'Jesus, this is a creepy book,' she said with a shudder. 'I wouldn't read these stories to *my* kid. Take this one, "The Story of Chen O". It's about a massacre at a ferry crossing, and the only survivor is a pregnant woman who's captured by the killers.'

He brought the teapot to the table and sat down across from her. All night he had been subdued.

'Jane, I can't get it out of my head. The way you looked when you came home the other night. Shell-shocked. The blood all over your clothes.'

'You do remember what I do for a living?' she said.

He nodded. 'And I knew there'd be days like this. I just didn't realise how hard it would be to live with.' He got up to answer the phone when it rang.

'I don't much like it, either,' she said.

'It's for you.' Gabriel stood with the phone in his hand and a look of concern in his eye. 'He won't give me his name.'

She took the phone. Felt her husband watching her as she answered, 'Detective Rizzoli.'

'I know you've been asking about me, so I figured I'd cut to the chase. Let's you and me talk, face to face. Four o'clock tomorrow, my house. Just you and no one else. And tell your husband he has nothing to worry about.'

'Who is this?' she demanded.

'Kevin Donohue.'

She looked up sharply at Gabriel. Barely managed to keep her voice even as she said: 'What is this about, Mr Donohue?'

'The Red Phoenix. Your investigation's going way off the rails. I think it's time to set a few things straight.'

ALTHOUGH BOTH Frost and Tam sat watching her from their cars, Jane felt dangerously exposed as she rang the bell at Kevin Donohue's front gate. A moment later, two beefy men strode towards her down the driveway, sidearms bulging under their jackets. They asked her no questions, merely admitted her through the gate. As she passed under the arch, she spotted a surveillance camera overhead: every move she made was being monitored. She noted the absence of trees and shrubbery. There was only a lawn and a concrete driveway lined with lampposts with more security cameras: stark evidence that being a prince of the Irish mob had its downside.

Her escorts led her into a living room where an enormous man sat in an extra-large armchair. He was in his sixties, clean-shaven and balding, with blue eyes that glared from beneath heavy lids. She already knew that this was Kevin Donohue, known for his impressive appetites and his equally impressive bad temper.

'Scan her, Sean,' someone said. She hadn't noticed there was another man in the room, a skinny and nervous-looking fellow in a business suit.

One of her escorts moved towards her, holding a radio frequency scanner, and Jane snapped, 'What the hell's this all about?'

'I'm Mr Donohue's attorney,' the skinny man said. 'We need to make sure you're not bugged. And you'll have to hand us your cellphone.'

'This wasn't part of the agreement.'

'I don't want any recording of this conversation,' rumbled Donohue.

For a moment Jane and Donohue traded stares. Then she handed her cellphone to the attorney and stood motionless while the bodyguard scanned her. When Sean pronounced her clean, Donohue invited her to sit. She chose an armchair, so that she would be at his eye level.

'Your reputation precedes you,' said Donohue. 'Detective Jane Rizzoli. Smart-ass tongue. Bulldog.'

'I'll take that as a compliment.'

'Which is why I'm telling you to dig somewhere else for your bones. You've been asking questions about me. So has your husband, Mr Special Agent Gabriel Dean. Quite the law enforcement couple. I'm not worried that you're gonna find anything useful, mind you. But it makes me look weak to my rivals. And if I look weak, that brings the vultures out.' He leaned forward. 'There is nothing that can link me to the Red Phoenix.'

'What about Joey Gilmore?'

'Small stuff. Not worth the price of a bullet.'

'Can't be that small if you're bringing in outside people to mop up now.'

'What?'

Jane glanced at Donohue's bodyguards. 'I'm going to reach into my pocket for some pictures, OK?' She pulled out two morgue photos and slid them across the table towards Donohue. 'Your hired help just can't keep their heads on straight.'

Jane had chosen the two most graphically grotesque morgue photos: Jane Doe with her slashed throat gaping open; John Doe's severed head lying beside his torso on the autopsy table. The images had their desired effect: Donohue's face turned as pasty as the corpses.

'Why the fuck are you showing me this?' he demanded.

'Why did you hire these two killers?'

The lawyer cut in. 'This conversation has come to an end. Sean, Colin. Escort Detective Rizzoli out of the house.'

'Shut up,' said Donohue. 'I'm gonna answer her question, OK?' He looked at Jane. 'I didn't hire 'em. I don't even know who that woman is.'

'And the man? Do you recognise him?'

'Maybe. Looks a little familiar. What do you think, Sean?'

Sean eyed the photo. 'I think I seen him around. Don't know his name, but he's local. Ukrainian or Russian.'

Donohue shook his head. 'Bad news, those boys. I can tell you, this guy never worked for me. So you might wanna think of backing off.'

'Are you threatening me, Mr Donohue?'

'You're a smart girl. What do you think?'

'You called me a bulldog, remember? Well, I'm going to keep on digging in your back yard because that's where I'll find Joey Gilmore's bones.'

'Come on. The cook killed those people but Joey's old hag of a mother just can't let it go. That's why she sent me that note.'

Jane went very still. 'You got one?'

'Few weeks ago, I got a copy of Joey's obit. Plus some stupid message she wrote on the back.'

'If Mrs Gilmore is the reason you're investigating Mr Donohue,' said the attorney, 'don't waste your time.'

'How do you know Mary Gilmore's sending these notes?' Jane asked. 'Did she sign yours? Was there a return address?'

The attorney frowned as he suddenly registered what Jane had said. 'Notes, as in plural? She's sent more than one?'

'Mailings have been sent to all Red Phoenix family members. The notes are similar to what Mr Donohue received.'

The attorney and Donohue looked at each other. 'We need to rethink this,' said the attorney. 'If Mary Gilmore isn't doing this . . .'

Donohue's fingers rolled into fists. 'I want to know who the hell is.'

MAURA AWAKENED just after dawn, and was happy to see that the sun was shining. She pulled on jeans and a T-shirt and walked down the hall to the kitchen. She sat in front of the laptop computer that she'd left on the kitchen table the night before.

When Detective Tam had dropped off the material, she had not welcomed the extra work and had put it off until last night, when she'd only glanced at the photos briefly: it had been late and she'd had a long day. Now, with a few mouse clicks, she reopened the digital image of Wu Weimin's body, lying in the Red Phoenix kitchen, focusing more intently on the images of the dead cook and on the weapon that was clasped in his hand. Near his shoulder lay a spent bullet casing and, at the periphery of the photo, something she hadn't noticed the evening before: a second casing.

Maura paused. The report said that there was only one bullet in the cook's head, so why had he fired twice? She knew this was not unusual in suicides: the victim often had to build up the courage to kill himself, and could miss the first time. Or the gun had misfired. Under the circumstances, she knew the police had probably seen no reason to go searching for the second bullet.

But still something nagged at her: the fact that nothing in the report had really offered a reason as to why the cook had killed those four people.

She decided to come at the problem from another angle. She began to imagine that the cook hadn't killed himself; that his death had been staged to look like a suicide. Which meant that someone else had shot those other four people, and then killed the cook. She imagined him, working in the kitchen when someone had started shooting in the other room. She knew from the photos that the gun had had no silencer . . . so why did the report detail that the people in the three apartments upstairs had only heard one bang? Her sixth sense tingling, she flipped through the report, until she found what she had been looking for: seven different witnesses stated that they'd heard only one bang, yet a total of nine bullet casings were found in the Red Phoenix restaurant.

Something was *not* right.

She opened Wu Weimin's autopsy report. The cook was found lying on his side, his back wedged up against the closed cellar door. His right hand—the one still clutching the gun—was later found positive for gunshot residue. She clicked through the photos. The fatal bullet had been fired into the right temple, and a close-up showed it to be a hard contact wound, the edges seared and blackened by gases rushing out of the barrel. There was no exit wound. She clicked on the skull X-ray and saw metallic fragments scattered throughout the cranium. *A hollow-point bullet*, she thought. *Maximum damage with minimum penetration.*

She moved on to the other files.

James Fang had been shot once in the head. The bullet had entered above his left eyebrow. Joey Gilmore had been shot once in the back of the head. The last two victims, Arthur and Dina Mallory, were found at the corner table where they had been sitting. Arthur was shot twice, once in the back of the head, once in the spine. His wife was hit three times, the bullets punching into her cheek, her mid-back and her skull. Scanning down to the pathologist's summary, she saw that he'd concluded the same thing she did: that Dina Mallory had been moving when she was shot the first two times, probably trying to flee her attacker.

Maura was about to set the report aside when she noticed a sentence describing the dissection of the stomach and duodenum: Based on volume of gastric contents, which appear to include spaghetti fragments with a tomato-based sauce, the post-prandial period is estimated to be one to two hours. Arthur Mallory's stomach contents included cheese and meat, with partially digested fragments of lettuce.

This did not make sense, either. Why would the Mallorys, their bellies full of what appeared to be an Italian meal, be sitting in a Chinese restaurant?

None of it makes sense, she thought. But then she paused suddenly, thinking about the extra bullet casing. The gun was fired twice in the kitchen, but only one blast was heard. And the Glock had a threaded barrel, so it *could* be fitted with a silencer. She imagined again an alternate sequence of events: an unknown killer executes Wu Weimin. Removes the silencer and places the weapon in the dead man's hand. Fires randomly one last time to plant gunshot residue on the victim's skin. It would explain why only one blast was heard and why there were two bullet casings in the kitchen.

But there was one last detail she couldn't explain: why Wu Weimin, given the chance to flee out of the back exit, had chosen to remain in the kitchen.

She focused on the cellar door. On the cook's body, lying in front of it. Blocking it. Suddenly she thought, *Maybe he couldn't flee.*

Because he had a very good reason to stay.

FIVE

'Luminol's probably going to make this whole place light up,' said Jane. 'According to the realtor, all they did after the event was wash down the walls and mop the floors. The linoleum was never replaced. So I'm not sure what this exercise is going to prove.'

'We won't know until we look, will we?' said Maura.

They stood outside the old Red Phoenix restaurant, waiting for the crime scene unit. Total darkness was needed to properly examine the interior, and dusk was just now deepening, bringing with it a damp chill.

Jane peered through the restaurant window. 'We've already been in there, you know. Just bare walls and empty rooms.'

'The blood will still be there,' said Maura. Soap and scrubbing erased only the visible evidence; the chemical ghost of blood remained on floors and walls. Luminol could reveal old smears and footprints that may have been missed during the original investigation.

A vehicle rounded the corner and Frost and Tam stepped out.

'You got the key?' Jane called out.

Frost pulled it from his pocket and unlocked the door. He felt for the light switch. Nothing happened. 'Bulb must've burned out.' Their four flashlight beams sliced back and forth, crisscrossing in the darkness.

'Hello?' a voice called from the alley. 'Detective Rizzoli?'

A new pair of duelling flashlight beams joined theirs as two men from the crime scene unit entered. One of the men squatted and examined the floor. 'This is the same linoleum?'

'That's what we're told,' said Tam.

'Looks it, too. Should light up really well.' He grunted as he stood up, his belly as big as an eight-month pregnancy.

His much thinner associate said, 'What are you hoping to find? Must be a reason you're looking after nineteen years.'

Jane said, 'We have reason to believe it wasn't a murder-suicide.'

'So we're looking for unexplained footprints? Evidence of an intruder?'

'That would be a start.'

The men carried in lighting equipment and video gear. The power outlets were still live, and when they plugged in the cord to illuminate the dining area, the glare of the lamps was as harsh as sunlight. While one of the criminalists videotaped the room, his partner unpacked boxes of chemicals from a cooler. Maura recognised both men from the rooftop crime scene.

Slowly, the videographer panned the room with the camera and straightened. 'OK, Ed? You ready to start?'

Tam handed Maura a pair of goggles and a respirator, which she pulled over her face to protect against the luminol fumes. Only after everyone was masked did Ed, the taller of the two, begin mixing chemicals. He swirled the solution in a jar, then decanted it into a spray bottle. 'Where do you folks want to start?'

'This section,' said Jane, pointing to the area near the cash register.

Ed moved into position, then glanced at Frost. 'Lights.'

The room went black, and the darkness seemed to magnify the sound of Maura's breathing in the respirator. Only faintly did she hear the hiss of the spray bottle as Ed released a mist of luminol. A geometric pattern of blue-green suddenly glowed on the floor as the luminol reacted with the traces of old haemoglobin.

'Light.'

Frost flipped the switch and they all stood blinking in the glare. The blue-green glow had vanished; in its place was the same patch of floor they had seen earlier. Tam looked up from his laptop, on which he'd loaded the crime scene photos. 'Corresponds with what I see here,' he said. 'No surprises. That's right where Joey Gilmore's body was found.'

They moved to the nook behind the counter where James Fang died, and again the lights went out. The floor and wall lit up, glowing splatters where traces of the waiter's blood had splashed, like the fading echoes of a scream.

They moved on to the corner where the Mallorys had perished. Two bodies meant twice as many splatters, and here was a horror show of splashes and smears that flared in the darkness.

Frost turned on the lights and they all stood silent for a moment. Nothing had surprised them so far, but what they'd seen was nonetheless unsettling.

'Let's move on to the kitchen,' said Jane.

It seemed colder in the next room. It didn't help that the floor was concrete, designed for easy swabbing in an area where grease and sauces would splatter. *And blood, too,* Maura thought. She stood shivering by the cellar door.

'Right here is where the cook was found,' she said.

'So we'll find more blood. Big surprise,' said Ed, his note of sarcasm unmistakable. 'Do you want to tell us what you're looking for, Dr Isles? So this might actually make sense?'

'I'll tell you when I see it. Let's start with that doorway leading into the dining room.'

Ed nodded to Frost. 'Lights off.'

The sudden blackness in the kitchen was complete. The spray bottle hissed, and glowing streaks of blue-green magically spread on the floor.

'I see footprints here,' said Ed. 'Maybe a woman's size five, six?'

'Those are in the crime scene photos, too,' Tam said. 'The cook's wife lived right upstairs. When she heard the gunshot, she walked in through the alley door and found her husband. Tracked his blood into the dining room, where she found the other victims.'

'Well, that's what it looks like here.'

Maura heard more spray, and new footprints appeared, a luminous record of the wife's movements that night. They followed the prints backwards, until suddenly a bright pool bloomed. Here was where Wu Weimin's blood had collected, spilling from the wound on his temple.

'Lights, please,' said Ed. 'We'll finish up over there.' He pointed towards the kitchen exit leading to the alley. 'Did the wife leave the same way she came in?'

'No,' said Tam. 'According to Ingersoll's report, she ran out of the front exit, down Knapp Street. Headed towards Beach Street to call for help.'

'So there shouldn't be any blood at this end.'

Tam peered at his laptop. 'I don't see any in this crime scene photo.'

What they had captured so far on video was exactly what they'd expected to find. *Was this a mistake, a wild goose chase?* Maura wondered. *Have I just wasted everyone's evening?*

'Let's wrap this up and go home,' said Jane, sounding weary.

The lights went out and Maura heard the spray bottle once again deliver its mist of luminol.

Suddenly Ed blurted: 'Hey, are you seeing this?'

'Lights!' Jane called out, and Frost turned on the lamp.

In the glare, they all stood silent for a moment, staring at bare concrete.

Ed was frowning. As they crowded round the camera, he rewound and hit Play. Glowing in the darkness were three blue-green patches that moved in a line towards the alley exit. Two were smeared and misshapen, but the third was unmistakably a tiny footprint.

'How do we explain the fact that these footprints aren't in any of the crime scene photos?'

'Because someone cleaned them up,' said Maura softly. 'Before the police arrived.' *Yet the traces remain*, she thought. *Invisible to the human eye, but not to luminol.*

The others looked stunned. A child had been in this kitchen, a child who had stepped into blood and had tracked it out of the door, into the alley.

'The cellar,' said Jane. She swung open the cellar door and shone her flashlight down the steps. From the blackness below rose the smell of damp stone and mould.

'The cook died right here, blocking this door,' said Jane. She turned to Ed. 'Let's look at these top steps.'

There were no impatient looks this time. The criminalists moved swiftly to reposition the camera, aiming it down the cellar stairs. They all crowded in as the lights went out, and Ed unleashed a final hiss of luminol. They saw that blood had trickled from the kitchen above and had dripped down onto the top step.

A step where they could see the treadmark of a small shoe.

'A CHILD WAS IN the kitchen cellar that night, Mrs Fang,' says Detective Rizzoli. 'Do you know who that child was?'

The policewoman studies me, monitoring my reaction as I absorb what she has just told me. Through the closed door I can hear my students as they diligently practise their combat manoeuvres, but here in my office it is silent as I weigh my possible responses. I allow no emotions to ripple the surface of my face. Between the two of us, this has become a chess game played with moves of which Detective Frost, who is also watching, is probably not even aware.

I ask: 'How do you know?'

'There were footprints in the kitchen and on the steps in the cellar. A child's footprints.'

'Even after many years, Mrs Fang, blood leaves traces,' says Frost, patiently explaining what he believes I do not understand. 'We know that a child came out of the cellar, stepped in Wu Weimin's blood, and walked out of the kitchen, into the alley.'

'Detective Ingersoll never said anything.'

'By the time the police arrived that night, the prints were wiped away,' says Detective Rizzoli. 'Who would do that, Mrs Fang? Who would want to hide the fact that a child was in the cellar?'

'Why ask me? I was in Taiwan visiting my family when it happened.'

'But you knew Wu Weimin and his wife. The child in the cellar was their little girl, wasn't it? Mei Mei, five years old. Where did they go, the mother and daughter?'

'I have no idea.'

'Why did they run? Was it because the wife was illegal?'

I glare at her. 'Are you surprised that she would run? If I were illegal, Detective, and you thought my husband had just killed four people, how quickly would you put me in handcuffs and have me deported? Li Hua wanted her daughter to grow up in America, so can you blame her?'

'If she wiped away those footprints, then she destroyed evidence.'

'Maybe it was to protect her daughter.'

'The girl was a witness.'

'And would you put a five-year-old girl in a courtroom? Do you think a jury would believe a child of illegal immigrants, when the whole city has already called the father a monster?'

The policewoman falls silent, thinking about the logic of what I've said. It is the logic of a mother desperate to protect herself and her child from authorities she did not trust.

Frost says, gently: 'We're just trying to learn the truth, Mrs Fang.'

'I told the truth nineteen years ago,' I point out. 'I told the police that Wu Weimin would never hurt anyone, but it was so much easier for them to think he was a crazy Chinaman.' I hear the bitterness in my voice. 'Searching for the truth is too much work. That's what the police thought.'

'It's not what I think,' says Frost quietly.

I stare back at him and see sincerity in his eyes.

'If Mei Mei was in that cellar,' says Detective Rizzoli, 'we need to find her. We need to know what she remembers. What can you tell us about her?'

I think about this for a moment. 'I remember she was afraid of nothing. She was never still, always running and jumping. When my daughter, Laura, would babysit, she'd come home exhausted. She told me she never wanted to have children if they were going to be as wild as Mei Mei.'

'An intelligent girl?'

I give her a sad smile. 'Do you have children, Detective?'

'I have a two-year-old daughter.'

'And you probably think she's the cleverest child ever born.'

Now it was Rizzoli's turn to smile. 'I know she is.'

'Because all children seem clever, don't they? Little Mei Mei was so quick, so curious . . .' I swallow hard. 'When they left, it was like losing my own daughter all over again.'

'Where did they go?'

'There was a cousin in California, I think. Li Hua could have married again. She could have a different name.'

'You have no idea where she is now?'

'I don't even know if she's alive.'

There is a knock on the door, and Bella steps into the office. '*Sifu*, the last class of the day has left. Will you need me?'

'Wait a moment. We are just finishing here.'

The two detectives turn to leave. Rizzoli pauses and regards Bella. I can almost see the thoughts whirring in her head. Mei Mei was five years old when she vanished. How old is this young woman? Could it be possible? But Rizzoli merely nods goodbye and walks out of the studio.

After the door shuts, I say to Bella: 'We are running out of time.'

'Do they know?'

'They're closer to the truth.' I draw in a deep breath, and it worries me that I cannot cast off the new fatigue that now drags me down. I am fighting two battles at once: one of them against the enemy that smoulders in my own bone marrow. I know one of these enemies will take my life.

The only question is, which one will kill me first?

NOW THERE WERE THREE missing girls. On Jane's desk were files on Jane Doe, the Red Phoenix massacre, and the disappearances of Laura Fang and Charlotte Dion. She'd started a new file on Mei Mei, the cook's daughter. She would be twenty-four years old now, perhaps married and living under a different name. They had no photos, no fingerprints, no idea what she looked like. She might not even reside in the country. Or she could be right under their noses, teaching martial arts in a Chinatown studio. Jane pictured Iris's stony-faced assistant, Bella Li, whose background they were already looking into.

Jane turned her attention back to Laura Fang and Charlotte Dion. To the startling connection between them, despite the gulf that separated their lives. Two such different girls, yet both had lost parents in the restaurant shooting. Paging through their files, she heard the echo of Ingersoll's last words to her: '*It's all about what happened to those girls.*'

Were these the girls he'd meant?

PATRICK DION'S ESTATE looked no less impressive the second time Jane saw it. She drove between the twin stone pillars onto the private road that took her past birch trees and lilacs and up the rolling lawn towards the massive house. As she pulled up under the porte-cochère, Patrick emerged from the house to greet her.

'Thank you for seeing me again,' she said as they shook hands.

'Is there news about Charlotte?' he asked.

'I'm afraid I don't have anything new to report. This is in connection to our current investigation, the murder in Chinatown.'

'What does that have to do with my daughter?'

'There've been developments that make me think Charlotte's disappearance is connected with another missing girl. I'd like to look at it again. Even though it's been nineteen years, I won't let your daughter be forgotten.'

She saw him blink away tears, and she knew that for him the pain was still alive.

With a weary nod, he said: 'Come inside. I've brought her things down from the attic, as you requested.'

She followed him into a formal dining room. On the rosewood table, large enough to seat a dozen guests, was a collection of cardboard boxes.

'This is what I saved,' he said sadly. 'I finally gave most of her clothes away to charity. Charlotte would have approved, I think.' He reached into one of the boxes and lifted out a pair of frayed blue jeans. 'Funny, how I never could bring myself to give these away. Blue jeans never go out of style. If she ever comes back, I know she'll want them.'

'Would it be easier for you if I looked through these boxes on my own?'

'No, I'll need to explain things.' He pulled out a photo album. 'This is what you probably want to see.'

On the first page was a photo of a young blonde woman holding a red-faced newborn. *Our Charlotte, eight hours old*, was written beneath it. So this was Dina when she was still Patrick's fresh-faced bride. Before Arthur Mallory stepped into their lives.

'Charlotte was your only child?' Jane asked.

'Dina insisted. At the time, I was fine with it. But now . . .'

Now he regrets it, she thought. She turned the pages and studied other photos of Charlotte as a golden-haired toddler.

Patrick handed her the next volume. The years seemed to accelerate in this second album. Suddenly that cherubic toddler transformed into a glum-faced adolescent, posing in her school uniform at the front gate of the Bolton Academy.

'She hated that uniform,' said Patrick.

'Did she not want to go to Bolton?'

'She certainly did want to go. But I had a hard time losing my little girl to boarding school. Dina insisted, because it was a school where a girl could meet all the right people. Dina was completely focused on Charlotte making the right friends and marrying the right man.' He paused and added, ironically, 'As it turned out, it was Dina who met a husband at Bolton.'

'That must have been hard for you when Dina left.'

Patrick gave a resigned shrug. 'I accepted it. And oddly enough, I rather liked Arthur Mallory. Liked the whole Mallory family, in fact: Barbara; their son, Mark. All of them were decent people.'

Jane studied the final image in the album. It was a wedding photo, and standing at the centre were the new bride and groom, Dina and Arthur Mallory. Flanking them were their respective children, Mark at his father's side, Charlotte at her mother's.

'Charlotte looks a little lost,' said Jane.

'It happened so fast. We'd met the Mallorys only a year before, when Charlotte and Mark both performed at the Christmas pageant. A year later, Dina had left me for Arthur. And I was just another single father, raising a daughter on my own.'

'Charlotte stayed with you after the divorce?'

'Dina and I felt it was best if I had custody so that Charlotte could stay in the house where she'd grown up.'

'And there was no tug-of-war over your daughter?'

'Just because two people get divorced doesn't mean they don't care about each other. We were now all part of an extended family. Arthur's ex-wife, Barbara, remained bitter. But I saw no point in hanging on to resentments.'

Jane knew that Ingersoll had written in his report that Patrick Dion and his ex-wife had stayed cordial after the divorce. Now, hearing it from Patrick Dion himself, she could believe it.

'They even spent their last Christmas here, with me,' he said. 'Arthur and Dina and Mark. We had dinner together in this room. I remember Charlotte asking Mark about Harvard. Dina gave her a pearl necklace. We had pumpkin pie for dessert. And afterwards, I took Mark downstairs to my woodshop, because he loved working with his hands.' Patrick looked at her, as if suddenly remembering she was there. 'Now they're gone. And there's only Mark and me left.'

'You two seem close.'

'He's a fine young man.' Patrick paused. 'Mark's thirty-nine, but at my age, anyone under forty still seems like a young man.'

Jane pulled another book out of the box, a Bolton Academy yearbook.

'She was a sophomore that year,' said Patrick. 'That was the year before she . . .' He paused, his face darkening. 'I thought about suing the school for negligence. They took my daughter on a field trip without adequate supervision. The teachers didn't pay attention, and suddenly my girl was gone. I was an ocean away, where I couldn't do a damn thing to save her.'

'I understand you were in London.'

He nodded. 'Adding to my goddamn fortune. I'd throw this all away, if only I could . . .' Suddenly he stood up. 'I think I could use a stiff drink right now. Can I pour you one?'

'Thank you, but no. I'm driving.'

'If you'll excuse me,' he said, and walked out.

Jane opened the yearbook and spotted Charlotte. She was a beautiful girl, but tragedy already seemed stamped into her features. Printed beneath her photo was a list of her interests and activities: DRAMA CLUB, ART, ORCHESTRA, TENNIS TEAM.

Orchestra. She remembered that Laura Fang had played the violin. The girls might have grown up in different universes, but they had music in common. She spotted Charlotte, posing with two dozen other music students. The caption read: CANDACE FORSYTH, MUSIC DIRECTOR, AND THE BOLTON ACADEMY ORCHESTRA.

She heard Patrick return to the dining room. 'Did your daughter know a girl named Laura Fang?' Jane asked.

'Detective Buckholz asked me that same question, after Charlotte disappeared. I told him I hadn't heard the name before. I only found out later that Laura Fang was a girl who vanished two years before Charlotte. That's when I understood why he asked me about her.'

'You can't think of any link between the girls? Charlotte never mentioned Laura's name?'

'Your child comes home from school and talks about this girl or that boy. How can any parent possibly remember all the names?'

He was right; it was an impossible thing to expect of a parent.

Jane flipped to the senior students, and scanned the photos of clean-cut boys dressed in their uniforms of blue blazers and red neckties. There was Mark Mallory, a handsome young man, bound for Harvard. His interests were listed: LACROSSE, ORCHESTRA, CHESS, FENCING.

Orchestra again. That was, after all, how the Dions and Mallorys had met; through their musical children at the Christmas pageant.

'I'm not quite sure how any of this is going to help you,' said Patrick. 'Detective Buckholz asked me all these questions nineteen years ago.'

She looked up at him. 'Maybe the answers have changed.'

As JANE DROVE WEST on the Massachusetts Turnpike, the afternoon sun was in her eyes. By the time she reached the Bolton Academy, it was nearly 5 p.m. She drove through the front gate, onto a curving drive shaded by ancient oak trees. Three girls sat chatting on the stone steps.

'Excuse me. I'm looking for Mrs Forsyth, the music director,' said Jane.

'She's in Bennett Hall,' one of the girls said, extending a graceful arm to point at the stately building across the lawn. 'There.'

'Thanks.' As Jane walked across the lawn, she felt their eyes following her, the alien specimen from the world of merely ordinary people. She came to the steps and gazed up at the white columns. *It's like scaling Mount Olympus* she thought, as she climbed the stairs into the central hall.

The sound of a scratchy violin drifted from the corridor to her left. She followed it to a classroom where a teenage girl sat bowing with fierce concentration, while a white-haired woman frowned at her.

The woman turned and said, 'Yes?'

'Mrs Forsyth? I called earlier. I'm Detective Rizzoli.'

'We're just finishing up here.' The teacher turned to her student and sighed. 'You're all tensed up today, so there's no point continuing the lesson. Go back to the dorm and practise.'

Resignedly, the girl packed up her instrument. As she turned to go, she said to Jane: 'Are you, like, with the police? I want to be an FBI agent someday.'

'Then you should go for it. The Bureau could use more women.'

'Tell that to my parents,' she muttered and slouched out of the room.

'That girl is never going to be much of a musician,' said Mrs Forsyth.

'The last I heard, playing the violin isn't a requirement for the FBI.'

Mrs Forsyth eyed her coolly. 'You said you had questions, Detective?'

'About one of your students from nineteen years ago. She was in the school orchestra. Played the viola.'

'You're here about Charlotte Dion, aren't you?' The woman sighed. 'The one student no one ever lets us forget. Mr Dion still blames us, doesn't he?'

'It would be hard for any parent to accept. You can understand that.'

'Boston PD never considered our school negligent. We had more than enough chaperones on that excursion: a ratio of one to six. And these weren't toddlers on the outing, these were teenagers. We shouldn't have to baby-sit them. But with Charlotte, maybe we should have.'

'Why?'

'Have you ever noticed the way misfortune seems to target certain people? They'll lose their spouse, their job and get cancer all in the same year. That was Charlotte, always gloomy, always attracting bad luck. Which may be why she didn't seem to have a lot of friends.'

'In the school yearbook, she seemed to have a healthy list of activities,' Jane said. 'Music, for instance.'

Mrs Forsyth nodded. 'She was a decent violist, but her heart never seemed to be in it. Only in her junior year did she finally manage to pass the auditions for the Boston summer orchestra workshop.'

'How many of your students attend that workshop?'

'A few every year. It's very selective.' Mrs Forsyth paused. 'I know who you're going to ask about next. That Chinese girl who disappeared, right?'

Jane nodded. 'You read my mind. Her name was Laura Fang.'

'I understand she was a talented girl. That's what I heard after she vanished. A number of my students attended the workshop with her.'

'But not Charlotte?'

'No. Charlotte didn't pass the audition until the year after Laura disappeared, so they wouldn't have met each other. Another question you were about to ask, I'm sure.'

'You remember all these details, even after nineteen years?'

'Because I went over it again just recently with that other detective.'

'Which detective?'

'I can't remember his name. I'd have to check my appointment book.'

'I'd appreciate it if you looked it up right now, ma'am.'

A look of irritation flickered in the woman's eyes but she crossed to her desk and rummaged through a drawer until she came up with a daily planner. 'I thought he looked a bit old to be a detective, but I guess experience counts for something.'

'Was his name Detective Ingersoll?' Jane asked.

'So you know him.'

'Detective Ingersoll is dead. He was shot to death last week.'

The appointment book tumbled from Mrs Forsyth's hands.

'Why was he here, Mrs Forsyth? Why was he asking about Charlotte?'

'I assumed it was her father pushing for it, still hoping for answers.'

'Did you ask Mr Dion?'

She flushed. 'The Bolton Academy avoids any contact with Mr Dion. To avoid dredging up . . . bad feelings.'

'Tell me exactly what Detective Ingersoll said to you.'

The woman sank into the chair behind her desk. She swallowed. 'He didn't ask very much about Charlotte. It was more about the other girl, Laura Fang, and others. He had a long list with maybe two dozen names. He asked if any had attended Bolton. I told him no.'

'Do you remember any of the names on that list?'

'No. I didn't know any of them. He told me they were all girls who'd gone missing like Laura.' Mrs Forsyth straightened and looked up at Jane. 'Girls who've never been found.'

THE SILENT GIRL | 99

'THESE ARE INGERSOLL'S phone records for the past thirty days,' said Tam, spreading out the pages on the conference table for Jane and Frost. 'At first glance, nothing jumps out. It's mostly mundane stuff. Calls to his daughter, his dentist, his credit card company. A call to a fishing camp where he stayed in Maine.'

'Geez. He sure ate a lot of pizza,' observed Frost.

'You'll notice that he called family members of the Red Phoenix victims. Those calls were made around the anniversary of the massacre.'

'Mrs Gilmore and Mark Mallory confirmed that Ingersoll called to find out if they received the anonymous mailing,' said Frost.

'But there are a few that don't make sense,' said Tam. 'This one, April 6th, to My Best Friend dog groomers in Lowell. As far as we know, Ingersoll never owned a dog. I called the number. They'd never heard of him, and he wasn't on their client list. I thought maybe he'd called a wrong number.' He pointed to another entry. 'Then there's this, April 8th, to Worcester. It's the number for the Shady Lady Lingerie store.'

Jane grimaced. 'I'm not sure I want to know the details.'

'When I spoke to the store,' said Tam, 'no one recognised the name Ingersoll. So I assumed it was just another wrong number.'

'A reasonable assumption.'

'But incorrect. His phone call wasn't for the Shady Lady at all, but for the party who used to have that number.'

Jane frowned. 'How did you figure that out?'

'After your visit to the Bolton Academy, I pulled up the state database of missing girls, as you asked. I put together a list of every girl who's vanished in Massachusetts over the past twenty-five years.'

'You went that far back?' said Frost.

'Charlotte vanished nineteen years ago. Laura Fang twenty-one years ago. I chose twenty-five as the cut off, to give myself a good margin, and I'm glad I did.' Tam pulled a page from a bulging folder and slid it across the table. Midway down the page was a phone number circled in red ink. 'This is the Shady Lady number Ingersoll called. Twenty-two years ago, that same number was listed under the name Gregory Boles in Worcester. Phone numbers turn over all the time. I think that's the party Detective Ingersoll was actually trying to reach. But Boles moved out of state twelve years ago.'

'Who is Gregory Boles?' asked Frost.

Scanning down the page of phone numbers, Jane suddenly felt a thrill of comprehension. 'These are the contact numbers from the missing children's database.' She looked up.

Tam nodded. 'Gregory Boles is the father of a missing girl. I was planning to review all the cases that are currently open but I realised it was a monumental task, trying to find any links with Charlotte or Laura. I got the idea of cross-referencing all the phone numbers from Ingersoll's phone log. Judging by the numbers on his call log, he started tracking down certain families in early April. Then he stopped making any phone calls at all. From either his cellphone or his landline.'

'Because he thought he was being monitored,' said Jane.

'Based on the calls he made before he stopped, these are the missing girls he was homing in on.' Tam slid a page in front of her.

Jane saw only three names. 'What do we know about these girls?'

'They were thirteen, fifteen and sixteen. They all vanished within a hundred and fifty miles of Boston. Two were white, one was Asian. A- or B-grade students. No delinquency, no reason to think they'd be runaways. Maybe that's why Ingersoll grouped them together.'

'How old are these cases?' asked Frost.

'These girls all vanished more than twenty years ago.'

'So he was just looking at old cases? Why not more recent ones?'

'I don't know. Maybe he was just getting started. The thing that puzzles me is why he got himself involved in the first place. He didn't work these disappearances when he was with Boston PD. Was retirement so boring?'

'Maybe someone hired him to do PI work.'

'That was my first thought,' said Tam. 'I've been able to reach all three families, but none of them hired Ingersoll.'

Jane looked at the names of the three new girls. 'And now he's dead,' she said softly. 'What the hell did he get himself into?'

'Kevin Donohue's territory,' said Tam.

Jane and Frost stared at him. Although Tam had been working with them for barely two weeks, he had already acquired a hint of cockiness. In his suit and tie, with his neatly clipped hair and icy stare, he could pass for Secret Service.

'Word on the street,' said Tam, 'is that Donohue's been running girls for years: prostitution's just one of his sidelines. What if this is how he obtains those girls?'

'By kidnapping A-grade students?' Jane shook her head. 'Somehow, it seems like a risky method of picking up underage prostitutes.'

'But it would tie everything together: Joey Gilmore, missing girls and the Red Phoenix. Maybe Ingersoll discovered the link to Donohue, and that's when he stopped using his phones. If Donohue got wind of it, Ingersoll knew he'd be a dead man.'

'Ingersoll *is* a dead man,' said Jane. 'What we don't know is why, after all these years in retirement, he suddenly got interested in missing girls.'

JANE SAT at her desk, reviewing what she knew about the three new names on the list. The first to vanish was Deborah Schiffer, aged thirteen, from Lowell, Massachusetts. Twenty-five years ago, she vanished somewhere between her middle school and her piano teacher's house.

A year and a half later, Patty Boles, fifteen, was last seen at a shopping mall, where she'd been dropped off by her mother. Like Deborah Schiffer, she was an above-average student who had never been in trouble. Her disappearance no doubt contributed to the subsequent break-up of her parents' marriage. Her mother died seven years later; her father, whom Jane was finally able to reach in Florida, scarcely wanted to talk about his long-lost daughter. 'I'm remarried and I have three kids now. It hurts too much to even hear Patty's name,' he told Jane over the phone. He confirmed he'd spoken to Detective Ingersoll recently.

More than a year passed before the next girl went missing. Sherry Tanaka, sixteen, vanished from her own home one afternoon, leaving the front door ajar. Her mother, now living in Connecticut, had recently received a letter from Ingersoll asking about Sherry. It was dated April 4, and had been forwarded through a series of old addresses.

Having three Massachusetts girls go missing over a period of six years was not in itself surprising. Dozens of girls in Massachusetts had vanished during that same time period, girls in the same age group, who had not made it onto Ingersoll's list. Why had he focused on these particular victims?

And then there was seventeen-year-old Charlotte Dion. Unlike the other girls, she'd been older and a disinterested C-minus student. How did she fit into the pattern?

Jane turned her attention to the folder on Charlotte compiled by Detective Buckholz. It was a great deal thicker than Laura Fang's file, and she had to assume it was because of the Dion name. Wealth did count, even in matters of justice.

Jane opened the envelope containing what were probably the last images ever recorded of Charlotte, obtained from the *Boston Globe* photo files. There were a dozen photos taken at the double burial service of Arthur and Dina Mallory. The horrific nature of their deaths, and the extensive publicity surrounding the Red Phoenix massacre, had drawn nearly 200 people to the cemetery according to the *Globe* article, and the photographer had taken several shots of the sombrely dressed gathering.

The most arresting images were the close-ups of the family. Charlotte, with her pale features and long blonde hair, was the fragile embodiment of grief. Her hand was lifted to her mouth, as though to stifle a sob, and her face was contorted in a look of physical pain. Standing on her right was her father, looking at her with concern. But her body was turned away from him, as though she did not want him to see her distress.

At the periphery stood Mark Mallory, his dark hair now longer and more unruly. He towered over the gaunt, middle-aged woman seated in a wheelchair. His mother, Barbara, Jane assumed. Here was the discarded wife, staring at the graves of her ex-husband and the woman who had stolen him. Did she feel some trace of satisfaction at that moment?

Jane flipped to the next photo, taken from the same vantage point, but Charlotte's face was blurred as she turned even further from her father. By the next shot, she was halfway off the frame, only her back still in view. One more click of the shutter, and Charlotte was no longer visible at all; neither was Mark. Patrick Dion and Barbara Mallory remained in place, both their faces registering puzzlement that their children had slipped away from the gathering.

What had been going on between Mark and Charlotte? Had he followed her to offer his support?

The final shot was of the crowd as it dispersed, their backs turned from the grave sites. Charlotte was again visible, walking beside her father, Patrick's arm round her waist. But Charlotte's head was turned in a backward glance towards her mother's grave. That same mother who had walked out of her life five years earlier.

AT LUNCHTIME, Jane went downstairs to the cafeteria for coffee and a ham sandwich. She brought both up to eat at her desk, and turned to her computer to review the file of crime scene photos from the Ingersoll residence. *That was the night I should have died.* She took a deep breath and forced herself to focus. She studied the kitchen, where Ingersoll lay with blood pooled round his head. Clicked to his home office with the ransacked drawers, the bare desktop where a computer must have been. This was the chaos that he'd found when he got home from his fishing trip: the evidence of a burglary. Finally she clicked on the bedroom, where Ingersoll's suitcase still sat on the floor. He'd not had the chance to unpack.

She advanced to the photos of his Ford Taurus, parked on the street. That night she'd been so shaken by what had happened in the alley, she had not personally searched the car. Frost reported finding a week-old receipt from a Greenville, Maine, gas station. It corroborated the daughter's statement that Ingersoll had left for a fishing trip.

She went back through all the photos again, clicking through image after image. When she did not find what she was searching for, she called Frost.

'Did you find a tackle box anywhere in the house?' she asked.

'Um, no. I don't remember seeing one.'

'Who goes fishing without a tackle box?'

'Maybe he rented everything up at the camp where he was staying.'

'You talked to the manager up there?'

'Yeah. But I didn't ask him about fishing gear. Why?'

'Just strikes me as odd, that's all.' She hung up and pulled out the page with Ingersoll's call log. Scanning down it, she spotted a Maine area code and dialled the number.

A male voice answered with a no-nonsense: 'Loon Point.'

'Detective Jane Rizzoli, Boston PD. May I ask who I'm speaking to?'

'Joe. Someone else called from Boston PD yesterday. Spoke to my son.'

'That would have been Detective Frost. You had a guest up there recently, name of Ingersoll.'

'Yes, Will said you folks were asking about him. My wife checked him into the cabin, but she's not here today. He stayed five days, pretty much kept to himself.'

'Was that the first time Mr Ingersoll stayed at Loon Point?'

'Don't remember seeing him before.'

'How long have you worked there?'

'Since it opened. I own the place. Look, I gotta help some guests.'

'One last question. Did Mr Ingersoll rent any fishing gear?'

'Yeah. Will helped him choose a rod and reel. Don't think he caught much, though.'

As she hung up, her cellphone was ringing. It was Erin.

'I've seen some pretty surprising things over the years, but this might just top them all.'

'What are we talking about?'

'That metallic fragment that was embedded in the neck of Jane Doe.'

'Yeah. A fragment from the blade.'

'It's unlike any metal I've ever come across.'

FROST AND TAM were waiting for Jane in the crime lab. So was a soft-spoken African American gentleman whom Erin introduced as Dr Calvin Napoleon Cherry, from Harvard's Arthur Sackler Museum.

'When I realised what this metal might be, I asked Dr Cherry to take a look at it,' said Erin. 'If anyone has an answer, it'll be him.'

Dr Cherry responded with an embarrassed laugh. 'You make me sound far too impressive.'

'What is your role at the Sackler Museum, Dr Cherry?' asked Jane.

'I'm curator of their weapons collection. I wrote my doctoral thesis on the metallurgic analysis of blades. Specifically, the blades of China and Japan. They're closely related.'

'So you think this blade was made in Asia?'

'I'm almost certain it was.'

'Here,' said Erin, settling down in front of her computer. 'Let me show you the images I sent to Dr Cherry earlier this week. These are micrographs of the fragment.' On the monitor they saw an image of grey swirls and waves.

'What you're looking at,' said Dr Cherry, 'is called lamellar or Damascus steel. It forms this wavy pattern when different layers of metal are folded and hammered again and again. The more layers you see beaten together, the finer the workmanship, and the stronger the sword. In China, the best steel is called *bailian jinggang*, or "hundred-times-forged steel". And that produces these patterns you see here, which we call the blade's veins.'

'But it's not from Damascus at all,' said Frost.

'No, it's originally from India. But good ideas are bound to spread, and once the technique reached China, sword making truly advanced to an art.' Doctor Cherry warmed to his theme: 'With every new conflict, weapons always evolve. When the Mongols invaded during the Song dynasty, they introduced sabres. The Chinese adapted that sabre into their own curved sword. It's known as the *dao*, and it was used by cavalry to cut and slash while on horseback. We're talking about blades that were razor-sharp, so you can imagine the carnage on the battlefield. There would have been mass dismemberment and decapitation.'

It was a gruesome image that Jane could picture only too vividly. She remembered the alley. The whoosh of the blade, the spray of hot blood on her face.

'For much of ancient history, armed conflict was part of life in China,' said Dr Cherry. 'Warlord was pitted against warlord. And there were invasions by Mongols and pirates.'

'Pirates? In China?'

Dr Cherry nodded. 'During the Ming dynasty, Japanese pirates terrorised the Chinese coast. Then a hero named General Qi defeated them.'

'I remember hearing about him,' said Tam. 'My grandmother told me that General Qi cut off the heads of five thousand pirates.'

'General Qi's elite soldiers were renowned for their ingenious tactics,' said Dr Cherry. 'And their weapon of choice was the *dao*. The Chinese sabre.' He pointed to the magnified image on Erin's computer screen. 'It's amazing to think that's what this fragment probably came from.'

'How can you tell from that little piece? Couldn't it be from a Japanese samurai sword?'

'That's possible, I suppose, since the Japanese learned their sword-making techniques from the Chinese.'

'And samurai swords are for sale in speciality knife stores.'

'Ah, but those stores don't sell swords like this one,' said Dr Cherry.

'What's so special about it?' asked Jane.

'Its age. Based on carbon-fourteen dating.'

Jane frowned. 'I thought that was only used for dating organic material. This is steel.'

'Let's go back to how ancient swords were made,' said Dr Cherry. 'The traditional technique was to melt iron sand in a forge. That iron was then combined with carbon to form steel. But where do you get the carbon? They used wood ash.'

'And wood is organic,' said Tam.

'Exactly. We extracted the carbon component of this specimen using sealed-tube combustion,' said Erin. 'And that carbon was then analysed.'

'And that's where the big surprise came in,' said Dr Cherry. He pointed to the micrograph. 'That steel you see there was crafted during the Ming dynasty. Carbon-fourteen dating narrows it down to sometime between the years 1540 and 1590.' He looked at Jane, his eyes aglow. 'That just happens to be the era of General Qi's legendary army. A sabre with this degree of craftsmanship could have been wielded by one of his elite soldiers. Maybe it even cut off the heads of a few pirates.'

Jane stared at the image on the computer. 'This weapon is over four hundred years old? And it's still usable?'

'It's possible to preserve such a sword for a long time, but it takes special care, especially if this weapon actually saw use on the battlefield. Blood corrodes steel, even if it's assiduously wiped away. The blade would need repeated cleaning and polishing and that alone abrades the metal, making the cutting edge brittle. That may be why this particular blade chipped off in the victim's neck: it's simply reached the end of its useful life as a killing tool.' He gave a wistful sigh. 'What I'd give to examine it! A *dao* from General Qi's era would be priceless, if you could just find it.'

Frost said, softly, 'I know where to find that sword.'

ONCE AGAIN, Detectives Rizzoli and Frost have invaded my studio, and this time they've brought along a well-dressed black gentleman whose soft-spoken diffidence indicates that he is not a policeman. The sudden interruption startles my class, and the dozen students stand frozen. Only Bella strides into action, planting herself beside me. She acts as my fierce guardian, all five foot four inches of her.

Detective Rizzoli assumes command of the conversation. 'We understand you're in possession of an antique sword, Mrs Fang,' she says. 'We ask you to surrender it to us now.'

I look at Detective Frost and shame darkens his eyes. On the night we shared dinner, I allowed him to hold Zheng Yi and I shared the sword's history with him. That night, I saw kindness in his face. Now that face tightens into a mask that closes off our earlier connection. It is clear that he is a policeman above all, which poisons any possibility of friendship between us.

'And if I give you my sword, what will you do with it?' I ask.

'Examine it to determine if it was used in the commission of a crime.'

'Will it be returned to me undamaged?'

'Mrs Fang, we're not here to negotiate. Where is the sword?'

Bella steps forward, fury radiating off her like the hum of a high-voltage wire. 'You can't just confiscate it!'

'The law says I can.'

'Zheng Yi has been in my family for generations,' I say. 'It has never left my possession.'

Detective Rizzoli frowns at me. 'The sword has a name?'

'Why are you surprised? Don't you have a legend in Western culture, about a sword named Excalibur?'

'Madam Fang,' says the black man. 'Believe me, I don't want the sword damaged in any way. I promise I'll treat it with care.'

'And why should I believe you?' I ask.

'Because it's my job. I'm Dr Calvin Cherry from the Arthur Sackler Museum, and I've examined many ancient swords.' He dips his head, a gesture of regard that impresses me. 'I would be honoured if you'd allow me to see Zheng Yi.'

This man pronounces the name with a perfect accent, so I know he speaks Mandarin. Even more importantly, he understands that a fine weapon is to be revered.

'Come with me,' I say. 'Bella, please take charge of the class.'

I lead the visitors into the back room and unlock the closet to reveal the bundle that lies on the shelf. With both hands, I present it to Dr Cherry.

He receives it with a bow. Detectives Rizzoli and Frost watch as he peels back the layers of red silk, exposing the sheathed weapon. He pauses for a moment to examine the scabbard, which is made of lacquered wood with bronze fittings. When he pulls out the sword, the blade makes a musical whine that sends a thrill across my skin.

'*Liuye dao*,' he says softly.

I nod. 'A willow-leaf sabre.'

'And you say this comes from your family?'

'It was my mother's. And before that, her mother's.'

'How many generations does it go back?'

'All the way to General Washi.'

Detective Rizzoli asks, 'Who was he, this general?'

'General Washi was a woman,' says Dr Cherry. 'A warrior who fought with a sword in each hand. She commanded thousands of soldiers against those Japanese pirates I told you about.' He looks at me in wonder. 'And you're her descendant.'

Smiling back at him, I nod. 'I'm pleased you know of her.'

'Dr Cherry,' cuts in Detective Rizzoli. 'What about the sword?'

'Of course.' He slips his glasses on his nose. 'This has the typical curve of a willow-leaf *dao*. This one is somewhat shorter than usual, but I guess you'd expect that if this weapon was designed specifically for a woman's hand. Look at these etchings in the steel! I'm amazed how deep they still are! And this grip, you'd almost think it was original, if you didn't know it has to be at least four hundred . . .' He pauses. For the next few moments he says nothing at all. He brings the *dao* close to his glasses, minutely studying the cutting edge of the blade. Finally, he reaches into his pocket for a magnifier, through which he examines the etched panels.

At last he straightens, and when he looks at me, I see a strange sadness in his eyes. A look that is almost regretful. He slides the *dao* back into the scabbard and holds it out to me. 'Madam Fang, thank you for allowing me to see Zheng Yi.'

'Then you are finished with her?' I ask.

'There's no need for us to take it after all.'

Detective Rizzoli protests. 'Dr Cherry, the crime lab needs to examine it.'

'Trust me, this is not the weapon you're looking for.'

Rizzoli turns to Detective Frost. 'Is it the same sword you saw?'

Frost looks confused. 'I'm not sure. I mean, I only saw it for a moment.'

'Detective Frost,' I say coldly, 'the next time you visit, I hope you'll be courteous enough to tell me what it is you really want from me.'

My barb finds its mark, and he flinches as though stung.

Detective Rizzoli sighs. 'Mrs Fang, regardless of what Dr Cherry says, we still need to take the sword for further study.'

I place it in her hands. 'I expect it returned to me undamaged.'

As the visitors leave, I see Detective Frost cast a regretful look back, but I wear my disdain like a shield.

'*Sifu?*' Bella says softly, stepping into my office.

In the next room, the students continue sparring. She closes the door so they cannot see the look of satisfaction that passes between us.

The chess game continues.

JANE WAITED until they were halfway down the block before she confronted Dr Cherry. 'How can you be so sure this isn't the weapon?'

'That sword you took from her isn't the one you're looking for. It's certainly well made, and it has the proper heft and balance of a Ming dynasty sabre. But it is just a very good reproduction. At most, maybe fifty, seventy-five years old.'

'Why didn't you say any of this while we were there?'

'Because it's clear that she believes it's real. I didn't have the heart to disillusion her, not when it means so much to her. At the museum, I'm often asked to evaluate family heirlooms. People bring in things with all sorts of mythology attached to them. Almost always, my verdict is disappointing because what they bring aren't treasures, but worthless reproductions. It forces people to question everything they were ever told as children. People want to believe their family has a unique story to tell, and for proof they point to Grandma's antique ring, or Grandpa's old fiddle. Why force them to hear the brutal truth?'

'Mrs Fang believes she's descended from warrior women,' said Frost. 'Do you think that's just another family fantasy?'

'Anything's possible, Detective Frost. You could be descended from King Arthur or William the Conqueror. If that's important to you, then go on believing. Family mythology has far more meaning to us than the truth. It helps us cope with the insignificance of our own lives.'

Jane snorted. 'My family mythology was all about how much beer Uncle Lou could chug at one sitting.'

Dr Cherry smiled. 'I'm talking about heroes. There must be at least one of those in your family. Think about it, Detective.'

Jane did think about it as she drove home; about a great-aunt who was a nun in Africa. Another great-aunt who struggled to feed eight children in Italy during the war. They could be called heroes, but nothing like Iris Fang's legendary ancestor who fought with two sabres. A fable was what that sounded like: no more real than Sun Wukong the Monkey King, who

battled demons and river monsters. And who could blame Iris for retreating
into such a fantasy? She was dying of leukaemia. Her husband and daughter
were gone. Alone in her sad home, did she dream of battlefields and glory?
Wouldn't I?

As she braked at a stoplight, her cellphone rang. An angry voice blasted
her ear.

'Why didn't you tell me?' said her brother Frankie. 'We can't let her do it.'

She sighed. 'I take it this is about Mom's engagement?'

'I had to hear the news from Mike. She can't marry that guy. You gotta
stop her.'

'You wanna tell me how I should go about that?'

'Fuck's sake, Jane, I can't believe you're letting this happen. Families
oughta stick together. And what do we know about this Korsak guy,
anyway?'

'He's a decent human being. And he's a good cop.' She paused, struck by
the fact that she was defending the same man whom she had not relished as
a stepfather. But everything she'd said about Korsak was true. A woman
could do much worse.

'And it's fine with you that he's bonking Ma?' said Frankie.

'You have no problem with Dad bonking the Bimbo.'

'That's different. He's a guy.'

That pissed her off. 'Mom's not dead yet, Frankie. She's good-looking
and fun, and she deserves another chance at love. Instead of harassing her
about this, you go and talk to Dad. He's the reason she went out with
Korsak in the first place.'

She tossed the phone on the seat, angry that this was yet one more thing
to worry about.

The phone rang again. Abruptly, she pulled over to the kerb to answer it.

'I don't have time for this, Frankie,' she snapped.

'Who the fuck's Frankie?' came an equally irritated retort. 'Listen,
Rizzoli, I've had enough of this Red Phoenix crap and I want you to make it
stop.' There was no mistaking Kevin Donohue's gravelly voice.

'I don't know what you're talking about, Mr Donohue,' she said.

'I got another one this afternoon. Joey's obituary. "Survived by his
loving mother and sister", blah blah blah. And there's a message on the
back. It says, "It's coming for you."'

'And you think it's worth taking seriously?'

'Two people have been chopped up by some freak monkey creature, and you think I shouldn't take this seriously?'

She said, evenly, 'That information isn't public.'

'I ain't the public, OK?'

So he does have a channel into our investigation, she thought. A man as powerful as Donohue could buy eyes and ears everywhere, including City Hall and Schroeder Plaza.

'Do your job, Detective,' said Donohue. 'You're supposed to serve and protect, remember?'

She took a breath and managed to sound civil. 'I'll need to examine the latest note. Where are you right now?'

'I'm at my warehouse on Jeffries Point. Get here soon.'

SIX

Darkness had fallen when Jane drove through the open gate of Donohue Wholesale Meats and parked between a BMW and a silver Mercedes. Mobsters did seem to like their flashy imports. As she climbed out of the car she heard the roar of a jet taking off from nearby Logan Airport.

'Detective Rizzoli.'

Turning, she recognised one of the burly bodyguards she'd met at Donohue's residence a few days ago. Sean.

'He's waiting inside,' Sean said, and eyed her holstered weapon. 'First, you're gonna have to hand that over.'

'Mr Donohue didn't mind me carrying the other day.'

'He's more nervous now on account of that message.'

'I don't surrender my weapon to anyone. So you tell Mr Donohue he can come see me at police headquarters.' She turned back towards her car.

'OK,' the man relented. 'But I'll be watching you like a hawk.'

'Whatever.'

She followed him into the warehouse, and as the insulated door swung shut behind her, she suddenly wished she'd brought a heavier jacket. It was so cold in there she could see her own breath. Sean led her through a curtain of slitted plastic, into the refrigerated area beyond. From ceiling hooks hung enormous sides of beef, row upon row of them, a forest of suspended corpses. They walked through to an office at the rear of the building, and her escort knocked on the door.

It swung open and she recognised the second bodyguard. Jane walked into the windowless room, and the door gave a solid thud as it closed behind her. She was trapped in a fortress within a meat locker, guarded by armed thugs, yet she felt less nervous about the situation than her host appeared to be. Wielding power meant always dreading the moment when you'd lose it.

Kevin Donohue sat behind his desk, his sausage-like fingers resting on the ziplock bag containing the latest message. 'Unfortunately,' he said, 'my brilliant associates got their fingerprints all over it.'

'These notes never have any fingerprints,' she said, taking the bag. She looked at the photocopied side, the *Boston Globe* obituary of Joey Gilmore, published nineteen years ago. Flipping it over, she read the message, written in block letters: IT'S COMING FOR YOU.

She looked at Donohue. 'What do you think the "it" refers to?'

'Obviously, it's that thing playing vigilante with a sword. I want this crap to stop, before any more blood gets spilt.'

'You mean your blood, specifically.' She glanced at the two men flanking her. 'Looks to me like you've already got plenty of protection.'

'Not against that thing. Word round town is, it sliced up those two professionals like lunch meat. And then it vanished without a trace.'

'Were they your professionals?'

'I told you the last time. No, I didn't hire them.'

'Any idea who they were working for?'

'I'd tell you if I knew. I hear the contract went out on that cop weeks ago.'

'A contract on Detective Ingersoll?'

Donohue nodded. 'Must've made someone really nervous.'

'Ingersoll was retired.'

'But he was asking a lot of questions.'

'About girls, Mr Donohue. Girls who've gone missing.' Jane stared into his eyes. 'Now, that's a subject that should make you nervous.'

'Me?' He leaned back, his massive weight setting off a loud creak in the chair. 'No idea what you're talking about.'

'Prostitution? Trafficking underage girls?'

'Prove it.'

She shrugged. 'Gee, now that I think about it, maybe I should just let the monkey creature do its thing.'

'It's coming after the wrong guy! I had nothing to do with the Red Phoenix! Sure, Joey was a weasel. I didn't shed any tears when he got whacked, but I didn't order it.'

She looked down at Joey's obituary. 'Someone thinks you did.'

'It's that crazy lady in Chinatown. Gotta be her behind it.'

'You mean Mrs Fang?'

'I'm thinking she hired Ingersoll to find out who killed her husband. He got too close to the truth and that's how this war started. If you think the Irish play rough, you haven't seen what the Chinese can do. They have people who can practically walk through walls.'

'Are these people or fairy tales we're talking about?'

'Didn't you see that movie *Ninja Assassin*? They're trained to kill since childhood.'

'Ninjas are Japanese.'

'Don't split hairs! It's the same skills, the same training. I've been look-ing into Iris Fang's background. She grew up in some secret monastery up in the mountains, where they train kids for that sort of thing. And now she has all those students working for her.'

'She's a fifty-five-year-old widow.' *An ailing woman who believes she's descended from a mythical general and has a fake sword to prove it.*

'There are widows, and then there's her.'

'Do you know for a fact that Iris Fang is threatening you?'

'I'm just telling you what it smells like to me. She lost her husband that night, and figures that I ordered the hit. I'm being blamed, and for once I didn't do it.'

A loud bang suddenly rocked the building. Jane caught a glimpse of Donohue's face, frozen in surprise, just before the room went pitch-black.

'What the fuck?' yelled Donohue.

'I think the power's out,' one of his men said.

'Get the generator going!'

'If I can find a flashlight . . .'

A noise overhead made them all fall silent. Jane looked up as a rapid thump-thump-thump pattered on the roof. She felt her palms slicken with sweat as she unsnapped her weapon holster. 'Where's the generator switch?' she asked.

'It's in the warehouse,' one of the men responded. 'Electrical box is against the back wall. But I ain't gonna be able to find it in the dark—' He stopped as they heard the sound again, light as raindrops across the roof.

Jane pulled out her flashlight. The beam landed on Donohue, his face gleaming with sweat and fear. 'Call nine one one,' she ordered.

He grabbed the phone on his desk. Slammed it down again. 'It's dead!'

She pulled her cellphone from her belt. No signal.

'These walls are bulletproof and blastproof,' said Donohue.

'Great. The ultimate dead zone.'

'You'll need to go outside to get a signal.'

I don't want to go outside. And neither does anyone else, Jane thought. *But we can't stay in here for ever; someone has to step out and make the call, and it doesn't look like it's going to be anyone but me.* She drew her weapon and went to the door. 'I'll lead,' she said. 'I need back-up.'

A moment passed. 'All right,' Donohue said. 'Take Colin with you. But Sean stays.'

She only hoped Colin had enough functioning grey cells not to accidentally shoot her in the back.

At the door Jane paused, listening for sounds beyond it, but the barrier was too thick.

She pulled the door open a crack. Through a high warehouse window shone the dim glow of the city; just enough light for Jane to make out dark rows of hanging meat. Anything could be lurking in that gloom.

Jane swung her flashlight and quickly scanned the perimeter. In one sweep she registered hanging carcasses, the concrete floor, the fog of her own breath. She heard Colin behind her, his breathing shaky with fear.

An armed and terrified man was not the sort of back-up she'd had in mind.

'Where's the closest exit?' she whispered.

'Straight ahead. Far end of the building.'

Swallowing hard, she started down the row of carcasses. She swept the light back and forth, scanning for movement. The flashlight felt slippery in her trembling hand. *Whatever you are*, she thought, *you spared me once before*. But that didn't mean it would repeat the favour, not when it saw the company she was keeping.

More carcasses loomed. Aiming her light straight ahead, she could not see the end of the row. Abruptly she halted. 'Listen.'

It was just a faint creak, the sound that a tree makes when a rising wind causes it to sway. *It's coming from above us*. Jane lifted her light towards the ceiling and saw a carcass swinging back and forth, as if shoved by an invisible hand.

They heard another creak to their left. 'There!' said Colin, and Jane swung her light. Found herself staring at a second carcass moving like a giant pendulum back and forth across the narrow beam of her flashlight.

'Behind us!' said Colin, voice rising to shrill panic now. 'No, over there!'

Jane spun, her light catching movement everywhere as the darkness came alive with a noisy chorus of clanks and squealing metal.

'Where the fuck is it?' yelled Colin, wildly swinging his weapon as carcasses swayed all round them. He fired and somewhere in the darkness metal clanged. He fired again and the bullet thunked into cold meat.

'Will you stop it, before you kill us both!' Jane yelled.

He ceased fire but was still jerking one way and then the other in search of a target. No doubt he imagined the creature everywhere, just as she did. *Over there, was that the flash of a face, the gleam of an eye?*

She and Colin stood, backs pressed against each other, both of them frantically scanning the shadows. The darkness seemed to be watching them. *And with this light in my hand*, she thought, *whatever is here knows exactly where we are*.

'Keep moving,' she whispered. 'To the door.'

He was not about to be left behind. As she moved towards the door, she could almost feel the man's breath on her neck. For a guy like Colin, a gun was enough to transform a coward into a bully and a killer. But put that man in the dark where he can't see the enemy, the coward is stripped bare again.

Only after they'd reached the exit and stepped outside did she hear him give a relieved sigh. She pulled out her cellphone, but hesitated before making the call. What would she say? *The power failed and we all freaked out. Heard things in the dark and imagined monsters.*

'You gonna call or what?' said Colin. The bully was back.

She lifted her phone and went instantly still, her gaze riveted on the warehouse rooftop. A figure squatted there, silhouetted like a gargoyle against the night sky. It was watching her, just as she was watching it. *Does it see me as friend or enemy?*

'There it is!' yelled Colin.

As he raised his gun to fire, Jane grabbed his arm. The bullet went wild, flying harmlessly into the sky.

'What the fuck?' Colin yelled. 'It's right there, kill it!'

On the rooftop, the figure didn't move; it simply sat staring at them.

'If you don't take it down, I will,' said Colin. Once again he lifted his gun, scanning the rooftop. 'Where is it? Where'd it go?'

'It's gone,' said Jane, staring up at the empty rooftop. *You saved my life once; now I've saved yours.*

'DONOHUE'S A DIRTBAG,' said Tam. 'I say we just let the thing take him out.'

The thing. They had no other name for whatever it was that had perched on the warehouse last night. In the battle between good and evil, the thing had clearly staked its position. Already it had cut down two hired killers. Now its gaze was fixed on Donohue.

It spared me, thought Jane. *How does it know I'm one of the good guys?*

'Whatever it is,' said Frost, 'it's pretty damn clever at avoiding surveillance cameras.'

The three detectives had spent all morning reviewing video footage from cameras mounted throughout the neighbourhood where Donohue's warehouse was located. The feed from one of Donohue's cameras was now playing on the monitor, and it showed an evening view of his parking lot. Jane watched her own car pull in through the gate.

'Smile. You're on *Candid Camera*,' said Frost.

On the video, Jane stepped out of her car. Donohue's man Sean appeared, and they had their conversation about Jane's weapon.

'Why didn't you ask us to go there with you?' said Tam.

'I was just there to pick up the note. It was nothing.'

'Turned into a lot more than nothing. You could have used us.'

On the screen, Jane and the bodyguard disappeared into the warehouse and the view went static. Frost fast-forwarded the video ten minutes. The image suddenly went blank.

'And that's it,' said Frost. 'The same thing happens in all of his surveillance cameras. The power cuts out, and the picture goes blank.'

'So we don't have a single shot of the thing,' said Tam.

'Not on Donohue's cameras.'

'Is this thing invisible?'

'Maybe it just knows what it's doing.' Frost brought up thumbnail photos of the warehouse exterior. 'I took these pictures this morning. You can see the cameras are focused on entrance points. But the back side of the building is just uninterrupted wall, so it wasn't under surveillance. Nor was the rooftop.' He looked at Jane. 'It is physically possible to evade the cameras. This doesn't have to be some supernatural creature.'

'Last night, it was easy to believe it was,' said Jane softly. 'Donohue has a security system and bodyguards. He's armed to the teeth. But against this thing, he has no idea how to protect himself.'

'Why should we care, exactly?' said Tam. 'The thing's doing our job for us. When it comes to cleaning up the bad guys, I say let it rip.'

Jane stared at the photos of Donohue's warehouse. 'You know, I have a hard time disagreeing with you. I owe that thing my life. But I want to know how it penetrated the building. I didn't see it until the end when it allowed me to see it. When it sat up on the roof.'

'Why would it do that?' said Frost.

'Maybe to prove to us it actually exists? Funny thing is, I'm not afraid of it anymore. I think it's here for a reason' She looked at Tam. 'What do you know about *wushu*?'

He sighed. 'Of course you'd turn to the Asian guy.'

'Come on, Tam, you know a lot about Chinese folk tales.'

'Yeah,' he conceded. 'Courtesy of my grandmother.'

'Donohue thinks that ninja warriors are after him. I looked it up last night and I found out ninja techniques actually come from China. Donohue says these guys are raised from childhood to kill, and they can penetrate any defences.'

'We both know half of that is fantasy.'

'Yeah, but which half?'

'The half that made it into *Crouching Tiger, Hidden Dragon*.'

'I liked that movie,' said Frost.

'But did you ever once believe that warriors can fly through the air and fight in treetops? Of course not, because it's a fairy tale. Just like all the other tales about monks who could walk on water or immortals who came down from heaven to mingle with men.'

'But legends sometimes have an element of truth to them,' said Jane. 'And there really were fighting monks in China.'

'OK,' admitted Tam. 'Maybe that part is real. There actually were fighting Shaolin monks from a mountain temple. They got famous for their combat skills after they defended the emperor against an uprising. But the art of *wushu* goes back long before those monks. It's thousands of years old, so old that no one really knows its true history. And with every century that goes by, the tales get more and more outlandish. That's how you end up with people thinking that *wushu* warriors are like ghosts: impossible to kill.'

'After last night, I'd almost believe it's true,' said Jane.

'I'd almost believe it's a ghost, too,' Frost said as he studied another video on the screen. 'I pulled footage from cameras all over that neighbourhood, and so far I haven't caught a glimpse.'

'If it's flesh and blood, it's going to turn up somewhere,' said Jane.

Frost switched to a different video. 'OK, this camera's about a block away.' He hit Play, and a view of an alley appeared, a chain-link fence blocking the far end. Minutes passed and nothing changed. 'Again, nothing.'

Jane stood up. 'Happy viewing. Call me if you spot anything.'

She was almost out the door when she heard Frost suck in a sharp breath. She turned. 'What?'

'It went by so fast!'

Jane moved back to the monitor and watched as Frost rewound and hit Play again. The same dimly lit alley with the chain-link fence at the far end.

'There,' said Frost.

The figure seemed to materialise out of darkness, its back to the camera as it moved in a blur down the alley. In one swift leap it launched itself up and over the fence and landed in a crouch on the other side. There it paused and straightened to its full height.

Frost froze the image.

It was garbed head to toe in black. They could not see a face, but the figure clearly stood out in silhouette, revealing a slender waist and the unmistakable curve of hips.

'It's a woman,' said Frost.

BELLA LI strode into Boston PD's Schroeder Plaza wearing low-slung blue jeans and a black leather jacket. Before stepping through the metal detector, she made a show of peeling off the jacket, revealing a skintight T-shirt that hugged every curve of her bra-less breasts. She returned the stares of the watching cops and swaggered through Security to meet Jane.

'Didn't know I'd have to pass inspection,' Bella said.

'Everyone does. Even the mayor.' Jane waved her towards the elevator.

As they rode up to the second floor, Bella stood with hip cocked, jacket slung over her shoulder. *This is one gal who could probably take me down*, Jane thought. Bella might not be big, but she was all muscle and as lithe as a panther. Staring at her, Jane wondered, *Are you the creature who saved my life in that alley?*

Jane escorted Bella to the interview room. 'I'll let Detective Frost know you're here,' she said, and left the young woman alone.

In the adjoining room, Jane joined Frost, who was watching Bella through the one-way mirror. Their guest appeared not in the least nervous, and was leaning back in her chair, boots propped up on the table.

'Did she say anything interesting on the way up?' asked Frost.

Jane shook her head. 'Never even asked why we called her in. I think she's trying to show us that she doesn't give a damn. Let's go rattle her cage.'

Bella answered Jane's questions in a monotone. The easy queries came first: Name? Date of birth? Occupation? Bella sighed loudly, the picture of disinterest. But the next question made the muscles in her forearm twitch.

'Where were you last night, between the hours of six and nine?'

Bella shrugged. 'I was home.'

'Alone?'

'I consider my love life private. I don't see why I should have to share names with anyone.'

'So someone was with you?' asked Frost. 'Could you tell us his name?'

'Why do you assume I'm interested in men?' She smiled at Jane.

'OK,' Jane said with a sigh. 'What was her name, then?'

'There was no one. I was home alone.'

'Did you leave your residence at any time?'

'I don't remember.'

'Maybe if we showed you a photo, you would remember.'

'What photo?'

Frost said, 'From a security camera on Jeffries Point. You're very good at eluding surveillance cameras, Ms Li. But you didn't spot all of them.'

For the first time, Bella didn't have a ready response.

'We know it's you in the video,' Jane lied. 'We know you were there at the warehouse. The question is, why?'

The girl laughed. 'You tell me. Since you seem to know everything.'

'You went there to scare Kevin Donohue.'

'Why would I?'

'You broke into his warehouse. Disabled his security system and his phone line.'

'I did that all by myself?'

'You have extensive martial arts training. You were taught at one of the best academies in the world, in Taiwan.' Jane slapped a folder on the table. 'The file on your travel records for the past five years.'

'So I've been in and out of the country. Aren't we Americans free to travel where we want?'

'Not many Americans spend five years in a Taiwan monastery, studying an ancient art like *wushu*.'

'Different strokes for different folks.'

'And here's the interesting part. You were sponsored by Mrs Fang. She's not wealthy, yet she paid for those years of training. Why?'

'She saw that I had talent. I was seventeen and living on the streets when she took me on, maybe because I reminded her of her daughter.'

'Is that what you're doing in Boston? Playing her surrogate daughter?'

'I teach at her studio. We practise the same style of martial arts. And we share the same philosophy.'

'What philosophy would that be?'

Bella looked her in the eye. 'That justice is a responsibility shared by all.'

'Justice? Or vengeance?'

'Some would say that vengeance is simply another word for justice.'

Jane stared at Bella, trying to read her. Looking into those eyes, Jane glimpsed an animal spirit that made her suddenly draw back. As if she'd glimpsed something in those eyes that was not quite human.

Frost broke the silence. 'Ms Li, it's time to tell us the truth about why Iris Fang chose you in particular.'

'She could have chosen anyone.'

'But she flew all the way to San Francisco to find one particular seventeen-year-old girl whose mother had just died. What was so special about you?'

When Bella didn't answer, Jane said, 'We have your school records from California. They don't mention your mother's immigration status.'

'My mother's dead. What does it matter now?'

'She was an illegal immigrant.'

'Prove it.'

'What about you, Bella?'

'I have a US passport.'

'Which says that you were born in the state of Massachusetts. Six years later, you're registered in a public school in San Francisco. Your mother is working as a hotel maid with a fake Social Security number. Why did you two suddenly up stakes and run to California?' Jane leaned in closer. 'I have a pretty good idea of who you really are. I just can't prove it yet. But I will.' She glanced at Frost. 'Show her the search warrant.'

Bella frowned. 'Search warrant?'

'Detective Tam is at your address now, with the search team.'

'What do you think you're going to find?'

'Evidence that will link you to the deaths of an unidentified female Jane Doe on the night of April 15th, and an unidentified male John Doe on the night of April 21st.'

Bella shook her head. 'Sorry to disappoint you, but I was onstage at a *wushu* demonstration in Chinatown on April 15th. There were at least two hundred witnesses.'

'We'll verify that. In the meantime, if you want an attorney, now is the time to call one.'

'You're arresting me?' Bella snapped forward, a move so sudden that Jane flinched. 'This is a very bad mistake.'

'Tell us why it's a mistake, and maybe we'll reconsider,' said Jane.

Bella stared back with eyes as cold as polished stone. 'I have nothing more to say.'

BELLA'S APARTMENT was clean. Far too clean.

'This is the way we found it,' said Tam. 'It's like no one lives here. Either she's obsessive-compulsive about housecleaning, or she was scouring away any trace evidence.'

'How did she know we'd be coming here?'

'Anyone who gets a call to visit Boston PD is going to figure they're a suspect. She must have realised we'd be coming.'

Jane went to the window. It was quiet on this corner of Tai Tung Village, at the south end of Chinatown. Iris Fang's residence was a minute's walk away. She went into the bathroom, where Frost was on his knees scanning the cabinet beneath the sink.

'Nothing,' he said. 'Not a single hair in the shower or sink. It's like no one lives here.'

'Are we sure she does?'

'Tam spoke to the old guy next door. Says he hardly ever sees her, but he does hear voices in here every so often.'

'Voices, as in plural?'

'Could be the TV. She lives alone.'

Jane looked round the pristine bathroom. 'Looks like someone's also been through here with the bleach and a vacuum cleaner.'

'Funny thing about the vacuum cleaner. We can't find one, so we have no bag to look at, no trace evidence.'

Jane headed into the bedroom, where she found Tam talking on his cellphone and a Boston PD criminalist looking at the mattress.

'You didn't see anything like a sword?'

'No, ma'am. We went through the closets and drawers. Pulled out all the furniture.' He paused, glancing round at the bare walls. 'I'm guessing she hasn't been here very long. Didn't bring much in the way of clothes, either.'

Jane opened the closet and saw no more than a dozen items hanging there. Three pairs of black trousers, a few dark sweaters and blouses: the wardrobe of a temporary visitor. A girl who remained a mystery to them.

'Sorry to tell you this,' said Tam, holding up his cellphone. 'But her alibi for April 15th is solid. I just spoke to the programme director at the cultural centre. That night they hosted a martial arts demonstration. Bella Li performed with eight students from the academy. The group arrived at six, ate dinner, and went onstage about nine. They were there for the whole evening.'

'She has no alibi for April 21st.'

'That's not a reason to hold her.'

'Then let's find a reason. Something about her trips my sensors. I know she's involved, but I don't know how.'

'So what do we have, besides your gut feeling?' Tam asked.

'It's served me well before.'

'You know, Tam's right,' said Frost. 'We have to release her.'

'Not till I know more about who she really is,' said Jane. 'There has to be a trail somewhere.' She crossed to the bedroom window and looked down at an alley. The sash was unlocked and a fire escape landing was right outside. Any other female tenant would feel nervous about this lack of security, but Bella Li was fearless, striding through life ready for battle.

Jane turned from the window and suddenly stopped, her gaze on the curtain. The fabric was a print of beige bamboo stalks against a forest of green. On that multicoloured background, the silvery streak was almost invisible. Only at that angle, with the light glancing across the fabric's surface, did Jane see the strand clinging to the fabric.

She pulled an evidence bag out of her pocket and delicately plucked the strand from the curtain. Holding the bag up to the light, she stared through the plastic at the single hair. Then she looked at the window, and at the fire escape just beyond it.

It was here. The creature was in this room.

THE HUNTER WALKS in the woods, rifle in hand, eyes alert for his quarry's prints on snow-dusted ground. It never occurs to him that his prey might be watching him, biding its time until he makes a mistake.

The hunter who stalks me now would see little to fear. I appear to be a middle-aged woman, my hair streaked with grey, my gait slowed by weariness and the weight of the grocery bags I carry. I keep my head down, my shoulders drooped, so that anyone who sees me will think: Here is a victim. Not a woman you need to fear.

But by now my opponent knows he should be wary, just as I am wary of him. So far we have never actually connected, except through his surrogates. We are two hunters still circling each other, and he must make the next move. Only when he emerges into the light will I know his face.

As I draw near my home, I see the light over the porch is dark. Deliberate sabotage or merely a burned-out bulb? My nerves hum with alarm and my heart accelerates. Then I spot the parked car and see the man who steps out to greet me, and my breath rushes out in a sigh of relief and exasperation.

'Mrs Fang?' says Detective Frost. 'I need to speak with you.'

I stare at him without smiling. 'I'm tired tonight. And I have nothing more to say.'

'At least let me help you with those,' he offers. He takes the grocery sacks from my hands and carries them up the steps. He waits for me to open the door. He looks so earnest that I don't have the heart to reject his offer.

I unlock the door and let him in.

As I turn on lights, he carries the sacks into the kitchen and sets them on the counter.

'I wanted to apologise,' he says. 'And to explain.'

'Explain?' I ask, sounding as if I really don't care what he has to say.

'The sword, and why we took it. The weapon we've been looking for is a very old sword, and I knew you owned one.'

'By now you must have realised the mistake you made.'

He nodded. 'The sword will be returned to you.'

'And when will Bella be released?'

'That's more complicated. We're still looking into her background. Something I was hoping you could help us with, since you know her.'

I shake my head. 'The last time we spoke, Detective, I ended up being considered a suspect. You're a policeman, first and foremost.'

'What else would you expect me to be?'

'I don't know. A friend?'

That makes him pause. 'I would be your friend, Iris,' he says. 'If only . . .'

'If only I weren't a suspect.'

'I don't consider you one.'

'Then you aren't doing your job. I could be that killer you're searching for. Maybe you should search my house. There could be another sword hidden here somewhere.'

'Iris, please.'

'Maybe you'll report back to your colleagues that the suspect is not going to be charmed into giving away any more information.'

'That's not why I'm here! The night we had dinner, I wasn't trying to interrogate you. I felt like we both needed a friend, that's all. I know I do.'

He can't bring himself to look me in the eye. He may be a policeman, but he's afraid of my opinion. There's nothing I can offer him now, not comfort or friendship or even a touch on the arm.

'You need a friend your own age, Detective Frost,' I say quietly.

'I don't even see your age. I see a woman who'll never get old.'

'Tell me that in twenty years.'

He smiles. 'Maybe I will.'

The moment trembles with unsaid words. He is a good man; I see that in his eyes. But it's absurd to think we could ever be more than mere acquaintances. Not just because I am nearly two decades older but because of the secrets that place us on opposite sides of a chasm.

As I walk him to the door, he says, 'Tomorrow I'll bring the sword back.'

'And Bella?'

'There's a chance she'll be released in the morning.'

'She's done nothing wrong.'

He stops. 'It's not always clear what's right and what's wrong. Is it?'

I stare back at him, thinking, *Could he know? Is he giving me permission for what I'm about to do?* But he merely smiles and walks away.

I lock the door behind him. The conversation has left me off-balance. What to make of such a man, I wonder, as I head up the stairs to change my clothes. Yet again, he makes me think of my husband.

I am distracted, mulling over the conversation, and I miss the clues that should have warned me: the tremor in the air; the faint scent of unfamiliar flesh. Only when I flip my bedroom light switch and nothing happens do I suddenly realise I am not alone.

The bedroom door slams shut behind me. In the sudden darkness, I cannot see the blow hurtling towards my head, but my instincts spring to life. Something whooshes just above me as I duck and spin towards the bed, where my sword is concealed. Not the decoy reproduction that I surrendered to the police, but the real Zheng Yi. For five centuries, she has been passed down from mothers to daughters, a legacy meant to protect us.

Now, more than ever, I need her.

My attacker lunges, but I slip away like water and roll to the floor. Reach under the box spring for Zheng Yi. She fits into my hand like an old friend and makes a musical sigh as she slides from her scabbard.

In one fluid motion I rise and whirl to face the enemy. The creak of the floor announces his location, to my right. Just as I shift weight to attack, I hear the footfall, but this one is behind me.

Two of them.

It's the last thought I have before I fall.

JANE CROUCHED beside Iris's bed, reading the evidence and not liking what it said to her. There were red splatters on the floor and on the edge of the sheets where a body had fallen. The blood loss was minimal; certainly not enough to be fatal. She stared down at smeared drops, across which a body had been dragged. She had already spotted more blood on the stairs and on the front porch where the door had been left wide open. Something was very wrong.

Jane turned to Frost. 'You're sure it was nine o'clock when you left here last night?'

He nodded, a dazed look in his eyes. 'I didn't see anyone else around when I came out of the house. And I was parked right outside.'

'Why were you here?'

'To talk to her. I felt bad about what happened. About taking the sword.'

'You came to apologise for doing your job?'

'Sometimes, Rizzoli, the job makes me feel like an asshole, OK? Here's a woman who's already a victim. She lost her husband and her daughter. And we turn her into a suspect.'

'All I know is that Iris Fang has been at the centre of this from the beginning. Everything seems to revolve round her.' Jane's cellphone rang.

It was Tam on the line. 'Donohue has an alibi for last night.'

'And his men?'

'All three swear they spent the evening together watching TV.'

'So we can't rule them out.'

'We can't prove it in court, either.'

She turned to Frost. 'Maybe Bella will finally talk to us.'

BELLA LOOKED even more hostile today. 'It's *your* fault this happened,' she said. 'I should have been there. I would have stopped it.'

Jane kept her voice calm as she said, 'So you knew they would take her?'

'We're wasting time! She needs me.'

'How will you help her when you don't even know where she is?'

Bella opened her mouth to speak, then glanced at the one-way mirror, as if aware that others were watching.

'Why don't we start with who you really are,' said Jane, placing a photocopy of a birth certificate on the table. 'You were born right here in Boston. A home birth, at a Knapp Street address. Your father's name was Wu Weimin.'

Jane read the acknowledgment in Bella's eyes. Not that she needed it; the document was only exhibit number one. Jane brought out other photocopied documents. Her records from the San Francisco public schools. Her mother's death certificate. It was all there in black and white, the paper trail that Jane's team had doggedly pursued over the last forty-eight hours.

'Why did you come back to Boston?' asked Jane.

Bella looked her in the eye. '*Sifu* Fang asked me to come. She's not well, and she needed another instructor at her school.'

'Yes, that's the story you keep telling us.'

'Is there a different story?'

'It has nothing to do with what happened in the Red Phoenix? Nothing to do with your father killing four people?'

Bella's face snapped taut. 'My father was innocent.'

'Not according to the official report.'

'And official reports are never wrong.'

'If it's wrong, then what's the truth?'

Bella glared back. 'He was murdered.'

'Is that what your mother told you?'

'My mother wasn't there!'

Jane paused, registering the unspoken meaning of those last words. 'But someone was there,' she said quietly. 'Someone who was hiding in the cellar when it happened.'

Bella went absolutely still. 'How did you . . .'

'The blood told us. Decades later, with a chemical spray, we can still see it. We found your footprint on the cellar steps, and on the kitchen floor, leading towards the exit. Footprints that someone had wiped away by the time the police arrived.' Jane leaned in closer. 'Why did your mother try to erase the evidence?'

Bella didn't answer.

'She did it to protect you, didn't she?' said Jane. 'Because you saw what happened, and she was afraid that someone would come after you.'

Bella shook her head. 'I didn't see it.'

'You were there.'

'But I didn't see it!' Bella cried. For a moment her outburst seemed to hang in the air between them. She whispered: 'But I heard it.'

Jane waited for the story to be told.

Bella took another breath. 'My mother was asleep in bed. But I wasn't tired. So I went downstairs to see Daddy.'

'In the restaurant.'

'He was annoyed with me, of course.' A sad smile tugged at her mouth. 'There he was, juggling pots and pans. And I was whining for attention. He told me to go back upstairs. He was busy, and Uncle Fang didn't have time for me, either.'

'Iris's husband?'

Bella nodded. 'He was in the dining room. I looked through the door and saw him sitting at a table with a man and woman. They were drinking tea.'

Jane wondered why the waiter would be sitting with two patrons.

'What were they talking about?' she asked.

Bella shook her head. 'It was too noisy in the kitchen to hear anything in the dining room. My father banging his pots. The fan blowing. All I remember is my father, working at the stove. Sweating. He always worked in his old T-shirt . . .' Her voice faltered. 'My poor father. Always working.'

'What happened then?'

Bella's mouth twisted in a rueful smile. 'I was demanding attention, while he was trying to fill the take-out cartons. Finally he told me to go downstairs and choose an ice cream from the freezer.'

'In the cellar?'

She nodded. 'I'd been down there many times. There was a big chest freezer, tucked in the corner. I had to climb onto a chair to lift the lid. I remember looking inside for the flavour I wanted, the one with stripes of chocolate and vanilla and strawberry. But I couldn't find any. They were all vanilla.' She took a deep breath. 'And then I heard my father shouting.'

'At whom?'

'At me.' Bella blinked away tears. 'He was screaming at me to hide. He said it in Chinese. The killer couldn't understand, or he would have come looking for me.'

Jane glanced towards the one-way mirror. She couldn't see Frost and Tam, but she imagined their astonished faces. Here was the tale's missing chapter. 'And you hid?' asked Jane.

'I didn't understand what was happening. I started to go up the steps, but then I stopped. I heard him pleading for his life, in his broken English. That's when I understood this wasn't a game.' Bella swallowed. 'So I did what he told me to do. I didn't make a sound. I ducked underneath the stairs. I heard something fall. And then a loud bang.'

'How many gunshots in all?'

'Just one. That single bang.'

Jane thought of the weapon found in Wu Weimin's hand: a Glock with a threaded barrel. The killer had used a silencer to muffle the sound of those first eight gunshots. Only after dispatching his victims did he remove the silencer, place the grip in Wu Weimin's lifeless hand, and fire the final bullet, ensuring that gunshot residue would be found on the victim's skin.

The perfect crime, thought Jane. *Except for the fact that there was a witness. A silent girl, huddled under the cellar steps.*

'He died for me,' whispered Bella. 'He should have run, but he wouldn't leave me. So he died right in front of the cellar door. Blocking it with his body. I had to step in his blood to get past him. If I hadn't been there that night, my father would still be alive.'

Jane understood it all now. Had the staged suicide been a last-minute idea, something that occurred to the killer as he stood over the cook's body? It was such a simple thing, to wrap a dead man's fingers round the grip and fire the last round. Leave the gun behind and walk out of the door.

'You should have told the police back then,' said Jane. 'It would have changed everything.'

'No, it wouldn't. Who would believe a five-year-old girl? And my mother wouldn't let me say a word. She was terrified of the police.'

'Why?'

Bella's jaw tightened. 'My mother was here illegally. What do you think would have happened if the police focused on us? My father was dead. Nothing we could do would change that. All she could think about was keeping us both safe. If the killer knew there was a witness, he might come looking for me. That's why she wiped up my footprints. That's why we packed our suitcases and left two days later.'

'Did Iris Fang know?'

'Not until years later, when my mother was dying of stomach cancer. She wrote to *Sifu* Fang and told her the truth. Apologised for being a coward. But after so many years, there was nothing we could prove, nothing we could change.'

'Yet you've been trying, haven't you?' said Jane. 'For the past seven years, either you or Iris has been mailing obituaries to the families. Telling them that the truth hasn't been told.'

'It *hasn't* been. They need to know that. That's why the letters were sent, so they would keep asking questions. It's the only way we'll find out who the killer is.'

'So you and Iris have been trying to draw him out into the open. Sending notes, taking out that ad in the *Boston Globe*, hoping the killer will get worried and finally attack. And what was the plan then? Take justice into your own hands?'

Bella laughed. 'How could we possibly do that? We're only women.'

Now it was Jane's turn to laugh. 'As if I'd ever underestimate *you*.' She reached into her briefcase and pulled out her copy of *Monkey*, the ancient Chinese folk novel. 'I'm sure you've heard of the Monkey King.'

'Chinese fairy tales. What do they have to do with anything?'

'One particular chapter caught my attention: "The Story of Chen O". It's about a scholar who travels with his pregnant wife. They're attacked by bandits and the husband is killed. His wife is abducted.'

Bella shrugged. 'I've heard it.'

'Then you know the wife gives birth to a son while in captivity and secretly places him on a wooden plank, with a letter explaining her plight. Like baby Moses, the child's set adrift on the river. He floats to the Temple of the Golden Mountain, where he's raised by holy men. He grows to manhood and learns the truth about his parents. About his butchered father and his imprisoned mother.'

'Is there a point to this?'

'The point is right here, in the words spoken by the young man.' Jane read the quote. '"He who fails to avenge the wrongs done to a parent is unworthy of the name of man." That's what this is about, isn't it? You're like the son in this story. Haunted by the murder of your father. Honour-bound to avenge him.' Jane slid the book in front of Bella. 'It's what the Monkey King would do: fight for justice. Protect the innocent. Avenge a father. Monkey may wreak a bit of havoc in the process. But in the end, justice is done. He always does the *right thing*.'

Bella said nothing.

'I understand completely,' said Jane. 'You're not the villain in this. You're the daughter of a victim, a daughter who wants what the police can't deliver:

justice.' She lowered her voice to a sympathetic murmur. 'That's what you and Iris were trying to do. Draw out the killer. Tempt him to strike.'

Was that the hint of a nod she saw?

'But the plan didn't work out so well,' said Jane. 'When he did strike, he hired professionals to do the killing for him. So you still don't know his identity. And now he's taken Iris.'

Bella looked up, fury burning in her eyes. 'It went wrong because of you. I should have been there to watch over her.'

'She was the bait?'

'She was willing to take the risk.'

'And you two were going to deliver justice all by yourselves?'

'Who else is going to do it? The police?' Bella's laugh was bitter. 'All these years later, they don't care.'

'You're wrong, Bella. I sure as hell do care.'

'Then let me go, so I can find her.'

'You have no idea where to start.'

'Do you?' Bella spat back.

'We're looking at several suspects.'

'While you keep me locked up for no reason.'

'I'm investigating two homicides. That's my reason.'

'And I have an alibi. You know I didn't kill that woman on the roof.'

'Then who did?'

Bella looked at the book and her mouth twitched. 'Maybe it was the Monkey King. You do know how the folk tale starts, don't you? How Sun Wukong emerges from stone and transforms into a warrior? The night my father was killed, I emerged from that stone cellar just like Monkey. I was transformed, too.'

Jane tried to imagine Bella as a frightened five-year-old, but she could see no trace of that child in this fierce creature. *If I'd witnessed the murder of someone I loved, would I be any different?*

Jane stood up. 'You're right, Bella. I don't have enough to hold you. You can leave.'

'And I won't be followed? I'm free to do what I have to?'

'What does that mean?'

Bella rose from her chair, like a lioness uncoiling herself for the hunt. 'Whatever it takes,' she said.

SEVEN

I can hear him breathing in the darkness, beyond the blinding glare that shines in my eyes. He has not allowed me to see his face; all I know is that his voice is as smooth as cream. He is starting to grow angry because he realises I am not easily broken.

He is worried as well, because of the personal tracking device he found strapped to my ankle. A device that he has disabled by removing the battery.

'Who was tracking you?' he asks.

Despite my bruised jaw, my swollen lips, I manage to answer in a hoarse whisper: 'Someone you never want to meet. But you soon will.'

'Not if they can't find you.' He tosses down the tracking device, and when it hits the floor it is like the sound of shattering hope. I was still unconscious when he took it from me, so I don't know when the device ceased its transmissions. I don't even know where I am.

My wrists are trapped by manacles bolted to the wall. The floor beneath my bare feet is concrete. There is no light. Perhaps it is night. Or perhaps this is a place where light never penetrates. My hands twitch, aching to close round a weapon.

'You're looking for your sword, aren't you?' he says, and waves the blade in the light, so that I can see it. 'A beautiful weapon. Is this what you used to kill them?' The blade hisses past my face. 'I hear her hand was sliced off clean. And his head came off with a single stroke.' He brings the blade to my neck. 'Shall we see what this can do to *your* throat?'

I hold still. I've been ready to die these past nineteen years, and with a slash of the blade he'll free me at last to join my husband. What I feel isn't fear but regret that this man will never feel my sword's bite against his own throat.

'There was a witness, in the Red Phoenix,' he says. 'Who was it?'

'Do you really think I would tell you?'

'So someone was there.'

'And will never forget.'

The sword digs deeper into my neck. 'Tell me the name.'

'You're going to kill me anyway. Why should I?'

A long pause, then he lifts the blade from my skin. 'Let's make a deal,' he says calmly. 'You tell me who this witness is. And I'll tell you what happened to your daughter.'

He sees my confusion, and laughs.

'You had no idea, did you, that this was always about her? Laura, wasn't that her name? Pretty little thing. Long black hair, skinny hips. And so trusting. It wasn't hard to talk her into the car.'

'I don't believe you.'

'Why would I lie?'

'Then tell me where she is.'

'First tell me who the witness is. Tell me who was in the Red Phoenix. Then I'll tell you what happened to Laura.'

I am trying to understand why this man knows my daughter's fate. She disappeared two years before my husband died in the shooting. I never imagined any connection between the events.

'She was such a talented girl,' the smooth voice says. 'That first day we rehearsed, I knew she was the one I wanted. Vivaldi's "Concerto for Two Violins". Do you remember her practising that piece?'

His words are like a blast of shrapnel through my heart because I know now he's telling the truth. He heard my daughter play. He knows what happened to her.

'Tell me the name of the witness,' he says.

'This is all I'll tell you,' I say quietly. 'You are a dead man.'

The blow comes without warning, so violent that it whips my head backwards and my skull slams against the wall. Through the roaring in my ears I hear him speaking to me, words that I don't want to hear.

'She lasted seven, maybe eight weeks. Longer than the others. She looked delicate, but oh, she was strong. Think of it. For two whole months, while the police were searching for her, she was still alive. Begging to go home to her mommy.'

My control shatters. I cannot stop the tears, cannot suppress the sobs that rack my body. They sound like an animal's howls of pain, wild and alien.

'I can give you closure, Mrs Fang. I can answer the question that's been tormenting you. Where is Laura?' He leans in closer. 'Tell me what I want to know, and I'll put your mind at rest.'

It happens before I even think about it: a feral reaction that surprises us both. He flinches away, gasping in disgust as he wipes my spit from his face. I expect that another blow will follow. But it does not come. Instead, he picks up my tracking device. 'Really, I don't need you at all,' he says. 'I'll replace this battery and wait to see who shows up.'

He leaves. I hear the door shut, and footsteps thud up stairs.

I cry and flail against the manacles. He had my daughter. He kept her. I remember after Laura vanished, when my husband and I clung to each other, neither daring to say what we were both thinking. What if she is dead? Now I realise there was a far worse possibility, something that we had not imagined: that she was still alive. That during those two months, as James and I felt hope die and reluctant acceptance take its place, our Laura was still breathing. Still suffering.

I slump back, exhausted. Leaning against the wall, I try to reconcile what he has just told me with what I already know, which is this: Two years after my daughter's abduction, my husband and four other people were massacred in the Red Phoenix restaurant. How could these events be related? This he never explained.

I struggle to remember everything he said. One sentence suddenly comes back to me, words that instantly freeze the blood in my veins: *She lasted seven, maybe eight weeks. Longer than the others.*

My head lifts at the revelation. *The others.*

My daughter was not the only one.

WHAT DID INGERSOLL KNOW, and why was he killed? Those were the two questions that consumed Jane as she sat late into the afternoon, sifting through her notes. According to Donohue, a contract had gone out on Ingersoll when he began asking questions about missing girls.

And what do missing girls have to do with the Red Phoenix?

All the victims were pretty and petite. All were good-to-excellent students. All were multitalented. Patty Boles and Sherry Tanaka played in tennis tournaments. Deborah Schiffer played the piano in her school orchestra. But none of the three knew one another, at least according to their parents. And they were different ages at the times of their disappearances. Jane thought about this for a moment.

She jotted down the order in which the girls disappeared.

Deborah Schiffer, aged thirteen.

Laura Fang, aged fourteen.

Patty Boles, aged fifteen.

Sherry Tanaka, aged sixteen.

Charlotte Dion, aged seventeen.

Every year, a different girl, a different age. As if the kidnapper's taste had matured as the years passed.

She reached for the last photos of Charlotte, taken at the funeral. She flipped through the sequence until she came to the last image: Mark walking behind Charlotte. Tall and broad-shouldered, he could easily have overpowered his stepsister.

Every year, an older girl.

The year that thirteen-year-old Deborah Schiffer vanished was a year after Dina and Arthur Mallory married, forming a new and reconstituted family, with all the joint activities that this would have entailed. School assemblies. Orchestra performances. State tennis tournaments.

Is that how the victims were chosen? Through Charlotte?

Jane rang Patrick Dion. 'Would it be possible for me to take another look at Charlotte's school yearbooks?'

'You're welcome anytime. Perhaps I could help you.'

'I've been thinking a lot about Charlotte. About whether she's the key to everything that's happened.'

'My daughter has always been the key, Detective. There's nothing I want more than to know what happened to her.'

'I understand, sir,' Jane said gently. 'I know you want the answer, and I think I might be able to provide it.'

PATRICK ANSWERED the door wearing a baggy pullover sweater, chino slacks and bedroom slippers. His face, like his sweater, was sagging and careworn, every crease etched with old grief. And here was Jane to bring back the awful memories. When they shook hands, she held on longer than necessary: a grasp meant to tell him that she was sorry.

He gave her a sad nod and led the way into the dining room, his slippers shuffling across the wood floor. 'I have the yearbooks waiting for you,' he said, pointing to the volumes on the dining table.

'I'll just bring these out to my car and be on my way. Thank you.'

He frowned. 'If it's all right, I'd rather you didn't take them out of the house.' He placed his hand on the stack of books. 'This is what I have left of my daughter. And I worry that they'll get lost or damaged. You're perfectly welcome to sit here as long as you need and look through them. Can I get you something? A glass of wine? Coffee?'

Jane smiled. 'I have to drive: coffee would be wonderful.'

She sat down and spread out the books on the table. She opened the volume from Charlotte's first year at the Bolton Academy. Her photo showed a fragile-looking blonde with braces. Jane flipped through the book to the older students and found Mark Mallory. He would have been fifteen.

'Here you are,' said Patrick, carrying in a tray with a coffeepot. 'You must be hungry, too. I can make you a sandwich.'

'No, this is perfect,' she said. 'I'll eat supper when I get home. Which reminds me.' She pulled out her cellphone and tapped out a quick text message to Gabriel: Home late. Start dinner without me.

'Are you finding what you need here?' Patrick asked. 'If you tell me what you're looking for, I might be able to help.'

'I'm looking for connections between your daughter and these girls.' Jane opened the file she'd brought with her and pointed to the list of names.

Patrick frowned. 'I know about Laura Fang, of course. But I'm afraid I'm not familiar with these other girls.'

'They disappeared from different towns, in different years. I'm wondering if Charlotte knew any of them. Maybe through music or sports.'

'Why are you looking at these girls in particular?'

Because a dead man named Ingersoll pointed the way, thought Jane. What she said was: 'These names have come up in the course of the investigation. If a link with Charlotte exists, I might be able to find it here.'

'In her yearbooks?'

She flipped through the student activity pages. 'The Bolton Academy's very good about chronicling everything their students do. I'm hoping to reconstruct Charlotte's school years. Where she was, what activities she participated in.' Jane looked at Patrick. 'She played the viola. That's how you got to know the Mallorys. At the kids' musical performances.'

'How does that help you?'

Jane turned to the section for the music department. 'Here. This was the year she first played in the orchestra.' She pointed to a photo of the musicians,

which included Charlotte and Mark. Below it was the caption: THE ORCHES-
TRA'S JANUARY CONCERT BRINGS A STANDING OVATION!

Just the sight of the photo made Patrick wince. He said softly, 'It's hard,
you know. Looking at these photos.'

Jane touched his hand. 'I'll go through these books on my own. If I have
any questions, I'll ask.'

He nodded. 'I'll leave you alone, then,' he said, and retreated from the
dining room.

Jane poured another cup of coffee. Opened the yearbook for Charlotte's
eighth-grade year, when she would have been thirteen and Mark sixteen.
His photo now showed a square jaw and those broad shoulders. Charlotte
still had a delicate child's face. Jane flipped through the school activities
section, searching for photos of either one. She found them in a group portrait, taken at the statewide 'Battle of the Orchestras', March 20, in Lowell,
Massachusetts.

Deborah Schiffer lived in Lowell, and she played the piano. Two months
after that photo was taken, Deborah had vanished.

Jane's head was humming with excitement and caffeine. She searched
the volumes for Charlotte's ninth-grade yearbook. She flipped to the photo
of eight music students: BOLTON'S BEST QUALIFY FOR BOSTON SUMMER
ORCHESTRA WORKSHOP. She did not see Charlotte in the photo, but there was
Mark Mallory, a darkly handsome seventeen-year-old. That year, Laura
Fang had been fourteen. She too had attended the orchestra workshop. Had
Laura been dazzled by one particular boy's good looks and wealth, a boy for
whom a girl of Laura's humble upbringing would be invisible? Or was
Laura very much on his radar?

Jane's throat felt parched, the buzzing in her head louder. She took
another sip of coffee and reached for Charlotte's tenth-grade yearbook.
When she opened it, the words seemed smudged, the faces indistinct. She
rubbed her eyes, turned to the activities section. There was Charlotte in the
orchestra, but Mark had graduated.

She turned to the athletics pages. Again she rubbed her eyes, trying to clear
away the fog that seemed to hang over her vision. The photo moved in and out
of focus, but she could still pick out Charlotte's face in the line-up of tennis
players. BOLTON TEAM TAKES SECOND PLACE AT OCTOBER'S REGIONALS.

Patty Boles had been a tennis player, too. Had she competed at those regionals? Had she caught someone's eye, someone who could easily learn who she was, and which school she attended? Six weeks after that tournament, Patty Boles vanished.

Jane gave her head a shake, but the fog seemed to thicken before her eyes. *Something is wrong.* She tried to call for help, but no sound came out.

Struggling to her feet, she heard her chair topple over. All feeling was gone from her legs: they were like wooden stilts, senseless and clumsy. As she lurched towards the doors, they opened, and Patrick appeared.

'Help me,' she whispered.

But he didn't move. He simply stood watching her, his expression coldly dispassionate. Only then did she realise what a mistake she'd made.

JANE TRIED TO SWALLOW, but her throat was parched, her tongue as dry as leather against the roof of her mouth. Slowly she registered the tingling in her left arm from lying too long in one position. The gritty surface beneath her cheek. And the woman's voice that would not let her sleep.

'Wake up. You must wake up!'

Jane opened her eyes—or thought she did. The darkness was impenetrable. She tried to roll onto her back and strained to move her hands and feet, but met the unyielding resistance of duct tape. She did not know how she'd come to be in this cold, black place. The last she remembered was sitting in Patrick's dining room, sipping coffee.

Coffee that he served me.

'Detective Rizzoli! *Please* wake up!'

Jane recognised Iris Fang's voice. 'How . . . where . . .'

'I cannot help you. I'm here, against the wall. Chained to the wall. We are in a cellar, I think. Maybe in his house. I don't know because I can't remember how I got here.'

'Neither can I,' groaned Jane.

'He brought you here hours ago. We don't have much time. He's just waiting for the other one to return.'

The other one. Jane struggled to think through the fog in her head. Of course Patrick was not working alone. At sixty-seven, he would need someone to help him. That's why he'd hired professionals to kill Ingersoll, to attack Iris.

'We have to prepare,' said Iris. 'Before they come back.'

'Prepare?' Jane couldn't help a desperate laugh. 'I can't move my arms or legs. I can't even feel my hands!'

'But you can roll towards the wall. I saw a set of keys hanging near the door when he turned on the light and brought you down. They might unlock my handcuffs. You free me, then I'll free you.'

'Which way is the door?'

'It's to my right. Follow my voice. The keys are hanging on a hook. If you can get to your feet, grab the keys with your teeth—'

'That's a lot of ifs.'

'*Do it.*' The command pierced the darkness. But the next words were soft. 'He took my daughter,' she whispered, sobs suddenly stuttering through. 'He's the one.'

Jane fought against her bonds, but the duct tape was indestructible.

'The keys. You have to reach them.'

Jane twisted, rolled across the floor. Her face scraped on the concrete. How was she going to do this? She couldn't even make it across the floor, much less rise to her feet and reach the keys.

'You have a daughter,' said Iris softly.

'Yes.'

'Think of her. Think of what you'd do to hold her again.'

She thought of Regina in the bathtub, dark curls clinging to pink skin. Regina, who would grow into a young woman, never knowing her own mother except as a ghost reflected in her own face. And she thought of Gabriel, growing old and grey. *A lifetime we'll never have together if I don't survive this night.*

'Think of her.' Iris's voice drifted through the darkness. 'She'll give you the strength you need to fight.'

'Is that how you did it all these years?'

'It was all I had. It's what kept me alive: the hope that my daughter might come home to me. I lived for that, Detective. I lived for the day I'd see her again. Or if it never happened, for the day I would see justice done. At least I'll know that I died trying.'

Her head clearer now, Jane rolled again and suddenly her back collided with a wall. She lay briefly, on her side, resting for what would be the most difficult challenge. 'I've reached the wall,' she said.

'Get to your feet. The door's at the far end.'

Jane tried to squirm up to a kneeling position, but lost her balance and collapsed face-down, her mouth slamming against the floor. Pain shot into her skull.

'Your daughter,' said Iris. 'What is her name?'

Jane licked her lip and tasted blood. 'Regina,' she said.

'And you love her very much.'

'Of course I do.' With a grunt, Jane struggled to her knees. No, she would not be kept away from her daughter. She would survive this night, the way Iris had survived these past two decades, because nothing mattered more to a mother than seeing her child again.

Get to your feet, Jane thought. *Get those keys.*

She rocked forwards on her knees and sprang up. Landed on her feet, but only for a few tottering seconds before she lost her balance and fell forwards again, her kneecaps slamming onto concrete.

'Again,' ordered Iris. 'The keys.' No hint of sympathy in her voice. Was she as ruthless with her students? Was this the way real warriors were honed: without mercy, pushed beyond their limits?

Jane tensed and sprang up. She wobbled, but the wall was right beside her. She propped her shoulder against it. 'I'm up.'

'Get to the far corner. That's where the door is.'

Another hop, another wobble. She could do this. 'Once we get free, we still have to get past him,' said Jane. 'He has my gun.'

'I don't need a weapon.'

'Oh, right. Ninjas just fly through the air.'

'You don't know anything about me. Or what I can do.'

Jane hopped again. 'Tell me—since we're probably going to die, anyway—are you the Monkey King?'

'The Monkey King is a fable.'

'It leaves behind real hair. It kills with a real sword. So who is it?'

'He's inside you and me. He's inside everyone who believes in justice.'

'I'm not talking mystical mumbo jumbo,' Jane panted and hopped again. 'I'm talking about something real. Something that saved my life.' She said quietly: 'I just want to thank him—or her—for that.'

Iris answered, just as softly: 'It already knows.'

Jane's forehead banged against a door. Jane felt metal brush her cheek. Heard the soft clink of the hanging keys. 'Found them!'

'Please don't drop them.'

Jane gripped the keys in her mouth and lifted the ring off the wall hook. *We're going to do this. We're going to beat them* . . .

The squeal of the opening door made her freeze. Lights blazed on, so bright that she shrank back, blinded, against the wall.

'Well, this is a complication,' said a voice she recognised. She opened her eyes and saw Mark Mallory beside Patrick. *It has always been the two of them*, she thought. Hunting together. Killing together. And the bond that linked these men was Charlotte. Poor Charlotte, whose every interest, every activity, had introduced predators to their prey, turning something as inno- cent as a tennis meet or an orchestra performance into an opportunity for killers to glimpse and choose fresh faces.

Mark wrenched the keys from Jane's mouth and shoved her to the floor. 'Does anyone know she came here?'

'We have to assume so,' said Patrick. 'That's why we need to get rid of her car. We should have done it hours ago, if only you'd gotten back sooner.'

'I wanted to see if anyone would show up.'

'No one came for her?' He looked at Iris.

'Maybe the tracker's broken. Or maybe no one cares about her. I waited for four hours, and not a soul turned up.'

'Well, someone's going to be coming for this one,' said Patrick, looking at Jane.

'Where's her cellphone?'

Patrick handed it to Mark. 'What are you going to do?'

He began to tap out a message. 'Let's tell her husband she's headed to Dorchester and won't be home for a while.'

'Then what?'

'It has to look like an accident. Or a suicide.'

Patrick nodded. 'Her gun's up in the dining room.'

'My husband will know,' said Jane. 'He knows I'd never kill myself.'

'The spouse always says that. And the police never believe them. Do they, Detective?' said Mark, and he smiled.

Jane thought of how it would probably happen: a bullet to her head to kill her, followed by a second gunshot to plant residue on her hand, the way Wu Weimin's suicide had been staged. What Mark said was true: it was too easy to ignore the denials of a victim's family. She'd been guilty of it herself.

'You've made so many mistakes,' said Iris. 'You have no idea what's about to happen.'

Mark turned to her and laughed. 'Look who's talking. The lady chained to the wall.'

Iris regarded him with an eerily calm gaze. 'Before it all ends for you, tell me. Why did you choose my daughter?'

Mark crossed towards Iris until they were face to face. Though he was far taller, though he held every advantage, Iris revealed not a flicker of fear.

'Pretty little Laura. You remember her, Patrick?' Mark said. 'The girl we offered a ride to.'

'Why?' said Iris.

Mark smiled. 'Because she was special. They all were.'

'We're wasting time,' said Patrick, stepping towards Jane. 'Let's get her out of here.'

But Mark was still looking at Iris. 'Sometimes I chose the girl. Sometimes Patrick chose. You never know what will catch your eye. A ponytail. A cute little ass. Something that makes her stand out.'

'Charlotte must have known,' said Jane, looking at Patrick in disgust. 'She must have realised what you were. Jesus, her own *father*. How could you kill her?'

'Charlotte was never part of this.'

'Never part of it? She was at the centre of it!'

The men ignored her and bent down to grab her. Patrick picked up her feet and Mark hauled her up under her arms. Though Jane squirmed, they lifted her easily and carried her towards the door.

'You've already lost,' said Iris. 'You just don't know it yet.'

Mark snorted. 'I know who's chained to the wall.'

'And I know who followed you back here.'

'No one followed me—' His voice suddenly cut off as the lights went out.

In the pitch black, both men released Jane and she fell to the floor, skull slamming against concrete. She lay stunned.

'What the fuck?' said Mark.

Iris's voice whispered through the gloom: 'Now it begins.'

'Shut up! Just shut up!' Mark yelled.

'It's probably nothing,' said Patrick, but he sounded unnerved. 'Look, maybe we just blew a fuse. Let's go upstairs and check.'

The door banged shut and their footsteps faded up the stairs. Jane heard only the thumping of her own heart. 'What's happening?'

'What was always meant to happen.'

'You knew? You expected this?'

Iris did not answer. In the silence, Jane felt, rather than heard, the brush of air against her cheek. *Something else is here with us.*

She heard the soft clatter of handcuffs falling. And a whisper: 'Apologies, *Sifu*. I would have come sooner. Here is Zheng Yi. I found her upstairs.'

Jane knew that voice. 'Bella?'

A hand was pressed across her lips and Iris murmured: 'Stay.'

'You can't leave me like this!'

'You're safer here.'

'At least cut me free!'

She felt a tug on her hands, heard the hiss of the blade slicing through her duct tape bindings. Another slice freed her ankles. 'Just remember,' Iris whispered into her ear. 'This is not your battle.'

It is now. But Jane stayed silent as the two women melted into the darkness. She reached out, felt the wall nearby, and propped herself up, as unsteady as a newborn foal.

A gunshot made her chin snap up.

I can't be trapped down here, she thought. *I have to get out of this house.*

She felt her way to the door. It softly creaked open. Upstairs, she heard heavy footsteps running. Two more gunshots.

Get out now. Before the men come back for you.

She started up the steps, moving slowly, afraid to make a sound. She was the noncombatant trying to slip through a war zone to safety, wherever that might be. She didn't have her car keys, so she'd have to run to the neighbours. She remembered the long driveway, the tall hedge. By daylight, it had looked like a private garden, enclosed to keep the world out. Now she knew that the gate, with its spiked posts, was also meant to keep people in. This was no garden of Eden; it was a death camp.

She reached the top of the stairs and felt another closed door. Pressing her ear against it, she heard nothing. How many gunshots had there been? At least three: enough to have taken down both Iris and Bella. Were the women lying dead beyond the door? Were Patrick and Mark now on their way back to the cellar to find her?

The door swung open soundlessly, to darkness every bit as thick as in the cellar. She slowly inched her way across the floor, arms outstretched. She collided with an edge that hit her hip—a table. Jagged metal suddenly bit her fingers and she pulled back, startled. It was a table saw. She hit another obstacle: a drill press. This was Patrick's woodworking shop. She wondered if mahogany and maple were the only things this equipment had sliced into.

More gunshots. Four in a row. *Get out, get out!*

At last she located the door and wasted no time slipping through it, to find yet another set of steps to climb. How far below ground had she been?

Deep enough so that no one would have heard my screams.

At the top of the stairs, she found herself in a carpeted hallway. She could barely make out shapes in the darkness. Hand brushing across a wall, she inched ahead. All she wanted to find was a way out.

On the landing above, footsteps started down the stairs.

She ducked through the first open doorway to her left. An office. She scrambled forwards and her shoes crunched across broken glass. Suddenly her foot snagged and, as she went sprawling, her palm slid through something sticky. By the glow of moonlight, she stared at the dark form lying on the floor right beside her. A body.

Patrick Dion.

She scrabbled away, sliding backwards across the floor. Felt something heavy spin away from her hand. A gun. She reached for it, and the instant her fingers closed round the grip, she knew it was her own weapon. The gun that Patrick had taken from her. *My old friend.*

Footsteps creaked behind her and came to a halt.

Jane was framed by moonglow that seemed as bright and inescapable as a searchlight. She looked up to see Mark's silhouette.

'I was never here,' he said. 'When the police come to talk to me, I'll tell them I was home in bed the whole time. Which makes it Patrick who killed all those girls and buried them in his yard. Patrick who killed you. And then shot himself.'

Behind her, hand concealed in shadow, she clutched her weapon. But Mark already had his gun pointed at her. Even as she lifted her weapon, she knew she was too slow, too late.

But at that instant Mark gasped and turned away from her, his gun swinging towards someone—something—else.

Jane fired. Three shots, four; her reflexes on automatic. The bullets slammed into his torso.

Pulse whooshing in her ears, Jane rose to her feet and stood over his body. He did not move. But the shadows did. It was just a whisper of air. A flutter of black against black at the periphery of her vision. Slowly she turned towards the figure that stood cloaked in darkness. Though she could have fired, she did not. She simply stared at a face crowned with silvery fur. At jagged teeth that gleamed in the moonlight.

'Who are you?' she whispered. 'What are you?'

A breath of wind brushed her face and she blinked. When she opened her eyes again, the face was gone. *Was it really here, or did I imagine it?* She looked out at the moonlit garden and saw it, then, darting across the lawn and vanishing into the cover of trees.

'Detective Rizzoli?'

With a start, Jane whirled round to see Bella and Iris in the doorway, Iris sagging heavily against the younger woman.

'She needs an ambulance!' said Bella.

'I am not as young as I once was,' groaned Iris. 'Or as swift.'

Gently, Bella lowered her teacher to the floor. Cradling Iris in her lap, she began to murmur in Chinese, words that she repeated again and again, as though chanting a magical spell.

JANE STOOD in Patrick Dion's driveway and watched the sun come up. She had not slept in twenty-four hours and, suddenly dizzy, she swayed backwards against a police cruiser. When she opened her eyes again, Maura and Frost were walking towards her.

'You should go home,' said Maura.

'That's what everyone tells me.'

Frost frowned as Jane bent down to pull on shoe covers. 'You know, you probably shouldn't go in the house,' he said.

'Like I haven't already been in there?'

'That's the point.'

He didn't need to explain. She'd been the one to take down Mark Mallory, and it was almost certainly her gun that had fired the bullet into Patrick Dion's brain. Her weapon was now in the custody of ballistics.

The front door opened and the first stretcher came out.

'The older man had one bullet wound. Right temple, close range,' said Maura. 'I have a feeling we're going to find gunshot residue on his right hand. Does that remind you of another crime scene?'

'The Red Phoenix,' said Jane softly. 'Wu Weimin.'

Maura sighed. 'We have no witnesses, do we?'

Jane shook her head. 'Bella said that she and Iris didn't see it.'

'But there was another intruder in the house,' Frost pointed out. 'You said you saw him.'

'I don't know what I saw.' Jane looked towards the garden.

Maura said, 'I could call Patrick Dion's death a suicide, but it's too similar to the Red Phoenix. It feels staged.'

'I think it's meant to be similar. Justice completing its circle.'

'Justice doesn't qualify as a manner of death.'

Jane looked at her. 'Maybe it should.'

'Hey, Frost! Rizzoli!' Tam called to them from a grove of trees, where he stood with a team of criminalists. 'Cadaver dog's just scented on something.'

They walked over. *The missing girls.* Surely there were other girls who'd vanished in the years since Charlotte Dion disappeared? And what more convenient place to hide the bodies than in this private sanctuary? The CSU team stood silent and grim-faced. The dog was the only cheerful one among them.

'The soil's been disturbed here,' Tam said, pointing to a patch of bare earth under the trees. 'It was covered with loose brush.'

Jane looked round at the tree-shaded grounds and the dense shrubbery. This was evil on a scale she could scarcely comprehend. *How many bodies are lying here?* she wondered. *How many silent girls who will finally be able to speak?*

'Frost, I think I'll leave this to you. I'm going home,' she said and walked away, back across the lawn. Back into the sunshine.

'Rizzoli.' Tam followed her. 'Just wanted to let you know, I spoke to the hospital a little while ago. Iris Fang is out of surgery.'

'Is she going to be OK?'

'She took a bullet to the thigh and lost a lot of blood, but she'll recover.'

'We should all be so tough.'

'Should I head over to the hospital? Get a statement from her?' he asked.

'Later. Right now, I need you here.'

'So I'm staying with the team?'

'Yeah. That is, if you want to stay with homicide.'

'Thanks. I'd like that a lot,' he said simply.

As he turned to leave, she suddenly noticed a bright streak reflecting off the back of his head. Clinging to his jet-black hair, the lone strand stood out like glitter. A silver hair.

'Tam?' she said.

He turned. 'Yeah?'

For a moment she just looked at him. She remembered how he'd slipped so quickly and silently through Ingersoll's window. Remembered how the Knapp Street surveillance camera had captured her and Frost but not Tam. *'Maybe I'm a ghost,'* he had joked. *Not a ghost*, she thought, *but someone who knew what was being said and what was being planned at every step of the investigation.*

'Never mind,' she said. And walked away.

IT WAS HAPPY HOUR at J. P. Doyle's and the bar was packed. Jane finally spotted Vince Korsak in a booth keeping company with a fried seafood platter and a pint of ale.

'Sorry I'm late,' she said, and ordered a small salad.

'That all you're eating?'

'I'm going home for supper. Haven't spent much time there.'

'Yeah, I hear it's been a real circus. How many bodies they dig up so far?'

'Six, all females. We're looking at Mark Mallory's residence as well. There's just one fly in the ointment,' she said as she picked up her fork. 'There's no way I'll ever close the files on either John Doe or Jane Doe. And it was her death that set off the whole thing.'

'Never found the sword that killed her?'

'Vanished. But I have a pretty good idea who did it.'

'Enough to convict?'

'Honestly? I don't want to convict. Sometimes, just doing my job means I'd have to do the wrong thing.'

Korsak laughed. 'Don't ever let Dr Isles hear you say that.'

'No, she wouldn't understand,' Jane agreed. What Maura understood was facts, and those facts had led to the conviction of Officer Wayne Graff a few days ago. Yes or no. Black or white. For Maura, the line was always perfectly clear. But the longer that Jane was a cop, the less certain she was of where that line between right and wrong was drawn.

She dug into her salad. 'So what'd you want to talk to me about?'

He sighed and put down his fork. Jane knew it was serious: very few things, other than an empty plate, could make Vince Korsak surrender his fork. 'You know I love your mom.'

'Yeah, I think I got that part figured out.'

'I mean, I really love her. She's fun and smart and sexy.'

'You can stop right there.' She set down her own fork. 'Just tell me where this is going.'

'All I want is to marry her.'

'And she's already said yes. So?'

'The problem is your brother. He calls her three times a day, trying to talk her out of it. It's pretty clear he despises me.'

'Frankie doesn't like any kind of change, period.'

'He's got her all upset and now she's thinking of calling off the wedding, just to keep him happy.'

'It's OK,' she said. 'I'll talk to Frankie.' If that didn't work, she'd also give her brother a good whack upside the head.

His head lifted. 'You'd do that for me? Really?'

'Why wouldn't I?'

'I got the idea you weren't crazy about me and your ma.'

'I just don't want to hear the sweaty details, OK?' She gave him an affectionate punch on the arm. 'You make her happy. That's all I care about.'

'I love her. You know that. I love you, too. But not your brother.'

'That I totally understand.'

They chatted a bit more, then she left him to his seafood platter. Exiting through the crowded bar, she suddenly heard someone call out: 'Rizzoli!'

It was retired Detective Buckholz, who had investigated Charlotte Dion's disappearance nineteen years ago. 'I gotta talk to you,' he said.

'Could we talk tomorrow, Hank?'

'No. I got something to say, and it's really bugging me.' He drained his glass. 'Let's step outside. Too damn noisy in here.'

They walked out of Doyle's and stood in the parking lot. It was a cool spring evening, the smell of damp earth in the air. Jane zipped up her jacket and glanced at her parked car, wondering how long this would take.

'You know your case against Patrick Dion and Mark Mallory? You got it wrong,' he said.

'What do you mean?'

'Two rich guys hunting girls together for twenty-five years? The whole country's wondering why we didn't stop them.'

'They were smart about it, Hank. They didn't escalate and they didn't get sloppy. They managed to stay in control.'

'Patrick Dion had alibis for some of those disappearances.'

'Because they took turns snatching the girls. We've already found six bodies on Dion's property, and I'm sure we'll find others.'

'But not Charlotte's. I guarantee you won't find her there.'

'How do you know?'

'It may have been nineteen years ago, but I remember the details. I pulled out my old notes, just to be sure. I know Patrick Dion was in London the day Charlotte went missing. He flew home right after he got the news.'

'OK, so you're right about that detail.'

'Mark Mallory couldn't have snatched Charlotte, either, because he was visiting his mother in a rehab hospital after a stroke.'

She eyed him in the fading daylight. Buckholz was defending his own record, so he couldn't possibly be objective. *Humour the old guy.* She gave him a sympathetic nod. 'I'll review the case file and get back to you.'

'You think you can just brush me off? I was a good cop, Rizzoli. I checked out every move he made that day. There was no way Mark Mallory could have snatched Charlotte.'

'Because he said he was visiting his mother? Come on, Hank. You can't take his word, or his mother's. She would have lied.'

'But you can trust the medical record.' He reached into his jacket and pulled out a folded paper. 'It's a photocopy of the nurses' notes from Barbara Mallory's hospital chart. Look at the entry for April 20th, one in the afternoon.'

Jane scanned down to what the nurse had written: '*Patient resting comfortably. Son here visiting and requests that his mother be moved to a quieter room, away from nurses' station.*'

'At one o'clock,' said Buckholz, 'Charlotte Dion was with her school group in Faneuil Hall. The teachers first noticed her missing around one fifteen. So tell me how Mark Mallory, who's sitting in his mom's hospital room twenty-five miles away, manages to snatch his stepsister only fifteen minutes later?'

Jane read and re-read the nurse's entry. There was no mistaking the date and time. *This is all wrong*, she thought. Except there it was, in black and white.

'It's obvious that your two perps didn't take Charlotte,' said Buckholz.

'Then who did?' Jane murmured.

'I'm betting it was just some guy who made an opportunistic grab.'

Some guy. A perp they had yet to identify.

She drove home and thought about the odds. Two killers in her family, and Charlotte gets snatched by an unrelated stranger? She thought about what they knew for certain: that Dion and Mallory had been stalking and killing girls together. Had Charlotte discovered her father's secret? Was that the real reason they had to dispose of her? Had it been arranged through a third party, so that both Patrick and Mark had solid alibis?

Once again, the mystery revolved round Charlotte. She thought of the last photos ever taken of Charlotte, at the funeral. She remembered how Charlotte had been flanked by her father and Mark. Surrounded by enemies and unable to escape.

Jane sat up straight, suddenly struck by the answer that should have been obvious from the beginning.

Maybe she did.

JANE CROSSED the New Hampshire border and drove north, into Maine. By the time she reached Moosehead Lake in the late afternoon, the air had turned chilly. She wrapped a scarf round her neck and walked to the landing, where a motorboat was moored.

A boy of about fifteen waved at her. 'You Mrs Rizzoli? I'm Will, from the Loon Point Lodge.' He took her overnight bag. 'Is this all the luggage you brought?'

'I'm only staying for one night.' She glanced round the dock. 'Where's the skipper?'

Grinning, he said. 'Right here. Been driving this boat since I was eight.'

Still dubious about the kid's skills, she climbed aboard. As he started up the engine, she asked: 'How long have you worked at the lodge?'

'All my life. My mom and dad own it.'

She took a closer look at the boy. Saw a strong jaw and sun-bleached hair. He seemed utterly at ease as he guided the boat away from the pier. Before she could ask him any more questions, they were skimming across choppy water, the motor too noisy for conversation. By the time they reached the opposite shore, the sun was dropping towards the horizon. She saw rustic cabins and a cluster of canoes pulled up on the bank. On the pier, a towheaded girl of about eight or nine stood waiting to catch the mooring line. Jane knew at once that these two were brother and sister.

'This troublemaker here is Samantha,' Will said with a laugh, as he affectionately mussed the girl's hair. 'She's our general gofer round here. You need a toothbrush, extra towels, whatever, just give her a shout.'

The girl went scampering ahead up the pier with Jane's bag. Will led her to one of the cabins. 'Mom put you in this one. It's got the most privacy.'

They climbed the steps to the screened porch, and the door squealed shut behind them. Samantha had put Jane's bag on a rustic luggage rack at the foot of the bed. A fire was already crackling in the stone hearth.

'I wish I'd brought my husband here. He'd love this place.'

'Bring him back next time.' Will turned to leave. 'Once you get settled in, come over to the lodge for dinner.'

After he left, she sank into a rocking chair on the porch and watched the sunset. The sound of lapping water made her drowsy. She closed her eyes and did not see the visitor approach her cabin. Only when she heard the knock did she look out to see the blonde woman standing outside the screen door.

'Detective Rizzoli?' the blonde woman said.

'Come in.'

The woman stepped inside. Jane could see the resemblance to Will and Samantha, and she knew that this was their mother. She also knew, without a doubt, what her name was. It was Ingersoll's oddly timed fishing trip that had made Jane focus on Loon Point, a trip on which he'd brought no tackle box. This was the real reason Ingersoll had come to Maine: to visit the woman who now stood on the porch.

'Hello, Charlotte,' said Jane.

The woman glanced through the screen, scanning the area for anyone within earshot. 'Please don't ever use that name. I'm Susan now.'

'Your family doesn't know?'

'My husband does, but not the children. It would have been too hard to make them understand. And I never want them to know what kind of man their grandfather . . .' Her voice trailed off. With a sigh she sank into one of the rocking chairs. For a moment the only sound was the creak of her chair on the porch.

Jane stared at the woman's profile. Charlotte—no, Susan—was only thirty-six, yet she looked older. Years in the outdoors had freckled her skin, and her hair already had silvery streaks. But it was the pain in her eyes that aged her the most.

Leaning her head back against the rocker, Susan stared off at the darkening lake. 'It started when I was nine years old,' she said. 'One night, he came into my room. He told me I was old enough to learn what all daughters were supposed to do. We're supposed to . . . please our daddies.' She swallowed. 'So I did.'

'Didn't you tell your mother?'

'My mother?' Susan's laugh was bitter. 'My mother's concerns never extended beyond her own interests. After she started her affair with Arthur, it took her only two months to fly the coop. She never looked back. I'm not sure she even remembered that she *had* a daughter. So I was left behind with my father, who was only too happy to retain custody. Uncontested, of course. Oh, a few times a year, I was scheduled to spend weekends with Mom and Arthur, but she pretty much ignored me. Arthur was the only one who showed me any real kindness. I didn't know him well, but he seemed like a decent man.'

'What about his son?'

There was a long silence. 'I didn't realise what Mark was,' she said softly. 'He seemed perfectly harmless when our families first got together. We all got along so well. The trouble was, my mom and Arthur were getting along better than I realised at the time.'

'It seems that your father and Mark were getting along rather well, too.'

Susan nodded. 'It was as if my dad had finally found the son he'd always wanted. Even after my parents divorced, Mark would come over and they'd go downstairs to Dad's workshop. I had no idea what was really going on down there.'

A lot more than woodworking, thought Jane. 'You didn't think it was strange, the two of them spending so much time together?'

'I was mostly relieved to be left alone. It was around then, when I was thirteen, that my dad stopped coming to my room at night. Now I realise that was when the first girl disappeared. When my dad found someone else to amuse him. With Mark's help.' Susan sat very still, her gaze fixed on the lake. 'If I'd known what Mark really was, my mother and Arthur would still be alive.'

Jane frowned. 'Why do you say that?'

'They went to the Red Phoenix because of something I told them.'

'You?'

Susan took a deep breath. 'It was the weekend for my visit with Mom and Arthur. I'd just got my licence, and I drove myself to their house for the first time in my father's car. That's when I found the pendant. It had fallen between the seat and the console, where nobody noticed it for two years. It was a gold dragon with a name engraved on the back. Laura Fang.'

'Did you recognise the name?'

'Yes. The story was in the newspapers when she disappeared. I remembered the name because she was my age, and she played the violin. And at Bolton, some of the students talked about her because they knew her from the summer orchestra workshop.'

'Mark attended that workshop.'

Susan nodded. 'He knew her. But how did Laura's pendant end up in my father's car? Then I started thinking about what he'd done to me. If he'd abused me, maybe he'd done it to other girls. Maybe that's what happened to Laura. Why she disappeared.'

'And then you told your mother?'

'That weekend, it all came out. I told her and Arthur everything. What my dad had done to me years earlier. What I'd found in his car. At first, Mom couldn't believe it. Then, in her usual self-centred way, she started worrying about the bad publicity and how her name would get dragged into the newspapers. But Arthur took it seriously.'

'Why didn't they go straight to the police?'

'My mom didn't want to attract any attention until they knew this wasn't some weird coincidence. Maybe there was another Laura Fang, she said. So they were going to show the pendant to Laura's family.' Susan's next words were almost inaudible. 'That's the last time I saw them alive: when they left to meet with Laura's father, at the restaurant.'

This was the final piece of the puzzle: the reason why Arthur and Dina had gone to Chinatown that night. Not to eat a meal, but to speak with

James Fang about his missing daughter. Gunfire had ended the conversation, a bloody massacre that was blamed on a hapless immigrant.

'The police said my mom and Arthur were just in the wrong place at the wrong time,' said Susan. 'But I kept wondering if it was connected: Laura and the shooting. The pendant was never found, so I had no evidence. And then there was Mark. He was home with us that weekend, so he knew what was going on.'

'He called Patrick. Told him your mother and Arthur were going to Chinatown.'

'I'm sure he did. But it was only at the funeral that I put it all together. My father and Mark, working together. But without the pendant, I couldn't prove a thing. And I knew how easy it would be for my dad to make me disappear.'

'So you made yourself disappear.'

'I didn't plan it ahead of time. But I was with my class, walking Boston's Freedom Trail.' She gave a sad laugh. 'And suddenly I thought, *I* want to be free, too! So I slipped away from the teachers. To throw everyone off track, I dropped my backpack and ID in an alley. I had enough cash to buy a bus ticket north. When I got to Maine, I suddenly felt like . . .' She sighed. 'Like I'd arrived home.'

'And you stayed.'

'I got a job cleaning cabins. I met my husband, Joe. And that was the biggest gift of my life, finding a man who loves me, no matter what.' She lifted her head. Sat up straight. 'I remade my life. Had my children. Together, Joe and I built these cabins. Built the business. I thought I'd be happy, just hiding away here for ever.'

The sound of laughter drifted from the lake where Will and his sister were splashing in the water. Susan rose from her chair and stared at them.

'Samantha's nine years old. The same age I was when my father first came into my bedroom.' Susan kept her back turned to Jane, as if she could not bear to let her see her face. 'You think you can put the abuse behind you, but you never can. It pops up when you least expect it. When you smell gin and cigars. Or hear your bedroom door creak open at night. Even after all these years, he's still tormenting me. And when Samantha turned nine, the nightmares got worse, because I saw myself at her age. I thought of what he did to me, and what he might have done to Laura. And I wondered if there were other girls I didn't even know about. But I didn't know how to bring him down, not by myself. Then on March 30th I opened the *Boston Globe*.'

'You saw Iris Fang's ad. About the Red Phoenix massacre.'

'"*The truth has never been told*,"' Susan whispered. 'That's what the ad said. And suddenly I knew that someone else was searching for answers. For justice.' She turned to face Jane. 'That's when I finally got the nerve to call Detective Ingersoll. I knew him because he'd investigated the Red Phoenix massacre. I told him about Laura's pendant. About my dad and Mark. I told him there might be other missing girls.'

'So that's why he started asking questions,' said Jane. Questions that had put him in danger, because word got back to Patrick that Ingersoll was gathering evidence. Patrick would have assumed that Iris Fang was behind it, because she'd placed the ad in the *Globe*. Killing Iris and Ingersoll would eradicate the problem, so he had hired professionals. But the killers had underestimated what they were up against.

'I was terrified that my father might find me,' said Susan. 'I told Detective Ingersoll not to say anything that could be traced back to me. He promised that no one would know what he was working on.'

'He kept his word,' said Jane. 'We had no inkling that you were the one who hired him. We assumed it was Mrs Fang.'

'A few weeks later, he called me. He said we had to meet, and he drove up here. He'd come up with the names of three girls who might have met me before they vanished. It turned out I was the link. I was the reason they were chosen.' Her voice broke and she sank into the chair again. 'Here I've been living with my little girl, safe and secure. I never knew there were other victims. If only I'd been braver, I could have stopped this a long time ago.'

'It has been stopped, Susan. And you did have a role in that.'

Susan looked at Jane, her eyes glistening. 'Only a minor role. Detective Ingersoll died for it. And you're the one who finished it.'

But not alone, thought Jane. *I had help.*

'Mom?' The girl's voice drifted in from outside. 'Dad said to come and get you. He's not sure if it's time to take the pie out of the oven.'

'I'm coming, sweetheart.' Susan rose to her feet. 'Dinner's ready. Come when you get hungry,' she said, and she stepped out.

From the porch, Jane watched Susan take Samantha's hand. Together, mother and daughter faded into the twilight.

THREE MONTHS LATER
Fujian Province, China

The scent of incense wafts across the courtyard where Bella and I stand before the tomb of her father's ancestors. It is an ancient cemetery. For at least a thousand years, generations of the Wu family have been interred here, and now Wu Weimin's ashes lie with his forefathers. No longer does his tormented soul wander the spirit world, crying out for justice. Here he will finally lie, for an eternity, in peace.

Bella and I light candles and bow to her father's memory. Suddenly, I sense the presence of someone else, and I turn to see a figure step through the courtyard gate. I know by the grace with which he moves that it is Wu Weimin's son by his first wife, the son who has never forgotten him and has continued to honour him.

As the man moves into the glow of candlelight, Bella nods to her half-brother and he returns the greeting with a sad smile. They are so alike, these two, both as unyielding as the stone that entombs their father's ashes. Now that their duty has been fulfilled, I wonder what will become of them. When you have devoted half your young life to a single goal, and you finally reach it, what is left to be accomplished?

He gives me a respectful bow. '*Sifu*, I am sorry to be late. My flight from Shanghai was delayed because of weather.'

I study his face and I see more than fatigue in the lines round his eyes. 'Are there problems in Boston?'

'I believe she knows. I feel her watching and probing. I sense her suspicion every time she looks at me.'

'What will happen now?'

He stares at the burning candles. 'I think—I hope—that she understands. She wrote me a glowing commendation. And she wants me to work with her on another Chinatown investigation.'

I smile at Johnny Tam. 'Detective Rizzoli is not so different from us. She may not agree with the way we accomplished our objective, but I believe she understands why we did it. And she approves.'

I touch a match to the courtyard fire pit, lighting the tinder. Flames leap up and we feed them joss papers of spirit money. As the smoke lifts, it carries comfort and fortune to the ghosts of those we love.

There is one final item we must burn. As I pull the mask from its sack, the silvery hair suddenly seems alive, as if the spirit of Sun Wukong himself has sprung from the shadows. But the mask hangs limp in my grasp, merely a mouldering prop of leather and monkey fur. All three of us have worn the mask. I, while defending myself on the rooftop against a woman assassin. Bella, while saving a policewoman's life. And Johnny last of all, when he fired the bullet into Patrick Dion's head, completing the circle of death.

I drop the mask into the flames and, in one bright flare, the mask is consumed, returning Sun Wukong to the spirit world where the Monkey King belongs. But he is never truly far away; when we need him most, each one of us will find him within ourselves.

The three of us stare into the fire pit, seeking in those glowing ashes what we each want to see. For Bella and Johnny, it is their father's smile of approval. They have done their filial duty; now their lives are their own.

And what do I see in those ashes? I behold the face of my daughter, Laura, whose remains were recovered ten weeks ago from a corner of Patrick Dion's property. I see the face of my beloved husband, his hair as black as the day we married. Though they do not age, here I linger on this earth, my health faltering, my hair turning silver, the years etching their lines ever more deeply into my face. But with every year that I grow older, I draw closer to James and Laura, to the day when we will once again be together. So I march through the deepening shadows, unafraid.

Because I know that, at the end of my journey, they will be waiting for me.

tess **gerritsen**

Were the Chinese aspects of *The Silent Girl* inspired by your own heritage?

Very much so! My mother is an immigrant from China, and she filled my head with stories about ghosts and fighting monks in China, so the world of *Crouching Tiger, Hidden Dragon* was a very familiar one. I've wanted to write about those tales for years, but only with this book did I feel ready to integrate my Asian-American past into a story.

Are both your parents Chinese?

My father was second-generation Chinese-American, born in 1923 in California. His parents were immigrants from a Cantonese-speaking province of China. My mother emigrated to the States from China when she was in her early twenties, in part to escape the political turmoil in China.

Do you feel that Chinese culture is very much a part of your life?

Throughout most of my life, I've tried to downplay my Asian heritage because I wanted so much to be an American. I was the only Asian kid in my elementary school, and I longed to be like everyone else. I insisted on American food; I was embarrassed by my mother's poor English. Only with maturity did I come to appreciate my own Asian roots: not just the food and the ancient history, but also the philosophy of child-rearing and the respect for education and knowledge.

How did you first come across the legend of the Monkey King?

As a child, hearing the tales from my mother. I also vaguely recall watching a cartoon series about the Monkey King on TV.

Do you believe, as many Chinese do, that the spirits of our ancestors are all around us, watching over us?

No, I'm afraid I'm too much an evidence-based person. My background in science makes me demand proof before I'll believe anything. It may also be my rebellious response to the fact that my mother was a big believer in parapsychology. She threw some pretty interesting dinner parties with spiritual mediums who'd occasionally go into trances right in the middle of a conversation.

Could you describe your home and its location?

I live in a small town of 5,000 people on Maine's mid-coast. It's gorgeous here, with a rocky shoreline and mountains looking out over the sea. My home is right on the ocean, and from my office I need only glance sideways to see the water and the seabirds.

Your books have ranged widely across so many settings and topics—from nuns and space stations to mummies and biblical stories. What, in particular, sparks your imagination?

I never know what will capture my curiosity. I'm interested in many things, and when I run across an interesting bit of information, I'll often want to delve more deeply. Which then gets a story going in my head and, the next thing you know, I'm writing a book about it.

You studied anthropology before deciding on medical school—what attracted you to the subject?

It embodied everything I loved: travel to foreign lands, history, and unfamiliar cultures. I also delved into physical anthropology as an undergraduate and spent many hours in the museum basement, measuring and examining human bones. I still think that, if I weren't a writer, I would be working very happily in some field of anthropology or archaeology.

You've said that you like to tap into something that raises the hairs on the back of your neck when writing . . . Where does that taste for chills come from, do you think?

It comes from my mother's love of horror films. When I was small, she used to take my brother and me to every scary film that Hollywood ever made. I learned to associate entertainment with thrills and chills, and I think that's what makes me gravitate towards writing scary stories.

How did you meet your husband and was it love at first sight?

We met in medical school in San Francisco, and yes—I'd have to say that it was love at first sight!

How old are your two sons and what are they into right now?

They're twenty-nine and twenty-seven years old. My older son is now in China, earning his credentials to teach Mandarin in American schools. My younger son works as a professional photographer in New York.

If your family had to pick three adjectives that are quintessentially 'Tess' what would they be?

Persistent (some would say obsessive!). Curious. Solitary.

What is your most cherished dream or ambition?

To write the stories that I want to tell—and not just what the market demands.

And if you could offer one piece of wisdom or life-advice to our readers, from your own heart, what would it be?

No experience in life is wasted; learn from your mistakes and move on.

The
Little Village
School

Gervase Phinn

Elisabeth Devine causes quite a stir on her arrival in Barton-in-the-Dale. Not only is she wearing red shoes with silver heels—not the usual head teacher attire—but she's also been in charge of a big inner-city school. Why would she want to come to a little village primary school with more problems than school dinners?

But Elisabeth Devine has her reasons, and a woman who would wear red shoes to an interview is obviously capable of tackling anything . . .

1

'She was wearing red shoes?' gasped the caretaker, incredulity creeping across his face.

'That's what I said, Mr Gribbon. She was wearing red shoes with silver heels and black lacy stockings,' continued Mrs Scrimshaw, the secretary of Barton-in-the-Dale Parochial Primary School. 'Not the sort of outfit I would have thought suitable for someone coming for an interview for a head teacher's position.'

It was the end of the school day. Mrs Scrimshaw looked up at the clock on the wall and made a small clucking noise with her tongue. She was obliged to wait until all the staff and pupils were off the premises, and there was still a child in the entrance waiting to be collected, so she couldn't get off home. For her to remain in her office after school each afternoon was something Miss Sowerbutts, the head teacher, insisted upon. Mrs Scrimshaw couldn't for the life of her understand why it was the head teacher who was out of the door a minute after the bell sounded for the end of school, and herself who had to remain, but she didn't say anything.

No one argued with Miss Sowerbutts.

In the thirty minutes after school, the caretaker frequently called in to see her, usually to grumble about something or other. Mr Gribbon was a tall, gaunt man with a hard beak of a nose and the glassy protuberant eyes of a large fish. The school secretary sometimes considered telling the caretaker to stop his moaning and get on with his work, but she bit her tongue. *It is important*, she thought, *to keep on the right side of him*. Caretakers could be extremely useful, but they could also be very difficult if crossed.

Mrs Scrimshaw peered over the top of her unfashionable, horn-rimmed spectacles, brushed a strand of mouse-coloured hair from her forehead and nodded. 'And she had earrings the size of onion rings and bright blonde hair,' she disclosed.

'And you say she got the job, Mrs Scrimshaw; the woman with the red shoes?' clarified Mr Gribbon.

'Yes, she did,' the school secretary told him, before adding, 'Of course, there wasn't much to choose from. Between you and me, there were very few applicants for the post.'

'And that dreadful report from them pokerfaced school inspectors must have put a lot of people off,' observed the caretaker.

'Actually, the report never got a mention in the information I sent out to the candidates,' divulged the secretary. 'I don't think any of the candidates were aware of it. I suppose the governors wanted to keep it under wraps.'

'Aye, well, the new head teacher will find out soon enough,' said the caretaker grimly. 'She'll have a job on her hands, and no mistake.'

'Yes, she will,' agreed Mrs Scrimshaw, glancing up at the clock again.

The caretaker sniffed noisily. ''Course, I came out of the report not too badly. They said the premises were clean and well kept, as I recall, despite the fact it's an old building in need of a lot of work.'

Mrs Scrimshaw gave a slight smile. She had read the school inspectors' report in some detail, and the section on the state of the premises had hardly been as positive as the caretaker maintained—it had contained a number of issues that needed addressing. There was the question of the cockroaches, for a start, which crawled out from under the skirting boards in the night. Many times she had arrived in the morning to discover several of the large black beetles wriggling on their backs in their death throes after the caretaker had sprinkled dreadful-smelling white powder down the corridor. She didn't say anything about that or the other recommendations of the inspectors, but turned her attention back to the appointment of the new head teacher.

'Evidently the governors were split. Dr Stirling wanted to re-advertise the position, from what I gathered, but the major, with the help of that objectionable councillor with the fat face and the red nose, the officious man from the Education Office, and the vicar, pushed it through. He said the school needed a new head teacher straight away to get things moving.'

'Well, they couldn't have picked anyone more different from the present head teacher,' observed the caretaker. 'And that's the honest truth.'

The school secretary thought for a moment of the present incumbent, Miss Hilda Sowerbutts, dressed in her thick, pleated tweed skirt, crisp white blouse buttoned up to her thin neck, heavy tan brogues and that silly knitted hat like a tea cosy perched on top of her head. She allowed herself another small smile. She tried to imagine her wearing red shoes, a short skirt and black lacy stockings. Yes, the new head teacher was certainly very different.

'So what did Miss Sowerbutts have to say about the appointment?'

'Nothing,' Mrs Scrimshaw told him. 'I was taking the candidates a cup of coffee before the interviews when Miss Sowerbutts walks down the corridor, stares at them for a moment, gives this dry little smile, nods and then leaves the school, telling me she'll be back when the interviews are over. When she got back, she never said a word, not one word. Never asked who got the job or anything. Went into her office, closed the door and carried on as normal. Of course, she was not best pleased that the governors hadn't seen fit to involve her in the appointment; that's why she was in such a black mood.'

'That must have stuck in her craw,' remarked the caretaker.

'Oh, it did,' said the school secretary. 'She went off alarmingly the week before when she met the chairman of governors. She gave the major a piece of her mind and no mistake.'

Mrs Scrimshaw had left the office door slightly ajar at the time of the major's visit, the better to hear the exchange. The chairman of the governing body, Major C. J. Neville-Gravitas, had informed Miss Sowerbutts that it was not really appropriate for her to take part in the appointment process, and this had not been received very well. The head teacher had argued with him, but to no avail. He had explained that, although he personally had no objection to her sitting in on the interviews, Mr Nettles, the education officer from County Hall, had raised an objection and was adamant that she should not attend.

'Well, what did she expect?' said the caretaker now. 'After that damning report from the school inspectors, she'd be the very last person to take any advice from. I mean, let's face it, she's well past her sell-by date, is Miss Sowerbutts. She was teaching in this school when I was a lad. She should have retired years ago. School's been going from bad to worse; parents complaining, children leaving to go to other schools like nobody's business, behaviour not all it should be and poor standards to boot, and her walking round the school with a face like a death mask.'

'You don't need to tell me, Mr Gribbon,' said the secretary. 'I've read the school inspectors' report as well. They said the senior management was "lacklustre" and the school "moribund", and there were "serious weaknesses that needed addressing urgently".'

The caretaker chuckled, jangling his keys. 'So how did Miss Brakespeare take it, then?' he asked. 'I suppose as the deputy she thought she was in with a chance of getting the job.'

'I think she found it a bit of a relief not to have got it, to be honest,' replied the school secretary. 'I guess she didn't want it anyway, what with having that disabled mother to look after and her near retirement. She came into the office after the interviews in quite a jolly mood. If you want my opinion, she only applied for the post because Miss Sowerbutts pushed her into it. You know how forceful she can be.'

'Tell me about it,' muttered the caretaker. 'So did you meet her then, the new head teacher?'

'Yes,' replied Mrs Scrimshaw. 'She seemed very pleasant and chatty, and certainly had more about her than the other candidates. She popped into the office after the interview to say she looked forward to working with me and would be calling in to the school next week to look round and meet people.

'One wonders, of course,' she said, 'why someone so well qualified and already a successful head teacher in a large city primary school should want to move to a village in the middle of the country. I saw her references and they were very good indeed. I mean, there's a drop in salary for a start, then the cost of moving house.'

'Is she married then?' asked the caretaker.

'Well, she's "Mrs" on the application form,' the school secretary said, 'but where it asked for marital status she had written, "Single".'

Just then, a small voice could be heard in the corridor: 'Excuse me, Mr Gribbon, I'm sorry to interrupt your conversation but may I have a quick word with Mrs Scrimshaw?'

The caretaker moved away from the door to let a small boy into the office. He was a bright-eyed, rosy-cheeked child of about eight or nine, his hair cut in the short-back-and-sides style with a neat parting. Unlike the other junior boys in the school, who wore jumpers in the school colours, open-necked white shirts and long grey flannel trousers, this child was attired in a smart blue blazer, a hand-knitted pullover, grey shorts held up by an elastic belt with a snake clasp, a white shirt and tie, long grey stock-ings and sensible shoes. He could have been a schoolboy of the 1950s, except for the brightly coloured frames of his glasses.

'Hasn't your mother arrived to collect you yet, Oscar?' asked the school secretary irritably.

'No, not yet, Mrs Scrimshaw,' replied the child cheerfully, 'but I am sure she will be here directly. She said she would be a little late today.' He had a curiously old-fashioned way of speaking.

'Yes, well, I have to get home,' Mrs Scrimshaw told him sharply. 'I really shouldn't have to wait around until your mother decides to collect you.' She drew in a deep breath. 'Well, what do you want, Oscar?'

'I just wanted a quick word with you about the new head teacher,' replied the boy. 'Miss Sowerbutts told us yesterday in assembly that the governors would be appointing a new head teacher today, and that whoever gets the job will probably be calling in at the school some time next week.'

'Well, what about it?' asked Mrs Scrimshaw.

'Well, it occurred to me,' said the child, 'that it would be a really good idea to make a big poster that we could put in the entrance hall to greet our new head teacher for when he or she visits. It would make them feel wel-come, don't you think? I could do it over the weekend.'

'I think you would need to ask Miss Sowerbutts about that, Oscar,' said the school secretary, imagining the expression on the face of the head teacher when such an idea was suggested. 'Now, why don't you go and wait in the entrance for your mother and read your book?'

'So, *did* the governors pick a new head teacher, Mrs Scrimshaw?' asked the boy, without moving.

Mr Gribbon had had enough: 'Go on now! Off you go!' said the caretaker. 'Do as you're told.'

'Actually, I'm glad I've seen you, Mr Gribbon,' said the boy, ignoring the instruction. 'I've noticed that one or two of the paving slabs on the school drive have cracked, and could be a health and safety hazard.'

'Have you indeed?' The caretaker grimaced.

'It's just that if someone trips up and falls over they could break a bone and then the school could get into a lot of trouble. I think it would be a really good idea, Mr Gribbon, if you replaced those paving slabs.'

The caretaker opened his mouth to reply but the boy smiled widely and said, 'Well, I think I can see my mother at the school gates. I'll get off then.'

'Goodbye, Oscar,' sighed the school secretary, slowly shaking her head.

'Goodbye, Mrs Scrimshaw,' the boy replied. He turned to the caretaker. 'Goodbye, Mr Gribbon, and you won't forget about the broken paving slabs, will you?'

'Now look here, young man—' started the caretaker, scowling, but before he could complete the sentence, the child was out of the door.

'I do hope the lady in the red shoes is our new head teacher,' shouted the boy from the corridor. 'She looked nice.'

MISS HILDA SOWERBUTTS, to avoid being there at the time of the interviews, had left the school that morning before the first candidate had been called into her room to face the appointment panel. She had been curious to see the candidates, though, so she had looked them over as they sat in the corridor. *A motley group*, she had thought to herself. She had left the school and arrived back after the candidates and governors had departed at lunchtime, had not asked Mrs Scrimshaw who had been offered the position, and had closeted herself in her room for the remainder of the day.

At the sound of the bell signalling the end of school she strode down the path, seething malevolently, without saying 'Good afternoon' to the school secretary. She was furious with the governors, of course, but Mrs Scrimshaw had annoyed her with the excessive attention she had paid to the candidates, and by the obsequious way she had followed the chairman of governors around like some fussy little lap dog.

Miss Sowerbutts walked briskly through the village, past the village store and post office and the Blacksmith's Arms, to arrive at her small cottage at the end of the high street.

After pouring herself a large, extra dry sherry, she sat in the small, tidy living room, simmering. To be treated like this by the governors after all her years of loyal service to the school, to be slighted in such a way, was quite unforgivable. When the chairman of governors had informed her the week before that she was not to be involved in the interviewing process, she had, for one of those rare moments in her life, been lost for words. She had not been allowed to see the application forms or give an opinion about the short list. She felt extremely angry. Lifting the sherry glass to her lips, she emptied the contents in one great gulp.

The phone rang.

'Yes?' she answered sharply.

'It's me,' a small voice came down the line. It was the deputy head teacher. 'I didn't get a chance to see you after school and I just wanted—'

'Did you get it?' Miss Sowerbutts asked quickly.

'No. The woman in the red shoes got it, a Mrs Devine.'

Miss Sowerbutts received the news with a face as hard as a diamond. 'Well, I think it is disgraceful,' she said angrily. 'Disgraceful!'

'She seems very nice,' Miss Brakespeare told her. 'She took the time to have a word with me both before and after the interviews.'

'I'll see you tomorrow, Miriam,' said Miss Sowerbutts, and without a word of commiseration, she banged down the receiver.

What was surprising to her was that the deputy head teacher had not sounded at all disappointed that she had not got the job; in fact, she had sounded distinctly light-hearted.

THE REVEREND ATTICUS, rector of Barton, surveyed his tea, which had just been placed before him, through the thin lenses of small, steel-framed spectacles. In the centre of the plate was a weeping chunk of boiled ham, half a hard-boiled egg with a blob of sickly-looking mayonnaise on top, two circles of dry cucumber, a radish, an overripe tomato and a fan-shaped piece of wilting lettuce edged in brown.

'Is there something the matter with your tea, Charles?' asked his wife.

She was a plain woman with a long oval face and skin the colour of the wax candles on the altar in the church, but her redeeming features were the most striking jade-green eyes and her soft titian hair.

'No, no, my dear,' the vicar replied, raising a smile. 'I was just thinking.'

'About what?' asked his wife, spearing a radish.

'Oh, what I might make the theme of my sermon on Sunday.'

'Well, I hope you will make it a great deal shorter than last week's sermon,' his wife said, rather petulantly.

He stared out of the window at the pale green pastures, dotted with grazing sheep and crisscrossed by grey stone walls, that rolled upwards to the great whaleback hills and gloomy grey clouds in the distance. The scene had a cold and eerie beauty about it. He recalled a snatch of text: '*I will lift up mine eyes unto the hills, from whence cometh my help*.'

'My father, the bishop, always made his sermons short and sweet,' his wife continued. 'The church was invariably full when he spoke.'

Here we go again, thought the vicar, forcing a piece of tasteless lettuce into his mouth. The Reverend Atticus knew soon after his marriage that he was something of a disappointment as a son-in-law. But Marcia had taken to the rather serious and intense young man when she had first met him at one of her father's soirees and had been attracted by his warm, attentive manner and kindly eyes.

For his part, the young Charles Atticus was drawn to the striking, almond-shaped green eyes and golden auburn hair of the young woman who introduced herself as the bishop's daughter. They had talked for most of the evening and he had been invigorated by her company.

But, he thought, *over the years, the lovely, interesting woman has become increasingly dissatisfied with her lot; more critical and tetchy, and certainly more outspoken.* She'd dreamed of ending her days in the bishop's palace, surrounded by her children. Sadly, he recalled the time when they had come to realise that they would never be blessed with children. His wife, more than he, had felt the great sense of loss.

'And, of course,' continued his wife now, 'my father spoke in the sort of plain and simple language that people understood. I do think your sermons are way above their heads, with all these biblical quotations, classical references and theological opinions. You are not lecturing to divinity students.'

'I do try to stimulate some thought in those who hear me,' said the vicar, having succeeded in swallowing the lettuce.

'My father, though you did not share his stance on a number of theological matters, imagined that you might go far in the Church when you married me,' she said. 'He said you had great potential if you could only be less serious and more sociable and mix with the right people. Yes, and I too thought you might go far.'

'I am very content here,' said the vicar.

'Well, I am not,' his wife retorted. 'I imagined that you would, at the very least, have been offered the dean's position, but it went to that fussy, shrill-voiced Peacock man, who no doubt ingratiated himself with the bishop.'

The Reverend Atticus raised his eyes heavenwards and the snatch of verse again came to mind. He sighed inwardly and examined his plate. He had never revealed to his wife that the present bishop had tried to persuade him that his name should be put forward for the said position, and that in every likelihood he would have been offered it; or that he had told the bishop he was honoured, but he was quite content to be the vicar of the small, rural parish of Barton-in-the-Dale.

His wife, having consumed her salad, placed her knife and fork together on her plate. 'And then there's the bishop,' she said.

'And what about the bishop, my dear?' enquired the vicar, predicting what she was about to impart.

'"Call me Bill," he says, with that irritating laugh of his and his hearty handshake and happy-clappy services. The confirmation service was like a revivalist meeting, all that loud singing and clapping.'

'"A merry heart doeth good as medicine",' observed the vicar.

'I beg your pardon?' asked his wife.

'The Song of Solomon,' murmured her husband.

His wife gave a weary sigh.

He was saddened by his wife's resentful words and by the fact that he had not lived up to her expectations. 'You are not at all happy today, are you, Marcia?' he asked, putting down his knife and fork and resting his white, well-cared-for hands on the table with priestly precision.

'No, Charles, I am not,' she replied.

'Has something upset you?' he asked.

'If you really want to know, it's this village that has upset me. I can't walk down the high street without a curtain moving. I get stopped by parishioners all the time asking about church functions and services, and what are we doing about the Harvest Festival and the summer fête. I am always the vicar's wife. People seem to forget that I am a person in my own right.' She bit her lip momentarily and looked down at her empty plate. 'It's so very claustrophobic here. I imagined that when the dean's position came up we would be moving to that lovely Georgian house in the cathedral precinct and be at the centre of the city; meet different and interesting people and have something of a life.'

The vicar rubbed his forehead. 'I am sorry you feel this way, Marcia,' he said. 'My one ambition was to be a country parson and serve a small community and hopefully to make some difference to people's lives: it was never my intention to climb up some ecclesiastical ladder. You knew that when you married me.'

'Yes, Charles, you may be very happy being just a country parson, but what about me?' She dabbed her eyes with her napkin. 'What sort of life is this for me?'

'Perhaps if you involved yourself in the life of the village a little more,' he suggested, with a harassed look on his face.

'You mean become a morris dancer?' she said. 'Attend the local history society meetings? Join the WI? I don't think so.'

The couple sat in silence for a while.

'We appointed the new head teacher at the school this morning,' he said, changing the subject and trying to sound cheerful.

'Well, I hope you picked someone different from Miss Sowerbutts,' replied his wife. 'That sour-faced woman should have gone years ago.'

The vicar thought for a moment and recalled the surprise on the faces of his fellow governors when the attractive, blonde-haired woman with the red shoes and the black stockings had walked through the door at the interviews that morning. As soon as she spoke, he had been immediately impressed by her confident manner, her sensible views on education and her obvious enthusiasm and good humour.

'Are you listening, Charles?' asked his wife. 'I said, I hope you have picked someone different.'

'Oh, yes,' he replied, 'the new appointment is very different, indeed.'

'The head teacher who's at the school at the moment is a most disagreeable woman,' the vicar's wife informed him. 'And before you spring to her defence and tell me she has all these good points and I shouldn't be so unkind, I have not heard one person in the village say a good word about her.'

'I was about to say,' said the vicar, 'that Miss Sowerbutts does have something of a joyless disposition and a somewhat disconcerting countenance, I have to admit.'

'In simple language, Charles,' said his wife, 'she's a miserable, bad-tempered gorgon of a woman. I don't think I've ever seen her smile. She walks about the village with a permanent scowl. One good thing that came out of that inspection of the school was getting her to retire. Although it's a pity that it had to be the inspectors and not the governors who got rid of her. I mean, one wonders what you governors are for; you should have grasped the nettle years ago.'

The vicar sighed with weary sufferance and felt it better not to pursue this line of conversation. He could have told his wife that the governors had discussed a number of times the possibility of suggesting to Miss Sowerbutts that she might consider retiring early, when parents began to move their children to other schools, but that they had discovered it was extremely difficult to remove a head teacher—unless of course he or she ran off with the dinner money or behaved inappropriately with a child.

'So what's the new head teacher like?' asked his wife.

'She's a very amiable and experienced person,' the vicar told her. 'Extremely well qualified and with excellent references. She's at present the head teacher of a large and very successful inner-city primary, which received a glowing report from the school inspectors. I feel certain she will change the school for the better.'

'Why on earth would she want to come to a backwater like Barton-in-the-Dale?'

That very thing had been raised by one of the governors on the appointment panel, but the vicar said nothing and turned his attention to the circles of cucumber on his plate.

THE GOVERNORS HAD convened in Miss Sowerbutts's room for the interviews at nine o'clock that morning: the chairman, Major C. J. Neville-Gravitas, Royal Engineers (Retd); the Reverend Atticus, rector of Barton; Mr Nettles, an education officer from County Hall; Dr Stirling, a local GP; Mrs Pocock, a parent governor; Mrs Bullock, a foundation governor; and Councillor Cyril Smout, the Local Education Authority representative.

The first candidate, Miss Brakespeare, the deputy head teacher, had proved singularly unimpressive, and it was clear that her heart was not in her application. She had smiled a great deal, sighed a great deal and nodded a great deal, but said very little. When asked if she would accept the position were it offered, she had replied that she would need to think about it.

The second candidate, a thin woman with a pained expression, had explained that she was looking for a quieter, less stressful life at a little country school. When the vicar mentioned the negative school report, the candidate's mouth had tightened.

'Negative school report?' she repeated. 'That was not made clear in the information sent out.' She awaited a response, but no one on the governing body decided to elaborate. The candidate had folded her hands together in a slow, controlled manner. 'Well, bearing in mind this critical report, of which I was not aware, I shall have to reconsider whether or not I want the position.'

'She's out of t'runnin',' observed Councillor Smout after the woman had left the room. 'She's a carbon copy of t'head teacher we've got at t'moment. Out o' frying pan, into t'fire, if we was to appoint 'er.'

The penultimate applicant was a tall, pale-faced man in his late twenties with an explosion of wild, woolly ginger hair, a small goatee beard and a permanently surprised expression.

'Do take a seat,' the chairman told him, gesturing to the hard-backed chair facing the crescent of governors. It was clear to all from the major's expression that he was less than impressed with the outfit this candidate was wearing: a crumpled linen jacket, crushed strawberry corduroy trousers, a pink shirt and a wildly colourful and clumsily knotted tie.

'Now, Mr Cuthberton,' the major had asked, 'could you tell us why you applied for this position?'

The candidate leaned forward earnestly in his chair, steepled his hands and launched into a carefully prepared monologue.

Councillor Smout had then asked the stock question he always asked at head teacher appointments: 'So, what makes a good head teacher, then?'

This was a question the candidate had clearly been expecting, for he delivered a statement that he had obviously rehearsed. He concluded: 'And so, it goes without saying, a head teacher should be dynamic, dedicated and hard-working.'

'Well, why bother sayin' it then?' said Councillor Smout under his breath.

When this applicant had left the room, the chairman had shaken his head. 'I was not keen on that chappie, I have to say. Not the sort of person we want for this school.'

The final candidate, an attractive woman in her late thirties, wearing a tailored grey suit, cream blouse, black stockings and red shoes with silver heels, had brought the chatter of the governors to an abrupt halt when she walked through the door.

'Good morning,' she said cheerfully.

The major had moved forward in his chair, stroked his moustache and smiled widely. 'Good morning,' he said. 'Do take a seat, Mrs—er . . .'

'Devine,' she told him, returning the smile. Her eyes were clear and steady. 'Elisabeth Devine.'

There was an expression of absolute wonder on the major's face, as if he had just discovered a rare and beautiful butterfly on a leaf.

The last candidate had considerable presence and gave an outstanding interview, answering the questions clearly, fully and confidently and looking each of the governors in the eye.

Councillor Smout had then asked his stock question: 'What makes a good head teacher, then?'

'Someone who believes that all children matter,' she told him, 'and that includes the bright and the talented, those with special educational needs, and the damaged, disaffected and ill-favoured. The good head teacher never writes a child off. I think the good head teacher is keen and enthusiastic; respectful of children's backgrounds and culture; somebody who has a vision that a school should be cheerful and welcoming and optimistic, where children love to learn and learn to love. She is a leader who involves the governors, staff, parents and to some extent the pupils in the decisions, who manages with openness and fairness and has a sense of humour; indeed, a sense of fun. Shall I continue?' she asked.

'No, no,' Councillor Smout had said. He had sat throughout her answer as if transfixed, his legs apart, his arms comfortably crossed over his chest, his head tilted a little to the side and his mouth open. 'That's quite sufficient, thank you.'

The vicar had then mentioned the inspectors' report. 'You are perhaps not aware, Mrs Devine, that this school has received a particularly critical report from the school inspectors. In the light of this, are you still disposed to be considered for the post?'

The candidate had clearly been surprised with the revelation, but she had already realised, she told him, having looked round the school and spoken to the deputy head teacher, that there were problems that needed addressing. She went on to say that she really wanted the post and that she would welcome the opportunity of working with the governors and staff in turning things round. Looking at Mr Nettles, she had smiled and told him she assumed the Education Office would give her a deal of support in making the necessary changes.

'Of course,' the education officer had assured her, though in the tone of one humouring a child.

'Do we need to vote on this?' the chairman asked when Mrs Devine had left the room. 'It seems to me the last candidate is head and shoulders above the rest.'

There were grunts of agreement and nods of heads. The one dissenting voice came from Dr Stirling, who, apart from asking each of the candidates a short question, spoke now for the first time.

'I will grant you, Mr Chairman, that the last candidate was extremely impressive,' he said. 'Rather too impressive, perhaps. Mrs Devine is clearly in a different league from the other applicants, none of whom I think is suitable for this position, but what I would ask is this: why does she want to come here?'

'There may be many reasons why Mrs Devine might wish to come here,' the vicar argued. 'For example, perhaps there is nothing left for her to do at her present school and she wishes to take on a fresh challenge.'

'Or she's looking for a quiet life in the country, like the other candidate,' observed the doctor.

'I think that is quite unfounded, Dr Stirling,' said the vicar. 'Mrs Devine is fully aware that this school is experiencing some difficulties. She said as much in her interview.'

'An' if she were looking for a quiet life in t'country,' added Councillor Smout, 'she'd 'ave backed out when she were told about t'report.'

'Well, I thought she gave an excellent performance,' said the major.

'Perhaps you have made my point, Mr Chairman,' the doctor said. 'It was indeed something of a performance. Rather too polished for my liking.'

'I for one think she's t'ideal replacement for Miss Sowerbutts,' Councillor Smout said, wishing to escape the small, cramped room. 'She's a striking-looking woman with a lot about 'er. What do you think, Mr Nettles?'

'I think Mrs Devine seems eminently suitable,' he replied.

'Mr Chairman—' Dr Stirling started.

'Dr Stirling,' the education officer now said in a deeply patronising voice, 'as the representative of the director of education, here to advise the governors, I feel it incumbent upon me to point out that we need to expedite the matter of appointing with some urgency. It appears you are the only dissenting voice, so I think that the governors should put it to a vote.'

And so it was that Mrs Elisabeth Devine was appointed the new head teacher of Barton-in-the-Dale Parochial Primary School.

2

Mrs Sloughthwaite, proprietor of the village store and post office, stood at the door of her shop the morning after the interviews. It was a bright, sunny, summer Saturday, and Mrs Sloughthwaite, a round, red-faced woman with a large fleshy nose, pouchy cheeks and a great bay window of a bust, hoped the good weather would encourage visitors to the village. Tourists passing through on their way to more picturesque spots sometimes stopped to patronise her shop, and she enjoyed passing the time of day and regaling them with a potted history of the place—though nothing of great import had happened there.

Barton-in-the-Dale had a timeless quality about it that suited Mrs Sloughthwaite. Former inhabitants long since dead and buried in St Christopher's churchyard, were they to be resurrected, would recognise it immediately, for little had changed. Mrs Sloughthwaite had lived there all her life, and she loved the village with its pale stone and pantile-roofed cottages, the old walls of greenish-white limestone enclosing the solid Norman church with its square tower, the black yews and elms in the graveyard, the two pubs and the proud monument built in honour of the second Viscount Wadsworth, a long-dead local squire. Nothing of any real note happened there, but that was the way she liked it—predictable and undisturbed, well away from the noise and the bustle of town and city life. *Mind you*, she thought, folding her arms under her substantial bosom, *there is a bit of interesting news*. A new head teacher had been appointed up at the school. A glimmer of private amusement passed across her face as she thought of Miss Sowerbutts, the present holder of the post. That long beak of a nose had been well and truly put out of joint, or so she had heard.

It was as if the very thought of the said woman had conjured her up, for there she suddenly stood, body stiffly upright and wearing that silly knitted hat and mothball-scented skirt, with a battered canvas shopping bag hanging loosely from her arm.

'I take it you are open?' asked Miss Sowerbutts, without a smile.

'Oh, I didn't see you there, Miss Sowerbutts,' replied the shopkeeper in an overly friendly way. She smiled insincerely. 'I was in a world of my own. Yes, indeed we are open.' She led the way inside and positioned herself behind the counter. 'It's a beautiful day, isn't it?'

'Yes, indeed,' replied Miss Sowerbutts, scanning the shelves.

'I love this time of year when all the buds come out and the flowers appear. June is my favourite month, although I have to say—'

'Are these the only biscuits you have?' interrupted Miss Sowerbutts.

'I'm afraid so. We don't have much call for any others. The custard creams are nice and there's a very popular Venetian selection box.'

'They are not to my taste,' replied the customer. 'I don't have a sweet tooth. I want rich tea or plain digestives. I shall have to go into town.'

Suit yourself, you miserable old crone, thought Mrs Sloughthwaite, before going on to remark casually: 'I gather they've appointed the new head teacher up at the school.'

It was a carefully and cleverly aimed provocation. She had heard from Mrs Pocock how displeased Miss Sowerbutts had been at not being consulted in the appointment of her successor.

'Yes, so I hear,' was the murmured reply. The thin smile conveyed little more than feigned interest. 'I'll take a jar of that coffee; the roasted blend.'

Mrs Sloughthwaite reached up to the shelf behind her. 'Yes, Mrs Pocock called in for her order yesterday afternoon and said the governors had appointed someone.'

'Did she? I'll have a packet of brown sugar as well.'

'Very colourful character by all accounts.'

'Who is?'

'The new head teacher.'

'Well, I wouldn't know,' Miss Sowerbutts told her with quick indifference. 'I've not met her.'

'You'll be able to put your feet up now, won't you, and enjoy your retirement,' Mrs Sloughthwaite added. It was a comment guaranteed to annoy.

Miss Sowerbutts stiffened, fixing Mrs Sloughthwaite with a piercing stare. 'Retirement?' she repeated.

'Well, now that you've finished at the school, you'll have time on your hands, I should imagine.' The shopkeeper's smile was a mask on her face.

'Mrs Sloughthwaite,' Miss Sowerbutts replied with a bleak smile, 'I am *not* the sort of person who puts her feet up, and I will most certainly not have "time on my hands". I shall be as busy as ever.' She dug into her canvas bag for her purse. 'How much for the coffee and the sugar?'

MARCIA ATTICUS was digging in the herbaceous borders of the rectory garden when she caught sight of the lone figure wandering among the gravestones, pausing here and there to examine the inscriptions. The visitor was an attractive-looking woman with bright blonde hair, dressed in a stylish cream raincoat and a pale, silk scarf of eau de nil.

'Are you looking for someone in particular?' asked the vicar's wife, leaning over the low stone wall that surrounded the rectory garden.

Elisabeth turned and smiled broadly. 'No, I was just looking. I find epitaphs fascinating. It's a beautiful church, and so peaceful.'

'A little too peaceful for my liking,' said Mrs Atticus, smiling ruefully.

'And your garden is quite delightful.'

'One tries one's best. It's such an effort keeping the lawn in this condition. The dandelion seeds blow over from the graveyard. Such a nuisance. I do so wish Mr Massey would do something about the weeds. He is supposed to keep it tidy but he spends most of his time in the Blacksmith's Arms and comes and goes as he pleases.'

'Is the church open?' asked Elisabeth.

'Oh, yes, my husband never locks it. I have told him that one day when the brass candlesticks disappear from the altar, and the poor box goes missing, he will finally decide to lock the door. My husband is a very trusting man. He tends to see the good in everyone.'

'Well, he is a priest, after all,' Elisabeth commented. 'I think that is what priests are supposed to do.'

'That is exactly what he says,' said the vicar's wife wryly. 'And, speak of the devil—if you will pardon the expression—here he comes.'

The Reverend Atticus had emerged from the rectory. He was a tall man with a thin-boned face, skin as smooth as parchment, high arching brows and a long, prominent nose. When she had first set eyes upon him at her interview the day before, Elisabeth had thought he had the appearance of someone who was likely to be a severe and uncompromising individual, but he had proved to be very different: as soon as he had opened his mouth, she had decided that she liked the Reverend Atticus, with his soft voice and solicitous and kindly manner. Unlike the stony-faced doctor who had said very little, and the bellicose, red-faced councillor with the loud voice, the Reverend Atticus had smiled a great deal throughout her interview and listened attentively to her answers. He had been the first to extend a hand to congratulate her when she had been offered the job, and he had expressed the hope that she would settle into the school and be happy in her new role.

The clergyman's smile broadened when he caught sight of her talking to his wife.

'Ah,' he said breezily, addressing his wife, 'you have become acquainted with our new head teacher, my dear?'

'Oh!' exclaimed Mrs Atticus. 'I didn't realise.'

'I'm Elisabeth Devine,' said Elisabeth, extending a hand across the wall.

Marcia Atticus removed her gardening glove. 'I'm very pleased to meet you,' she said.

'I thought I would spend a day in the village; have a look round and get a feel for the place,' Mrs Devine explained. 'It's quite a delightful spot, so unspoilt and tranquil.'

'We like it,' replied the vicar, glancing at his wife. 'Don't we, my dear?'

His wife gave a small and unconvincing smile, but didn't reply.

'I'm just about to have an interlude from writing tomorrow's sermon,' announced the cleric cheerfully. 'I'm considering the Parable of the Lost Sheep—sheep always go down well in this part of the world. I feel sure my wife would enjoy a cup of coffee and a break from her labours in the garden. Perhaps you might like to join us, Mrs Devine?'

The rectory was an unprepossessing building that had been erected in the late nineteenth century. With its shiny, red brick walls, greasy grey slate roof, small square windows, towers and turrets and enveloping high, black iron fence, the building resembled more a workhouse than a vicarage. Inside it was cool and unwelcoming, with its black-and-white patterned tiles in the hallway, plain off-white walls, high ceilings and heavy oak doors. The place smelt of old wood and lavender floor polish.

'Come through into the sitting room, Mrs Devine,' urged the vicar. 'My wife will entertain you while I get the coffee.'

Elisabeth followed Mrs Atticus into a sombre and spartan space with heavy, old-fashioned furniture, dark faded carpet and thick, plain green curtains. Her eyes were immediately drawn to a large watercolour painting of St Christopher's, which hung above the mantelpiece. It was one of the rare bits of colour in the room.

'So what brings you to Barton-in-the-Dale?' asked the vicar's wife, gesturing to her visitor to take a seat in a heavy and threadbare armchair.

Elisabeth Devine did not know the questioner sufficiently well to confide in her as to why she had decided to leave such a comfortable, well-paid and rewarding position in the city to move to a small village in the Yorkshire Dales. She knew that whatever she divulged would spread like wildfire throughout the small community. *It would be best*, she thought, *to be evasive.*

'Oh, I felt like a change,' she replied, casually. 'City life has become increasingly hectic and noisy, and I decided it was time to move on.'

Mrs Atticus looked for a moment at her visitor, studying her carefully. She was certain there was more to it than merely a change of scenery and the desire for a quiet life. 'It might not be as quiet and uneventful as you imagine,' she replied. 'You will be well aware that the school is in something of a crisis.'

Elisabeth had not known things were quite that bad, but decided to remain quiet.

'As you will know, it had a dire report from the school inspectors,' continued Mrs Atticus, 'and parents are taking their children away and sending them to the school at Urebank. It will be a real challenge for you.'

Elisabeth felt it had been rather underhand of the governors that the report had only been mentioned by the vicar at her interview the day before, but she maintained her composure and smiled. 'I like a challenge,' she said.

'Here we are with the coffee.' The vicar arrived, carrying a tray.

'I was telling Mrs Devine, Charles,' said his wife, 'that she will have her work cut out taking on the village school. It will be a real challenge turning it around.'

'I am sure Mrs Devine is most capable, my dear.'

'I hope so,' replied Elisabeth. 'I mentioned to the chairman of governors after the interview that I would like to call in to the school on Wednesday to meet the staff and the children. I am sure Miss Sowerbutts will fill me in on what I need to know then.'

Mrs Atticus gave a hollow laugh. 'Oh, I am sure she will do that. She is very adept at filling people in. Wouldn't you say so, Charles?'

Her husband smiled the tolerant, patient smile of the sort a teacher might employ when explaining things to a small child, and decided to disregard the question.

'Milk and sugar, Mrs Devine?' he asked.

'Just milk, please,' she replied. The vicar passed her her cup.

'Of course,' continued Mrs Atticus, quite enjoying her husband's discomfiture, 'Miss Sowerbutts is something of a sad figure. She's taught in the school all her career. They made her head teacher, I reckon, as some sort of long-service award. I guess there has been little passion in her uneventful life, and numerous disappointments. Why else should she be so ill-tempered with people, and so crotchety?'

The vicar raised an eyebrow in wordless contradiction.

Marcia Atticus reached for her coffee and took a small sip from the china cup. 'She has lived in the same cottage in the village where she grew up, a place where nothing ever happens, ruling the roost in the school like some Victorian school ma'am and—'

'My dear,' interrupted the vicar, shuffling on his chair with obvious embarrassment, 'I feel sure Mrs Devine does not wish to hear this.'

There was a distinct coldness in his wife's reply. 'I am merely telling Mrs Devine what everyone in the village thinks, and preparing her for meeting Miss Sowerbutts. If she is expecting the red-carpet treatment and a warm welcome, then she is in for a rude awakening.'

There was an awkward silence. Elisabeth glanced in the direction of the vicar's wife. There was something dark and troubling in those green eyes.

'What a delightful picture,' she commented, placing her coffee cup on the small table next to her and rising to look more closely at the watercolour above the mantelpiece.

'You think so?' asked the vicar's wife.

'Oh, yes,' replied her visitor, 'it's superbly painted. The artist has captured so well the atmosphere of autumn. The mist and colours of the leaves are quite wonderful, and the detail on the church is remarkable.'

'You know about art then, do you, Mrs Devine?' asked the vicar's wife.

'Not a great deal,' Elisabeth replied, 'but I can recognise a good painting when I see it, and this is exceptionally well painted.'

'I did it,' announced Marcia Atticus, deciding that she quite liked the new head teacher at Barton-in-the-Dale.

MRS SLOUGHTHWAITE'S menacing bosom and large hips carried as much weight in the village as she did structurally. She knew everything there was to know in Barton-in-the-Dale, and was a most efficient conduit of gossip and information. She knew that the major had an eye for the ladies, that the vicar's wife was not a happy woman and that her poor, henpecked husband had to put up with her moods and sharp tongue. She knew that Mrs Pocock's husband was a bit too fond of his drink and that Mrs Stubbins's son—that disagreeable, badly behaved Malcolm—had to be watched, for she had discovered sweets had gone missing when he had been in the shop. She knew that Councillor Smout's relationship with his brassy secretary was not as platonic as he imagined people thought, and she could have predicted that the sad, timorous little Miss Brakespeare would never have got the post of the new head teacher in a month of Sundays.

The door of her shop opened and an elegant woman entered.

'Good morning,' she said pleasantly.

''Morning, love,' replied the shopkeeper, rising to her full height and then stretching over the counter to get a glimpse of the woman's shoes. They were not the expected red with silver heels but of copper-brown leather.

Mrs Sloughthwaite turned to her other customer and dismissed her with the words, 'Well, if there's nothing else, Mrs Widowson.' She wanted no other person privy to the conversation she was going to have with the new head teacher of Barton-in-the-Dale School, and she considered Mrs Widowson a terrible gossip. If there was any information to glean, *she* was to be the one to get it first.

When Mrs Widowson had departed, the shopkeeper gave Elisabeth her undivided attention. 'Now then, love, what can I get you?'

'I would just like the local paper, please.'

'You're the new head teacher up at the school, aren't you?' said Mrs Sloughthwaite, reaching under the counter for the newspaper. The question was academic, for she knew who this well-dressed woman was.

'That's right,' replied Elisabeth.

'I thought so,' said the shopkeeper, nodding. She peered at her customer with more than a little interest. 'One of the governors popped in yesterday and mentioned in passing what you looked like.'

Elisabeth laughed. 'I see.'

'Well, I hope you are going to be happy at the school.'

'I am sure I will.'

'Are you intending to live in the village?' asked the shopkeeper bluntly.

'Yes, that's why I want the local paper,' Elisabeth told her. 'I thought I'd spend the afternoon looking at some properties.'

'There's not much on the market in the village. There's a new block of flats at Ribbledyke, and some houses the size of egg-boxes in Urebank, but if you have a family, I don't think one of those would be suitable.'

Elisabeth smiled to herself. Like the vicar's wife, here was another person determined to find out as much about her personal life as she could. 'I was thinking of something rather older and with a bit of character; perhaps a stone cottage,' she said.

Mrs Sloughthwaite thought for a moment. 'The only place like that round here what I know of is Wisteria Cottage, old Mrs Pickles's place up Stripe Lane, but it's been empty for a couple of months and will need a lot doing to it. Nice position though, overlooking fields and in walking distance of the school, and it has a good bit of garden and a paddock at the side.'

'That sounds promising,' said Elisabeth.

'I'll point you in the right direction before you go,' said Mrs Sloughthwaite, feeling pleased that she had at least extracted some information about the new head teacher that she could impart to those who called in at the shop. 'Will you still be wanting the paper?' she asked.

'Yes, please,' Elisabeth replied, reaching into her handbag.

'I had the present head teacher in the shop only this morning,' said the shopkeeper. 'Have you met her?'

'Not really, no,' replied Elisabeth, 'but I'll look forward to meeting her when I call in at the school.'

I bet you will, thought Mrs Sloughthwaite, dropping the coins that had been passed over the counter into the till. *I wish I could be a fly on the wall.*

BARTON-IN-THE-DALE Parochial Primary School was a small, solid, stone-built Victorian structure with high mullioned windows, a blue patterned slate roof and a large oak-panelled door with a tarnished brass knocker in the shape of a ram's head. Set back from the main street, which ran the length of the village, it was tucked away behind the Norman church of St Christopher and partially hidden by a towering oak tree with branches reaching skywards like huge arms. It was an imposing if rather neglected building. The small garden to the front was tidy enough but, apart from a few sad-looking flowers and a couple of overgrown bushes, it was bereft of plants. The paint on the window frames was beginning to flake and the path leading up to the entrance had several cracked and uneven flagstones.

It was later the same afternoon, and Elisabeth was sitting on a bench by the oak tree, considering whether she had done the right thing in applying for the post of head teacher there. She should have found out more about the school before applying, and then she might have learned of the problems she would have to face. Of course, there was a good reason for her wanting to come to this particular school, but she certainly had had second thoughts when she had first seen the building, and got such a cold reception from Miss Sowerbutts. Then there was Miss Brakespeare, the dowdy, serious and dull deputy head teacher, who, despite her friendly demeanour after the interview, would no doubt be resentful that she had not been offered the post and would not take kindly to any changes Elisabeth would wish to implement. She sighed, and chased the thought from her mind.

She closed her eyes and let the sun, breaking through the overhanging branches of the ancient oak, warm her face. She thought for a moment, considering how she might start to make the necessary changes. The state of the building was the first priority. The school was in need of a coat of paint, the flagstones on the path wanted replacing, the hedge trimming, the garden to the front tending and the fence round the perimeter repairing. It needed to look cheerful and welcoming. She would put some large tubs of bright geraniums by the door, have vivid flowers in window boxes and a bird table on the small lawn. This was cosmetic and would be the easy part. Her main challenges, she knew, were to raise the standards; gain the confidence of the teachers, the governors and the parents; and stem the haemorrhaging of children to other schools. It would not be easy.

She stood, breathed in deeply and smoothed the creases in her coat. She would go in search of the little stone cottage that she had heard about from the shopkeeper.

It took quite a while for Elisabeth to discover Wisteria Cottage. It stood along a track of beaten mud overgrown with nettles, a small, pale stone building with a sagging roof, peeling paint and a neglected garden. Rough, spiky grass sprouted like clumps of green hair from the guttering, and dandelion, daisies and ragwort, left to go to seed and disperse in a sudden wind, sprouted between the broken paving slabs leading to the porch. Great plumes of wisteria hung from the wall. The front door, partially covered by dense holly and laurel bushes, was colourless, the paint having peeled away many months ago. To the side was a heavy horse-chestnut tree, its leaves fanning out like fingers and one huge branch split and charred by lightning. Somewhere in a distant field, a tractor chugged.

Elisabeth knew that she had to have this cottage. She stood on the tussocky lawn with its bare patches and seemingly hundreds of molehills, bordered by waist-high weeds, tangled brambles and rampant rosebushes, and gazed through the trees at a vista of green, undulating fields crisscrossed with silvered limestone walls that rose to the craggy fellside, and she marvelled at the view.

She knew she could transform this old cottage into her dream home.

Beyond the five-barred gate at the end of the track was a small boy of about ten or eleven, lifting a dry cow pat with a stick and disturbing a buzzing cloud of yellow horseflies. He stopped when he caught sight of Elisabeth and, having watched her for a moment, came over.

''Ello,' he said cheerfully, climbing up onto the gate, sitting on the top and letting his spindly legs dangle down. He was a small boy with large, low-set ears, a mop of dusty, dark blond hair and the bright brown eyes of a fox. He was dressed in a faded T-shirt, baggy khaki shorts and Wellington boots that looked sizes too big for him.

'Hello,' replied Elisabeth.

'Grand day, i'n't it?' said the child, grinning broadly. 'I likes this time o' year,' he said, scratching a muddied knee.

'So do I,' said Elisabeth. 'I hope this weather continues.'

'Oh, it will that,' said the boy. He waved his stick like a conductor with a baton. '"If t'rooks build low, it's bound to blow, if t'rooks build 'igh, t'weather's dry." That's what mi granddad says, and 'e's never wrong.'

'He sounds a clever man, your granddad,' said Elisabeth.

''E is,' the boy agreed. 'I've seen a nuthatch in that 'orse-chestnut tree,' he told her, pointing with the stick. 'We gets all sooarts o' birds in this garden—bluetits, jays, redstarts, hawfinches, linnets, magpies and t'odd pheasant from t'big estate—and when that buddleia's out you should see t'butterflies—red admirals, peacocks, tortoiseshells and some reight rare species an' all.'

'You're fond of this garden, aren't you?' asked Elisabeth, charmed by the boy's cheerful good humour.

'Aye, I love comin' 'ere,' he said. 'Mrs Pickles who used to own it, she used to let me come 'ere. She's deead, tha knows.'

'Yes, I heard.'

'She were nice, Mrs Pickles,' said the boy. 'She used to give me a drink of 'er 'omemade ginger beer an' a biscuit when I called.'

'I'm afraid I don't have any ginger beer or biscuits,' Elisabeth told him.

'Oh, I weren't 'intin'. I were just sayin'.' He looked at her closely. 'You thinkin' o' buyin' this place, then?'

'Yes, I'm thinking about it,' replied Elisabeth.

He sucked in a breath. 'Lots to do. You've got moles underneath your lawn, rabbits in your borders, rooks in your chimney, swallow nests under your gutterin', bees beneath your eaves and frogs in your cellar. It'll tek some fettlin', I can tell you.'

'I think you're trying to put me off,' said Elisabeth, smiling.

'Nay, missis,' said the child with a grin, 'just purrin' you reight. It'll be champion when it's done up. Best view in t'village.'

'It's a lovely aspect, right enough,' said Elisabeth, looking at the view before her.

'That's where I live, ovver yonder in t'caravan.' The boy pointed with his stick. 'Mester Massey lets us purr it on 'is field. We 'ave to pay 'im rent, mind. Mi granddad says 'e's a tightfisted old so-and-so and allus on t'make. I live wi' mi granddad.'

Elisabeth wondered why the child was not with his mother and father, but decided not to pry.

''Course, if ya do buy t'cottage,' the child continued, winking, 'you'd be wanting somebody to give you an 'and to get rid o' all them pesky creatures, wouldn't you?'

'Yes, I suppose I would,' said Elisabeth.

'Aye, well tha knows where to come. Best leave your bees and your swallows. They don't do no 'arm. Mi granddad can sweep your chimney, if you've a mind, an' I can set mole traps, and sort out your rabbit problem.'

'What's your name?' she asked.

'Danny.'

'I'm Mrs Devine, Danny, and I'm pleased to meet you.'

'Bloody 'ell,' the boy said under his breath, then spoke up: 'Are you t'new 'ead teacher up at t'school?'

'I am,' said Elisabeth, stifling a laugh.

'We were telled last week in assembly that we were gunna gerra new 'ead teacher. Mi granddad were talkin' to 'is pals in t'pub last neet and they said you were picked yesterday and that you 'ad a fancy name. He said it means 'eavenly an' 'e says they said you were a bit of all right.'

'Did he?'

'And that you wore these fancy red shoes.' The boy glanced down at Elisabeth's feet as if to confirm his grandfather's observation.

'Is that so?' She bit her lip to hide a smile.

'Aye, but 'e telled me I'd berrer be watchin' me p's and q's because you'd likely be reight strict.'

'Things seem to get round the village pretty quickly,' said Elisabeth, amused by the revelations.

'Oh, tha can't keep owt secret round 'ere. And if tha wants owt broad-castin' fast, just tell Mrs S who runs t'post office an' t'village shop.' The boy suddenly sat up on the gate and threw his stick away. 'Hey up, miss, I 'opes you dunt think I was bein' cheeky, and I din't mean to swear, or owt. I was only tellin' you what folk were sayin'.'

'No, Danny,' said Elisabeth, 'I don't think you were being cheeky. The information is very interesting.'

The boy looked embarrassed. 'If I'd 'ave known you were t'head teacher, miss, I'd 'ave kept mi gob shut.'

'I'm glad you didn't.'

'Mi granddad sez I open mi gob too much sometimes bur I can't seem to 'elp it. He says a closed gob catches no flies. And tha's what gets me into trouble at school, talkin' too much.'

'And how is school, Danny?' she asked.

The boy blew out noisily. 'I'm not gerrin' on reight well at t'moment, to tell ya t'truth. All this learnin' dunt suit me. Any road, miss, I'd best get back. Mi granddad's cookin' rabbit for us dinner. There's no shortage of rabbits round here. They breed like . . . like—'

'Rabbits?' suggested Elisabeth.

The boy laughed. 'Aye, like rabbits.' He jumped down from the gate. ''Bye, miss,' he said and started to run off across the field, leaping over the cow pats, but he stopped to call back: 'And I don't think tha's strict or stuck-up, either.'

'Goodbye, Danny,' said Elisabeth under her breath, thinking about the first impression she had made on the residents of Barton-in-the-Dale.

THE FOLLOWING WEDNESDAY found Elisabeth outside the entrance of the village school. It was another bright, clear June day and the air was full of birdsong and the smell of blossom. She had telephoned the head teacher on Monday to confirm the visit she had agreed with the governors following the interview, but Miss Sowerbutts had instructed the school secretary to deal with it rather than talk to Elisabeth herself. She was far too busy.

Mrs Scrimshaw mused to herself that the head teacher was blessed with the ability to appear very busy while actually avoiding work of any kind.

'Mrs Devine.'

Elisabeth looked round to see a head, with a beak of a nose and large glassy eyes, appear over a bush.

'I'm Mr Gribbon, the school caretaker. I just thought I'd make my presence known.' He emerged from behind the bush, clutching a spade. He had heard from Mrs Scrimshaw that the new head teacher was to visit that day, and had positioned himself at a vantage point so he could catch her prior to her entering the building. 'Just giving the garden a bit of a tidy up,' he said, holding up the spade. She noticed that he glanced down at her shoes.

'Good morning, Mr Gribbon,' said Elisabeth, going over to him and shaking his hand. She appeared much brighter than she actually felt.

'It's a lovely little school,' he told her. 'You'll be very happy here, I'm sure.'

'I'm certain I will,' replied Elisabeth.

'Needs a bit doing to it, of course,' he said.

'Yes, I can see,' said Elisabeth, looking at the building, 'but I am sure that together we can make it nice and bright and welcoming. It just needs a coat of paint on the windowsills and a couple of new flagstones on the path. Nothing very drastic.'

'Yes,' he said, suddenly deflated. 'I suppose it does. I do try my best, Mrs Devine, but there's only so many hours in the day and Miss Sowerbutts is always telling me we don't have the money for improvements, and there's quite—'

Elisabeth held up her hand as if stopping traffic. 'Please, Mr Gribbon, I did not mean to sound critical. I am sure you try your best.' She saw disappointment written across his face. 'I could tell when I came for the interview that you keep the interior of the school clean and well looked after. The floor in the hall is quite splendid.'

The caretaker was clearly mollified. 'I do take pride in my floor,' he said, relieved to see that the new head teacher was wearing flat-soled shoes and wouldn't be leaving marks on it.

'I can tell,' said Elisabeth. 'And now, if you will excuse me, I have an appointment with Miss Sowerbutts.'

Elisabeth was kept waiting for ten minutes in the drab entrance hall before being shown into the head teacher's office. Miss Sowerbutts sat stiffly behind the large desk, her eyes dramatically narrowed. She wore a prim, white blouse buttoned up high on her neck and a hard, stern expression on her face. *So this is my successor*, she thought, examining the woman who sat with legs crossed opposite her, dressed up to the nines and wearing enough make-up to shame a cosmetic counter. This was the person the governors deemed appropriate to replace her, someone who would, no doubt, overturn everything she had established over the years, who would introduce all those modern approaches and trendy initiatives and undo all she had achieved. Well, she need not expect her to be warm and welcoming.

'I have to say from the outset, Mrs Devine,' said the head teacher, removing her glasses slowly and placing them carefully on the desk, 'that it seemed to me very discourteous of the governors to agree to you coming into the school this morning without consulting me first.'

'I did telephone the school on Monday to check if it was convenient,' Elisabeth told her. 'The school secretary said it would be all right. I believe you were busy at the time and unable to speak to me.'

Miss Sowerbutts pursed her thin lips. 'You will, no doubt, have heard that the school received a most unfair and inaccurate report from the school inspectors,' she said.

'I had heard so,' Elisabeth replied.

Miss Sowerbutts snorted. 'The inspectors were a group of disorganised, disparaging and disagreeable people, and had no understanding of the problems we face here.'

'What are the problems?' asked Elisabeth, hiding her rising irritation.

'I beg your pardon?'

'You mentioned the problems you have to face.'

Miss Sowerbutts retained her chilly and disapproving composure and gazed at Elisabeth balefully, folding her cold-looking and bloodless hands before her as if in prayer. 'People might imagine that in a small country primary school like this one, we are free of problems; that all the children are hard-working, well behaved and value education, and that their parents are supportive and appreciative of one's efforts.' This observation was clearly made for Elisabeth's benefit. 'Well, if they think that, then they are sadly misguided. Most of them come from farming families and their parents want nothing better for them than to work on the farm when they leave school. The children have limited prospects and little ambition. In consequence, they are at best lethargic and, at worst, uncooperative and truculent.' A red rash had appeared on Miss Sowerbutts's neck and her face was flushed with displeasure. 'The inspectors clearly did not appreciate this, and advised that I should be more proactive in raising the standards and be more supportive of the children who were difficult and disruptive, and that I should pay more attention to pupils with special educational needs.' She sniffed. 'As I told them, I have always been of the opinion that one has to have the raw material before one can achieve anything of note, and that one cannot make a straight beam out of a crooked timber.'

Elisabeth was filled with an intense but unexpressed anger. She felt like giving this woman a good shake or striking her. She had no business teaching children.

Miss Sowerbutts took a small embroidered handkerchief from her sleeve and dabbed the corners of her thin mouth. 'Then there're the offspring of the incomers to the village,' she continued, now well into her stride. 'Most send their children to St Paul's, the preparatory school at Ruston, but we have a number of affluent parents who commute to the city each day and are so busy making money that they spend little time with their children or exert the appropriate discipline in the home. They think taking them abroad and letting them have televisions in their bedrooms is all they have to do. These children have too much at home, are indulged by their parents and have far too much to say for themselves. You will find their parents pushy and demanding.'

'I see,' said Elisabeth. She considered for a moment tackling this virago and telling her that in her opinion, the keys to educational achievement were self-esteem and expectation, and that all children mattered and deserved the best a teacher could give. Clearly this woman spent little time building up the children's confidence in their own worth and expected little of them. It was no wonder that the inspectors had been so damning and that parents were taking their children away.

'Why do you think so many parents have decided to send their children to other schools?' she asked.

Miss Sowerbutts smiled a wintry smile and regarded her successor through half-closed eyes. 'Mrs Devine,' she replied, 'I am not privy to the motivations of parents. I run a well-disciplined and orderly school, employing traditional, tried-and-tested teaching methods. I make no apology for doing so. It does not go down well with some of the parents, any more than it did with the inspectors, and if they decide to send their children elsewhere then that is their concern.'

Elisabeth sighed inwardly but refrained from commenting on Miss Sowerbutts's statement.

'I would like to look round the school, if you have no objection,' she said.

The head teacher stared at her blankly for a moment. 'I didn't imagine that you would want to go into the classrooms,' she said.

'I think it would be good to learn a little about the school before I start next term,' Elisabeth told her, 'and to meet the teachers.' She paused and looked the woman straight in the eye. 'Don't you?'

'I suppose it is all right,' the head teacher responded. 'I did mention to the teachers that you would be visiting this morning. Miss Brakespeare teaches the older juniors and has been a stalwart in this school for as long as I. Miss Wilson is in her first year of teaching and takes the infants. She's young and inexperienced and has a great deal to learn. Mrs Robertshaw takes the lower juniors and, I have to say, can be very trying and not a little difficult at times. We do not see eye to eye on a number of matters. This, of course, will be of no interest or importance to you as Miss Wilson and Mrs Robertshaw are both on temporary contracts and will be leaving at the end of the term.'

'I wasn't aware of that,' said Elisabeth. She was soon to learn that there were several other things of which she was unaware.

Miss Sowerbutts gave a small smile. 'Oh, didn't the governors mention that?' she said. There was an air of triumph in her voice. 'Well, I am sure you are keen to look round, so I won't delay you.' She replaced her glasses and looked down at the papers on her desk. 'You will forgive me if I do not accompany you. I have quite a lot of paperwork to deal with.'

Elisabeth gave an inward sigh of relief that Miss Sowerbutts would not be coming with her. She stood, and said in a pleasant voice, 'Thank you for your hospitality.'

The sarcasm was not missed by the head teacher, who continued, tight-lipped, to stare at the papers on her desk.

3

Before calling in at the classrooms, Elisabeth looked round the building of which she would soon have charge. It came as no surprise to her that the school had come in for such heavy criticism. The small entrance, with its shiny, green wall tiles and off-white paint, was cold and unwelcoming. It was bare of furniture save for a wooden chair and a small occasional table in the centre, on which was an ugly vase containing some dusty plastic flowers. Pinned to a notice board on a plain wall were various warning notices about head lice and scabies. From it the corridor, lined with old cupboards and with a floor of pitted linoleum the colour of mud, led to the four classrooms, three of which were used for teaching. The fourth, a cluttered, general-purpose room, was where equipment and materials were stored. All four rooms were small and square, with high beams, large windows and hard wooden floors.

Elisabeth knocked on the door and entered the first classroom, the windows of which gave an uninterrupted view of the dale that swept upwards to a belt of dark green woodland, distant purple peaks and an empty blue sky. Ranks of wooden desks of the old-fashioned lidded variety, heavy and battle-scarred and with holes for inkwells, faced the blackboard. At the front of the room, on a dais, was a sturdy teacher's desk made of pine with a high-backed chair, while at the side was a bookcase containing a tidy stack of books and folders, a set of dictionaries and some reference texts. A colourful if rather unimaginative display decorated the walls, and a few pieces of children's writing were pinned alongside lists of key words, the rules of grammar and various arithmetical tables.

All eyes looked in Elisabeth's direction as she entered the room. Miss Brakespeare, a stick of chalk poised between finger and thumb, swallowed nervously, blinked rapidly and gave a small, uneasy smile. 'Oh, Mrs Devine,' she said, startled.

'May I come in?' asked Elisabeth, standing by the door.

'Yes, of course,' replied the deputy head teacher hurriedly. 'I was telling the children you would be calling into school this morning.'

Elisabeth moved to the front of the class and surveyed the faces before her. They were indeed a mixed group: large, gangly boys; fresh-faced boys; lean, bespectacled boys; girls with long plaits; girls with frizzy bunches of ginger hair; girls thin and tall, dumpy and small. They filled the room, which was hot and stuffy.

'Good morning, children,' she said pleasantly.

'Good morning, Mrs Devine,' chorused the pupils in subdued tones, staring at her as if she were some rare specimen displayed in a museum case.

'Now, you must be the oldest children in the school,' she said.

'That's right,' Miss Brakespeare told her. She gave an almost apologetic smile. 'These are the nine- to eleven-year-olds.'

'It's a large class,' observed Elisabeth.

'Thirty-eight,' Miss Brakespeare informed her. 'It is rather a crush in here, but we manage.'

'Well, it is really good to meet you all,' Elisabeth told the children in a cheerful voice, 'and I am so looking forward to coming to your school next term.' She noticed Danny sitting at the back looking warily at her. *I imagine he's worried that I might say something to him*, she thought, *and embarrass him in front of the other children.* Elisabeth met his eyes steadily, smiled but said nothing.

The children continued to stare with blank expressions.

'I don't wish to disturb your lesson, Miss Brakespeare,' said Elisabeth, breaking the silence. 'I just wanted to introduce myself. Perhaps one of the children could tell me what you are doing this morning?'

A red-faced girl with curly ginger hair and formidable silver braces on her teeth raised a hand and waved it like a daffodil in a strong wind.

'Miss, we're doing a worksheet on verbs,' she said.

'That sounds interesting,' said Elisabeth, thinking the very opposite.

Miss Brakespeare recalled the inspector's comment that her teaching was on the dull side and lacked vitality, and that she should endeavour to make her lessons more interesting. She knew in her heart that she was just about competent as a teacher, but she did try her best. Since the inspection, she had thought hard about the report and had made a serious effort to make her lessons more interesting: planning them more carefully and picking topics that the inspector had suggested might appeal to the children, but on this occasion, with a visitor in school, she'd thought she would play safe. Worksheets tended to keep the children quiet and fully occupied, and there was less chance of any disruptions.

'Perhaps this is not the most interesting of topics,' admitted Miss Brakespeare, 'but we try to do some very interesting things in this class, Mrs Devine. Don't we, children?'

There were a few murmurs of assent.

'I must have been away that day,' mumbled a large-boned individual with tightly curled hair, short, sandy eyelashes and very prominent front teeth.

'That's not a very nice thing to say, Malcolm Stubbins,' said Miss Brakespeare, colouring a little. 'We do some very interesting things.'

'Most of the stuff we do is boring,' he said peevishly.

'That will be quite enough,' said Miss Brakespeare. 'I don't think Mrs Devine will be very impressed with that sort of comment, Malcolm.'

Elisabeth noted the boy. He stared back at her defiantly, almost inviting her to say something, but she remained silent. *He will prove to be a bit of a handful, this young man,* she thought, *but I can handle him.* She had dealt with boys much more difficult in her time.

'And what is your name?' Elisabeth asked the girl with the bright ginger hair and braces, when the children had settled back down to work.

'Chardonnay,' replied the child. 'I'm named after a drink.'

Elisabeth smiled. 'May I look at your work?' she asked.

The exercise book was slid across the desk. The work it contained was untidy and inaccurate and the spellings were bizarre, but the girl's stories were quite imaginative and well expressed.

'I don't like doing worksheets,' whispered Chardonnay. 'I like writing poems and stories best, and using my own words.'

'You're a good story writer,' said Elisabeth.

'I know,' said the girl. 'Miss Brakespeare says I have a talent for story writing. She says I have a wild imagination, a bit too wild sometimes. I like writing about vampires. It's just that I need to be more careful with my spelling, but I just can't get my head round words. They're right tricky, aren't they, miss?'

'They certainly can be,' agreed Elisabeth, trying to decipher some of the words the girl had written. 'What is this word: "yrnetin"?' she asked.

'Wire-netting,' replied the girl. 'We've had to put it round the hencoop to keep the fox out.'

Elisabeth nodded. 'I see.'

'Miss Brakespeare does do some interesting things,' continued Chardonnay, 'but when she does, Malcolm Stubbins always spoils it. He shouts out and acts the fool. He's a real nuisance and he stops people getting on with their work.'

'And he spits and swears,' divulged the child sitting next to Chardonnay, a large girl with huge bunches of mousy brown hair.

'Her name's Chantelle,' Chardonnay told Elisabeth. 'She's my best friend.' The girl then lowered her voice to a whisper. 'You had better have a look at the display on the wall. Miss Brakespeare's been in at the weekend putting it up.'

'And she's had her hair done specially,' said Chantelle, 'and she's got a new dress on.'

Elisabeth smiled and moved on, thinking how blunt and honest children could be. She arrived at Danny's desk. 'Hello,' she said.

The boy looked embarrassed. 'Hello, miss,' he replied quietly.

The boy sitting next to Danny was a small, pale-faced boy with curly blond hair, his head bent over his work.

'Hello,' Elisabeth said to him.

The child lowered his head further and closed his exercise book with a snap, before placing both his hands firmly on the top. It was clear he was not going to share his work.

'And what is your name?' she asked.

The boy looked up at her furtively with deep-set eyes that seemed in search of something. There was an air of vulnerability about him which she guessed set him apart from the other children.

'James dunt say owt, miss,' said Danny. 'He never does.'

AT MORNING BREAK, Elisabeth joined the teacher of the lower juniors, who was on playground duty. Mrs Robertshaw was a broad, ruddy-complexioned woman with a wide, friendly face and steel-grey hair gathered up untidily on her head. She was dressed in a brightly coloured floral dress and a shapeless pink cardigan beneath her raincoat, and wore a rope of pearls and matching earrings.

'We are being observed,' confided the teacher, her lips almost pressed together, as she walked with Elisabeth round the playground. 'They're both watching us from the head teacher's room, no doubt wondering what we're talking about.' Elisabeth had noted herself that the head teacher and her deputy were peering through a window.

'Miss Brakespeare's pleasant enough, well intentioned and harmless, but she's well and truly under the thumb of Miss Sowerbutts and can't sneeze without asking her permission. I've been too long in the profession to be browbeaten by that sort of head teacher. I suppose I'm speaking out of turn, but I'm the kind of person to speak my mind.' Elisabeth could tell that but didn't reply. 'Anyway, things were made even worse for me after the inspection,' she continued, 'particularly when Miss Wilson and myself received some very positive comments from the inspectors. Miss Sowerbutts was not best pleased. You will be like a much-needed breath of fresh air.'

'I believe you are thinking of leaving?' said Elisabeth.

'I am leaving, yes,' Mrs Robertshaw replied. 'My contract terminates at the end of term, so I am looking for another position. I shall miss the children but little else.'

'Would you consider staying if there was a permanent job?'

Mrs Robertshaw stopped and faced Elisabeth. 'Are you serious?'

'Yes, of course I am.'

'Well, it's not something I have given a lot of thought to.' Mrs Robertshaw fingered the pearls at her throat. 'Miss Sowerbutts made it quite clear that you would probably be keen to bring in some new teachers—"a clean sweep", as she termed it.'

'Then Miss Sowerbutts is mistaken,' Elisabeth replied. 'I should like to ask you to delay applying for any posts until after I start here. Give me a chance to settle in and see how we like working together. Will you do that?'

'Well,' said Mrs Robertshaw, smiling, 'that's come as a bit of a shock. I was thinking of applying for a post at Urebank, but after I had a look round I decided not to. I can't say that I was overly impressed with the head teacher when I visited the school. You are aware that he's been poaching children from this school?'

'No, I wasn't.'

'He even put an advert in the local paper singing Urebank's praises and saying there were plenty of spare places at his school. Cheek of the man.'

Elisabeth decided this was neither the time nor the place to enquire into this with a woman she had only just met. 'So you will think again about applying for other jobs?' she asked.

'Thank you, Mrs Devine,' Mrs Robertshaw replied. 'I will.'

Elisabeth suddenly became aware of a small boy standing next to her. He was a child of about eight or nine, with a thatch of straw-coloured hair and dressed in an old-fashioned outfit. His hands were clasped behind his back.

'I'm sorry to interrupt your conversation, Mrs Robertshaw,' he said, 'but I thought I would come and introduce myself to the new head teacher.'

The teacher shook her head, smiled and placed a hand on the boy's shoulder. 'This is Oscar, Mrs Devine,' she said, 'and he's one of my star pupils. Aren't you, Oscar?'

'I should like to think so,' said the child, seriously. 'I have been identified as one of the G and T pupils after we did the verbal reasoning tests, haven't I, Mrs Robertshaw? G and T means gifted and talented, you know.'

'Hello, Oscar,' said Elisabeth, trying to restrain herself from laughing.

'Good morning, Mrs Devine,' he replied seriously.

'And how are you today?' she asked.

'Well, to tell you the truth, I'm not a hundred per cent,' he said. 'I woke up with quite a nasty headache this morning. My mother thinks there's a bug going round and suggested that I stay at home, but I knew you were coming into school today and didn't want to miss you.'

'Oscar likes to know what's going on,' explained the teacher, giving Elisabeth a significant look.

'I do like to keep up to speed with things,' said the boy. He looked up at Elisabeth. 'I painted a poster over the weekend welcoming you, but Miss Sowerbutts wasn't too keen on the idea when I asked her if I could put it up. If you are coming into our class later this morning, I'll give it to you.'

'That was very nice of you, Oscar,' said Elisabeth, amused by his adult way of speaking.

'Well, I'll let you continue your conversation,' said the boy. 'Maybe I will see you later, Mrs Devine.'

'He keeps me on my toes, does Oscar,' Mrs Robertshaw confided. 'Quite a little character, isn't he?'

ELISABETH LEFT MRS ROBERTSHAW and went in search of Miss Wilson. The infant classroom was neat and tidy, and children's paintings, collages and poems had been carefully mounted and displayed. A large, bright alphabet poster and a list of key words for children to learn decorated one wall, and an attractive reading corner contained a range of colourful picture and reading books, and simple dictionaries. She learned later that the young teacher had purchased most of the books herself.

Elisabeth thought how very youthful-looking Miss Wilson was. A slender woman with short, raven-black hair, a pale, delicately boned face and great blue eyes, she looked decidedly nervous.

'Your classroom is delightful,' said Elisabeth. 'I always think the environment in the early years should be particularly bright and cheerful.'

The blue eyes surveyed her for a moment. 'Thank you.'

'I wasn't aware that you and Mrs Robertshaw were both on temporary contracts,' continued Elisabeth. 'I mentioned to Mrs Robertshaw that she might like to stay on. Perhaps you might consider that, too. I can't promise anything until I've discussed it with the governors and been in touch with the Education Office, but it may be possible to make your contract a permanent one. Would you like to stay if I can arrange it?'

'I should love to,' replied the teacher quickly. 'It's just that I imagined that you would want to appoint some new staff.'

'Why should I want to do that?' asked Elisabeth.

'Mrs Sowerbutts said—'

'Ah, yes,' interrupted Elisabeth, 'I think I know what Miss Sowerbutts said.'

Noise in the corridor indicated that the children were returning from morning break. The little ones lined up outside the classroom chattering excitedly.

'Come along in, children, quickly and quietly,' Miss Wilson told them.

When the infants were finally settled at their tables, the teacher turned to Elisabeth.

'This is Mrs Devine, our new head teacher,' she said with a smile.

ELISABETH DECIDED TO CALL into the school office before departing but paused for a moment in the drab entrance hall to consider what she had seen that morning. Through the door, the magnificent oak tree seemed to embrace the building with its spreading branches. The ancient Norman church, illuminated by a bright sun and beneath a cloudless azure sky, looked like the backdrop for a medieval drama. A lone sheep grazed by the village green and from some distant field there came a curlew's fitful cry. *Barton-in-the-Dale*, she thought, *has much to offer*.

There was a great deal to be done, of course, but she felt confident she could turn this school around. She was much happier having met the staff. The success of a school, she knew, depended on the calibre of the teachers as much as on the strong and purposeful leadership of the head teacher. Elisabeth felt that she could work with Mrs Robertshaw and Miss Wilson, who seemed personable, committed and enthusiastic teachers. Miss Brakespeare, however, was a different matter. She appeared amenable and good-natured, but the lesson Elisabeth had observed that morning was one the inspectors would undoubtedly have described as less than satisfactory.

'Pensive.'

Elisabeth's thoughts were interrupted by a small voice.

'That's what my mother says,' said Oscar, 'when I look out of the window daydreaming.'

'Well,' said Elisabeth, smiling down at the bright face which looked up at her, 'I *was* lost in thought. I was just thinking how beautiful it is—the trees and the sky and the church.'

'Yes, it's very picturesque, isn't it,' agreed the child, cocking his head and following her gaze. He turned and looked up again. 'I hope you have had a pleasant morning, Mrs Devine.'

'Very pleasant, thank you, Oscar.'

'You forgot your poster,' he said, holding out a rolled-up piece of paper with a pale blue ribbon around it.

'Thank you. It is a lovely thought, and when I start next September it will be the first thing I shall put up on the wall.'

Oscar smiled widely. 'You know, Mrs Devine,' he said, nodding sagely like a professor in front of his students, 'I think that you and I are going to get along famously.'

'I'm sure we are, Oscar,' Elisabeth replied.

'I HOPE YOU'VE HAD a pleasant morning,' said the secretary cheerfully when Elisabeth entered the school office.

'Very pleasant, thank you, Mrs Scrimshaw,' she replied, laughing.

'Something's amused you, anyway,' said the secretary.

'I've just been having a conversation with Oscar and he asked me exactly the same thing.'

'Oh, you've met our Oscar, have you? Old beyond his years is that young man. Some would say too clever by half. His mother's a psychologist and his father's a barrister, so you might guess where he gets it from.'

Elizabeth smiled. 'I thought I might just say goodbye to Miss Sowerbutts before I leave,' she said.

'Oh, she's gone out,' said the secretary. She smiled, in an attempt to cover her embarrassment. She had thought to herself how blatantly rude it had been of Miss Sowerbutts to leave the premises before the newly appointed head teacher had left, but of course that was just like her: she was making a point. 'She often pops out at lunchtime,' she lied.

'I see,' said Elisabeth. 'Well, I wonder if I might have a copy of the school report? I would like to see what the inspectors said.'

The secretary looked uncomfortable and smiled awkwardly. 'Miss Sowerbutts keeps the report in her room,' she replied.

Elisabeth looked at her calmly. 'I am sure she won't mind me borrowing it,' she said in a determined voice. 'Of course, had Miss Sowerbutts been here I would have asked for it, but she isn't. You will understand, I am sure, that I need to get a view of what needs to change before I start.' She stared at the secretary with penetrating blue eyes. 'So if you wouldn't mind . . .' She left the end of the sentence unspoken.

The secretary swallowed nervously. The last thing she wanted was to get on the wrong side of the new head teacher. 'Yes, of course, Mrs Devine,' she replied, rising from her chair and imagining what Miss Sowerbutts would say when she returned. *It's just as well she is out of the school*, she thought. 'I'll get it.'

'Thank you.'

'And Miss Brakespeare said she would like a quick word before you go, Mrs Devine,' said the school secretary, 'if you could spare her a few minutes.'

Elisabeth found the deputy head teacher in her classroom, tidying up after her class.

'Oh, there you are, Mrs Devine,' said Miss Brakespeare, as Elisabeth entered the room. 'I'm glad my message caught you before you left. I just wanted to apologise for Miss Sowerbutts's behaviour this morning. She's not been herself of late and has been feeling very hurt and depressed, what with the school inspection and then not being involved in the interviews for her successor. I . . . I . . . want you to know that I harbour no resentment whatsoever about you getting the position of head teacher here.' Her tone was genuine. 'To be frank, I didn't want the job and I was very pleased when you were appointed. I will be supportive of all your efforts and I look forward to working with you.' She breathed out heavily. 'There, I needed to say that before you left.'

'Thank you, Miss Brakespeare,' said Elisabeth, rather touched by the woman's simple and unpretentious comments. 'I appreciate your honesty and I, too, look forward to working with you.' She held out her hand and smiled reassuringly. 'I think that if we all pull together, we can make Barton-in-the-Dale Primary School the best in the county.'

Miss Brakespeare shook her hand lightly and returned the smile. 'I hope so,' she replied.

ON ARRIVING HOME after her visit to Barton-in-the-Dale, Elisabeth read the school inspectors' report. It was indeed damning of the leadership and management of the school, critical of Miss Brakespeare's lessons, which were described as 'poorly planned and uninspiring', but had many positive things to say about the other two teachers. Elisabeth, referring frequently to the findings in the report, penned a long letter to the chairman of governors outlining in some detail what changes she wished to implement when she took over the following September. A copy was sent to the director of education and to the inspector who had written the critical report of the school. She asked the chairman of governors to convene an extraordinary meeting of the governing body, at the beginning of the school's summer holidays, so she could outline her plans.

Her second letter was to the teaching and non-teaching staff, saying how much she was looking forward to joining them in September and asking them to attend a short meeting a week prior to the start of the new term to discuss her proposals. Elisabeth then turned her attention to other pressing matters.

WHEN SHE HAD RECEIVED confirmation of her appointment at Barton-in-the-Dale, Elisabeth had resigned from her position at the school at which she was head teacher, put her house on the market, sold it within a fortnight, and started making plans for her new life.

One Saturday, she had returned to the village to view the cottage she was determined to buy. It was quite an ordeal getting to the rear of the building. Accompanied by the estate agent, a rather dapper young man in a smart grey suit and designer sunglasses, she had found the path to the side of the cottage blocked by a herd of heavy-uddered cows, jostling and pushing at each other, lowing in complaint at the narrowness of the track. A black-and-white sheepdog ran at their heels, snapping to keep the bumbling beasts moving forward, and behind it ambled a red-faced, narrow-eyed farmer with a bearded chin, his greasy cap set on top of a mane of thick, ill-cut hair. He had touched his cap as he passed them and growled, 'Nice day.'

'It appears that some of the farmers have started using this as a means of access to their fields,' the estate agent had explained, 'but the path belongs to the property, and should you buy it you will need to make this clear. I noticed, too, that the paddock, which also belongs to the cottage, has sheep grazing on it. You will need to find out whose they are if you become the owner of the cottage.'

Inside, the cottage had looked damp and cheerless with its thick and faded curtains, threadbare carpet, windowpanes that had been broken and replaced by cheap glass and a naked light bulb dangling from a yellowing electric flex, but Elisabeth immediately saw its potential.

To the estate agent's surprise, she had made an offer there and then and was informed the following day that it had been accepted.

AT THE BEGINNING of the summer holidays, Elisabeth had moved in. Now she stood in the small front room of the cottage, a bucket, sweeping brush, mops and dusters before her, looking round and wondering where to start.

'What have you done, Elisabeth Devine?' she murmured to herself. 'What have you let yourself in for?'

'Quite a bit, by t'looks of it.'

Elisabeth jumped as if ice-cold water had been flicked in her face, and she swung round. In the doorway stood an old man. The visitor had a friendly, weathered face, grizzled, smoky-grey hair and an untidy beard, while his smiling eyes rested in a net of wrinkles. He was dressed in a clean, long-sleeved, collarless shirt that was open at the neck, baggy corduroy trousers and heavy boots.

'Gosh, you startled me,' Elisabeth said, placing a hand on her heart.

'Beg pardon, missis,' said the speaker. 'I din't mean to frit you. I'm Danny's granddad. 'E telled me 'e'd met you. We live in t'caravan on t'yonder field. I 'eard that tha 'ad bought t'cottage and thowt tha might welcome a bit of an 'and. Tha's a fair bit to do.'

'That's very kind of you, Mr—' began Elisabeth.

'Just Les, Mrs Devine,' he told her. 'Everyone 'ereabouts calls me Les.'

'Well, I'm very pleased to meet you, Les,' said Elisabeth, extending her hand, which he shook vigorously.

'Our Danny told me abaat thee. 'E said tha were reight tekken wi' this owld place when 'e fust met thee and that 'e 'ad an idea that tha'd buy it. Builders in t'village will be queuin' up to get crackin' on t'place soon as they 'ear it's been sold, but between thee and me and t'gatepost, there's some of 'em who 'ud tek thee for a ride. Charge t'earth for doin' nowt. Now, I do charge for mi services but I can promise thee that I'm reasonable, fair, 'ard-workin', tidy and punctual. Ask anyone in t'village and they'll tell thee that Les Stainthorpe is an 'ard worker and won't let thee down.'

Elisabeth smiled. She had warmed to the man straight away. 'Well, Mr Stainthorpe . . . Les,' she said, 'if you are as good a worker as you are a salesman, I think I've found a builder in a million. So, where do we start?'

The next month and a half saw a transformation in the cottage. Danny's granddad was true to his word and worked tirelessly and painstakingly. He replastered the bulging walls, repointed the stonework, exposed the beams and stained them a lustrous brown, replaced the broken guttering, sanded down and varnished the old pine doors, repaired the rotten window frames and fitted some shelves. When Elisabeth had looked doubtful at the times when he had scratched his beard and come up with suggestions for improvement, he had smiled, winked and told her, 'Trust me.' So she had trusted him and it had paid off.

'You see, Mrs Devine,' the old man told her one bright sunny August afternoon, as they sat at the table in the newly decorated kitchen, 'I've been in this cottage many a time when old Mrs Pickles were alive and thowt to missen that if I owned it, I knew just what I'd change.'

Elisabeth had the oak floors polished, new carpets laid, put up some bright curtains and hung some colourful prints and pictures on the walls, arranged her chairs and sofa and the old oak dresser in the sitting room and put the longcase clock in the hall. The place looked like home—warm and cosy.

She invited Les round for a drink to celebrate the completion of the work. As she stood with the old man at the door of the cottage she suddenly began to cry.

'Hey, hey, Mrs Devine,' said Les Stainthorpe, 'I din't reckon I'd done that bad a job.'

'It's wonderful,' she told him, wiping her eyes. 'It's just what I imagined.'

DURING THE TIME of the cottage's restoration, Danny had kept his distance. He seemed embarrassed to be in Elisabeth's company and spent most of the time in the garden, hacking away at the overgrown bushes, mowing the lawn and digging the borders.

'He's quite a little worker, is Danny,' Elisabeth told his grandfather as they watched him through the kitchen window.

'Aye, 'e's a good lad,' said the old man, nodding.

'He's been keeping out of my way these past few weeks,' she said. 'Have I said something to upset him?'

'Gracious me, no, Mrs Devine,' said the man. 'It's just that t'lad dunt want to be ovverfamiliar like, what with you being t'new 'ead teacher at 'is school an' all. 'E reckons tha not like the last 'un, owld Miss Sowerpuss. Nivver liked 'er an' I can't say as 'ow I blames 'im. Always at 'im, she was, about 'is work. Our Danny might not be t'brightest apple in t'orchard when it comes to readin' and writin' and arithmetic an' such, but 'e's good-natured an' 'e can turn 'is 'and to owt if it's practical.'

'Yes, he's a nice young man,' Elisabeth told the boy's grandfather. 'He's a credit to you.'

The old man coloured up. 'I tries mi best, Mrs Devine. Danny's mi daughter's lad. She were a bit of a tearaway was my Tricia. Stubborn she was, and wayward. I reckon I was a bit soft with 'er after 'er mother up and left. She 'ad Danny at seventeen. No father in sight, of course. Any road, one neet police called and said she'd been knocked down on t'way 'ome. Driver never stopped. 'It an' run, it were. She were walking down some dark lane, pushing 'er babby in 'is pram. I mean, you expect that you'll outlive yer children, don't you, but it 'appens they sometimes go afore you.' The old man rubbed his beard. 'Social worker passed little Danny to me and 'e's been wi' me ever since. There's just 'im and me now. We're like two peas in a pod.'

'So Danny doesn't see anything of his grandmother?' asked Elisabeth.

'Tricia's mum? No, no, Maisie's not been in touch. She came to t'funeral, of course, but I've not seen 'ide nor 'air of 'er since. Danny sometimes asks about 'er, but what can I say?'

The boy looked up from digging as if he knew they were talking about him. He waved. 'Just 'im and me,' his grandfather repeated under his breath, waving back.

MRS SLOUGHTHWAITE straightened her overall as Elisabeth walked through the door. 'Good morning, Mrs Devine,' she said.

'Morning,' said Elisabeth. 'I have a list here. Quite a lot, I'm afraid.'

'I'm not complaining,' said the shopkeeper. 'Keeps me in business. Them who come to live here in the village usually shop at the new supermarket at Gartside.'

'Well, I won't be,' said Elisabeth. 'I think it's important to support the local businesses. I shall be placing an order each week.'

Mrs Sloughthwaite glowed. The more she saw of the new head teacher, the more she liked her. She glanced down the list. 'As regards the biscuits, Mrs Devine, could I interest you in a box of my special Venetian selection?'

'Why not,' said Elisabeth.

'I hear you're doing up old Mrs Pickles's cottage,' said the shopkeeper as she placed the various items on the counter.

'Yes,' replied Elisabeth. 'That's one of the reasons for calling in, to thank you for drawing my attention to it. It's exactly what I wanted.'

'I'm very pleased. I always try to be of help. I also heard you've got old Les Stainthorpe doing the place up for you.' Elisabeth opened her mouth to answer but the shopkeeper rattled on. 'He's a good worker and he'll not take you for a ride.'

'I've been delighted with the work he has done. He's really transformed the place.'

''Course, he's had a rough time of it what with his wife running off and then his daughter getting killed.'

'Yes, I heard,' said Elisabeth. 'Very sad.'

'Rumour was,' continued Mrs Sloughthwaite, leaning over the counter and lowering her voice, 'that the child wasn't his, but I'm not one for gossip.' She straightened up. 'You wouldn't like another box of Venetian biscuits, would you? They're on special offer.'

'No, thank you,' replied Elisabeth.

'Mind you, he's done a good job, has the lad's grandfather, bringing up young Danny. It'll be an upheaval for him having to move his caravan.'

'I didn't know that,' said Elisabeth.

'Oh, I should have thought that you would have heard. Fred Massey, who owns the field the caravan is on, has told Les Stainthorpe to shift it before the week's out. They had a right set-to in the Blacksmith's Arms. Nearly came to blows, so I heard.'

'Mr Stainthorpe never mentioned it,' Elisabeth told her.

'Well, that does surprise me. I mean the argument was about your cottage, in a manner of speaking.'

'My cottage?' Elisabeth asked.

'Evidently Les Stainthorpe told old Massey that he shouldn't be grazing his sheep on your paddock without your permission or using your track as a thoroughfare for his cattle. Fred Massey told him to mind his own business and they were at it hammer and tongs.'

'Oh dear,' sighed Elisabeth, 'I've hardly moved into the village and I'm causing trouble.'

'It's not you, Mrs Devine,' said the shopkeeper, 'it's that Fred Massey taking liberties. He's a nasty piece of work and no mistake, and is so fond of hard work he lies down beside it. You want to tell him to shift his sheep.'

The following week, Les Stainthorpe moved his caravan into the paddock next to Elisabeth's cottage.

ON THE AFTERNOON when Les and two of his pals were moving the caravan, Elisabeth looked out of the kitchen window to see Danny with the small, pale-faced boy with curly blond hair she had met when she had visited Miss Brakespeare's lesson the previous month. She went into the garden.

'Hello, you two,' she said brightly. Danny smiled and waved, while the other child lowered his head shyly.

'Hello, miss,' said Danny.

'You're not helping your grandfather with the move, then?' she asked.

'No, miss,' replied the boy, "'e said I'd only get under 'is feet. 'E telled me to pack all my things in some boxes and 'e said to mek missen scarce. I'm showin' Jamie my mole traps, if that's all right, then we're goin' rabbitin'.'

'And how are you going to catch this persistent little mole of mine, Danny?' asked Elisabeth, surveying the chains of molehills on her lawn.

'Catch him!' cried the boy, throwing his head back. 'Catch him? I'm gunna kill him.' He reached down, dug into a sack at his feet and produced a vicious-looking, scissor-like contraption with springs. 'I'm purrin this down 'is run. That'll stop 'is little game.'

'I don't like the idea of killing him,' Elisabeth said. She turned to his solemn-faced friend, who was listening. 'What do you think, James? Do you think we should let Danny put his trap down?'

The boy looked up and shook his head. *What a sad child*, Elisabeth thought, *wrapped in his protective shell, never speaking, never smiling.*

'It's t'only way. I'm tellin' thee, miss,' said Danny, returning the trap to the sack and putting it down.

'Well, I think your friend and I have outvoted you, Master Stainthorpe,' said Elisabeth. 'Haven't we, James?' The boy gave a slight smile and nodded. 'Now, you take that dreadful piece of equipment away, Danny Stainthorpe, and I'll get you two some lemonade and one of the special chocolate biscuits I bought at the village store.'

'Not that Venusian selection?' asked Danny, shaking his head and laughing. 'She's been trying to get rid of them for weeks.'

'Is there something wrong, James?' asked Elisabeth, seeing the boy suddenly wriggling as if he had a terrible itch.

'It's mi ferret, miss,' laughed Danny. "'E gets a bit lonely if 'e's left in t'dark for too long. Ger 'im out, Jamie.'

James reached into his pocket and produced a little, sandy-coloured, pointed-faced creature with small, bright, black eyes. He held the animal under its front chest, his thumb under one leg and, using his other hand, gently stroked the creature down the full length of its body.

'I've shown Jamie 'ow to 'old 'im, miss,' explained Danny. 'They have to be held special, like, so as they feel relaxed and comfortable. 'E's champion, i'n't 'e?'

'I'm not so sure I agree with you about that,' replied Elisabeth, looking at the creature suspiciously. 'Aren't ferrets known for being vicious?'

The boy laughed. 'Nay, miss. Yer ferret meks a gradely pet. 'E don't bark, 'e's clean as a whistle and is a reight mischievous little beggar.'

'Does he bite?' she asked.

'Only a bit,' replied Danny, nonchalantly. 'Do you want to 'old 'im, miss?'

'Not on your life!' exclaimed Elisabeth. She turned to Danny's friend. 'And what about you, James? Do you like ferrets?'

The boy looked up shyly and nodded, but didn't speak.

'So you're giving your ferret some exercise this morning?' she said to Danny, smiling at him warmly.

'I am that,' replied Danny. ''E's a workin' ferret as well as a pet and 'e's goin' down t'rabbit 'oles today. 'E'll stop them rabbits, I can tell thee.'

'Poor rabbits,' said Elisabeth. She decided not to enquire what the ferret would be doing but she had a good idea. 'Well, when you two have finished, come and have some lemonade,' she said.

As she walked towards the house, Elisabeth heard Danny whisper: 'I telled thee she were all reight, Jamie. She's really nice, is Mrs Devine.'

AT THE GOVERNORS' extraordinary meeting, Major Neville-Gravitas apologised for the absence of so many of his colleagues.

'Mr Nettles, the education officer, and Councillor Smout are both on holiday,' he explained. 'Mrs Bullock, the foundation governor, is not well and Mrs Pocock is also indisposed, so that just leaves myself, Dr Stirling and the vicar and, of course, your good self, Mrs Devine.'

'I quite understand,' Elisabeth replied, rather disappointed with the turnout. At her last school the governors had been keen and supportive and attended meetings religiously. 'It is a busy time of year. I do appreciate you giving up your time.'

'I hope we are not going to be too long,' said the major, glancing at his watch. 'I have an important appointment scheduled later today.' He had arranged to play a round of golf that afternoon.

'No,' replied Elisabeth, 'I shouldn't think this will take too long.'

'Well now, Mrs Devine,' said the major, 'perhaps you would like to tell us why we are here.'

'As I outlined in my letter to you, Mr Chairman,' Elisabeth told him, 'I felt it would be prudent to let the governors know early on my intentions and seek their approval for the changes I wish to make. Here is a copy of my proposals.' She passed round a folder containing a sheaf of papers. 'First, I intend to convert the head teacher's room into a staff room. I think you will agree that the teachers should have somewhere to take a break and have a little privacy. This room will house all the confidential material, documents, guidelines and files, which will be moved from the school office to give the secretary more space. It is very cramped in there at the moment.'

'Where will you go?' enquired the vicar.

'This brings me on to the next change I wish to make. I intend to teach, and shall use the spare classroom. The top juniors, who will number over forty at the start of the next term, is too large a class in my opinion. I would like to split this with Miss Brakespeare.'

'You're going to teach?' asked the major, incredulously. 'Miss Sowerbutts never taught.'

'Yes, Mr Chairman, that is my intention. I shall ask Miss Brakespeare to take the nine-year-olds and I shall teach the ten- and eleven-year-olds.'

'That's all very well,' said the major, 'but when will you do all the administration and deal with the letters and such?'

'At home, before and after school,' Elisabeth told him. 'I shall be the first to arrive at the school and the last to leave. Parents, should they wish to see me, can make an appointment for when I am not teaching.'

'I noted,' said the major, flicking through the folder, 'that in your letter to me there were some resource implications. I guess the Local Education Authority will baulk at expending any money, if you follow my drift.'

'That is why I hope, Mr Chairman, that the governors will lobby the Local Education Authority for such resources. The old desks must go, as they are entirely unsuitable. We need tables, and the dreadful linoleum in the corridor needs replacing. A carpet would be good. There are also damp patches on the ceiling and I wish to refurbish the entrance hall. All this is outlined in my report. Finally, I come to the most important request, and that is to make the two teachers, Miss Wilson and Mrs Robertshaw, permanent members of staff. As you will be aware, they are at present on temporary contracts.'

'I didn't know that,' said the vicar. 'Were you aware of that, Dr Stirling?'

'No, I wasn't,' the doctor replied, his expression blankly impersonal.

'Yes, yes,' said the major quickly. 'Miss Sowerbutts felt it was best that they be offered temporary contracts to see how well they got on and if they were suitable.'

'Nevertheless—' began the Reverend Atticus.

'It's water under the bridge now, Vicar,' said the major, irritably.

'As to the question of the teachers' suitability,' said Elisabeth, 'both Miss Wilson and Mrs Robertshaw seem very capable and I should be sorry to lose them. I think it would have an adverse effect on the school if there was a change of staff at this time. They have proved themselves, and I think they should be offered permanent positions.'

'I shall have to talk this over with Mr Nettles at the Education Office before making any decision,' said the major. 'And now I have an important meeting to attend, so I will close the meeting.'

'Before you do, Mr Chairman,' said Elisabeth, 'I take it, then, that you and the governing body are supportive of the proposals and you will inform the Education Department at County Hall?'

'Yes, yes,' said the major, in a less than enthusiastic tone of voice, which indicated that this woman might be a little too forceful for his liking.

4

Dr Stirling was waiting for Elisabeth as she made her way out of the school. He was a tall, not unattractive man, aged about forty, with a firm jawline and a full head of dark hair greying at the temples and parted untidily. What was most striking about him were his pale blue eyes. Elisabeth noticed that he stooped a little, that his suit was unfashionable and had seen better days, that his shirt was frayed around the collar and that his shoes could do with a good polish. He spoke in a quiet, sometimes almost inaudible voice, not that he had said much that morning. He had been less than friendly at the interview and it was clear to Elisabeth that he found something about her that he did not like.

He shifted nervously in the small entrance area of the school, like a schoolboy sent to the head teacher for misbehaving. 'Might I have a word with you, Mrs Devine?' he said.

'Yes, of course, Dr Stirling,' she replied.

'I felt it only fair to let you know that my son will not be returning to this school after the summer holidays, and that therefore I shall also be resigning as a parent governor.'

'I see,' said Elisabeth.

'I can assure you that it's nothing personal. James is a quiet, rather sensitive boy and I feel that St Paul's Preparatory School in Ruston will suit him better. The classes are smaller, there are more specialist teachers and it has better facilities.'

So the small, pale boy who never spoke was the doctor's son. 'Well, Dr Stirling,' said Elisabeth, 'I am obviously disappointed with your decision but you are entitled to do what you feel is best for your son. I might have hoped that you would have kept him here and given me a chance to make the necessary changes. Maybe I could have brought James out of his shell.'

The doctor bristled. 'Bring him out of his shell?' he retorted. 'There are people in the world, Mrs Devine, who are quiet. James is one of them. He is a thoughtful child, a little withdrawn at times, but he is intelligent and interested in things around him. He is indeed a quiet boy, but that is understandable. He still misses his mother a great deal. You probably are not aware that he lost his mother a couple of years ago. My wife had a riding accident and, of course, her death distressed him greatly.'

'I am very sorry to hear about your wife, Dr Stirling,' Elisabeth told him. 'You must both have been devastated.'

'We were,' he said sadly, 'but time is a great healer, and James will, I am sure, eventually come to terms with it.'

'I think there is more to it than that, Dr Stirling,' Elisabeth told him. Her voice was level and cautious.

His blue eyes flashed. 'In what way, more to it?'

'I think that James has a condition that needs to be addressed,' she said.

'A condition?' he repeated. 'And what condition would this be?'

'James, I gather from Miss Brakespeare, is fully capable of speech and understanding language, but is completely silent in lessons. Despite her efforts he just doesn't speak. This, of course, is of concern, and perhaps—'

'He speaks quite happily and indeed expressively at home,' interrupted Dr Stirling sharply. 'He can communicate perfectly normally in a situation in which he feels comfortable and, to be frank, I don't think he feels comfortable in this school—hence my decision to send him to St Paul's.'

'Dr Stirling, it is not quite as simple as that. James may indeed converse freely at home but he is completely silent in class. He never asks or answers a question and, from what I gather, only speaks to one other pupil.'

'And how would you know all this, Mrs Devine?' asked the doctor.

'From what I have been told by his teacher and by observing it myself,' she replied.

'And when have you met my son?' he asked.

'I met James when I visited the school and later when he came into my garden with his friend, Danny.'

'The boy who lives with his grandfather in the old caravan? Yes, I knew he was a friend of James's.'

'Although the boys were at my cottage for some time, your son never spoke one word, not even to say hello. It must be clear to you, a doctor, that your son has a communication disorder, and his consistent unwillingness to speak at school will inevitably interfere with his emotional development and his educational achievement. At my last school there was a boy with a similar problem and—'

'Mrs Devine,' interrupted Dr Stirling again, 'James has no condition, disorder or problem. He is just a quiet, underconfident little boy who is still grieving for his mother. He will soon grow out of it. I did discuss his unwillingness to talk in school with the previous head teacher here and she was of the same opinion. Miss Sowerbutts felt it was a stage many children go through; something to draw attention to themselves.'

'Well, I don't agree, Dr Stirling,' said Elisabeth. 'Most children do not go through this stage, and the very last thing James wants to do is draw attention to himself. Quite the opposite, in fact. I believe James has a condition that is called selective mutism.'

Dr Stirling sighed noisily. 'I might have guessed there would be some fancy educational label to describe it,' he said, without looking at her.

'And if his condition continues,' Elisabeth told him, 'and if it is ignored, then it tends to be self-reinforcing and those around such a person may eventually expect him or her not to speak, so they don't bother talking to them. This makes the prospect of his speaking seem even more unlikely. Sometimes in this situation a change of environment, such as a change of school, may make a difference, but the upheaval could also be distressing and harmful. Providing love, support and patience, offering emotional encouragement, which James clearly gets at home, is all important but—'

'Mrs Devine, I am grateful for your concern over my son but it is academic, since he will be moving to St Paul's next term.'

'If I could get you to talk to an educational psychologist—'

'No, Mrs Devine, that will not be necessary,' said Dr Stirling abruptly. 'I really do not feel we have anything further to discuss.'

She looked into the pale blue eyes. *Here is a man*, she thought, *with a sense of unswerving purpose, a man used to asking questions and telling people what to do; a stubborn man who is not prepared to listen.* 'I sincerely hope you are right and that your son will be very happy at St Paul's.'

ELISABETH FOUND THE MEETING of teachers and non-teaching staff that took place the week before the start of the school term an altogether more reassuring affair than the meeting with the governors. In the newly designated staff room she outlined to those present—Miss Brakespeare, Miss Wilson, Mrs Robertshaw, Mrs Scrimshaw and Mr Gribbon—what she intended. The staff had arrived at the school amazed at the changes that had already taken place, and sat in silence, too stunned to speak. When Elisabeth explained that she would be teaching half the upper juniors, Miss Brakespeare broke her silence.

'Split the class?' she said in disbelief. 'You intend to teach the top half of the juniors?'

'That's right,' Elisabeth confirmed. 'I think it is unreasonable for you to have to teach so many children. The classroom is small and cramped for so many pupils, and the marking of the children's work must be very time-consuming for you. Quite apart from that, it must be difficult for you to differentiate the work for so wide an age and ability range.'

'It is,' acquiesced the deputy head teacher, looking astonished.

'Does this meet with your approval, then?' asked Elisabeth.

'Well, it has come as a bit of a shock, Mrs Devine,' said Miss Brakespeare, 'but I must say, a very welcome one.'

'That's settled, then,' Elisabeth told her. She turned to the two other teachers. 'I hope to hear from the Education Office early next term about your contracts. The governing body was unanimous in supporting my request for you to become permanent members of staff if you wish to stay and we are happy working together.'

'That's wonderful,' said Mrs Robertshaw.

'Thank you,' said Miss Wilson, looking pleased.

'Now, as you can see,' continued Elisabeth, 'the former head teacher's room has become our staff room, which gives you, Mrs Scrimshaw, more space in the school office.' The school secretary was too dumbstruck to say anything. 'Mr Gribbon has done an excellent job,' continued Elisabeth.

Following the meeting with the governors, Elisabeth had talked through with the caretaker the changes she wanted to make. Inwardly, Mr Gribbon's heart had sunk into his boots at the thought of all the work it would entail, but he had smiled weakly and said he would start immediately. The following week he had opened up the fourth classroom and moved half the desks from Miss Brakespeare's room, to be used until the new tables arrived.

'Thank you for all your hard work, Mr Gribbon,' said Elisabeth now.

The caretaker smiled, nodded and rubbed his chin, pleased with the recognition of his efforts.

'And I told the governors,' continued Elisabeth, 'that *I* shall be the first into the school in the morning and the last to leave in the afternoon.'

The school secretary looked startled. 'You will?'

'I will,' said Elisabeth firmly. 'Now, I am sure that there must be quite a few issues some of you wish to raise, and suggestions you want to make, and I am very willing to listen to them.'

The five colleagues stared back at the new head teacher but remained silent. None of them had anything to suggest, for any requests they might have had in their minds had been answered.

Then Miss Brakespeare spoke: 'Welcome to Barton-in-the-Dale, Mrs Devine,' she said. Her tone was sincere. 'I hope you will be very happy here.'

IT WAS A BRIGHT EARLY September morning when Elisabeth arrived for her first day as the new head teacher of the village school. She noticed that the windows had been cleaned, the broken flagstones on the path replaced, the hedge trimmed and the fence round the perimeter repaired.

Mr Gribbon, wanting to make a good impression, was there early, dressed in a new pair of bright blue overalls and busy at work digging in the border surrounding the tussocky lawn at the front of the school.

'My goodness, Mr Gribbon,' Elisabeth exclaimed, standing at the gate, 'you've transformed the place. What a difference.'

'I try my best, Mrs Devine,' he replied, clearly pleased with the praise. He had seldom received any commendations from the previous head teacher, so had made little effort apart from with his floors, which he prized. *It's nice*, he thought, *to receive some recognition*. 'I just need to give the window frames a lick of paint and sort the lawn out now.'

'Well, I am very grateful for all your hard work,' Elisabeth told him. 'It is much appreciated.'

It wasn't long before the school secretary and the teachers arrived. The many doubts Elisabeth had harboured about taking on this post seemed suddenly dispelled when she saw the people she would be working with. There was a cheerfulness and buoyancy in the air; a lively, genial chatter and a real sense of optimism.

Before the start of school, Elisabeth called a meeting in the new staff room, at which she provided coffee and biscuits. She welcomed everyone and said she looked forward to what she knew would be a successful term.

She noticed there was a visible difference from the Miss Brakespeare she had met previously. Like the caretaker, the dowdy, serious and conventional deputy head teacher she had encountered on her visits to the school had made a real effort, and now looked and sounded quite a different person.

Miss Brakespeare indeed felt quite a different person, and was in a particularly jaunty mood that morning. With hair newly permed and tinted, dressed in a bright floral dress and with a rope of large amber beads draped round her neck, she chatted away amiably. She had been into the school following the staff meeting that had taken place before the start of term to mount displays in her classroom and found, after Mr Gribbon's efforts, that her room was bright and clean. Now, with half the desks gone, it was veritably spacious. When she looked down the list of pupils she would have in her depleted class, she found, to her delight, that the new head teacher, as she had said, was to teach the oldest children, who included the two most difficult and disruptive pupils. She would no longer have to contend with the likes of Malcolm Stubbins and Ernest Pocock, or with the local GP's son, that strange, hypersensitive, disturbed little boy who never said a word.

Miss Brakespeare, on that first morning of the new term, smiled wryly when she saw Elisabeth arranging some chocolate biscuits on a plate.

'Join the club, Mrs Devine,' she said, amiably.

'I beg your pardon?' asked Elisabeth.

'I see Mrs Sloughthwaite has managed to sell another packet of her Viennese biscuits or, as she likes to tell people, her Venetian selection box,' she said. 'I think everyone in the village must have a box somewhere.'

Later that morning, when she saw the parents arriving with their children, Elisabeth straightened the creases in her skirt discreetly, buttoned her jacket, took a deep breath and walked slowly down the school path to meet them. It was an unusually large turnout of mothers and fathers standing at the gate that morning, no doubt there to see the new head teacher about whom they had heard so much. Elisabeth had deliberately dressed for the part, in a stylish red turtleneck sweater, navy-blue jacket and skirt and the famous red shoes with the silver heels she had worn at the interview. She smiled and greeted each parent with a friendly, 'Good morning.'

One mother approached her. She was an extremely thin and intense-looking woman dressed in a charcoal-grey suit with narrow chalk stripes.

'This is my mother, Mrs Devine,' said Oscar brightly. He gestured with a small hand. 'Mumsie, this is Mrs Devine, the new head teacher. I've told you all about her.'

'Good morning, Mrs Devine,' the woman said. 'I hope you will be very happy here.'

Elizabeth smiled her thanks as Oscar continued blithely: 'You can go now, Mumsie,' proffering a rosy cheek to be kissed. 'You won't be late this afternoon, will you? Remember I have piano practice at four fifteen.'

'No, Oscar,' said his mother. 'I won't be late.' She gave Elisabeth a weary smile. 'I don't know where he gets it from,' she confided quietly.

'I see Mr Gribbon has replaced the broken paving slabs,' observed the child when his mother had departed. 'I did mention it to him.'

IN ASSEMBLY THAT MORNING, the children, silent and wary, sat cross-legged on the highly polished floor in the school hall as Elisabeth introduced herself and said how much she looked forward to getting to know everyone. She then described the changes that would be taking place. Later, as her class lined up outside the classroom door, she explained that she had placed name cards on the desks to show where children would sit and so that she could learn their names. The placing of each pupil was strategic: boy next to girl and the two potentially disruptive children—Malcolm Stubbins and Ernest Pocock—seated at the very front, but well away from each other.

Malcolm Stubbins was, as Elisabeth expected, the first to object. 'Can't we sit with our pals?' he asked tetchily, slouching in his chair.

'Do call me "miss" when you speak to me, Malcolm,' replied Elisabeth pleasantly. 'And sit up.'

The boy grimaced, shuffled forward and repeated the question: 'I asked if we could sit with our pals,' he said, and then added loudly, 'Miss.'

'No, you can't,' replied Elisabeth. 'You can see your friends at break and lunchtimes; that is, of course, if you behave yourself and are not kept in. In the classroom you are here to work, and I want no distractions.'

The boy muttered something.

'What did you say?' snapped Elisabeth.

'Nothing,' he said.

'I have asked you to call me "miss",' said Elisabeth, standing over him and looking him straight in the eyes. 'Please do so in future, or you and I will fall out. Do I make myself clear, Malcolm?'

'Yes, miss,' he grumbled.

AFTER SCHOOL THAT DAY, Elisabeth went into the office and dialled the number of the Education Office.

'Hello.' It was a young woman's matter-of-fact voice.

'I'd like to speak to Mr Nettles, please.'

'He's tied up at the moment,' came the reply.

'When might he be free?'

'I've no idea. He's in a meeting.'

'This is Mrs Devine, head teacher at Barton-in the-Dale Primary School. I shall be here for the next hour, so if he could ring me, I should be very grateful. It is important.'

'I'll tell him,' said the young woman curtly, and put down the receiver.

'Hello, miss.' Danny stood at the office door.

'Hello, Danny,' she replied. 'Come in.'

'Is it reight that Jamie's not comin' to this school no more, miss?'

'It is,' replied Elisabeth. 'His father thinks St Paul's will suit him better.'

''E dunt want to go,' said the boy. 'We were at t'duckpond and 'e said 'e weren't comin' back 'ere. 'E were really upset, miss.'

Elisabeth thought for a moment. 'James talks to you quite a lot, doesn't he, Danny?'

'Yea, I suppose 'e does,' replied the boy.

'Why doesn't he talk to anyone else, do you think?' she asked.

Danny shrugged. 'I dunt know, 'e just dunt. Jamie stopped talkin' to other people after 'is mum 'ad t'accident. 'E talks to 'is dad sometimes, but it's mainly me 'e talks to.'

'He must feel really comfortable with you, Danny,' said Elisabeth. 'I guess he thinks of you as a very special friend.' The boy nodded and looked embarrassed. 'And James told you he doesn't want to go to another school?'

'Yeah, 'e did, miss.'

'And has he told his father this?'

'No, miss, 'e dunt want to upset 'im. 'E thinks if 'e tells 'is dad it'll make 'im unhappy. 'E says 'is dad gets real sad these days.'

'I see.'

'Will you speak to 'is dad then, miss?' asked the boy. 'Please.'

'All right, Danny,' she said, 'I'll try.'

ELISABETH CALLED at the surgery on the way home, explaining to the receptionist that she would wait until Dr Stirling had seen all his patients, as this was a personal matter of some importance.

Eventually the waiting room emptied and Elisabeth was told by the receptionist that the doctor was now free to see her.

'Ah, Mrs Devine,' said Dr Stirling, managing a small smile. He rose from his desk. 'Do come in.'

Elisabeth noticed again how neglectful he was of his appearance. His hair had been combed untidily and it was clear he hadn't shaved that day. His linen jacket was creased and had a button missing, and his shirt had not been ironed properly.

'Now,' he said, 'what seems to be the problem?'

'I'm here about James,' Elisabeth told him.

The mention of his son's name resulted in a change to the doctor's countenance. He inhaled noisily, scratched his tousled hair and tapped his fingers impatiently on the top of his desk. 'Look, Mrs Devine, I have made my decision. If you are here to ask me to let James stay at the school, you are wasting your time.'

'Have you asked your son if he wants to go to St Paul's, Dr Stirling?' asked Elisabeth.

He sighed and continued to tap his fingers on the desk. 'James and I have discussed it,' he replied, 'and he sees the sense in what I have decided; that the move is in his best interests.'

'I don't think he does,' said Elisabeth.

Dr Stirling bridled. 'Excuse me?'

'I said I don't think James wants to move school.'

'And how would you know that?' he asked.

'Because his friend, his only friend and the one he speaks to the most, told me so.'

'This would be the young man who lives in the caravan?'

'That's right,' she replied. 'Danny seems to be the only one in the school James speaks to, and he confides in him.'

'Look, Mrs Devine, I appreciate your interest—' began the doctor.

'If I thought James would be happier at another school,' Elisabeth told him, 'I would be the first to suggest it because, believe it or not, I do have the child's best interests at heart, as I have for all the children in my care. In my opinion, a move to another school, one to which he doesn't wish to go, could set him back. Dr Stirling, your son has a problem that you seem unable to accept. I ask you—'

'Mrs Devine,' the doctor said, a slight tremble in his voice, 'we have had this conversation before. Please let it rest.'

Elisabeth sat there for a moment looking at the sad, distressed figure who refused to meet her eyes and suddenly felt desperately sorry for the man. He had lost a wife he obviously had dearly loved and had a son with emotional problems; he was living a cheerless, empty life. If anyone was in need of a doctor's help, it was the man sitting before her.

'Very well, Dr Stirling,' said Elisabeth softly. 'Thank you for seeing me. As I said to you before, I genuinely hope that James will be happy in his new school.'

IT WAS EARLY on Friday morning when Elisabeth, sitting opposite Mrs Scrimshaw in the school office, managed at long last to speak to Mr Nettles. When she mentioned that she had left several messages for him requesting that he call her back, he sounded dismissive.

'Yes, yes, Mrs Devine, I do appreciate that you wished to speak to me but the first week of a new school term is always a very busy time and I have had many pressing matters to deal with. What can I do for you?'

'I wanted to know if the chairman of governors has been in touch with you?' asked Elisabeth.

'I did speak to Major Neville-Gravitas after the Education Sub-committee meeting earlier in the week,' he told her.

'So you are aware of the requirements that I set out in my letter to him? I sent a copy to the Education Office for your information. I hope you received it.'

'Yes, yes, I did receive your letter.' He remembered that he had put it at the bottom of the pile in his in-tray.

'Then you will be aware of the refurbishments required and the equipment which I need, in particular new tables and chairs.'

'I have considered your request regarding the tables, and the thing is, Mrs Devine, it might prove difficult, in the present economic climate, to meet it.'

'Why is that?' Elisabeth asked.

'As you will no doubt be aware, we have to make savings, and expenditure of this nature needs to be budgeted for. Indeed, the Education Sub-committee meeting this week was to discuss the proposed savings. It will be lean times for us all, I am afraid.'

'So, other schools in the authority are making do with desks that are old and unsuitable like the ones at this school, is that what you are saying, Mr Nettles?' Elisabeth asked.

'Miss Sowerbutts liked the old-fashioned desks,' Mr Nettles told her.

'I do not,' said Elisabeth, 'and neither did the school inspectors, and the sooner they are replaced the better. And I am sure I don't need to remind you that the inspectors also made comments about the need for some renovations in the school, and the need for more up-to-date reading material.'

'I have read the report, Mrs Devine,' said Mr Nettles, 'and these things take time and money.'

'And while you are on the line,' said Elisabeth, 'perhaps you can explain to me why the teachers at this school are on temporary contracts?'

'Ah, well, Miss Sowerbutts requested that, so she could be entirely sure they were suitable.'

'Mr Nettles,' said Elisabeth, getting increasingly irritated by the man's evasive answers, 'Miss Sowerbutts is no longer the head teacher here: I am. And I would like the contracts made permanent. The governors were unanimous at the meeting, which you were unable to attend, in supporting this.'

'That, too, might prove a little tricky in these stringent economic times,' the education officer told her.

Elisabeth took a deep breath. 'So, Mr Nettles, let me get this clear. You are not going to provide me with the necessary resources, you are ignoring the inspectors' recommendations and you do not intend to make the teachers' contracts permanent. Is that what you are saying? Because if it is, I do need to know this so I can inform my governors, the parents and the school inspectorate.'

'No, no,' replied Mr Nettles, clearly rattled. 'I am not saying that at all. I think this matter needs to be discussed at the next full governors' meeting.'

'Which will be when?'

'Generally the school governors meet a few weeks into the new term,' he told her. 'I guess it will be some time in mid-October.'

'And you will be attending the meeting this time, Mr Nettles?' Elisabeth enquired.

'I shall endeavour to do so,' he replied.

'And in the interim, you will seriously consider these requests?'

'Indeed. Now, I *do* have a number of urgent matters to deal with . . .'

'Until the next governors' meeting, then,' said Elisabeth, putting down the receiver.

'I did say that you would get nowhere with that man,' observed Mrs Scrimshaw. 'He's a waste of space.' She paused. 'And I think there is more to this than meets the eye. A few tables wouldn't cost anything, and I bet none of the teachers in other schools are on temporary contracts.'

'Yes, that had occurred to me,' replied Elisabeth. 'I have my suspicions that there is another agenda here.' She was soon to discover that her suspicions were warranted.

'I WILL NOT TOLERATE fighting in this school!' Elisabeth leaned over her desk, her nose a few inches from the boys' faces. It was the following Monday morning and two miscreants stood before her desk. 'Is that clear?'

'Yes, miss,' said Danny.

'We will start with you, Malcolm,' said Elisabeth. 'What have you got to say for yourself?'

'It was him what started it,' grumbled the boy. 'He told me to put my hand in his bag and when I did, it bit me.' He held up his index finger.

'What bit you?'

'His ferret.'

'Why did you bring your ferret to school, Danny?'

''E were a bit under t'weather, miss.'

'It bit my finger,' huffed the other boy, 'and hung on. It hurt.'

''E 'ad no need to hurt him, miss,' said Danny. ''E was stranglin' 'im. If 'e 'ad kept still, Ferdie would 'ave let go.'

'But you told Malcolm to put his hand in your bag, didn't you, Danny?' clarified Elisabeth.

'No, miss,' replied the boy. 'I didn't. Malcolm thought there were some sweets in there and grabbed mi bag and run off wi' it. Then when 'e put 'is 'and inside, 'e frightened Ferdie and 'e bit 'im. 'E were really rough tryin' to pull 'im off and that's when I thumped 'im and 'e thumped me back.'

Elizabeth breathed in deeply. 'I do not like children who don't tell the truth,' she told a glowering Malcolm Stubbins. 'Danny did not tell you to put your hand into his bag as you claimed, did he?'

'Yeah, he did,' replied the boy, stubbornly.

'Please don't make it worse by telling lies, Malcolm,' said Elisabeth. 'You ran off with his bag, and perhaps you have learned a hard lesson not to go into other people's things. Danny is not blameless in all this either, because he brought the ferret to school, and hit you, which he should not have done. Now I am telling you both that should anything like this happen again you will be in deep trouble, and I shall be having words with your mother, Malcolm, and your grandfather, Danny. Is that clear?'

'Yes, miss,' replied Danny.

'Yes, miss,' muttered the other boy.

IT WASN'T LONG, of course, before news of the fight circulated in the village.

'There were no fights in the school when I was head teacher,' announced Miss Sowerbutts in the village store the following afternoon. She was sharing her observations with another customer. 'I prided myself on keeping very good discipline in the school.' She was clearly revelling in the news that there were problems at the school.

Mrs Sloughthwaite, listening to the diatribe from behind her counter, didn't like Miss Sowerbutts and her preening self-satisfaction.

'Oh, you know what they say, Miss Sowerbutts,' she said, deliberately being provocative, 'a bit of rough and tumble is to be expected in growing lads. My Nigel was always getting into scraps when he was a boy. It's part of growing up, and you know yourself what Malcolm Stubbins is like. From what I've heard, when you were head teacher, he was always outside your room for misbehaving, wasn't he?'

Miss Sowerbutts didn't deign to answer. 'And all these changes,' she grumbled to no one in particular. 'I'm told the school is not the same. Everything's been changed. I feel sorry for poor Miss Brakespeare, having to endure it.' She purred with satisfaction.

'She seems very happy,' remarked Mrs Sloughthwaite, smiling indulgently. 'She called in the shop last week and she looks years younger. The changes the new head teacher is making seem to have gone down very well with her, by all accounts.'

'I very much doubt it,' scoffed Miss Sowerbutts. She wore an expression a stranger might mistake for a smile. 'And I hear the doctor has taken his son away,' she remarked, clearly rejoicing in the bad news. Mrs Sloughthwaite saw something like triumph flash across her customer's face. *It's strange*, she thought, *how the misfortunes of others bring solace to sad and gloomy people like Miss Sowerbutts*. 'Well, of course, that doesn't surprise me in the least,' the former head teacher added.

Mrs Sloughthwaite folded her dimpled arms and pictured the silent little boy who sometimes came into the shop with his father. 'I suppose Dr Stirling reckons the lad needs more specialist help with his communication problem that the school can't—and didn't—provide.' There was a heavy emphasis on the word 'didn't'.

'The boy was perfectly happy when I was head teacher,' retorted Miss Sowerbutts, acidly.

'Well, I don't suppose you knew, Miss Sowerbutts,' said the shopkeeper, with the fixed smile she had perfected over the years, 'what with him never speaking a word.' She chuckled inwardly at the evident consternation that her words caused.

'I'll just have some tea bags,' announced the former head teacher, looking sharply at the shopkeeper and placing the exact money on the counter.

'Are you sure I can't interest you in a Venetian selection box?' asked the shopkeeper.

MISS SOWERBUTTS DECIDED to call in on Miss Brakespeare later that day. She was keen to learn first-hand about all the changes that had taken place at the school.

She found her former colleague in the small garden to the front of her cottage, sitting in the late-afternoon sunshine marking exercise books. She was dressed in a bright summer frock and pink cardigan, in contrast to her visitor, who wore an outfit better suited to midwinter.

'I just thought I'd call, Miriam,' she said, 'and see how you are getting on. I heard there was a fight.'

'Oh, hello,' said Miss Brakespeare.

Miss Sowerbutts noticed that there was something of a change in her former colleague. She seemed somehow brighter and more self-assured.

'Young Danny Stainthorpe had brought his ferret to school and it bit Malcolm Stubbins. It couldn't have chosen a better victim. He lies easier than he breathes, that boy, and was such a pain when he was in my class.' Miss Breakspeare paused. 'As you well know.'

'What do you mean *was* in your class?' asked Miss Sowerbutts, staring at her former colleague uncomprehendingly. 'He still is, is he not?'

'Oh, no, Mrs Devine teaches the oldest children now and he's in her form.'

'She teaches?' Miss Sowerbutts exclaimed, incredulity creeping across her face.

'It works very well,' explained Miss Brakespeare, nonchalantly. 'We've split up the older children. I have a smaller class, and don't have Malcolm Stubbins and Ernest Pocock to contend with.'

Miss Sowerbutts gave a sniff of disapproval. 'It would not have happened in my day,' she announced stiffly.

'What wouldn't?' asked Miss Brakespeare. Her face was impassive.

'A head teacher teaching.' She sniffed again, self-righteously.

'No, I don't suppose it would,' replied Miss Brakespeare. She gave a quiet little smile. 'Of course, you never taught, did you?' *There's something rather pointed in that remark*, thought Miss Sowerbutts, *and completely out of character*. Miss Brakespeare would never have spoken to her in that tone of voice when she was her deputy head teacher. However, she let it pass.

'In my opinion,' stated Miss Sowerbutts, pompously, 'a head teacher's role is not to teach: it is to lead and to manage, and to deal with problems.'

Miss Brakespeare was about to reply but hesitated. She wanted to tell this woman whom she had put up with for more years than she cared to recall that she found the changes in the school liberating and had never felt happier. She refrained from doing so, however, and merely remarked: 'Mrs Devine manages to do that as well.'

'Do what?'

'Teach *and* manage the school.'

'I see,' said Miss Sowerbutts, annoyed by the inference. She smiled grimly. 'Well, I am pleased you find the new arrangements are to your liking, Miriam. Let us hope that you remain as content.' She could not resist a final observation. 'Of course, things might very well alter if many more children leave. Dr Stirling's decision to move his son will, no doubt, have repercussions.' A triumphant smile was on her face.

'I think it's time I was getting Mother's tea,' said Miss Brakespeare.

WEDNESDAY AFTER SCHOOL found Mrs Stubbins in Elisabeth's classroom. Malcolm's mother smoothed an eyebrow with a little finger and shuffled uncomfortably in her seat. She was sitting, wedged sideways, in one of the small desks used by the children, and looked a comical character: a round, shapeless woman with frizzy, ginger hair, an impressive set of double chins and immense hips. Her mouth was turned downwards in perpetual hostility.

'Well, he says you're picking on him,' she told Elisabeth angrily.

'Malcolm never sees himself in the wrong,' said Elisabeth calmly. 'It is always someone else's fault.'

'He told me—'

Elisabeth held up a hand and stopped the woman in her tracks. 'One moment, please, Mrs Stubbins. Now that you are here, and I have to say I am very pleased to see you, there are one or two things I have to say about your son. Malcolm can be a disruptive and difficult boy and, what is more, he is lazy. He doesn't like to work and will not apply himself, or do as he is told, and he disturbs the other children. His behaviour is unacceptable.'

'Well, that's not what he says,' blustered the woman. 'He says as how you're always picking on him and you called him a liar.'

'Do you want your son to be a success in life, Mrs Stubbins?' asked Elisabeth suddenly. 'Do you hope he will get good results in his school examinations, secure a good job that he will enjoy doing, and grow up into a polite, well-adjusted and caring young man and be a credit to you?'

''Course I do, but he says you're picking on him. Soon as you started here he says you've had it in for him. He liked it better in Miss Brakespeare's class.'

Elisabeth could have told the woman that he liked it better in Miss Brakespeare's class because he was allowed to do as he pleased. She remained calm and motionless. 'I am telling you I am not in the habit of picking on children. And as long as your son is in this school,' she said, 'he will behave himself.'

'If that's your attitude,' replied Mrs Stubbins, 'I don't think he will be staying in the school for much longer.' She smoothed the eyebrow again and creaked in the desk. 'Tomorrow I shall go and see Mr Richardson, the headmaster at Urebank, and get a place for my Malcolm at his school. I've heard that Dr Stirling for one has taken his son away, so he can't be happy with the way things are going here, no more than I can.'

'Then there is nothing more to say, Mrs Stubbins,' Elisabeth said, rising from her chair. 'I hope that Malcolm settles at his new school and that no one picks on him there.' The hint of sarcasm in the tone of her reply was not lost on Mrs Stubbins, who, with a stony expression on her face, eased herself out of the desk and left the classroom, wordlessly brushing past Mrs Scrimshaw who was coming in to give Elizabeth some paperwork.

'That woman,' said the school secretary. 'You can see where her Malcolm gets his bad manners from.'

5

The telephone rang.

'Mrs Devine?'

'Yes.'

'This is Robin Richardson here,' came a cheerful voice down the line. 'I'm the headmaster at Urebank Primary School in the next village. I just thought I'd give you a call to see how you are settling in.'

'That's very thoughtful of you,' said Elisabeth. 'I'm settling in really well, thank you.'

'Good, good. I know it must be a little daunting taking the helm at a new school, so please don't hesitate to call me if I can give any help or advice. Of course, you will discover that being a head teacher is very different from being deputy head. Where were you deputy head teacher?'

'I wasn't a deputy,' Elisabeth told him. 'I was head teacher at a large inner-city school prior to moving here. But thank you for the offer.'

'No problem,' he said. The arrogance had disappeared from his voice. 'I read your inspection report,' he said, 'and I must say that the leadership and management at the school came in for heavy criticism. Your predecessor, I gather, was extremely angry.'

'Yes, I believe so.'

'Of course, Miss Sowerbutts was of a different age,' he continued. 'I don't wish to speak out of turn, but she harked back to a golden age when bobbies walked the beat, people stood up for the national anthem and children did as they were told. Of course, she could be very difficult at times, rather remote and unapproachable and not the most accommodating of people. I have to admit our relationship was rather strained. Some would say she was a rather autistic character: cool and distant and subject to quite angry outbursts.'

'Mr Richardson,' said Elisabeth, her hand tightening on the receiver, 'in my experience autism does not mean cool and distant, and not all autistic people are subject to angry outbursts. It is a condition with a wide spectrum. No two autistic people are alike. In my experience they can be warm and affectionate and most accommodating.'

'Yes, yes, of course they can,' he said quickly. Mr Richardson was not a man who liked to be put in his place, and his voice betrayed his irritation. 'I was using the term in a generic sense.' There was a silence. 'Actually, while I'm on the phone, Mrs Devine, I would like to have a word with you about another matter.'

'Is it about Malcolm Stubbins?' she asked, knowing full well that it was.

'As a matter of fact, it is,' he replied. 'I have had a request from his mother. She wants her son to come to my school here at Urebank. I didn't go into all the ins and outs of why she wants to move the boy,' he continued, 'but she feels her son will be better suited at my school.'

'I think she may be right,' replied Elisabeth. 'You might be able to cater for Malcolm's needs better than we can.'

'We will, of course, do the very best for him.' There was another moment's silence. 'I have to admit, Mrs Devine, that I find the situation of these departures of children from your school somewhat embarrassing. I want to assure you that in no way do I encourage it.'

Apart from putting advertisements in the local paper advertising your school, Elisabeth thought to herself, recalling her conversation with Mrs Robertshaw.

'Are you still there?' he asked.

'Yes, I'm still here.'

'I was just saying that if a parent wishes to move a child from one school to another, there is little one can do about it.'

'Quite,' agreed Elisabeth.

'I just thought I would let you know,' he said.

'That was very thoughtful of you, Mr Richardson,' Elisabeth told him.

He appeared oblivious to the sarcasm in her voice and cleared his throat. 'I suppose if your numbers decrease any more, the Education Committee will have to consider whether or not it is viable to keep the school open. I do so hope that they don't decide to close Barton.' When Elisabeth didn't reply, he continued. 'I don't suppose you have heard anything?'

'No, I haven't,' replied Elisabeth.

'That's good to hear,' the headmaster remarked unconvincingly. 'It's just that I have heard rumours. Probably nothing to get too concerned about.' He cleared his throat. 'Well, it's been good talking to you, Mrs Devine. Do come and have a look round my school if you have the time.'

She thumped down the receiver. *Odious man*, she thought. Elisabeth stared out of the office window for a moment. So that was why the chairman of governors and the education officer had been so evasive about expending money on the equipment, and the reason for the temporary contracts. They were intent on closing the school. Well, if that was their intention, they had another think coming. She would fight them all the way.

Walking back to her classroom, Elisabeth was surprised to see the deputy head teacher still at her desk this late on a Friday afternoon.

'You seem very happy in your work.'

'I am,' replied Miss Brakespeare, with a sudden smile. 'It's been so much easier with the smaller class, and the children are better behaved without a certain unruly element to distract them.' She sighed. 'I wish Malcolm

Stubbins's mother had moved her son to another school before now.'

'Well, let us hope no more parents decide to take their children away.'

'They won't,' said Miss Brakespeare, and smiled again. 'You know, Mrs Devine, you've made a great difference to the school in the short time you've been here. It's a happier place. The children are happier now, and the staff are, too. You've been a tonic.'

'Thank you,' Elisabeth said. She could feel tears pricking her eyes. 'After a long, dispiriting day I can really do with that encouragement.' She thought for a moment. 'I think they want to close the school.'

'Close the school?' Miss Brakespeare repeated. 'They've been talking about it for as long as I can remember.'

'I have an idea that they are serious about it this time,' Elisabeth told her. 'I've just had Mr Richardson from Urebank on the phone and he certainly gave me the impression that the Education Committee is keen on the idea. I think he knows more than he was letting on.'

'That man is devious,' cried Miss Brakespeare. 'He's got contacts at the Education Office, you know. As thick as thieves with that bumptious Councillor Smout.' She saw Elisabeth's gloomy expression. 'Anyway,' she said reassuringly, 'I shouldn't worry. I can't believe that they would close Barton-in-the-Dale.'

'IT'S VERY GOOD to see you, Mrs Devine,' said Mr Williams, resting his elbows on the desk and steepling his fingers. He was a small, dapper, dark-complexioned, silver-haired Welshman with shining eyes.

It was the following morning, and Elisabeth sat with the head teacher of Forest View Residential Special School in his study. 'John's an easy-going young man and copes as well as he can. He's a grand lad, no problem at all, and is already very popular with the staff.'

'I'm so glad,' replied Elisabeth. 'He seemed happy enough last Saturday when I saw him, but of course with his condition, it's difficult to tell.'

'Oh, I think I can safely say your son is a happy enough boy and has settled in here remarkably well.'

'I cannot tell you, Mr Williams,' said Elisabeth, 'how relieved I was when he was offered a place here. His teachers at his last school did their best, but I wanted the specialist care for him that you provide here. Even in the short time John has been at Forest View, he seems to have made progress.'

'Indeed he has, but like many autistic children, progress can be slow, and John still seems to be content in his own world. As you know, there is no disorder as confusing to comprehend or as complex to diagnose as autism, and I have no idea how much John understands. The main thing is that we assume that he has some comprehension and we try to give him the best possible care and education, and the richest of experiences, that we can.'

'Do you think he knows who I am?' Elisabeth asked. 'Sometimes he looks at me and I think I see some recognition in his eyes.'

'That I cannot answer for certain,' replied the head teacher, 'but I think it is very likely that he does. He just doesn't feel inclined to display any recognition, that's all.' He rested his hands on the desktop. 'I should like to think that the visits from parents and visitors are beneficial and I should be delighted to see you at any time, not just on the Saturday visits. You really don't have to make an appointment, just call in.' He smiled and coloured a little.

'I shall take you up on that,' said Elisabeth. 'I intend to visit John as much as I can.'

'Then you will be one of the very few parents who do frequently visit their children. Most telephone to see how their child is getting on but rarely spend much time with them.'

Elisabeth found it hard to understand why a parent should take such little interest in their child; not to visit regularly, watch them grow, see what progress they were making. 'They know, I suppose,' she said, 'that in this school their child will be well looked after; that they get the best attention and care. I think you do an amazing job here.'

'Thank you,' said the head teacher. 'That's what the school inspectors said, although they used the word "outstanding" rather than "amazing". They visited last week, and you, as a parent, will be very pleased, as indeed we on the staff were, with the findings in the report.' He paused and gave a fleeting smile. 'Actually, one poor inspector was in quite a state during the visit. When he was observing a lesson, one of the children managed to get hold of a metal paperclip that was on his clipboard. Little Rebecca put it in her mouth and spent the whole of the morning poking out her tongue with the paperclip on it, making a game of it. We had the devil's own job trying to get the paperclip off her. Anyway, Dr Stirling, who was in school, managed to retrieve it. I think Rebecca has a bit of a soft spot for the good doctor, as indeed do many of the children.'

'Dr Stirling visits here, does he?' asked Elisabeth.

'Yes, he's the local doctor on whose services we frequently call. Nice man. Do you know him?'

'Yes,' she said, 'I know him. He's on my governing body—well, for the time being. I can't say that I have found him very nice. He's a cold fish.'

'He's not, actually,' Mr Williams told her. 'He was a very gregarious man until his wife's death. Then he became much quieter and more thoughtful. Outwardly, Michael Stirling might appear a bit distant, but I reckon his demeanour is a covering to protect the sensitive man beneath.' Mr Williams changed the subject: 'So, you are just down the road from us now, and you won't have a long journey when you wish to visit us.'

'That was the main reason for moving,' she told him, 'so I could see more of John. As soon as he got a place here I started looking for jobs in the area, and Barton was the first school that came up.' She paused. 'Sometimes I think I was a bit impetuous and should have waited rather longer.'

'You sound as if you have some regrets,' said Mr Williams.

'I have mixed feelings at the moment,' she said. 'The children and staff are fine, but some of the governors and the parents will be hard work, and I think I am going to cross swords with those at the Education Office. I have a sneaking suspicion they want to close the school.'

'I have to say that I've had battles with the education people over resources,' the head teacher told her. 'They always want to cut costs. You want to try and hang on to Dr Stirling. He was massively supportive when we put in a bid for more equipment and extra staffing.'

'I don't think I can rely on Dr Stirling's support,' Elisabeth told him. 'I am afraid we don't see eye to eye on a number of matters. He's taken his son away from the school and is sending him to St Paul's.'

'I'm sorry about that,' said Mr Williams, pushing back his chair and standing up. 'Well, I'll take you to see John.'

ELISABETH, LIKE MOST MOTHERS with their newborn baby in their arms, had thought her son the most beautiful child in the world. Baby John had great blue eyes and a dazzling smile, tiny fingers like sticks and nails as pink and shiny as seashells. Simon, his father, had held him high in the air and told him he would be a son in a million, go to Cambridge as he had done, and make everyone so proud of him.

The baby had smiled early and fed easily, but when he had made no effort to walk like other children of his age, or to speak, and began increasingly to reject physical contact, Elisabeth had known something was wrong. The doctor and health visitor had reassured her that the child was fine.

'Oh, he's just a bit slower than other children,' Simon had said dismissively, when she had tried to talk to him about her worries. 'Stop fussing.' She had seen in his eyes that he refused to believe that there was anything wrong with his son.

But Elisabeth had known that things were not right. At three, and still not speaking, John had stiffened when touched, avoided eye contact and was happiest when left alone sorting out shapes. He had been meticulous in arranging things, and would spend hours organising his bricks and making sure everything was exactly in order. He had become quite obsessive about neatness and routine.

The meeting with the specialist, which Elisabeth had insisted upon, had confirmed her misgivings. The parents had learned that their son was a child with a disorder called autism, which meant he would likely never speak, interact with others, embrace them, kiss them, never understand humour or irony and could be subject to seizures and maybe violent outbursts. He would never lead a 'normal' life, if this meant going to the local school, passing examinations, finding a job, getting married and having children. Her husband had been devastated and, on hearing this diagnosis, had stared out of the window as if in a trance. She had reached out to hold his hand. It had felt cold and dead.

Simon had spent less and less time at home. There was always an excuse why he had to be away on business, always some reason why he couldn't go with her to see the specialist or spend time with his son. Whereas she wanted to find out more about her son's condition, desperate to know about education and diet and therapy, her husband was reluctant even to talk about it. Then the illusion that nothing was wrong gradually disappeared. He felt guilty and hopeless, unable to cope with this silent little boy who lived in his own closed world. Although he denied it furiously, Elisabeth knew Simon found the child an embarrassment.

There were arguments and simmering silences and, one day, when John was five, Simon packed his things and left. Following the divorce, Elisabeth heard that Simon had remarried. She had telephoned him once to tell him how John was getting on, and had been told it would be for the best if she didn't get in contact again. It distressed Simon's new wife. Since then, Elisabeth had heard nothing from him.

Determined to give her son the best possible education, she had enrolled John at a local special school with an excellent reputation. Here the teachers were committed and hard-working and seemed able to handle autistic children who struggled to communicate and interact. Elisabeth, by now a head teacher, would drop him off in the mornings and a carer would collect him in the afternoons and stay until she arrived home. When her son reached eleven, his head teacher took her aside. John, he felt, could make greater progress and receive more help at a school that could offer more specialist care for young people with his condition. Forest View, a residential special school for young people with autism, was suggested. Elisabeth managed to secure her son a place. Here the teaching was simple, coherent and structured to meet the individual needs of the pupils. It was a calm and secure environment with soft lighting and no strident bells sounding every hour, and there was plenty of space. The school was surrounded by beautiful countryside and the air was fresh and clean.

The problem was that it was over fifty miles away, in the heart of the Yorkshire Dales.

Elisabeth had realised that the long journey each weekend to Forest View to see John would inevitably begin to take its toll. She knew she would feel guilty when a conference or training course came up that she would have to attend, and which would mean she couldn't make the journey to see her son. So she had scoured the educational papers looking for a head teacher's position in a school near Forest View, and when the post came up at Barton-in-the-Dale, a small rural primary school only a few miles away, she had applied for the post, got it and started her new life.

Elisabeth now found John sitting at a table carefully arranging small coloured beads in straight lines. His forehead was furrowed with concentration. She sat next to him and watched for a moment. He was a good-looking eleven-year-old boy, with large dark eyes, long lashes and blond hair.

'Hello,' Elisabeth said cheerfully. 'What are you up to?'

Her son continued to arrange the beads. He seemed oblivious to her.

'You used to love playing with my beads when you were younger. I remember once when I broke a rope of pearls and they scattered all over the floor and you managed to find every one and arrange them in the exact order. Quite a feat.'

John stopped what he was doing for a moment, as if recalling a distant memory, and then returned to the beads.

'The cottage is just about finished,' she said, placing her hand next to his. 'Carpets are down, curtains are up, walls painted and the garden is taking shape. I did have moles in the garden but they have mysteriously disappeared. I have an idea Danny, who I told you about last week, has been putting down traps.' Her son didn't look round but edged his fingers towards hers until they touched.

Elisabeth talked for some time, telling her son about the teachers at her school, the changes she was making and her niggling worry about a possible closure. He continued to arrange the beads, never looking up. His face was expressionless.

'Oh, John,' Elisabeth sighed. She remained silent for a moment. 'I love you so much, you know,' she told him. 'I hope that you know that.' How she wished she could hold him, smooth his hair and kiss his cheek, but she knew she couldn't. To do so would distress him greatly. It broke her heart that he would probably never know how much she loved him.

'Mrs Devine.' Elisabeth jolted in her chair as if she had been bitten. She looked round to find Dr Stirling at the door. 'Mr Williams told me you were here,' he said, glancing at her nervously. 'I'm sorry if you were startled. I hope I'm not disturbing you.'

'No, no. I'm just having a few quiet moments. I find it very therapeutic to get away from everything. School and parents and governors' meetings and all the paperwork.'

'Yes, I know what you mean. Life can be very hectic at times.' He gave a reassuring smile.

He sat down next to the boy and watched him. John, head down, face fierce with concentration, continued to meticulously arrange the beads.

'Hello,' said the doctor, resting his hand gently on the boy's. John quickly pulled his hand away.

'Sometimes he doesn't like to be touched,' Elisabeth told him, 'particularly when he's engaged in some activity.'

'I'll remember that,' said the doctor, and smacked the back of his own hand playfully.

Perhaps the man is human after all, thought Elisabeth, smiling. He certainly seemed to be a great deal calmer and more pleasant than when she had last seen him.

'I didn't know you had a son at Forest View,' the doctor said. 'Mr Williams has just told me.'

'Yes, this is John,' she said. 'He's just started here.'

'It's an excellent school,' he told her. He turned to look at her son, seemingly fascinated by what the boy was doing. 'You're making a great job of that,' he said.

Elisabeth studied the man's profile. Seeing him from this angle, with his untidy hair and his lopsided smile, he had something of the small child about him: careless of his appearance, innocent, vulnerable. She had a powerful urge to reach out and touch his cheek.

'Of course, now that I have moved closer to him,' she said quickly, trying to cover her embarrassment, 'it means I can visit John whenever I like. He loves to arrange things. I think he finds the repetition comforting and reassuring. I come on Saturdays to see him and during the week if I can manage it.' She looked down at her hands and for some unaccountable reason her heart began to gallop. *What is it about this man*, she thought, *that puts me in such a state?*

'I am sure he looks forward to seeing you,' said the doctor. 'John's about James's age, isn't he?'

'He is,' she replied, thinking what a pity it was that the man sitting next to her didn't understand that his own son was in need of help. 'And how is James settling in at St Paul's?'

'Oh, he's not started yet,' Dr Stirling told her. 'The independent schools tend to begin the term a couple of weeks later than the state ones. But, you probably know that. He starts on Monday.'

There was an embarrassing silence.

'I had better be making tracks,' he said, getting to his feet. 'I have quite a list of patients to visit today.' He held out his hand. 'Well, goodbye then, Mrs Devine.'

'Goodbye, Dr Stirling,' she replied.

Why is it, he thought, *that this woman makes me feel so uneasy and awkward? Why is it that she's in my thoughts so much of the time?* He stopped at the door and thought for a moment, then he turned to look at Elisabeth with searching, worried eyes. 'I was a little short with you when you called in at the surgery,' he said. 'I said things which I now regret. I'm sorry if I appeared rude and dismissive. I'm sure that your comments were well intentioned.'

Elisabeth looked into his face, which seemed to wear a dejected expression, and felt a great surge of sympathy for him. Her lips moved slightly, as if she was about to say something, but the words would not come.

'It was good to see you again, Mrs Devine,' said Dr Stirling, and with that he was gone.

THE REVEREND ATTICUS, rector of Barton, surveyed his usual Saturday breakfast. He sometimes said a silent prayer that he would be given a lightly fried egg, a rasher of crispy bacon, a slice of black pudding and some wild mushrooms. In the centre of the plate was an insipid-looking, undercooked poached egg on a square of burnt toast.

'Is there something the matter with your breakfast, Charles?'

'No, no, my dear,' he replied, smiling wanly, 'I was just thinking about what I might say in my sermon tomorrow.' He cut a corner from the toast. 'I thought I could focus on the Good Samaritan.'

'Well, don't make it too long,' she told him.

'I shall endeavour not to,' replied her long-suffering husband. The vicar chewed thoughtfully and nodded. 'I was prompted to think of this theme when I was told that the new head teacher has let old Mr Stainthorpe, the odd-job man, site his caravan on the field adjoining her property. That was very good of her, was it not?'

'Yes, I'd heard,' replied his wife. 'I met Mrs Devine in the village, actually, and she has asked me to go into the school. She's trying to encourage people with some expertise to go in, and wondered if I might give a helping hand with the artwork there. Evidently the children have had little experience of any sort of painting and Mrs Devine would like some advice. As you know, she was quite taken with my work. I have to say I was somewhat reluctant at first, but she persuaded me and, you know, I think I might enjoy it. It's a while since I picked up a paintbrush.'

'I think that is an excellent idea,' said her husband, deciding not to tackle the egg. 'It will take you out of yourself.'

'Charles,' sighed his wife. 'I do not wish to be "taken out of myself". I am quite content as I am, to some extent, anyway, although I still would like to have moved to the city. It is merely one afternoon of my time. I am not taking on a permanent teaching position there.'

MISS BRAKESPEARE DABBED perfume on her wrists and behind her ears and stared at herself in the mirror.

'Are those new shoes?' asked her mother. 'They're a bit fancy, aren't they? And I've not seen that dress before, either. You're splashing out a bit, aren't you?'

'As you know, I spend little enough on myself,' replied Miss Brakespeare. There was an edge to her voice.

Her mother gave her a quizzical look. 'And where are you going?'

'Into town.'

'Into town,' Mrs Brakespeare repeated. 'It'll be chock-a-block on a Saturday. It's so crowded at the weekends these days that people don't go there any more.' She paused. 'And what about my lunch?'

'There's a salad in the fridge.'

'You know I'm not that partial to salads.' Her mother's lips were set in a thin line. 'I can't eat tomatoes, and cucumber gives me wind. What time will you be back?'

'I'm not sure.'

The old lady shuffled irritably in her chair. 'I really don't know what has got into you these days, Miriam,' she said. 'You've been acting very strangely of late, ever since that new head teacher took over. You go earlier to school and come home later and have been quite sharp with me, and now you're spending money like there's no tomorrow on new clothes and all this gallivanting.'

Miss Brakespeare turned to face her mother. 'I hardly think buying a few new clothes is extravagant and that going into town is "gallivanting". And if I have been behaving differently, it is because I feel different. Actually, Mother, for once in my life, I feel valued and listened to. Mrs Devine has been like a breath of fresh air. She has introduced some very welcome changes and has given me responsibility. It suits me very well.'

'I can't say that I like the change, Miriam,' complained her mother.

'Well, I am afraid you are going to have to put up with it. And I have to say, now that you have raised the matter, that you, like Miss Sowerbutts, have rather taken me for granted and put upon my good nature.' Her mother opened her mouth to speak but paused, as if searching for the right words. Her daughter continued blithely, 'I know you have various ailments and it can't be all that pleasant spending all day by yourself, and that there are things you can't manage and I am sorry for that, but you must understand that I do have a life outside this house. Now, the salad is in the fridge, and an egg custard. I shall be back sometime this afternoon. Is there anything you want from town?'

'No,' said her mother, at last finding her voice. 'Nothing.'

ELISABETH HAD BARELY returned from Forest View that Saturday when there was a sharp rap on the door. Outside in the porch was a man in a greasy cap and soiled blue overalls.

'May I help you?' she asked.

'Aye, could you move your car, missis? I need to get my beasts down the track and back to yonder field.'

'It's Mr Massey, isn't it?'

'Aye, that's me.'

'I was hoping I might meet you,' said Elisabeth. 'I would prefer that in future you do not bring your cows down there. As you can see, I park my car on the track and your cows do make a mess.'

'Look here, missis,' said the man, 'I've brought my cows down that track as long as I can remember. It's a right of way.'

'No, Mr Massey, it is not a right of way,' Elisabeth told him. 'It belongs to me. It is private property; something of which I think you are well aware.'

'Well, I'm telling you, missis, that it's a right of way,' the man said belligerently, 'and I've lived in this village a damn sight longer than you have. It always has been a right of way and I have the right to bring my beasts down it. I don't know what you've been told by old Les Stainthorpe, but I'm telling you that track is for anyone's use.'

'Would you care to see the deeds of this cottage, Mr Massey, in which it states quite clearly that the track is part and parcel of this property?'

'I don't believe what I'm hearing,' growled the man.

'And, while you are here, it gives me the opportunity of asking you to remove your sheep from my paddock.'

'Move my sheep?' The man's face became flushed with anger.

'Had you asked my permission to graze your sheep there and not been so mean-minded as to evict Mr Stainthorpe from your field, I might have been more inclined to let your sheep stay in the paddock but, as it is, I would like them removed.'

The man stared at her for a moment and then moved closer. 'I've heard about you,' he said.

'And I you, Mr Massey,' Elisabeth replied, not at all daunted and looking him straight in the eye.

'If you think you can come here into our village and start laying down the law then you've another think coming. I shall carry on using that track and grazing my sheep as I've done before, and nobody will stop me.'

'I think they will, Mr Massey,' Elisabeth informed him. 'If you continue to trespass on my property, I shall have to resort to taking legal action to prevent you. Good day.'

'You've not heard the last of this!' he shouted, stabbing the air with a finger. 'Not by a long chalk.' He turned and stomped off.

ELISABETH, SITTING in the sunshine the following morning, looked up. A small hairy head was poking through the bushes to the rear of the cottage garden. The dog observed her for a moment with small, bright eyes, cocked its head, and then, sensing she was not a threat, eased its body through the shrubs and scampered towards her, wagging its tail frantically.

'Hello,' said Elisabeth, lowering the book she had been reading and reaching down to pat the bristly body. 'And who are you?'

'His name's Gordon,' came a strident voice from the gate.

The speaker was a large woman in an old tweed skirt, shapeless waxed jacket and heavy green rubber boots. Her voice had echoes of cut-glass chandeliers and silver salvers, nursemaids and governesses.

'He's called Gordon,' she informed Elisabeth, 'because when I got him he reminded me so much of my dear grandfather, who sported sandy whiskers and had the same bright eyes.'

'He's a fine dog,' said Elisabeth.

'He is, isn't he?' agreed the woman. 'Border terrier. Good at ratting. I often take my Sunday constitutional by this cottage. Mrs Pickles, who used to live here, gave him scraps. I think he was hopeful you might have something for him. He has a remarkable memory when it comes to food.'

Elisabeth went over to the gate. 'I'm afraid he's out of luck this morning.'

The woman put the dog on a lead. 'You are Mrs Devine, I take it?' she said. 'The new head teacher at the village school? I'm Helen Wadsworth.' She held out her hand which Elisabeth shook. 'I live up at Limebeck House. On a fine day like this you can see it from here. This was originally a tied cottage, you know. Mr Pickles was my father's gamekeeper for many years, and when he retired it was given to him. I'm so glad someone's bought it at long last.'

'Would you care to come in and have a look at what I've done inside?' asked Elisabeth. 'You are very welcome.'

'Well, you know, I might just do that,' said the woman. 'By nature, I am a terribly nosy person.' She tied the dog up to the gate.

'I hope you approve of the changes,' Elisabeth told her, as she led the way to the cottage.

The interior, with its polished floors, thick red curtains, pale cream sofa and chairs and exposed beams, came as a surprise to Elisabeth's visitor.

'My goodness!' she exclaimed. 'You've transformed the place. Not a humble gamekeeper's cottage any more, is it?'

Elisabeth, listening to the observation, couldn't tell whether the woman approved of the changes or not.

The visitor looked round the room, taking everything in. 'And I see that you have smartened up the exterior of the school as well,' she said. 'You may not be aware, but it was my grandfather who endowed the building. It was originally intended for the children of the estate workers. The school was given over to the Local Education Authority in the 1920s. I am afraid that I did not get along with the former head teacher, and we had words over the plaque.'

'The plaque?' repeated Elisabeth.

'Yes, there was an ornamental tablet fixed to the wall in the entrance commemorating the school's opening. I was most upset when Miss Sowerbutts removed it. I went in to see her and she refused my request to reinstate it. I took the plaque home with me, in the end. I'm afraid that after that, I have had nothing to do with the school, and have not spoken to the woman since.'

'Perhaps you might like to visit the school again now,' Elisabeth said.

'I should like that very much,' replied the woman.

'And show me where the plaque should go?'

The woman's face broke into a great smile. 'I should be delighted,' she said.

LATER THAT MORNING, Danny appeared. Elisabeth saw him from the window, mooching around by the bushes with his hands pushed deep into the pockets of his jeans. She went out to see him.

'Hello, Danny,' she called. 'What are you up to today?'

'Oh, nowt much,' replied the boy. 'I were supposed to be meetin' Jamie down by t'millpond this mornin', but 'e never turned up.'

'I think he'll probably be a bit busy today,' Elisabeth told him. 'He'll be getting ready to start at his new school tomorrow.'

'Miss, did you 'ave a word with 'is dad about 'im not wantin' to go to that new school?' asked Danny. 'You said you would.'

'I did, yes.'

'Did you tell 'im that Jamie dunt want to go?'

'I did. I told him what you told me, but I'm afraid I wasn't able to change his mind,' she told him. 'I did try my best.'

The boy looked deflated. ''E won't like it there, miss. I know 'e won't. There'll be all these strange teachers and new kids and Jamie won't know anybody and they won't understand about 'im not speakin' and that.'

'I should imagine his father has told them all about that, Danny,' said Elisabeth. 'They will all be aware of how quiet James can be. I am sure he will be fine and soon make friends and settle there.'

I wish I could be certain of that, she thought.

'Thanks for tryin' anyway, miss,' Danny said. He looked up. 'Miss, I'm sorry about bringin' mi ferret to school. I won't do it again, even if Ferdie's off-colour.'

'That's water under the bridge,' said Elisabeth, 'and I don't think you'll be getting into any more fights now that Malcolm is at another school.'

'No, miss. I'm glad 'e's not at t'same school. Malcolm used to pick on Jamie,' Danny told Elisabeth.

'Did he?'

'He din't do it when I was around, though,' Danny said. ''E knew I'd smack 'im one.'

Elisabeth shook her head. 'Well, now Malcolm's left, I hope there will be no more fighting, young man.'

'I 'ope Jamie still wants to be mi friend,' Danny said, shuffling his feet.

'I'm sure he will,' Elisabeth told him, thinking that James needed friends like Danny.

6

Barton-in-the-Dale had two public houses: the Mucky Duck and the Blacksmith's Arms. The former, once called the Dog and Duck, was a bright, brash and noisy place with loud music, happy hours and pub quizzes. In contrast, the Blacksmith's Arms hadn't changed in years. The outside looked dark and run-down, with its dull brick walls, sagging roof of odd-shaped tiles and brown-painted window frames. It was here that some of the farmers, shopkeepers and businessmen of the village gathered in the evening and at Sunday lunchtimes to argue about sport and politics, and put the world to rights.

The interior of the pub was dim, reeking of beer and wood smoke: despite the mildness of the weather, a blazing fire crackled in the inglenook fireplace. The walls were bare save for a few hunting prints, a pair of old bellows and a couple of antique shotguns. Sticky-topped tables were arranged on the grey flagstone floor with an odd assortment of chairs and stools. When the landlord had once foolishly suggested that the place could do with some refurbishment, the regulars had protested strongly.

At the public bar Fred Massey, dressed in his ill-fitting Sunday suit—a bargain from a charity shop—finished his pint of bitter in one great gulp.

'I'll tell you what, Albert,' he told his companion, a round-faced individual of immense girth and several impressive chins, 'if that woman thinks she can start laying down the law to me, she's in for a bloody shock.'

'Don't start all that again, Fred,' interrupted the landlord, leaning over the bar and pointing. 'Or you'll have to drink at the Mucky Duck.'

Fred was quiet for a while. 'I reckon it were Les Stainthorpe what put the idea in her head, telling her it were her track. I had a right argument with him in here about it.'

'Aye, so I heard,' said Albert, shuffling off the bar stool, ready to depart. He had come into the pub for a quiet Sunday lunchtime drink and interesting conversation, and had heard quite enough.

'She comes into this village all la-di-da, as if she owned the place,' continued Fred, 'and I'll tell you this, it's not only me she's upsetting. I hear

Mrs Stubbins and Dr Stirling have taken their kids away from the school and Miss Sowerbutts is outraged at all the changes this woman's making.'

Fred Massey's diatribe had been overheard by two customers at the other end of the bar. Major C. J. Neville-Gravitas smoothed his moustache with an index finger before finishing his single malt.

'Interesting,' he remarked to his companion.

'Aye, I 'eard,' replied Councillor Smout. 'Bit of a rum do this, i'n't it?'

'She seems to have made a few enemies since starting at the school, our Mrs Devine,' observed the major. 'By the sound of it, it appears more children are leaving,' he said, 'including the son of one of our governors. It does not bode well.'

The councillor gave a small smile. 'Well, in a way, it does,' he said. 'I mean, if we are to close t'school, as was proposed at t'last Education Sub-committee meeting, it sort of plays into our hands.'

'In what way?' enquired his companion.

'Well, if t'school is continuing to lose children and t'community as a whole don't 'ave no confidence in t'head teacher, *and* she's ruffling a few feathers, well, it does make it rather easier to go ahead wi' closure, dunt it?'

'Ah, yes, I see,' said the major. 'I follow your drift.'

The councillor tapped his fleshy nose with his forefinger. 'Any road, we shall have to play it a bit on t'careful side at t'next governors' meeting.'

THERE WAS AN urgent rapping on the cottage door. It was early Sunday evening and Elisabeth was in the kitchen preparing her supper. She opened the door to find Dr Stirling looking dishevelled and clearly distressed.

'Mrs Devine,' he said breathlessly. 'I'm sorry to trouble you at this hour, but I wonder if you've seen James? Is he here?' he asked, looking around.

'No,' Elisabeth replied, 'he's not.'

'Oh dear,' he sighed. 'I thought perhaps he might have come over here. You did mention that he had been to your cottage before and I thought he might have come here and forgotten about the time.'

'I'm afraid I haven't seen him.'

'I had an afternoon call, an emergency out at Littlebeck, and left James at home around five,' the doctor told her. 'Mrs O'Connor, my housekeeper who lives close by, usually calls round to keep an eye on James when I go out but she was at church. James said he would be all right by himself, this once. When I arrived home he wasn't there. Do you think he's with the boy he's friendly with? Danny, isn't it?'

'I don't think so,' said Elisabeth. 'James was to meet Danny by the mill-pond earlier today, but he never showed up.'

'The millpond!' exclaimed the doctor. 'Oh God, I hope—'

'Dr Stirling,' said Elisabeth calmly, 'I am certain there is nothing to worry about. James has probably just forgotten about the time.' She glanced at the longcase clock in the hall. 'It's only a little after seven and still light. Maybe he went for a walk. It is a lovely evening and—'

'But he's never done anything like this before,' the doctor told her. 'He always tells me or Mrs O'Connor where he's going and he's always back home at the time I tell him. Could we have a word with this friend of his?'

'Of course we can,' said Elisabeth.

Dr Stirling followed Elisabeth down the path and across the paddock to the caravan. Elisabeth knocked lightly on the door.

Les Stainthorpe poked his head out of a window. 'Oh, hello, Mrs Devine. Come on in.'

Elisabeth entered the caravan. She had not been inside before and was surprised to see how clean and tidy everything was. The beds had been neatly made, and pots and pans had been tidied. There wasn't a thing out of place. Danny, sitting writing at the table, looked up anxiously.

'You'll be pleased t'lad's doin' 'is 'omework, Mrs Devine,' said the old man. He caught sight of Dr Stirling waiting outside, a worried expression on his face. 'Hello, Doctor,' he said. 'There's nowt up, is there?'

'I wonder if Danny has seen anything of James?' asked Elisabeth.

'No, miss,' said the boy getting up from the table. 'I telled you I was supposed to meet 'im this mornin' down by t'millpond but 'e never turned up.'

'The thing is, Danny,' explained Dr Stirling, coming into the caravan, 'James is missing.'

'Missin'!' the boy exclaimed.

'He's not at home,' said the doctor, 'and I don't know where he is. You haven't seen him at all today?'

'No.'

'Have you any idea where he might be?' asked Elisabeth.

'No, I don't,' said Danny, 'but I know why 'e's run off.'

'Run off!' repeated the doctor. 'What do you mean, he's run off?'

'It's because of that bloody school yer sending 'im to!'

'Hey, hey, Danny Stainthorpe,' said his grandfather sharply. 'Less of that sort of language and don't be so rude to t'doctor.'

'Well, it is, Granddad,' said the boy angrily. 'Jamie din't want to go to that school; 'e wanted to stay where 'e was and 'e was real upset that 'is dad was makin' 'im go. I told you that, Granddad. Jamie tried to tell Dr Stirling but 'e wouldn't listen and then Mrs Devine tried to tell 'im and 'e wouldn't listen to 'er, either.' He breathed out heavily. 'I don't know why adults don't listen.' The boy began to rub his eyes.

'Now, don't get upset, Danny,' said Elisabeth calmly. 'I'm quite sure James is all right. Shall we go and have a look and call in at some of the places you and James like to go to and see if we can find him?' Elisabeth turned to Dr Stirling. 'It might be a good idea if you were to go back to your house in case James returns. Leave your number and if he turns up, I'll give you a ring.'

'Yes, I'll do that,' said Dr Stirling, rubbing his forehead. 'And thank you.'

'If we don't find him,' said Elisabeth, 'I think you should call the police.'

IT WAS GETTING DARK. There was a drizzle of rain and a cold white moon in a gunmetal-grey sky, and still no sign of the missing boy.

They sat on heavy chairs round the large oak table in the gloomy dining room at the Stirlings' home, Clumber Lodge: Dr Stirling, Elisabeth and two young police officers.

The young policeman with the red nose, colourful acne and greasy black hair flicked his notebook shut and leaned back in his chair.

'I wouldn't worry too much, Dr Stirling,' he said casually. 'Children run off all the time. I've known a number of cases when kids have had a bit of a tiff with their mums and dads and run off. We soon find them.'

Elisabeth knew that this was not the case, but she remained silent.

'I have not had a "tiff" with my son, Officer,' said Dr Stirling. His face was drawn and troubled. 'There was no argument.'

The young policeman looked at his colleague, a thin-faced woman with her hair scraped back on her scalp into a small bun, and rolled his eyes.

'What I mean,' he said, 'is that children leave home for a number of reasons. There was a girl who couldn't face sitting her school exams and took herself off to her grandma's in Halifax, and a lad who went looking for his dog and got lost. We soon find them. Now, you say you have looked in all the places he might have gone?'

'Yes,' said Elisabeth, resisting the temptation to ask him if he was taking the situation seriously.

She and Danny and the boy's grandfather had searched for a good hour, looking in the boys' den, down by the millpond, in the small copses and hedgerows, the deserted barns and round the village, getting increasingly worried as the evening drew on and there was no sign of the missing boy.

'Well, I've got a picture of your son,' said the young policeman, rising from his chair. 'I'll alert all my colleagues to keep an eye out for him and if he's not turned up by tomorrow, we'll organise a proper search.'

Dr Stirling stared into the distance as if looking for something.

'The boy is only just eleven,' said Elisabeth, 'and he should not be out all night at that age. I suggest you start a search immediately.'

'As I said, we will certainly keep an eye out for the boy,' the officer replied. 'Let's not get too overanxious at this stage.'

'Thank you for that,' said Dr Stirling to Elisabeth after the police officers had gone. 'You had better go. There's nothing more you can do. I'll stay here and hope James comes home.' He was close to tears. 'I don't know what I'll do if anything has happened to him.'

Elisabeth rested a hand on his arm. 'Are you going to be all right?'

'Not really,' he replied.

'Mr Stainthorpe and some of the men in the village are out looking. If you like, you could join them and I'll stay here in case James returns.'

'Yes,' replied Dr Stirling, 'I'd like to do that. Thank you.'

THE SEARCH PARTY returned after a couple of hours. Elisabeth saw from the dejected expressions on the men's faces that they had not found the boy.

'Well, we've looked everywhere for t'lad,' Les told Elisabeth in a lowered voice, 'but there's no sign. 'Appen 'e's fallen asleep somewhere. I pray to God 'e 'as and that nowt's 'appened to 'im.'

Elisabeth left Dr Stirling sitting staring out of the window. The clock in the hall struck eleven. She had tried again to reassure him but she was now as worried as he was about his son.

She walked slowly through the village towards home. Despite the mildness of the night, she felt cold. When she arrived at the cottage she didn't feel like going inside. She negotiated some fresh cow pats that spattered the track, came to the gate and looked down the shadowy garden that she had brought to life again; it was now a place of order and fruitfulness and beauty. She breathed in deeply, aware of the stillness of the night. The wind had dropped and the clouds had moved away, leaving bright stars and a crescent moon curved silver and as bright as a sabre in the sky. Soft rain sifted through the treetops and the wet grass glittered in the moonlight.

As her eyes became more accustomed to the darkness, she saw a small, hunched figure on the bench at the corner of the lawn. She ran through the gate and bent before the child and rested her hand on his.

'James?' she said quietly.

The boy looked up. His hair was wet and his cheeks were smeared where he had been crying, and his small lip trembled. Suddenly the tears came welling up, spilling over. The boy began to sob, great heaving sobs, and he fell into Elisabeth's arms and hugged her.

'It's all right,' she said. 'You're safe. It's all right.' She stroked his hair and held his shuddering shoulders and thought of her own son, unreachable, shut away in his own private world. How she longed to hold *him* in her arms, stroke *his* hair and comfort *him*. She snuffled. 'My goodness, you've got me crying now,' she said.

They sat there in the darkness holding each other. The wet slates on the cottage roof glistened, the crescent moon shone in a coal-black sky and the stars winked. In the distance she heard the howl of a fox.

'Shall I take you home?' asked Elisabeth.

There was a small, imperceptible whisper. 'Yes.'

DR STIRLING STOOD by the fireplace in the sitting room. Elisabeth sat opposite him on the large padded sofa, a glass of brandy cupped in her hands. James had been tucked up in bed, and the evening's drama was over.

'I've been a bloody fool,' he said, taking a gulp from his glass.

Elisabeth didn't answer.

'A bloody fool,' he repeated. 'I never realised how much James disliked the idea of moving school. Young Danny was right: I should have listened, talked to him about it more.' He thought for a moment. 'And I should have listened to you.'

'Well, I'm as guilty as anyone for listening but not hearing—if that makes any sense. Perhaps this has been a salutary lesson,' Elisabeth said, 'that we should listen more to what children try and tell us.'

Dr Stirling looked at her for a moment before speaking. He had been wrong about her, judged her unfairly. That evening she had been there for the boy, and for him, too.

'You know I was against you being appointed at the school,' he told her.

'I guessed as much,' said Elisabeth. 'You scowled all the way through the interview.'

'Scowled?' he cried. 'I never scowl!'

'You looked like a bulldog with toothache.'

He laughed. 'Really?'

'I could tell you were not impressed.'

'Actually, I was very impressed with your answers,' he told her. 'It's just that I couldn't understand why someone who was a head teacher of a large and successful school, on a good salary and with a wonderful inspectors' report and excellent references, should want to come to a small school in a remote village. I had the idea you were coming here for a quiet life. If you had explained about your son and the reason—'

'Why should I?' Elisabeth interrupted. 'It's not anyone else's business, and I can't be doing with those overly sympathetic, "Oh, you poor dear, it must be so hard for you" comments. Anyway, there were other reasons for wanting to move. I needed a fresh start, a challenge; a break from the past.'

'I see.'

'My husband left me,' Elisabeth said suddenly. She had not told anyone about her past since moving to the village, but for some inexplicable reason she wanted to tell him. 'Simon wanted a "normal" son, whatever that means. He couldn't cope with his son's disability and left when John was five.'

'I'm sorry,' Dr Stirling said. 'Does he see John at all?'

'No,' she said. 'He married again and started a new life. I don't feel any bitterness or anger; in fact, I hope he's happy.' She looked into the quiet, watchful eyes, blue as china marbles, which stared into her own. 'As happy as *I* am.'

Dr Stirling smiled. 'I'm glad,' he said. 'I can't tell you how grateful I am for what you have done tonight.' He continued to look into her eyes. 'I hope we can be friends, good friends, and that you'll have James back at Barton.'

'Do you need to ask?'

'No, I don't suppose I do,' he said. 'And your suggestion that James should see the psychologist . . .'

'Yes?'

'Perhaps you could arrange that.'

'Of course,' she replied.

They looked at each other for a moment, and both realised they had changed from being combative strangers to becoming friends.

THE NEXT MORNING, Dr Stirling brought his son into school early, before the other children had arrived. James sat with his father in Elisabeth's classroom as quiet as ever, but she noticed, as she spoke, that on a number of occasions the boy lifted his dark eyes shyly and looked at her. She would smile at him and he would give a small smile back before averting his eyes.

'It was quite a drama,' Dr Stirling said. He put an arm round his son's shoulders. 'We were really worried about you, young man,' he said to him. 'Anyway, it's sorted out now and there will be no more running away. And you'll be a good boy for Mrs Devine.'

'He will be,' Elisabeth said. 'From what Miss Brakespeare has told me, he's never been anything other than a good boy, and I am looking forward to teaching him.'

She walked with James's father to the entrance hall.

'Before you go, there are a couple of favours I would ask of you, though, Dr Stirling.' There was a twinkle in her eye.

'Oh dear, this sounds ominous.' His face broke into a smile. 'Come along then, what are they?'

Elisabeth smiled. 'Nothing too onerous, I can assure you. Firstly, I want you to remain as a governor at the school.'

'Done,' he replied. 'What next?'

'Sex.'

'Sex!' he spluttered.

'The older pupils need a few sex education lessons,' Elisabeth told him.

The doctor laughed. 'And you want me to do them? I think there are people much better qualified to talk to children about sex than I.'

'Oh, I think I can manage talking to the girls on this topic, but I think the boys might be less embarrassed and better informed, and be prepared to ask questions, if their lessons were from a man.'

'OK, I'll do it. But if I do, you must start calling me Michael. I think we can dispense with the "Dr Stirling" bit, don't you?

'Very well, Michael,' she said, and felt a small rush of blood to her face.

When James's father had gone, Elisabeth returned to the classroom. The boy looked a sad little figure, sitting at his desk staring out of the window.

'Come along, James,' she said cheerfully, 'you can have a walk round the school with me. I often do this before everyone arrives, to make sure it's clean and there's no litter.' As they toured the school, Elisabeth outlined the plans she had for extracurricular activities. James listened but said nothing.

They stopped and looked across the school field to the vast, white expanse of sky, the undulating green pastures dotted with sheep, and distant sombre peaks. They stood there in silence. 'And you know, James,' Elisabeth said after a while, 'if there's anything that troubles you again, you must tell your father. He loves you very much and wants the best for you.' The boy reached out and touched her hand, and then he rested his head on her arm for a moment.

AT ASSEMBLY, Elisabeth looked at her pupils as they filed quietly into the school hall. Things had certainly changed since she had taken over as head teacher two weeks ago, and not just in the appearance of the building and in the morale of the staff. Her insistence during the first week on silence as the children entered and left the hall at assembly time (with a few practice runs until they got it right), that they should make less noise at dinnertime and move around the school in a more orderly fashion, had been accepted by the children, and they had responded surprisingly well.

Miss Brakespeare attributed the improvement of the children's behaviour to the fact that the head teacher, when she was not teaching, spent most of her time round the school, unlike her predecessor, who had tended to keep herself closeted in her room. Her commitment and enthusiasm began rubbing off on her staff, who, like her, started arriving at school early, leaving later and spending only a little time in the staff room.

'If you had a magic wand,' Elisabeth would ask a child, as she walked round the playground or sat with him or her at dinnertime, 'what changes would you make in the school?'

The answers were predictable. Many of the children bemoaned the fact that there was little happening out of lessons: no sports teams or after-school clubs, lunchtime activities and trips out of school; needs that Elisabeth had identified herself and ones she was determined to meet.

When the children had assembled that morning, sung the hymn and said a prayer, Elisabeth addressed them.

'Now, I have some quite exciting news,' she said. 'I have been having a word with people in and around the village and I have asked some of them to come into school and offer a number of activities during the lunch-hour and after school, for those who are interested. Mrs Atticus, who is a very fine artist and who lives at the vicarage, will be coming in on Tuesday lunchtimes to take an art class. Mr Tomlinson, who plays the organ in the chapel, has agreed to help Mrs Robertshaw start a choir. I have also persuaded Mr Parkinson, who is a Scout leader, to take those boys and girls who are keen for football practice for an hour on Thursdays after school. I also have in mind to organise some school trips and, for the older children, perhaps a visit to France next year.' There was a hubbub of excited chatter. 'Quietly, please.' The noise subsided. 'Now, all these things will be put in a letter that each of you will take home to your parents or guardians. I know you will make all our visitors very welcome when they come into our school and be on your best behaviour.' She paused. 'Won't you?'

'Yes, Mrs Devine,' the children chorused loudly.

DURING THE WEEKS that followed, the school became a hive of activity at lunchtime and after school. The clubs and extra classes, the sports activities and the music took off to such an extent that Elisabeth started to receive many positive comments from parents at the school gates about how pleased they were with these initiatives.

Mrs Robertshaw and Mr Tomlinson had recruited a good number of pupils for the choir, and the children, who delighted the minister and the congregation at the Methodist chapel at their first performance, became regular features at the services. The finest singer had been Chardonnay, who had a clear and powerful voice and who had sung a solo. Mr Parkinson had formed a football team in which Chantelle had turned out to be the star player, and Miss Wilson's rounders team had very nearly won its first match against St Paul's. The Reverend Atticus had started to visit the school each week and had agreed to teach some religious education lessons in addition to taking assemblies.

Elisabeth was delighted with the response and had been surprised at how much talent and enthusiasm there was among the children. The greatest revelation had come in the form of Ernest Pocock.

'He has a natural aptitude,' Marcia Atticus informed Elisabeth over a cup of coffee in the staff room one Tuesday morning. 'The boy has an excellent eye for detail and colour, and a great sense of perspective. I think he has a real chance of getting an award in the County Art Competition.'

Mrs Scrimshaw came scurrying into the playground to find Elisabeth, with news that Lady Wadsworth wanted to see her.

Elisabeth found her visitor in the staff room. She wore a ridiculously colourful checked tweed suit as shapeless as a sack of potatoes, and a wide-brimmed green felt hat sporting two long pheasant feathers held in place by a silver brooch in the shape of a fox's head. The outfit was complemented by thick brown stockings and shoes of the heavy, sensible brogue variety with little leather acorns attached to the front. She looked magnificently outlandish.

'Mrs Devine,' she said heartily, rising to her feet as Elisabeth entered the room. 'I do hope I have not come at an inconvenient time.'

'It's good to see you, Lady Wadsworth.'

'Helen, please,' she said. 'I feel I know you already, and now we are neighbours, so to speak, we will no doubt see a deal of each other.' She pointed to a large brass plaque leaning against the wall. 'After our very pleasant conversation on Sunday, I thought I would drop it off before you change your mind. I can show you where it used to go.'

The plaque was rather large—at least three feet square. 'I'll get Mr Gribbon to fix it to the wall,' said Elisabeth, wondering if she had done the right thing in agreeing to have it reinstated.

'Splendid,' said Lady Wadsworth.

'Perhaps, while you're here, you might like to have a look round,' suggested Elisabeth.

'I told you I was a rather inquisitive person,' Lady Wadsworth replied, 'and I should like that very much. I have to say I didn't recognise the place when I walked through the door. You have certainly made some changes, as you have at the cottage.' Again, Elisabeth wondered if her visitor altogether approved: it was her rather sharp tone of voice and the way she scrutinised everything. However, it was clear after her tour of the school that Lady Wadsworth did indeed approve, and was suitably impressed with the changes that had been made.

'I have an idea,' Elisabeth told her as they viewed a dark corner near the toilets, 'that if I can squeeze some funding out of the Education Office we could have a small library here, with a carpet and cushions, a small table and chairs, and a good selection of books.'

'It's a splendid idea,' agreed Lady Wadsworth. 'I am all in favour of children reading. "Books are the architecture of a civilised society," as my grandfather used to say, "and reading is the very protein of growth in learning." He was a very erudite man, the second Viscount, you know.'

THAT AFTERNOON Elisabeth's class, having heard a story she read to them about a man who lost the winning lottery ticket, was asked to write an account of something valuable or precious that had been lost.

'I'm writing about the time my mum lost her ring,' said Chardonnay, when Elisabeth went to look at her work. 'It was her engagement ring and she took it off last Christmas to try on a ring my gran had given her and it got thrown out with all the wrapping paper.'

'Oh dear,' said Elisabeth.

'We had a rotten Christmas as well,' said Chantelle. 'My dad bought my mum this red silk underwear and she stuffed it back in the box and told him that only tarts wear red underwear and she'd not be seen dead in it and she wanted a deep fat fryer.'

'And did your mother find her ring, Chardonnay?' Elisabeth asked, eager to change the subject from the red silk underwear. 'No, she never did,' replied the girl. 'Anyway, she's got another now, and it's a bigger one.'

That evening, Elisabeth sat down to mark the children's exercise books. Her pupils had really made an effort to write interesting accounts on the topic she had set for them and they had taken care with their writing. Chantelle's account of the time her mother had lost her contact lens in the cinema made her laugh out loud. Danny's detailed and informative account, predictably about his ferret, described the time Ferdie had disappeared down a rabbit hole and had been missing for three days. Then Elisabeth got to James's piece of work.

'*The most precious thing I have lost is my mum*,' he wrote. Elisabeth's heart missed a beat. '*Sometimes when I'm in bed at night I try and think of her face but I can't see it and it makes me upset. The next morning I have to look at the picture on the shelf in the kitchen and the one in the sitting room to remind me. Sometimes a piece of music she liked reminds me of her and I begin to cry. I remember too the way she laughed. It used to make my dad laugh. He doesn't laugh much any more. He spends a lot of time staring out of the window. It makes me feel very sad. The most precious thing that I've lost is my mum and I shall never forget her.*'

He had written underneath, '*Please don't read this out to the class.*'

Elisabeth closed the exercise book. 'Oh, James,' she said aloud.

THE FOLLOWING MONDAY, Elisabeth arranged for Dr Stirling to see Mrs Goldstein, the educational psychologist. He listened intently as the condition of selective mutism was explained to him.

'James has a relatively rare condition,' Mrs Goldstein told him, 'but I have every reason to believe that he can be helped and that things will improve. From what you have told me, he is perfectly capable of speech and understanding language and can read well, but in certain social situations he is silent. At school, I gather he doesn't say anything except to his best friend. Is there anyone else he speaks to?'

'He sometimes speaks to Mrs O'Connor, my housekeeper.'

'But he speaks quite freely at home to you?' she asked.

'Yes, he's still a little quiet, but then, as I've said, he's been rather reticent since my wife died.'

'It's not uncommon for a child to withdraw into himself like this after some trauma that gives a sense of incredible loss. However, thankfully it is a fact, and I am sure I don't need to tell a doctor this, that time is a great healer.'

'So what do we do?' asked the doctor.

'Well, there's no magic cure for a start, but lots of love and support and patience from family and friends can have a real impact on any success in treating this condition. He should never be prompted to speak, but attention should be taken to making him feel comfortable and relaxed and confident in social settings. I think your son is in very good hands here, and is well placed to make real progress. Mrs Devine strikes me as a very competent and capable head teacher.'

And she's much more than that, thought Dr Stirling.

MRS ATTICUS'S TUESDAY lunchtime art class proved very popular and successful, and the school corridors and classrooms soon became richly colourful, with vibrant paintings and sketches, delicate watercolours and line drawings. The vicar's wife turned out to be a natural teacher. Elisabeth called in at the art class and found Mrs Atticus well organised, enthusiastic and with a firm, no-nonsense approach with the children.

'I can see you have really taken to this,' Elisabeth told her one morning.

'Do you know,' replied Mrs Atticus, 'I have to say I had some misgivings about coming in to teach the children, but I am really enjoying working with them.'

'Perhaps you ought to think of training as a teacher,' suggested Elisabeth. 'I've checked—there is a course at St John's College and you could do your teaching practice here. We should be delighted to have you.'

'Thank you, Elisabeth,' replied Mrs Atticus. 'I might just do that. Do you know, I have to admit that I've felt quite liberated since coming here. I've been stuck in that dark and depressing vicarage for so long with very little to do, it really got me down.' Her eyes glinted with pleasure.

Dr Stirling arrived at the school the following Tuesday to take the lesson on sex education as he had promised. He entered the classroom with Elisabeth, who introduced him and explained to the children what the lesson that day would be about. She imagined that James would be embarrassed by seeing his father at the front of the classroom talking about such a delicate subject, but he seemed unconcerned. Elisabeth appreciated that the subject of sex required very sensitive and careful handling, and seeing several of the boys smirking and nudging one another, she felt it appropriate that she should stand eagle-eyed at the front of the classroom. She noticed that a large grin had appeared on the face of Ernest Pocock.

The children listened attentively as Dr Stirling explained, simply and clearly, the human reproductive system and the changes that would be taking place in their bodies as they grew older. Elisabeth then took over to talk about the moral implications of sexual relationships. At the end, she asked if there were any questions.

She was met with silence.

'There must be some questions you would like to ask Dr Stirling,' she prompted, looking round the classroom.

Ernest Pocock raised a hand. He had a cheeky smile right across his face.

I might have guessed it would be him, thought Elisabeth. What deeply embarrassing question had he thought up?

'Yes, Ernest, what would you like to ask?' she said, bracing herself.

'Will there be the art class this lunchtime, miss?' he asked.

7

'So, how are you liking it at your new school then, Malcolm?' asked Mrs Sloughthwaite. She kept a wary eye on the items displayed on the counter as she asked the question. The boy might not be very good at much, but at sleight of hand he was the master.

'It's all right,' mumbled the boy.

It was the following afternoon, and Mrs Stubbins had called in at the village store to do her weekly shopping. She smoothed an eyebrow with a little finger. 'Oh, he's settled in really well,' she told the shopkeeper. 'Best thing I ever did was move him.'

If truth be told, Malcolm had not settled in at Urebank. He found the work hard and tedious, and he didn't like his teacher. The new boy was made to sit at the front by himself; he soon found that the teacher was less than impressed with the work he produced. Any attempts on Malcolm's part to make friends with some of the other boys in his year proved unsuccessful. One thing he knew, he was good at was football, but the team was well established and successful, and his offer to play in a match fell on deaf ears.

'Oh, I'm sure he is better off where he is,' said Mrs Sloughthwaite. 'It's surprising, though, that Malcolm didn't get on at the village school. All the parents who come into the shop since Mrs Devine took over seem very content with the way things are, and very happy with the changes that the new head teacher is making. And from what I hear, some of those parents who sent their kiddies to Urebank are regretting it now they've heard about the improvements. I reckon some of them will be sending them back before too long.' She smiled to herself at the evident dismay her comments were creating. 'They've got a choir there, now, as well,' Mrs Sloughthwaite continued. 'The children sang in the Bethesda chapel on Sunday and Mrs Widowson said they sounded lovely, and she's not one to give out compliments easily.'

'I've never been one for hymns and such myself,' disclosed Mrs Stubbins, rather scornfully.

'And a football team,' announced the shopkeeper as she leaned over and rested her Amazonian bosom and arms on the counter. She looked down at the sulky boy. 'Are you in the football team at Urebank, then, Malcolm?' she asked.

'No,' he muttered, scowling.

'THE THING IS,' said Mr Richardson over the telephone, 'it's not working out.'

'Oh, I'm sorry to hear that,' said Elisabeth, trying not to sound pleased.

She had received the call on the day of the governors' meeting, and was busy preparing papers in the office with Mrs Scrimshaw.

'Yes,' said the head teacher of Urebank School. 'I was not aware when I agreed to accept this boy of his track record. You gave me no indication that he was a particularly difficult and disruptive individual.'

'Mr Richardson, you never asked about Malcolm Stubbins or why his mother wished to move him. You said that if a parent comes to you wanting to move his or her child, then there is nothing you nor I can do about it.'

Mr Richardson decided not to respond to that comment. 'Mrs Devine, I am asking you to take this boy back. I should like to inform his mother that I feel he is better suited to return to Barton. After all,' he continued, 'he is in your catchment area and should by rights attend your school.'

'Like the other children who live in the village but who attend Urebank,' replied Elisabeth. She felt like telling him that already several parents were intending to move their children back to Barton, but she thought it judicious not to do so. He would soon find out.

There was a silence. 'So you will not have the boy back?' he asked.

'If Malcolm's mother wants him to attend your school rather than mine, Mr Richardson, then there is really nothing I can do.'

'I see,' he said sharply. 'Well, I shall not be letting this matter rest and shall be contacting the Education Office.' He thumped down the phone.

Mrs Scrimshaw, who had been listening intently to this exchange, put down the papers she had been stapling together and pulled a face. 'My goodness, Mrs Devine, you certainly told him where to go.'

The head teacher was in particularly high spirits that day. Before Mr

Richardson's telephone call she had shown two sets of parents round the school and been assured by them that their children would be starting there the following week, while a growing number of parents of children from outside the catchment area were enquiring about sending their sons and daughters to the school. All this was ammunition for the governors' meeting that evening, when she would raise the question of the school's future.

THE THREE CONSPIRATORS met in the corner of the Blacksmith's Arms, prior to the meeting of the governing body.

'I think it might be best, Major,' said Mr Nettles, 'if you let me take the lead when we come to the first item on the agenda, about the school closure. I am fully conversant with the various procedures and processes for closing a school, and the meeting, in my experience, could be a little controversial.'

'Oh, I think not, Mr Nettles,' remarked Councillor Smout, draining his pint glass. 'I don't think there'll be that much opposition. 'Owever, we need to tread carefully.'

'I wish I could be as confident, Councillor,' observed the education officer smugly, before taking a sip of his slimline tonic. 'In my experience, these meetings can be quite heated.'

'Look, Mr Nettles,' said Councillor Smout, 'let's be clear about this. T'school is small by any standards; it's losing pupils 'and-over-fist; and this new 'ead teacher 'as, from what I can gather, caused a lot of waves in t'village, upsetting t'locals. And, I might add, she's also got on t'wrong side of other 'ead teachers. I've 'ad a call only today from Mr Richardson at Urebank about some spat 'e's 'ad with 'er. I don't expect Dr Stirling will show 'is face now that 'is lad's at t'other school, so I can't see as 'ow there'll be all that much controversy.'

'And then there's the critical school report,' added the major. 'We shouldn't forget that.'

'I mean,' said Councillor Smout, 'everyone comes out of this smelling of roses as far as I can see. Miss Brakespeare gets early retirement, a lump sum and a pension, t'school can be sold off and t'field at t'back used for a much-needed 'ousing development—bringin' in a tidy sum to t'authority to boot—and we can easily transfer Mrs Devine to another school. I can't see as 'ow she'll be all that bothered.'

'I'm not so sure about that,' ventured the major. 'I think you underestimate

Mrs Devine. She is quite a formidable character and might not take too kindly to having the school close, particularly when she's only just been appointed. She is a strong-minded woman and may put up quite a fight.' He paused, pursing his lips. 'It did seem to me to be a little unethical to appoint her when we had every intention of closing the school.'

'Major, it was not finally decided until the Education Sub-committee met, so I don't think we need to worry on that score. And I have dealt with strong-minded head teachers before,' said Mr Nettles, a confident smile on his face. 'I think I can manage Mrs Devine.'

ELISABETH WAS WAITING to greet the governors on their arrival for the meeting. When all the members of the board had gathered in the entrance hall, she invited them to join her on a tour of the school.

'I see that you have reinstated the plaque,' observed the major, staring at the large brass tablet set in a prominent position in the entrance.

'Lady Wadsworth was very keen to have it restored to its former place,' Elisabeth told him, 'and I was only too happy to oblige.'

'You are acquainted with Lady Wadsworth, then?' remarked the major, raising an eyebrow.

'She is a neighbour of mine,' Elisabeth told him. 'Do you have any problem with the plaque being displayed again?'

'No, no,' said the major quickly, 'not at all. In fact, I was somewhat upset when Miss Sowerbutts refused to put it back.'

Dr Stirling arrived. 'I'm sorry I am late,' he apologised to Elisabeth, 'I had a call-out.'

'Dr Stirling,' said Councillor Smout, looking startled. 'I'm surprised to see you 'ere.'

'And why is that, Councillor?' he was asked.

'Well, I understood that you 'ad taken your son away from t'school and under those circumstances, I thought that—'

'Whatever gave you that idea?' enquired the doctor. 'James is still here, and very happy.'

'I see,' said the councillor, giving the major and Mr Nettles a look.

'Shall we proceed?' asked Elisabeth.

The building was immaculate: clean, bright walls; highly polished floors; and well-mounted displays of work. Children's paintings and poems, posters, pictures and book jackets covered every available space. Shelves held attractive books, tables were covered in shells, models, photographs and little artefacts, and there were coloured drapes at the windows.

'Very impressive,' said the major, in a somewhat subdued tone of voice. He could see that there would be problems ahead.

'Yes, indeed,' murmured Councillor Smout, thinking to himself that he had been perhaps rather premature in assuming that the matter of the school closure would be plain sailing.

'And what about you, Mr Nettles?' asked Elisabeth. The education officer had remained silent, but, having seen the remarkable changes, shared his colleagues' opinions that closing the school would not be such an easy task as he had imagined.

'Yes, yes,' he replied unenthusiastically. 'Very nice.'

'Nice!' repeated Dr Stirling. 'That's something of an understatement, isn't it? The change in the school is quite extraordinary.'

'It's fantastic,' said Mrs Pocock. 'I've never see the place look so lovely.' She pointed to a large painting of a rural scene displayed to good effect on the wall at the end of the corridor. 'That's my Ernest's,' she said proudly to Mrs Bullock.

'You are to be congratulated, Mrs Devine,' enthused the vicar, rubbing his long hands together. 'Quite a remarkable transformation. The school looks wonderful.'

The major glanced at Mr Nettles. The education officer gave a weak smile but said nothing.

The first topic for consideration on the agenda—one sent from the Education Department—was, of course, the proposed closure of the school. The item was couched in the rather ambiguous phrase of, 'The future of the school'. Elisabeth had a shrewd idea what this meant and was determined to pre-empt any discussion about proposed closure. She therefore deliberately misinterpreted it.

'I'm delighted to see this as the first item on the agenda,' she said in an ingenuous voice. 'In preparation, I have put together for the governors my first report on the changes I have made and a detailed outline of my short- and long-term development plans. I think the future of the school is looking very bright.'

The major stroked his moustache. 'I . . . er . . . thank you for that, Mrs

Devine,' he said. He looked towards the education officer. 'I believe Mr Nettles has something to say on this matter.'

There was no complacent look on the education officer's face now. He gave a small cough. 'The thing is, Mrs Devine, the Education Sub-committee is of the opinion that we need to consider the viability of the school,' said Mr Nettles.

'Viability? May I ask exactly what that means?' asked Dr Stirling.

'As you are well aware, Doctor, the school is losing pupils,' began Mr Nettles, 'and—'

'If I might come in there,' said Elisabeth. 'The school is no longer losing pupils. In fact it is quite the reverse. The parents of two children who live in Gartside, which is out of this catchment area, have decided to send their two daughters here, and a new family has moved into the village and their three children will start next week. In addition, a former pupil of the school, who moved to Urebank, will be joining them. I think the numbers are looking very healthy.'

'Really,' said the vicar, smiling. 'That is excellent news.'

'That's as may be, Mrs Devine,' said the education officer, getting rather hot under his collar, 'but it is a fact that the school has been losing pupils and—'

'But as I have just explained, Mr Nettles,' said Elisabeth, 'not any more.'

The education officer looked to the major. 'Mr Chairman,' he said, irritated by the interruptions, 'if I might be allowed to finish. Barton-in-the-Dale is just one of the many small schools in the county which possibly might close.'

'Close!' exclaimed the vicar.

'Nonsense!' added Mrs Pocock.

'Perhaps I might ask Councillor Smout to come in here,' said Mr Nettles. 'He is a member of the Education Sub-committee and can acquaint you with the situation better than I.'

Councillor Smout, leaning back expansively on his chair and sucking his teeth, announced, 'The thing is, this is a small school and expensive to maintain and t'Local Education Authority 'as to make financial savings.'

'Are you saying you want to close the school?' demanded Mrs Pocock.

'We are considering it,' replied the councillor.

'You close this school, Cyril Smout, over my dead body!' she cried.

'It's outrageous!' said the vicar.

'They can't do that,' said Mrs Bullock. 'We have our Countrywomen's meetings here.'

'Might I ask, Mr Chairman,' enquired Dr Stirling, 'if Mrs Devine has been consulted on this matter or, indeed, been given any indication that the school might close? As far as I remember there was no mention of this at her interview, and we governors have certainly heard nothing about it before this afternoon.'

'No, this is the first occasion it has been raised,' the major told him.

'And were you aware of the proposal?'

The major was becoming increasingly uncomfortable. 'Councillor Smout might have mentioned it.'

'Look,' said the councillor, 'I don't like the idea of closing t'school any more than anyone 'ere, but as everyone is aware, we need to cut t'education budget and t'savings must come from somewhere. I know that some people may be upset—'

'Upset!' huffed the Reverend Atticus. 'I think "upset" is something of an understatement, Councillor. The people in the village, if they think their school is to close, will not be merely upset, they will be up in arms. I tell you now, it will not be countenanced.'

'If I could finish,' said Councillor Smout. 'I appreciate, I really do, that there will be some strong feelings, but small schools like this are expensive to maintain and, as I 'ave said, we need to make savings.'

'May I ask what the chairman has to say on the matter?' asked the vicar.

'Well, I . . . er . . . quite understand the . . . er . . . governors' reaction, and indeed I share it with them, but er . . . it does seem to me that, we need to . . . er . . . consider what the Education Department is suggesting.'

'It sounds, Major,' said Dr Stirling, 'as if you are in favour of considering this proposal and, if you are, it seems to me that your position as the chairman of the governing body at this school is untenable.'

'I never said I was in favour of the proposal,' replied the major, weakly.

'If I might come in here, Mr Chairman?' said Mr Nettles loftily. 'The governing body is obliged to consider this proposal.'

'Nonsense!' exclaimed Mrs Pocock. 'I, for one, don't intend considering anything. This school has improved no end since the beginning of term and it's madness to think of closing it.'

'Indeed,' said the vicar, raising his voice, 'I think you will find a great deal of opposition to any attempt to close the school.'

'Hear, hear,' echoed Mrs Bullock.

'And, what is more,' added the vicar, 'to appoint a head teacher and then announce that the school might close as soon as she is in post is tantamount to gross dishonesty.'

The major looked appealingly at Mr Nettles, who sat stony-faced.

'I suggest,' said Dr Stirling, 'we put it to the vote with the motion that we, the governors of Barton-in-the-Dale Primary School, strongly oppose any effort on the part of the Education Authority to close the school.'

'I think we are a little premature in this,' observed Mr Nettles. 'I would urge you to consider what the Education Department is suggesting before taking any such premature and impulsive action. After all, we haven't discussed the proposal yet.'

'And we are not going to,' announced Mrs Pocock.

'Mr Nettles,' said Dr Stirling, 'as I understand it, your function in attending the governors' meetings is to advise. You are an officer of the authority and not a governor, and, as such, you do not have a vote.' He glanced at the major, who looked bewildered. 'I propose we vote on the matter.'

And so it was that, with one abstention from the chairman and one against from the councillor, the motion was carried.

THE FOLLOWING WEEK, Elisabeth received two unwelcome letters in the post. The first was from Mr Richardson, accusing her of unprofessional conduct. The second was from Mr Nettles, informing her curtly that a public meeting was to be called at which a representative of the Local Education Authority would address 'governors, parents and teachers, and any others who might have an interest in the school'.

Elisabeth threw this letter down on the desk. 'There is no way that I am going to be intimidated by that awful man,' she told Mrs Scrimshaw. 'If he thinks he can ride roughshod over everyone, he is making a big mistake.'

'What are we going to do?' asked the school secretary.

'We will make a plan of action,' Elisabeth told her. 'We will rally support, display posters throughout the village, write letters and get items in the local papers. We shall fight this tooth and nail.'

'I have an idea what's in this one,' said Mrs Scrimshaw, holding up an official-looking brown envelope with an elaborate crest on the rear. 'It's them. They're coming back. They said they would be calling again after the holidays and they couldn't be coming back at a worse time.'

Elisabeth, too, knew only too well what the brown envelope contained when she examined it herself. It would be a letter informing her of an impending visit straight after half-term by one or two of Her Majesty's Inspectors of Schools. 'Not necessarily,' she said. 'This could very well work to our advantage.'

'In what way?' asked Mrs Scrimshaw.

'If we come out of this visit with a good report, which I don't doubt we will, we will have some powerful ammunition.'

'I hope so,' said the secretary. 'And I do hope we don't get that inspector with the face like one of those gargoyles on the church, and the dandruff and bad breath. He looked as if he'd been dug up. I don't think he knew how to smile.'

'Can you recall his name?' asked Elisabeth, tearing open the envelope and scanning the contents.

'Mr Steel,' Mrs Scrimshaw told her.

'Oh dear, the letter's from Mr Steel,' Elisabeth told her. 'He will be coming in on the 31st of October.'

'Halloween,' remarked Mrs Scrimshaw. 'That figures.'

They both burst out laughing.

THE HALF-TERM HOLIDAY CAME. Danny appeared in Elisabeth's garden for the first two days to help his grandfather clear away the dead flowers, dig over the soil, weed the borders and prune the bushes, but then wasn't seen again for the rest of the week.

''E's gone off with 'is pal and 'is dad,' explained Les to Elisabeth when she asked where Danny was. 'Doc Stirling's arranged some trips out for 'is lad an' asked if our Danny wanted to go along. 'E were as chirpy as a songbird this morning. They're goin' swimmin' and then to t'cinema in Clayton.'

IT WAS INEVITABLE that the meeting would eventually take place. On the Wednesday, Elisabeth entered the village store to do her weekly shopping to find Miss Sowerbutts at the post office counter.

She took a deep breath. 'Good morning,' she said cheerfully.

''Morning, Mrs Devine,' said the shopkeeper. It was clear from the expression that came over her round face that Mrs Sloughthwaite was going to relish this confrontation.

The former head teacher swivelled round. Her face was hard and set. She fixed Elisabeth with a piercing stare but managed a cool acknowledgment before turning back to the counter.

'I was just telling Miss Sowerbutts here,' said the shopkeeper, 'about all the changes at the school. She wouldn't recognise the place now, would she, Mrs Devine?'

Elisabeth gave a weak smile but felt it politic to say nothing.

'No, I don't suppose I would recognise it,' said Miss Sowerbutts in an aggrieved tone, 'and frankly I am not that interested.'

'Oh, there're all sorts of things going on now,' continued the shopkeeper. 'They've got an art class, chess club, football and rounders teams, a choir, a drama club—'

'Yes, well, that's all very well,' said the former head teacher, with a downturn of her mouth, 'but I never allowed my professional priorities to be distracted by frills and furbelows when I was in charge.' Her features were alien and hostile.

Elisabeth felt her throat tightening. 'I must take issue with you there, Miss Sowerbutts,' she retorted, her voice calm and measured. 'Such activities are not "frills and furbelows", as you call them; they are an essential part of a broad and balanced curriculum and are very important in a school. Indeed, they add immeasurably to the richness of a child's experience.'

Miss Sowerbutts gave a small, cynical smile. 'Please don't lecture me, Mrs Devine,' she said. 'I have heard all this before. No doubt such changes go down well with some, but I have been in education long enough to believe that such things—art and drama and choirs and suchlike—merely decorate the margins of the more serious business of teaching children how to read and write and add up.'

It is pointless arguing with this woman, thought Elisabeth. 'Well, let us agree to differ,' she said.

But Miss Sowerbutts had not finished, and played her trump card with great satisfaction. 'And, of course, should the school close, all these changes will have been for nothing.' She turned away. 'I'll just have two second-class stamps,' she told the shopkeeper.

MR STEEL, HMI, arrived at the school the following week, on an overcast, drizzly morning. Mrs Scrimshaw's description was apt, for Mr Steel was a tall, cadaverous man with sunken cheeks, greyish skin and a mournful countenance. He was dressed in a black suit, wore shiny black shoes that creaked when he walked, and carried a black briefcase with a gold crown embossed on the front.

He spent the first part of the morning looking through various documents: guidelines, lesson outlines, teaching strategies, development plans, pupil profiles, attainment details and test results, which had all been carefully presented in a series of folders. Elisabeth had spent every evening that week making sure everything was in place.

The school inspector's first port of call was the infants at morning break. He found the children, unable to go out to the playground on such a rainy day, involved in various activities in their classroom. Some were playing in the sand tray, others were measuring water in jugs and beakers; some were sitting, looking at picture books in a corner, and others were creating buildings with wooden blocks. A small group was in the home corner, dressing up and acting out parts.

Following the morning break, Mr Steel made notes in a small, black book, while Miss Wilson read the children a story.

She found it quite unnerving seeing him sitting in the corner of the classroom scribbling away, and wondered what he could possibly find to write about, but she carried on with the story and the class listened attentively, and behaved impeccably. When she had set the children writing, the inspector looked through her lesson plan, questioned the children and selected several to read to him.

Then he headed for Miss Brakespeare's classroom. He was particularly interested in the work her pupils were undertaking, since it was their teacher of whom the inspectors had been most critical on their last visit.

With a smaller, younger and better-behaved group of children, and minus the one difficult pupil, Miss Brakespeare felt she taught a very good lesson. She had discussed the topic with Elisabeth and planned it carefully.

In Mrs Robertshaw's class, once she had introduced the inspector, the lower juniors had settled down quietly to write their description of a Viking settlement. Mr Steel decided to examine the children's work and question them. The first child he quizzed was a bright-eyed child of nine with a thatch of straw-coloured hair and very colourful glasses. Oscar was staring out of the window, his elbow on the desk and his chin cupped in his hand.

'Have you finished your work?' asked the inspector.

'No,' replied Oscar seriously. 'I've not started yet. I'm contemplating.'

'Perhaps you would like to tell me what you are doing,' said Mr Steel.

'I'm about to start my account about the Vikings,' Oscar told him. 'Do you know anything about Vikings?'

'A little,' replied the inspector. He was unused to children asking him questions. It was his job to ask *them* questions.

'Some people think they wore helmets with horns on,' said the boy. 'Well, they didn't.'

'No, so I understand,' said the inspector. 'What do you—'

'They were good sailors and navigators and travelled long distances. Do you know what they came in when they went to other countries?'

'Longboats?' suggested the inspector wearily.

'What else?'

'I don't know,' the inspector admitted.

'They came in *hordes*,' the boy told him. 'The word is spelt differently from "hoards".' He wrote two words on his jotter and pointed with a pencil. '"Hordes" are large groups of people like invaders; "hoards" are stores of money. Did you know that?'

'Yes, I did,' replied the inspector, intrigued by this strange, articulate, old-fashioned boy who observed him over the top of his coloured frames.

Oscar slid his exercise book across the desk. 'I imagine you wish to see my book,' he said. 'One of the inspectors looked the last time. He told me that I had a lot to say for myself.'

Mr Steel sympathised with his colleagues. 'What is your name?' he asked.

'Oscar,' the boy replied. 'And you are called Mr Steel.'

'And how would you know that?'

'You are wearing a badge,' said the boy.

'We have had a very interesting conversation, haven't we, Mr Steel?' Oscar remarked.

'Yes, we have,' replied the inspector.

'We can continue it at lunchtime if you like,' said the boy.

'I shall look forward to that,' said Mr Steel, making a mental note to avoid this particular pupil.

Mr Steel reported back to Elisabeth at the end of the day.

'There has been a remarkable improvement in all aspects of the school,' he said, 'and you are to be congratulated. The teaching is good or better, and the quality of the children's work has greatly improved. Particularly impressive is the range of extracurricular activities on offer and which the children were at pains to describe to me. The leadership and management are more than satisfactory; the documentation is thorough and appropriate; and the environment for learning is very good. I do not envisage that I will be calling again in the foreseeable future.'

Elisabeth glowed inside. 'That is good to hear,' she said. 'I am very relieved you are happy with what you have seen.'

'More than happy. I shall be writing a report for your governors, a copy of which will be sent to the Education Office in due course,' said the inspector.

'And were you aware, Mr Steel, that the Local Education Authority has it in mind to close the school?' asked Elisabeth.

'No, I wasn't,' replied the inspector.

'Well, it has. A public meeting is to be called in the next few weeks. I should be most grateful if you were able to send your report before then.'

Mr Steel smiled for the first time that day. It was a small, tightlipped smile. 'I don't envisage any problem with that,' he said.

THE REVEREND ATTICUS, rector of Barton, surveyed his dinner.

'What is this, my dear?' he asked his wife.

'Beef cobblers. I got the recipe from the secretary at the school.'

'It's a substantial meal,' the vicar said, staring at the mound before him.

'Well, you could do with building up, Charles. You've looked decidedly pale and peaky of late.'

The vicar carefully posted a mouthful of fatty meat into his mouth and chewed slowly.

'It occurred to me,' said Mrs Atticus, 'that in your efforts to prevent the school from closing, you might enlist the support of the bishop. Knowing him, he will have cultivated some important and influential people and it's just the sort of campaign he would like.'

'That sounds an excellent idea,' replied her husband, having managed to swallow a gobbet of fat. 'I shall most certainly drop him a line. We need all the support we can get.'

Since his wife had started the art class at the village school, she had been altogether more good-humoured, and he welcomed this change in her temperament. 'You appear to be enjoying your time at the school, my dear,' observed the vicar.

'Yes, Charles, I am,' she replied. 'I have to say that when it was first suggested by Mrs Devine, I was chary about trying to teach a group of children, but the class has proved very popular and I have uncovered some real talent. I have also found Mrs Devine very accommodating. Actually, she recommended that I might consider training as a teacher.'

The Reverend Atticus did not wish to appear overly enthusiastic, but the thought of his wife occupied all day filled him with delight.

'That sounds an excellent idea,' he said. 'I think you would make a splendid teacher, Marcia.'

'Why, thank you, Charles,' she replied, smiling. 'Do hurry up with your dinner. There's spotted dick for pudding.'

OVER THE NEXT TWO WEEKS leading up to the public meeting, everyone opposed to the closure of the village school worked hard to draw the community's attention to the situation. Elisabeth wrote to all parents, enclosing a copy of Mr Nettles's letter and urging the recipients to write in protest to the Education Office, members of the Education Sub-committee and other influential people. Miss Brakespeare was industrious in making sure the shops, pubs and houses in the village displayed the large and colourful posters painted by the children, with 'SOS: Save Our School' emblazoned at the top. The vicar and the local Methodist minister raised the matter at their services and Mrs Pocock organised a petition. Local newspaper feature writers, always on the lookout for newsworthy items, were only too pleased to report the story.

MR PRESTON, the director of education, sat behind the large mahogany desk in his office, drumming his fingers and contemplating what to do about the large pile of strongly worded letters he had received, and the several critical newspaper articles concerned with the closure of Barton-in-the-Dale School that lay before him.

There was a tap at the door.

'Enter!' he shouted.

Mr Nettles appeared, smiling inanely. Mr Preston disliked the man, with his obsequious manner and irritatingly nasal voice.

'I think you could have handled this matter rather better, Mr Nettles,' he said. 'I have been inundated with letters and petitions from vicars and ministers, doctors and shopkeepers, governors and parents and every Tom, Dick and Harry in that wretched village. I've even had the local MP on the phone. Now we have the local newspapers up in arms, too. Whatever happened at the governors' meeting?'

'The trouble, Mr Preston,' the education officer whined, 'is that the governors were not at all receptive to the idea.'

'Well, I don't imagine that they would be delighted when they were told we are thinking about closing the school but I understood, from the memoranda you sent to me and the latest briefing, that there was likely to be very little opposition.'

'The thing is,' the education officer explained, 'the situation has rather changed at the school since it was first mooted that it be closed.'

'In what way?' asked Mr Preston.

'The school has improved quite dramatically with the arrival of the new head teacher,' the education officer told him. 'She's turned the school around, and some of the governors and a great many parents are now very keen to keep the school open.'

'I assume that she was aware it was an interim contract when she accepted the position?' asked the director of education.

'Well, no, she wasn't. We felt—that is, Councillor Smout and the chairman of governors—felt that if we advertised it as a temporary post, there would be few applicants.'

'Mr Nettles,' said the director of education, crossly, 'why did you not ask the present deputy head to take over in the interim?'

'We did consider that, but she was thought unsuitable. The inspectors' report was quite critical of her. Indeed, it singled her out for criticism. So we made no mention to the candidates for the headship of the possibility that the school might close when we advertised the position.'

'Something of an oversight, that, wasn't it; not to say unethical?'

'Well, it had only just been broached at the Education Sub-committee, and only Councillor Smout and the chairman were privy to this.'

'And you.'

'Yes, and myself. Councillor Smout was very insistent that we should not mention anything about a possible closure to any of the applicants and indeed to the other governors, apart that is, from the chairman.'

The director of education thought for a moment and stared out of the window. *Here's a pretty kettle of fish*, he thought. It sounded to him that it was too far down the road to turn back now. The school had been identified by the Education Sub-committee as the first to close and, as far as he was concerned, it should go ahead. He was not a man to bow to pressure groups. He would have to take charge.

'I've arranged a public meeting at the school for me to explain the situation and answer any questions,' explained Mr Nettles.

'When?' asked the director of education.

'Next Thursday,' came the reply.

'I shall go myself,' said the director of education. 'I do not want this to escalate. The national media will get in on the act if we are not careful.'

'Very well,' said the education officer.

'And in future, Mr Nettles, perhaps you might consult me on such matters as this, and also exercise a little more tact in your dealings with governors and head teachers.'

8

The school hall was packed for the public meeting. It seemed that everyone in the village and many from without were there. Councillor Smout had sent his apologies for his absence: a pressing engagement had arisen that necessitated his attendance. He had, of course, heard on the grapevine that the meeting was likely to be highly contentious and he, being the only one to vote for the closure of the school, knew he would be the most unpopular person there.

Elisabeth glanced at her watch and noticed that the time had very nearly arrived for the start of the meeting. She was disappointed to see that Dr Stirling had decided not to attend. She had thought, at the very least, that he would have come and lent his support, particularly since he had been so impassioned at the governors' meeting against the proposed closure. She also wondered why Les Stainthorpe had decided to stay away.

Mr Nettles and his superior were the last to arrive: one minute before the five o'clock start. Elisabeth had never met the director of education, but knew who he was immediately when she saw a suave-looking man in a dark suit and crisp, white shirt and silk tie walk through the door.

'This is Mrs Devine,' said Mr Nettles, ushering the director of education in the direction of the head teacher.

Mr Preston gave a most disarming smile and pressed Elisabeth's hand warmly. 'I am delighted to meet you, Mrs Devine,' he said. 'It is a great pity that we have to meet under these circumstances.' He then turned his attention to the major. 'I felt, Mr Chairman, that it would be appropriate if I came to the meeting myself.' He glanced at his expensive wristwatch. 'I think we are about ready to start, are we not?'

The chairman of governors mumbled a few words of introduction to a stony-faced hall of people and then retreated to the side, relieved to be out of the firing line.

'Good evening,' said the director of education. He stared down at the sea of grim faces before him. It did not deter him, so confident was he in his powers of persuasion. 'I am so pleased to see that so many of you have been able to make it today. I should like to say at the outset that it is important for me to hear what you have to say. This is a consultative meeting in which you will have the opportunity of asking questions and giving your views. But,' he continued, 'first of all, I need to explain what the Education Department's overall plan is for the future of the service. I wish to stress that nothing has been decided about the future of this school or any other in the authority. It is being considered, no more. It is a hard fact that the authority has to tighten its belt and make drastic savings, and one of the ways is to close some of the smaller and least viable establishments. It is very regrettable that we have to do this, but we do have to reduce our spending. The Education Sub-committee has identified a number of small schools, Barton-in-the-Dale being one, which we might consider closing.'

There were grumbles and inaudible comments from the assembly.

'Let me be perfectly clear about this, and repeat that nothing has been decided yet and that we are still looking at all options.'

There followed a series of testimonials. The Reverend Atticus stressed the positive changes that had taken place since the beginning of term, and pointed out how all in the village were massively supportive of the head teacher. Mrs Pocock and a number of other parents spoke of their satisfaction with the education provided.

The meeting proved to be less heated and noisy than Elisabeth had expected, thanks to the adept handling of his audience by the director of education. He had reiterated that no decision had been made, that he would consider all representations, and that he would look at other options.

The director of education thanked Elisabeth as she walked with him to the door. She placed a red folder in his hand. 'You might wish to read my plans for the development of the school,' she said, 'and the most recent report from Her Majesty's Inspector, who recently made a return visit.'

Mr Preston looked Elisabeth full in the face, not with a smile but with an intense gaze. 'Thank you,' he said. 'I shall read it with great interest.'

IT WAS EIGHT O'CLOCK when Dr Stirling knocked on the cottage door later that evening.

'Come in,' said Elisabeth.

'I thought I had better come and explain why I wasn't at the meeting,' he said. 'You might have heard already from Mr Stainthorpe what happened.'

'No,' replied Elisabeth. 'I've just got in myself and I haven't seen him. Come through.' She led her visitor into the small sitting room and gestured to a chair for him to sit down.

'I was called out on a rather grisly emergency,' Dr Stirling explained, sitting down and taking a deep breath. His face looked deathly pale.

'Would you like a drink?'

'A brandy would be good,' he said.

Elisabeth poured him a large brandy and sat opposite him. 'So, what happened?' she asked.

Dr Stirling took a sip and began to talk.

Fred Massey, having attached the sugar-beet cutter to his ancient tractor, had proceeded to feed the edible roots down the long funnel for them to be mashed for cattle feed. At the foot of the machine was an auger, a corkscrew-like rod that pulped the sugar beet, which frequently got stuck and required encouragement to go down the funnel. Mr Massey, rather than using a piece of wood as any sensible person would have done, had used his foot, which had descended into the machine to be pulverised along with the sugar beet. The engine had cut out, but the farmer had been trapped.

It was fortunate that Les Stainthorpe had been in hearing distance of the man's screams and was able to go to his assistance. The emergency services and Dr Stirling had been called, and the fire crew had cut the farmer out.

'And how is Mr Massey?' asked Elisabeth now.

'He's a very lucky man. If Mr Stainthorpe hadn't heard him shouting for help he could very well have bled to death. I think that he might lose part of his foot, but it could have been a whole lot worse.' He took another sip of brandy and said, 'Anyway, how did the meeting go?'

When he had heard Elisabeth's account of the meeting, Dr Stirling nodded. 'It sounds rather more optimistic.'

'I think they listened,' Elisabeth told him, 'but I would be surprised if the meeting meant that they will reconsider. The director of education was very plausible and charming and reassuring and all that, but I pride myself on being a pretty good judge of character on first meeting someone, and I think he's as slippery as an eel.'

'A good judge of character,' the doctor repeated. 'I'm a terrible judge of character—but you know that, anyway.' He thought for a moment, looking at the woman whom he had come to like and respect . . . and more. 'I wonder how you judged me at our first meeting?'

Elisabeth smiled. 'I sometimes get it wrong,' she replied.

'I think the fault was with me, to be honest,' he said. 'I'm not that good with words.'

'I thought you did very well when you took the sex education lesson.'

'Ah, well, I was on my own ground then,' he told her. His face suddenly became flushed. 'I didn't mean I'm an expert on sex, but on medical matters relating to sex . . . You know what I mean.'

Elisabeth suddenly threw back her head and covered her mouth, snorting and spluttering. 'I'm sorry,' she cried, weeping with laughter.

'Was it that funny?'

She nodded, still laughing uncontrollably.

He began laughing, too.

They were interrupted by a loud knocking at the cottage door.

It was Danny. He stood on the step, clearly upset.

'Whatever is it, Danny?' asked Elisabeth.

'It's . . . it's mi granddad,' the boy stammered. ' 'E's been taken badly. 'E's really poorly, miss.' He gripped Elisabeth's arm. 'Please, Mrs Devine, will you come and look at 'im and will you phone the doctor?'

'Dr Stirling's here,' she told the boy. 'Come along, we'll go and see your grandfather, and don't worry, I'm sure he'll be all right.'

LATER THAT EVENING, after Danny's grandfather had been taken to hospital and the boy was tucked up in her spare room, Elisabeth sat down with Dr Stirling. She rested her head on the back of her chair and sighed.

'What a day,' she said. 'I think it's me who needs the brandy now. Will Les be all right?' she asked.

'From what the registrar said at the hospital, Mr Stainthorpe is a very sick man. We'll know more when he's had the tests. I'll call in at the hospital tomorrow and see how he's getting on. He's as stubborn as a mule and not one to go to the doctor. I have a feeling he's known for some time that he's not well.'

'Poor Danny,' said Elisabeth. 'He'll be lost without him.'

'He'll be all right with you tonight?' asked Dr Stirling.

'He will. Tomorrow I'll contact Social Services and I guess they can arrange for him to be fostered for a time while his grandfather is in hospital. He must feel so lonely and afraid. He's lived with his grandfather all his life. They've never been apart.'

'He could stay with me and James for a time,' suggested Dr Stirling.

'Really? That would be so much better for him,' said Elisabeth.

'I'll see if it can be arranged,' replied the doctor. 'You have enough on your plate at the moment. I'm sure James would like to have him stay with us. Danny needs his friends now.'

Elisabeth looked at the good-natured, unaffected man in the crumpled suit and scuffed shoes who sat before her. 'Thank you,' she said. 'That's very kind of you.'

'It's the least I can do,' he replied, and she noticed for the first time how his eyes lit up when he smiled.

MRS SCRIMSHAW APPEARED at the classroom door the following morning.

'He's in the entrance,' she told Elisabeth.

'Who?'

'Major Double-Barrelled,' the secretary said, pulling a face. She lowered her voice so she was not overheard by the children. 'I don't know how he has the nerve to make an appearance after yesterday.'

'I'll come now.' Elisabeth turned to her class. 'I want you to get on with your work quietly while I am away. Is that clear?'

'Yes, miss,' chorused the class.

The chairman of governors stood waiting in the entrance, staring at the large plaque on the wall. He smiled rather sheepishly on seeing Elisabeth.

'Mrs Devine,' he said, extending a hand.

'It's good to see you, Major,' said Elisabeth cheerfully, shaking his hand. 'Have you read Mr Steel's new report?'

'Yes, I have. It shows a great deal of improvement.'

'So why should they wish to close such a successful school?' Elisabeth asked bluntly.

The major sighed. 'Mrs Devine,' he said, 'as was explained at the governors' meeting, there need to be some savage cuts and sadly some schools will have to close.'

'I rather expected, Major, that you, as the chairman of the governing body, would have given your whole-hearted support in opposing such a move. I have to say I was very disappointed that you chose not to.'

The major stroked his moustache. 'I am in a very difficult position,' he said. 'I, along with Councillor Smout who, incidentally, phoned me this morning to inform me that he wishes to resign from the governing body, am a nominee and a representative of the Education Authority, and I have to act in its best interests. Then, as chairman of governors, I have to be supportive of the school. I'm in a sort of no-man's-land, if you follow my drift. That is why I abstained from the vote, which, in retrospect, was the wrong decision.'

'So, what are you saying?' asked Elisabeth.

'I'm saying that, having thought over the matter, I should have supported the other governors and that now maybe I should, like Councillor Smout, resign as the chairman of the governing body. It was remiss of me not to support Dr Stirling's motion. I very much regret that.'

'If, from what you have said, Major,' Elisabeth told him, 'you are now going to support the other governors in opposing the closure, I think you should stay on as the chairman. I know I can work with you and I hope that you can work with me.'

The major's face brightened. 'Well, if you really think so—' he began.

'And I will draft a letter to the parents, with a copy to the Education Department, informing them that the head teacher, staff and all the governors are now unanimous in wanting Barton-in-the-Dale Parochial Primary School to remain open.'

IT WAS ARRANGED that Danny should stay with Dr Stirling. The social worker, having spoken to the boy's grandfather and interviewed the doctor, agreed that the boy could remain there for the time being.

Elisabeth saw a great change in Danny over the next few days. The bright-eyed, chatty boy became a retiring, uncommunicative, sad little figure who sat staring out of the window in class and could often be found crying when out of sight of the other children.

Danny had been with Elisabeth to the hospital the afternoon after the boy's grandfather had been admitted. The old man had sat propped up in bed, trying to appear cheerful, but he had looked pale and drawn and his eyes had lost the brightness Elisabeth had been used to seeing. It was clear to her that he was a very ill man.

The boy had buried his head in his grandfather's arms and wept.

'Hey, hey,' Mr Stainthorpe had said, patting his grandson's head gently. 'You're supposed to be cheering me up, young Danny. Come along and tell me what you've been up to.'

'When will you be comin' 'ome, Granddad?' the boy asked.

The old man's gaze met Elisabeth's. His face had looked furrowed and bleak. 'Oh, it's early days yet,' he had replied breathlessly. He changed the subject. 'I 'ear you stayed with Mrs Devine last night?'

The boy had sniffed and nodded.

'We are hoping—that is, Dr Stirling and myself—that Danny could stay at the doctor's for the time being, if that's agreeable to you, of course,' Elisabeth said.

'Well, if you do, I 'opes you'll be a good boy, Danny Stainthorpe, and not put t'doctor out.'

'He's a very good boy,' Elisabeth told the old man, her face soft with concern. 'He's never any trouble and he's a real credit to you. Don't you worry, we'll take very good care of him.'

'Thank you, Mrs Devine,' Mr Stainthorpe had said, his eyes filling with tears. 'I really appreciate that.'

IT WAS THE FOLLOWING WEEK that Les Stainthorpe had an unexpected visitor. Fred Massey was wheeled in and parked by the side of the bed.

''Ow are you then?' asked Les.

'How am I? Well, I've just had my foot nearly cut off so I'm not dancing for joy.'

'It could have been worse.'

'Aye, it could. Any road, I wanted to see you to thank you. I wouldn't be here now if you hadn't have helped—calling the emergency services and Doc Stirling—and stopping with me until they came. I appreciate that. I thought I was a goner and no mistake. Any road, I wanted to thank you.'

'You should 'ave been more careful.'

'Aye, I know. I'm sorry to see you in here, Les Stainthorpe, and I mean it. I didn't want to give you a heart attack.'

'It weren't an 'eart attack.'

'Well, whatever it were, I'm sorry you're here. I know we've had our differences over the years, but I want bygones to be bygones, and when you come out, I'll take you for a pint in the Blacksmith's Arms.'

'That'll be a first, Fred Massey, you buyin' somebody a pint.' The old man lay back on his pillow. He caught his breath.

There was silence until Massey asked, 'Is there anything you want?'

'Aye, there is,' said Les. 'I want you to shift them sheep of yours from Mrs Devine's paddock and stop usin' 'er track.'

An unaccustomed smile spread across Fred Massey's face. He chuckled and shook his head. 'Aye, I reckon I could do that.'

And the two old men, who had been enemies for years, shook hands.

'MISS, WILL YOU SPELL "GIRAFFE"?' asked Chardonnay. When she had started teaching the class, Elisabeth had asked the children to keep a weekly journal and write an entry in it each Monday morning. It had proved very successful. The children enjoyed describing what they had been doing over the week, and Elisabeth had learned a great deal about her pupils; their interests and their activities out of school.

Elisabeth wrote the word on the blackboard. 'And did you see one at a zoo?' she asked.

'See what, miss?'

'A giraffe.'

'I haven't seen any giraffes, miss.'

'Well, why do you want the word?' asked Elisabeth, intrigued.

'For my journal, miss.'

'Read out what you have written,' said the teacher.

The girl read out her entry: 'My mum said I could join the choir at St Christopher's. I asked her if giraffe to go to all the services.'

'I think you need three words,' said the teacher, smiling. '"Do you have".'

'Thanks, miss,' said Chardonnay. 'I always get my knickers in a twist when it comes to spellings.'

Elisabeth looked at her class. There were some real success stories. Chantelle had scored the winning goal against a rival football team the week before, and Chardonnay's solo performance with the choir at the Methodist chapel had gained her much praise. Ernest Pocock also seemed a very different boy from the truculent and uninterested pupil she had first met. His coming second in the County Art Competition, and the display of his paintings down the corridor, had made him something of a celebrity in the school.

After break, before the children settled down to work, Chardonnay waved a hand in the air and asked, 'Miss, is the school going to close?'

'Miss, that's what I've heard,' said Chantelle. 'Miss Sowerbutts told my mum in the post office.'

'They are thinking about it,' Elisabeth told her, 'but I don't intend to let that happen. You don't want the school to close, do you?'

The class loudly chorused, 'No, miss.'

The most poignant entry in the children's journals that week was from Danny. His account spoke of his grandfather's illness and how worried and frightened he felt: '*There is no one in the world like my granddad. He brought me up when my mum was killed and we do everything together. He doesn't shout at me and he's never hit me. I can tell him anything and he can tell me anything. If my granddad gets it wrong, he says so. He says an apology costs you nothing and it's not being weak to admit you don't always get things right or that you don't know something. Now he's in the hospital and I think he's really ill and I don't know what to do. I'm lost without him.*'

Later that morning, Elisabeth found Danny sitting with James in the hall, his lunch uneaten before him.

'You're very quiet these days, Danny,' said Elisabeth. She rested a hand on his arm. 'It's hard for you, isn't it?' she said. He nodded. 'I'm so sorry about your grandfather.'

The boy looked up and into her eyes. Perhaps he expected her to say what most adults would say—that things would turn out all right and that his grandfather would soon be home and life would return to normal. He knew in his heart that this would not be the case. 'I'm frightened, miss,' he said.

'I know,' she replied. 'It's a worrying time for you.'

'I really miss Granddad, Mrs Devine,' the boy told her, quietly.

'I know you do,' she said, patting his hand. 'After school we'll go to the hospital and see your granddad, shall we?'

'Yes, miss,' he replied. 'Thank you, miss.'

'Now, you eat your lunch.'

THEY FOUND Danny's grandfather in a side ward on his own. He was ashen-faced but raised a smile when he saw them.

'Now then,' he said, trying to sound cheerful. 'I thought you might be calling in to see me.'

Danny ran to the bed and gave his granddad a tight hug. He began to cry.

'Hey, lad, come on, what's all this?' asked Les gently. 'I wants cheerin' up and to 'ear what you've been up to! You run down to the shop and get me a newspaper and yourself some sweets. There's some small change in the drawer. Then I want all your news.'

When the boy had gone he asked Elisabeth to come and sit beside him. His face was gaunt and he breathed with difficulty.

'How are you, Les?' asked Elisabeth.

The old man shrugged. 'I think you've probably guessed, Mrs Devine,' he said, 'that t'future's not lookin' too bright for me.'

'Yes,' Elisabeth replied quietly. 'I'm so sorry.'

'Aye, well, it comes to all of us in t'end. The thing is, I'm not afeared o' dyin'. What does worry me is what'll 'appen to Danny. 'E's got no one in t'world, Mrs Devine. I reckon 'e'll end up bein' fostered out or put in a children's 'ome and I know it'll 'appen not suit t'lad.' He wiped his eyes. 'I want to ask you summat, Mrs Devine.'

'You don't need to ask me, Les,' Elisabeth told him, taking his leathery hand in hers. 'I'll make sure that Danny is well cared for. I shall be looking out for him all the time. You can be certain of that.'

The old man sighed and smiled. He resettled his head on the pillow. 'Thank you,' he said. 'Thank you.'

They sat there in silence for a while. 'I 'ave to tell 'im,' said the old man. 'I can't put it off. It'll be t'most difficult thing I've ever done in mi life but I 'ave to do it. I've never kept nowt from t'lad and he's allus telled me t'truth. I think it's best if I tell 'im today. Better sooner than later.'

When Danny returned, Elisabeth made an excuse and sat in the corridor outside, thinking about the dying man talking to his grandson.

DANNY WEPT all the way back to Dr Stirling's house and then ran up to his bedroom. James was about to follow him, but Elisabeth told him that she thought Danny would want to be alone for a while and to leave him for ten minutes before going up.

'His grandfather told him,' Elisabeth said quietly as she followed Dr Stirling into the sitting room.

He nodded. 'I guessed as much.' He moved a pile of papers from a chair. 'Do sit down,' he said.

'Poor Les,' said Elisabeth. 'His main worry is what will happen to Danny. I guess I need to inform Social Services so they can arrange things for when his grandfather . . .' Her voice tailed off.

'Yes, they will need to know,' agreed Dr Stirling. 'Of course, the boy can stay here until something is sorted out. I spoke to the specialist this morning and she thinks it's a matter of days rather than weeks.'

'Oh dear,' sighed Elisabeth. 'He'll be lost without him.'

Dr Stirling looked across at her. 'You've been very good,' he said. 'I can't imagine what they would have done without you.'

'It's what anyone would have done.'

'No, it's not,' he said. He was about to say something more, but stopped.

'Well, I had best be going,' Elisabeth told him. 'I'll take Danny along to the hospital tomorrow and drop him off later. Good night.'

'Good night, Elisabeth,' said Dr Stirling.

'THEY SAY HE'S NOT LONG for this world,' remarked Mrs Sloughthwaite in a matter-of-fact tone of voice.

The shopkeeper was in discussion with Mrs O'Connor, who had called in to the general store for the week's provisions.

'No,' agreed the housekeeper. 'I heard Dr Stirling on the phone to the hospital, and from what I can gather he won't last out the week, poor man. I feel sorry for young Danny. Not much of a Christmas to look forward to, has he, poor child?'

'I hear that Mrs Devine has been very good, taking the lad to the hospital,' said Mrs Sloughthwaite.

'To be sure, she has,' agreed the housekeeper. 'Every day she's been driving him there and back and she's been such a comfort for the boy. Sure she's a grand woman. It was a fine day when they appointed her to the school.'

'And I hear she's getting on well with Dr Stirling these days,' said Mrs Sloughthwaite determinedly.

'Who is?'

'Mrs Devine. I mean, from what Mrs Pocock told me,' continued Mrs Sloughthwaite, 'Dr Stirling was very much against her getting the job at the school. He took against her from the start for some reason. She said he was the only one at the governors' meeting who voted not to appoint her.'

'She had no business telling you that.'

'Then they had a difference of opinion about a number of things and he was going to take his son away. The next thing I hear, he's changed his mind, the lad's back at the school and they're getting on like a house on fire.' Mrs Sloughthwaite allowed her customer the time to reply, but when nothing was forthcoming she continued to probe. 'From what I've heard, Mrs Devine spends as much time at Dr Stirling's as she does at her own cottage. They seem to be on very good terms these days.'

Mrs O'Connor had learned to be very circumspect when talking to the shopkeeper on certain matters. 'You know Dr Stirling,' she replied nonchalantly. 'Sure, doesn't the man get on with everybody. I think I'll take a box of those Viennese chocolate biscuits. Dr Stirling has a sweet tooth.'

INCOMPREHENSION CREPT across Lady Helen Wadsworth's face.

'Close the school!' she exclaimed.

'That's their intention,' replied Elisabeth.

Her neighbour, who had been on holiday at the time of the public meeting, and who had only just learned from the font-of-all-knowledge at the village store of the plans to close the school, had hurried round to Elisabeth's cottage to hear first-hand of the proposals.

'It's quite out of the question!' she cried, her face decorated with fury. 'I've just got my grandfather's plaque back on the wall and they want to go and close the school! He built and endowed the village school for the welfare and education of the children, and there is not the slightest possibility of it closing!'

'I wish I had your confidence,' said Elisabeth, 'but they appear determined to go ahead. Whenever I phone the Education Office for an update, they are particularly evasive.'

Lady Helen gave a dismissive grunt. 'We'll see about that.'

LATER IN THE WEEK, Lady Wadsworth made her grand entrance at County Hall. She had booked an appointment to see the director of education and had dressed for the encounter in her brightest tweeds and heaviest brogues, and decorated herself with a variety of expensive-looking jewellery. Her lipstick was as thick and red as congealed blood.

As she was shown into his office, Mr Preston rose from his chair, came to the door to greet her and proffered her a hand.

'My dear Lady Wadsworth,' he began, with his polished smile.

'Don't "Lady Wadsworth" me, Mr Preston,' she retorted, waving away his hand and plonking herself down straight-backed in the nearest chair. 'I am extremely angry!' she exclaimed.

'I am assuming you are here to see me about Barton-in-the-Dale School,' said the director of education, retreating behind his desk and sitting down.

'You assume correctly,' Lady Wadsworth replied frostily. 'It is quite outrageous that you are contemplating closing the school that my grandfather founded and endowed.'

'I assure you, Lady Wadsworth,' replied the director of education, 'I very deeply regret having to go down this road, but the Education Department has to cut costs and—'

'Mr Preston,' Lady Wadsworth said, holding up a gloved hand, 'the school is at the very centre of village life. Furthermore, the new head teacher, Mrs Devine, is a most accomplished and hard-working woman. She has *transformed* the school since her arrival, and I do not use that word lightly. I find it amazing that you should appoint her and then decide to close the school.'

'I am merely an officer of the local authority, Lady Wadsworth,' he told her. 'It is the councillors on the Education Sub-committee who decide on the schools earmarked for closure. I just carry out their directives.'

'On your advice,' said his visitor sharply.

'I beg your pardon?'

'The councillors act on your advice, do they not? They are guided by you. It is you who recommends which schools should be closed and which should remain open. I assume that that is one of your functions.'

'I am not in favour of any school closing,' he replied evasively. 'But sometimes needs must.'

Lady Wadsworth curled a lip. 'Mr Preston, I need to point out a consideration of which you and the members of the council may not be aware. Should the school close, then the buildings and adjacent land revert to the Limebeck Estate. There is a codicil in the endowment document to that effect. So, if the councillors think they can sell the buildings and the land in the misguided belief that they can raise money, then they are very much mistaken.' She stood. 'I bid you good day, Mr Preston.'

At her departure, an angry director of education reached for his telephone. 'Tell Mr Nettles I wish to see him immediately!'

9

Elisabeth knew why Dr Stirling had called at the school that morning. He stood outside her classroom door looking tired and ill at ease.

'Excuse me for a moment, children,' she told her class. 'I have to pop out. Get on with your reading quietly, and best behaviour, please.'

She joined her visitor in the corridor. Dr Stirling rested a hand on her arm. She didn't need to be told.

'It's Danny's grandfather, isn't it?' she asked.

'Yes,' replied Dr Stirling, 'he died this morning.' Elisabeth gave a great heaving sigh. 'Are you all right?' he asked.

She looked through the small window in the classroom door at Danny, who was sitting by the window reading quietly. 'I suppose it falls to me to tell him,' she said softly.

'I think it would be best coming from you,' he said. 'I'll stay if you wish.'

'Thank you, I would appreciate that, but this is not the best time to tell him. Perhaps you could call back at lunchtime and we'll see him then.'

'You'll be much better at it than I,' he said. 'Having to tell someone that the person they love has died I find the most difficult part of being a doctor.'

'I'll tell him,' said Elisabeth. 'He knew that his grandfather had little time left, not that that makes it any easier. I promised his grandfather I would take care that Danny was well looked after, but I really don't know what will happen to the boy now. Since he has no family I suppose he'll end up in care. Anyhow, I'll let Social Services know.'

At lunchtime, Dr Stirling returned and joined Elisabeth and Danny in her classroom. The boy looked utterly wretched, for he knew why they had asked to see him.

'Danny,' said Elisabeth, a hollow feeling in her heart, 'I'm afraid I have some very sad news.' Danny began to cry. She put her hand round his shoulder and held him to her.

ELISABETH ARRIVED at Forest View the following Saturday afternoon. She found John at his favourite table by the window, rocking gently backwards and forwards and staring intently at a large coloured poster. When she sat next to him he held out his hand, which she grasped and squeezed.

'Oh, I see that you're in the mood to hold hands today, are you?' she said. 'I'm sorry I couldn't make it this morning. I had somewhere really important to go to. Mr Williams tells me you were a model pupil this week on the trip to see the Christmas lights at Clayton, and is really pleased with the way you've been this week.'

That morning she had been at Les Stainthorpe's funeral. The crematorium had been packed and the Reverend Atticus's homily had moved his congregation to tears.

'I reckon there will be snow before too long,' said Elisabeth now. 'Do you remember how you used to like the snow? I remember your face when you first saw those big flakes falling from the sky and how you loved to scoop them up when they had settled and watch them melt in your hands. We built a snowman, remember?' John, not looking at her, continued to rock. 'Work is as hectic as ever and I'm still waiting to see if the school has a future.' The boy stopped rocking and examined a tiny insect that scurried across the table. He touched it gently with his finger. 'I never imagined that this job was going to turn out like this,' continued Elisabeth. 'Apply for a post at a quiet country school in a picturesque little village, I thought, lovely scenery, lots of peace and quiet, no worries and no problems.' She sighed. 'Still,' she said, trying to sound cheerful, 'I'm able to come and see you as often as I want now, and that's the main thing.'

'Well, that is good to hear.'

Elisabeth turned to find Mr Williams standing in the doorway.

'I'm sorry, I couldn't help but eavesdrop. For what it's worth, I think you made the right decision. You know, I look forward to your visits as much as I hope John does.'

'I don't know what benefit there is for him,' said Elisabeth, 'with me rattling on out loud like this, but I should like to think he understands something of what I say and I find it therapeutic. He's the only one I can be really honest with and share all my hopes and fears and feelings.'

Mr Williams had liked this attractive, intelligent, good-humoured woman from their first meeting a few months ago, when she had brought her son to the school. 'I'm a good listener,' he said, 'and I promise not to interrupt or disagree with you. Actually, I wanted to have a word with you about something that has arisen. Could you call into my office on your way out?'

Later, Mr Williams explained his own worry. 'The head teachers of the special schools were called to a meeting with Mr Preston last week,' he told Elisabeth, 'and it looks likely that your school is not the only one to be threatened with closure. They have to make quite stringent cuts and it appears they want to shut one of the special schools. I have an idea that it might be this one.'

'But John's barely started here and settled in. I've never seen him so contented. It can't close!' cried Elisabeth angrily. 'It just can't!'

'I assure you that I shall fight until my last breath to resist any moves to close the school, but they are keen on integrating children with special needs into mainstream schools.'

'But John couldn't cope in a mainstream school!' she exclaimed.

'Nothing may come of it, of course,' Mr Williams reassured her, 'but if it does and I end up in the same boat as you, with a proposed closure on my hands, I would appreciate your support.'

'That goes without saying,' she replied.

'Thank you, I appreciate that,' said Mr Williams. 'And if you do want to talk anything through with me I should be delighted to listen. Perhaps I might take you out for a drink one evening?'

'That would be nice,' she replied smiling, but not really listening.

JAMES WAS WAITING outside the staff room the following Monday morning.

'Hello, James,' said Elisabeth. 'Did you want to see me?'

He nodded. 'Let's go into the entrance where it's quiet and we won't be disturbed. Then you can tell me what's on your mind.'

They sat on the small bench beneath the brass plaque. Elisabeth took a small notebook and a pencil from her handbag and gave them to the boy. This was the means by which the boy communicated with her in class.

The boy shook his head and passed the notebook and pencil back.

'Well, you know, James, I can't help you unless I know what it is that's making you unhappy.'

The boy, looking at his feet, thought for a moment. She could see him struggling to speak, twisting his small fingers and mouthing words. Then he took a deep breath and whispered, 'It's Danny.'

'Danny,' Elisabeth repeated. 'Are you worried about Danny?'

He nodded.

'I see. Well, I'm worried about Danny, too. He's had a very difficult time lately and I know how upset he is about his grandfather, but we are doing our very best for him and we'll see he is all right.'

The boy shook his head. He struggled to find the words. 'He doesn't want to leave,' he whispered, still looking down at his feet. He began to tremble. He raised his voice. 'He wants to stay here. He doesn't want to go away. I don't want him to go away.'

'James,' said Elisabeth. 'I don't want Danny to go away either, but he will need to be looked after and it may mean that he is going to go to a family that lives away from here.'

The boy looked up at her, then he gripped her arm. '*Please,*' he said.

AFTER SCHOOL, Elisabeth called at Dr Stirling's. Mrs O'Connor made them tea and, as she brought it into the sitting room, announced: 'Upstairs has all been cleaned, the ironing's done, the boys have been fed and your dinner's in the oven. Now I'm off.'

'Thank you, Mrs O'Connor,' the doctor said, pouring the tea.

'I have some good news,' Elisabeth told him.

'They're not going to close the school!' he exclaimed.

'No,' she replied. 'I'm afraid things have gone very quiet in that direction. It's about James. We had a conversation this morning.'

'He spoke to you!' He put down the cup with a clatter, causing the tea to spill over onto the saucer. 'Good gracious. Whatever did he say?'

'It was Danny, in effect, who prompted him to speak. James came to see me to tell me how unhappy Danny was about leaving the village and the school. I think he felt that speaking to me rather than writing it down as he usually does would have greater effect.'

'James had the same conversation with me yesterday,' replied Dr Stirling. 'I got to thinking, and this morning I got in touch with Social Services and asked if it was possible for me to become his foster carer initially but, if things work out, to adopt him.'

'Adopt him? You mean you would adopt him?' She was stunned. 'Michael, it's a very big step to take. Have you looked into exactly what adoption involves?'

'Of course I have. It might appear a spur-of-the-moment decision to you, but I have discussed things pretty thoroughly with Social Services. They thought it was an excellent idea. They usually like to place children with couples, of course, but they said it was hard to find homes for adolescent boys. To be honest, I'm really excited about having him here and I don't think I'll make too bad a father to him.'

'You'll make a great father to him and you know it.'

Dr Stirling gave a big smile. He ran his hand through his untidy hair. 'I know Mrs O'Connor will be pleased. She's been fussing around him like a mother hen since he arrived and moaning to me like a banshee about the "poor, wee orphaned child". I've not mentioned anything to Danny or to James yet, because there are a few formalities that have to be taken care of before it is agreed. They also need to speak to Danny. I meant to phone you to let you know I'll be going to the children's department at County Hall with Danny tomorrow to sort things out. So Danny won't be at school. Also, I think they might want a reference from you.'

'Of course,' said Elisabeth. She felt like reaching over and hugging him. *You're a good, good man, Michael Stirling*, she thought.

THE NEXT MORNING, Danny stood in the hall of Clumber Lodge looking clean and smart in a white shirt, tie, grey jumper and trousers, and polished shoes.

'Well now,' said Mrs O'Connor, brushing the boy's shoulder with a hand, 'don't you scrub up well?' She looked down at the sad face.

'Thank you for lookin' after me, Mrs O'Connor,' he said. He looked like someone on his way to his execution.

'It's been a pleasure,' she replied. 'And whatever it is you're worried about, sure, it may never happen.' She looked at Dr Stirling and winked.

'Will I need to pack mi things?' the boy asked.

'Not for the moment, darlin',' she said.

'Well, come along, young man,' said the doctor cheerfully. 'Let's be off.'

In the car Danny was very quiet. 'Will I meet t' people who are goin' to look after me today?' he asked finally.

'Maybe,' said Dr Stirling evasively. He smiled inwardly.

Miss Parsons, senior social worker, came out of her office to meet them. She was a handsome woman with bright eyes and light sandy hair tied back to reveal a finely structured face. 'Good morning, Dr Stirling,' she said, shaking his hand. She turned to the boy. 'Hello, Danny.'

'Hello, miss.'

'Dr Stirling, I would like to have a little chat with Danny on his own, so if you wouldn't mind waiting . . .? We won't be long.'

Danny followed the woman into her office and was introduced to her colleague, Mrs Talbot, a small, smiling woman with cropped white hair. The boy sat nervously on a hard wooden chair facing the desk, his hands locked beneath him. He bit his bottom lip.

'Now then, Danny,' said Miss Parsons, giving him a reassuring smile, 'don't look so frightened, I'm not going to eat you. We're just going to have a little chat.' She sat behind her desk. 'I was very sorry to hear about your grandfather. He sounded like a very special man.'

''E was,' Danny replied, a tremble in his voice.

'And I know how difficult it is for you at the moment, wondering what will happen to you and where you will go.'

Danny nodded.

'How are you getting along at Dr Stirling's?' she asked.

'OK, miss,' he replied in a small voice.

'Just OK?'

'Well, no. I really like it there.'

'What's the best thing about living at Dr Stirling's house?' she asked.

'Well, there's mi bes' friend James there, an' Mrs O'Connor.'

'She's the housekeeper.'

'Aye, she looks after Dr Stirling, cooks an' cleans an' that. She's really nice. Dr Stirling's really nice as well. And I can keep mi ferret in t'back garden.'

'And what about Dr Stirling?' asked Miss Talbot. 'How are you getting on with him?'

'I like 'im.'

'Let's get Dr Stirling to come and join us,' she said, rising from her chair. Dr Stirling came in and sat down next to Danny. 'Now, Danny, at the moment you are being fostered by Dr Stirling. Do you know what I mean by the word "fostering"? It means that someone looks after a child or young person until they can go back to their parents. In this case, it would have been your grandfather. Well, sadly you can't go back to your grandfather, so we have to make other arrangements.'

The boy's eyes were brimful of tears and his face became twisted in anxiety. His small body looked as loose and floppy as a puppet's. 'Where will I go?' he asked, his breath coming with difficulty.

The senior social worker reached across the desk and patted the boy's hand. 'Well now, Danny, Dr Stirling wants to continue to foster you,' Miss Parsons told him. 'And if it works out and you are happy there, he wants to adopt you. Do you know what that means?'

Danny sniffed and rubbed his eyes. He tried to speak but the words wouldn't come.

'Would you like to stay with me and James?' Dr Stirling asked him, resting his hand gently on the boy's shoulder.

'Stay wi' you?' Danny asked quietly. 'You mean, come an' live wi' you and James and not go anywhere else, not never?'

'Not never,' said the doctor. 'So what about it?

Danny looked at Dr Stirling for a moment. Then his small body shook and tears bubbled from his eyes.

'Good gracious,' said Dr Stirling, feeling tears welling up in his own eyes. 'I didn't think the thought of living with me and James would have this effect.'

'I'm just 'appy,' sobbed the boy.

'EXCUSE ME, MRS DEVINE.' Oscar had marched across the playground. 'I think you ought to know that there is a man in a car at the front of the school. He looks to me like a suspicious character and you can't be too careful these days.'

'Thank you, Oscar,' Elisabeth replied.

The man in the car was in the entrance hall when Elisabeth arrived back in the school, staring at the brass plaque on the wall. Tall and precise-looking, he was dressed in an expensive-looking light grey suit and silk tie and wore highly polished shoes.

'Mr Preston,' said Elisabeth.

'Good morning, Mrs Devine,' he said, putting on his professional smile. 'I trust it is not an inconvenient time for me to call.' He was perfectly courteous but his voice was slightly flat. 'The reason for my visit is to tell you that the decision to close this school has been deferred.'

'Deferred,' repeated Elisabeth.

'That is correct. The Education Sub-committee has, on my advice, decided to put on hold any closure plans with regard to Barton-in-the-Dale. I have examined the inspector's report and the various representations from those in the community and have recommended that the school remains open for the foreseeable future.'

'I have your assurance on that?' she asked.

He regarded her steadily. 'Of course,' he said, his eyes revealing nothing of the thoughts that lay behind them.

'Thank you,' Elisabeth said. 'Can I assume that the two teachers here will be offered permanent contracts?'

'Yes, of course.'

'And the desks will be replaced?'

'I shall ask Mr Nettles to see to it.'

'And we can have a library?'

'Mrs Devine,' said the director of education, holding up a hand. 'It will be considered all in good time. I shall leave it to you to inform your chairman of governors and you will, no doubt, wish to tell the staff and parents.' He paused. 'By the way, you might be aware that the post of head teacher has come up in the north of the county in a large, purpose-built school. It's an excellent salary. You might consider applying.'

'No, Mr Preston,' she told him. 'I am more than happy here.'

Mrs Stubbins was sitting in the teacher's chair in the classroom, her sullen-faced son standing next to her. She made a move to get up when Elisabeth entered.

'No, no, Mrs Stubbins, don't get up,' said Elisabeth.

'Thank you for seeing me, Mrs Devine,' said Mrs Stubbins obsequiously. Gone was all the anger and bluster Elisabeth had witnessed when the woman had come into the school the last time.

Elisabeth stood by the teacher's desk and looked down at her visitor, her hands clasped before her. 'What can I do for you, Mrs Stubbins?' she asked.

'The thing is, Mrs Devine, he never settled at Urebank. He was picked on by the other kids and by the teachers something dreadful. You was, wasn't you, Malcolm?'

'Yeah, I was,' grumbled the boy.

'I do recall you telling me that you felt that I picked on your son.'

'Well, no, not in the same way. You were much nicer about it.' She smoothed an eyebrow with a little finger. 'So I'd like Malcolm to come back here,' Mrs Stubbins said. 'He can start next Monday or after the Christmas holidays, if that's all right with you, Mrs Devine.'

'The thing is, Mrs Stubbins,' she was told, 'I am really not inclined to have Malcolm back. You were very critical of this school, refused to cooperate and you ignored my advice by sending Malcolm to Urebank. I don't feel it would be a good idea to move him again and I suggest that your son stays where he is.'

The woman's bottom lip began to tremble. 'He was excluded from Urebank and now they've expelled him. I know what I did was wrong and I'm sorry for what I said. I want him to come back here.'

'And what do you have to say, Malcolm?' Elisabeth asked the boy.

Malcolm jumped sharply, as if he had been jabbed with a cattle prod. 'Me?'

'Yes, you,' said Elisabeth. 'Do you want to come back here?'

'Yeah.'

'Pardon?' snapped Elisabeth.

'I mean, yes, miss, I do,' he mumbled.

Elisabeth thought for a moment. 'If I do have Malcolm back, it will be for a trial period to see how he behaves himself. I expect to receive your full support, Mrs Stubbins, and should Malcolm step out of line, I shall contact you immediately and ask you to take him home.'

Mrs Stubbins cheered up. 'That's very good of you, Mrs Devine,' she said. 'Does that mean he can come back?'

'Malcolm Stubbins,' said Elisabeth, turning to the boy, 'do you understand what I have said to your mother?'

'Yes, miss.'

'And you are going to be on your best behaviour if you return?'

'Yes, miss.'

'Say thank you to Mrs Devine,' said Mrs Stubbins, poking her son.

'Thank you, Mrs Devine,' he said unenthusiastically.

'That's settled then,' said Elisabeth. 'And we have a place on the football team, if you are interested.'

The boy suddenly came to life and his face lit up. 'In the team?' he cried.

'If you are interested.'

'You bet!' exclaimed the boy.

'I THINK YOU'RE A SAINT,' observed Mrs Scrimshaw as she watched Elisabeth pick up the receiver and dial the number for Urebank, 'having that ne'er-do-well back. I would have told that Mrs Stubbins where to get off.'

'I have an idea young Malcolm will be a changed boy when he returns,' Elisabeth told her. 'I think he's learned his lesson.'

'Robin Richardson, headmaster, speaking,' came a voice down the line.

'Good afternoon, Mr Richardson,' Elisabeth said pleasantly. 'This is Elisabeth Devine here, from Barton-in-the-Dale School.' There was a silence. 'Are you still there?'

'Yes, I am still here,' he replied coldly.

'I wanted to let you know that I have just seen Malcolm Stubbins and his mother. I understand he has now been expelled from Urebank and I am sure you will agree that it's not really a good idea to have a child sitting at home all day and missing his education. I have agreed to take the boy back.'

'As I explained to you, Mrs Devine,' he said haughtily, 'the boy was a most difficult and disruptive pupil. Had I known this, I should never have considered taking him.'

'So you will, no doubt, be pleased that he is returning here,' she said. There was another silence. 'Well, that is all I wanted to say.'

'One moment, Mrs Devine,' came the sharp voice down the line. 'I was intending to get in touch with you. I am actually extremely angry about the situation, as I gather several other parents are considering taking their children away from my school. It is just not acceptable.'

'I believe that most of the children involved were originally at this school,' Elisabeth told him, 'and that they live in this catchment area. So, technically, they should be here.'

'Some are,' he told her, 'but there are other parents who have been in touch whose children are not. These pupils live in *my* catchment area and should by rights go to *my* school.'

'Do you recall our conversation over the matter of parents choosing to send their children to another school, Mr Richardson?' asked Elisabeth.

'No, I can't say that I do,' he replied.

'Well, let me remind you: I think we agreed that one has to accept that parents have the right to send their children to another school if they so wish. As you said yourself, if they are insistent, then there is very little one can do about it.'

'I see. Well, I have to say, Mrs Devine, that I find your attitude at the very least surprising, and at most unprincipled,' he said angrily, 'and I shall be contacting the Education Office over this matter.'

Elisabeth remained calm and courteous. 'Well, that, of course, is up to you, Mr Richardson,' she said. 'Good afternoon.'

'That's telling him,' said Mrs Scrimshaw, smiling gleefully.

'WE'RE JUST GIVIN' your garden a last tidy-up before winter sets in, aren't we, James?' said Danny.

His friend nodded.

It was Saturday morning and Elisabeth was off to see her son at Forest View as usual. She was dressed in a smart camel-hair coat and green woollen scarf and matching gloves, as the November days were cold. She smiled with pleasure at seeing the two boys so obviously happy.

'Thank you, Danny,' she replied. Elisabeth had turned to go when James spoke. It was a quiet, hesitant voice but she heard him clearly enough. 'Are you going to see your son, Mrs Devine?' he asked.

Elisabeth's heart missed a beat. This was the first time she had heard the boy speak since he had been to see her about Danny.

'Yes, I am,' she replied, trying to conceal her surprise.

The boy stared at her with wide eyes and a serious expression. 'You have a son at Forest View,' he said. 'My father told me. He visits the school.'

'I din't know you 'ad a son, Mrs Devine,' said Danny, in a loud and cheerful voice.

'Yes, I have a son. His name's John and he's about your age. He has special needs. I go to see him every Saturday.'

'My father said he doesn't speak,' said James shyly.

'No, he doesn't, and sadly, he probably never will.'

'I'm sorry about that, Mrs Devine,' he said. There was a genuine concern in his voice.

'Fancy you 'avin' a son, miss,' said Danny, putting his hands on his hips. 'I was only sayin' to James last week that you'd make a super mam.'

Elisabeth smiled at the boy with his floppy fringe of dark blond hair and bright brown eyes. It was good to see him so happy.

'You're a little charmer, Danny Stainthorpe,' she said. 'When you grow up, you'll have all the girls running after you if you go flattering them like that.'

The boy screwed up his face. 'I don't want any lasses runnin' after me,' he said. 'I'm 'appy as I am wi' mi ferret. You know where you are wi' ferrets. There's them two lasses at t'school who won't leave me be. Everywhere I go there's that Chardonnay, and t'other 'un, Chantelle, is allus sending me notes. They're drivin' me barmy.'

'Danny Stainthorpe!' came a loud voice from the track down the side of the cottage.

'Hey up, miss,' said Danny, tilting his head to one side, 'it's Mester Massey. I wonder what 'e's after.'

'Danny Stainthorpe!' shouted the man again. 'I wants a word with you.' The boy ambled over to the gate. 'Now then, young fella-me-lad, I hear you've got a ferret. Well, is this any good to you?' He pointed down to a fancy-looking cage. 'Do you want it?'

'Yes, please,' said Danny. 'Thanks very much, Mester Massey.'

'And, if you've a mind, you can come up to the farm. I've a few jobs wants doing. Paid work, mind you. I don't want owt for nowt.' The old man wiped his nose on the back of his hand. 'He were a grand man, was your granddad. I can't say as how we always saw eye to eye, but he was a grand man.' He waved at Elisabeth. 'Now then, Mrs Devine. I was glad to hear that the school's stopping open,' he shouted. 'You'll be pleased to know I'm here to move the sheep from your paddock.'

James followed Elisabeth as she headed for the cottage. She stopped. 'Is there something else you wanted to say, James?' she asked.

The boy nodded. He touched her hand and looked up into her eyes. 'Thank you,' he said.

10

The Reverend Atticus sat at his desk in his study that afternoon. His half-finished sermon had been put aside and he was in a thoughtful mood. The theme of his homily was self-interest and the unwillingness of some people to see the other's point of view. He felt a twinge of guilt as he thought of his wife and her desire to move to the city: something he had refused to contemplate. With hindsight, he felt he had failed in his obligation to his wife. *It was selfish of me*, he thought, *to deny Marcia the life she craved.*

Then, as if in answer to a prayer, came a telephone call from the bishop. He was told that his name had been put forward as the most suitable candidate for the position of archdeacon.

'My lord,' the Reverend Atticus replied, 'I am, of course, deeply honoured that you should deem me suitable—'

'Now, don't go turning this down, Charles,' the bishop interrupted sharply. 'I won't hear of it. We need someone of your calibre, so I want you to give the matter some serious thought, and to talk it over with your wife.'

'My lord,' the vicar replied, 'I don't need to give it any serious thought. I should be honoured to accept.'

'Splendid,' said the bishop, rather taken aback at the speed of the vicar's acceptance. 'I shall be in touch. Oh, by the way, on the matter of the school closing: I had a word with the right people.'

'We are all very grateful, my lord,' said the Reverend Atticus.

The sermon can wait, the vicar told himself. He needed to tell his wife the good news.

Marcia Atticus was arranging some flowers when he entered the drawing room. She looked in a particularly good mood and was humming to herself.

'Oh, there you are, Charles,' she said brightly. 'I think these will be the last of the roses. Sermon finished?'

'Not quite,' her husband replied. 'My dear, I wanted to have a word with you, if I might,' he said.

'Before you do, let me tell you my good news. I have just received a letter from St John's College informing me that I have been accepted to do teacher training. Isn't that wonderful?'

'Congratulations,' said the vicar, bending to peck at her cheek.

'I'm really quite excited about starting,' she trilled, 'and I must go into the city on Monday to get the books on the reading list. It's all worked out so well. You know, you were quite right, Charles; going into the village school each week has given me a new lease of life. I have felt useful and valued.' She linked her arm through his. 'I know I go on about you being more ambitious and assertive, but I have come to realise that I have been rather selfish.'

'No, no, not at all, my dear,' began the vicar. 'In fact—'

She placed a finger over his lips. 'Yes, Charles, I have,' she said determinedly. 'I now realise that being a country parson is your vocation and it is what you are so good at. I know how very well regarded and respected you are in this community and that you would be very unhappy with all the politicking and social gatherings at Cathedral Close. So, in future, I won't go on about you not becoming a dean or an archdeacon or a bishop.'

'Thank you, Marcia,' said the prospective Archdeacon of Clayton, with a wan smile.

'Now, you wanted to speak to me about something?'

ELISABETH WAS LEAVING Forest View after visiting John when the head teacher approached.

'I was hoping to catch you before you left,' Mr Williams said. 'I wanted you to be one of the first to know. I had a telephone call from the Education Office yesterday and we are safe, thank goodness.'

Elisabeth sighed, 'What a relief.'

'And I hear you have a reprieve, too?'

'That's right. Mr Preston came to see me personally. Any decision on the future of Barton-in-the-Dale has been put on the back burner.'

'Perhaps . . .' started Mr Williams, 'er . . . perhaps you might like to take me up on that offer of a drink—as a way of celebrating our two pieces of good news. Perhaps this evening?'

It seemed churlish of Elisabeth to refuse. 'Well, yes,' she replied.

Mr Williams smiled widely. 'Excellent. Shall we say seven thirty? What about the Royal Oak at Gartside?'

'That would be fine,' said Elisabeth. He was a pleasant enough man: easy to talk to and good company. *What harm can there be*, thought Elisabeth, *in having a drink with a colleague?*

ELIZABETH ARRIVED at the pub to find David Williams waiting for her at a corner table in the lounge.

'Good evening, Elisabeth,' he said, rising to his feet. 'What can I get you?'

'Just an orange juice, please,' she said.

'How do, Mrs Devine,' came a loud voice from the public bar. She looked up to see the weather-reddened face of Fred Massey. He waved.

'Hello,' she called back, then sighed. He was heading in her direction.

'Out on the town, I see,' he said.

She gave a small, pained smile. It was just her luck that Fred Massey of all people should be there. It would be round the village now like wildfire.

Mr Williams returned with the drinks.

'How do,' said Fred, eyeing the man up and down.

Elisabeth decided not to introduce her companion, but Fred Massey was determined to discover as much as he could.

'I'm a neighbour of Mrs Devine's,' he explained, smiling and revealing a set of yellow teeth. 'Fred Massey's the name. I have a farm in Barton.'

'Williams. David Williams.'

'And might I ask what do you do for a living, Mr Williams?' asked Fred.

'I'm a head teacher,' he replied, surprised at the man's bluntness.

'Well, we've got here the best head teacher in Yorkshire, bar none,' said Fred Massey, nodding in Elisabeth's direction. 'I'm pleased to meet you. 'Course when I was at school, head teachers—'

'It is good to see you, Mr Massey,' interrupted Elisabeth. 'I'll let you get back to your pint.' She gave him a tight smile of dismissal.

'Aye, well, good to see you too, Mrs Devine, and to have met you, Mr Williams. I hope you both have a very pleasant evening.' With a smile on his face and a flash of the yellow teeth, he departed.

ELISABETH DEVINE sat in an easy chair by the window in her sitting room later that night. The evening with David Williams had not gone well. Unable to stand being under observation by Fred Massey, she had invited the head teacher back to her cottage for a coffee. He had sat on the sofa, his hands cradling the cup, and had suddenly launched into a most unexpected and deeply embarrassing speech.

'I'm so glad I have this opportunity of speaking to you,' he had said.

Elisabeth had felt her stomach lurch. She had prayed he was not going to say what she imagined he would.

'Although we have only known each other for a short time, Elisabeth,' he had continued, 'it's as if I have always known you. When my wife and I divorced, I went through a very bad patch. I've felt pretty lonely these last few years, as I guess you have, too.'

'David,' Elisabeth had interrupted, 'please don't say any more. You know how much I appreciate all you do for my son. I think a lot of you and—'

'I guess there's going to be a "but" at the end of this sentence,' he had said sadly.

'I'm afraid there is,' Elisabeth had said. 'I would not wish to give you any expectation. I am afraid I don't share the feelings you may have for me.'

'I see.'

'We can remain friends?' she had asked.

'But of course.' He had looked down, deflated, and, replacing the cup on the table, had stood up. 'Well, I should be going. I shall see you as usual at Forest View next week.' He had reached forward and shaken her hand. 'Good night, Elisabeth.'

'Good night, David,' she had said, and when the door had closed behind him, she had taken a deep, deep breath.

'DO YOU KNOW who the mystery man is then?' asked Mrs Pocock when she called into the village shop the following day.

'Mystery man?' the shopkeeper repeated.

'Him who was out with the new head teacher last night. I've just seen Edith Widowson on her way to chapel and she said Mrs Devine was out with a man last night. Fred Massey told her.'

Mrs Sloughthwaite settled herself more comfortably against the counter. 'All I know is that Fred Massey come in here for his Sunday paper this morning and told me he'd seen Mrs Devine sitting at a corner table in the Royal Oak at Gartside with this man, and very cosy they looked too.'

'Do you think it was the husband?'

'No, this chap's name is Williams. He's a Welshman. He's a head teacher by all accounts,' confided the shopkeeper. 'About the same age as her and friendly enough, according to Fred Massey.'

'Do you think he's married?'

'Couldn't say, but it struck me as a bit furtive, them meeting in the corner of a pub in another village.'

The topic of their conversation walked through the door.

'So as I was saying, Mrs Pocock,' said Mrs Sloughthwaite, deftly changing the subject, 'the Venetian chocolate biscuits are on special offer this week. Oh, hello, Mrs Devine.'

'Good morning, Mrs Sloughthwaite,' said Elisabeth. 'Good morning, Mrs Pocock.'

''Morning, Mrs Devine,' said the other customer.

'I've just called in for my order,' said Elisabeth.

'It's all ready for you,' said Mrs Sloughthwaite, making no effort to get it.

'And to thank you for all the support you have given over the proposal to close the school,' added Elisabeth. She turned to Mrs Pocock. 'The governors, of course, have been splendid. Thank you for all your sterling work.'

Mrs Pocock gave a self-satisfied smile, and nodded appreciatively.

The shopkeeper began her interrogation: 'It was good of Dr Stirling to take on young Danny, wasn't it?' she asked.

'It was,' replied Elisabeth.

'He's a very compassionate man is Dr Stirling.'

'Yes, he is.'

'It was tragic when his wife was killed.'

'Yes,' agreed Elisabeth, 'it must have been very hard for him.'

'Time can be a great healer,' added Mrs Pocock.

'It's a pity that he's never got married again,' remarked Mrs Sloughthwaite. 'From what his housekeeper tells me, Clumber Lodge needs a woman's touch about the place.'

'Well, I'll be on my way,' said Elisabeth. 'If I could have my order.'

Mrs Sloughthwaite disappeared behind the counter and reappeared with a box of groceries. 'Goodbye, Mrs Devine,' she said. 'Have a nice day.'

MICHAEL STIRLING STOOD at the window in the sitting room, looking out across the garden. The boys had done a grand job pruning, weeding and tidying. *I should be happy*, he told himself. The battle to keep the village school had been won, young Danny had found a home, and his once quiet and distant son was coming out of his shell and looked much happier of late. But he was miserable. The medical journal he had been reading had been set aside. The person most on his mind was Elisabeth Devine.

Mrs O'Connor appeared at the door.

'Will you be wanting a cup of tea, Doctor?' she asked.

'Yes, thank you, Mrs O'Connor, that would be very welcome,' he replied.

'I'll put the kettle on.' The housekeeper paused at the door and heard him sigh. 'You look miles away. Is there something wrong?'

He sighed again. 'Not at all, everything is fine. Danny seems to have settled here very well, all things considering.'

'It was very good of you to take the lad in, Dr Stirling,' said the housekeeper. 'You're a decent man, so you are.'

He smiled. 'I don't know about that, Mrs O'Connor,' he said. 'I'll let you get the tea.'

The housekeeper was not yet ready to depart, for she had things to say. 'I saw Mrs Devine today,' she said casually.

'Oh, yes?' replied Dr Stirling, equally casually.

'She's a lovely woman, to be sure. From what Mrs Sloughthwaite says, she's got a gentleman friend.'

Dr Stirling took a sudden interest. 'Has she?'

'Another head teacher. A Welshman. Quite the dapper man, so I heard.' Having sown the seed, she said, 'I'll get the tea,' and left the room.

Michael Stirling felt even more wretched. So Elisabeth had an admirer in David Williams.

Mrs O'Connor returned with a large, brown-glazed teapot, a china cup and saucer and a jug upon a tray. She poured the strong black liquid. 'Why don't you give her a ring?' she asked.

'I'm sorry?'

'Mrs Devine,' said the housekeeper. 'Why don't you give her a ring?'

'And why would I want to do that, Mrs O'Connor?' he asked.

'A fire in the heart makes smoke in the head, as my owld Grandmother Mullarkey used to say.'

'I'm sorry,' said Dr Stirling, 'I don't quite know what your Grandmother Mullarkey meant by that.'

Mrs O'Connor gave a small smile. 'Oh, I think you do, Dr Stirling,' she said, leaving the room. 'I think you do.'

As ELISABETH SAT in her sitting room thinking over the events of the evening before, the telephone rang shrilly.

'Hello. It's Michael Stirling here.' His mouth was dry. 'I'm not disturbing you, am I?'

'No, not at all,' replied Elisabeth. Her heart missed a beat. 'You must be a mind-reader. I was just thinking about you.'

'Thinking about me?'

'Yes.'

He took a breath. 'I was wondering if you might . . . if you are free, that is . . . that you might consider letting me . . . coming out . . . that is . . . with me . . . for a meal.' He sounded nervous and embarrassed.

'I'd love to,' Elisabeth replied quickly. 'When have you in mind?'

'Tonight?'

'Tonight will be fine,' Elisabeth told him, her heart beating like a drum in her chest. 'I shall look forward to that. Where shall I meet you?'

'Oh,' he said, trying to catch his breath. 'I'll collect you at about seven.'

'Right,' she said.

'Right,' he replied, 'I'll see you then.' He put down the receiver and flopped back in his chair.

'IT'S VERY GOOD of you to look after the boys for the evening,' Dr Stirling told Mrs O'Connor later.

'It's a pleasure,' she replied. 'Are you going anywhere nice?'

'Frederico's, the Italian place in Limebeck.'

'With anyone special, or shouldn't I ask?' She gave a knowing smile.

'Yes, Mrs O'Connor, I am going out with someone very special.'

'Well, do give Mrs Devine my best wishes, won't you.'

'And how do you know it's Mrs Devine?' he asked.

'Oh, come along, Dr Stirling, I do have eyes in my head. I've seen the way you look at her.'

'Do you think she—'

'Feels the same about you?' Mrs O'Connor finished the sentence. 'Of course she does. I've seen the way she looks at you as well.'

The two boys appeared at the door.

'Where are you going?' asked James.

'Just out for a meal,' replied his father. 'I shan't be long.'

'Can we come?' James asked.

'No, not tonight,' said his father, smiling and ruffling the boy's hair.

'You've got your new suit on,' said James, frowning. 'And you're wearing aftershave. I can smell it. Who are you meeting?'

'All these questions,' said Dr Stirling, colouring a little. 'I'm just meeting someone for a quiet meal, that's all.'

The two boys looked at each other and Danny whispered in his friend's ear. They both giggled. Then Danny nudged James and winked at him before turning to the doctor.

'Give Mrs Devine our best wishes, won't you, Dr Stirling,' he said, a great smile filling his face.

It was the last day of term at Barton-in-the-Dale School. Ernest had painted a large, smiling Santa riding on a golden sleigh pulled by prancing reindeers and laden with presents. Mrs Atticus had supervised the transformation of the entrance hall, where the children had stuck different shapes of coloured tissue paper on the windows to give it the effect of stained glass. Lady Wadsworth had donated a large fir tree from the Limebeck Estate, which had pride of place at the front of the hall.

The air was icy fresh that day. Great flakes of snow began to fall in the morning and soon walls, paths, trees, road signs, letterboxes and rooftops were shrouded in white. The whole area around the small school was a vast silent sea. Rays of watery winter sunlight pierced the high feathery clouds, making the snow glow a golden pink. The scene was magical.

Of course, the school caretaker was not in the best of moods as he surveyed the scene from the school office.

'I hate this weather,' he moaned to Mrs Scrimshaw. 'I've been out since dawn chucking sand and salt all over the path and shovelling mountains of snow. And my back's giving—'

'Happy Christmas, Mr Gribbon,' interrupted the school secretary.

'Beg pardon?'

'What a lovely time of year it is,' she said, maintaining her overly upbeat demeanour. 'A time of peace and goodwill, when everyone sounds happy and full of good cheer and enters into the spirit of the season.'

'What?' he asked, missing the sarcasm in her voice.

She changed her tone. 'For goodness' sake cheer up. You're like the Prophet of Doom. It's the end of term and it's nearly Christmas. You can rest your back over the next two weeks.'

A small voice could be heard in the corridor.

'Excuse me, Mr Gribbon, I'm sorry to interrupt your conversation but may I have a quick word with Mrs Scrimshaw?'

The caretaker breathed through his nose like a horse and moved away from the door to let a small boy into the office.

'Oh, it's you, Oscar,' said the school secretary, looking up.

'As you know, I am the narrator at the nativity play and I just wanted to make sure that the carol sheets are ready to put on the chairs. If they are, I could do that at lunchtime if you like.'

'Everything is in hand, Oscar,' said Mrs Scrimshaw.

'Shouldn't you be in your classroom doing some work instead of wandering around the school?' asked the caretaker.

'Miss Brakespeare said I could pop out,' the boy told him.

'Well, you want to pop back in,' said Mr Gribbon. 'Go on, off you go.'

'Actually, I'm glad I've seen you, Mr Gribbon,' said Oscar, ignoring the instruction. 'I've noticed that the path leading up to the school entrance is covered in snow again.'

'Have you indeed?' The caretaker stiffened.

'I nearly slipped and I could have hurt myself,' continued the boy. 'I think it would be a really good idea, Mr Gribbon, if you did a bit of shovelling.'

The caretaker opened his mouth to reply but the boy smiled widely and said, 'Well, I must press on.'

IT SEEMED THAT the whole of Barton-in-the-Dale had turned out for the nativity play, for the school hall was packed that afternoon. Mrs Sloughthwaite, Mrs Widowson and Mrs O'Connor arrived early and commandeered seats in the centre of the front row; the shopkeeper had closed the village store early so she could attend. The Reverend Atticus, the prospective Archdeacon of Clayton, arrived smiling widely and joined the three women on the front row. He was soon followed by Lady Wadsworth and the major.

'It's so good to have the nativity play performed again in the school,' remarked the cleric. 'As I recall, Miss Sowerbutts was not that keen when I broached the matter with her.'

'She was not very keen on anything that involved any extra work,' observed Lady Wadsworth.

There wasn't an empty seat in the hall. When Dr Stirling finally arrived he had to stand at the back of the hall with Elisabeth. Mr Tomlinson took up his position at the piano, and the school choir filed in and stood beneath the small stage. Silence descended. From behind the makeshift curtains could be heard the excited whispering of the children. Oscar, dressed in a dark blue blazer with a red bow tie, slipped through the curtains. He cleared his throat and then, tilting his coloured glasses slightly on the bridge of his nose, announced: 'We would like to welcome you all to our nativity play.'

As Oscar narrated, the pupils re-enacted the age-old story without mishap until the Angel of the Lord nearly missed her cue: 'I said!' Oscar shouted, 'Then the Angel of the Lord appeared again.' Chardonnay, her halo askew and one of her cardboard wings bent, rushed onto the stage.

Then, as the angels and shepherds left the scene, the Three Kings arrived: Melchior was in flashing trainers; Chantelle clutched a blue shampoo bottle to represent her gift of myrrh; and the third king was James. He was dressed in a velvet cloak made from a faded red curtain that still had the hooks in, and he was sporting a cardboard crown that covered half his face.

Elisabeth turned to see the expression on Dr Stirling's face. He moved his head forward as he looked intently at his son. James shuffled nervously to the centre of the stage and stared round, wide-eyed and frightened. There was a long silence. The children in the choir turned their heads and the other two kings looked at each other and shrugged. Oscar, feeling he should take charge of the situation, moved forward and was about to speak, but he stopped when he saw James hold up a hand. The boy closed his eyes for a moment, then he took a deep breath and in a loud and confident voice he spoke: 'I am Balthazar, king of the west, and I bring frankincense.'

When he had delivered his lines, a flash of pure pleasure lit up his face. With his eyes shining, he looked over the heads of the audience to where his father was standing and smiled a triumphant smile.

THAT EVENING, a white moon lit up the landscape, luminous and still. Cars growled along the road through the soft snow, throwing cascades of slush in their wake. No wind blew, no birds called, no animal moved and, save for the sporadic, soft thud of snow falling from the branches of the towering oak tree which stood before the school, all was silent.

Elisabeth sat at her desk in the classroom. Everyone had gone home and the school was silent. There was a stillness, as if life itself had been suspended. A figure appeared at the door.

'I saw the light on,' said Dr Stirling.

'I wasn't quite ready to go home yet,' Elisabeth told him. 'I'm just having a quiet few moments, unwinding before tidying things up.'

'It was a wonderful nativity,' he said, coming over to the desk. She could smell the aftershave on his collar.

'Yes, it was. I was very proud of the children.' She looked down at her hands, almost afraid of meeting his eyes. 'And what about James? Didn't he do well?'

'He did,' replied the doctor. 'I was very proud of him.' A silence fell. 'Elisabeth,' he hesitated, searching for the right words to use. 'I . . . I . . . wanted to say . . .'

Then, seeing a sprig of mistletoe on the desk, he picked it up.

'One of the girls who has a bit of a crush on young Danny brought it into school,' Elisabeth told him. She chuckled. 'She chased the poor lad round the yard but he was having none of it. Then in the classroom she—'

'Happy Christmas, Elisabeth,' interrupted Dr Stirling, leaning forward and holding the mistletoe above her head.

She looked at him for a moment, then smiled. 'Happy Christmas, Michael,' she said, lifting up her face.

gervase **phinn**

You have quite an unusual Christian name for a Yorkshire lad.

Yes, I was born to parents with a sense of humour. My mum liked the name and thought it was a bit posh, but we certainly weren't. I went to school in Rotherham and did my O levels then went to Trinity and All Saints College in Leeds to do my English degree and then onto Sheffield University to do a Masters. I have stayed in Yorkshire all my life.

What do you love most about Yorkshire?

I love the industrial side and the rich dales and moors, but also all the incredible abbeys and churches.

Do you have a favourite place?

Roche Abbey near Rotherham, it's a hidden gem. It's in a little valley near Maltby, a mining town. It is the most wonderful remains of an abbey in a beautiful green hollow surrounded by thick woodlands and nobody ever goes there. In winter it is magnificent, you could be in another world.

And are you a lover of Yorkshire pudding?

Yes, of course. As a starter though. But my favourite Yorkshire dish is rhubarb. Yorkshire is famous for the rhubarb triangle, so I like rhubarb crumble—especially my wife's granny's recipe.

You were a teacher for fourteen years before becoming a schools' inspector. Was it a relief to get out of the classroom?

No, it wasn't a relief. I always missed the classroom very much. I only moved jobs because I was invited to apply for the post of English adviser for the local authority of Rotherham. Throughout my career, whether I was working as an adviser or an inspector, I always grasped any opportunity to do some teaching—either in primary and infant schools, or at adult night classes.

What do you think makes a good teacher?

Good teachers are immensely enthusiastic, and their enthusiasm is infectious. Stanley Matthews, the footballer, once said, 'Wrinkles appear on the face with age, but cynicism and lack of enthusiasm wrinkle the soul.' I think teachers have to be enthusiastic, hard-working, caring, dedicated, sensitive and supportive. They must have the interests of every child, however damaged or repellent, at heart. It's a very demanding job, but I do think it is a most important role in society because you can actually transform a child for good or for ill.

How did you get started as a writer?

I had a wonderful, inspirational, gentle teacher, Miss Wainwright, who taught me to love books and reading. My mother, too, loved books and read to me every evening, and we'd talk about the stories and characters. I then went on to read English at Leeds University. Like any person studying English, I'd always wanted to write a book, and my great ambition was to be the author of a Penguin paperback. Which has come about! And what I've done over the years is what many writers do: I've written things down about people and places. They're often insignificant little trifles, but I've always kept a writer's notebook.

And how did your Dales series of books come to be published?

The charities Childline and NSPCC were opening a big new Childline office in Leeds and I was asked to do an after-dinner speech. Esther Rantzen came along and heard me talk, and later invited me onto her television show. I was on it three times in all, and my future editor at Penguin, Jenny Dereham, happened to see the programme and rang up to ask if I'd like to show her some examples of my work. It all went from there.

How different did you find writing fiction to nonfiction?

Not a great deal, to be frank. You still have to engage the reader with your characters, and include poignant pieces as well as amusing anecdotes. Fiction does, however, offer greater scope because you're inventing the characters and you can take them in any direction you wish. By taking a step back, you can sympathise with them more. It's the only occasion where I have actually wept at my own writing.

Who is your favourite character in *The Little Village School*?

Surprisingly, not the main character, the delightful Mrs Devine of the red shoes with silver heels. It is the owner of the village store, Mrs Sloughthwaite. She knows everybody's business in the village and everything that goes on. I really enjoyed writing about her.

Can you describe a typical day in the life of Gervase Phinn?

No. Every day is different. I have just returned from visiting schools and lecturing in Northern Ireland, tomorrow I am working in an infant school, reading stories and poems, the day after I am speaking at a charity event. Next week I am presenting prizes at a Speech Day, speaking at a literary lunch, giving an after-dinner address, visiting two more schools and appearing on stage as part of my theatre tour. I fit the writing in when I can.

Do you have a favourite saying?

I think my favourite saying is one that I came across in a little Catholic school in the Midlands and it was: 'In this school we learn to love and we love to learn.'

BURIED
SECRETS

Joseph Finder

It's happening again.

The nightmare.

A few years ago teenager Alexa Marcus was abducted in a parking lot and driven around for a few hours before being released.

It was intended as a warning to her father, Marshall Marcus, one of the richest men in Boston.

But now it's happening again, and Alexa is terrified the kidnappers are not just sending a warning . . . that this time their intentions are far more deadly.

1

If this is what a prison is like, Alexa Marcus thought, I could totally live here. Like, for ever. She and Taylor Armstrong, her best friend, were standing in line to get into the hottest bar in Boston. The bar was called Slammer, and it was in a luxury hotel that used to be a jail. They'd kept the bars in the windows and the central rotunda ringed with catwalks, that whole cell-block effect.

'I'm loving the smoky eye,' Taylor said, studying Alexa's eye make-up. 'See? It looks amazing on you!'

'It took me, like, an hour,' Alexa said. The fake eyelashes, the black gel eyeliner and charcoal eye shadow—she was sure she looked like a hooker who'd been beat up by her pimp.

'Takes me, like, *thirty seconds*,' Taylor said. 'Now look at you—you're this totally hot babe instead of a suburban prepster.'

'I'm *so* not suburban,' Alexa protested. 'Dad lives in Manchester.' She'd almost said, '*I* live in Manchester,' but she no longer thought of the great rambling house she grew up in as her home, not since Dad had married that gold-digger Belinda.

'Yeah, OK,' Taylor said. Alexa caught her tone. Taylor had grown up in a town house on Beacon Hill—her dad was a United States senator—and considered herself urban and therefore cooler than anyone else. Plus, the last three years she'd been in rehab, attending the Marston-Lee-Academy, the tough-love boarding school the senator had sent her to get cleaned up.

'Oh, God,' Alexa murmured as the line drew closer to the bouncer.

'Just relax, OK, *Lucia*?' Taylor said.

'Lucia . . .' Alexa began, and then she remembered that Lucia was the name on her fake ID. Actually, it was a real ID, just not hers—she was 17, and Taylor had just turned 18, and the drinking age was 21. Taylor had bought Alexa's fake ID from an older girl.

'Just look the bouncer in the eye and be casual,' Taylor said. 'You're totally fine.'

Taylor was right, of course.

The bouncer didn't even ask to see their IDs. When they entered the hotel lobby, Alexa followed Taylor to the old-fashioned elevator. Taylor got in. Alexa hesitated, slipped in, shuddered—God, she hated elevators!—and just as the accordion gate was knifing closed, she blurted out, 'I'll take the stairs.'

They met up on the fourth floor and managed to snag a couple of big cushy chairs. A waitress in a halter top took their order: a couple of Ketel One vodka sodas.

Models in black leather shorts and vests were parading around like it was a catwalk. An MIT frat boy tried to hit on Alexa and Taylor, but Taylor blew the guy off: 'Yeah, I'll give you a call—next time I need tutoring in, like, differential calculus.'

Alexa felt Taylor's eyes on her.

'Hey, what's wrong, kid? You've been acting all depressed since you got here.'

'I'm fine.' Alexa shook her head. 'Dad's just being all weird.'

'Nothing new about that.'

'But, like, he's all paranoid all of a sudden. He had these surveillance cameras put in, all around the house.'

'Well, he is the richest guy in Boston. Or one of the richest.'

'I know, but it's not his normal control-freak mode, you know? It's more like he's scared something's going to happen.'

'Try living with a father who's a United States senator.'

'May I join you?' A male voice.

Alexa looked up, saw a guy standing there. Not one of the frat boys, though. *Definitely* not. He had dark hair and brown eyes, a day's growth of beard. Black shirt with white pinstripes, narrow waist, broad shoulders. He was totally a babe.

Alexa smiled, blushed, and looked at Taylor.

'Do we know you?' Taylor said.

'Not yet,' the guy said, flashing a dazzling smile. Late twenties, early thirties, maybe? He had some kind of Spanish accent.

'There's only two chairs,' Taylor said.

He said something to a couple seated next to them, slid a vacant chair over. Extended a hand to shake Taylor's, then Alexa's.

'I'm Lorenzo,' he said.

THE BATHROOM had Molton Brown hand soap and real towels. Alexa re-applied her lip gloss while Taylor touched up her eyes.

'He's totally into you,' Taylor said.

'What are you talking about?'

'Like you don't know it.'

'How old do you think he is?'

'I don't know, thirties? Go for it,' Taylor said. 'It's totally cool.'

WHEN THEY FINALLY SUCCEEDED in elbowing their way back to their chairs, Alexa half expected Lorenzo to be gone.

But he was still there, sipping his vodka. Alexa reached for her second drink—a Peartini, at Lorenzo's suggestion—and was surprised it was half gone. Man, she thought, I am truly wasted.

'If you kids'll excuse me,' Taylor said, 'I need to get going.'

'Taylor!' Alexa said.

'Why?' said Lorenzo. 'Please, stay.'

'Can't,' Taylor said. 'My dad's waiting up for me.' With a conspiratorial sparkle in her eye, Taylor gave a little wave and disappeared into the crowd.

Lorenzo moved to Taylor's chair, next to Alexa's. 'Tell me about you, Lucia. How come I never see you here before?'

For a moment she forgot who 'Lucia' was.

NOW SHE WAS DEFINITELY DRUNK. She felt like she was floating above the clouds, smiling like an idiot, while Lorenzo was saying something to her. The room swam. Her mouth was dry. She reached for her glass of San Pellegrino, knocked it over. Smiled sheepishly. Lorenzo reached over and dropped his napkin over the puddle to blot it up.

She said, 'I think I need to go home.'

'I take you,' Lorenzo said.

He tossed a bunch of twenties on the table, stood. She tried to stand, but it felt like her knees were hinged and the hinges didn't work. He took her hand, his other hand round her waist, half lifted her up.

'My car . . .'

'You shouldn't drive,' he said. 'I drive you home. You can get your car back tomorrow. Come, Lucia.' He steered her through the crowd. People were staring at her, the lights streaky rainbow and glittery, like being underwater and looking up at the sky.

NOW SHE FELT the pleasant coolness of the late-night air on her face. Traffic noise, the bleat of car horns, the sound smearing by.

She was lying down on the back seat of a strange car, her cheek pressed against the cold, hard, cracked leather. The car smelled like stale cigarette smoke and beer. A Porsche, she was pretty sure, but old and filthy inside. Not what she'd have imagined Lorenzo driving.

Do you know how to get there? she tried to say, but the words came out slurred. She wondered: how did he know where to go?

A FEW MINUTES LATER she heard the car door open and close. The engine had been shut off. When she opened her eyes, she noticed it was dark. No streetlights. No traffic sounds, either. Her sluggish brain registered a faint, distant alarm.

The door opened, and the light came on, illuminating a man's face. Shaved head, piercing blue eyes, sharp jaw, unshaven.

'Come with me, please,' the new man said.

SHE AWOKE in the back seat of a big new SUV.

She looked at the back of the driver's head. He had shaved black hair. On the back of his neck, a strange tattoo crawled up from beneath his sweatshirt. Her first thought was, Angry eyes. A bird?

'What happened to Lorenzo?' she tried to say, but she wasn't sure what came out.

'Just stretch out and have yourself a nice rest, Alexa,' the man said. He had an accent, too, but harsher, more guttural.

That sounded like a good idea. She felt herself drifting off, but then her heart started to race: he knew her real name.

2

'Here's the thing,' the short guy said. 'I always like to know who I'm doing business with.'

I nodded, smiled.

Philip Curtis, as he called himself, was an inch or two above five feet, bald, and wore enormous black-framed glasses. The Patek Philippe watch on his wrist had to be sixty years old. It said inherited money and had been passed down, probably from his dad.

'I checked you out.' His brow arched. 'Did the whole due-diligence thing. Seems you've got an unusual background. Went to Yale but never graduated. Did a couple of summer internships at McKinsey, huh?'

'I was young. I didn't know any better.'

His smile was reptilian. But a small reptile. A gecko, maybe. 'The part I don't get is, you dropped out of Yale to join the army. What was *that* all about? Guys like us don't do that.'

'Go to Yale?'

He shook his head, annoyed. 'You know, I thought the name Heller sounded familiar. Your dad's Victor Heller, right?'

I shrugged as if to say, You got me.

'Your father was a true legend.'

'Is,' I said. 'He's doing twentysome years in prison.' My father, Victor Heller, the so-called Dark Prince of Wall Street, was serving a twenty-eight-year sentence for securities fraud.

'I was always a big admirer of your dad's. He was a real pioneer. Then again, I bet some potential clients, they hear you're Victor Heller's son, they're gonna think twice about hiring you. But not me. Way I figure it, that means you're probably not going to be too finicky about all the fussy legal stuff. Know what I'm saying?'

'Gotcha,' I said. I found myself looking out of the window. I liked the view. You could see right down High Street to the ocean.

I'd moved to Boston from Washington a few months ago and was lucky to find an office in an old building in the financial district, a rehabbed nineteenth-century lead-pipe factory. From the outside it looked like a Victorian poorhouse straight out of Dickens. But on the inside, with its bare brick walls, exposed ductwork and factory-floor open spaces, you couldn't forget it was a place where they actually used to make stuff. And I liked that. The other tenants were consulting firms, an accounting firm and several small real-estate offices. On the first floor was the showroom for Derderian Fine Oriental Rugs. My office had belonged to some high-flying dot-com that had gone bust and broken their lease, so I caught a break on the price.

'So you say someone on your board of directors is leaking derogatory information about your company,' I said, turning round slowly, 'and you want us to—how'd you put it?—"plug the leak". Meaning you want their phones tapped and emails accessed.'

'Hey,' he said, winking. 'I'd never tell you how to do your job.'

'Of course. Obviously, you know that what you're asking me to do is basically illegal.'

Just then my phone buzzed—an internal line—and I picked it up. 'Yeah?'

'OK, you were right.' The smoky voice of my forensic data tech, Dorothy Duval. 'His name isn't Philip Curtis.'

'Of course,' I said.

'Don't rub it in.'

'Not at all,' I said. 'It's a teachable moment. You should know by now not to question me.'

'Yeah, yeah. Well, I'm stuck. If you have any ideas, just IM me and I'll check them out.'

'Thanks,' I said, and I hung up.

The man who wasn't Philip Curtis had a strong Chicago accent. Wherever he lived now, he was raised in Chicago. He had a rich dad: the hand-me-down Patek Philippe confirmed that.

I had a vague recollection of an item I'd seen on BizWire about troubles in a family-held business in Chicago. 'Will you excuse me for just one more minute?' I said. 'I have to put out a fire.' Then I typed out an instant message and sent it to Dorothy.

The answer came back less than a minute later: a *Wall Street Journal* article. I skimmed it, and I knew I'd guessed right.

I leaned back in my chair. 'So here's the problem,' I said. 'I'm not interested in your business.'

Stunned, he looked at me. 'What did you just say?'

'If you'd really done your homework, you'd know that I do intelligence work for private clients. I'm not a private investigator, I don't tap phones, and I don't do divorces. And I'm not a family therapist. This is clearly a family squabble, Sam.'

'I told you my name is—'

'Don't even bother,' I said wearily. 'Your family troubles aren't exactly a secret. You were supposed to take over Daddy's company until he heard you were talking to the private-equity guys about taking Richter private and cashing out.'

His father, Jacob Richter, had gone from owning a parking lot in Chicago to creating a company valued at ten billion dollars.

'So Dad gets pissed off,' I went on, 'and appoints Big Sis CEO and heir apparent instead of you. But since you know all of Dad's dirty laundry, you figure you'll get him on tape offering kickbacks and bribes and you'll be able to blackmail your way back in.'

Sam Richter's face had gone purple. 'Who did you talk to?'

'Nobody. Just did the whole due-diligence thing. I always like to know who I'm doing business with. And I really don't like being lied to.'

Richter lurched to his feet. 'You know, for a guy whose father's in prison for fraud, you sure are acting all high and mighty.'

'You've got a point,' I conceded. 'Mind showing yourself out?' Behind him Dorothy was standing, arms folded.

'Victor Heller was . . . the *scum of the earth!*' he sputtered.

'Is,' I corrected him.

'YOU DON'T TAP PHONES,' Dorothy said, moving into my office.

I smiled, shrugged. 'I always forget you listen in.' Our standard arrangement was for her to monitor all client meetings via the IP video camera built into the monitor on my desk.

'You *hire* guys to do it.'

'Exactly.'

'What the *hell* was that all about?' she snapped.

Dorothy and I had worked together at Stoddard Associates in DC before I moved to Boston and stole her away. She knew digital forensics inside and out. More important, no one was as stubborn as Dorothy. She simply did not give up. She loved telling me off and showing me up and proving me wrong, and I enjoyed that. You did not want to mess with her. And there was no one more loyal.

'You heard me. I don't like liars.'

'Get over it. We need the business.'

'I appreciate your concern,' I said, 'but you don't need to worry about the firm's cash flow. Your salary's guaranteed.'

Dorothy was a striking woman, with mocha skin, liquid brown eyes and an incandescent smile. She always dressed elegantly, and she wore her hair extremely short.

'I think we need to have regular update meetings like we used to do at Stoddard. I want to go over the Garrison case,' she said.

'I need coffee first. And not that swill that Jillian makes.'

Jillian Alperin, our receptionist and office manager, was a strict vegan and a 'green' fanatic. The coffee she ordered for the office comprised organic fair-trade beans grown by a small co-op of indigenous peasant farmers in Chiapas, Mexico. It would probably have been rejected by a death-row inmate.

'Well, aren't you fussy,' Dorothy said.

The phone rang—the muted internal ring. Jillian's voice came over the intercom: 'A Marshall Marcus for you.'

'*The* Marshall Marcus?' Dorothy said. 'As in the richest guy in Boston? You turn this one down, and I'm gonna whip your butt.'

'Probably personal.' I picked up. 'Marshall. Long time.'

'Nick,' he said. 'I need your help. Alexa's gone.'

MARSHALL MARCUS LIVED on the North Shore, about a forty-minute drive from Boston, in the quaint town of Manchester-by-the-Sea. His house was enormous and handsome, a rambling shingle-and-stone residence perched on a promontory above the jagged coastline. Marcus lived there with his fourth wife, Belinda. His only child, a daughter named Alexa, was away at boarding school, would soon be away at college, and—from what she'd once told me about her home life—wasn't likely to be around much after that.

Marshall Marcus had grown up poor in Mattapan, in the old Jewish working-class enclave. He had learned to play blackjack as a kid and figured out pretty early that the house always has an advantage, so he started coming up with all sorts of card-counting schemes. He got a full scholarship to MIT, where he taught himself Fortran on those big old IBM 704 mainframes. He came up with a clever way to use the computers to improve his odds at blackjack.

The story went that one weekend he won ten thousand bucks in Reno. He opened a brokerage account and was a millionaire by the time he graduated, having devised some complicated investment formula. Eventually he perfected this proprietary algorithm and started a hedge fund and became a billionaire many times over.

My mother, Frankie, who was his personal assistant for years, tried to explain it to me, but I didn't get it. All I needed to know about Marshall was that he was good to my mother when things were bad.

After my father disappeared—Dad had been tipped off that he was about to be arrested, and he chose to go fugitive instead—we had no money, no house, nothing. We had to move in with my grandmother, Mom's mother, in Malden, outside of Boston. Mom, desperate for money, took a job as an office manager to Marshall, who was a friend of my father's. She ended up working for him for years, and he always treated her well.

Despite the fact that he'd been a friend of my father's, I liked him. He was gregarious and affectionate and funny, a man of large appetites—he loved food, wine, cigars and women, all to excess.

Almost everything about Marcus's house was the same as the last time I'd visited: the Har-Tru tennis court, the Olympic-sized swimming pool. The only thing new was a guard booth. A drop-arm beam barricade blocked the narrow roadway. A guard came out of the booth and asked my name, even asked to see my driver's licence. This surprised me. Marcus, despite his enormous wealth, had never lived like a prisoner. Something had obviously changed.

Once the guard had let me through, I parked in front of the house, crossed the broad porch, and rang the bell. A minute or so later the door opened and Marshall Marcus came out, his arms extended.

'Nickeleh!' he said, his customary term of endearment for me. He engulfed me in a bear hug. When I last saw him, he was mostly bald on top and wore his grey hair down to his shirt collar. Now he was colouring it brown, and the hair on the top of his head had magically grown back.

I couldn't tell if it was a toupee or very good implants. He was wearing a blue robe over pyjamas, and he looked exhausted.

He released me, then leaned back to examine my face. 'Look at you. You keep getting more and more handsome! I bet you gotta beat off the girls with a stick.' He put a pudgy arm round me. 'Thank you for coming, Nickeleh, my friend. Thank you.'

'Of course,' I said.

'This new?' he said, jerking his head towards my car.

'I've had it for a while.'

I drive a Land Rover Defender 110, which is boxy and Jeep-like and virtually indestructible. Not a very comfortable ride, and pretty noisy inside when you exceed thirty miles an hour. But it's the best car I've ever owned.

'Love it. *Love it.* I drove one around the Serengeti once on safari. Annelise and Alexa and me . . .' His smile disappeared abruptly, his face drooping as if worn out by the effort of keeping up the façade. 'Ahhh, Nick,' he whispered, 'I'm scared out of my mind.'

WE SAT IN A BIG L-shaped eat-in kitchen/sitting room, in comfortable chairs covered in slouchy off-white slipcovers.

'Last night she drove down to Boston.'

'When was this? What time did she leave the house?'

'Early evening, I think. I was on my way back from work. She was gone by the time I got home.'

'What was she doing in Boston?'

He heaved a long sigh. 'Oh, you know—she's always partying.'

'She drove herself? Or did she get a ride with a friend?'

'She drove. Loves to drive.'

'Was she meeting friends, or was this a date? Or what?'

'Meeting a friend, I think. Alexa's not dating. Not yet, anyway.'

I wondered how much Alexa told her father about her social life. Not much, I suspected. 'Did she say where she was going?'

'She just told Belinda she was meeting someone.' Marcus shook his head, then put a hand over his eyes.

After a few seconds, I asked softly, 'Where's Belinda?'

'She's upstairs lying down,' Marcus said. 'She's just sick about it. She didn't sleep all night. She's a wreck. She blames herself.'

'For what?'

'For letting Alexa go out, not asking enough questions—I don't know. It's not easy being the stepmother. Any time she tries to, you know, lay down the law, Alexa bites her head off. She cares about Alexa like she was her own. She really does. She loves that girl.'

I nodded. Then I said, 'Obviously, you tried her cell.'

'A million times.'

'Do you have reason to believe something happened to her?'

'Of *course* something happened to her. She wouldn't just run off without telling anybody!'

'Marshall,' I said, 'I can't blame you for being scared. But don't forget, she does have a track record for acting up.'

'That's all behind her,' he said. 'She's a good kid now.'

'Maybe,' I said. 'But maybe not.'

SOME YEARS BACK, as a kid, Alexa had been abducted in the Chestnut Hill Mall parking lot, right in front of her mother, Annelise, Marcus's third wife.

She hadn't been harmed. She'd been driven around and, a few hours later, dropped off at another parking lot. She insisted she hadn't been sexually assaulted; they hadn't even spoken to her.

So the whole thing remained a mystery. Marcus was known to be rich; maybe it had been an aborted kidnapping-for-ransom attempt. That was my assumption, anyway. Then her mother, Annelise, left, telling Marcus she couldn't bear to live with him anymore. Maybe that was precipitated by her daughter's kidnapping, her realisation of how vulnerable she was, married to a rich man like Marcus.

Who knows what the real reason was. She died of breast cancer last year, so she wasn't around to ask. But Alexa was never the same after that. She got even more rebellious—smoking at school, breaking curfew, doing whatever she could to get into trouble.

So one day, a few months after it happened, my mother called me—I was working in Washington at the Defense Department at the time—and asked me to drive up to New Hampshire and have a talk with Alexa at Exeter.

She wasn't easy to talk to, but since I was Frankie Heller's son, and she loved my mom, and I wasn't her dad, eventually I broke through. She still hadn't metabolised the terror of the abduction. I told her that was normal and that I'd worry about her if she hadn't been so deeply frightened by that day. I said it was great she was being so defiant. She looked at me with disbelief, then suspicion.

I said I was serious. Defiance was great. That was how you learn to resist. I told her that fear was a tremendously useful instinct, because it's a warning signal. We have to listen to it, use it. I even gave her a book about 'the gift of fear', though I doubt she read it.

Whenever I came to Boston and she was home from school, we'd make a point of getting together. And even, after a while, talking.

But she continued doing stuff that she knew would get her into trouble—smoking, drinking, whatever—and Marcus had to send her to some kind of reform school for a year. It might have been the trauma of the abduction. It might have been a reaction to her mother's running off. Or maybe it was just being a teenager.

'What's with all the security?' I asked.

Marcus paused. 'Times have changed. More crazies out there. I have more money.'

'Have you received any threats?'

'Threats? No. But I'm not going to wait.'

'I just want to know if you had any specific warning—a break-in, what-ever—anything that inspired you to tighten your security.'

'I made him do it,' a female voice said.

Belinda Marcus had entered the kitchen. She was a tall, slender blonde, beautiful. Maybe forty. She was all in white: white ankle-slit trousers, a white silk top with a low neckline. She was barefoot. Her toenails were painted coral.

'I thought it was absolutely *mad* that Marshall didn't have any guards. A man who's worth as much as Marshall Marcus? As prominent as he is? And after what happened to Alexa?'

'They were out *shopping*, Belinda. That coulda happened even if we'd had an armed battalion surrounding the house.'

'You haven't introduced me to Mr Heller,' Belinda said. She approached, offered me her hand. Her fingernails were painted coral, too. She had the vacant beauty of your classic trophy-wife bimbo, and she spoke with a sugary Georgia accent.

I stood up. 'Nick,' I said. All I knew about her was what I'd heard from my mother. Belinda Jackson Marcus had been a flight attendant with Delta and had met Marcus in the bar at the Ritz-Carlton in Atlanta.

'Pardon my manners,' Marcus said. 'Is she not a gorgeous creature?' A wide smile—he'd had his teeth capped, too. That and the new hair. Marcus had never been vain, so I assumed he'd done all this work out of insecurity at having a wife so much younger and so beautiful. Or maybe she'd been pushing him to renovate.

Belinda said, 'How about I fix y'all some coffee?'

'Sure.'

She glided over to the long black soapstone-topped island and clicked on an electric kettle. 'I'm not really much for making coffee,' she said, 'but we have instant. It's quite good, actually.'

'You know, I've changed my mind,' I said. 'I've had too much coffee this morning already.'

Belinda turned round suddenly. 'Nick, you have to find her.'

She was freshly made up, I noticed. She didn't look like she'd been up all night. Unlike her husband, she looked refreshed. I knew enough to know that you didn't roll out of bed looking like that.

'Did Alexa tell you who she was meeting?' I asked.

'I didn't—She doesn't exactly tell me everything.'

'She didn't tell you what time she'd be back?'

'Well, I assumed by midnight, maybe a little later, but you know, she doesn't take it too well when I ask her that sort of thing.'

'Have you called the police?' I said.

'Of course not,' Marcus said.

'Of course *not*?' I said.

Belinda said, 'The police aren't going to do anything. They'll come and take a report and tell us to wait until twenty-four hours is up, and then it's just gonna be file-and-forget.'

'She's under eighteen,' I said. 'They take missing-teenager cases pretty seriously. I suggest you call them right now.'

'Nick,' Marcus said, 'I need *you* to look for her.'

'Have you called any of the hospitals?' I said.

The two exchanged an anxious look before Belinda replied, 'If anything had happened to her, we'd have heard by now, right?'

'Not necessarily,' I said. 'Let's start there. Just to rule that out. I want her cellphone number. Maybe my tech person can locate her that way. And I want you to call the police. OK?'

Marcus shrugged. 'They won't do *bupkes*, but if you insist.'

None of the hospitals between Manchester and Boston had admitted anyone fitting Alexa's description, which didn't seem to give Marcus and his wife the sense of relief you might expect.

Instead, it seemed that the two of them were holding back something important, something dire. I think that gut instinct was the reason I took Marcus's request seriously. Something was very wrong here. It was a bad feeling, and it only got worse.

Call it the gift of fear.

3

Alexa stirred and shifted in her bed.

Knife stabs of pain pierced the backs of her eyeballs. It felt like someone was pounding an ice pick into her skull.

Where was she? *She couldn't see anything.*

The darkness was absolute. She wondered whether she'd gone blind. Maybe she was dreaming. It didn't feel like a dream, though. She remembered drinking at Slammer with Taylor. Everything else was blurry. She had no recollection of how she'd got home, how she'd ended up in her bed with the shades drawn.

She inhaled a strange, musty odour. Unfamiliar. *Was* she at home? It didn't smell like her room in Manchester. Had she crashed at someone's house? Not Taylor's, she didn't think. Her sheets were always too crisp, and the house smelled like lemon furniture polish.

She knew only that she was sleeping on top of a bed. No sheets covering her. They must have slid off. Her hands were at her side. She fluttered her fingers, feeling for the hem of a sheet, and the back of her hand brushed against something smooth yet solid. She felt a satiny material over something hard, like the slatted wooden safety rails on the sides of a bunk bed.

She still couldn't see anything. She could feel the soft yielding mattress below her and felt the pyjamas on her legs, which didn't feel like the sweatpants she usually wore to bed. She was wearing something different. Like hospital scrubs? Was she in a hospital? Had she got hurt, maybe been in an accident?

The ice pick was driving deeper into her brain, and she just wanted to roll over and put a pillow over her head. She raised her knees to flip over—and her knees hit something hard.

Startled, she lifted her head, and her forehead collided with something hard, too. Both hands flew outwards, striking hard walls. Fingers skittering up the sides and then the top, satin-covered walls barely three inches from her lips.

Even before her brain was able to make sense of it, some animal instinct within her realised, with a dread that crept over her and turned her numb and ice cold: she was in a box.

She started breathing fast. She *had* to be in a nightmare—the worst nightmare she'd ever had. Trapped in a box. Like a . . .

Satin lining. Walls of wood, maybe steel. Like being in a coffin.

That light-headed feeling that accompanied the hardness in her stomach and the coldness throughout her body, which she always felt before she passed out. And she was gone.

BY THE TIME I got back into the Defender and headed towards Boston, it was after noon. I couldn't shake the feeling that Marcus really did have a serious reason to fear that something had happened to his daughter. Not just something he wasn't telling me, but something he'd actually anticipated. In other words, not an accident.

Maybe it was nothing more than a fight between Alexa and her stepmother, which ended with Alexa making a threat—*I'm leaving, and I'm never coming back!*—and then taking off.

Though it didn't really make sense that Marcus would withhold that sort of thing from me. It wasn't like Marcus to be discreet. This was a guy who happily discussed his constipation and how Viagra had improved his sex life.

I was about to call Dorothy and ask her how we might be able to locate Alexa's phone, when my BlackBerry rang. It was Jillian.

'Your son's here,' she said. 'He says you two were supposed to have lunch?' In the background I could here cacophonous music playing.

'Whoops. Right. He's my nephew. Not my son.' I'd promised Gabe I'd take him to lunch, but I'd forgotten. 'Tell him I'll be there soon. And could you put me through to Dorothy?'

GABE HELLER WAS my brother Roger's stepson. He was sixteen, a very smart kid but definitely a misfit. He had hardly any friends at the private boys' school he attended in Washington. He dressed all in black. Recently he'd even started dyeing his hair black, too.

Roger, my estranged brother, was a jerk, not to put too fine a point on it. He was also, like our father, in prison. Gabe, luckily, was genetically unrelated to his stepfather or he'd probably be in juvie. I seemed to be the only adult he could talk to.

Gabe was spending the summer at my mother's condo in Newton. He was taking art classes in a summer programme for high-school students at the Museum School. He loved his nana and wanted to get away from his mother, Lauren.

But I think the main reason he wanted to be in Boston was that it gave him an excuse to see me, though he'd never admit it.

He was sitting at my desk chair, drawing in his sketchpad. Gabe was a scarily talented comic-book artist.

'Working on your comic book?' I said as I entered.

'It's a graphic novel,' he said stiffly. 'And hey, thanks for remembering our lunch.' He was wearing a black hoodie, zipped up.

'Sorry about that, Gabe. How's the summer going for you?'

'Boring.'

For Gabe, that was a rave. 'Wanna grab some lunch?' I said.

'I'm only about to pass out from hunger.'

I noticed Dorothy hovering. 'Listen, Nick,' she said. 'That number you gave me? I'm not going to be able to locate her phone.'

'That doesn't sound like you. That sounds . . . defeatist,' I said.

'Nothing to do with my ability. It's a matter of law.'

'Like that ever stopped you?'

'Here's the deal. The person whose phone you want me to locate . . .' She glanced at Gabe. 'Can we speak in private, Nick?'

'Gabe, give me two minutes,' I said.

'Fine,' he snapped, and left my office.

'Sounds like you're actually taking the case,' Dorothy said. 'Couldn't pass up the money?'

'No, it's . . . it's complicated. This is not about Marshall Marcus. I happen to like his daughter. I'm worried about her.'

'Why is he freaking out? I mean, she's seventeen, right?'

'I don't get it, either. I think he knows more than he's telling me.'

'Maybe you need to ask him some direct questions.'

'I will. Tell me about Facebook. Alexa must be on Facebook, right?'

'I think it's a legal requirement for all teenagers,' she said. 'I'll look into it.'

'So what's the problem with locating Alexa's iPhone? I thought there was some way for iPhone owners to track down lost phones.'

'We'd need her Mac username and password. And I'm guessing she doesn't share things like passwords with Daddy.'

'Can't you crack it, or hack it, or whatever you do?'

'That takes time. And even if I do succeed, odds are we won't get anything, because she'd had to have activated the MobileMe finder on her phone, and I doubt she did. Fastest way is ask AT&T to ping the phone through their network.'

'Which they'll do only for law enforcement,' I said. 'There's got to be some other way to find this girl's phone.'

'Not that I know of.'

'You giving up?'

'I said not that I know of. I didn't say I'm giving up.' She looked up and noticed Gabe lurking outside my office door. 'Anyway, I think your son is getting hungry,' she said with a wink.

MOJO'S, A TYPICAL BOSTON BAR—five flatscreens all showing sports, lots of Red Sox and Celtics memorabilia. The patrons were a mix of stockbrokers and cab drivers.

'I like that new girl you hired,' Gabe said.

'Jillian? She's different.'

'Nah, she's cool.'

Herb, the owner, took our order. He was a large-framed pot-bellied guy.

'Yo, Nicky,' he said. 'How's the accounting business? You got any tips for me, like how to stop paying taxes?'

'Do what I do. Just don't pay 'em.'

He laughed loudly. It didn't take much to amuse him.

'Truth is, I'm an actuary.' The sign on our office door said, HELLER ASSOCIATES—ACTUARIAL CONSULTING SERVICES. This was an excellent cover. As soon as I told people I was an actuary, they stopped asking questions.

'Gotta hand it to you, man,' Herb said kindly, 'I don't know how you do it. Crunching numbers all day? I'd go out of my mind.'

I ordered a burger and fries. Gabe looked up from the menu. 'Do you have veggie burgers?'

'We have turkey burgers, young fella,' Herb said.

Gabe furrowed his brow and tipped his head to the side. I recognised that look. It was the supercilious expression that got him beat up at school on a regular basis and sometimes even thrown out of classes. 'Oh,' he said, 'I didn't know turkey was a vegetable.'

Herb gave me a quick sideways glance, as if to say, *Who the hell is this kid?* But he liked me too much to give it back to my guest.

'I'll just have a plate of fries and ketchup. And a Coke.'

When Herb left, I said, 'Looks like Jillian has a new recruit.'

'She says that eating red meat makes you aggressive,' Gabe said. 'Hey, Uncle Nick, you know, that was a good idea you had about Alexa's Facebook.'

I froze. 'What are you talking about?'

'Alexa Marcus? Her dad is scared something happened to her?'

I slowly smiled. 'You were eavesdropping!'

'Did you know Dorothy has an audio feed on her computer that lets her listen in to everything you say in your office?' he said.

'Yes, Gabe. That's our arrangement. So what were you thinking about Alexa's Facebook page?'

'I'm pretty sure I know where Alexa went last night. It was on her Facebook wall.'

'How were you able to see that?'

'We're Facebook friends. Well, I mean, she has, like, eleven hundred Facebook friends, but she let me friend her.' He sounded proud. 'She came over to Nana's a couple of times. She's cool. And it's not like she has to be nice to me.'

I nodded. Beautiful rich girls like Alexa Marcus usually weren't nice to nerdy boys like Gabe Heller. 'So where'd she go?'

'She and her friend Taylor went to Slammer. Some fancy bar in that hotel that used to be a jail? I think it's called the Graybar?'

'Taylor—is that a boy or a girl?'

'A girl. Taylor Armstrong? She's the daughter of Senator Richard Armstrong. Taylor and Alexa went to school together.'

I glanced at my watch, put my hand on his shoulder. 'How about we ask them to pack up our food to go?' I said.

'You're going to talk to Taylor?'

I nodded.

'She's at home today,' Gabe said. 'Probably sleeping it off. I bet you find Alexa there, too. Uncle Nick?'

'What?'

'Don't tell Alexa I told you. She'll think I'm a stalker.'

I FOUND THE JUNIOR SENATOR from Massachusetts picking up his dog's poop.

Senator Richard Armstrong's standard poodle was trimmed in a full Continental clip: shaved body, pompoms on his feet and tail, and an Afro atop his head. The senator was groomed just as carefully, his silver hair perfectly coiffed. He leaned over, his hand inside a plastic CVS bag, grabbed the dog's excrement, and deftly turned the bag inside out. He stood and noticed me standing there.

'Senator,' I said.

'Yes?' A wary look.

We stood in an oval park, enclosed by a wrought-iron fence, in one of the most elegant neighbourhoods in Boston.

'Nick Heller,' I said. 'Is this a good time?' I'd reached him through a mutual friend, told him what was going on, and asked if I could come by.

'Walk with me,' he said. I followed him to a trash bin, where he dropped his bundle. 'So, I'm sorry to hear about the Marcus girl. Any news? I'm sure it's just a family quarrel. She's at that age.'

Armstrong had a Boston Brahmin accent; he was descended from an old Boston family. We stood before his house—bow-front, freshly painted black shutters, American flag waving. 'Well, if there's anything I can do to help, just ask,' he said. He gave me his famous smile, which had got him elected to the Senate four times. A journalist once compared the Armstrong smile to a warm fire. Up close, it seemed more like an artificial fireplace.

'Excellent,' I said. 'I'd like to talk to your daughter.'

'My daughter? I doubt Taylor has seen the girl in months.'

'They saw each other last night.'

'News to me,' he said. 'Anyway, I'm afraid Taylor's out.'

'You might want to check again,' I said. 'She's upstairs.'

Gabe was monitoring her incessant Facebook postings for me and texting me updates. I didn't know how, since he wasn't a Facebook friend of Taylor's, but he'd found some way.

'I'm sure she and her mother—'

'Senator,' I said. 'Please get her for me. This is important. Or should I just call her cell?'

Of course, I didn't actually have Taylor Armstrong's cellphone number, but it turned out I didn't need it. Armstrong invited me in, no longer bothering to conceal his annoyance. No more election-winning smile. The electric fireplace had been switched off.

TAYLOR ARMSTRONG ENTERED her father's study like a kid summoned to the principal's office, trying to mask her apprehension with sullenness. She sat down in a big kilim-covered chair.

I sat in a facing chair while Senator Armstrong skimmed papers at his simple mahogany desk. He was pretending to ignore us.

The girl was pretty. Her hair was black, obviously dyed, and she wore heavy eye make-up. She was wearing a brown suede tank top, skinny jeans and short brown leather boots.

I introduced myself and said, 'I'd like to ask you a few questions about Alexa. She's missing. Her parents are extremely worried.'

She looked up, a petulant expression on her face.

'Have you heard from her?' I said.

She shook her head. 'No.'

'When did you last see her?'

'Last night. We went out.'

I was glad she didn't try to lie about it.

'How about we go for a walk?' I said.

'A walk?' she said, as if I'd asked her to eat a live bat head.

'Sure. Get some fresh air.'

Her father said, 'You two can talk right here.'

For a few seconds she looked trapped. Finally, to my surprise, she said, 'I wouldn't mind getting out of the house.'

FROM LOUISBURG SQUARE we made our way down the steep slope of Willow Street. 'I figured you could use a cigarette.'

'I don't smoke.'

But I could smell it on her when she first came downstairs. 'Go ahead, I'm not going to report back to Daddy.'

Her expression softened almost imperceptibly. She shrugged, took a pack of Marlboros and a gold S. T. Dupont cigarette lighter from her little black handbag.

'I won't even tell Daddy about the fake IDs,' I said.

She gave me a sidelong glance as she opened the lighter. She flicked it, lit a cigarette, and drew a lungful of smoke. She exhaled twin plumes from her nostrils, like a movie star from the old days.

We crossed over to West Cedar, down a tiny alley called Acorn Street. 'You and Alexa went to Slammer together,' I said. I waited.

'We just had a couple of drinks,' she said finally.

'Did she seem upset? Pissed off at her parents?'

'No more than usual.'

'Did she say anything about getting out of the house, just taking off somewhere?'

'No.'

'Does she have a boyfriend?'

'No.' She sounded hostile, like it was none of my business.

'Did she say she was scared of something? Or someone? She was once grabbed in a parking lot—'

'I know,' she said scornfully. 'I'm, like, her best friend.'

'Was she afraid that something like that might happen again?'

She shook her head. 'But she said her dad was acting weird. Like maybe he was in trouble? I really don't remember.'

'Did you two leave the bar together?'

She hesitated. 'Yeah.'

She was so obviously lying that I hesitated to call her on it outright for fear of losing any chance of her cooperation.

Suddenly she blurted out, 'Did something happen to Lexie?'

We'd stopped at the corner of Mount Vernon Street. 'Maybe.'

'*Maybe?* What's that supposed to mean?'

'It means I need you to tell me everything.'

She threw down her cigarette. 'Look, she met a guy, OK?'

'Do you remember his name?'

She avoided my eyes. 'Spanish guy, maybe. I don't remember.'

'Were you with her when she met this guy?'

I could see her running through a series of mental calculations. If this, then that. If she said she wasn't with Alexa, why not? Where was she? Two girls go to a bar, they almost always stay together.

'Yeah,' she said. 'But I didn't really catch his name. And I was definitely sideways by then, and I just wanted to go home.'

'Did they leave together?' I said.

I waited so long I thought she might not have heard me. When I was about to repeat the question, she said, 'I guess. I don't really know.'

'How could you not know?'

'Because I left first.'

I didn't point out the contradiction. 'You went straight home?'

She nodded.

'You haven't heard from her since you left Slammer last night?'

'Right.'

'Have you tried to call her?'

She shook her head.

'Text her?'

She shook her head again.'

'You didn't check in with her for an update on how the night went? I thought you guys are, like, BFFs.' Somehow I knew that was chat-speak for 'best friends for ever'.

She shrugged.

'Do you understand that if you're lying to me, if you're covering something up, you might be endangering your best friend's life?'

She shook her head, then started walking down the street away from me. 'I haven't heard anything,' she said without turning back.

My gut instinct told me she wasn't lying about not having heard from Alexa. Obviously, though, she was lying about something. Her guilt flashed like a neon sign.

I called Dorothy. 'Any progress in locating Alexa's phone?'

'No change. We're going to need the assistance of someone in law enforcement, Nick. No way round it.'

'I have an idea,' I said.

WHEN YOUR JOB INVOLVES working with the clandestine, as mine does, you learn the power of a secret. Knowing one can give you leverage, even control, over another, whether in the halls of Congress or the halls of high school, in the boardroom or at the racetrack.

When I worked at Stoddard Associates in DC, I did a project for a freshman congressman from Florida who was fighting a nasty re-election battle. His opponent had got hold of a copy of the lease on an apartment in Sarasota he'd rented for his girlfriend, a hostess. This was news to his wife, the mother of his six children, and definitely inconvenient for the congressman, given his strong family-values platform. I did some cleanup work, and the whole paper trail disappeared. The congressman won the election easily.

It wasn't a job I was proud of, but now the congressman was the ranking member on the House Judiciary Committee, which oversees the FBI. He didn't owe me any favours, since he'd paid well for Stoddard's 'research services', but I knew certain things about him, which was even worse. I reached him on his private line and asked him to make a call for me to the Boston field office of the FBI.

I told him I needed to talk to someone senior. Now.

THE FBI's BOSTON FIELD OFFICE is located in One Center Plaza, part of the Government Center complex, which most Bostonians consider a blight, a concrete scar on the face of our beautiful city.

When I got out of the elevator on the sixth floor, I saw a huge gold FBI seal on the wall and a Ten Most Wanted poster. A couple of receptionists sat behind a bulletproof glass window. I pushed my driver's licence into a slot like a bank teller's, and they made me surrender my BlackBerry. One of the women behind the glass spoke into a phone and told me someone would be out in a few minutes.

When they make you wait ten or fifteen minutes, it's probably because a meeting is running late. When you're past the forty-five minute mark, they're sending you a message.

It was close to an hour before the FBI guy emerged.

He wasn't what I expected. He was a hulking guy, entirely bald, the kind of shiny bald that takes work. He wore a knockoff Rolex, a grey suit that was too short in the sleeves, a white shirt too tight at the neck and a regimental striped tie.

'Mr Heller?' he said in a deep voice. 'Gordon Snyder.' He offered me a hand as huge and leathery as an old baseball mitt. 'Assistant special agent in charge,' he added.

That meant he was one of the top guys in the FBI's Boston office, reporting directly to the special agent in charge. I had to give credit to my philandering congressman from Sarasota.

He led me to his office, which overlooked Cambridge Street. A desk, two computer monitors, a flatscreen TV with the sound off, set to CNN. He sat behind his perfectly clean desk. 'I understand you work in the private sector these days, Mr Heller.'

'Right.' I suppose that was his not-so-subtle way of letting me know he'd read a dossier on me and knew what I used to do.

'So what can I do for you?'

'I'm helping a friend look for his daughter,' I said.

He furrowed his brows. 'What's the girl's name?'

'Alexa Marcus.'

He nodded. The name didn't seem to mean anything to him.

'Her father is Marshall Marcus. Hedge-fund guy in Boston.'

'How old is she?'

'Seventeen.'

He nodded. 'She's been kidnapped?'

'Possibly.'

'Well, is there a ransom demand?'

'Not yet. But given the circumstances and her own history—'

'So you're saying the father's concerned his daughter *might* have been kidnapped.'

There was something strange about Snyder's expression. A look of confusion so exaggerated it was almost comical. 'See, what baffles me, Mr Heller, is why the Boston police never reached out to us.'

'They sure should have.'

'I know, right? Normally that's the first thing they'd do in a case like this. Kidnappings are FBI business. Gotta wonder why not.'

'Well, if you could arrange to ping her phone—'

But Snyder wasn't finished. 'I wonder if the *reason* they never reached out to us is that no one notified them about the missing girl in the first place.' He clasped his hands, looked down at his desk, then up at me. 'See, Marshall Marcus never called it in to them. Interesting, isn't it? You'd think he'd be all *over* the police and the FBI to locate his daughter, wouldn't you? If it was *my* daughter, I wouldn't wait two seconds. Would you?' His eyes pierced mine, his upper lip curled in disgust.

'He called the police,' I said. 'A couple of hours ago.'

He shook his head and said firmly, 'Never happened.'

'You have bad information.'

'We have *excellent* information on Marcus,' he said. 'We know for a fact that neither he nor his wife placed a call to the police. Not from any of his four home land lines. Neither of his two cellphones. Nor his wife's cellphone. Nor any land line at Marcus Capital.'

I said nothing.

He gave me a long look. 'That's right. We've had Marshall Marcus under court-ordered surveillance for quite some time now. As I'm sure he knows. Did he send you here, Mr Heller? Please don't bother trying to deny the fact that you met with Marcus at his house in Manchester this morning. Is this why you're here? Acting as his agent? Trying to see what we've got on him?'

'I came here because a girl's life may be in danger.'

'The same girl who had to be sent away to a special disciplinary school because of repeated behaviour problems?'

It was all I could do to keep from losing it. 'That's right. After she was abducted. Stuff like that can really screw with your head. You don't get it, do you? We're on the same side here.'

'You're working for Marcus, right?'

'Yeah, but—'

'Then we're on opposite sides. We clear?'

4

Alexa felt her heart thud faster and faster. She could hear it. In the terrible silence, her heartbeat was like a kettledrum.

'You can hear me, Alexa, yes?' said the tinny voice.

A wash of acid scalded her oesophagus. She gagged, retched. A little vomit splashed on her damp shirt, settled back in her throat.

She needed to sit upright to empty her mouth, but she couldn't raise her head more than a few inches. *She couldn't move.*

'Please take care of yourself,' the voice said. 'We cannot open your coffin if something happens to you.'

'Coffin . . .' she gasped.

'There is no reason for you to die. We don't want you to die. We only want you to convince your father to cooperate with us.'

'How much money do you want?' she whispered.

'Why do you think we want money, Alexa? And even if we did want money, your father has nothing.'

'My father is . . . He has an obscene amount of money, OK? He can pay you anything you want. He'll give it all to you if you please, please, please let me out now.'

'Alexa, now you must listen to me very, very carefully, because your survival depends on it.'

She swallowed. A lump had lodged in her throat.

'I'm listening,' she whispered.

'Good. Now, Alexa? We must talk about your breathing, OK? Are you listening?'

She shuddered and moaned. 'Please . . .'

'You have air in your coffin, but it is not so much. If we just put you in the casket and put it in the ground, you would not last half an hour. But we know this is not enough time for you.'

'*The ground?*' she whispered.

'Yes. You are in a steel casket buried under ten feet of earth. You have been buried alive. But I'm sure you already know this.'

Something exploded in her brain: bright sparkles of light. She screamed with vocal cords so raw that the only sound that came out was a wheezing gasp, but in the darkness it was thunderously loud.

A FLUORESCENT ORANGE parking ticket was tucked under the Defender's windshield wipers. Damn Snyder. If he hadn't kept me waiting so long, the time on the meter wouldn't have run out.

I had my BlackBerry out, about to call Marcus, when I heard a female voice behind me. 'Nico?'

The nickname that hardly anyone used anymore except a few people I knew in DC a long time ago.

I sensed her, maybe even smelled her, before she touched my shoulder. Without even looking round, I said, 'Diana?'

'You still have the Defender, I see,' she said. 'You don't change much, do you?'

'Hey,' I said, and I gave her a hug. For a moment I didn't know whether to kiss her on the mouth—those days were long gone—but she resolved the dilemma by offering her cheek. 'You look great.'

I wasn't lying. Diana Madigan had on tight jeans and worn brown cowboy boots and an emerald-green top that brought out her amazing pale green eyes.

I'd never met a woman quite like her. She was tough and empathetic and elegant. And beautiful. She had a taut, lithe body with a head of crazy wavy hair. It was light honey brown with auburn highlights. Her nose was strong yet delicate. The only sign of the years that had passed were faint laugh lines etched round her eyes.

We hadn't seen each other in five or six years, since she was transferred from the FBI's Washington field office to Seattle and she'd declared she didn't want a long-distance relationship. Our relationship had been a casual one—not 'friends with benefits', exactly, but no pressure, no expectations. This was the way she wanted it, and given my work hours and how much I travelled, I was fine with the arrangement. I enjoyed her company, and she enjoyed mine.

Still, when I got a call from Diana telling me that she'd moved to Seattle, I quickly went from baffled to wounded. I'd never met anyone like her before and was convinced I never would again, and I was surprised she didn't feel the same. I was disappointed in myself for having misread her so badly. Until then, I'd always considered my ability to read others one of my natural talents. The end of my relationship with Diana went into my mental cold-case file.

But I've always found unsolved cases irresistible.

'I look like a wreck, and you know it,' she said. 'I've been up all night texting predators, pretending to be a fourteen-year-old girl.'

'So you're still working CARD?'

'Believe it or not.'

CARD stood for the FBI's Child Abduction Rapid Deployment unit. It was heart-wrenching work. I never knew how she could keep doing it. I thought by now she'd have burned out.

She wasn't wearing a wedding ring, and I could only assume she didn't have kids, either. I wondered whether she ever would, having seen what could happen to them.

'Why don't I give you a lift,' I said.

'How do you know I don't have my car here?'

'Because you'd have parked in the underground garage like all FBI employees do. Plus, you'd be carrying your car keys in your left hand. Don't forget, I know you.'

She looked away. Embarrassed? Unreadable, in any case. As always, the emotional equivalent of Kryptonite. 'My apartment's in the South End. I was going to take the T.'

I opened the passenger-side door for her.

As I DROVE I caught the faintest whiff of her perfume: rose and violet and cedar, sophisticated, haunting and unforgettable. Neuroscientists tell us that nothing brings back the past as quickly and powerfully as a smell. Diana's perfume brought back a rush of memories. Mostly happy ones.

'How long have you been in Boston?' I asked.

'A little over a year. I heard you might be here. Did Stoddard send you here to open a satellite office or something?'

'No. I'm on my own now.'

'You like it?'

'It would be perfect if the boss weren't such a hard-ass.'

She laughed ruefully. 'Nick Heller, company man.'

'You said Pembroke Street, right?'

'Right. Off Columbus Ave. Thanks for doing this.'

'My pleasure.'

'Listen, I'm sorry about Snyder.'

'How did you know I met with him?'

'I saw you storm out. Looked like it didn't go too well.'

'Did he tell you what we talked about?'

'Sure.'

I wondered whether she'd followed me out, too. Maybe this meeting wasn't a coincidence. Maybe she'd heard I was in the building and wanted to say hi. Maybe that was all she wanted. I dropped another note into the cold-case file marked MADIGAN, DIANA.

'So what's with his fixation on Marshall Marcus?'

'Marcus is his great white whale. Guys like that, the more elusive the target, the more obsessed they become.'

Tell me about it, I thought. 'Well, he seemed a whole lot more interested in taking down Marcus than finding his daughter.'

'Maybe because he's in charge of financial crimes.'

'Aha.'

'I don't understand why you were meeting with the head of the financial crimes unit if you were looking for a missing girl.'

I was beginning to wonder the same thing. 'That was the name I was given.'

'Is Marshall Marcus a friend of yours?' she said.

'Friend of the family. My mother worked for him,' I said. 'And I like his kid. But apparently you guys are investigating him for something. What can *you* tell me about him?'

'Not much. It's a sealed investigation. And I'm on the other side of the firewall.'

I pulled up in front of her narrow bowfront brownstone, double parking in front of a space easily big enough for the Defender to fit.

'Well, thanks again,' she said, opening the door.

'Hold on. I need to ask you a favour. You think you can put in a request to locate Alexa Marcus's cellphone?'

'It's not so easy to do an end run round Snyder. What makes you think something happened to her?'

I was about to answer, when she looked around and said, 'Look, if you want, you can come up for a sec, explain this all to me.'

I shrugged, playing it cool. 'Hell, seems a shame to waste a perfectly good parking space.'

HER APARTMENT on the second floor wasn't very big, yet it felt lush and rich and textured. The walls were painted various shades of chocolate brown and earth tones. Every single piece of furniture, every object, had been carefully selected.

She pointed me to a big corner sofa while she made fresh coffee. She served it in a big mug that looked hand-painted: it was dark and strong and perfect. She didn't have any, though, because she needed to sleep.

A woman invites you up to her apartment, you usually know what to expect. But not in this case. We'd both moved on. We'd gone from Friends with Benefits to Just Friends.

Being Just Friends didn't change the way I felt about her. But we were here to talk about Alexa Marcus. I told her what I knew about what had happened to Alexa and about Taylor Armstrong.

'I hate to say it, but Snyder has a point,' she said. 'It hasn't even been twelve hours, right? So she met a guy, and she's sleeping it off in some BU dorm. That's entirely possible, right?'

'Possible, sure. Not likely. It's not like a girl her age to go dark. She'd have checked in with her friends.'

'She's an overprotected girl with a troubled home life, and she's testing the limits,' Diana said. She was sitting in an overstuffed easy chair, and she'd removed her cowboy boots. The only make-up she had on was lip gloss. Her skin was translucent.

'I don't think you really believe that,' I said. 'With the kind of work you do.'

The shape of her mouth changed so subtly that you'd have to know her well to see it. 'You're right,' she said. 'I'm sorry. I was playing devil's advocate. Given what the girl's gone through—that attempted abduction a few years ago—she's not likely to go home with a strange guy no matter how much she's drunk.'

'It wasn't an *attempted* abduction,' I said. 'She *was* abducted. Then released.'

'They just . . . grabbed her, drove her around for a few hours, and then released her? All that risk of exposure with no payoff?'

'Apparently so.'

'And you believe this?'

'I have no reason not to. I've spent a lot of time talking with Alexa about it.'

She leaned back in her chair. 'If her father secretly paid a ransom and didn't want to tell anyone, would she really know?'

She was smart. I'd forgotten how smart. 'If he had a reason to keep it secret, maybe not. But that was never the sense I got.'

'Maybe he doesn't tell you everything.'

'Maybe there's something *you're* not telling.'

She turned to me. 'You know I'd never divulge confidential details of an ongoing investigation, and I'm not going to start now.'

'I know.'

'So the speculation seems to be that Marshall Marcus is laundering money for some very bad guys.'

'Laundering money? That's ridiculous. The guy's a billionaire. Maybe he's managing money for some questionable clients.'

'I'm just telling you what I hear. And I should warn you: Gordon Snyder is not a guy you want for an enemy. If he thinks you're working against him, against his case, he'll come gunning for you.'

'Consider me warned.'

'OK. Now, do you have a picture of Alexa?'

'Sure,' I said, reaching into my breast pocket for one of the photos Marcus had given me. She came over and sat next to me on the couch, and I felt my heart speed up a little. I handed her a picture of Alexa in her field-hockey uniform, her blonde hair tied back in a headband, her cheeks rosy, her blue eyes sparkling.

'Pretty,' she said. 'She looks like she's got fight.'

'She does. She's had a rough patch last few years.'

'Not an easy age. I hated being seventeen.'

Diana never talked much about growing up, besides the fact that she was raised in Scottsdale, Arizona, where her father was with the US Marshals Service and was killed in the line of duty when she was a teenager. After that her mother moved them to Sedona and opened a New Age shop.

I noticed her body shifting slightly towards me. 'You know, I recognise that shirt,' she said. 'Didn't I give it to you?'

'You did. I haven't taken it off since.'

'Good old Nico. You're the one fixed point in a changing age.' She gave me one of her inscrutable smiles. 'All right, I'll put in a request to AT&T. I'll find a way to push it through.'

'I appreciate it.'

'Look, it's not about you. Or us. It's about the girl. As far as I'm concerned, Alexa Marcus is legally a minor, and she may be in some kind of trouble, and that's all I need to hear.'

'So does this make it officially an FBI matter?'

'Not necessarily. Not yet, anyway. But if I can help out on this, you know where to find me.'

'Thanks.' A long, awkward silence followed. Neither one of us was the type to pick at emotional scabs. Yet there we were, sitting in her apartment, just the two of us, and if ever there was a time to talk about the elephant in the room, this was it.

'So how come . . .' I began, but stopped. *How come you never told me you were posted in Boston?* I wanted to say. But I didn't want it to sound like a reproach. Instead, I told her, 'Same here. You ever need anything, I'll be there. Right on your doorstep.'

She smiled and turned to look at me, but as soon as I met those green eyes and felt her breath on my face, my lips were on hers. They were warm and soft and her mouth tasted of lime.

A phone started ringing.

Diana pulled away. 'Hold on, Nico,' she said, drawing her BlackBerry from the holster on her belt.

She listened. 'OK,' she said. 'I'll be right in.'

'What is it?'

'My predator,' she said. 'He's been texting me again. I think he's getting a little suspicious. He wants to change our meeting time. They need me back at work. I'm—I'm sorry.'

'Me, too,' I said.

She was on her feet, looking for her key card and her house keys. 'What the hell did we just do?' she said, not looking at me.

'What we just did—I don't know, but . . . let me drive you back.'

Suddenly she was all business. She shook her head and said firmly, 'My car's right here.'

It felt like jumping out of a sauna into four feet of snow.

I DROVE TO THE FOOT of Beacon Hill and pulled into the drive in front of the Graybar Hotel, the last place I knew Alexa had been.

The negative energy at the front desk was so thick I felt like pointing a 9mm semiautomatic pistol at the supercilious front-desk clerk just to get his attention. He seemed to be caught up in a conversation with a female desk clerk.

I cleared my throat. 'Can someone call Naji, please? Tell him it's Nick Heller.' Naji was the hotel's security director.

The guy sullenly picked up his phone and spoke softly into it. 'He'll be up soon,' he said. He had artfully messy hair with a lot of gel in it. I stood at the desk, waiting. He went back to his conversation but noticed me out of the corner of his eye and turned round again, saying with annoyance, 'Um, it might be a while?'

So I strolled through the lobby and saw a sign for Slammer. I took the elevator to the fourth floor and looked around. Flatscreen TVs mounted on the brick walls. Leather couches and banquettes. A long bar. Lights in the floors. A fair number of security cameras.

When I returned to the front desk, a good-looking dark-haired guy was waiting for me. Classic Arab facial features. He smiled as I approached. 'Mr Heller?'

'Thanks for meeting me, Naji,' I said.

'Mr Marcus is a very good friend of the Graybar,' he said. 'Anything I can do, please, I am at your service.' Marshall Marcus was not just a 'friend' but one of the original, and biggest, investors. He'd called ahead, as I'd asked.

Naji produced an oblong key fob with a BMW logo: the keyless entry fob to the four-year-old M3 Marcus had given Alexa to drive. Attached to the key chain was a valet ticket.

'So she never claimed the car?'

'Apparently not. I made sure no one touched the vehicle, in case you needed to run prints.'

The guy was clearly experienced. 'The police might,' I said. 'Any idea what time she valeted the car?'

'Of course, sir,' Naji said, and he showed me the valet ticket, which was time-stamped 9.37, the time Alexa had given the BMW to the valet.

'I'd like to look at the surveillance video,' I said.

'In the parking garage, do you mean? Or at the valet station?'

'Everywhere,' I said.

The Graybar's security command centre was a small room in the business offices in the back. It was outfitted with twenty or so monitors showing views of the exterior, the lobby, the kitchen, the halls outside the restrooms. A chunky guy with a goatee was sitting there watching the screens. Actually, he was reading the *Boston Herald*, but he hastily put it down.

'Leo,' Naji said, 'can you pull up last night's video feeds from cameras three through five?'

Naji and I stood behind Leo as he opened several windows on a computer screen.

'Start from around nine thirty,' I said.

Leo advanced the frames at double and triple speed. At nine thirty-five a black BMW parked and Alexa got out. The valet handed her a ticket, and Alexa joined a long line waiting to get into the lobby as the valet drove off with her car.

'Can we zoom in?' I said.

Leo moved the mouse, clicked a few keys. I saw Alexa hugging another girl who was already in line. Taylor Armstrong.

'Can we follow her into the hotel?' I asked.

'Of course. Leo, pull up nine and twelve,' Naji said.

From another angle, just inside the lobby, I could see the girls approach the elevator. Then the elevator doors came open and the two girls got in. Abruptly, Alexa got out. Taylor remained.

Alexa was claustrophobic. She couldn't bear to be in enclosed spaces, especially elevators.

'Ah,' I said. 'I want to see where that one's going, the one who didn't get in the elevator.'

From another camera, I watched Alexa climb the stairs. Another camera showed her arriving at the fourth-floor bar, where she met up with Taylor. We continued watching as they found some chairs.

For a stretch, nothing much happened. The bar got increasingly crowded. A waitress in a skimpy outfit took their order. A guy approached. He had his shirt-tails untucked. Blond, ruddy face. He didn't look Spanish. Alexa smiled, but Taylor didn't look at him.

After a few seconds, he left. I actually felt sorry for the kid.

The girls kept talking. They laughed, and I surmised it was about the guy with the untucked shirt.

'You can fast-forward,' I said.

Another guy approached. This one was dark-haired. Mediterranean— maybe Italian, maybe Spanish. The girls smiled. This was a side to Taylor I hadn't seen—no sullen pout. Lively and animated.

'Is there a different angle on this?' I said.

Leo opened another window, and I could see the man's face in profile. Leo zoomed in. A handsome guy in his early thirties.

The guy pulled a chair over and sat down, apparently having been invited. He signalled for a waitress.

'This man, he comes here often,' Naji said.

I turned to him. 'Oh? What's his name?'

He shook his head. 'I don't know.'

I turned back to the monitor. The guy and the two girls were talking and laughing. The waitress came, took their drink orders.

The man was sitting next to Taylor but was much more interested in Alexa. He kept leaning towards her.

Interesting, I thought. Taylor was at least as pretty as Alexa. But Alexa's father was a billionaire. Yet how would he know that—unless he'd picked out his target in advance?

The drinks came, served in big martini glasses. After a while both girls got up. The man remained at the table by himself.

'Can we follow the girls?' I said.

Leo switched to an already open window, made it bigger. The girls were walking together, holding on to each other, both looking a little tipsy. I watched them enter the ladies' room.

Then something in the other computer window caught my eye. The camera in which you could see the Latin man sitting alone. He was doing something. He reached out a hand and slid Alexa's half-full martini glass across the table towards himself.

'What the hell?' I said. 'Enlarge this window, could you?'

Once Leo did so, we could see everything he was doing. The man slipped his right hand into his jacket, glanced around, then nonchalantly dropped something into Alexa's martini glass. He took the swizzle stick from his own drink and stirred hers. Then he pushed her cocktail back in front of her place.

'Oh, God,' I said.

In the other window on the monitor, the girls emerged from the restroom and returned to their table. Alexa took a drink.

A few minutes later Taylor stood up, said something. Alexa looked upset, but the guy didn't. Taylor left. Alexa stayed.

She drank some more, and the two of them laughed and talked.

Alexa began to exhibit signs of serious intoxication. She slumped back in her chair, smiling gamely. But she looked sick.

The man pulled out a billfold, put down some cash, then helped Alexa to her feet. She looked as if she could barely stand.

'Cash,' I said, mostly to myself.

But Naji understood. 'He always pays in cash.'

'That's why you don't know his name?'

He nodded. 'I can't say for sure, but I think he may be a dealer.' He quickly added, 'But he never deals here.'

This wasn't good.

Now the guy walked Alexa to the elevator. He pushed the button. A minute later the elevator arrived and they got in. She had an elevator phobia, but I doubted she knew where she was.

The lobby camera captured the guy escorting Alexa towards the front door, almost dragging her. She was stumbling. People entering the hotel saw this and smiled. They probably figured the guy's girlfriend had had too much to drink.

The man handed a ticket to the valet.

An older black Porsche arrived: a classic but not in very good shape. The rear panel was dented, and there were dings and scrapes all over it. The dealer helped Alexa into the back seat, where she lay flat.

My stomach clenched. The car pulled away from the front entrance and out of the circular drive. 'I need another angle,' I said.

'Certainly, sir,' Naji said. 'His face?'

'No,' I said. 'His licence plate.'

Of course, the plate number would be recorded on the man's valet ticket, but I wanted to be absolutely certain. A camera directly in front of the valet station had captured his licence plate with perfect clarity.

The name on the ticket was Costa. He'd arrived at 9.08, before the girls did.

Naji burned a bunch of still frames of Alexa and Taylor with the guy, including close-ups of his face from several different angles, to a CD. I had him make me a couple of copies. Then I borrowed his computer and emailed a few of the stills of Costa to Dorothy.

The Defender was parked in one of the short-term spaces out front. I got in and called Dorothy. I gave her a quick recap, then read her the licence plate number and asked her to pull up the owner's name and address and anything else she could get. I gave her the name 'Costa', warned her it was probably fake, and asked her to check her email. She already had. I told her that the hotel's security director suspected he was a narcotics dealer.

I pulled out of the hotel drive. About three blocks away I suddenly had another thought, and drove back to the hotel. I found Naji in the hall.

'Sorry,' I said. 'One more thing. The Porsche. The valet records show an arrival time of 9.08. I'd like to see all video from the valet station around that time.'

It took Leo a minute to call up the video I wanted: the Porsche pulling up to the kerb earlier in the evening and Costa getting out.

Then I saw something I didn't expect. Someone getting out of the passenger's side. A woman.

Taylor Armstrong.

5

'Alexa,' the voice said, 'please do not scream. No one can hear. Do you understand this?'

She tried to swallow.

'You see, when you panic or scream, you hyperventilate, and this only uses up your air supply much quicker.' His accent was thick and crude, but his voice was bland and matter-of-fact, and it was all the more terrifying for it.

'*No no no no no,*' she chanted in a little voice, a child's voice.

'Carbon dioxide poisoning is not pleasant, Alexa. You feel like you are drowning. You will die slowly and painfully.'

She gasped desperately for air. She was trapped ten feet underground, under tons of dirt, in this tiny box in which she could barely move, and the air would soon run out.

'You are listening to me, Alexa?'

'Please,' she whispered. 'Please don't do this. Please.'

'Alexa?' the voice said. 'I can see you. A video camera is mounted right over your head. It gives infrared light you cannot see. I can also hear you through the microphone. Everything comes to us over the Internet. And when you speak to your father, he will see and hear you, too.'

'Please, let me talk to him!'

'Yes, of course. Soon. But first let us make sure you know what you must say. If you say your lines correctly and your father gives us what we want, you will be free in a matter of hours, Alexa.'

'He'll give you anything. Please let me out now. You can lock me up in a room or a closet if you want. You don't need to do this. Please, oh, please, don't do this . . .'

'If you do exactly as we ask, you will be out of there right away.'

'You are a *monster!* Do you know what's going to happen to you when they catch you? Do you have any idea, you *psychopath?*'

There was silence.

'Do you *hear* me, you creep?'

More silence.

Only then did she understand how much she depended on the man with the owl tattoo on the back of his head. The Owl was her lifeline to the world.

She must never again offend the Owl.

'I'm sorry,' she said. '*Please talk to me.*'

Nothing. Now she understood that phrase 'the silence of the grave.' She shuddered and cried softly, 'I'm sorry. Come back.'

'Alexa,' the voice said finally, and she felt sweet relief. 'Do you want to cooperate with us?'

'Oh, I do, I do. Please, tell me what you want me to do.'

'Alexa, I want you to reach under your mattress.'

Obediently she lowered both hands to the thin mattress and discovered that it rested on a series of metal bands that ran crosswise, spaced a few inches apart. Her hands found a space between the bands and plunged into an open area below. Her left hand touched an object, a cluster of objects, and she grasped the cap and narrow neck of what felt like a plastic bottle. There were many. She grabbed one and pulled it up and through the bands. A water bottle.

'Yes, very good,' said the voice. 'You see, I have given you some water. You must be thirsty.'

She twisted the cap with her other hand, and it came off with a satisfying snap. She put it to her parched lips and drank greedily.

'There is water to last you a few days,' the voice said. 'Perhaps a week. There are protein bars, too. Enough for a few days. Then you will starve to death. But before that, you will suffocate.'

She kept drinking.

'Now you must listen to me, Alexa.'

She pulled the bottle away from her mouth. She gasped, '*Yes.*'

'If you say exactly what I tell you, and your father does exactly what I ask, you will be free from this torture.'

'He'll give you whatever you want,' she said. 'He *loves* me.'

'I guess you will now learn if this is true,' the voice said. 'Because if your father does not love you, you will die terribly down there. I will watch you die, Alexa. And I will enjoy it.'

AFTER A QUICK STOP at a great old tobacco shop on Park Square, I made a pit stop at home. I called a friend of mine and asked him to do a quick job for me. A little while later my BlackBerry rang.

Without preface, Dorothy said, 'The Porsche is registered to a Richard Campisi. He reported his car stolen over a week ago.'

'I take it you've looked at his photo.'

'Of course. And he's not Costa. Not even close.'

'So our guy stole the car. So he couldn't be traced, I assume. This isn't good, Dorothy. It's been more than twelve hours since she disappeared. No one's heard from her. It's like what happened to her a few years ago, only this time it's for real.'

'A kidnap for ransom, you think? I hope that's all it is.'

'You hope it's a kidnapping?'

'I hope it's a kidnap for ransom. Because that means she's alive and all her dad has to do is pay money. The other possibility . . .'

'Yeah,' I said. 'I know what the other possibility is.'

I called Diana and asked her to put a rush on her request to locate Alexa Marcus's phone.

THIS TIME THE DOOR to Senator Armstrong's town house was opened by a housekeeper. 'The senator not here,' she said.

'I'm here to see Taylor, actually,' I said. 'Please tell her it's Nick Heller.' She asked me to wait outside and closed the door.

The door opened again five minutes later. It was Taylor, dressed to go out, her small black handbag slung over her shoulder.

'Time for a walk,' I said.

Halfway down Mount Vernon Street, I said, 'The guy Alexa left Slammer with last night—what's his name?'

'I told you, I don't remember. Is that what you came back for?'

'I just wanted to be sure I understood. Does your daddy know you got a ride with some guy whose name you don't even know?'

For a split second I could see the panic in her eyes, but she covered smoothly. 'I didn't get a ride with him. I got a cab home.'

'I'm talking about how you got to the bar in the first place.'

'I took a cab.'

'No,' I said softly, 'you arrived with him in his Porsche.' Before she could dig herself in deeper, I said, 'It's on the surveillance video at the hotel. You sure you want to keep lying to me?'

'Look, I didn't . . .' She started off defiant, but she seemed to crumple in front of me. 'I met this guy at a Starbucks, OK? Yesterday afternoon. And he really, like, came on to me.'

She waited for a reaction, but I made my face unreadable.

'We just started talking, and he seemed like a cool guy. He asked if I wanted to go to Slammer with him, and I . . . I was sort of nervous, 'cause I'd just met him. I said OK, but I wanted my friend to join us so it wouldn't be so intense. Like not really a date, you know?'

'Alexa knew all this?'

She nodded.

'His name?'

A beat. 'Lorenzo.'

'Last name?'

'He might have told me, but I don't remember.'

'So you two came to the Graybar together, and Alexa met you—where? Upstairs in the bar? Or in front of the hotel?'

'In line, in front. There's always a line there like a mile long.'

'I see.' The surveillance video was fresh in my mind: Alexa joining Taylor in line, no guy with her. The guy had approached the two of them in the bar an hour later. Acting as if he'd never met either one of them before. So: a total set-up.

'You got a smoke?' I said.

She shrugged, took the pack of Marlboros from her handbag.

'Light?' I said.

She pulled out the gold Dupont lighter.

As I took it from her, it slipped out of my hand and clattered to the cobblestones. I picked it up, lit a cigarette, handed the lighter back. 'Thank you. Now tell me about Lorenzo. Did he give you his cellphone number?'

'No,' she said. 'I gave him mine.'

'Did he ever call you? To make arrangements?'

'No.'

'How'd you feel when he went home with your best friend instead of you?'

She said unconvincingly, 'He wasn't my type.'

I'd led her down Mount Vernon across Charles Street, then left on River Street. I didn't want to walk down Charles. Not yet.

'Huh. When you met him at Starbucks earlier in the day, you must have been intrigued enough to agree to see him again.'

'Yeah, well, he turned out to be kind of—I don't know—sleazy? Anyway, he was definitely more into Alexa.'

'So when you met Lorenzo at Starbucks, were you sitting at one of those big, soft chairs in the window? He sat down next to you?'

She nodded.

'Which Starbucks was this?'

'The one on Charles Street, on the corner of Beacon.'

'And you were just sitting alone?' I said. 'Sitting by yourself in one of those big, soft chairs by the window?'

Her eyes narrowed. She didn't like the way I repeated the bit about the big, soft chairs. 'Yeah. What's your point?'

We'd stopped at the corner of Beacon and Charles. Across the street was the Starbucks she was talking about. 'Take a look.'

'What?'

'That Starbucks doesn't have any big, soft chairs, does it? And see? There sure as hell aren't any chairs in the window. Right?'

She stared, but only for show, because she knew she'd just been caught in another lie. 'Look, he was just going to show her a good time,' she said in an emotionless voice. 'I was doing her a favour.'

'Man, what a friend you are,' I said. 'You knew Alexa had been abducted once before and was still traumatised by it. Then you meet a guy, or maybe you already knew him, and you set him up with your so-called best friend. A guy you thought was sleazy. A guy who put a date-rape drug in your best friend's drink, probably with your full knowledge. And abducted her. Maybe killed her.'

A long black limousine pulled up to the red light next to us.

She blew out a plume of smoke. 'All you can prove is I went to Graybar with some guy. All that other crap? You're just guessing.'

The rear passenger's window in the limousine rolled smoothly down. A man I recognised stared at me, a natty fellow in a tweed jacket with a bow tie and round horn-rimmed glasses. His name was David Schechter. He was a well-known Boston attorney and power broker. He was utterly ruthless.

Next to him in the back seat was Senator Richard Armstrong.

'Taylor,' the senator said, 'get in.'

'Senator,' I said, 'your daughter is implicated in Alexa Marcus's disappearance.'

Armstrong turned to his attorney, as if deferring.

Taylor Armstrong opened the limo door and got in. I made one last attempt. 'Man, and I thought you were her best friend,' I said.

'Yeah, well, I don't think I'm going to have a problem finding a new one,' she said with a smile, and I felt a chill.

Then David Schechter gestured for me to come closer.

'Mr Heller,' said Schechter, speaking softly. 'The senator and his daughter do not wish to speak to you again.' He slammed the door, and the limo pulled away from the kerb and into traffic.

I pinched out my cigarette and tossed it into a trash can. I'd given up smoking a long time ago and didn't want to start again.

My BlackBerry started ringing. I pulled it out, saw it was Marcus. 'Nick,' he said. 'Oh, thank God.' There was panic in his voice, something I'd never heard before.

'What is it?' I said.

'They have her . . . They . . .'

He broke off. Silence.

'Marshall? You got a ransom demand?'

'No. It's just an email with a link to some—Oh, please God, Nick, get out here now.'

I looked at my watch. Soon it would be rush hour. The drive to Manchester would take even longer than usual.

'Did you click on the link?'

'Not yet.'

'Don't open it until we get there. I'm on my way.'

I PICKED UP DOROTHY at the office. We made better time than I expected and got to the security booth at Marcus's before six.

Marcus met us at the door. Ashen-faced, he showed us in. Belinda threw her arms round me, a display of affection I'd never have expected. I introduced Dorothy, and Marcus led us to his study.

The shades were drawn. The only illumination was a circle of light cast by a banker's lamp with a green glass shade. It sat in the middle of a massive refectory table that served as his desk. The only other objects on the table were a large flatscreen computer monitor and wireless keyboard.

He sat in a black leather chair and tapped a few keys. His hands were trembling. Belinda stood behind him. We stood on either side and watched him open an email message.

'As soon as this came in, I told him to call you,' Belinda said to me. 'I also told him not to do *anything* until y'all got here.'

'This is my personal email account,' he said quietly. 'Not many people have it. That's the weird thing—how'd they get it?'

Dorothy noticed something else. 'They used an anonymiser. A disposable anonymous email address. Untraceable.'

The subject line read 'Your Daughter.' The message was brief:

Mr Marcus:

If you want to see your daughter again, click here:

www.CamFriendz.com

Click on: Private Chat Rooms

Enter in search box: Alexa M

User name: Marcus

Password: LiveOrDie?

You may log in only from your home or office. No other location. We monitor everyone who signs in. If we detect any other incoming IP addresses, including any law-enforcement agencies, local or national, all communications will be severed and your daughter will be terminated.

He turned round to look at us. 'Belinda wouldn't let me click on the link.' He sounded depleted and resigned.

'What's CamFriendz-dot-com?' Belinda said.

'It's a live video site,' Dorothy said. 'Social networking.'

Marcus said, 'What should I do?'

'Wait a minute,' Dorothy said. She took out her laptop and hooked it up to a cable in the back of his computer. 'OK.'

'What are you doing?' Belinda said.

'A couple of things,' she said. 'Screen-capture software so we can record anything they send you. Also, packet-sniffing software so I can log network activity remotely.'

'They say if anyone else tries to look at this, they're going to cut off all communication! Are you trying to get her killed?'

'No,' Dorothy said. 'All I'm doing is setting up, in effect, a clone of this computer. I'm not logging in. No one's going to detect it.'

'Well, you can just look at Marshall's computer,' Belinda said. 'I will not have you compromise Alexa's safety in any way.'

'They have no way of knowing that's what I'm doing.' I could see Dorothy's patience was running out. 'Also, we need to make sure they're not trying to infect this computer with malicious code. May I?' Her fingers were poised over Marcus's keyboard. He nodded.

'Don't touch that!' Belinda said, alarmed.

'Can I talk to you for a moment?' I said to her, and I took her out into the hall. 'I'm worried about your husband. He'd be panicking by now if it weren't for you. You did the right thing by telling him to call me and by not letting him click on that link.'

She looked pleased.

'And I hate to impose on you further at a time like this,' I said, 'but I need you to go into another room and make an evidentiary compilation for me.'

'An . . . evidentiary . . .'

'Sorry, that's the technical term for an exhaustive description of all potential evidence that might help lead to her whereabouts,' I said. I'd made it up on the spot, but it sounded plausible.

'What sort of evidence?'

'Everything. I mean, what Alexa was wearing when she left. The make and size of her shoes and each item of clothing, her handbag, anything she might have been carrying in it. You're far more observant than Marshall, and it's extremely important. We need the compilation as soon as possible. Within the next hour.'

'Y'all want me to use a computer or write it out?'

'Whatever's fastest for you,' I said.

I went back in. Dorothy had positioned herself in front of Marshall's computer, standing. She tapped, moved the mouse, and after a minute she said, 'OK. Open the hyperlink.'

In seconds a new window opened. It showed a web site with a banner across the top: CAMFRIENDZ—THE LIVE COMMUNITY!

Within it were moving video windows. In some of them were second-tier celebs like Paris Hilton. In others, teenage girls wearing low-cut tank tops and a lot of eye make-up.

Dorothy tapped and moused again, entered some text, scrolled down, clicked some more. A still photo of Alexa popped up.

A school portrait, it looked like, from when she was younger.

Green letters at the top of Alexa's photo said ENTER CHAT.

Dorothy clicked on it, and a log-in window appeared. She entered the username and password they'd supplied. For a while nothing happened. She sidled over to her laptop, and Marshall and I came closer to the screen to watch.

Then a big window popped up, with another still photo of Alexa.

Only this looked like it had been taken recently. Her eyes were closed, with dark smudges of make-up that made her look like a raccoon. Her hair was scraggly. She looked terrible. Then I realised this was video. You could see slight motion as she shifted in her sleep, and the light was strange, green-saturated, as if taken with an infrared camera, indicating that she was in the dark.

A loud metallic voice: 'Alexa, it's time to say hello to your father.' A man's voice. An accent: eastern European, maybe.

Alexa's eyes came open, her eyes staring wide, her mouth agape.

Marcus gasped. 'She's alive. God almighty, she's *alive*.'

Alexa's eyes were shifting back and forth. She said, 'Dad?'

Marcus stood up, shouted, 'Lexie. Baby! I'm here!'

'She can't hear you,' Dorothy said.

The amplified voice said, 'You may speak, Alexa.'

Her words came all in a rush in a high-pitched shriek. 'Dad, oh please, they've got me in this—'

The sound of her voice abruptly cut out, and the accented voice said, 'Follow the script exactly, Alexa, or you will never talk to your father, or anyone else, again.'

Now she was screaming, her eyes bulging, face flushed, head moving side to side, but there was no sound, and after ten more seconds the window went black.

Marcus said, '*No!*' and he catapulted himself out of his chair.

'The link's gone down,' Dorothy said. The video image had once again become Alexa's school portrait. 'She didn't cooperate.'

I glanced over at Dorothy's laptop, saw a column of white numbers whizzing by on a black background. 'What'd you get?' I asked her. 'Can you tell where the signal's coming from?'

She shook her head. 'Looks like CamFriendz is based in the Philippines. So that's a dead end. These guys could be anywhere in the world.'

Marcus began to teeter, I caught him. 'They killed her,' he said.

'No,' I said. 'They need her for ransom.'

Dorothy excused herself and said she wanted to give us privacy to talk. She took a second laptop from her Gucci bag and went to work in the sitting area off the kitchen to try to trace the IP address.

'You were expecting something like this, weren't you?' I said.

'Every day, Nick,' Marcus said sadly.

'After what happened to Alexa at the Chestnut Hill Mall.'

'Right,' he said softly. He stared straight ahead.

I spoke quietly to him. 'If they contact you and demand money, I know you'd do it in a heartbeat. But I need you to promise me you won't. Not until you consult with me and we make sure it's done the right way.'

He kept staring straight ahead.

'You never did call the police, did you?' I said.

'I—'

I interrupted him before he could go on. 'I don't like being lied to by my clients. I took this job because of Alexa, but if I find out you're lying or holding anything back, I'll walk away. Got it?'

He looked at me for a long time, blinking fast.

'I'll give you amnesty for anything you did or said up till now,' I said. 'But from here on out, any lie and I'm off the case. So let's try again: did you call the police?'

He paused. Then, eyes closed, he shook his head. 'No.'

'OK. This is a start. Why not?'

'Because I knew they'd just bring in the FBI.'

'So?'

'All the FBI cares about is putting me in prison.'

'And why's that? Do they have a case?'

He hesitated. Then, 'Yes.'

I looked at him. 'If you don't tell me everything now, I'll walk.'

'You wouldn't do that to Alexa.'

I stood up. 'I'm sure the FBI will do everything possible to find her.'

'Wait!' Marcus said. 'Nick, listen to me.'

I turned back. 'Yes?'

'Even if they asked for a ransom, I couldn't pay it.' His face was full of humiliation and anger and deep sadness all at once. 'I have nothing. Completely wiped out. I'm ruined.'

'You have ten billion dollars under management.'

'Had. It's all gone.'

'That's not possible.' I cocked my head. 'What happened?'

'About six or seven months ago my CFO noticed something so bizarre he thought we'd accidentally got the wrong statements. He saw that all of our stock holdings had been sold. All the proceeds were wired out, along with all the rest of our cash on hand.'

'Wired where? By whom?'

'If I knew, I'd have it back.'

'Well, you have a prime broker, don't you, that does all your trading? If they screwed up, they have to unwind it.'

Slowly he shook his head. 'All the trades were authorised using our codes and passwords. Our broker says they're not responsible.'

'Isn't there one guy there who's in charge of your account?'

'Of course. But by the time we discovered what had happened, he'd left the bank. A few days later he was found in Venezuela. Dead. He and his entire family had been killed in a car accident.'

'What brokerage firm do you use?'

I was expecting to hear one of the major players, and I was surprised when he answered, 'Banco Transnacional de Panamá.'

'*Panama?*' I said. 'Why?'

He shrugged. 'Half of our funds are offshore, you know. Arabs and the like—those are the ones with the real money.'

But I was dubious. Panama was the Switzerland of Latin America: the land of bank secrecy, an excellent place to stash money with no questions asked. Panama meant you had something to hide.

'Suddenly Marcus Capital Management had no capital to manage. We had nothing. *Nothing.*'

'I think I see where this is going. You couldn't tell your investors they'd lost all their money, right?'

'Some of them had hundreds of millions of dollars with me. What was I going to tell them? I screwed up? I never had a losing quarter all those decades. No one's ever had a record like that.'

'So what'd you do, Marshall?'

'I needed cash. Lots and lots of it. Massive infusions. And no bank in the world would lend me money.'

'Ah, gotcha. You took in new money so you could make it look like you hadn't lost anything. So who'd you take money from?'

'You don't want to know, Nickeleh. These are bad men.'

'Let me hear some names.'

'You ever hear of Joost Van Zandt?'

'Are you out of your mind?' Van Zandt was a Dutch arms dealer whose private militia had supported Liberia's murderous dictator, Charles Taylor.

'Desperate, more like,' he said. 'How about Agim Grazdani? Or Juan Carlos Santiago Guzman?'

Grazdani was the head of the Albanian mafia. His portfolio included gunrunning, human trafficking and counterfeiting. Guzman, the leader of Colombia's Norte del Valle cartel, was one of the most violent narcotics traffickers in the world.

'And the damned Russians,' he said. 'Stanislav Luzhin and Roman Navrozov and Oleg Uspensky.'

'My God, Marshall, what the hell was the idea?' I said.

'I thought I could get the ship righted with all the new cash and I'd be back on my feet. But it wasn't enough to meet all the margin calls. My whole firm went down the crapper anyway.'

'The new money with the old.'

He nodded.

'Guzman and Van Zandt and Grazdani and the Russians,' I said. 'You lost all their money. Which one of them took your daughter?'

'I have no idea.'

'I'm going to need a complete list of all of your investors.'

'You're not walking away? Thank you, Nick.'

'I also want a list of all your employees, past and present. Including household staff, past and present. Personnel files, too.'

There was a knock on the door.

'I'm sorry to interrupt,' Dorothy said, 'but the video stream is back online.'

WE CROWDED AROUND the monitor while Dorothy worked the keyboard.

'It just started up,' she said.

The same still photo of Alexa as a girl. Superimposed over it, in green letters: LIVE and ENTER CHAT. Dorothy moved the mouse and clicked. Alexa's face appeared again. That same extreme close-up. Tears ran down her cheeks.

'Dad?' she said. She was looking slightly off to the side, as if she didn't know for sure where the camera was. 'Daddy, they're not going to let me go unless you give them something, OK?'

The picture was sort of stuttery and jittery. Not very high quality. 'Um . . . first, they say if you contact the police or anything, they're just going to . . .'

She blinked rapidly, tears streaming down. 'I'm so cold, and I'm so afraid that I'm too weak and I can't change,' she said suddenly, almost in a monotone. 'I—I twist and turn in the darkest space and . . . I don't want to be here anymore, Daddy.'

There was a low rumble, and suddenly the image pixellated: it froze, turned into thousands of tiny squares that broke apart, and a second later the image went dark.

But then the video was back. Alexa was saying, 'They want *Mercury*, Daddy, OK? You have to give them *Mercury* in the raw. I—I don't know what that means. They said you will. Please, Daddy, I don't think I can hold out any longer.'

And then the image went dark once again. We waited a few seconds, but this time it didn't come back.

'Is that it?' Marcus said, looking wildly from me to Dorothy and back. 'That's the end of the video?'

'I'm sure it's not the last,' I said.

'IR camera for sure,' Dorothy said. Infrared, she meant. The reason for the video's monochrome, greenish cast.

'They're holding her in total darkness,' I said.

Marcus shouted, 'What are they doing to her? Where is she?'

'They don't want us to know yet,' I said. 'So what happened to the image at the end?'

'Some kind of transmission error, maybe,' Dorothy said.

'I'm not so sure. You notice that low-pitched sound? Sounded like a car or a truck nearby.'

Dorothy nodded. 'They're probably near a highway.'

'Nope,' I said. 'Not a busy street. That was the first vehicle we heard. So that tells us she's near a road, but not a busy one.' I turned to Marcus. 'What's Mercury?'

His eyes flooded with tears. 'No idea.'

'And what was all that about "I'm too weak and I can't change" and "I twist and turn in the darkest space"?'

'Who the hell knows,' he said, his voice phlegmy. 'She's terrified. She was just babbling!'

'It sounded like she was reciting something. A book? Maybe something you used to read to her when she was a little kid?'

'I . . . you know . . .' He faltered. 'You know, her mother read to her. And your mother. I—I never did. I really wasn't around very much.'

And he put a hand over his eyes.

AS WE DROVE AWAY from Marcus's house into the starless night, I told Dorothy about how Marshall Marcus had lost it all.

She reacted with the same kind of slack-jawed disbelief that I had. 'You telling me he lost ten billion dollars like it dropped behind the sofa cushions?'

'Basically.'

She shook her head. She was multi-tasking, tapping away at her BlackBerry as she talked. 'You have any idea what Mercury is?'

'Marshall doesn't know. Why should I?'

'Marshall *says* he doesn't know. Maybe it's one of his offshore funds or something. Money he's stashed somewhere.'

'No. If the kidnappers know they lost their whole investment, they also know he's broke. So Mercury *can't* refer to money.'

'All these guys hide chunky nuts of money away. Like evil squirrels.'

'But why not just say wire three hundred million dollars into such-and-such offshore account or we kill the kid?'

'I don't know,' she admitted.

'Well, what's more valuable than money? Some proprietary trading algorithm, maybe. Some investment formula he invented.'

'You think he knows but he's not telling us? Even if it gets his daughter killed?'

For a long time I said nothing. 'Hard to believe, isn't it?'

'You know him,' she said. 'I don't.'

'No,' I said. 'I thought I knew him. Now I'm not so sure.'

'Hmph,' she said. Then she said it again.

'What?'

'Oh, please don't let this be true.'

'What are you talking about?'

I glanced at Dorothy. She was staring at her BlackBerry. 'That stuff Alexa was saying? "I twist and turn in the darkest space"?'

'Yeah?'

'I Googled it. Nick, it's a lyric from a song by a rock group called Alter Bridge. The song's called "Buried Alive".'

6

By the time I'd dropped Dorothy off at her apartment and found a parking space near my loft downtown, it was almost nine at night. I found a space a few blocks away, cut through the alley and up the stairwell to the back entrance on the fifth floor.

The loft was one large open space with a fifteen-foot ceiling. The bedroom was in an alcove on the opposite side of the apartment from the bathroom. Bad design. In another alcove was a kitchen with high-end appliances, none of which I'd ever used, except the refrigerator. There were cast-iron support columns and exposed brick. The place was spare and functional. Uncluttered.

I went straight to the bathroom, stripped, and jumped in the shower. I stood there feeling the hot water pound my back. Unable to get the image of poor Alexa Marcus out of my head. I wondered what she meant by 'buried alive'. Maybe she was locked in an underground bunker or vault of some kind.

When I shut off the water and reached for the towel, I thought I heard a noise. A snap or a click. Or nothing.

I listened for a moment, then began towelling myself off.

And heard it again. Definitely something. Coming from inside the apartment. A *scritch scritch scritch*.

I let the towel drop and nudged the bathroom door open a bit wider. Listened harder.

It was definitely inside the loft, at the front.

Both of my firearms were out of reach. The SIG SAUER P250 semi-automatic pistol was under my bed. But to reach the bedroom alcove, I'd have to pass them first. I cursed the idiotic layout of the place, putting the bathroom so far from the bedroom. The other weapon, a Smith & Wesson M&P 9mm, was in a safe under the kitchen floor. Closer to them than to me.

The recently refinished wooden floors were solid and silky smooth, and they didn't squeak when you walked on them. Barefoot, I was able to take a few noiseless steps into the room.

Two men in black ambush jackets. One was large and heavily muscled, with a Neanderthal forehead and a black brush cut. He was sitting at my desk doing something to my keyboard, even though he didn't look like the computer-savvy type. The other was small, with short mouse-brown hair, sallow complexion. He sat on the floor right beneath my huge wall-mounted flatscreen TV. He was holding my cable modem and doing something with a screwdriver.

Both of them wore latex gloves, jeans and dark jackets. If you'd ever worked undercover, you'd know their clothing was as conspicuous as an electronic Times Square billboard. It was carry-conceal attire, with hidden pistol pockets and magazine pouches.

I had no idea who they were or why they were here, but I knew immediately they were armed. And I wasn't. I wasn't even dressed.

I wasn't scared, either. I was pissed off, outraged at the audacity of these two intruding into my living space. I wanted to know who had sent them, and why.

So I backed into the bathroom and stood there for a moment, dripping on the floor, considering my options, thinking.

Somehow they'd got in without setting off the alarm. They'd managed to defeat my security system, which wasn't easy. Obviously they hadn't expected me to be home. Nor did they see or hear me come in through the service entrance at the back of the loft. They hadn't heard me showering at the other end of the apartment: in this old building, water constantly flowed through the pipes.

My one advantage was that they didn't know I was here.

This was a time when a little clutter might have been useful. At first glance, I saw nothing promising. Toothbrush and toothpaste, water glass, mouthwash, towels.

Then I saw my electric razor. Its coiled cord was about two feet long. Stretched to its full length, it would probably reach six feet. I slipped on my trousers, unplugged the razor, then padded silently, stealthily, into the main room.

I had to go for the muscle first. The computer guy wasn't likely to be much of a threat. Once Mongo was out of the way, I'd find out whatever I could from Gigabyte.

I approached slowly.

In a few seconds, I was ten feet away from the intruders, hidden behind a column. Holding the shaver in my right hand and the plug in my left, I pulled my right hand back, stretching out the coiled cord like a slingshot. Then hurled it, hard, at the side of his head.

It made an audible crack. The man screamed, tipped back in the chair, and crashed to the floor. I jerked at the cord, and the shaver ricocheted back to me.

Meanwhile, the computer guy was scrambling to his feet. But I wanted to make sure the big one stayed down. I launched myself at him, landing on top of him, and jammed my knee into his solar plexus. The wind came out of him. He managed to land a hard punch on my jaw, painful but not disabling. I aimed a drive at his face with everything I had. It connected with a wet crunch. He screamed, writhed in agony. His nose was broken, maybe a few teeth as well.

In my peripheral vision, I noticed that the weedy computer guy was pulling what appeared to be a weapon from his jacket.

During the brief struggle, I'd dropped the electric razor, so I reached for the weighted sticky-tape dispenser on my desk and in one smooth arc hurled it at him. He ducked, and it clipped him on the shoulder. The weapon in his right hand, I saw now, was a black pistol with a fat oblong barrel. A Taser.

Tasers are meant to incapacitate, not kill, but take my word for it, you don't want to get hit with one. They send fifty thousand volts and a few amps coursing through your body, paralysing you, disrupting your central nervous system.

He took aim like an expert. I leaped to one side, and something grabbed my ankle, causing me to stumble. It was the beefy guy.

The thin one smiled at me. I heard the click of the Taser being armed. I swept a big black Maglite flashlight from the edge of my desk and swung it at his knees. He dodged, but the Maglite struck his legs just below his kneecaps with a satisfying crack.

I reached up to grab the Taser, but instead I got hold of the black canvas tool bag on his shoulder. He spun away and fired.

The pain was unbelievable. Every single muscle in my body cramped tighter and tighter. I was no longer in control of my body. I went rigid as a board, and toppled to the floor.

BY THE TIME I COULD MOVE, two minutes or so later, both men were gone. Far too late to attempt to give chase, even if I were able to run. Which I certainly wasn't.

I got up gingerly and surveyed the mess, my anger building, wondering who had sent these men to do a black-bag job on me.

I gathered the things the intruders had left behind in their haste to leave, including the black canvas tool bag and my dismantled cable modem. And one thing more: a little white device connected between one of the USB ports on the back of my computer tower and the cable to my keyboard. It almost looked like it belonged there. The colour matched exactly. If you weren't looking for it, you'd never have noticed it.

I'm no computer expert, but I knew this little doohickey was called a keylogger. It contained a miniature USB drive that captured every single keystroke you type and stored it on a memory chip.

Inside the case to my cable modem, I found a little black device that I recognised as a flash drive. I had a feeling it didn't belong there. I called Dorothy on my BlackBerry.

'They knew you were meeting with Marcus,' she said. 'They didn't think you'd be home.'

'Well, if so, that means they weren't watching us.'

'You'd have detected physical surveillance, Nick. They're not stupid. I want you to put that keylogger back in the USB drive.'

I did.

'Do you know how to open a text editor?'

'I do if you tell me how.'

She did, and I opened a window on my computer and read off a long series of numbers. Then I took the keylogger out of the USB port and inserted the little device from the cable modem. And repeated the process, reading off more numbers.

'Hang on,' she said.

I waited. The two spots where the Taser prongs had sunk in, on my right shoulder and my left lower back, were still twitching and were starting to get itchy.

'Huh,' she said. 'Oh, now, this is interesting. The serial numbers you just gave me come from law enforcement-grade equipment. Whoever broke in was working for the US government.'

'Or at least was using government equipment,' I pointed out. 'They weren't necessarily government operatives themselves.' Though now I had a fairly good idea about who might have sent them.

Even before I arrived at the Boston field office of the FBI, Gordon Snyder knew why I wanted to talk with him, and he knew I was working for Marshall Marcus, who was the target of a major high-level FBI investigation. And I, as someone employed by Marcus, was probably an accomplice. Which made me a target, too.

Snyder had flat out told me that the FBI was tapping Marcus's phones. Which meant he knew I'd driven up to Manchester. He knew I wasn't home, that it was safe to send his black-bag boys.

I recalled Diana's warning: *If he thinks you're working against him, against his case, he'll come gunning for you.* 'Can you pull up the video for my home cameras? I want to see how they got in.'

When I moved in, I'd hired a security firm to put digital surveillance cameras outside the doors to my loft. They were all motion-activated and were networked into a video server at the office. The surveillance video was stored on the office network.

She said she'd call me back. While I waited, I searched the apartment for more traces left by Gordon Snyder's team.

When Dorothy called back, she said, 'I'm afraid I don't have the answer for you. Take a look at your computer.'

I walked back to my desk and saw what looked like four photographs on my screen of the stairwells outside the front and back doors to my loft. Each, I saw, was the video feed from a different camera. Somehow she'd put them on my computer remotely.

'How'd you do that?' I said.

'A good magician never reveals her secrets.' The cursor began moving, circling the first two windows. 'These first two didn't get any action, so forget them.' They disappeared. 'Now watch.'

The remaining two windows grew bigger so that they took up most of the monitor. 'They entered your apartment at eight twenty-two p.m. So here we are, eight twenty-one and . . . thirty seconds.' Both windows advanced a few frames, and suddenly a red starburst appeared in the middle of each image, obliterating them.

'Laser zapper,' I said.

'Exactly.'

The red cloud disappeared after a minute, and the picture returned.

'So we still don't know how they got in,' I said. 'But this tells us they knew where the cameras were.'

'Why do you say that?'

'You can't blind the cameras if you don't know where they are. But both cameras are concealed,' I said. 'One in a smoke detector and one in an air vent. The smoke-detector camera isn't all that original. But the air vent one—that's unusual. It takes some serious skill to hit that one first time.'

'So what's your point?'

'They got hold of the schematics. As well as my password.'

'Maybe from the security company that put them in.'

'Possibly. Or maybe from my own files, there in the office.'

'Not possible,' she said. 'I'd have detected the intrusion, Nick.'

'Put it this way,' I said. 'Not only did they know exactly where my cameras were, but they were able to disarm the system. Meaning they knew the code.'

'From your security company.'

'They don't know my code.'

'Who does?'

'Just me.'

'You don't keep your code written down anywhere?'

'Just in my personal files at the office,' I said. 'On my computer. Stored on our server.'

'Oh,' she said. 'Someone's got into the office network.'

'Or else we've got a leak,' I said. The other line rang. I saw from the caller ID it was Diana. 'Let me take this.' I clicked over.

'Nick,' Diana said, her voice tight. 'I just heard from AT&T. I think we've found our girl. Her phone's on and transmitting.'

'Where is she?' I said.

'Leominster.'

'That's an hour away.' I looked at my watch. 'Maybe less, this time of night. How precise a location did they give you?'

'They're emailing me lat-and-long coordinates, in degrees and minutes. Give me ten minutes.'

'Go back to bed. I got this.'

'Technically, I put in the request. I'm not allowed to pass on the information to someone outside the Bureau.'

'OK,' I said. 'I'll drive; you navigate.'

I QUICKLY GATHERED some equipment, including the Smith & Wesson and a handheld GPS unit, a Garmin eTrex.

As we drove, I told Diana what had happened since I'd seen her last: the surveillance tape at the Graybar Hotel, the guy who'd spiked Alexa's drink and driven her away. Her 'friend' Taylor Armstrong, who'd cooperated in the abduction for some reason I didn't yet understand. The streaming video. Marshall Marcus's admission that he'd taken money from some dangerous people in a last-ditch attempt to save his fund, though he'd lost it all anyway.

Diana furrowed her brow. 'Let me check the phone detail records.' She began scrolling through her BlackBerry. 'The last outgoing call hit the tower in Leominster at two thirty-seven a.m.'

'Almost twenty-four hours ago,' I said. 'How long did it last?'

More scrolling. 'About ten seconds.'

I heard her scroll some more, and then she said, 'The last number dialled was nine-one-one. Emergency. But it doesn't look like the call went through. It hit the tower, but it must have been cut off.'

'I'm impressed. She must have been pretty spaced out from the drugs, but she had the wherewithal to try to call for help. What calls did she receive around then?'

'A bunch of incoming, between three in the morning to around noon today. Two land lines in Manchester-by-the-Sea.'

'Her dad.'

'One mobile phone, also Marcus's. The fourth is another mobile phone, registered to Taylor Armstrong.'

'So Taylor did try to call. Interesting. If she was trying to reach Alexa, that may indicate she was actually worried about her friend. Which indicates she might not have known what happened to her.'

'Or that she was feeling guilty about what she'd done and wanted to make sure Alexa was OK.'

'Right,' I said.

For a time we didn't talk. It had started to rain. I switched on the wipers. I began to sense her looking at me. 'What?' I said.

'Why is there blood on your collar? And please don't tell me you cut yourself shaving.'

I explained about the break-in at my loft. Gave her my theory that Gordon Snyder was behind it. When I was done, she said, 'That's not FBI. That's not how we work. If Snyder wanted to monitor your email, he'd do it remotely.'

I thought for a moment. 'You may have a point.'

We went quiet again. I was on the verge of asking her about what had happened between us earlier in the day when she said abruptly, 'Why is her phone still on?'

'Good question. They should have turned it off or destroyed it. Anyone who watches crime shows knows a cellphone can give up your location.'

'Maybe she hid it somewhere. Like in the vehicle she was abducted in.'

'Maybe.'

A black Silverado was weaving between lanes without signalling.

'I'm glad we reconnected,' I said. It came out a little stiff. 'Funny to think we've both been in Boston all these months.'

'I meant to call.'

'Nah, where's the fun in that? Keep the guy guessing.'

She was silent for a moment. 'Did I ever tell you about my dad?'

'A bit.' I knew he'd been killed while tracking down a fugitive, but I waited to see what she'd say.

'You know he was a US Marshal, right? I remember how my mom always lived with that knot in her stomach, you know—when he left for work in the morning, would he come home safe?'

'Yet you risk your own safety every day,' I said gently, not sure what she was getting at.

'Well, that's the life I signed up for. But always having to worry about someone else? That's more than I can stand, Nico.'

'What are you saying?'

'I'm saying we had an understanding, and I knew I wasn't abiding by it. We were supposed to be casual—no pressure, no commitment, right? But I was starting to get in a little too deep, and I knew that wasn't going to be good for either one of us.'

I couldn't help thinking about all that had been left unsaid between us, but all I managed was, 'You never said a word about it.'

She shrugged, went quiet. The only sound was the highway hum, a faint rhythmic thrumming.

'They didn't ask me to go to Seattle,' she said softly. 'I put in for a transfer. I had to pull myself out, because I saw what my mom went through. I should probably marry a chartered accountant, you know?'

For a long time no one spoke.

Now we were zooming along Route 12 North through Leominster. On the other side of the street was a Staples and a Marshall's. A Bickford's restaurant. A Friendly's restaurant. All closed and dark. I pulled over to the shoulder and put on the flashers.

She looked up from the GPS. 'This is it,' she said. 'We're within a thousand feet of it right now. Right there.' Diana pointed. 'That's 482 North Main Street.'

Behind the Friendly's was a four-storey motel built of stucco and brick in the classic American architectural style best described as Motel Ugly. A tall pole-mounted road sign out front had the yellow-and-red Motel 12 logo brightly illuminated.

I pulled into the motel parking lot. There were maybe a dozen cars parked. None of them was the Porsche I'd seen on the surveillance video, not that I expected to see it here. On the other side of the motel loomed a tall self-storage building. Nothing seemed quite right.

'Dammit,' I said, 'we need more precise coordinates. Can you call AT&T back and ask them to ping the phone again? I want the GPS coordinates in decimal format.'

While she called, I walked back towards the road. No construction lots that I could see, no fields or private homes.

'Got it,' Diana called out, running towards me. She held the Garmin out, and I took it. A flashing arrow represented us. A dot indicated Alexa's iPhone, and it was extremely close. I walked closer to the road, and the flashing arrow moved with me.

I crossed the street to a scrubby shoulder beside a guardrail. Now the arrow and the dot were almost aligned. I stepped over the guardrail and onto a steep downward grade that rolled into a drainage ditch, then rose sharply. I scrambled down the hill. At the bottom, I looked again at the GPS. The arrow was precisely on top of the dot. I looked up, then to my right and to my left.

And there, in the yellow light of the street lamp, I saw it. Lying in the ditch, a few feet away. An iPhone in a pink rubber case.

Instead of finding Alexa, we'd found her discarded phone.

But it told us she was probably within a hundred miles of Boston. We knew from the hotel's surveillance tape what time she'd been abducted. We knew from the 911 call that she'd gone through Leominster, north of Boston, less than an hour later.

Only fourteen hours had elapsed between her abduction and the first time her kidnappers had contacted Marshall Marcus. That included trans-porting her and then—if her clues were to be taken literally—burying her in some sort of crypt or vault. And setting up cameras that could broadcast over the Internet. An arrangement like that was complicated and must have taken several hours. So they couldn't have gone too far. But that didn't narrow it down much.

I DROPPED DIANA OFF at FBI headquarters. It was barely six in the morning. She'd grab the techs as soon as they got in and ask them for a complete work-up of Alexa's phone.

After she got out, I sat in the Defender and thought about going home to catch a few hours' sleep. Until I checked my email.

I found a long series of emails not from a name but from a number I didn't recognise. It took me a few seconds to realise that they'd been sent automatically by the miniature GPS tracker concealed in Taylor Armstrong's gold S. T. Dupont lighter.

Well, not *her* lighter, but the one I'd switched with hers when I'd 'accidentally' dropped it. I'd bought it at the tobacco shop in Park Square, the exact same S. T. Dupont Ligne 2 Gold Diamond Head lighter. A classic, and ridiculously expensive. But a lot cheaper than hiring someone to tail her.

The tiny tracking device had been installed by an old Special Forces buddy of mine who had his own business in technical surveillance counter-measures. He had wedged a nano GPS device inside the fluid reservoir and programmed the thing to send out signals when it was moved more than a thousand feet. Now I could see that immediately after Taylor and I had our little talk on the corner of Charles and Beacon, she went home—or was driven home in David Schechter's limousine—and then she drove to Medford, five miles northwest. So who might she be meeting with such urgency?

I had a pretty good idea.

TWENTY MINUTES LATER I was driving down Oldfield Road in Medford, a pleasant street lined with graceful old trees and clapboard houses. Some were two-family homes, some apartment buildings, most of them well maintained. The Tufts University campus was a short walk away.

The house where Taylor Armstrong had spent forty-three minutes last night was a white three-storey wooden house. At six thirty in the morning, there wasn't much going on in the neighbourhood.

I got out and, with a quick glance around, I climbed the front porch quietly but casually and saw a stack of five buzzers with a stack of matching names. Five apartments. Five surnames. Schiff, Murdoch, Perreira, O'Connor and Unger. I memorised them, went back to the car, hit a speed-dial button on my BlackBerry, and woke Dorothy up.

She called back five minutes later. 'Margaret O'Connor is seventy-nine years old, a widow, and has owned the house since 1974. The other four rent. One works for Amnesty International. Two of them are Tufts graduate students. The fourth is our guy.'

'Which one?'

'Perreira. His full name is Mauricio da Silva Cordeiro-Perreira. I pulled up his pic. It's the same guy from the hotel surveillance tape.'

'His surname's on his doorbell. So Taylor knew his last name. What's his connection to her?'

'Here's what I found out: thirty-two years old. Born in São Paulo, Brazil. Rich family—we're talking major money. Daddy's with the UN in New York. He's a member of Brazil's permanent mission. Mauricio grew up in one of those gated compounds in Morumbi, on the outskirts of São Paulo.'

'So how'd a rich boy like that end up living in a walk-up apartment in Medford?'

'Looks like he spent a few lazy years as a grad student at the Fletcher School of Law and Diplomacy at Tufts. But he's a dealer—mostly coke and weed, some meth.'

'Now it gets interesting. What do you have on that?'

'A couple of years ago there was this joint DEA/ICE investigation on the theory that the kid was using his father's diplomatic pouch to bring in controlled substances.'

'Dad must not have been too pleased with that,' I said.

'Wouldn't surprise me if Daddy disowned him. He's been busted a couple of times, but nothing sticks.'

'If his dad's at the UN, he's protected by diplomatic immunity.'

'They can't get arrested for drugs?'

'They can't get arrested for murder,' I said.

'Man, I picked the wrong life. I shoulda been a diplomat. What I'd give for a loaded gun and ten minutes of diplomatic immunity.'

'Now this is starting to come together,' I said. 'Taylor has a record of drug problems, and Mauricio is probably her dealer.' His family background gave him entrée to the right social circles—well-off college kids. And prep-school kids like Taylor Armstrong.

'Daddy disowns him, there goes the trust fund,' Dorothy said. 'And the diplomatic pouch. Supply drops; money stops flowing in so fast; it gets hard to pay the rent. Guy like that might get desperate for money. Take on a high-risk job like kidnapping a rich girl.'

'Or maybe he was hired because he was Taylor's dealer,' I said.

'Hired by who?'

'Well, Mauricio is from Brazil. One of Marcus Capital's unhappy investors is Juan Carlos Guzman.'

'Who is . . . ?'

'Colombian drug lord who lives in Brazil.'

'Oh, God, a drug cartel has that girl? And you think you're gonna get her back?'

'With your help I have a chance.'

'Nick, there's no way I or anyone else is gonna trace that video feed. I've talked to everyone I know.'

'They went to a lot of trouble to send Marcus a ransom demand.'

'You think our guy's still in that apartment or he took off?'

'I don't know. If he is, he was just the courier—he picked Alexa up and handed her off to someone else,' I said.

'What if he's not there?'

'I'll ransack his apartment and see what I can find that might lead me to Alexa. Talk later.' I clicked off.

Drug dealers tend to live in a state of paranoia. He probably had a gun close to the bed—under it or behind the headboard.

The only workable plan was to take him by surprise.

I kept an assortment of tools in my car's glove box and reached for the EZ snap gun, a good old manual lock pick. Unfortunately, lock-pick guns aren't particularly quiet.

I mounted the apartment building's side stairs, which provided exterior entry to the separate units. I ascended to the top level, sidled along the railing for a few feet, and assessed.

A small window, curtains drawn, next to the apartment door. A simple pin tumbler lock. Some no-name brand. That was a relief.

And a pinpoint LED light: a security system. But the light was dark. He probably disarmed the system when he was at home.

So he was here. Good. I worked quickly. A loud snap. I had to squeeze the lock-pick gun's handle ten or eleven more times. Unless Perreira was deep asleep, he must have heard it. Finally, I felt the lock turn, and I was in.

An air conditioner was on somewhere, in another room. All the curtains were drawn. In a few seconds, my eyes became accustomed to the dark. I approached the loud snoring that came from an open bedroom door. Mouth gaping, snoring like a buzz saw, was the man I recognised as Lorenzo. The guy from the security video at Slammer. The guy who'd abducted Alexa. No question about it.

I came round to the side of the bed where Perreira lay under the rumpled sheet. In my left fist I grabbed the end of the sheet. With a swift jerk I yanked it up and over his head, then under, trapping his head in the sheet. He began to flail. But he was wrapped as tight as a mummy. My right hand gripped his throat and squeezed.

He shouted, and thrashed his arms and legs. I clambered on top of his writhing body, pinning him down with my knees. I was afraid he might pass out, so I eased up a bit on his throat.

He gasped, then said hoarsely, '*O que você quer?*'

I had no idea what he was saying. I don't speak Portuguese. 'Where is she? Speak English,' I said.

'I deliver'—he gasped—'the package. I *deliver* the package!'

'*Package?*' A white-hot anger crackled in my blood like a live wire. It took great restraint to keep from crushing his windpipe.

Clearly he thought I was connected to the kidnapping. And he *was* just the delivery boy—he'd been hired to abduct Alexa and hand her over to someone else.

He thought I was one of his employers. That meant he probably hadn't met them. Which could be useful.

'I'm going to let you go so you can answer a few questions,' I said. 'If you lie about anything at all, I'm going to slice your ear off and send it to your father at the UN for his office wall.'

'No! I tell you everything! What do you want? I do everything you say! I gave you this girl, and I shut my mouth.'

'Where is she?'

'Why you asking me this? You tell me to pick the bitch up and drug her and bring her to you. I do it. I got the money. I say nothing. We're all done here. It's all good.'

It's all good. A phrase I really hate.

'For you I'd say it's pretty much all bad right now.'

On his bedside table was a Nokia cellphone. I grabbed it with my free hand and pocketed it.

Then I reached behind the headboard and found what felt a lot like a gun duct-taped back there. A very expensive STI pistol. I pocketed that, too, then released my grip on his throat entirely.

'All right.' I climbed off and stood beside the bed. 'Get up.'

Weakly, he shifted his legs over the side of the bed. He gasped, 'What you want from me, man? I gave it to—the guy.'

'Which guy?'

'The guy who gave me the phone. I don't know anyone's name, man! I can't talk. The guy got eyes on the back of his head!'

I was about to ask what he meant when I heard the thunder of footsteps on the stairs outside. He heard it, too. His face was tight with fear. Then came a crash and the splintering sound of his door being broken down with a metal ram.

The men who burst into the room were wearing green uniforms with green ballistic vests and black Kevlar helmets and goggles that made them look like giant insects. They all had FBI patches on their shoulders and chests.

The expression on Mauricio's face changed. He looked relieved.

7

The man was slowly crossing the bare earthen field towards the farmhouse when the satphone on his belt began to trill. He knew who it was, because only one person had this number.

As he answered the phone, he stopped at the centre of the hump of earth and made a mental note to take another run at it with the pneumatic backfill tamper. Or a few passes with the backhoe tyres. Not that the girl was going anywhere, ten feet down.

But in rural New Hampshire, neighbours sometimes got curious.

'Yes?' Dragomir said.

'Nothing yet,' said the man who called himself Kirill. They spoke in Russian.

Kirill was an intermediary who passed messages back and forth between Dragomir and the very rich man Kirill called only the Client. Never a name. This was fine with Dragomir. The less he and the Client knew about each other, the better.

But Kirill worried that some detail might go awry. He seemed to think that his daily check-ins would keep everything running smoothly. He didn't know that Dragomir rarely made mistakes.

'What do you think, the father went back to sleep? He should have sent the file immediately. His daughter—'

'Patience,' Dragomir said.

A plane roared overhead, and the line went staticky. Jets flew by every hour or so, mostly at night, from the air base.

'—hostage is in good health?' Kirill was saying.

The iridium phone was encrypted, so Kirill spoke fairly openly. Dragomir never did. His reply was curt, 'Is there anything else?'

'Nothing.'

He disconnected the call. The setting sun gave a golden cast to the raked soil. He had a fleeting memory of the hard dirt prison yard, where no grass could grow. He'd liked lawns ever since.

Dragomir mounted the porch, past the air compressor on its long yellow extension cord, and pulled the screen door open. There were holes in the screen, so he opened and closed the wooden back door swiftly to keep out the bugs. The whole farmhouse was falling down. But he had no right to complain. The house and the land it sat on, nearly three hundred acres in a remote part of New Hampshire, was owned by an old man who'd moved to Florida. The property hadn't had a visitor in four years. Not even a caretaker. So he'd appointed himself caretaker. Even though the family trust had no idea.

As he went through the converted sun room, he could hear the girl's pathetic mewling over the computer speakers. The noise irritated him, so he hit a key to mute it.

AN HOUR LATER I was on the sixth floor of One Center Plaza with Diana, who looked exhausted, her eyes red-rimmed and bleary. Yet she was still the most beautiful woman I'd ever seen.

'So how'd that happen?' I said quietly as we walked.

'All I was told was a CI tipped them off.'

A confidential informant. 'Whose?'

We reached a warren of cubicles, most of them empty, but it was still early. Her cubicle was unmistakable.

It was the grade-school photos taped to the cubicle walls that marked it as her workspace: sweet-looking kids who obviously weren't relatives of hers. And the curling newspaper clips with headlines like SEX OFFENDER CHARGED IN GIRL'S DISAPPEARANCE.

'I have no idea,' she said. 'I'm not cleared at that level.'

'So who gave the order to roll the SWAT team?'

'The only person who can mobilise tactical is the SAC. But how did *you* know where to find Perreira?'

'I put a tracker on Taylor Armstrong.'

She smiled, nodded. 'Nice.'

'Whoever did this just screwed up our best chance to find Alexa,' I said. 'Where is he?'

'Downstairs in a locked interview room.'

'I want to talk to him.'

'You can't. He's invoking diplomatic immunity. A legal attaché from the Brazilian consulate in Boston is on his way in. A man named'—she glanced at a Post-it pad next to her desk phone—'Cláudio Duarte Carvalho Barboza. Until he's finished consulting with Perreira, no one can even *enter* the interview room.'

I stood up. 'Do me a favour and show me where he is,' I said.

'Why?'

'Just curious,' I said.

Diana led me down a flight of stairs to a closed, windowless door. A plain white door with a metal knob. No one standing around outside keeping watch.

'Any cameras or one-way mirrors?'

'Never. It's not Bureau policy.'

'Huh. You know, I'd love a cup of coffee.'

Her face was impassive, but there was a glint in her eyes. 'I may need to brew a fresh pot. Might take me a while.'

MAURICIO WAS LEANING BACK in a metal chair behind a Formica-topped table, looking bored. When he recognised me, he slowly grinned a broad smile of victory.

'I'm not talking, man. I got the . . . the *imunidade diplomática*.'

'So as soon as the legal attaché from the Brazilian consulate shows up, you're a free man. You go home. I like that.'

He found this amusing. 'You like that, huh?'

I joined him in a laugh. 'Oh, yeah. Definitely. Because out there, you don't have any diplomatic immunity. As soon as they let you go, it's going to be a feeding frenzy out there. The guys that hired you? They're going to assume you told us everything.'

A quick head shake. 'I don't cooperate with FBI.'

'Sure, you did.' I pulled out his Nokia mobile phone and showed it to him. 'You gave us a bunch of phone numbers, for one. And the US government is extremely grateful to you. In fact, I'm going to see to it personally that we issue you a commendation for all your help.'

'No one believe I talk,' he said. But he didn't sound so confident anymore. He'd assumed I was with the FBI, and I didn't plan to correct the impression.

'Yeah? I wonder what they'll think when I leave a message on your voicemail with the name of your contact at the Bureau. Telling you how to arrange our next meeting. Maybe talking about how you'll be wearing a wire next time you meet with your Colombian friends. Ever hear what they do to people who betray them?'

'They not gonna kill me.'

'True,' I said. 'They like to torture and mutilate first. But you know what? Today's your lucky day. Because I'm prepared to offer you a deal. You tell us what we want to know, and you'll never hear from us again.' I waited a beat. 'It's all good.'

'What do you want?' he whispered, his voice cracking.

'The name of the guy who hired you to pick up the girl. A full description. How he contacted you in the first place. Where you delivered the . . . "package" . . . to them.'

'I don't *know* the name, man,' he whispered. 'He was some big dude. Real strong. Real scary.'

He was telling the truth, I was now convinced. His terror had yanked away his habitual scrim of dishonesty. He had just one objective right now, which was to stay alive.

I heard what sounded like footsteps approaching, voices becoming louder. Mauricio heard it, too. He froze, looked at the door.

'Where did he take her?' I said.

'The guy's got eyes on the back of his head,' he whispered.

'What do you mean, eyes *in* the back of his head?'

But then the door came open, and a squat, hulking man in a grey suit with a gleaming bald head stared in. 'What the hell are you doing in here?' came the rumbling voice of Gordon Snyder.

Before I could reply, a loud voice came from behind him. 'No one is allowed to talk to my client! I made that clear on the phone.'

Someone shoved his way past Snyder into the interview room: a large, elegant man, probably six foot two. He had long grey hair, deep-set eyes and acne-gouged cheeks. He was wearing a dark suit and a burgundy foulard tie and an air of authority.

The legal attaché from the Brazilian consulate, of course.

'Remove this person at once,' he said, his English impeccable. 'My discussions with my client must be absolutely privileged.'

'Understood, Mr Barboza,' Snyder said. His eyes flashed with fury at me. 'Get the hell out of here,' he said.

A DOG WAS BARKING in the yard.

Dragomir's first thought was of hunters. It wasn't hunting season, but that didn't deter some people. He'd posted NO TRESPASSING/NO HUNTING signs, but not everyone could read, or chose to.

Hunters meant intruders, and intruders meant scrutiny.

People in rural areas were always getting involved in their neighbours' business. Are you the new owner? Are you an Alderson? What's with the Caterpillar backhoe loader out back?

He'd bought all the equipment with cash. The backhoe came from a farm-supply store in Biddeford, the air compressor from the Home Depot in Plaistow. The casket he'd picked out at a wholesale casket company in Dover. The sturdiest one they had was sixteen-gauge carbon steel. Groundwater seepage was always a problem, which might cause the girl to drown slowly before they were done with her, and that wouldn't do. Fortunately, the model he'd purchased was equipped with a water-resistant gasket. You turned a crank at the end of the box to seal it tight.

The refitting was quick work. He drilled a hole through the carbon steel at the end where the girl's head would be. There he welded a quarter-inch brass connector plug in place and attached it to a quarter-inch crushproof hose that ran several hundred feet to the air compressor on the porch. Air would flow in for a couple of minutes each hour, night and day, since it was on a timer switch. He trenched the hose into the ground, along with the Ethernet cable.

At the other end of the casket, he drilled a much larger opening with a hole saw. There he welded the brass bushing to attach the four-inch exhaust line. Now the grey PVC pipe stuck out of the ground in the middle of the dirt field. Its end curved down like an umbrella handle. It was the sort of thing used at a landfill to vent the methane gas that built up underground. So the girl would get a steady supply of fresh air, which was more than his father had had when he'd been trapped in the coal mine in Tomsk.

Each night his father came home caked in black dust so thick you could see only his eyes. Coal mining, he once told Dragomir, was the only job where you had to dig your own grave.

Dragomir listened, rapt, to his father's tales. How he'd seen a roof bolter come down on a friend of his and crush his face. Or watched a guy cut in half by the coal car. His mother, Dusya, raged at his father for filling a young boy's head with such frightening stories. But Dragomir always wanted to hear more.

The bedtime stories stopped when Dragomir was almost ten. A knock at the door to their communal apartment in the middle of the night. His mother's high, thin scream.

She brought him to the mine to join the crowds gathered there, pleading for news.

He was fascinated. He wanted to know what had happened, but no one would tell him. He overheard only fragments about how the miners had accidentally dug into an abandoned, flooded shaft. How the water rushed in and trapped them like rats.

But Dragomir wanted to know more. He wanted to know what it felt like to know that you were about to die and to be powerless to do anything about it, to know what his father knew in those last moments of his life. He'd always felt cheated somehow not to have seen the last seconds of his father's life.

All he had was his imagination.

The damned dog would not stop barking. Now he could hear it pawing at the screen door out back.

He opened the wooden door, his Wasp gas-injection knife at the ready. Just the screen between him and the cur. Startled, the dog backed away, bared its teeth, gave a low snarl.

He called to it softly in Russian, 'Here, pooch,' and opened the screen door. The dog lunged at him, and he plunged the blade into the beast's abdomen. With his thumb he slid the button to shoot out a frozen basketball of compressed air. The explosion was instantaneous, but he realised at once he'd done it wrong. He was spattered by the animal's viscera.

Once in a while he did make mistakes. Next time he would be sure to plunge the knife into the hilt before flicking the gas release.

It took him half an hour to sweep the ruined carcass into a trash bag and haul it into the woods to be buried later and then hose down the blood-slick porch and screen door.

He took a shower and got into clean jeans and a flannel shirt, and then he heard the doorbell ring. He looked out of the bedroom window, saw a Lexus SUV parked out front. He casually came down the stairs and opened the door.

'Sorry to disturb you,' said a middle-aged man with no chin. 'My dog ran off, and I was wondering if you might have seen it.'

'Dog?' Dragomir said through the front screen.

'Oh, now, where's my manners,' the man said. 'I'm Sam Dupuis, from across the road.'

'Andros,' Dragomir said. 'Caretaker.'

'Good to know you, Andros,' the neighbour said. 'I thought I saw Hercules run down your driveway, but maybe I was wrong.'

'Very sorry,' Dragomir said. 'Wish I could help. Hope you find him soon.'

I FOUND DIANA in a break room sitting by herself, just waiting.

'Your coffee,' she said, holding out a cup. 'Walk with me.'

I followed her out.

'They found Alexa's bag under his bed,' she said. 'He'd taken all her cash but was probably afraid to use her credit cards. The stolen Porsche was found in a Tufts garage. They found trace quantities of a white powder. A naturally occurring source of scopolamine.'

'A herbal date rape drug.'

She nodded. 'It's tasteless, odourless and water soluble. And it turns the victims into zombies. Lucid but totally submissive. And when it wears off, they have no recollection of what happened.'

On the way to the stairs, we passed the legal attaché from the Brazilian consulate, the guy with the long grey hair. Black curly chest hair sprouted out of his open shirt collar. He was walking briskly but seemed lost in thought, his head down.

As we climbed the stairs, I said, 'Any phone records in his apartment, cellphone records, any of that stuff?'

'They've collected everything, and they're working it.'

I stopped. 'Wasn't that guy wearing a tie?'

She looked at me in the dim light of the stairwell, then whipped round, and we went down the stairs at a good clip.

When we reached the interview room where I'd talked to Perreira, Diana opened the door and gasped. I can't say I was entirely surprised by what I saw, but it was grotesque all the same.

Mauricio Perreira's body was twisted unnaturally, his face frozen in a silent, agonised shriek. Fastened tightly round his neck like a tourniquet was the burgundy silk of the legal attaché's tie.

I raced down the four flights of stairs to Cambridge Street, but by the time I reached the sidewalk, there was no sign of him. There were at least a dozen ways he could have gone. It was hopeless. I'd failed at catching the man who'd just snuffed out my only lead to Alexa Marcus.

Diana greeted me in the sixth-floor lobby and didn't even ask. 'You never had a chance,' she said.

An alarm was sounding throughout the floor. Inside the interview room where Perreira had been detained, FBI crime-scene techs were already at work gathering prints and hair and fibre.

'Who cleared him in?' I said.

'That's the problem. Everyone assumed someone else had vetted him. He presented ID at the desk, claiming to be Cláudio Barboza from the Brazilian consulate, and who's going to question him?'

'Someone should call the consulate to double-check there's no one there with that name.'

'I just did. They don't even have a legal attaché in Boston.'

'Guys break into my loft to put a local intercept on my Internet. The SWAT team shows up in Medford minutes after I do. They grab a key witness, who's later murdered within FBI headquarters. Obviously, someone didn't want me talking to Perreira.'

'Don't tell me you're accusing Gordon Snyder.'

'I'd happily blame Snyder for the BP oil spill and global warming if I could. But not this. He's too obsessed with bringing Marshall Marcus down. But it's someone in the government. Someone at a high level who doesn't want me finding out who kidnapped Alexa.'

'OK. So if someone's really trying to stop you from finding Alexa, what's the reason?'

'No idea. But I feel like they're sending me a message.'

'Which is?'

'That I'm on the right track.'

MY OLD FRIEND George Devlin—Romeo, as we called him in the Special Forces—was the handsomest man you ever saw.

Not only was he the best-looking, most popular guy in his high-school class, as well as the class president, he was also the star of the school's hockey team. In a hockey town like Grand Rapids, Michigan, that was saying something. And he was a whiz at computers.

He could have done anything, but the Devlins had no money to send him to college, so he enlisted in the army. There he qualified for the Special Forces and was made a communications sergeant. That's how I first got to know George: he was the 18E, the comms sergeant in my detachment. I don't know who first came up with the nickname Romeo, but it stuck.

After he was wounded in Afghanistan and his veteran therapy ended, however, he told us to stop calling him Romeo and start calling him George.

I met him in the enormous white RV, bristling with antennas, that served as his combination home and mobile office. He'd parked it in an underground parking garage in a Holiday Inn in Dedham. That was typical for him. He preferred to meet in out-of-the-way locations.

I opened the van door and entered the dimly lit interior.

'Heller.' As my eyes adjusted, I could see him sitting on a stool, his back to me, before a bank of computer monitors.

'Hey, George. Thanks for meeting me at such short notice.'

'I take it the GPS tracker was successful.'

'Absolutely. It was brilliant. Thank you.'

I held out the Nokia cellphone I'd taken from Mauricio's apartment. He swivelled and turned his face towards me.

What was left of his face.

I'd never got used to seeing it. It was a horrible welter of ropy scar tissue. He had nostrils and a slash of a mouth, and the eyelids the army surgeons had laboured to give him were crafted from skin taken from his inner thigh.

I said, 'The only phone number on here, dialled or received, is for a mobile phone. That's probably his contact—whoever hired him to abduct the girl. If anyone can locate the bad guy from his phone, I'm guessing it's you.'

He spoke in a raspy whisper. 'Why didn't you ask the FBI for help?'

'Because I'm not sure who I can trust there.'

'The answer is no one. Why are you working with them?'

'Because I need them. Whatever it takes to get Alexa back.'

He breathed in and out noisily. 'No comment.'

He despised all government agencies. They were all too powerful and malevolent, and I think he blamed every one of them for the IED that had detonated his Humvee's gas tank.

He tilted his head to inspect the phone. 'Ah, a Nokla eighty-eight hundred.'

'You mean Nokia.'

He showed it to me. 'Can you read, Nick? It says NOKLA.' He slid off the back cover and popped the battery out. 'A Shenzhen Special,' he said, holding it up. The battery had Chinese characters all over it. 'Ever look on eBay and see a special sale on Nokia phones—brand new, half price? They're all made in China.'

I nodded. 'If you order mobile phones over the Internet, you don't have to risk going into Walmart or Target and having your face show up on a surveillance camera.'

Devlin looked at one of his screens. A green dot was flashing.

'Speaking of tracking devices, do you have one on you?'

'None that I know of.'

'May I see your handheld?'

I handed him my BlackBerry. He popped open its battery compartment. Lifted out the battery, then wriggled something loose with a pair of tweezers. Held it up.

'Someone's been tracking your every move, Heller,' he said. 'Any idea how long?'

I had no idea, of course. But at least now I knew how they were able to track me to Mauricio Perreira's apartment in Medford. Some 'confidential informant'.

'Looks like the FBI put a tail on you. And I thought you were cooperating. Did anyone have an opportunity to meddle with your BlackBerry without you noticing?'

I nodded. I remember checking in my BlackBerry at the FBI's reception desk in Boston, not once but twice.

'Now even *I'm* starting to get paranoid,' I said.

'In any case, you're absolutely correct about the Chinese knockoffs. Buying them over the Internet reduces their risk of exposure, yes. But there's an even better reason. Something only the best bad guys know about. The IMEI. The electronic serial number. Every mobile phone has one, even Noklas. But by using Shenzhen Specials, your bad guys have just made it *much* harder to be caught.'

'How so?'

'If the FBI has the serial number of a *real* Nokia phone, all they have to do is call Finland and Nokia's going to tell them where the phone was sold. Bad guys don't want that. But this baby, on the other hand—who're you gonna call, some factory in Shenzhen? They won't speak English and they sure as hell don't keep records and they probably don't even answer the phone. Good luck with that.'

'So these guys are pros,' I said.

He didn't reply. 'Here's your BlackBerry. Clean as a whistle.'

'I appreciate it,' I said. 'But I'd like you to put the GPS bug back in. First I'd like you to drain the battery on the bug, though. I want it to die a natural death in about, oh, fifteen or twenty minutes.'

He nodded. 'So they'll never know that you discovered it.'

'Right. I much prefer being underestimated.'

As I returned to the Defender, my BlackBerry was ringing.

'I thought I'd have heard from you by now,' Diana said.

'My BlackBerry was temporarily offline.'

'You didn't see what I sent you?'

'What did you send me?'

'A photograph of our kidnapper,' she said.

8

The town of Pine Ridge, New Hampshire (population 1,260), had a police force that consisted of two full-time officers, two part-time officers and one police chief.

Jason Kent, the rookie, entered the chief's office hesitantly. 'Chief?'

'Sam Dupuis keeps calling,' Chief Walter Nowitzki said. 'Got a bug up his ass about the Alderson property. Something about how his dog ran off. I didn't quite get it. But now he says he thinks they're doing work without a permit and who knows what else.'

'You want me to drive out and talk to Mr Dupuis?'

'Just head on over to the Alderson property and see what's up.'

'I didn't know any of the Aldersons even came here anymore.'

'Sam says it's a caretaker or something, works for the family.'

I CLICKED ON DIANA'S EMAIL and waited as it opened the attachment. A photograph. I could barely discern the back of a man's head and shoulders. So why was Diana so sure this was the guy?

I studied it more closely and saw what might have been the headrest of a car. The photo had been taken from the back seat.

The man's shoulders rose well above the headrest. His head appeared to be shaved. Something was obscuring a large area of his head and neck. As I looked closer, I realised it was a tattoo. A line drawing, highly detailed. Stylised feathers, a sharp beak, erect ears. An owl, maybe, with large, fierce staring eyes.

The guy's got eyes on the back of his head.

When Mauricio Perreira had babbled that to me, I assumed he meant to say, *He's got eyes in the back of his head.* Meaning: this man hears and sees everything, has sources everywhere; I can't give you his name—I'm scared of him.

He *was* scared. But it wasn't a metaphor. He meant it literally. There *were* eyes on the back of the man's head.

Diana answered on the first ring.

'Who took the picture?' I said.

'Alexa Marcus. This came from her iPhone, taken at 2.36 a.m. the night she disappeared.'

'That's an owl.'

'Right. The tattoo covers his head and neck and probably a good portion of his upper back as well.'

'You've probably already searched NCIC,' I said.

The National Crime Information Center is the computerised database of crimes maintained by the FBI and used by every police force and other law-enforcement agency in the country.

'Sure. No hits.'

'Isn't there some central database of criminal tattoos?'

'There should be, but there isn't. I've sent the photo to our seventy-five legal attachés around the world, asking them to run it by local law enforcement. Maybe we'll get lucky.'

'Yeah, maybe,' I said dubiously. 'You'd think a guy with an owl on his head and neck would be fairly memorable.'

'That's not smart. Owls are supposed to be smart.'

'It's not about smart. It's about scary. In some cultures an owl is a symbol of death,' I said. 'A bad omen. A prophecy of death.'

'Where? Which countries?'

I thought for a moment. 'Mexico. Japan. Romania, I think. Maybe Russia. Ever see an owl hunt?' I said.

'Oddly enough, I haven't.'

'It moves its head from side to side and up and down, looking and listening, triangulating on its prey. You really can't find a more perfect, more ruthless killer.'

'HI, MR HELLER,' Jillian said as I entered the office. 'Dorothy's looking for you.'

'You're allowed to call me Nick,' I said, for what must have been the twentieth time since she'd started working for me. I noticed the butterfly tattoo on her right shoulder. 'What does that mean, the butterfly?' I asked.

'It's a symbol of freedom and metamorphosis. I got it when I stopped eating meat. I also have a "meat is murder" tattoo on my lower back. Want to see it?'

Dorothy's voice rang out as she approached. 'Jillian, you can show your tramp stamps after work and on your own time.' She shook her head. 'I got that picture you sent,' she said to me. 'I've been Googling tattoos, but no luck so far.'

'My brother worked in a tattoo parlour in Saugus,' Jillian said.

'How about you replace the toner cartridge like I asked,' Dorothy said.

IN MY OFFICE, Dorothy said, 'I found spyware on our network. A molar virus. It burrowed into our intranet, injected code, and opened a back door. For a couple of days now it's been scanning all volumes for protected files and then sending them out.'

'That's how they got my security-system codes,' I said. 'Where did it send to?'

'Proxy servers so many times removed that they're just about impossible to find. But I rooted it out. It should be gone.'

My intercom buzzed, and Jillian said, 'You have a visitor.'

I looked at Dorothy, who shrugged. 'Name?' I said.

'Belinda Marcus,' Jillian said.

'I'M WORRIED *SICK* about Marshall,' Belinda said. She threw out her thin arms and embraced me.

'I'm sorry, Belinda. Did we have an appointment?'

She sat. 'No, we did not, Nick, but we need to talk.'

'Give me one quick second.' I turned my chair and typed out an instant message to Dorothy: NEED BKGD ON BELINDA MARCUS ASAP.

'I'm all yours,' I said.

'Nick, I know I should have called first, but I've been wanting to talk to y'all privately since this nightmare began.'

I nodded.

'I feel like I'm being disloyal, but I'm just at my wit's end, and *someone* needs to say something. Nick, you need to know that Marshall is under a great deal of pressure. All he wants is to get his beloved daughter back, but they . . . they won't let him give them what they want, and it's tearing him up inside.'

'Who's "they"?'

She looked at me anxiously. 'David Schechter.'

'How do you know this? Does he talk to you about it?'

'Never. I've just heard them arguing.'

'So you must know what Mercury is?'

She shook her head. 'I don't. I mean, it's a file of some sort, but I have no idea what it's about. We've got to give it to them.'

'So why are you telling me?'

She studied her fingernails. 'Marshall is in deep in some kind of trouble, and I don't know who to turn to.'

I looked at my computer screen. An instant message had popped up from Dorothy. A few lines of text.

'I'm sure he trusts you,' I said. 'You've been married for, what, three years, right?'

She nodded.

'You were a flight attendant when you met Marshall?'

She nodded, smiled. 'He saved me. I've always hated flying.'

'That's got to be a Georgia accent.'

'Very good,' she said. 'A little town called Barnesville.'

'Are you serious? I dated a girl from Barnesville. Cindy Purcell?'

Belinda shook her head. 'She must be a lot younger.'

'I'm sure you've eaten at her parents' restaurant, Brownie's.'

'Oh, sure. But Nick—'

'I've never had anything like their low-country boil.'

'Never had that dish, but I'm sure it's good. Southern cooking is the best, isn't it? I miss it so.'

'Well,' I said, standing, 'I'm glad you came in. I'm sure it wasn't easy, but it was very helpful.'

She remained seated. 'I know some people think I'm a gold-digger because I happened to marry a wealthy man. But I didn't marry Marshall for his money. I just want what's best for him. And I want that girl back, Nick. Whatever it takes.'

AFTER SHE LEFT, I called Dorothy in.

'You didn't really date a woman from Barnesville, did you?'

'No. And there's no Brownie's.'

'A good one about the low-country boil, Nick. If you've never had that, you're not from Georgia. What tipped you off?'

'Her accent's wrong. Words like "square" and "here"—she drops her Rs. Georgians don't talk like that. And then there's the way she keeps calling me "y'all".'

'Good point. "Y'all" is always plural. She's not from Georgia, is she?'

'I don't even think she's southern.'

'Then why's she faking it?'

'That's what I want to find out. Can you do a little digging?'

'Already started,' Dorothy said.

NOT LONG AFTER, my phone rang. I glanced at it: Dorothy. I picked up. 'What do you have?' I said.

'I talked to Delta Air Lines. Belinda never worked for them.'

'Why would she lie about that?'

'Because Marshall Marcus would never have married her if he knew her real employment background. She was a call girl.'

'Why does that not surprise me?' I said.

'I ran her Social Security number. Took acting classes in Lincoln Park. Employed as an escort with VIP Exxxecutive Service, based out of Trenton. That's three X's in Exxxecutive.'

'She's not southern, is she?'

'Southern Jersey. Woodbine.'

My BlackBerry emitted its text-message alert sound. I glanced at the message. It said '15 MINUTES' and gave the polar coordinates of what looked like a 7-Eleven parking lot 0.73 miles away.

The message was sent by '18E'. No name, no phone number. But he didn't need to use his name.

George Devlin was an 18E.

'Excuse me,' I said. 'I have to see an old friend.'

'HOW DID YOU KNOW I was close enough to make it here in fifteen minutes?' I said. 'You knew where I was?'

George Devlin ignored my question. Like it was either too complicated or too obvious to explain. He had his ways. He was preoccupied with angling a computer monitor so I could see it.

A greenish topographical map of Massachusetts appeared on the screen. A flashing red circle appeared, about fifteen miles northwest of Boston. Then three squiggly lines popped up—white, blue and orange—each emanating from the flashing red circle. The blue line came in from Boston, to the southeast. The orange line came down from the north. The white line followed the blue line from Boston, and then traced a path north with the orange.

'OK . . .' I said.

'If you look closely,' he said, 'you'll see that each line is made up of dots. The dots represent cell-tower hits from three mobile phones. Blue is for Mauricio. White is for Alexa. Orange is for the unknown person we'll call Mr X.'

I leaned forward. 'Mr X came down from close to the New Hampshire border, it looks like. So they all met fifteen miles northwest of Boston in . . . is it Lincoln?'

'Yes. Mauricio and the girl arrived together. They were there for seventeen minutes. Mr X stayed for only four or five minutes.'

They'd met in a wooded area, I saw. Near Sandy Pond, which was marked conservation land. Remote, isolated: a good place to bury someone. So Alexa's iPhone went from Boston to Lincoln and then north to Leominster. Which was where it was discarded.

Now I could see the pattern. Mauricio took her from the hotel to Lincoln, where he handed her to Mr X. While Mauricio went back to his apartment in Medford, Mr X was driving Alexa north. He tossed her phone out as they passed through Leominster. Presumably she stayed in the vehicle with him.

Then they crossed the border into New Hampshire.

'So the route stops in New Hampshire,' I said. 'Nashua.'

'No. Mr X's mobile phone falls off the grid in Nashua. That could mean that he shut it off. Mr X might have passed through New Hampshire on his way to Canada.'

'It's not a logical route if you're driving all the way to Canada.'

He nodded in agreement.

'They're in New Hampshire,' I said.

THE OFFICES of Marcus Capital Investment were on the sixth floor of Rowes Wharf, a harbour-front development. I gave the receptionist my name and waited in the luxuriously appointed lobby. I didn't have to wait a minute before Marcus's personal assistant appeared. She was a willowy redhead named Smoki Bacon, a stunningly beautiful, elegant young woman. This didn't surprise me. Marcus had a reputation for hiring only beautiful women as admins.

Smoki gave me a dazzling smile. 'Marshall's in a meeting right now, but he wants to see you as soon as it's over. It might be a while, though. Would you like to come back a little later?'

'I'll wait.'

'At least let me take you to a conference room, where you can use the phone and the computer.'

She showed me down a corridor. As we rounded a bend, we passed by what should have been the trading floor. There were thirty or forty workstations, all empty. 'I just can't tell you how worried we've all been about Alexa,' she said.

'Well,' I said, not knowing how to reply, 'keep the faith.'

At the threshold to an empty conference room, she put a hand on my shoulder. She leaned close and said through gritted teeth, 'Please get that girl back, Mr Heller.'

'I'll do my best,' I said.

INSTEAD OF WAITING, I decided to wander down to Marcus's office.

Smoki kept watch from her desk outside his office, I remembered. I also remembered that Marcus had a private dining room next to his office. When I'd had lunch there once, the waiting staff had appeared and disappeared through a back hallway.

It didn't take long to find the service hallway. One entrance was next to the men's room. It connected a small prep kitchen to the boardroom and Marcus's dining room, which looked like it hadn't seen much use in quite a while.

The door to his office was closed. But when I stood next to it, I could hear voices raised in argument. At first I could make out only fragments. Two men speaking, I was sure. One, of course, was Marcus. His voice was the louder, more emotional one. When he spoke I could mostly hear him. The other was soft spoken and calm and barely audible.

VISITOR: '. . . to go all soft now.'

MARCUS: 'If she dies, it'll be your doing, you understand? It'll be on your conscience! You used to have one of those, didn't you?'

VISITOR: '. . . damnedest to keep you alive.'

MARCUS: 'I don't care what you people do to me now. My life is over. My daughter is the only—'

VISITOR: (*a lot of mumbling*) '. . . years you've been the guy with all the solutions . . . they decide now you're the problem? . . . what their solution will be.'

MARCUS: '. . . on my side!'

VISITOR: '. . . want to be on your side. But I can't be unless you're on mine . . .'

MARCUS: '. . . you wanted, I did. *Everything!*'

VISITOR: '. . . have to spell this out for you, Marshall? "Grieving financier kills self at Manchester residence?"'

I pushed the door open and entered the office. Marcus was sitting behind a long desk heaped with papers.

Facing him in the visitor chair was David Schechter.

'NICKELEH!' Marcus rasped. 'What are you—didn't Smoki—'

'He was eavesdropping,' Schechter said. 'Isn't that right, Mr Heller?'

'Absolutely. I heard everything you said.'

Schechter blinked at me. 'As of this moment, your services are no longer required.'

'You didn't hire me,' I said.

'Schecky, let me talk to him,' Marcus said. 'He's a *mensch*.'

Schechter rose and said to Marcus, 'I'll expect your call.'

I watched him leave, then sat in the chair he had just vacated.

'What kind of hold does he have over you?' I said.

'Hold?'

'You hired me to find Alexa, and I can't do that unless you level with me. If you don't, you know what's going to happen to her.'

He looked like he'd aged twenty years since I'd seen him last. 'Nicky, you need to stay out of this. It's . . . personal business.'

'It took me a while to understand why you'd withhold the one thing that could get her back. Schechter is blackmailing you. He's the one who's keeping you from cooperating with the kidnappers.'

Marcus turned and stared out of the window. 'I hired you because I thought you were the only one who could find her.'

'No,' I said. 'You hired me because that was the only way you could get your daughter back without giving in to their demands.'

He wheeled slowly back round. 'Does that offend you?'

'I've been offended worse. But that's not the point. From the beginning you've been sandbagging me. You lied about calling the police. You didn't tell me how you were forced to take money from criminals, and you didn't tell me you'd lost it all. You've been keeping everything from me I needed to know to find her. Now they want the Mercury files—they are files, aren't they?—and you pretend you don't know what they are. So let me ask you this: whatever Schechter has on you, is it worth your daughter's life?'

His face crumpled, and he covered his eyes as he wept silently.

'You need to tell me what Mercury is. Then we'll figure something out.'

I got up and walked towards the door, then stopped. I hesitated a few seconds. 'Did you do a background check on Belinda before you married her?'

He lowered his hands. 'Belinda? What does Belinda have to do with anything?'

'I'm sorry to have to tell you this,' I said. 'But she was never a flight attendant. She's not from Georgia. She's from New Jersey. She was a call girl, Marshall. An escort. I think you should know.'

'Nickeleh, *boychik*. Grow up.' He sighed. 'She's a sensitive girl. She's kinda touchy about people knowing about our first date.'

A smile spread across my face as I headed again for the door. The old bastard. From behind me he called out, 'Please don't quit.'

I kept going and replied without looking back. 'Don't worry about it. You can't get rid of me. Though you might wish you did.'

DRAGOMIR WAS SITTING at the computer in the musty sun room at the back of the house when he heard the girl's cries.

Strange. He'd muted the computer's speakers. He rose and went to the back door. There he listened some more. The cries were coming from outside. Faint and distant and small. He didn't understand how he could be hearing them. She was ten feet underground.

On the porch, he cocked his head. The sounds were coming from the yard, maybe the woods beyond. Then he saw the grey PVC pipe standing in the middle of the field. The vent pipe carried not just the girl's exhalation but her cries as well.

When Dragomir had first come up with the idea of putting her in the ground, it seemed a stroke of pure genius. The Client's intelligence had turned up a psychiatrist's file indicating the target was afflicted with a debilitating claustrophobia. But that wasn't his real reason. Buried ten feet down, she was safely beyond his reach.

If the girl had been easily accessible, he wouldn't have been able to restrain himself. He would rape her and kill her as he'd done to so many other pretty young women. That wouldn't do at all.

He was listening so hard to the mewling that he almost didn't hear the crunch of a car's tyres on the dirt road out front. Back in the house, he strode to the front and looked out of the window. A police cruiser, dark blue with white lettering: PINE RIDGE POLICE.

A gawky young man got out. By the time the policeman rang the door buzzer, Dragomir was wearing a brown wig.

'How're you doing?' the policeman said. 'I'm Officer Kent. Could I ask you a few questions?'

IN THE LATE AFTERNOON, when I returned to the office, Jillian was on the floor packing boxes. She looked up as I entered. Her face was red and sticky with tears. 'Goodbye, Mr Heller.'

'What's going on?' I said.

'Before I leave, I want to apologise.'

'What are you talking about?'

'Someone emailed me a greeting card, and I opened it at work.'

'Did Dorothy fire you?'

'No, I'm leaving. I guess that e-card had some kind of software bug in it, like spyware? Dorothy says that's how people got onto our server and got into your personal files and the codes to your home security system?'

'It was you?'

'I . . . thought she told you,' Jillian stammered.

'Well, Jillian, I'm sorry, but you picked a bad time to quit, so you can't. Get back to answering phones, please.'

THE MORE I THOUGHT ABOUT Marshall and Belinda Marcus, the more I was convinced something wasn't right.

I knew a cyber-investigator in New Jersey, and I gave him a call.

'I want you to check on the dates of her employment by VIP Exxxecutive Service in Trenton,' I said. 'And I want you to trace her back as far as you can.'

I found Dorothy at her desk, staring at her computer screen. Alexa was speaking. '*I don't want to be here anymore, Daddy!*'

The image froze, then broke up into thousands of tiny coloured squares, like a Chuck Close painting. They scattered and clumped.

And then as the image redrew, she went on, '. . . *They want Mercury, Daddy, OK? You have to give them Mercury in the raw.*'

'I told Jillian she can't quit. What are you doing?'

'Cracking my head against a brick wall, that's what I'm doing.'

'Anything I can do?'

'Yeah. Fire my ass.'

'Nope. You're not allowed to quit, either. Tell me what's up.'

Dorothy replied quietly. 'I'm failing at the most important job anyone's ever given me.' Tears in her eyes.

Placing my hand on hers, I said, 'You're frustrated. I get that.'

'Nick, do you know how often I think of that girl and what she must be going through? And I just feel . . . powerless.'

'So tell me what you're stuck on.'

She hesitated only briefly. 'OK, listen to this.'

She clicked a key, and we were back to that same loop of Alexa speaking. Dorothy raised the volume. Under Alexa's words a hum grew louder. Then the image froze and broke up into tiny bits.

'Notice the noise is always followed by the picture breaking up? Every single time.'

'OK.'

'Thing is, a car or a truck or a train—they're not going to interrupt the video transmission like that.'

'So what's the significance of that?'

'What's the significance?' she said. 'It's going to tell us where Alexa Marcus is.'

'THERE IS SOME PROBLEM, Officer?'

Dragomir had learned that American policemen liked it when you used the honorific 'Officer'. They craved respect.

'We just like to introduce ourselves so you know who to call in case you need any help. So you, ah, work for the Aldersons?'

'Just caretaker. I do work for family. Fix up.'

'Oh, OK, right. So I guess one of your neighbours kinda noticed some construction equipment? Just want to make sure there's no infractions of the building code. You know, like, if you're building an extension without a permit?'

'No construction. Owner wants terraced gardens.'

'Mind if I take a quick look out back?'

Dragomir shrugged, said hospitably, 'Please.'

He followed the policeman round the back to the field of bare earth. The policeman seemed to be looking at the tracks in the hard soil, then the grey vent pipe in the middle of the field, and he approached it. 'That a septic tank, um, Andros?'

Dragomir hadn't told the cop his name. Obviously, the neighbour had. 'Is to vent the soil,' Dragomir said as they stood next to the pipe. 'From the landfill, the . . . compost pile.' An improvisation.

'Like for methane build-up or something?'

Dragomir shrugged. He didn't understand English. He just did what he was told. He was a simple labourer.

'Because you do need a permit if you're putting in a septic tank, you know.'

Dragomir smiled. 'No septic tank.'

Muffled distant screams came out of the vent pipe.

The policeman cocked his head. 'You hear something?' he said.

The girl's cries were louder now and more distinct.

'HELP GOD HELP SAVE ME PLEASE OH GOD . . .'

'That sounds like it's coming from down there,' the policeman said. 'How weird is that?'

'I'M LISTENING,' I said.

Dorothy sighed. 'Let's start with the basic question: how are they getting on the Internet, OK? I don't think it's your standard high-speed connection.'

'Why not?'

She leaned back. 'My parents live in North Carolina, right? So a couple of years ago they decided they wanted to get cable TV so they could watch movies. Only there wasn't any cable available, so they had to put one of those satellite dishes on their roof.'

I nodded.

'Once, I tried to watch a movie at their house and the picture kept fuzzing out. So I asked them what the problem was. And Momma said, Oh, that happens every time a plane flies by. See, they live close to the Charlotte/Douglas airport. And then I began to notice that, yeah, every time I heard a plane, the TV would crap out.'

'OK,' I said. 'If our kidnappers are deep in the woods somewhere, or in some rural area, satellite is probably their only way to get online. And you think a plane can break up the signal?'

'Easy. Satellite works by line of sight, so if something gets between the dish and the big old satellite up there in the sky, the signal's gonna break up. You got a big enough plane flying low enough, that thing can interrupt the signal.'

'So they're near an airport. But how near?'

'Hard to calculate. But close enough so when a plane lands or takes off, it's low enough to the ground to block the path to the satellite. It depends on how big the plane is and how fast it's going.'

'There are a hell of a lot of airports in the US,' I pointed out.

'That right?' she said drily. 'Hadn't thought about that. But if we can narrow down the search, it gets a whole lot easier.'

'I think we can.' I explained about George Devlin's cellphone mapping. How we knew that Mr X took Alexa across the Massachusetts border into New Hampshire.

She listened, staring into space, then said, 'That's helped a lot. I don't know how many airports there are in New Hampshire, but we've just narrowed it down to a manageable number.'

'Maybe we can narrow it down more than that,' I said. 'Does that creepy web site CamFriendz stream in real time?'

'They claim to. I'd say yes, within a few seconds.'

'So we match up those times with the exact flight times in the FAA's flight database. We're looking for airports in New Hampshire—hell, let's make it Massachusetts and Maine and New Hampshire, to be safe—with a flight schedule matching the times of our interruptions. And we can narrow it down more. Aren't there two separate interruptions during one of those broadcasts?'

'You're right.'

'So we have an exact interval between two flights.'

Her smile widened slowly. 'Not bad, Boss.'

I shrugged. 'Your idea.' One of the few things I've learned since going into business for myself: the boss should never take credit for anything. 'Can you hack into the Federal Aviation Administration's secure electronic database?'

'No.'

'The FBI will be able to. I'll give Diana a call.'

'Excuse me?' Jillian was standing there hesitantly. 'I forgot to take this out of the printer.' She held up a large glossy colour photograph. It was an enlargement of a section of the photograph from Alexa's iPhone of her kidnapper's tattoo.

'Thank you,' Dorothy said, taking it from her.

'I think I know what it is,' Jillian said.

'That's an owl,' I said. 'But thanks anyway.'

She held up something else, which she'd been holding in her other hand. A slim white paperback. On the front cover was a black-and-white line drawing of an owl.

It was identical to the owl tattoo in the photo.

'What's that?' I said.

'It's a book of tattoos my brother found.' She handed me the book. It was titled *Criminal Tattoos of Russia.*

'Dorothy,' I said, 'what time is it in Russia right now?'

ONE OF MY BEST SOURCES was a former KGB major general. Anatoly Vasilenko was a man in his sixties with an aquiline profile and the demeanour of a Cambridge don. By the time the Soviet Union had collapsed, he was already cashing in on his access and connections. For the right price, he could get you almost any piece of intelligence you wanted.

Tolya's English was better than that of most Americans I knew. 'Quite the interesting picture you sent. That tattoo? It's Sova.'

'Who?'

'Not "who". Sova is—well, *sova* means owl, of course.'

'Is it a Russian mafia tattoo?'

'Mafia? No,' he said. 'Sova is more like a loose confederation of men who've all survived the same prison—Prison Number One, in Kopeisk. Quite the nasty place. Why is this of interest to you?'

I told him.

When I was done, he said, 'This is not a good situation for you. Or for your client's daughter, more to the point. These are very bad people, Nicholas. Hardened criminals of the very worst sort. They're . . . untroubled by conventional standards of morality.'

'How bad are we talking?'

'I think you had a very unpleasant incident in the States not so long ago. Do you remember a brutal home invasion in Connecticut? Truly a nightmare. A doctor and his wife and three daughters were at home one night when a couple of burglars broke in. They beat the doctor with a baseball bat. Then they tied the girls to their beds and raped them for seven hours. After which—'

'All right,' I said, unable to hear any more. 'These were Sova members?'

'Correct. One of them was killed during an attempted arrest, I seem to recall. The other one escaped.'

'A burglary?'

'Entertainment.'

'Excuse me?'

'These Sova people will do things a normal person cannot begin to imagine. You couldn't ask for better enforcers.'

'Enforcers?'

'If you need outside talent for a dirty job, you might hire a couple of Sova members. Our newly minted Russian billionaires are often in need of hard men and are known to use Sova members.'

'Which ones?'

He laughed. 'Nicholas, we haven't even discussed a fee yet!'

He told me his fee, and I agreed to his usurious terms.

Then he said, 'Let me make some calls.'

THIS TIME DRAGOMIR USED the Wasp knife correctly. The young police officer didn't even have time to turn round before the blade went into his side, lightning fast, right up to the hilt.

Officer Kent died instantly.

DIANA AND I MET at the Sheep's Head Tavern, a sorta-kinda Irish pub in Government Center, right next to FBI headquarters. She'd told me she had to grab a quick dinner and then get back up to work. That was fine with me: I had a very long night ahead.

'I'm afraid I don't have anything for you,' she said. 'We didn't turn up anything in the FAA's flight log database.'

'Well, it was a brilliant idea,' I said. 'But not all brilliant ideas work out. Thanks for trying. I have something for *you*.'

I handed her Mauricio's mobile phone in a Ziploc bag.

'I don't understand,' she said. 'What is it?'

I told her.

'You took that from his apartment? Without telling me?'

'I'm sorry. I didn't trust Snyder.'

Her mouth tightened, and her nostrils flared.

'It was a mistake for me to withhold it from you. I know that.'

'So was it worth it, Nick? You know we can never use that as evidence in court, right? Since you disrupted the chain of custody?'

'I don't think the Bureau is going to be prosecuting a dead guy.'

'I'm talking about whoever's behind this thing. There's a reason we have procedures. We both want the same thing; we just have different ways to get there. But as long as you're working with me and the FBI, you have to respect the rules we play by.'

'I understand.'

She looked at me hard. 'Don't ever do this to me again.'

'I won't.'

'Good. Now, at least tell me you got something useful out of it.'

I nodded. 'His phone number and the only number on his call log, probably the guy who hired him to abduct Alexa. One of my sources plotted those numbers along with Alexa's phone number on a map of cellphone towers and was able to chart the route they travelled. The path seems to point to New Hampshire.'

'Meaning what? That Alexa's kidnapper came down from New Hampshire?'

'Yes, but more important, it means he's probably got her up there now. Somewhere in New Hampshire.'

'Well, that helps, I guess,' Diana said. 'But we're going to need more data points than that. Otherwise, it's a lost cause.'

'How about the tattoo?'

'Nothing came back on that from any of our legats.'

'Well, I've got an excellent source in Moscow who's making some calls for me right now. That owl is Russian prison ink. That owl tattoo identifies members of Sova, a gang of former Russian prison inmates.'

She took out a small notepad and jotted something down. 'If Alexa's kidnapper is Russian, does that mean he's working on behalf of Russians?' she mused aloud.

'Not for sure. But I'd put money on it. My source in Moscow says Sova members are often hired by Russian oligarchs to do dirty work when they need plausible deniability. Meanwhile, I want to find out what David Schechter's role in all this really is.'

'How's that going to help find Alexa?'

I told her about the exchange I'd overheard between David Schechter and Marshall Marcus.

'You think Schechter is controlling Marcus?' she said.

'Clearly. Maybe his wife's shady past has something to do with it.'

She cocked a brow, and I explained what I'd found out about Belinda Marcus's last profession. 'I have a PI digging into it right now. But I don't think that's it. It's too recent and too trivial.'

'Then what's the hold Schechter has over him?'

'That's what I plan to find out.'

'How?'

I told her.

'That's illegal,' she said.

I shrugged. 'As a great man once said, In certain extreme situations, the law is inadequate. In order to shame its inadequacy, it is necessary to act outside the law.'

'Martin Luther King?'

'Close. The Punisher.'

She looked confused.

'I guess you don't read comic books,' I said.

DRAGOMIR KNEW WHERE TO GO. Earlier he'd driven around the area, scouting escape routes in case it came to that, until he'd discovered a deserted stretch of narrow road that would do well.

He stopped at a place where the road curved sharply on the lip of a ravine at a point where he could see the traffic in both directions. There wasn't any. Then he drove a bit farther until he was about twenty feet from an edge where there was no guardrail.

Glancing around, he opened the trunk of the police cruiser, lifted Officer Kent's body out, and quickly carried it round to the open driver's side door. There he carefully positioned the body. Then he lifted the black plastic trash bags from the floor of the trunk.

An autopsy wasn't likely. Mostly likely they'd see a police officer killed in a tragic car crash and it would end there. Anyway, by the time any autopsy was done, he'd be long gone. He cared only about what might be found in the next twenty-four hours.

Before he pushed the car into the ravine, he put it in drive. If the gear selector were in neutral when the crash was discovered, any skilled investigator would immediately figure out what had really happened. He didn't make that kind of mistake.

9

At a few minutes after nine at night, the John Hancock Tower—the tallest building in Boston—was an obsidian monolith. A few lighted windows scattered here and there like a corncob with not many kernels remaining. Some of the building's tenants were open round the clock.

But not the law offices of Batten Schechter, on the forty-eighth floor. This was a sedate, dignified firm that specialised in trusts and estates and the occasional litigation, always resolved in back-room negotiations, perhaps a word whispered in the ear of the right judge. The sort of power exercised by Batten Schechter's attorneys was, like growing mushrooms, best done out of the light of day.

I drove the white Ford panel truck along the back of the Hancock Tower and up to the loading dock. A row of five steel pylons blocked my way. I got out, saw the sign—USE INTERCOM FOR ACCESS WHEN DOOR IS CLOSED—and I hit the big black button.

The steel overhead door rolled up, and a squat little man stood there. Stitched in script on his blue shirt was CARLOS. He glanced at the logo on the side of the van—DERDERIAN FINE ORIENTAL RUGS—nodded, hit a switch, and the steel columns sank into the pavement. He pointed to a space inside the loading dock.

'You here for Batten Schechter?' Carlos said.

I nodded, striking a balance between cordial and aloof.

All he knew was that the law firm of Batten Schechter had called the Hancock's property management office and told them that a carpet cleaner would be working in their offices sometime after nine o'clock. He didn't need to know that the 'facilities manager' of Batten Schechter was actually Dorothy.

Couldn't have been easier. All I had to do was promise Mr Derderian I'd buy one of his overpriced, though elegant, rugs for my office. In exchange he was happy to lend me one of his vans.

I pulled open the van's rear doors and wrestled with the bulky commercial carpet shampooer. Carlos helped me lower it to the floor, then pointed towards a bank of freight elevators.

I hit the button for forty-eight. As it rose, I adjusted Mauricio's STI pistol in my waistband. I'd been storing it in the Defender's glove box ever since I'd grabbed it from his apartment.

The steel elevator doors opened slowly on a small fluorescent-lit service lobby on the forty-eighth floor. I wheeled out the rug shampooer and saw four steel doors. Each was the service entrance to a different firm. The one for Batten Schechter was the only one with an electronic digital keypad mounted next to it.

From my duffel bag I drew a long, flexible metal rod bent at a ninety-degree angle, a hook at one end. This was a special tool called a Leverlock, sold only to security professionals and government agencies. I knelt down, pushed the rod underneath the door, and twisted it round and up until it caught the lever handle on the inside, then yanked it down. Thirteen seconds later I was in.

Now I found myself in some back corridor where the firm stored office supplies and cleaning equipment. I pushed the shampooer against a wall and made my way by the dim emergency lighting.

It was like going from steerage to a stateroom on the *Queen Mary*. Soft carpeting, mahogany doors with brass nameplates, antique furnishings.

David Schechter, as a named partner, got the corner office. In an alcove before the mahogany double doors to his inner sanctum was a secretary's desk and a couch. The double doors were locked.

Then I saw another digital keypad, mounted by the doorframe at eye level. Strange. It meant that Schechter's office probably wasn't cleaned by the crew that did the rest of the building.

It also meant there was something inside worth protecting.

From the duffel bag, I removed a black case. Inside, a flexible fibre-scope lay coiled in the form-fitted foam padding, like a metallic snake. I bent the scope into an angle, screwed on the eyepiece, and attached an external metal-halide light source, then fished it under the door. A lever on the handle allowed me to move the probe around like an elephant's trunk. Now I could see what was on the other side of the door. Angling it upwards, I inspected the wall on the far side of the doorframe. Nothing appeared to be mounted there.

When I swivelled the scope over to the other side of the doorframe, I saw a red pinpoint light, steady and unblinking.

A motion detector. A passive infrared sensor. It would detect minute changes in room temperature caused by the heat given off by a human body. A common device but not easy to defeat.

There were ways to get by these things. But this wasn't my expertise. The best I could do was guess. I considered abandoning the operation, but I'd come too far to turn back.

So I gathered a few items from the Batten Schechter offices. The first was easy. On the console behind Schechter's assistant's desk was an assortment of pictures. I slid the rectangle of glass out of a framed photograph of a little girl sitting on a shopping-mall Santa's lap.

In a storeroom, I found a carton of polystyrene sheets, used to line boxes or protect rolled documents, and a roll of packing tape.

When I returned to Schechter's office, I slid the Leverlock under the double doors and had them open in ten seconds.

Then came the tricky part.

Holding the polystyrene square in front of me like a shield, I advanced slowly towards the motion sensor. If I was remembering correctly, the foam would block my heat from being detected.

It took an agonisingly long time to reach the wall where the sensor was mounted. Like most state-of-the-art infrared sensors, this one had a built-in flaw. It was equipped with 'creep zone' coverage: if someone tried to slither on the floor underneath it, its lens would detect it right away. But it couldn't see above.

From behind the polystyrene scrim I took the small square of glass taped to my belt, lifted it slowly, and placed it against the sensor's lens. The strip of packing tape kept it securely in place.

Then I let the foam sheet drop to the floor.

The red light was steady. I hadn't triggered it.

I exhaled slowly.

Glass is opaque to infrared light. The sensor couldn't see through it, but it didn't perceive the glass as an obstruction.

I switched on the overhead lights. Two walls were panelled in mahogany. The other two were glass, nearly floor to ceiling, with views of Boston that were breathtaking. The lights twinkled like a starlit canopy fallen to earth. If this was the view from your office every day, you might start to believe you ruled the land below.

His desk was a small, delicate antique. There was a time when the more powerful an executive was, the bigger his desk. But now the more important you are, the smaller and more fragile your work surface.

Then I noticed a second set of mahogany double doors. They were unlocked. As I pulled them open, the overhead lights came on: Schechter's personal filing cabinets. The ones that contained documents too sensitive to be kept in his firm's central files. Each steel cabinet was secured with a high-security lock. The locks were unpickable, but not the cabinets. These were commercial-steel four-drawer filing cabinets. It was like putting a thousand-dollar lockset on a hollow-core door that even a kid could kick in.

I chose the one marked H–O, hoping to find Marshall Marcus's file. Kneeling, I inserted a metal shim between the bottom drawer and the frame, and sure enough, the locking bar slid up.

Then I pulled open the top drawer and scanned the file tabs. They looked like client files, past and present.

But these were no ordinary clients. There were files for some of the most influential public officials in the US in the past three or four decades. The names of the men (mostly, and a few women) who ran America. Not all of them were famous. Some—former directors of the NSA and the CIA, secretaries of state and treasury, certain Supreme Court justices, White House chiefs of staff, senators and congressmen—were dimly remembered if at all. But it wasn't possible that David Schechter could have represented a fraction of them. So why were these files here?

As I tried to puzzle out the connection among them, one name caught my eye: MARK WARREN HOOD, LTG, USA.

Lieutenant General Mark Hood. The man who'd run the covert operations unit of the Defense Intelligence Agency I'd once worked for. I pulled out the thick brown file folder. For some reason my heart began to thud.

I riffled through quickly until I noticed one word stamped in blue ink at the top of each page: MERCURY.

So here it was. And somehow it was connected, through my old boss, to me.

The explanation was here, if only I could make sense of the cryptic abbreviations or codes. I stopped at a photograph of a man clipped to a page of card stock. At the top were the words CERTIFICATE OF RELEASE OR DISCHARGE FROM ACTIVE DUTY. A military discharge form. It took a second before I recognised myself.

The shock was so profound that I didn't hear the tiny scuffling on the carpet behind me until it was too late, and then I felt a hard crack against the side of my head, and everything went black.

WHEN I CAME TO, I found myself in a panelled conference room, seated at one end of an immense cherry-wood conference table.

My head throbbed. When I tried to move my hands, I realised my wrists were secured with flex-cuffs to the steel arms of an office chair. My ankles were bound to the centre stem of the chair.

At the far end of the table, peering at me, was David Schechter.

He gave what was apparently his rendition of a smile. 'Did you know,' he said, 'that breaking and entering with intent to commit felony can land you in prison for twenty years? And that doing so with an unregistered weapon can get you life behind bars?'

'I assume the police are on the way.'

'I see no reason why we can't settle this without the police.'

I couldn't help but smile. He wasn't going to call the police. 'I find it hard to think when I'm losing circulation in my extremities.'

Skulking on either side of me were a couple of wide-bodied thugs. Security guards. Or bodyguards. Each held a Glock at his side. One of them was blond, with no neck and a vacant face.

The other one I recognised. He had a black crew cut and a muscle-bound physique. It was one of the two men who'd broken into my loft. Over his left eye, just below the brow, was a thin white bandage. A much bigger one was plastered next to his left ear. I remembered throwing my electric shaver into his face.

Schechter looked at me and nodded. 'Cut the man free.'

My friend threw his employer a look of protest but fished a strap-cutter from a pocket of his jacket and snipped the cuffs.

'Much better,' I said to Schechter. 'Now, if we're going to have a candid conversation, please tell these two muscle heads to leave.'

Schechter nodded. 'Semashko, Garrett, please. You can stand right outside.'

When the door closed, I said, 'Does Marshall Marcus know you arranged the kidnapping of his daughter?'

HE EXPELLED A PUFF OF AIR, approximately like a scoff. 'I'm sorry you think that. Nothing could be further from the truth.'

'Given your association with both Marcus and Senator Armstrong—both the father of the kidnapped girl and the father of a girl who assisted in that kidnapping—well, it seems quite the coincidence, don't you think?'

'Did it ever occur to you that we're all on the same side?'

'When you ordered me to stay away from the senator and his daughter, and when you announced that my services were no longer needed, it sort of raised a doubt in my mind. See, I'm on the side that wants to get Alexa Marcus released.'

'And you think I don't?'

I shrugged.

'Look at it statistically,' he said. 'What are the odds, truly, of Alexa coming home alive? She's as good as dead, and I think Marcus already understands this.'

'I'd say you tilted the odds against her by refusing to let Marcus hand over the Mercury files. Are they really worth two lives?'

'You have no idea. They are worth the lives of the one million Americans who have died defending our country. But I think you already know that. Isn't that why you had to leave the Defense Department?'

'I left because of a disagreement.'

'A disagreement with Mark Hood, your boss. Because you refused to halt an investigation that you were ordered to drop. An investigation that would have warned off parties who were unaware they were targets of the greatest corruption probe in history.'

'Funny, no one said anything about that back then.'

'No one could. Not then. But now we have no choice but to trust your discretion and your judgment and your patriotism.'

'You know nothing about me,' I said.

'I know plenty about you. I know all about your remarkable record of service to this country. Not just in the battlefield, but the clandestine work you did for DOD. General Hood says you were probably the brightest, and certainly the most fearless, operative he ever had the good fortune to work with.'

'I'm flattered,' I said sourly. 'And what got you so interested in my military record?'

He leaned forward and said heatedly, 'Because if *you* had been in charge of Marshall's security, this would never have happened. Yes, of course I've checked you out.'

'For what?' I said.

He paused. 'I'm sure you know about that "missing" 2.6 *trillion* dollars that an auditor discovered in the Pentagon a few years ago?'

I nodded. The story didn't get the kind of play in the mainstream media you'd have expected. Maybe such a sum of money was just too big to conceive of, like the weight of planet earth. 'The money was never found, right?'

He shrugged. 'Not my point. I'm saying that the Pentagon is a black hole. Everyone in the intelligence community knows that.'

'How would you know? Batten Schechter is a CIA front?'

'CIA? Please. Have you seen how far down they are on the org chart? Somewhere below the Bureau of Labor Statistics.'

'All right, then what the hell are you?'

'A middleman, nothing more. Just a lawyer who's helping make sure that no one "misplaces" three trillion dollars again.'

'Could you possibly be any more vague?'

'Who paid your salary when you worked for the DOD?'

'Black budget,' I said. That was the top-secret funding, buried in the US budget, for clandestine operations and classified research. All the stuff that officially doesn't exist. It's so well hidden that no one's ever sure how much there is or what it's paying for.

'Bingo.'

'Mercury refers to US black-budget funding?'

'Close enough. Any idea how big the black budget is?'

'Sixty billion dollars or so.'

'Let's say that's the figure that's leaked for public consumption.'

'So you're . . .' I stopped. Suddenly it all seemed clear. 'You're telling me that Marshall Marcus has been investing and managing the *black budget of the United States*. Sorry, I don't buy it.'

'Not all of it, but a healthy chunk. Quite a few years ago some wise men looked at the ebbs and flows of defence spending and realised that we were putting our national security at the mercy of public whims and political fads. One year it's "kill all the terrorists", the next it's "why are we violating civil liberties?" The CIA was gutted in the 1990s. Then nine eleven happens, and everyone's outraged—Where was the CIA? How could this have happened? Well, you *eviscerated* the CIA, folks, that's what happened.'

'And . . .'

'And the decision was reached at a very high level to set aside funds from the fat years to take care of the lean years.'

'And give it to Marshall Marcus to invest.'

He nodded. 'A few hundred million here, a billion or two there, and pretty soon Marshall had *quadrupled* our covert funds.'

'Brilliant. And now it's all gone. Doesn't sound like you did a whole lot better than the green eye-shades at the Pentagon.'

'Fair enough. But no one expected Marshall to be targeted.'

'So Alexa's kidnappers aren't after money at all, are they? "Mercury in the raw"—that refers to the investment records?'

'Let's be clear. They want some of our most sensitive operational secrets. This is a direct assault on American national security. And it wouldn't surprise me if Putin's people have a hand in this.'

'So you think the Russians are behind this?'

'Absolutely.'

That would explain why the kidnapper was a former Russian inmate. Tolya had said members of the Sova gang were often hired by Russian oligarchs. But now I wondered whether the Russian *government* might instead be behind it all.

'You're given access to classified information above top secret?'

'Look, it's no longer possible for the Pentagon to sluice money directly into false-front entities. You know all those anti-money-laundering laws aimed at global terror? They just give far too many bureaucrats in too many countries around the world the ability to do track-backs. Private funding has to originate in the private sector or else it's going to be unearthed by some corporate auditor.'

'I get that. So what?'

'If the wrong people got hold of the transfer codes, they'd be able to identify all sorts of cutaways and shell companies—and figure out who's doing what for us where. To hand all that over would be nothing less than a body blow to our national security. I can't allow it. And if Marshall were in his right mind, he wouldn't, either.'

'I wouldn't be so sure of that.'

'Believe me,' Schechter said, 'nothing would make me happier than if you were able to find Alexa Marcus and free her. But that's just about impossible now. We don't have any names of her captors. We don't have the slightest idea where she is.'

I didn't correct him. 'Are we done here?'

'Not quite. You've seen some highly classified files, and I want your assurance that it goes no further.'

'I really don't care what's in your files. My only interest is in finding Marshall Marcus's daughter.'

My head began thudding again as I got to my feet. I turned and walked out the door. His goons scowled at me. I smiled back.

'Nick,' Schechter called out, 'I know you'll do the right thing.'

'Oh,' I said, 'you can count on it.'

IT WAS ALMOST TEN THIRTY by the time I was back in Mr Derderian's van. As I drove, I powered on my BlackBerry, and it began to load up emails and make its voicemail alert sound.

One of the calls was from the PI in New Jersey who was looking into Belinda Marcus's past. I listened to his message with astonishment. Her employment as a call girl was by far the least interesting part of her history.

Then I noticed that four of the calls I'd received were from Moscow. I checked my watch. It was twenty minutes past six in the morning, Moscow time. I called and woke him up.

'I've been leaving messages for you,' he said.

'I was temporarily offline,' I said. 'Do you have names for me?'

'Yes, Nicholas, I do. I didn't think it prudent to leave this information on your voicemail.'

'Let me pull over and get something to write with.'

'Surely you can remember one name.'

IT WAS TOO LATE to catch a shuttle flight to New York's LaGuardia Airport. But an old friend flew cargo planes for FedEx. He got me on the eleven o'clock run from Boston to New York. In a little over an hour, I was walking into an adult entertainment club called Gentry on West Forty-fifth Street in Manhattan.

The carpeting inside was garish red. The music was bad and loud. There were red vinyl lounge chairs, red vinyl banquettes and booths, half of them filled with conventioneers and midlevel executives entertaining clients. Strobe lights rotated.

I found the VIP Room upstairs. Here the music was more sedate. A slightly higher class of clientele sat in tan suede clamshell banquettes that faced the stage. The guy I was looking for was sitting at a banquette with burly bodyguards on either side of him. You could tell they were Russian a mile away.

The boy was tall and skinny, with a pasty complexion and a patchy goatee. He wore a foppish black velvet jacket and was holding court for five or six equally scruffy-looking guys his age who were doing shots and generally acting obnoxious.

Arkady Navrozov looked fourteen, though he was almost twenty. Even if you didn't know that his father, Roman Navrozov, was obscenely rich, you could tell by the kid's entitled demeanour.

Roman Navrozov was said to be worth over twenty-five billion dollars. He was an exile from Russia, where he'd amassed a fortune as one of the newly minted oligarchs under Boris Yeltsin by seizing control of a few state-owned oil and gas companies and then taking them private. When Vladimir Putin took over, he threw Navrozov in jail on grounds of corruption.

He served five years in the notorious Kopeisk prison.

But he must have struck a deal with Putin, because he was quietly released from prison and went into exile, much of his fortune still intact. He had homes in Moscow, London, New York, Paris, Monaco. He owned a football club in west London. His yacht, usually docked off the French Riviera, was the biggest and most expensive in the world and was equipped with a French-made missile defence system.

Because Roman Navrozov lived in fear. He'd survived two publicly reported assassination attempts and probably countless others, thanks to his private army of some fifty bodyguards. He'd made the mistake of speaking out against Putin and the 'kleptocracy'.

He feared his son might be kidnapped and made sure that Arkady never went anywhere without his own matched set of bodyguards.

But Arkady was a modern kid, and he posted things on Facebook. Earlier in the day he'd posted: '@ Gentry: Rocking VIP Rm tonight!'

I was at Gentry, too, only I wasn't rocking it, and I didn't post it anywhere. It spoils the surprise.

My table was across the room but within view. Exactly on time the best-looking woman in the room sidled up to Arkady. His bodyguards didn't consider Cristal to be a mortal threat. She whispered something in the kid's ear and snuggled into his lap.

His friends sniggered. He got up and followed her through the drapes to one of the private areas. Arkady's bodyguards hustled over, but he waved them away. As I'd expected.

Before they returned to the banquette, I was gone.

The curtained-off private-dance area where Cristal had led Arkady had red velvet tufted walls and a large red velvet bed with a gold fringe. The lights were low.

From behind the red curtains, I could see the two of them enter.

'—nice and comfortable while I fetch us some champagne, all righty. You like Dom?'

She settled him down on the bed and put her tongue in his ear and whispered, 'Honey, when I get back, I'm gonna take the top of your head off.' She slipped out through the curtains, and I handed her a wad of bills, the second half of what I'd promised her.

Arkady didn't notice me sidling up to the bed from the other side. I lunged, quick as a cobra, clapped a hand over his mouth, jammed my revolver into the side of his head, and cocked the trigger.

'You ever see the top of a man's head come off, Arkady?' I whispered. 'I have. You never forget it.'

ROMAN NAVROZOV OWNED the penthouse condominium in the Mandarin Oriental, with one of the great views of the city. He felt safe in the Mandarin, according to my KGB friend Tolya. I was met in the lobby by a slim, elegant, silver-haired man of around sixty. He introduced himself as Eugene, an 'associate' of Mr Navrozov.

Even though he knew I had just kidnapped his boss's son, his demeanour was cordial. He knew I was here to transact business.

As he led me towards Navrozov's private elevator, I said, 'I'm afraid there's been a slight change in plans. We won't be meeting in his condo. I've reserved a room in the hotel.'

'I'm quite sure Mr Navrozov will not agree to that . . .'

'If he ever wants to see his son again, he might want to be flexible,' I said. 'But it's up to him.'

Fifteen minutes later the elevator on the thirty-eighth floor opened, and five men emerged. It was Roman Navrozov and a small army of body-guards. They moved with a military precision.

Roman Navrozov was a portly man, not tall, but he exuded authority. He had hawkish eyebrows and an unnaturally black fringe of hair round a great bald dome.

When they were halfway down the corridor, the lead guard made a quick hand gesture, and Navrozov and his entourage stopped. The first guard approached the door, weapon out. He saw at once that the door was ajar, propped open on the latch of the security lock. He made another gesture, and a second guard joined him, and the two moved swiftly into position on either side of the door. The first one kicked the door open, and they burst in, weapons drawn.

But since I was watching through the peephole in the room across the hall, they didn't find anyone inside. I hit a number on my phone. 'Moving into position one,' I said when it was picked up.

'Roger that,' a voice replied.

He was a member of my Special Forces detachment named Darryl Amos. While I was in flight, Darryl had driven into the city from Fort Dix, New Jersey, where he worked as a convoy operations instructor. He'd checked into a fleabag on West Forty-third. Right now Darryl was baby-sitting Roman Navrozov's son at the hotel.

I opened the door and crossed the hall.

A MINUTE LATER I was standing at the window a few feet away from the man who had masterminded Alexa Marcus's kidnapping.

We were alone in the room. He sat in a chair, legs crossed, looking imperious. 'You're a very trusting man,' he said.

'Because I'm unarmed?'

We both were. He rarely carried a weapon, and I'd surrendered mine. His guards were stationed in the hall right outside the door.

He replied without even looking at me. 'You say you have my son. Maybe you do, maybe you don't. In any case, now we have you.' He grinned. 'So you see, you haven't played this very well.'

'Maybe you'd like to tell your son you don't care what happens to him.' I turned to the laptop I'd set up on the desk and tapped at the keys to open the video-chat window.

On the laptop screen was a live video feed of Arkady Navrozov, hair matted, against a grimy white plaster wall, a wide strip of duct tape over his mouth. He wasn't wearing his black velvet jacket anymore. Instead, Darryl had put him in a medical restraint garment. It was an off-white cotton duck Posey straitjacket, with long sleeves that crossed in front and buckled at the back.

In the bad old days, Soviet 'psychiatric prison hospitals' used them on political dissidents. I knew the Posey wasn't strictly necessary, but the sight would strike fear into Navrozov's granite heart.

His son was cowering. You could see the barrel of a gun move into the frame and touch the side of his head. His eyes started moving wildly. He was trying to shout, but nothing was coming out.

His father sighed. 'What do you want?' he said.

'Simple,' I said. 'I want Alexa Marcus released immediately.'

'Is this a name I should recognise?' He smiled mirthlessly.

I sighed. 'Neither one of us has time for games. Where is she? I want exact coordinates.'

'When I hire a man to do a job, I don't look over his shoulder. They don't know who I am, and I don't know who they are.'

'Then how do you communicate with them?'

'Through an intermediary. A cut-out, I think is the term, yes?'

'But you have some idea where they are.'

A shrug. 'I think New Hampshire. This is all I know.'

'And where is your cut-out located?'

'In Maine.'

'And how do you reach him?'

He replied by pulling out his mobile phone. Wagged it at me.

'Call him,' I said, 'and tell him the operation is over.'

His mouth tightened. 'It's far too late for that,' he said.

'Cancel the operation,' I said.

He smiled. 'You are wasting my time,' he said.

Now I tapped a few keys on the laptop, and the video image began to move. Then, hitting another key to turn on the computer's built-in microphone, I said, 'Shoot him.'

Navrozov looked at me, blinked. He didn't believe me.

On the laptop screen there was sudden movement. The camera jerked. Now you could see only half of the kid's body, his shoulder and arm in the white duck fabric of his Posey straitjacket.

And the black cylinder of the sound suppressor screwed in to the end of Darryl's Heckler & Koch .45. Darryl's hand gripped the pistol, his forefinger slipping into the trigger guard.

Navrozov's eyes widened, watching the image on the screen.

Darryl's finger squeezed the trigger. The loud pop of the silenced round. A slight muzzle flash as the pistol recoiled.

Navrozov gave a strange, strangled shout.

His son's scream was muted by the duct tape. His right arm jerked, and a hole was blasted into his upper arm, a spray of blood. A large blotch of red on the white canvas. Arkady Navrozov's arm was twisting back and forth, his agony obvious, the chair rocking, and then I clicked the feed off.

'All right,' I said. 'Tell your cut-out the operation is over.'

He stared for a few seconds. Then he took out his mobile phone, punched a single button, and put it to his ear. After a few seconds, he spoke in Russian, quickly and softly.

He punched another button to end the call. He said, 'It is done.'

'And how long after he makes the call before Alexa is free?'

'He must do this in person.'

'You mean, he's going to eliminate the contractor.'

'Operational security,' Navrozov said.

'But he has to drive from Maine?'

'It will take thirty minutes, no more. So. We are done here.'

'Not until I speak to Alexa.'

'This will take time. My son needs medical treatment.'

'The sooner she's free, the sooner your son is treated.'

He exhaled. 'Fine. We have concluded our business here. Marcus will get his daughter, and I will get my son.'

'Actually, no, we're not done here.'

He squinted at me.

'Just a few questions about Anya Afanasyeva.'

He drew breath. I knew then I had him.

'Where did she pick up such a lousy Georgia accent?'

ROMAN NAVROZOV took from his breast pocket a slim black box with a gold eagle printed on the front, withdrew a black cigarette with a gold filter, and put it in his mouth. He took out a match and lit it, inhaled, and let out a plume of smoke.

'Anya Ivanovna really was not a bad actress at all,' he said. 'But she needed to do more research into the state of Georgia.'

I had no reason to think that Marshall Marcus was lying to me about how he'd met the woman who called herself Belinda Jackson. He was the victim, after all. When he'd met her at the Ritz-Carlton bar in Atlanta, he must have known that she was an escort. He just didn't know that she was employed by Roman Navrozov.

My investigator had checked on the dates of her employment by the escort service and confirmed my gut instinct. Then he was able to dig deeper. The woman who'd changed her name to Belinda Jackson, who'd dropped out of the School for the Performing Arts in Lincoln Park, New Jersey, had in fact enrolled under her real name: Anya Ivanovna Afanasyeva. She'd grown up in Woodbine, New Jersey, the daughter of Russian émigrés. That was about the sum total of the facts I knew. Everything else was informed guesswork.

'I assume you provided Anya with a complete dossier on Marshall Marcus,' I said.

Navrozov burst out laughing. 'Do you really think an attractive woman like Anya needs a dossier to capture the heart of such a foolish old man? Most men have very simple needs.'

'Your needs were simple, too,' I said. 'His account numbers and passwords, the way his fund was structured, where the critical vulnerabilities were.'

He gave a snort of derision that I assumed was a denial.

'Look, I'm familiar with the history of your career. The way you secretly seized control of the second-largest bank in Russia, then used it to take over the aluminium industry. It was extraordinary.'

He blinked, nodded, unwilling to show me how much he enjoyed the blandishment. But men like that were unusually susceptible to flattery. I could see that it was working.

'The way you stole Marcus Capital Management was nothing short of brilliant. You actually bought the Banco Transnacional de Panamá. Their broker-dealer. It was . . . genius.'

Strategic deception is a tricky thing. You never actually deceive your target. You reinforce beliefs he already has.

Roman Navrozov lived in a state of paranoia and suspicion. So he was automatically inclined to believe the staged video that Darryl had taped earlier, with the help of a buddy of his who'd agreed to put on a straitjacket wired with a squib and a condom full of blood. Roman Navrozov believed it was real. After all, he'd done far worse to the spouses and children of his opponents; such cruelty came naturally to him.

But what I was attempting now—trying to pull information out of him by convincing him I knew more than I did—was a much more risky game. Because, at any moment, I might slip and say something that would tip him off to the fact I was just plain lying.

He watched me for a few seconds. 'Well,' he said, and there it was, the proud smile that I'd been hoping to provoke.

In truth, it was sort of genius, in a twisted way. If there's some hedge fund you want to loot, all you have to do is buy the bank that controls its portfolio. Obviously, that's not going to happen with most normal hedge funds, which use the big investment banks in the US. But Marcus Capital wasn't a normal hedge fund.

'So tell me something,' I said. 'Why did you need to kidnap Marshall Marcus's daughter?'

'It was a desperation move. Because the original plan didn't work at all.' He sucked in a lungful of smoke, let it out.

'You wanted the Mercury files,' I said.

'Obviously.'

It made sense. Roman Navrozov was a businessman, and certain businessmen at the highest levels traffic in the most valuable commodities. And was there any commodity more rare than the deepest, darkest intelligence secrets of the world's remaining superpower?

'So were you planning on selling the black-budget files to the Russian government?'

'Black budget? You think the Mercury files have something to do with America's secret military budget?'

'They contain the operational details of our most classified intelligence operations.'

He looked at me in surprise. 'Is that what you were told? Next you will tell me you believe in Santa Claus.'

His mobile phone rang. He glanced at it. 'The cut-out.'

10

Kirill Aleksandrovich Chuzhoi drove up the long dirt road.

It had started to rain. He didn't enjoy wet work, but Roman Navrozov paid him extremely well, and if he wanted loose ends tied up, Chuzhoi would do whatever it took. He'd even gone down to Boston to take out a low-level drug dealer under the very nose of the FBI!

But the contractor—the *zek,* the convict who'd done time in Kopeisk— was reputed to enjoy killing so much that he preferred to draw out the process. In this man's line of work, such a disturbing streak of sadism was a qualification. Maybe even necessary. He was capable of doing anything.

He made Chuzhoi extremely uncomfortable.

With his shaved head and his staring eyes and his grotesque tattoo, the contractor viewed all others with contempt. So he would never imagine that a washed-up old KGB agent could possibly attempt what Chuzhoi was about to do. The element of surprise was his only advantage against this stone-hearted monster.

An overgrown lawn came into view, almost junglelike. In the midst sat a small, neat clapboard house. He parked his black Audi and approached the front door.

Chuzhoi wore the same suit he'd worn in Boston. His long grey hair spilled down to his shirt collar. His trusty Makarov .380 was concealed in a holster at the small of his back.

The green-painted door swung open, and a face loomed out of the darkness. The shaved head, the intense stare, the deeply etched forehead: Chuzhoi had forgotten how fearsome the man was.

The *zek* said nothing. He glared and turned round, and Chuzhoi followed him into the shadowed recesses.

'Sit.' The *zek* pointed to an armchair with a high back.

'The girl is here?' Chuzhoi said.

'No.' The *zek* remained standing. 'Why is this meeting necessary?'

'The operation has been terminated. The girl is to be released at once.' Chuzhoi pulled a sheaf of papers from his pocket. 'I will see to it that you are wired your completion fee immediately. All you have to do is sign these forms. Also, you will receive a bonus of one hundred thousand dollars as soon as the girl is handed over.'

'But terminated is not the same as concluded,' the *zek* said. 'Was the ransom not paid? Or were other arrangements made?'

Chuzhoi shrugged. 'I am only a messenger.'

The *zek* came near. 'You know, the girl's father is a billionaire. We can demand a ransom that will set us up for life.'

'The father has nothing anymore.'

'Men like that are never without money.'

A sudden gust of wind lashed the small window with rain.

The *zek* put his arm round Chuzhoi's shoulder in a comradely fashion. 'Think of how much we can make, you and I.' Then his hand slipped smoothly down Chuzhoi's back until it grasped the butt of his pistol. 'Last time you came unarmed.'

'The weapon is for my protection.'

'Do you know what this is?' the *zek* said.

Chuzhoi saw the wink of a steel blade, a thick black handle. Of course he knew what it was. In the calmest voice he could muster, he said, 'I am always happy to discuss new business opportunities.'

He felt the nip of the blade against his side.

The *zek*'s left hand slid back up his spine to his left shoulder. Suddenly Chuzhoi felt a deep twinge, and his left arm went dead.

'I know the Client's ransom demands have still not been met,' the *zek* said. 'I also know he has made a deal to give me up.'

Chuzhoi opened his mouth to deny it, but the blade had sunk in a little more, then pulled back. The pain was intense.

'I think you have some idea where the girl is located,' the *zek* said.

Chuzhoi hesitated, not wanting to admit he'd had the man followed after their last meeting. Chuzhoi had ordered the follower to keep the surveillance loose. In fact, he'd stayed back so far he'd lost him. But . . . was it possible the *zek* had detected the surveillance?

Even so, Chuzhoi had only an approximate location of the burial site. He didn't know the name of the town. The county, yes. Hundreds of square miles. So what? That was as good as nothing.

Before he could think of how to reply, the *zek* spoke. 'A man with your experience should hire better eyes.'

Chuzhoi felt the blade again, and the pain shot up to the top of his head and down to the very soles of his feet. In desperation he screamed, 'What do you want?'

'May I borrow your mobile? I'd like to make a phone call.'

'PUT IT ON SPEAKER,' I told Navrozov.

This was it. The call that told us either that the kidnapping had been successfully called off or . . .

Navrozov answered it abruptly, '*Da?*'

I heard something strange, something unexpected. A scream.

And then a man's voice, speaking calmly in Russian.

In the background was a continuous whimpering, a rush of words that sounded like pleading. I looked at Navrozov.

'Who's that?' I said.

The whimpering in the background abruptly got louder, turned into a high shriek that prickled the hairs on the back of my neck. Then a rush of words. Navrozov looked stricken as he listened.

'Who is it?' I demanded.

The calm voice was back on speaker. 'Someone is there with you?' the man said in English. 'Tell Mr Navrozov that his employee will no longer be able to report back to him. Goodbye.'

The connection was severed.

I had a sick feeling. I knew the worst had happened. So did Navrozov. He hurled the phone across the room.

'Who was that?' I said.

'This is the whole point of cut-outs!' he shouted. 'I don't *know* who it is.'

'*Where* is he, then?'

'I told you, somewhere in New Hampshire!'

'Within a thirty-minute drive from the Maine border, right? We know that much. But do you know if he was based in the north part of the state, or the south, or what? You have no idea?'

He didn't answer, and I could tell that he didn't know. That he was experiencing something he rarely felt: defeat.

'Wait,' he said, his voice hoarse. 'I do have something. A photograph. The cut-out was able to take a covert photograph of the contractor. For insurance purposes.'

'A face?'

He nodded. 'But no name. This man's face is not in any of your law-enforcement databases. It will not be easy to find him.'

'I want it,' I repeated. 'And I want one more thing. I want to know what Mercury really is.'

He told me.

Thirty minutes later, still numb with shock, I found my way to the street and into a cab.

JUST BEFORE SIX in the morning, the FedEx cargo flight landed in Boston. I desperately needed sleep. If I was to have any hope of locating Alexa Marcus, I needed most of all to rest my brain.

My phone rang as I was parking the Defender.

It was Tolya Vasilenko. 'The picture you just sent me,' he said. 'I am very sorry for you. This is a particularly bad egg. You remember this terrible murder of the family in Connecticut?'

'He was the one who survived? The one who escaped?'

'So I am told.'

'Name?'

'We haven't discussed a price.'

'How much do you want?' I said wearily.

'It's not money I want. Let's call it a swap of intelligence.'

He told me his demand, and I agreed to it without a moment's hesitation. Then he said, 'Dragomir Vladimirovich Zhukov.'

I mulled over the name, tried to connect it to the snapshot that Navrozov's security chief, Eugene, had emailed me: the hard-looking man with the shaven head and the fierce expression. 'What else do you have on him? Specifics about his background. His family.'

'You have decided to become a psychoanalyst?'

'The more I know about a target's personal life, the more effective I can be.'

'When he served in Chechnya with the Russian ground forces, he was disciplined for excess zeal in a "cleansing operation".'

'Is that why he was sent to prison?'

'No, no. He was sentenced to five years for theft of property. He'd got work on one of the oil pipeline projects in Tomsk, and apparently he "borrowed" one of the excavators for his own use.'

'Like getting Al Capone for not paying taxes.'

'That was all they could get him on. The Tomsk regional police were unable to connect him definitively to something far worse that they were sure he did. Which was the reason he borrowed the excavation equipment. An abandoned parcel of land outside the city was being developed for a housing project, and when the foundation was being dug, three bodies were unearthed. A middle-aged couple and their teenage son. The police forensic examiners found large quantities of dirt in their lungs. They were buried alive.'

'Which was why Zhukov borrowed the excavation equipment.'

'So it seems. But the case could never be proved. You see, he is very, very good. But if you are looking for a psychohistory, when Zhukov was a boy, his father died in a coal-mining accident.'

'Also buried alive?'

'Not quite. When some of the miners accidentally dug into an abandoned shaft that was filled with water, the tunnels were flooded. Thirty-seven miners drowned.'

'How old was Zhukov?'

'Nine or ten. His mother, Dusya, told our interviewer years ago that her son's chief complaint was that he never saw it happen. She says that was when she first realised that Dragomir wasn't like the other little boys.'

'He's not doing this for the money, is he?'

'I'm sure the money will come in handy, but no, I imagine he took this job because it offered him a rare opportunity.'

'Opportunity?'

'To watch someone drown before his eyes.'

As BADLY AS I NEEDED SLEEP, I needed to talk to Diana Madigan even more to tell her what I'd found out.

Six in the morning. She was an early riser. So instead of going home, I drove a few minutes out of my way. Her apartment lights were on.

'How about coffee?' she said warily.

'I think I'm past the point of no return,' I said. 'Any more caffeine's just going to put me in a coma.'

I sat on her couch, and she sat on the chair next to it. She was wearing a white T-shirt and sweatpants and was barefoot.

I told her as much of what I'd just learned as I could. It wasn't exactly a coherent presentation, but I managed to set out the basic facts. 'I've got Dorothy checking on every place in New Hampshire that rents excavation equipment, but she's not going to find anything until nine or ten, when the places open.'

'OK,' she said. 'Meanwhile, I've looked at the case files on that Connecticut home invasion.'

'Already? But how did you know . . .'

She smiled ruefully. 'Nico, you need sleep. You told me about that last night. It wasn't much use anyway. The husband survived but Zhukov left him seriously brain damaged. And there were no prints.' She came in close. 'If you don't give your brain and body a rest, you're going to start screwing up.'

'Don't worry about that,' I said. 'I don't screw up.'

'Now I know you're sleep deprived,' she said with a laugh.

And before I knew it, my lips were on hers. Then I was kissing her throat. 'Diana,' I said.

She silenced me with her mouth on mine and her legs wrapped tightly round my waist.

'I KNOW WE CAN'T GO BACK to the way things were,' she said.

'I wasn't thinking this was a do-over.'

She smiled and reached for me, and I held her for a long time.

My phone rang, and I glanced at it. Marshall Marcus.

'Nick,' he whispered, 'I just got a message.'

A beep indicated a call coming in on the other line. Dorothy.

'Hold on.' I clicked on Dorothy's call.

'Nick, Marcus just got an email from the kidnappers.'

'I know. He's on the other line. He was just telling me.'

'It's not good,' she said. 'Are you near your computer?'

I hesitated. 'I'm near *a* computer.'

'I'm going to send you an email right now.'

Diana brought her laptop over, and I signed on to my email. Meanwhile, I clicked back to the other line. 'Hold on, Marshall. I'm just opening it right now.'

> The rules are all change. Now demand is very simple for you to save your daughter. Five hundred 500 $US mil must be wired into account listed below by close of business 5.00 p.m. 1700 hours Boston time today.
>
> This is not open of negotiation. This is final offer.
>
> If $$$ received satisfactory by 5.00 p.m. 1700 hours Boston time today your daughter Alexa will be released. You will be notified of her location and can pick her up then.
>
> If $$$ not received you will get one last opportunity to watch your daughter Alexa on internet.
>
> You will watch when coffin is flood with water.
>
> You will watch your daughter drown before your eyes.
>
> You will watch last minutes of your daughters life.

Then followed a name and address of a bank in Belize, bank codes and an account number.

'Nicky,' Marshall Marcus said, his voice high, quavering. 'Dear God in heaven. Please, Nick, help. Five hundred million dollars? I don't have that kind of money anymore, thanks to those bastards, and they damned well know it.'

'Let me get off the phone,' I said. 'Maybe there's a way to pull this off.'

'How?'

But I just hung up.

I leaned over and gave Diana a kiss.

'Call me as soon as you know anything,' she said.

IN THE OFFICE half an hour later, I was on the phone with the Honorable Oliver Lindo, minister of national security in Belize.

When I was working at Stoddard Associates in DC, I'd helped him out with a sticky problem involving a boat, a rum factory, one of his ex-wives and a lot of angry Cubans.

'Do you know anyone at the Belize Bank and Trust Limited?'

'It is a shady bank, my friend. If you are thinking about hiding money . . . well, I can recommend— Actually, this is not a conversation we should be having on the mobile phone.'

'If I ever have money to hide away somewhere, you'll be the first person I'll call,' I said. 'But I'm calling about something else.'

'YOU WANT TO EXPLAIN to me how this is going to work?' Dorothy said.

'Just before the bank in Belize closes, Dragomir Zhukov is going to get a confirmation that five hundred million dollars has been deposited into his account,' I said.

'But it's all a trick, right? The bank is going to confirm a deposit that was never made?'

'Of course.'

'But what's the point? If this Zhukov guy has gone rogue, he doesn't answer to anyone. It doesn't make any difference whether he gets the money or not. He's never going to let Alexa go.'

'Not if he thinks he doesn't have to. That's why there's going to be a last-minute complication. Some screw-up in the number of his bank account that requires him to make a call.'

'And you'll be on the other end of that call.'

I shrugged. 'I'm going to let him know that he gets the five hundred million only after he releases Alexa.'

She looked at me. 'He'll just refuse. He'll say it's my way or the highway, and then he'll kill her.'

'You're probably right.'

'So what am I missing here?'

'He'll want to keep her alive until five o'clock. So I have until five o'clock today to find Alexa,' I said. 'Now I want you to go back to your idea about locating him based on the schedule of plane flights, the interruptions in the satellite signal.'

'What's to go back to? That's a dead end. Didn't you tell me the FBI didn't find any matches in the FAA database?'

'But there are military air bases in Maine and Vermont and New Hampshire. They each keep their own flight logs.'

'How do we get to them?'

I handed her the phone. 'The old-fashioned way.'

DOROTHY HAD ASSIGNED Jillian to pull up a list of companies in New Hampshire that rented construction equipment. There were almost nine hundred. Even after narrowing it down to just 'earth-moving equipment' and 'heavy construction equipment', we had close to a hundred. We'd have to get extremely lucky.

Meanwhile, Dorothy spent two hours on the phone with military air bases and Air National Guard air-traffic controllers. When she walked into my office with a wide grin on her face, I knew she had something.

'Each one of those interruptions in the video signal coincides exactly with a flight out of the Pease Air National Guard Base.'

'Portsmouth, New Hampshire.'

'No, no,' she said. 'Not that simple. The kidnap site could be anywhere from about five miles to forty miles away.'

'You can't narrow it down? Like, by triangulating?'

'Don't have enough data points. All I have is three cut-outs on the video, about ten seconds after three KC-One thirty-fives take off.'

'You've got plenty,' I said. 'You know the direction the planes took off towards, and you probably know the speed the planes take off at, right? You should be able to get within ten miles.'

My BlackBerry rang. I glanced at it, saw it was Diana. 'Hey,' I said. 'You got the photo I sent.'

'More than that, Nick,' she said. 'I think we found him.'

'You found Zhukov?'

Diana's voice was taut. 'We got a hit on his phone.'

'New Hampshire?'

'Just west of Concord. We're deploying up north.'

'You're deploying with the SWAT team?'

'They're calling in all assets, operational or not. They want me at a surveillance point outside the SWAT perimeter. I'm not actually going to be in the line of fire.'

'Give me the exact location.'

'It's a house on a country road. You can't be there. You know that. It's a Bureau operation.'

I inhaled slowly. 'Diana, listen. I don't want her to die in the middle of some big noisy SWAT team operation. I want her alive.'

'So do they. The number one priority is always victim recovery.'

'I'm not talking about intention. I'm talking about technique.'

'So what are you suggesting?'

'Is it just him, hiding out there? Or is that where he has Alexa buried? It makes all the difference in how you approach him.'

'We don't know if she's there or not.'

'As soon as he hears the snap of a twig or sees guys in ghillie suits coming through the woods, he's going to kill her. He's already threatened to flood the grave, and it wouldn't surprise me if he's set up to do it remotely.'

'That doesn't make sense. She's his bargaining chip.'

'Diana, this guy doesn't operate by normal rules. To assume he does would be a dangerous miscalculation. He wants to flood the grave or shut off her air supply, and he wants to watch it on his computer screen. He wants to watch her die.'

'Then why the ransom demand?'

'He figures he'll collect a load of money and kill her anyway. Tell your squad commander he wants me there on the scene. Tell him I'm the only one who knows anything about Dragomir Zhukov.'

As I DROVE NORTH ON 93, it started to rain, first a few ominous drops, then a torrential downpour. I could barely see the road. Normally I enjoy dramatic weather, but not then. It seemed to echo the feeling of anxiety that had come over me. My instinct told me that this was not going to end well.

So I blasted some music. By the time I reached the New Hampshire border, I was feeling more hopeful. I had to hit mute to answer the phone.

It was Diana, with directions to the SWAT staging area. 'We're mustering at a parking lot two miles from the house,' she said. 'You're going to join me on the perimeter surveillance team. But that means staying outside the hard perimeter.'

'Works for me. I'm maybe thirty miles away, no more.'

Forty-five minutes later I was sitting in the passenger's seat of a black Suburban. Diana was behind the wheel. Under her FBI sweatshirt, she was wearing a level III trauma vest, a concealable ballistic garment fitted with a trauma plate.

Rain sheeted down. We were parked at the end of the woods, stationed at what the SWAT team called 'phase line yellow', the last position before the action started. Phase line green was the imaginary line round the house. Phase line green meant game on.

In truth we were nothing more than observers. My role was limited and quite clear: if they were able to take the Russian alive, and if he resisted cooperation, I was to be put on the radio to communicate directly with him. Not in person, on the radio.

We waited. Everyone out there seemed to be waiting for a signal. The air was charged with tension.

Finally Diana said, 'You want to be up there, don't you?'

I didn't reply. I was still mulling things over. Something seemed *off* about the situation. I said, 'Can I borrow your binoculars?'

She handed me a pair. I dialled in the focus until the house came into view. It wasn't a farmhouse at all but a house in the woods. The grass was overgrown and wild, probably waist high. It was dark. No car or truck in the driveway that I could see.

I handed the binoculars back to her. 'Something's wrong.'

'How so? It's his phone number that came up, no question.'

'Only one way in or out, and we're sitting at it. The woods at the back of his house are overgrown. He can't walk for two minutes through that without getting stuck in thorn bushes. He's trapped. This isn't the sort of property he'd ever pick.'

'Maybe Navrozov's people chose it for him.'

'I don't think he'd ever let someone else make that kind of decision for him. He doesn't like to rely on anyone.'

'That's your assessment, based on a thirdhand evaluation in some old KGB file.'

'I don't see any generators, do you? So how the hell does he get on the Internet? Or a satellite dish,' I said. 'Also, it's sloppy.'

'What's sloppy?'

'Using his mobile phone. He shouldn't be using it again.'

'He doesn't know we have his phone number.'

'This guy never underestimates anyone.' I took out my cellphone and hit the speed-dial number for Dorothy.

'Where are you, Heller?'

'In the middle of what's beginning to feel a lot like a diversion,' I said. 'West of Nashua.'

'Nashua? That's something like forty miles south of the flight-path area. And I may have one more data point.'

'Let's hear it.'

'I've been combing NCIC for anything coming out of New Hampshire, and I came across a possible homicide.'

'And?'

'A rookie police officer was found in his car at the bottom of a ravine. At first it looked like he drove off the road. But the local police chief strongly suspects homicide, because of the victim's injuries. According to the county coroner, they're nothing like what you'd expect to see in a car accident. For one thing, all his internal organs in his chest cavity were destroyed. Like someone detonated a depth charge down there.'

My pulse started to race. 'Where was this?'

'Within the flight-path radius. Town of Pine Ridge, New Hampshire. Forty miles away, like I said.'

'WE'RE IN THE WRONG PLACE,' I said.

'What makes you so sure?'

'His phone's probably in there, but he's not. This is some sort of a diversion, maybe even a set-up. He knows Navrozov is trying to shut him down. Maybe he's trying to lure Navrozov's guys to the wrong site to conceal his true whereabouts.'

'The SWAT guys are about to launch an assault.'

'Which means that the FBI's best people are tied up forty miles away while our guy finishes the job. Come on, let's go.'

'I can't just leave the scene. You know that.'

'They don't need you here. This is a waste of your time.'

She looked agonised, wracked with indecision.

'Come on,' I said, opening the Suburban's door and getting out.

'Nick, wait.'

I turned back.

'Don't do it, Nick. Not by yourself.'

For a moment I looked at her: those green eyes, the crazy hair. I felt something inside me tighten. 'I've got to go,' I said.

I gently pushed the door closed.

THE WALK BACK to the parking lot where I'd left my car, a mile away, was dismal and slow. By the time I reached the Defender, my clothes were soaked through. I cranked the heat and headed north towards Pine Ridge. Dusk rapidly turned into night.

About fifteen minutes after I'd set out, Diana called.

'They found a body.'

'ID?' I asked.

'Yes. The name is Kirill Chuzhoi. In the US on a green card, residing in East Rutherford, New Jersey. Born in Moscow. He's on the payroll of Roman Navrozov's holding company, RosInvest.'

'And in his pocket you found a knockoff Nokia cellphone.'

'Right. Probably Zhukov's.'

'No. More likely his own phone, with Zhukov's SIM card inside. He knew if he put his SIM card in the other guy's phone, his phone number would pop up in your search and you'd think you'd found him. And he was right. Can you send me a photo of the body?'

'Hold on,' she said. A minute or so later she got back on. 'You should have it now.'

I put the call on hold, looked at my email, and found the picture. The bogus legal attaché from the Brazilian consulate who'd killed the drug dealer at the FBI office in Boston. Roman Navrozov had probably sent him to make sure Mauricio Perreira didn't give up any information that might tie him to Alexa's abduction.

When I got back on the call, I told Diana, 'Send this picture to Snyder, OK? It ties Navrozov to the murder at FBI headquarters.'

'Got it. Will do.'

'Can you get the team redeployed up here?'

'Where?'

I read off the GPS coordinates.

'Is that the exact location where you think he is?'

'No. That's the centre of the town of Pine Ridge. Dorothy's cross-checking property records against Google Earth satellite views. A sort of primitive kind of geographic profiling.'

'Looking for what?'

'Land that's big enough and private enough. Multiple points of egress. Unoccupied. Absentee owner goes to the top of the list. We're sort of running blind here, so try to get SWAT up here.'

'I'll do my best,' she said. 'I'll see you up there.'

A minute or so after I hung up, I had an idea. I reached Dorothy on her cell. 'Can you get me the home number of the chief of police in Pine Ridge?' I said.

'OH, BELIEVE ME,' the police chief's wife said, 'you're not interrupting dinner. Walter's out there sandbagging, and I don't know *when* to expect him. They're all out there. It's a mess. The river's swollen, and there's mud slides all over the place.'

'What's his cellphone?'

Chief Walter Nowitzki answered on the first ring.

'Chief,' I said, 'I'm sorry to bother you during such a difficult time, but I'm calling about Officer Jason Kent. He was on your force, reported as a homicide?'

'*Who's this?*' he said sharply.

'FBI,' I said. 'CJIS.'

He knew the jargon. Any cop would. CJIS was the FBI's Criminal Justice Information Services division, which maintained the central NCIC database of all reported crimes.

'How can I help you?'

'We've got a homicide in Massachusetts that seems to fit some of the basic parameters of the one you reported, so if you could answer just a couple of real quick questions—'

'Tell me what you wanna know,' he said.

'The day he was killed, what were his duties?'

'We got a fella called Dupuis. Kept calling to complain about one of his neighbours, and I asked Jason to go check it out.'

'What sort of complaint?'

'Oh, I dunno. Dupuis said he thought the guy down the road stole his dog and he mighta been doing work without a permit.'

'What kind of work?'

'Construction, maybe? All I know is, there hasn't been no one living on the Alderson farm for years, not since Ray Alderson's wife died and he moved down to Delray Beach. I figured maybe Ray had a caretaker getting the place ready to sell.'

'This caretaker,' I said. 'Has he been there a while?'

'Well, I'd have no way of knowing that. I've never met the fella. Foreigner, maybe. Ray's farm is a nice piece of land, more than two hundred acres, but the main house is all but falling down. Doesn't show well, which is why—'

'Where is it?' I cut in sharply.

'It's on Goddard, just past Hubbard Farm Road. You wanna talk to the owner, I can probably rustle up Ray's number down in Florida.'

'Don't bother. I know you've got your hands full. This is for the database. Routine data entry. It's what I spend my life doing.'

'Well, it's important work,' the police chief said kindly.

I thanked him and hung up before he could ask anything else.

'Dorothy,' I said fifteen seconds later, 'I need directions.'

11

By the time I drove into Pine Ridge, the rain had slowed to a drizzle. At the first major intersection, I took a left. About three miles down a narrow tree-choked road, I came to a roadblock. Hastily improvised: a couple of wooden sawhorses lined with red reflector disks. This was Goddard Road. About two miles down this way was the Alderson farm.

If I'd guessed right, it was also where Alexa Marcus was buried in the ground. And where I might find Dragomir Zhukov.

The road was rutted, deep mud. I got out, dragged a sawhorse out of the way, got back in the Defender, and ploughed ahead. It was like driving across a marsh. Gradually the road became a narrow lane.

Then my headlights illuminated a rusty metal mailbox that said ALDERSON. If there was a farmhouse down there, it was too far from the road to see. The driveway was the main access road. If this was indeed the right place, Zhukov was likely to have surveillance equipment in place, some sort of early-warning system.

So I drove on ahead, past the entrance, ploughing through the muddy river another half mile or so until it came to an abrupt stop. There I drove up the steep bank as deep into the woods as I could.

According to the map Dorothy had sent to my phone, this was the far end of the property. The house was a quarter-mile from here. Given the topography, the road couldn't be seen from the house.

I noticed the NO TRESPASSING/NO HUNTING signs posted to trees every fifty feet or so. They looked brand new. Someone had put them up recently to keep anyone from approaching the house.

I had some decent overhead satellite photos of the Alderson property, but nothing recent. The photos could have been three years old, for all I knew. I was at a real disadvantage.

At least I had a good weapon: my SIG SAUER P250 semiautomatic. I loaded several magazines with hollow-point bullets. They're designed to do a lot of damage to a person.

I stashed the Defender in a copse of birch trees and took my binoculars out of the back. I strapped on a side holster and jammed in the SIG, then clipped extra magazine holsters to my belt.

At the last minute I remembered something under the rear seat that I might need. It was an old military-spec Interceptor ballistic vest. It wasn't bulletproof—no such thing, really—but it was supposed to stop 9mm machine-gun rounds. I put it on. If I'd come to the right place, I needed to be prepared.

I set off through the woods. The ground was sodden and so slick in places I nearly lost my footing.

The land rose steeply and then plateaued. I spotted a small building in the distance. I peered through the binoculars and saw a windowless structure: a barn.

I came closer and finally saw the house. But it was dark. That wasn't promising. Either this was the wrong place or Zhukov had already left. Meaning that Alexa was dead.

I drew closer. I could see the long expanse of yard leading up to the house. The sky had begun to clear, and there was enough moonlight to make out a patchy lawn.

And midway between the barn and the house a neat oblong had been cut into the sorry-looking lawn. A rectangle about ten feet long by three feet wide. Like a freshly dug grave. But instead of the sort of earthen heap you see in a new grave, the ground was flat, crisscrossed with tyre tracks. At one end of the rectangular patch of dirt a grey PVC pipe stuck up like the sawn-off trunk of a sapling.

The house was an old brown tumbledown wreck. Mounted to the roof was a white satellite dish. It looked new.

In the shadows behind the barn, I began to discern the contours of a tall piece of equipment. I looked closer and saw that it was a Caterpillar back-hoe loader.

Peering through the binoculars, I focused on the house. Two floors, small windows. No light inside. On the wooden porch was another piece of equipment. An air compressor? That made sense. This was how he kept air flowing into her box, or whatever it was.

This had to be the right place.

For a minute or two I watched carefully, looking for some kind of movement in the darkness. I estimated I was about three hundred yards from the house, beyond the range of accuracy of my pistol. But if someone was inside with a rifle, three hundred yards was no problem. The moment I stepped into the clearing, I was a target.

I got on my cellphone and called Diana. In a whisper, I said, 'I think she's here. I'm looking at what may be a burial site. A vent pipe in the ground. Signs of recently excavated earth.'

'Zhukov?'

'The house is dark. I can't be sure if he's there. Tell your bosses that there's not much doubt. They need to get up here right away. Tell them to bring shovels.'

I hit END and made sure the ringer was off. Then I walked across the barren lawn towards what had to be the burial site. Suddenly the entire yard lit up, and I was blinded by the blaze of spotlights from two directions.

I flattened myself against the ground. Then in one quick motion I rolled over, facing up, and listened hard. Nothing.

I'd hit an invisible tripwire at ankle level. A low-tech motion detector. Was he waiting for me to get up so that, illuminated by the two spotlights, he could take aim? After two minutes, the spotlights went off and everything was black. No shot was fired.

The vent pipe was roughly a hundred feet from me. Would she hear me if I spoke into it? Then I realised if Zhukov were hiding in the house, monitoring Alexa over a remote connection, then whatever she heard, he'd hear, too. So I had to take him out first.

I sprang to my feet and started towards the house.

Round the side was a door. I kept going round to the front. No vehicles in the front of the house. He couldn't be inside or I'd be dead by now.

But what if Zhukov had simply abandoned the farmhouse? After all, he knew from Navrozov's cut-out that he was being actively hunted. Why stay here? Leave his victim in the ground, let her die.

A path had been worn across a scrubby front lawn to the front door. I detected no movement in any of the windows, so I pulled open the screen and tried the door. It came right open.

A small entryway, low ceilings, a musty odour. Cigarettes, too. I moved stealthily, the SIG in a two-handed grip, pivoted abruptly to my left, weapon pointed, ready to fire. Then to my right.

Nothing. Now there were three ways to go. A doorway on my right led to a small front room. On my left was a staircase. Straight ahead was another doorway, which I guessed led to a kitchen and the back of the house.

Then I heard a voice from the back of the house. A woman's voice, muffled, the tone rising and falling. A TV had been left on.

I stepped through the threshold, my body a coiled spring. I scanned the room, slicing with the pistol left to right.

The kitchen was windowless, carved out of an interior space. An old white GE stove, vintage 1940. A white porcelain sink. It was stacked high with plates and bowls that were crusted with food.

I heard the woman's voice again, much clearer now, coming from the next room. From the back of the house. Not from a TV.

The voice was Alexa's.

I burst into the adjoining room, gun extended.

'. . . bastard!' she was saying. Then her tone changed abruptly. 'Please, oh, God, please let me out of here. I can't stand it.'

Her voice was coming from computer speakers. A black Dell computer on a long wooden workbench. In the monitor, I saw that same close-up of Alexa's face, a greenish cast, just as we'd seen it in the streaming video. I almost didn't recognise her. Her face was gaunt, her eyes swollen to slits, deep purple hollows beneath them.

In front of the monitor was a keyboard. To the left of it was a small cheap-looking microphone. I switched it on.

'Alexa?' I said. 'It's Nick.'

'Who . . . who is this?'

'It's Nick Heller. You're going to be OK. I'm at the house. Nearby. Listen, Alexa, help is coming, but I need you to stay quiet and keep calm, all right? You're going to be OK. I promise.'

I saw a flash of light through the window. A car's headlights. I heard the rumble of a car's engine, then a door slamming.

Zhukov was here. It could be no one else. But I couldn't see him. He'd parked on the side of the house that had no windows.

'Nick! Get me out of here, Nick!' she screamed.

'He's back,' I whispered. 'Can you hear me?'

She stared up, and she nodded as she began sobbing.

'Everything will be fine,' I said. 'Really. As long as you don't say a word. OK? Not a word.'

I gripped the SIG in both hands.

He would enter the house through the front door, as I had. The worn path told me that. Yet he wouldn't expect anyone to be here. That would give me a temporary advantage. Time had slowed. I went into that strange, calm place I so often did when faced with grave danger: senses heightened, reactions quickened.

A door opened somewhere.

Not the front. Someone had entered the house, but from where? The side door I'd noticed earlier. Now I didn't know where in the house he'd be coming from. I didn't know the house.

I needed to conceal myself, but where? A door next to the kitchen entrance. A closet, probably, with a wooden kitchen chair next to it. I slid the chair a few inches out of the way. Opened the door with my left hand, stepped into the darkness—and plunged into space. Not a closet, but the basement stairs. I reached out and grabbed something to arrest my fall. A wooden banister. Swivelled myself round, pulled the door shut behind me. Lowering myself to my knees on the first step, I peered out through the keyhole.

Waited for him to appear.

DRAGOMIR ZHUKOV had parked at the side of the house just to vary the pattern. Never be predictable.

Before he opened the door, he glanced down at the baseboard and saw the tiny strip of transparent tape he'd placed between the door and the jamb. It was still in place. No one had entered here.

Long ago Dragomir had learned the importance of leaving nothing to chance. This was one of the many lessons he'd learned at the University of Hell, also known as Prison Number One, in Kopeisk.

The money transfer had been received in his account. The cut-out had been eliminated. The only chore that remained was hardly a chore at all.

He had rehearsed it countless times, savouring the prospect. He'd tell the young girl what was about to happen, because there was nothing as delicious as a victim's foreknowledge. Then he'd disconnect the air hose from the compressor and attach it to the garden hose with the brass coupler. Once he pulled up the lever on the farmer's hydrant, the water would begin to flow.

She would hear the trickle, and then she would know.

As the water level grew higher and the air pocket grew smaller, she would flail and pound and, most of all, beg. He would be watching in hypnotised fascination. She would drown before his eyes.

It was a terrible way to die. The way his father died. For years he could only imagine it. But now he would know.

As he entered the house, he stopped.

Something was different here. A shift in the air? A vibration? He had the finely tuned senses of a wild animal.

Now that the cut-out was dead, he wondered how long it would take for the Client to realise what had happened. But he was sure he hadn't been followed after the last rendezvous.

Still, something was *off*. He moved quietly through the parlour to the front door, where he'd placed another slice of sticky tape at the bottom of the door next to the jamb, both inside and out. A minuscule ribbon of tape lay on the floor.

Someone was here.

I COULD HEAR FOOTFALLS, the sounds louder, closer. Grasping the pistol in my right hand, the banister in my left, I looked through the keyhole and saw only the light from the computer monitor.

Someone had entered the room. I saw a leg. Walking towards the computer, or at least in that direction. Then, no more movement.

A man was standing a few feet from the door. I could see his back: large torso, broad shoulders, a dark sweatshirt, a black knitted cap on his head. And the hideous pattern on the back of his neck. The bottom half of an owl's face.

He entered the back room. A voice crackled from the computer speaker. 'Nick!' Alexa screamed. 'Please, don't go away!'

Zhukov turned swiftly, holding a weapon, an enormous steel semi-automatic with a barrel like a cannon. I recognised it at once. An Israeli-made .50-calibre Desert Eagle.

He turned slowly. He knew. He knew I was here somewhere.

Alexa's voice, steadily more frantic, 'Please, Nick, answer me! Don't leave me stuck here. Don't you go away!'

Zhukov's eyes scanned the room, up and then down, ticking slowly and methodically in a grid.

I'd come to rescue Alexa. But now it was a matter of survival.

The hollow-point ammo I was using wouldn't penetrate the thick old wooden door between us. Nor was my body armour meant to stop the .50-calibre Magnum rounds fired by the Desert Eagle.

I saw Zhukov's eyes shift towards the kitchen. He took a few steps in that direction. I could still see him through the keyhole.

As soon as I was sure he'd moved into the kitchen, I'd turn the knob silently and step out as noiselessly as I could. If I got the jump on him, I might be able to drop him with one well-aimed shot.

Reaching out slowly, I placed my left hand on the doorknob, ready to turn it once he was safely out of the room.

Then he swivelled round, back towards me. His gaze dropped to the floor, as if he'd just discovered something. I saw what he was looking at. The chair I'd moved out of the way of the basement door. It was out of place. Not exactly where he'd left it.

His gaze rose slowly. He smiled, raised the Desert Eagle, and pointed it at the basement door, directly at me, as if he could see through the wood. He squeezed the trigger—*blam blam blam*—and I lurched out of the way. Everything was happening in slow motion—the thunderous explosions and the muzzle flash, the splintering of the door—and as I let go of the doorknob and leaped backwards, I felt a bullet slam into my chest, and everything went black.

WHEN I CAME TO a few seconds later, my body was wracked with excruciating pain. Like something had exploded inside my chest while my rib cage was being crushed in some enormous vice. The pain in my left leg was even worse, sharp and throbbing. Everything moved in a sort of stroboscopic motion, like a rapid series of still images. Where was I?

On my back, I knew, crumpled on a hard, cold floor in the near darkness, surrounded by the dank odour of mould and old concrete. Pale moonlight filtered in from above, through a gaping hole in the underside of a wooden staircase.

In an instant I realised what had just happened.

A bullet had slammed into my ballistic vest, but it hadn't penetrated my body. I was alive only because two inches of solid oak had slowed the round's velocity. But I'd been shoved backwards down the stairs. Then I'd crashed through the termite-damaged rotten planks and landed on the concrete floor below.

I sensed blood seeping down my left leg. I reached down to feel the bullet wound. But there wasn't any. Instead, the jagged end of a broken plank almost a foot long was sunk into my left calf, through the denim of my jeans. I grabbed the board and wrenched it out.

I tried to recall the number of shots he'd fired at me. The Desert Eagle's magazine held only seven rounds. Had he fired four or five? Maybe even six. Maybe he didn't have any rounds left; maybe he had one.

I was short of breath and dazed. A creak overhead, then heavy footsteps on the top steps. Zhukov was coming downstairs. I felt for my weapon on the cold floor, but it was nowhere within reach.

A light came on: a bare bulb mounted to one of the rafters about ten feet away. He took another step. I lay absolutely still, held my breath. If I made a sound, he'd locate me, and he'd get a direct, unimpeded shot straight down. The vest wouldn't protect me.

Then I noticed the plank whose jagged end had sunk into my leg. I grabbed it, and in one hard swift throw I hurled it, smashing the bare light bulb, and everything went dark again.

In the dark the situation was more even.

But a few seconds later a flashlight beam shone down. I could hear him coming down the stairs, slowly and deliberately.

Then the beam went off. The only light was the faint trapezoid cast by the open door above. Maybe he'd stuffed the flashlight in a pocket. He needed two hands to hold the Desert Eagle.

I had to get to my feet to be ready to move, but do it silently. The timing was crucial. I could move only when he did, when the sound of his tread masked whatever slight noise I made getting up.

A dry whisking. A rat pattered across the floor towards me and paused, surveying the terrain. Directly overhead another step creaked. Startled, the rat skittered over my neck. I clapped both hands over its squirmy body, then hurled it across the room.

There was a shot. Zhukov had heard the rat's scuffling and assumed it was me.

But now he knew he hadn't hit me. No one can get shot with a .50-calibre round without giving a scream or groan or cry.

Was that his last shot? I couldn't be sure. Maybe he had one shot left. Or maybe he was on a new cartridge.

Through one of the missing risers, I could see the heels of his boots. Then I heard the unmistakable metallic *clackclack* of the pistol's magazine being ejected. The weapon was directly above me, close enough to wrench out of his hands if I moved fast enough, took him by surprise. *Now.*

I shoved against the floor with both hands, using the strength in my arms to get into a high pushup. Favouring my right foot, I levered myself up until I was standing. Then I grabbed his right boot and yanked it towards me. He lost his footing, stumbled down the steps, yelled out in surprise and anger. Something heavy and metal clattered near my feet. The Desert Eagle?

Should I go for the gun or launch myself at him?

I went for the gun.

But it was his flashlight: a long black Maglite. I leaned over and grabbed it, and when I spun round, he was standing maybe six feet away, pistol in a two-handed grip. He was aiming two feet to my left.

In the dark, he couldn't see me.

I arced the Maglite at his head. It struck him on the bridge of his nose. He staggered, and I lunged, knocking him to the floor, driving a knee into his stomach, my right fist at his head. I delivered a powerhouse uppercut to the side of his jaw. He dropped the gun.

I pinioned him to the floor with my right knee, but he had unexpected reserves of strength. As if the pain only spurred him on.

He levered his torso off the floor and slammed a fist at my left ear. I swung for his face, but then something large and steel came at me, and I realised he'd retrieved his weapon.

Holding the Desert Eagle by its long barrel, he swung the butt against my temple, like a steel blackjack. My head exploded. I careened to one side, and he was on top of me.

He flipped the gun round, then ground the barrel into the skin of my forehead, one-handed.

'Go ahead,' I panted. 'Pull the trigger.'

I saw the hesitation in his face. He was debating what to do. I knew then he had no more rounds left. He'd ejected the magazine but hadn't had the chance to pop in a new one.

He grimaced, and with his left hand he pulled something from his boot. A flash of steel: a five-inch blade, a black handle. A round steel button at the hilt. He whipped it at my face. I swung at him, but the tip of the blade was now under my left eye.

'Do you know what this is?' he said.

My KGB friend had told me about the Wasp knife.

'Dusya,' I said.

A microsecond pause. His mother's name seemed to jolt him.

That second was enough. I scissored my left leg over his right, behind the knee, pulling him towards me while I shoved my right knee up and into his abdomen. I grabbed his left hand at the wrist.

In an instant I'd flipped him back over onto the ground.

Jamming my right elbow into his right ear, I tucked my head in so it was protected by my right shoulder. My right knee trapped his leg. I gripped his left wrist, pushing against his fingers, which were wrapped round the knife handle. I kept pushing at them, trying to break his grip and strip the knife from his hand.

But I had again underestimated Zhukov's almost inhuman strength. He jammed his knee into my groin, and once again he was on me, the point of the knife inches away from my left eyeball.

I gripped his hand, trying to shove it away, but all I managed to do was keep it where it was, poised to sink in.

'If you kill me,' I gasped, 'it won't make any difference. The others are on their way.'

With a sneer, he said, 'And it will be too late. The casket will be flooded. And I will be gone.' The knife came in closer. 'I think you know this girl. Let me tell you what she did to me. She was a very dirty little girl.'

I roared in fury and gave one final, mighty shove with all the strength I had left. The knife moved backwards as he flipped onto his side, but he still didn't loosen his grip on the handle.

I drove my knee into his abdomen, sending his left arm backwards. The knife, still grasped tightly in his fist, sank into his throat, into the soft flesh underneath his chin.

Only later did I understand what happened in the next instant.

The palm of his hand must have slid inwards a fraction of an inch, nudging against the raised metal injector button, causing his Wasp knife to expel a large frozen ball of gas into his trachea.

There was a loud pop and a hissing explosion.

A terrible hot shower of blood and gobbets spat against my face, and in his bulging eyes I saw what looked like disbelief.

I WAS ABLE TO HOLD OUT until shortly after the casket came out of the ground.

It took five members of the FBI's SWAT team two hours of digging by hand, using shovels borrowed from the Pine Ridge police. The casket was almost ten feet down, and the earth was sodden and heavy from the recent deluge. They hoisted it out on slings of black nylon webbing, two on one side, three on the other.

It was dented in several places and had a half-inch yellow hose coming out of one end, which had been trenched into the ground for two hundred feet or so and was connected to the air compressor on the back porch. A much thicker, rigid PVC tube came out of the other end, the pipe I'd seen sticking out of the ground.

The team didn't believe my assurances that the casket hadn't been booby-trapped. I knew, though, that if Zhukov had placed a booby-trap in the casket, he would not have denied himself the opportunity to taunt me with it. Two of their bomb techs worked slowly and deliberately, making sure there were no triggering mechanisms.

Somehow they were able to ignore all the thumping and pounding and muffled screams from within. I wasn't.

Diana was supporting me. My legs had turned to rubber. Everything was moving in and out of focus, and I didn't understand why. True, the pain in my chest had grown steadily worse. The blunt-force trauma had been serious, but I'd thought the worst of it had passed. I was wrong. The escalating pain should have been the first sign. But I was preoccupied with getting Alexa out of her coffin.

'Nico,' Diana said, 'you weren't wearing trauma plates.'

'Hey, I was lucky I had a plain old ballistic vest with me,' I said between sharp gasps. Breathing was getting more difficult. I couldn't fill my lungs. That should have been the second sign.

'You should have waited for us.'

I looked at her, tried to smile.

'OK,' she conceded, nuzzling me on the neck. 'I'm glad you didn't wait. But do you always have to be the first one on the battlefield and the last one to leave?'

'I'll leave as soon as I see her.'

The hollow thumps, the distant, anguished cries that could have been half a mile away. I couldn't stand listening to it. Yet the bomb techs continued their inspection.

'There are no explosive devices,' I said. I staggered across the marshy field. 'He would have boasted about it.'

'Where are you going?'

'To get her out of there.'

When I got to Alexa's casket, I shoved aside one of the guys. He protested, and someone yelled, 'Back away!'

I shouted, 'One of you must have a set of Allen keys, right?'

Someone threw me a folding tool with a bunch of keys on it. I found the right one and inserted it in the hole at the foot of the casket and turned the crank anticlockwise four or five turns to unlock the lid. The rubber gasket had been mashed in places where the steel casket had begun to cave in under ten feet of dirt, but I managed to prise it up. A terrible odour escaped, like from a sewer.

Alexa had been lying in her own excrement, or just a few inches above it. She stared up, but not at me. Her hair was matted, her face chalk white, her eyes sunken in deep pits. She was wearing blue medical scrubs and was covered in vomit.

She didn't understand she was free.

I knelt over and kissed her forehead and said, 'Hey.'

She looked directly at me. I smiled at her, and she started to cry.

That was about the last thing I remembered for a long time.

12

I hate hospitals.

Unfortunately, I had to spend a couple of days at the Beth Israel Hospital in Boston, where my FBI friends were kind enough to helicopter me from New Hampshire. The ER doc told me I'd developed a tension pneumothorax as a result of the blunt-force trauma. He ordered up a lot of X-rays and put a chest tube in me, had the wound in my calf cleaned out and bandaged, gave me a tetanus shot. After three days they let me go.

Diana was there to give me a ride home.

'I want to see Alexa. Is she still in the hospital?'

'Actually, she got out a lot faster than you. She was treated for dehydration; they checked her out, and she's fine.'

'I doubt that. Is she at home?'

'Yeah. In Manchester. I don't think she's happy about it.' As we headed towards Massachusetts Avenue, she said, 'How about I cook dinner for you tonight? As a celebration.'

'I'd like that. A celebration of what?'

She gave me a sideways glance and pursed her lips. 'I don't know, maybe the fact you saved that girl's life?'

'If anything was a team effort—'

'You're doing that thing again. Where you give everyone else credit except yourself. You don't have to do that with me.'

I was too tapped out to argue with her.

'Let's make it my place,' she said. 'I don't want to be the first person to turn on your oven.'

THE WAVES CRASHED LOUDLY on the rocks below, and the wind howled along the point. The sky looked heavy, a mournful grey. The guardhouse was empty. I parked in the circular drive, crossed the porch, and rang the bell. After a minute the door opened.

'Nickeleh,' Marcus said, and he smiled, but it was not a happy smile. He was weary and defeated.

I followed him to the front of the house.

'She's still not talking?' I said.

Marcus heaved a long sigh as he sank into a chair. 'She hardly even comes out of her room. She sleeps all the time.'

'After what she's been through, she needs to see someone.'

'I know, Nick. I know. Maybe you can change her mind. She always seems to listen to you. So you're feeling better, Nickeleh?'

'Totally.' Then I said, 'You're doing the right thing.'

He gave me a questioning look.

'Meeting with the FBI.'

'Oh. Well, only because Schecky says he can get me a deal.'

'Give Gordon Snyder what he wants,' I said, 'and you'll have the FBI on your side. They have a lot of influence with the US Attorneys' Office.'

'But what does that mean? They're gonna put me in prison? My little girl, look what she's been through already—now she has to lose her daddy as well?'

'You might walk,' I said. 'It depends on how much you give them. You're going to have to tell them about Mercury.'

'Schecky says I have nothing to worry about if I do what he says.'

'How well has that worked out for you?' I said.

He looked stricken and said nothing for a long while.

Finally I broke the silence. 'Where's Belinda?'

'That's why I asked you to come,' Marcus said. 'She's gone.'

He handed me a pale blue correspondence card with BELINDA JACKSON MARCUS on the top. The note said:

Darling—

I think it's better this way. Someday we'll talk. I'm so happy Alexa is home.

I really did love you.

Belinda

'She said she was going out to meet a girlfriend in the city, and when I got up, I found this. What does it mean?'

It meant she'd been warned the FBI was about to close in on her. Though in truth, it would be difficult to prove Anya Afanasyeva guilty of any serious crime.

'Sometimes it takes a crisis to find out who a person really is.'

Marcus shook his head. 'Nick, I need you to find her for me.'

'I don't think she wants to be found.'

'What are you talking about? She's my wife. She loves me!'

'Maybe she loved your money more.'

'She knew I was broke for months. It never changed anything.'

'Well, Marcus, there's broke and there's *broke*, right?'

A long pause.

He then turned away.

'Come on, Marshall. Did you really think you could move forty-five million dollars offshore without anyone finding out? It's not so easy anymore.'

Marcus flushed. 'OK, so there was a little nest egg,' he said. 'Money I wasn't going to touch. Money I'll need if I'm ever going to get back in the game.' He sounded defensive, even indignant. 'Look, I'm not going to apologise for what I've got.'

'Apologise? What do you have to apologise for?' I said.

'Exactly.'

He didn't notice my caustic tone. 'I mean, you've been consistent from the beginning—you've never stopped lying to me. Even back when Alexa was kidnapped the first time and you told me you had no idea who was behind it. You knew it was David Schechter's people cracking the whip. Making sure you did what you were told.'

He hesitated a few seconds. 'Look, if this is about money, then fine. I'll pay your bill in full.'

I laughed. 'Like I said, Marcus, there's broke and there's broke. As of nine o'clock this morning, you're wiped out for real. Check with the Royal Cayman Bank and Trust. The entire forty-five million dollars was withdrawn this morning.'

'It's *gone?* How could this happen to me *again?*'

'Well,' I said, 'maybe it wasn't the smartest idea to put it all in Belinda's name.'

DAVID SCHECHTER WANTED to meet with me before the FBI arrived at his office. He said it was a matter of some urgency.

'I wanted to apologise to you.' He sat behind the antique desk.

'For what?'

'I overreacted. I'll be the first to admit it. I should have been upfront with you from the get-go. You're a true American hero.' He fixed me with a look of the deepest admiration.

'You're too kind,' I said. 'Apology accepted.'

'You of all people understand that our national security must never be compromised.'

'No question,' I said.

'I've already impressed upon Marshall the importance of not divulging to the FBI anything about Mercury that isn't germane to their investigation.'

'Why keep it secret from the FBI?'

'Nick, you know how Washington works. If it ever gets out that ten billion dollars in military black-budget funds has been lost because it was being privately invested—dear Lord, the sharks will come for miles. You were a soldier. Can you imagine what damage such a revelation would do to our nation's defence?'

'Not really.'

'You don't understand what a huge scandal would result?'

'Oh, sure. It'll be huge, all right. Lots of people are going to wonder how you stole all that money from the Pentagon.'

I'd finally learned the real story in a hotel suite at the Mandarin.

'You must realise,' Roman Navrozov had said to me, 'how frustrating it is for me to sit on the sidelines with billions of dollars ready to invest in the American economy, and yet every single one of my deals is blocked by the US government. While America sells itself off to every country in the world. Including its sworn enemies.'

'I think that's a bit of an exaggeration,' I'd said.

'Ten per cent of America is owned by the Saudis. And look what they did to your World Trade Center. The Communist Chinese own most of your Treasury bonds. Some of your biggest defence contractors are owned by foreign conglomerates. But when I try to buy an American steel company or an energy company, your government refuses. Some anonymous bureaucrats in the Treasury Department say it would harm your national security.'

'So you wanted the Mercury files for leverage? To force the US government to rubber-stamp your deals? There must be something in the Mercury files that a lot of powerful people want kept secret.'

He smiled.

'Let's hear it,' I said.

Now I leaned back in my fragile antique wooden chair. 'Turning a slush fund into a hedge fund to funnel secret payments to some of the most powerful people in America for three decades. That's genius.' I glanced pointedly at his ego wall. At all those photographs of David Schechter doing the grip-and-grin with former secretaries of defence and secretaries of state and four former vice presidents and even a few former presidents. 'But what was the point?'

'You don't have the slightest idea, do you?' He paused. 'You're probably too young to remember that there once was a time when the best and the brightest went into government work because it was the right thing to do.'

'Camelot, right?'

'Now where do the graduates of our top colleges end up? Law schools and investment banks. They go where the money is. The CEO of Merrill Lynch pockets a hundred million dollars for driving that company into the ground. The guy who almost destroyed Home Depot gets two hundred and ten million dollars just to go away. Yet a public servant who helps run the enterprise called the United States of America can't afford to send his kids to college?'

'This is good,' I said. 'I don't think I've ever heard a better rationalisation for graft.'

'Graft?' Schechter said, red-faced. 'How about calling it retention pay? The point of Mercury is to make sure that the best and the brightest aren't punished for being patriots. Yes, Nick, we diverted the money and guaranteed that our greatest public servants would never have to worry about money. So they could lead lives of public service. This sure as hell *is* about national security. It's about rewarding heroes and statesmen and patriots—instead of bankers and swindlers who'd sell out their country for two basis points.'

'Well,' I said softly, 'you make a good argument. And I'm sure you'll have the opportunity to make it before a jury of your peers.'

'I'll deny we ever spoke about it,' he said.

'Don't bother,' I said. I got up and opened the door to his office. Gordon Snyder and Diana Madigan were standing there, flanking Marshall Marcus. Behind them were six guys in FBI windcheaters. 'Marshall is cooperating.'

He shook his head. 'You son of a bitch.' He pulled open his desk drawer, and one of the FBI guys shouted, 'Freeze!'

But it wasn't a gun Schechter was after. It was a breath mint. He popped it into his mouth. Then he swallowed.

'Gentlemen,' he said with a beatific smile. 'Please enter.'

He didn't rise, though, which wasn't like him.

'David, I'm sorry,' Marcus said.

I turned and saw that Schechter was staring at me, his eyes fixed. His mouth was foaming. I could smell almonds.

I shouted, 'Anyone have a medical kit?'

A couple of the FBI agents rushed in. One of them checked his pulse, at his wrist and on his neck. Then he shook his head.

David Schechter liked to brag that he always had all the angles figured out. I guess he was right, after all.

EARLY IN THE FALL, I took Diana out for a drive. She wanted to see the New England foliage. She had no itinerary in mind. I suggested New Hampshire, where the leaves were further along.

Neither one of us spoke about the last time we'd been in New Hampshire together.

After we were on the road a while, I said, 'I have something for you. Look in the glove box.'

She gave me a puzzled look, then popped open the glove compartment and took out a small box, badly gift-wrapped.

'Aren't you a regular Martha Stewart,' she teased.

'Not my skill set,' I said. 'Obviously.'

She tore it open, gasped.

'I don't believe it,' she said, staring at the octagonal black perfume bottle. 'Where the hell did you get Nombre Noir? And a full ounce? And sealed? Are you out of your *mind*?'

'I meant to give it to you years ago,' I said.

She gave me a kiss. 'I thought I'd never have it again. Last time I checked eBay, a half ounce of Nombre Noir was selling for more than seven hundred dollars. Where'd you *get* this?'

'Remember my friend the Jordanian arms dealer? One of his clients is a sheikh in Abu Dhabi who had a stockpile in an air-conditioned storeroom. But by the time he handed it to me, you were gone.'

Diana once explained to me that Nombre Noir was one of the greatest perfumes ever created. But it was impossible to find. Apparently, the European Union decided to ban one of its main ingredients, because it causes sun sensitivity in some tiny percentage of people. The company recalled every bottle they could and then destroyed every one.

As soon as she told me it was impossible to find, of course, I made a point of tracking some down for her.

'Well, that serves me right for leaving without letting you know,' she said.

'Yeah, so there.'

'So, um, speaking of which? They've offered me a supervisory special agent job in Miami,' she said.

'Hey, that's a big deal,' I said with all the enthusiasm I could muster. 'Congratulations. Miami could be great.'

'Thanks.'

'Hard to turn down a job like that,' I said.

The awkward silence seemed to go on for ever.

'What about Gordon Snyder's job?'

Snyder's superiors weren't so happy about his planting an unapproved tracking device in my BlackBerry and then claiming that a confidential informant had tipped him off as to Mauricio Perreira's location—just about the time when I'd arrived at the dealer's apartment in Medford. He'd been demoted and transferred.

'Nah, they're looking for an organised crime specialist for that slot. So, mind if I ask you something about Roman Navrozov?'

'OK.'

'That helicopter crash in Marbella? A bit too convenient, don't you think?'

I shrugged. A deal was a deal.

'Let me guess. Putin's guys have been trying to get him for years, but he never made it easy for them. So you struck a bargain with one of your ex-KGB sources. Some sort of trade for information.'

After a long moment, I said, 'Sometimes stuff just happens.'

'Hmph.'

We both stared straight ahead for a while.

'You know,' she said, 'I probably shouldn't tell you this, but we're about to make an arrest in the Mercury case.'

'I was wondering if that would ever happen.' The weeks had turned into months, and not a single one of Marshall Marcus's 'investors' had even been brought in for questioning.

Marshall Marcus was still at liberty, since he'd cooperated fully with the FBI—and his new lawyers were still negotiating with the SEC. There were a lot of investors out there howling for his head. He'd certainly face some kind of prison time.

But apart from that, it was like nothing had happened.

'It's complicated,' she said. 'We're talking about some prominent individuals—senior government officials, elder statesmen. As the saying goes, if you shoot at a king, you must kill him.'

'But you have names and account numbers . . .'

'Suddenly there are a whole lot of very nervous people at the top of the Justice Department. They want everything completely nailed down before they'll go ahead with such a high-profile corruption sweep. They're insisting on all sorts of bank records, including from offshore banks that won't cooperate in a hundred years.'

'So who are you about to arrest?'

'General Mark Hood.'

I gave her a sideways glance. 'On what grounds?'

'Embezzlement, fraud . . . He was the one who supervised the illegal transfer of covert funds out of the Pentagon's black budget.'

I nodded. 'I figured as much.'

'You were onto him, weren't you? Before he fired you?'

'I guess so. Though I didn't know it at the time.'

I saw the exit sign and hit the turn signal.

'Where are we going?'

'Ever seen the Phillips Exeter Academy campus?'

'No. Why would I . . .' Then, realising, she said, 'You think she's ready to see you?'

'I guess we'll see.'

DIANA WAITED FOR ME in the car.

The girls' field hockey team was practising in the football stadium at the end of the campus. A few of the girls really stood out, one in particular, and when she turned, I saw it was Alexa.

She was wearing a headband, her hair tied back. Her arms were tanned and muscular, her legs long and lean.

Her blue mouth guard gave her a fierce appearance, but she looked healthy and happy.

The coach blew her whistle and shouted, 'Let's get some water,' and the girls all popped out their mouth guards. They talked loudly and squealed as they straggled towards the drinking fountain. A couple of them hugged Alexa and laughed about something.

Then Alexa turned, as if she'd sensed my presence without even looking, and caught my eye. She spoke quickly to one of her teammates and approached slowly.

'Hey, Nick.'

'You're really good, you know that?'

'I'm OK. I like it. That's the main thing.'

'You play hard. You're tough. Fearless, even.'

She gave a quick, nervous laugh. 'Gift of fear, right?'

'Right. So I wanted to say hi and make sure everything's OK.'

'Oh, um, OK, thanks. Yeah, everything's cool. It's good. I'm . . .' She

looked longingly over at her teammates. 'It's kinda not the best time. Is that
. . . that OK?'

'No problem.'

'I mean, like, you didn't drive all the way up here just to see me or anything, right? Like, I hope not.'

'Not at all. I was in the area.'

'So, um'—she gave me a little wave—'I gotta go. Thanks for coming by.
Nice to see you.'

'Yeah,' I said. 'You, too.'

I understood: just seeing me brought on all kinds of dark and troubling
emotions. I'd forever be associated with a nightmare. Her way of recovering
was to try to forget.

We all have our own ways of coping.

The coach blew her whistle again. I stood there watching for a few
minutes longer. Alexa charged down the field, dished it off to another
player, and kept on going. Suddenly everything was happening too fast to
keep track of. Just as she entered the striking circle, she somehow got the
ball back, and then I could see that the goalkeeper had been fooled and
Alexa had a clear shot, and she smiled as she flicked the ball up and it
soared towards the goal.

She'd take it from here.

joseph **finder**

Joseph Finder planned to be a spy. Or maybe a professor of Russian history. But while the career he stuck with—that of a best-selling thriller writer—is one he hadn't planned on, it does combine both of those vocations, and more.

Born in Chicago in 1958, Joseph Finder spent his early childhood living around the world, including in Kabul, Afghanistan, where his father set up centres for teaching English. Which makes it all the more interesting that English was not the young Finder's first language. While his parents were out working during the day, he spent time at home with domestic staff who spoke Farsi. 'I was speaking Farsi before I learned to speak English,' he says. The Finder family made several more moves to both international and domestic locales before finally settling back in America.

After taking a high school seminar on the literature and history of Russia, Finder was hooked. He went on to major in Russian studies at Yale, then completed a master's degree at the Harvard Russian Research Center, where he later taught. Just as he had dreamed, he was recruited to the Central Intelligence Agency—but he eventually quit in order to write. 'I wanted to be a spy for as long as I can remember,' the author says. 'The reality is that it's not as interesting as it sounds. I found the life of an intelligence analyst was very different from James Bond's. A career in a cubicle reading crop reports wasn't what I had in mind. Creating fictional characters is much more exciting.'

His first nonfiction book, published in 1983, when he was only twenty-four, was *Red Carpet: The Connection Between the Kremlin and America's Most Powerful Businessmen*, which revealed that Dr Armand Hammer, the CEO of Occidental Petroleum, had worked for Soviet intelligence in the 1920s and 30s. But *Red Carpet* could only tell part of the story, so Finder wrote his first novel—the only way he could legally tell the whole Armand Hammer saga. Published in 1991, *The Moscow Club* described events whose factual truth would only be revealed many years later. Ironically, Joseph Finder found that confidential sources were more willing to reveal classified information to him as a novelist than when he was working as a journalist and academic. Three more thrillers followed: *Extraordinary Powers*; *The Zero Hour*; and *High Crimes*, which was made into a film.

Then, in 2004, Finder turned to the ruthless drive, corruption and conspiracy of the corporate world for the plot of *Paranoia*. His next three novels, *Company Man*, *Killer Instinct* and *Power Play* followed suit and all became best sellers. His first series novel, *Vanished*, published in 2009, introduced Nick Heller, a high-powered intelligence investigator who exposes secrets that powerful people would rather keep hidden. He's a guy you don't want to mess with—and the man you call when you need a problem fixed.

For his research for *Buried Secrets*, Joseph Finder went to the extraordinary lengths of actually being buried alive. 'I discovered a few years ago that claustrophobia is one of my own fears. So when I had the idea for *Buried Secrets*—of a young woman, Alexa, held captive underground in a coffin—I felt I couldn't do that to one of my characters, much less a teenaged girl, unless I was willing to see what it was like for myself.

'It was harder than I expected to find a funeral director who was willing to let me "test drive" a casket (funeral directors don't say "coffin"). It's not exactly an everyday request, and I can only imagine what some of the people I talked to must have thought. But I found a very nice funeral director, Dennis Sweeney in Quincy, MA, who agreed to lock me into a casket.

'The first thing that surprised me was how comfortable it was. That's a real mattress in the casket; I almost thought I might be able to take a nap. But it didn't take long before I noticed how stuffy things were getting. I don't know whether a casket is actually airtight, but I quickly became aware of how little air I had.

'Then, to my horror, I realised I hadn't set up any kind of signal with Dennis to let him know when I was ready to come out. I started knocking on the inside of the lid, but at first they didn't hear me. Needless to say, I was relieved when they finally opened the lid. I probably only spent about ten minutes locked inside; it felt much longer. I sincerely hope I never have to do that again while I'm alive.'

Currently working on his third Nick Heller book, Finder does not want to say too much about it at this point, but does say that Nick is going to go international in the next book, and the story involves identity theft. 'Most people have no real idea of how easy identity theft can be,' says the author, 'or how badly it can wreck someone's life or business.'

Joseph Finder—'pronounced FINN-der,' he says. 'Rhymes with cinder and hinder'—lives in Boston, USA, with his wife and daughter and his 'needy golden retriever, Mia, a dropout from the seeing eye dog school.'

DARK MATTER

MICHELLE PAVER

January 1937.

Twenty-eight-year-old clerk Jack Miller is poor, lonely
and desperate to change his life. So when he's offered
the chance to be the wireless operator on an Arctic
expedition, he jumps at it.

Full of excitement, he and his four fellow explorers,
supported by a team of huskies, sail from Norway for
the remote, uninhabited bay where they will camp for
the next year—Gruhuken.

But as the darkness chases away the Arctic summer,
Jack begins to feel a creeping sense of unease.

Gruhuken is not uninhabited.

They are not alone . . .

Embleton Grange, Cumberland, 24th November 1947

Dear Dr Murchison,

Forgive me for this rather belated reply to your letter. You will, I am sure, understand why I found it hard to entertain your enquiry with any pleasure. To be blunt, you evoked painful memories that I have tried, for ten years, to forget. The expedition is not something I care to revisit.

You mentioned that you are working on a monograph on 'phobic disorders', by which I take it you mean abnormal fears. I regret that I can tell you nothing that would be of assistance. Moreover, I fail to see how the 'case' of Jack Miller could provide appropriate material for such a work.

You concede that you know little of Spitsbergen, or the High Arctic. This is to be expected. Few people do. Forgive me, though, if I question, therefore, how you propose to understand what it can do to a man to overwinter there, to battle the loneliness—even with the many comforts that our modern age affords—above all, to endure the endless dark. And, as circumstances dictated, it was Jack's misfortune to be there alone.

I don't think we will ever learn the truth of what happened at Gruhuken. However, I know enough to be convinced that something terrible took place. And whatever it was, Dr Murchison, it was real. It was not the result of some phobic disorder. I would add that, before entering politics, I undertook some years of study in the sciences, and thus feel entitled to be considered a reasonable judge of evidence.

I don't know how you came by the knowledge that Jack Miller kept a journal on the expedition, but you are right: he did. I saw him writing in it many times, although he never showed us its contents. No doubt the journal would, as you suggest, explain much of what happened; but it has not survived, and I cannot ask Jack himself.

Thus I fear that I am unable to help you. I wish you well with your work. However, I must ask you not to apply to me again.

Yours sincerely,
Algernon Carlisle

Jack Miller's Journal, London, 7th January, 1937

It's all over, I'm not going. I can't spend a year in the Arctic with that lot. They arrange to 'meet for a drink', then give me a grilling and make it pretty clear what they think of a grammar school boy with a London degree. The way they watched me when I entered the pub . . .

It was off the Strand, and full of well-to-do professional types, a smell of whisky and a fug of expensive cigar smoke. The four of them sat at a corner table, watching me shoulder my way through. They wore Oxford bags and tweed jackets with that elegant, yet worn, look that is acquired only at country house weekends. I was in my scuffed shoes and six-guinea Burton's suit. Then I saw the drinks on the table and thought, *Christ, I'll have to buy a round, and I've only got a florin and a threepenny bit.*

We said our hellos, and they relaxed a bit when they heard that I don't actually drop my aitches, but I was so busy wondering if I could afford the drinks that it took me a while to work out who was who.

Algie Carlisle is fat and freckled, with sandy-red hair; he's a follower rather than a leader, who relies on his pals to tell him what to think. Hugo Charteris-Black is thin and dark, with the face of an Inquisitor looking forward to putting a match to another heretic. Teddy Wintringham has bulging, penetrating eyes. And Gus Balfour is a handsome, blond hero straight out of *The Boy's Own Paper*. They are all in their mid-twenties, but keen to appear older: Carlisle and Charteris-Black with moustaches, Balfour and Wintringham with pipes clamped between their teeth.

I knew I hadn't a chance, so I thought to hell with it, give it to them straight: offer yourself like a lamb to the slaughter. So I did. Bexhill Grammar; Open Scholarship to University College London; the slump putting paid to my dreams of being a physicist; followed by seven years as an export clerk at Marshall Gifford.

They took it in silence, but I could see them thinking, *Bexhill, how frightfully middle class. And University College . . . not exactly Oxbridge, is it?* Gus Balfour asked about Marshall Gifford, and I said, 'They make high-quality stationery which they export all over the world.' I felt myself reddening. *God Almighty, Jack, you sound like Mr Pooter.*

Then Algie Carlisle, the plump one, asked if I shoot.

'Yes,' I said crisply. (Well, I can, thanks to old Mr Carwardine, DO, retired, of the Malaya Protectorate, who used to take me onto the Downs after rabbits; but that's not the kind of shooting this lot are used to.)

Carlisle asked, rather doubtfully, if I'd got my own gun.

'Service pattern rifle,' I said. 'Nothing special, but it does OK.'

That elicited a collective wince, as if they'd never heard slang before.

Teddy Wintringham mentioned wirelessing and asked if I knew my stuff. I said I should think so, after six years of night technical school, both the general and advanced courses; I'd wanted something practical that would keep me in touch with physics. *More Mr Pooter. Stop wittering, Jack.*

Wintringham smiled thinly at my discomfort. 'No idea what any of that means, old chap. But I'm told that we rather need someone like you.'

I gave him a cheery smile.

Gus Balfour—the Honourable Augustus Balfour—sensed that things were veering off track, and started telling me about the expedition.

'There are two aims,' he began, looking very earnest and more like a schoolboy hero than ever. 'One, to study High Arctic biology, geology and ice dynamics. To that end we'll be establishing a base camp on the coast, and another on the icecap itself—which is why we'll be needing a team of dogs. Secondly, and more importantly, we'll be working on a meteorological survey, transmitting observations three times a day, for a year, to the Government forecasting system. That's why we're getting help from the Admiralty and the War Office. They seem to think our data will be of use if—well, if there's another war.'

There was an uneasy pause, and I could see them hoping we wouldn't get side-tracked into discussing the situation in Spain and the neutrality of the Low Countries.

Turning my back on world politics, I said, 'And you're planning to achieve all that with only five men?'

This drew sharp glances, but Gus Balfour took it in good part. 'I know it's a tall order. But you see, we have thought about this. The plan is, Algie will be chief huntsman, dog-driver and geologist. Teddy's the photographer and medico. Hugo's the glaciologist for the icecap side of things. We'll all lend a hand with the meteorology. I'll be the biologist and, um, expedition leader. And you'll be—' He broke off with a rueful laugh. 'Sorry, we *hope* you'll be our communications man.'

He seemed genuinely keen to win me over, and I couldn't help feeling flattered. Then Hugo Charteris-Black spoiled it by demanding to know why I wanted to come.

'You do realise what the winter will be like?' he said, fixing me with his coal black stare. 'Four months of darkness. Think you can take it?'

I gritted my teeth and told him that that was why I wanted to go: for the challenge. They liked that. I expect it's the sort of thing you're taught at public school. I was glad I hadn't told them the real reason.

They'd have been mortified if I'd said I was desperate.

I couldn't put off buying my round any longer. Pints for Algie Carlisle, Teddy Wintringham and Hugo Charteris-Black (at sevenpence a go), a half for me (at another threepence halfpenny). I was thinking I wasn't going to manage it when Gus Balfour said, 'Nothing for me.' He made quite a convincing job of it, but I could tell that he was trying to help me out.

After that, things went OK for a while. We worked our way through our drinks, and then Gus Balfour glanced at the others and nodded, and said to me, 'Well, now, Miller. Would you care to join our expedition?'

I'm afraid I got a bit choked up. 'Um, yes,' I said. 'Yes, I should think I would.'

The others looked merely relieved, but Gus Balfour seemed genuinely delighted. He kept clapping me on the back and saying, 'Good show, good show!' I don't think he was putting it on.

We fixed our next meeting and then I said my goodbyes and headed for the door. At the last moment, I glanced over my shoulder—and caught Teddy Wintringham's grimace and Algie Carlisle's fatalistic shrug, as if to say: *Not exactly a sahib, but I suppose he'll have to do*.

Stupid to be so angry, but I wanted to march back and smash their smug faces into their overpriced drinks. Do you know what it's like to be poor? Hiding your cuffs, inking in the holes in your socks? Knowing that you can't afford more than one bath a week? Do you think I like it?

I knew then it was hopeless. I couldn't be part of their expedition. If I can't put up with them for a couple of hours, how could I stand a whole year? I'd end up killing someone.

Later

JACK, WHAT THE HELL are you doing? What the hell are you *doing*?

As I headed home, the fog on the Embankment was terrible. Buses and taxicabs creeping past, muffled cries of paper boys. Street lamps just murky yellow pools, illuminating nothing. God, I hate fog.

There was a crowd on the pavement, so I stopped. They were watching a body being pulled from the river. Someone said it must be another poor devil who couldn't find work. Leaning over the parapet, I saw three men on a barge hauling a bundle of sodden clothes onto the deck. I made out a wet, round head, and a forearm that one of the gaffs had ripped open.

I wasn't horrified: I've seen a dead body before. I was curious. As I stared at the black water, I wondered how many others had died in it, and why there weren't more ghosts?

You'd have thought that that brush with mortality would have put things in perspective, but it didn't. I was still seething when I reached the tube station. In fact, I was so angry that I overshot my stop and had to get out at Morden and backtrack to Tooting.

The fog was thicker in Tooting. It always is. As I groped my way up my road, I felt like the last one left alive. The stairs to the third floor smelt of boiled cabbage and Jeyes Fluid. It was so cold I could see my breath.

My room wasn't any better, but my anger kept me warm. I grabbed my journal and spewed it all out. *To hell with them, I'm not going*.

That was a while ago.

My room is freezing. The gas jet casts a watery glimmer that shudders whenever a tram thunders past. I've got no coal, two cigarettes, and twopence to last till payday. I'm so hungry my stomach's given up rumbling because there's no point. I'm sitting on my bed with my overcoat on. It smells of fog. And of the journey I've taken twice a day, six days a week, for seven years, with all the other grey people. And of Marshall Gifford, where they call me 'College' because I've got a degree, and where for three pounds a week I track shipments of paper to places I'll never see.

I'm twenty-eight years old and I hate my life. I never have the time or the energy to work out how to change it. On Sundays I trail around a museum to keep warm, or lose myself in a library book, or fiddle with the wireless. But Monday looms. And always I've got this panicky feeling inside, because I know I'm getting nowhere; just keeping myself alive.

Tacked above the mantelpiece is a picture called 'A Polar Scene' that I cut out from the *Illustrated London News*. A vast, snowy land and a black sea dotted with icebergs; a tent, a sledge and some husky dogs; two men in Shackleton gear standing over the carcass of a polar bear.

Nine years ago I cut the picture out and tacked it above the mantelpiece. I was in my second year at University College, and I still had dreams. I was going to be a scientist, and go on expeditions, and discover the origins of the universe—or the secrets of the atom. I wasn't quite sure which.

That's when it hit me, just now, staring at 'A Polar Scene'. I thought of the body in the river and I said to myself, *Jack, this is the only chance you'll ever get. If you turn it down, what's the point of going on? Another year at Marshall Gifford and they'll be fishing* you *out of the Thames.*

Now it's five in the morning and the milk floats are rattling past under my window. I've been up all night and I feel amazing. Cold, hungry, light-headed. But amazing.

I keep seeing old man Gifford's face. 'But Miller, this is madness! In a few years you could be export supervisor!'

He's right, it is mad. Chuck in a secure job at a time like this? A safe job, too. If there *is* another war, I'd be excused combat. But I can't think about that now. By the time I get back, there probably *will* be another war, so I can go off and fight. Or if there isn't, I'll go to Spain and fight.

It just doesn't seem *real*. But for this one year, I'm going to get away from my life. I'm going to see the midnight sun, and polar bears, and seals sliding off icebergs into green water. I'm going to the Arctic.

It's six months till we sail for Norway. I've spent the whole night planning, working out how soon I can hand in my notice and still survive till July. Going through the Army & Navy Stores pricelist, marking up kit. I've drafted a fitness plan and a reading list, because it occurs to me that I don't actually know very much about Spitsbergen. Only that it's a clutch of islands halfway between Norway and the Pole, and mostly covered in ice.

When I started this journal, I was convinced I wouldn't be going on the expedition. Now I'm writing because I need to record the exact moment when I decided to do this. The body in the river. If it hadn't been for that poor bastard, I wouldn't be going.

So thank you, nameless corpse, and I hope you're at peace now, wherever you are.

I am going to the Arctic.

THAT PICTURE above the mantelpiece—I've just noticed. There's a seal in the foreground. All these years and I thought it was a wave, but actually it's a seal. I can make out its round, wet head emerging from the water. Looking at me. I think I'll take that as a good omen.

The Grand Hotel, Tromsø, north Norway, 24th July

I didn't want to write anything more until we reached Norway, for fear of tempting Fate. I was convinced that something would happen to scupper the expedition. It nearly did.

Two days before we were due to set off, Teddy Wintringham's father died. He left a manor in Sussex, a tangle of trusts and a clutch of dependants. The heir was 'most frightfully cut up' and thought it simply wouldn't do for him to be gone a year, so he had to scratch.

The others actually talked about cancelling. Would it be 'responsible' to go without a medico?

I had a job keeping my temper. To hell with 'responsible': we're young, fit men! Besides, if anyone gets sick, there's a doctor at Longyearbyen— and that's only, what, two days away from camp.

It turns out that Hugo and Gus agreed with me, because when we took a vote, only tub-of-lard Algie voted against. And since he's the last person to stick his neck out, he backed down as soon as he realised he was outnumbered.

Afterwards, I went back to my room and got out my map of Spitsbergen. The map calls it 'Svalbard' because that's its new name, but everyone uses the old one, which is also the name of the biggest island. That's where we're going. I've marked our base camp in red. There, in the far north-east corner, on the tip of that promontory. Gruhuken. I think '*huken*' means hook, or headland. Not sure about '*Gru*'. There's nothing there. Just a name on the map. I love that. And I love the fact that none of the three previous expeditions to the area ever camped there. I want it to be ours.

Everyone was nervous on the train to Newcastle. Lots of hearty jokes from the 'varsity that I couldn't follow. Gus tried to explain them, but it only made me feel more of an outsider. In the end he gave up, and I went back to staring out of the window.

We had an awful crossing in the mail packet to Bergen and up the Norwegian coast, and Algie and Hugo were seasick. Thank God I've got a cast-iron stomach. But every night as I rolled in my berth, I dreamed I was back at Marshall Gifford. Every morning I woke up soaked in sweat, and had to tell myself it wasn't true.

And now here we are at Tromsø, where Amundsen took off in his flying boat nine years ago and was never seen again. Tromsø: 300 miles north of the Arctic Circle. My first encounter with the midnight sun.

Only there isn't any. A gentle, penetrating mizzle hasn't let up in days. Tromsø is a nice little fishing town: wooden houses painted red, yellow and blue, like a child's building blocks, and I'm told that it's backed by beautiful snowy mountains. I wouldn't know: I've never seen them. But I don't care. I love everything about this place, because it isn't London. Because I'm free. I love the clamour of the gulls and the sea slapping at the harbour walls. I love the salty air and the smell of tar. Above all, I love this soft, watery, never-ending light. There's no dawn and no dusk. Time has no meaning. We've left the real world, and entered a land of dreams.

Of course, the gulls mew day and night, as they can't tell the difference, but I don't even mind that. I'm writing this with the curtains open on the strange, pearly 'night' that is no night. I can't sleep. The expedition is really happening. Everything we do only makes it more real.

I was right about Gus being a *Boy's Own* hero. He doesn't have that square jaw or those clear blue eyes for nothing; he takes being expedition leader seriously. I sense that the expedition matters almost as much to him as it does to me.

Months ago, he engaged the British vice consul here as our agent. His name is Armstrong and he has chartered a ship to take us to Gruhuken. He's bought coal, boats and building materials for our cabin and had them dropped on the coast, to be picked up later. He's bought a sledge and a team of dogs, and got us permission from the Norwegian Government to over-winter. He's even engaged rooms for us at the Grand Hotel—which *is* actually quite grand.

He's been urging us to have a word with our skipper, Mr Eriksson, who's got some sort of problem with Gruhuken. Apparently he doesn't think it's 'right' for a camp. I'm glad to say that none of us is inclined to discuss the matter with Mr Eriksson, thank you very much, and Gus has quietly made Armstrong aware of that. We chose Gruhuken after weeks of poring over surveys from previous expeditions. It's not for some Norwegian sealer to mess up our plans. As long as he gets us there by August, so that we can set up a second camp on the icecap before the winter, Eriksson can consider his job done.

26th July

The amount of money we're spending, it's frightening!

In London, Hugo was in charge of drumming up finance, and I must say he's done a good job. He has an almost lawyerly ability to persuade, and has cadged discounts from firms hoping for endorsements, and talked the War Office into donating my wireless equipment for free. Everything else is coming out of the Expedition Fund, which is made up of grants from the University Exploration Club, the Royal Geographical Society and 'individual subscribers' (I suspect aunts). Total: £3,000. Gus says we have to 'be careful', but 'being careful' doesn't mean the same to him as it does to me.

In Newcastle we bought what we wouldn't be able to get in Norway: egg powder, Fry's eating chocolate, spirits, tobacco and cigarettes. That's when I learned that the rich have different priorities: third-class passages to Norway, but a crate of Oxford marmalade and two bottles of champagne for Christmas.

In Tromsø, we've been like children let loose in a sweetshop. We've bought mountains of jam, tea, coffee, flour, yeast, sugar and cocoa, tinned fruits, dried vegetables, butter (not margarine—I don't think the others have ever tasted it), and crates of something called 'pemmican', which is a kind of preserved meat: one grade for us, another for the dogs.

And our kit! Long silk underclothing (silk!), woollen stockings, mittens, mufflers and sweaters, kapok waistcoats, corduroy and waterproof Shackleton trousers, 'anoraks' (a kind of wind jacket with the hood attached), rubber boots, horsehide gauntlets and balaclava helmets. For the coldest weather, we've bought leather boots made by the Lapps, well tarred, and turned up at the toe. You buy them much too big, so you can stuff them with straw.

Hugo got the outfitter to take a photo of us in our winter gear. We look like real explorers. Algie's as round as an Eskimo; Hugo and I are both thin and dark, as if we've spent months on hard rations; and Gus could be Scandinavian: maybe Amundsen's younger brother.

But it was buying the rest of our equipment that really brought home to me what we'll be taking on. Tents, sleeping bags, ammunition, reindeer hides (as groundsheets). Above all, a formidable pile of paraffin lamps, headlamps and electric torches. It's hard to believe now, in this endless daylight, but there'll come a time when it's always dark.

Thinking of that gives me a queer flutter in my stomach. But, in a way, I can't wait. I want to see if I can take it.

Not that we'll be roughing it at Gruhuken. We've got a crate of books and a gramophone player, and even a set of Royal Doulton china, donated by Algie's mama.

In the morning, we're joining our ship, the *Isbjørn*, and its skipper, Mr Eriksson. He's a hardened sealer and trapper who's overwintered on Spitsbergen a dozen times. I've never met a trapper, but I've read about them and I know my Jack London. They're the real thing. Battling the elements, shooting seals and polar bears. In Norway, people look up to them as 'true hunters'. All of which I find a bit daunting.

The books say the golden days of trapping were when Spitsbergen was a no-man's-land. I still can't get over the idea that, until a few years ago, a wilderness not far from Europe belonged to no one; that a man could literally stake his claim wherever he liked, without seeking permission from a living soul. It sounds wonderful. But it came to an end in 1925, when the islands became part of Norway.

The stories they tell of that time! Marauding bears; lethal accidents on the ice; men going mad from the dark and the loneliness, murdering each other, shooting themselves. There's even a name for it. They call it *rar*. Armstrong shrugs it off as a 'strangeness' which comes over some people when they winter in the Arctic. He says it's simply a matter of a few odd habits, like hoarding matches or obsessively checking stores. But I know from the books that it's worse than that.

And they talk of something called *ishavet kaller*, which seems to be an extreme form of *rar*. It means 'the Arctic calls'. That's when a trapper walks off a cliff for no reason.

Rar. Ishavet kaller. Cabin fever. Nerve strain. I can understand why it used to happen in the old days, when men were utterly cut off, but it's different now. We'll have a gramophone and the wireless. And maybe, after all, that's for the best. I mean, compared to those trappers, we're amateurs. Algie's the only one who's ever been to the Arctic, and that was only six weeks' shooting in Greenland. No sense biting off more than we can chew.

The Isbjørn, somewhere in the Norwegian Sea, 27th July

I'm writing this in my cabin. *My cabin*. OK, it stinks of seal blubber and it's only slightly bigger than a coffin. But still. The *Isbjørn's* beautiful, a jaunty little sailing ship—just how I imagine the one in *Moby Dick*, only with a fifty-horse-power diesel engine that belches greasy black smoke. The ever-accurate Hugo tells me she's a ninety-foot sealing sloop (whatever that means), and that the crow's-nest, three-quarters of the way up her mast, is the mark of a true sealer. Inside, she's mostly hold, with four tiny cabins off the small saloon (I'm in one of these). I don't know where the crew sleeps, or even how many there are, as I can't tell them apart.

They're all splendid Nordic types with formidable beards and amazingly clean overalls.

Mysteriously, they don't stink of seal blubber, but everything else does. The rancid, oily smell has soaked into the woodwork. You can even taste it in the drinking water. Hugo and Algie are looking green, and I'm now feeling a bit queasy myself.

Somehow, we got everything on board, and the crew didn't drop any of my wireless crates. They're safe in the hold, thank God, not on deck with the dogs.

Those bloody dogs. I know we need them for the camp on the icecap, but I wish we didn't. According to Algie (our self-styled huntsman and dog-driver), Eskimo huskies are the toughest—best able to stand the cold—which is why we had them brought all the way from Greenland: eight of the brutes, filthy and over-excited after nine weeks cooped up in the holds of various ships.

To the upper classes, dogs are a religion, so Gus, Hugo and Algie already adore ours. They tell me they're 'really very friendly' and gave their new masters a rapturous welcome. I wouldn't know: I wasn't there. I don't like dogs and they don't like me.

Gus says this lot will win me over in the end, but I wouldn't bet on it. They look like a pack of wolves: shaggy, with teeth that can crunch through saucepans, and alarming ice blue eyes. Cunning, too. While the crew was getting them aboard, one clawed open the bolt on its crate and escaped. After an epic chase round the wharf, it fell in the harbour, where it swam in circles, yowling, until it was rescued. Algie says the only thing that scares a husky is the sea. Well, then, it shouldn't have fallen in, should it?

Later

WE HADN'T SEEN much of the skipper till he joined us for dinner, so to begin with, we were a little intimidated. He looks like a Viking: sharp grey eyes and a grizzled beard. He's got a handshake like a vice, and he calls me 'Professor'. In fact, he calls us all 'Professor'. I don't know if he's making fun of us or not.

We four sat like schoolboys dining with the headmaster. The saloon's cramped, warm and smelly, with a constant throb of engines, but extremely clean. Dinner was a tasty fish stew, with coffee the way Norwegians like it: viciously strong, with nothing so frivolous as milk or sugar.

Skipper Eriksson is a man's man, all right. Probably a hard drinker when you get to know him. But I like him. I respect him, too. He was born poor. Not middle-class poor, like me, but real, grinding, rural poor. He's been a sealer since he was eleven, and has worked his way up to being skipper and part-owner of the *Isbjørn*. To his credit, he treats us with neither envy nor scorn, but simply as rich young 'yentlemen' whose mystifying pleasure it is to spend a year in the wild, studying the weather.

The subject of Gruhuken only came up once, and it was Gus, as expedition leader, who introduced it. 'So, Mr Eriksson,' he said towards the end of the meal, 'we're delighted that your splendid ship is to be our home all the way to Gruhuken.' His tone was polite but firm, and his message was clear. We mean to go to Gruhuken, and we don't want any objections.

The Norwegian's smile faltered, but he didn't take up the challenge. Dropping his gaze, he rubbed his thumb across his lip. 'She is a good ship, *ja*. I hope you will like her.'

I exchanged glances with the others, and Gus gave a satisfied nod. But, later, while the others were talking, I caught Mr Eriksson watching them. His face was grave. Then his eyes shifted to me. I smiled. But he didn't smile back.

Whatever his reservations about Gruhuken, I'm glad he's keeping them to himself, because I don't want to hear them. I don't want anything to get in the way of our plans.

Over cigars (Hugo's diplomatic way of breaking the ice), I'd been planning to ask the skipper what it's like to overwinter in the wilderness, but somehow I couldn't. I had the same feeling I used to get when I was a boy, longing to ask Father about the Great War. I couldn't do it then and I couldn't now, maybe because I sensed that it wouldn't do any good; that he wouldn't tell me what I want to know.

Luckily, fat Algie wasn't nearly so scrupulous. Like a big russet labrador, he simply blundered straight in and asked. And, to my surprise, Mr Eriksson readily opened up. Or rather, he seemed to. But I noted that his stories were always about others, never himself.

The best one was about a trapper who was overwintering with a companion in a tiny hut on the coast of North-East Land. Halfway through what

Mr Eriksson calls 'the dark time', the other man fell sick and died. The trapper couldn't bury him, as the ground was frozen, and he couldn't build a cairn over the body for fear of attracting bears. So, instead, he simply kept it with him in the hut. Two months with a corpse. Then the spring came, and he was rescued by a passing ship.

When Mr Eriksson finished, there was a respectful silence. 'And when they found him,' I said at last, 'was he—the survivor—was he all right?'

'*Ja*, for sure.' Mr Eriksson's tone was brisk.

'But two months . . . How did he manage?'

'Singing songs. Reading his Bible.' His gaze skewered mine, and he chuckled. 'Not everyone go crazy, Professor.'

I flushed. 'I only meant it must have been hard.'

'Hard? *Ja*.' He said it in the Scandinavian way, on an in-breath, which makes it sound oddly like a gasp.

'But what I want to know,' said Hugo, leaning forward and fixing the Norwegian with his dark, inquisitorial gaze, 'is *why*? Why put yourself through it when the risks are so enormous, and the rewards so uncertain?'

Eriksson shrugged. 'Some men are poor. Some have troubles. Some want respect.'

'What about you?' I said. 'Why did you do it?'

His brow furrowed. 'Ach, I don't know. In the open country a man can breathe with both lungs.'

Gus nodded. 'And I suppose it must have been even better when it didn't belong to anyone.'

'No-man's-land,' I said. I asked Mr Eriksson if he missed that time.

That's when it happened. The Norwegian paused with his mug halfway to his lips and looked at me. His features went stiff. His small eyes drained of expression. It was unnerving. We all noticed it.

I wondered if the skipper was angry. I had the distinct impression that he suspected me of some hidden meaning. 'I only meant the freedom of it,' I said quickly. 'That is, to be able to go where you please. Surely that must have been wonderful?'

Mr Eriksson dropped his gaze. He shook his head. 'No.'

An awkward silence. Then Hugo turned the conversation, and shortly afterwards, Mr Eriksson set down his mug and went back to the bridge.

I've described this in detail because I'm trying to make sense of it. I like the skipper. The last thing I want is to offend him. But for the life of me, I can't see how I have. Did I touch some raw nerve? Or is it simply that he thinks we're fools, crazy young 'yentlemen' out of our depth? Maybe that's why he told the story about the trapper. As a warning.

But we're not ill-prepared, and we're not out of our depth. And no matter how many stories he tells, I'm not afraid of what's in store for us at Gruhuken. I'm looking forward to it.

The Barents Sea, 29th July

Now I know I'm really in the Arctic. Until this morning, it's been two days of rain, followed by fog. We kept bundling up and going on deck, but there was nothing to see except grey sky melting into grey sea. We haven't seen much of Mr Eriksson, either. Since dinner that first night, he's had most of his meals in his cabin. The sea has been calm, with only a gentle swell, and Hugo and Algie have found their sea legs. We've got used to the smell of blubber, and no one's been sick; but we've all been a bit subdued.

And now—the ice.

According to Mr Eriksson, it's a belt of drift ice a few miles wide, and nothing to worry about; the *Isbjørn* can take it in her stride. But that doesn't begin to convey what it's like. It's eerie, peering through the fog at the sea turned white. Huge, jagged floes like pieces of an enormous jigsaw, dotted with pools of meltwater, intensely blue. I hadn't expected it to be so beautiful. It brought a lump to my throat.

Mr Eriksson cut the engines, and I leaned over the side and gazed down at the rocking, jostling shards. Then I became aware of an odd, rapid popping sound; a brittle crackling, very low, but continuous.

The others came to see what I was looking at, and I asked, could they hear it? Hugo said, 'Oh, that's just air bubbles in the ice, being popped by the slapping of the waves.'

'Sounds as if it's talking to itself,' I said.

Gus threw me a curious glance. 'I was thinking the same thing.'

The others drifted away, but Gus and I stayed.

Gus leaned over the edge, his fair hair lifting in the breeze. 'Our first ice,' he said fondly.

I nodded. 'It's OK, isn't it?'

'Oh, yes. It's grand.'

'Sorry. That's what I meant.'

He sighed. 'You know, Jack, sometimes you can be a tad oversensitive.'

'Oh, really?'

'Yes, really. I don't care what words you use.'

'You might feel differently if you were me.'

'Perhaps. But Jack.' He turned to me, and his blue eyes were troubled. 'Do please believe me. I really don't care what words you use, I care what you mean. And doesn't all this'—a sweep of his arm—'make all that irrelevant?'

'It's a bit more complicated than that,' I said. 'Class matters because money matters.'

'I know, but—'

'No, you don't. You've got a twenty-five-bedroom house in the West Country and three cars. How can you know? How can you know what it's like to come down in the world, to miss your chance?'

'But you haven't missed your chance.'

'Yes, I have.' Suddenly I was angry. 'My family were all right once. Not like yours, but all right. My father was a Classics teacher. He was gassed in the War and couldn't work, so we had to move, and I had to go to a school where they say "OK" instead of "grand". Then he got TB and died, and the Army wouldn't give Mother a pension because he hadn't got TB from being gassed. Then the slump came and I had to give up physics and be a sodding clerk . . .' I broke off.

'I didn't know,' said Gus.

'Well, you do now. So don't brush it aside as if it doesn't matter.'

After that, we didn't talk. I felt embarrassed—and furious with myself for blurting things out. What's got into me?

Later

ALL DAY WE'VE BEEN making our way through the ice. I love it. The purity. The danger. A man in the crow's-nest calls directions, and Mr Eriksson steers the *Isbjørn* slowly through.

At one point, he cut the engine, and some of the crew lowered a boat and went fishing. Others let down a ladder and climbed onto a floe the size of a football pitch. While they were filling a barrel with meltwater, the dogs jumped down onto the floe and raced about. We quickly followed.

I couldn't believe it. A few days ago I was in London. Then I was standing on an ice floe in the Barents Sea.

While the others were playing with the dogs, I wandered off to the edge. According to the ship's thermometer, it's only a couple of degrees below freezing, but it was colder on the ice. My breath rasped in my throat. I felt the skin of my face tighten. And, for the first time in my life, I was aware of cold as a menace. The ice was solid beneath my boots, *And yet*, I thought, *a few inches below me, there's water so cold that if I fell in, I'd be dead within minutes. The only thing that's keeping me away from it is . . . more water*.

Moving closer to the edge, I peered down. The water was glassy green, extraordinarily clear. I experienced the feeling I sometimes get when I'm on a bridge or a railway platform. Rationally, you know that you've no intention of stepping off—but you're aware that you could, and that the only thing stopping you is your will.

As I write this, it's nearly midnight, and we're still not through the ice. I can feel each turn the ship makes. The shudder of impact, the change in the engine as we reach a clear patch, the subdued roar as we push the smaller floes aside. I think of those great shards rocking, talking to themselves.

I suppose what Gus was trying to say is that here in the Arctic, class doesn't matter. I think he's wrong about that: class always matters. But maybe up here it doesn't matter so much.

Spitsbergen, 31st July

By morning we were clear of the ice, and Mr Eriksson said we'd already passed the Sørkapp, the southern most tip of Spitsbergen. But the fog wouldn't let us see. All day we huddled on deck, waiting for a glimpse. It got colder. We kept running down to our cabins to pull on more clothes. And still nothing.

Some time after midnight, our patience was finally rewarded. The fog thinned, and although the sky remained overcast, the midnight sun behind the clouds cast a subdued grey radiance on an alien wilderness.

The Dutch whalers of the sixteenth century gave it the right name—Spitsbergen: the pointed mountains. I saw jagged peaks streaked with snow, looming over the mouth of a fjord where the black water was mirror-smooth, and dotted with icebergs. Further in, a vast, tormented glacier spilled into the sea. All of it so incredibly still.

Hugo shook his head in disbelief. Even Algie was impressed.

Gus said quietly, 'Do you realise, it's nearly one in the morning?'

I tried to speak but I couldn't. It was utterly unlike anything I'd ever seen. It was—intimidating. No, that's not the right word. It made me feel irrelevant. It made humanity irrelevant. I wonder if Gruhuken will be like this?

Hugo, the keen glaciologist, asked Mr Eriksson to head into the fjord to get nearer the glacier, and we craned our necks at fissured walls of ice and caverns of mysterious blue. From deep within came weird creaks and groans, as if a giant were hammering to get out. Now I know why people used to believe that Spitsbergen was haunted.

As we headed north up the coast, I realised that despite all my reading, I'd made the classic mistake of imagining the Arctic as an empty waste. Maybe a few seals and sea birds, but nothing like this. I never expected so much life. Great flocks of gulls perching on icebergs, rising in flurries, diving after fish. An Arctic fox trotting over a green plain with a puffin flapping in its jaws. Reindeer raising antlered heads to watch us pass. Walruses rocking on the waves; one surfaced right beneath me with an explosive, spraying *huff!*, and regarded me with a phlegmatic brown eye.

We passed a cliff thronged with thousands of sea birds. Gulls screamed, and the rock faces echoed with the strange, rattling groans of black birds with stubby wings, which Gus said were guillemots. He said that what I'd taken for gulls were kittiwakes, and that the Vikings believed that their cries were the wails of lost souls.

Many of the beaches are littered with driftwood, borne from Siberia by the Atlantic current, and weathered to silver. And bones: huge, arching whale ribs many decades old. According to Mr Eriksson, we're so far north that 'dead things' last for years.

There are other, less picturesque remains. Abandoned mines, and the broken-down cabins of prospectors long gone. In an inlet I saw a post rising from a cairn of rocks, with a plank nailed across the top. One of the seamen told me it was a claim sign.

I don't like these human relics. I don't want to be reminded that Spitsbergen has been exploited for hundreds of years, by whalers, miners, trappers, even tourists. Thank God there's only a handful of tiny settlements, and we're not going near any of them.

Just before dinner, Mr Eriksson spotted something on an island, and brought the ship in closer.

At first I couldn't see anything except a pebbly beach strewn with driftwood. Then I made out the blotchy, pinkish-brown carcass of a walrus, lying on its back. Something had gnawed a hole in its belly and eaten it from the inside.

Then a polar bear rose from behind a boulder and stretched its long neck to catch our scent. I couldn't see its eyes, but I sensed them. Until that moment, I'd never felt like prey. Never been so intensely watched by a creature that would kill me if it got the chance. I stared at it, and I felt death staring back.

Kill or be killed. That's what it comes down to. And yet somehow, I don't find that appalling. There's truth in it. A kind of stark beauty. I think that's what the Arctic means to me. I think that up here, I'll be able to 'breathe with both lungs', as Mr Eriksson says: to see clearly for the first time in years. Right through to the heart of things.

Advent Fjord, near Longyearbyen, 1st August

Disaster. Hugo tripped on a coil of rope and broke his leg.

Everyone went into emergency mode, very calm and stiff-upper-lip. 'Buck up, old chap, we'll soon set you to rights.' The consequences were too huge to be voiced out loud.

The first mate splinted the leg, and we carried Hugo down to his cabin. Mr Eriksson, face inscrutable, turned the ship about, and set course for Longyearbyen.

Gus, Algie and I squeezed into Hugo's cabin and tried to convince him that he hadn't let us down and endangered the whole expedition.

'Stupid, stupid, bugger, bugger!' He pounded his mattress with his fists.

His dark hair was plastered to his temples, his cheeks flushed after a dose of cocaine from the medicine chest.

'It's not your fault,' Gus said tonelessly.

''Course it isn't!' Algie robustly agreed, then gave an uneasy laugh. 'We seem to be jinxed, don't we? First Teddy, now Hugo.'

For a moment, no one spoke. Then Hugo said, 'Right. Here's what we do. You'll drop me off at Longyearbyen, where I'll get myself patched up, and find a berth on the next boat home. You chaps will carry on without me. Yes?'

Nobody wanted to be the first to agree.

Perplexed, Algie ran a hand through his carroty hair. 'But—you're our glacier fellow. Who'll man the camp on the icecap?'

'We'll have to scrap it, of course,' snapped Gus.

'What?' cried Algie. 'But the dogs . . .'

'Are now completely unnecessary,' said Hugo. 'God, you can be dim.'

'I don't understand,' said Algie. 'What do we do about the dogs?'

'It seems to me,' I said, 'that we'd be better off without them. I asked Mr Eriksson if we could sell them in Longyearbyen, but he said the mine manager's already got a team. He said . . .' I hesitated. 'He thinks we should put them down.'

A chorus of outrage. How could I even contemplate such a thing? The dogs would be useful in all sorts of ways: taking Algie about on his geological survey, warning us of bears. Suggestion emphatically over-ruled.

WE LEFT HUGO an hour ago in the *sykehus*—the hospital at Longyearbyen. Tomorrow, he'll board a tourist yacht and head back to Tromsø. I'll miss him: I think we could have been friends. I wish it was fat Algie who'd broken his leg.

Hugo didn't want us to stay, which was a relief, because in Longyearbyen I felt as out of place as the tourists from that yacht. God, what a dump. A ramshackle settlement of some 500 souls, it's all that's left of the great Arctic 'coal rush'. A few decades ago, a clutch of prospectors reported huge deposits, and greed took over. Nations scrambling to stake claims, companies sprouting like mushrooms, raising millions on expectation alone. Most have gone bankrupt, or were bought for a song by the Norwegians, who now run what remains. I saw ugly miners' barracks cowering at the foot of stark grey mountains, a cable railway strung along their flanks like a grimy necklace, its buckets dumping coal on the jetty in clouds of black dust.

On our way back to the ship, we passed a group of miners heading for 'town'. One turned his head and stared at me. His face was black with soot, his eyes angry and inflamed. He looked scarcely human. Capable of anything. I felt obscurely menaced. And ashamed. It feels wrong that there should be such places on Spitsbergen. I'm glad Gruhuken is far away from all this. I don't want it sullied.

Near Cape Mitra, north-west Spitsbergen, 2nd August

This morning, Algie and I were on deck when Gus called us down to the saloon. We knew at once that something was wrong. Eriksson sat in stony silence, his hands spread flat on the table.

Gus's face was set, his blue eyes glassy with anger. 'Ah, gentlemen.' He greeted us in clipped tones. 'It seems that Mr Eriksson here refuses to take us to Gruhuken.'

We stared at the skipper. He wouldn't meet our eyes.

'He says,' Gus went on, 'that he'll take us as far as Raudfjorden.'

'But that's forty miles short!' cried Algie.

'And he says,' continued Gus, 'that these were always his orders. That he's never heard any mention of Gruhuken.'

The blatancy of the Norwegian's lie astonished me. And he didn't back down. In fact, he put up quite a fight. He insisted that he'd been chartered to take us to Raudfjorden and no further. We said this was nonsense—our goal had always been Gruhuken. He said there was good camping on Raudfjorden. We pointed out that Raudfjorden has no icecap, and we'd hardly have gone to the trouble of bringing a sledge and eight dogs if we didn't need them. He said he knew nothing of that. His ship had been chartered for Raudfjorden, and to Raudfjorden she would go.

We reached stalemate. Algie muttered something irrelevant about legal action. Gus seethed. The Norwegian crossed his arms and glowered. Behind his granite demeanour, I sensed unhappiness. He hated reneging on his charter. So why was he doing it?

Gus placed both palms on the table and leaned towards the skipper. His usual genial manner was gone. In its place I saw the assurance which comes from generations of command. 'Now look here, Eriksson,' he said. 'You will carry out the job for which you were hired. You will take us to Gruhuken—and there's an end of it!'

Poor Gus. Maybe that works on his father's estate, but not with a man like Eriksson. The Norwegian sat like a boulder, immovable.

I decided it was my turn. 'Mr Eriksson,' I said. 'Do you remember our first night on board? I asked you why you chose to overwinter on Spitsbergen, and you said it's because there a man can breathe with both lungs. I took that to mean that you felt free. Free to make your own decisions. Was I right?'

He didn't reply. But I had his attention.

'Don't you see it's the same for us?' I went on. 'We thought long and hard about where to site our camp, and we chose Gruhuken. We chose it. We made a decision.'

'You don't know what you are doing,' he growled.

'Now look here,' cried Gus.

Without taking my eyes from Eriksson's, I signed Gus to silence. 'What do you mean by that? Come now, you're an honourable man. And yet you've gone back on your word. Why? Why don't you want to take us to Gruhuken? What's wrong with it?'

His face darkened. He glared at me. Then he leapt to his feet and struck the table with both fists. '*Helvedes fand!* As you wish! To Gruhuken we go!'

Off Gruhuken, 3rd August

We had a clear run up the coast and round the north-west cape, although the weather remained overcast and foggy. As we headed east, our anticipation grew. Only a few miles left to go. Gus and Algie leaned over the side, counting off landmarks on the map. I went to the wheelhouse to make one last attempt with the skipper.

'Mr Eriksson,' I began, with a poor attempt at geniality.

'Professor,' he replied, without taking his eyes from the sea.

'I don't wish to offend you,' I said carefully. 'And I'm not suggesting that you haven't been straight with us. But I'd count it a favour if you'd tell me, man to man, why you don't want to take us to Gruhuken.'

Still watching the waves, the Norwegian adjusted course. For a moment, his glance flicked sideways to me. Something in his expression told me he was wondering if I could be trusted.

'Please,' I said. 'All I want is the truth.'

'Why?'

I was startled. 'Well . . . isn't it obvious? We'll be there a year. If there's some problem, we need to know about it.'

'It's not always good to know,' he said quietly.

'I'm—not sure I agree with you. I think it's always best to know the truth.'

He gave me another odd look. 'Some places make bad luck.'

'What?' I was taken aback. 'What do you mean?'

'Gruhuken. It's . . . bad luck. Bad things happen there.'

'But what? Tricky currents in the bay? Bad weather off the icecap?'

He chewed his moustache. 'There are worse things.'

The way he said that. As if he couldn't bear to think of it.

For a moment I was shaken. Then I rallied and said, 'But Mr Eriksson, surely you don't believe that a place—a mere pile of rocks—can make bad things happen?'

'I didn't say that.'

'Then what?'

Another silence.

Exasperated, I blew out a long breath. That was my mistake. His face closed and I knew that I'd lost him.

Shouts from the deck. Gus and Algie were beaming and waving at me. 'Look, Jack, look!'

While I'd been talking to the skipper, the weather had undergone one of those sudden Arctic reversals. The clouds had lifted. The fog had cleared.

That first sight of it was like a blow to the heart. The desolation. The beauty. A fierce sun blazed in a sky of astonishing blue. Dazzling snow-capped mountains enclosed a wide bay dotted with icebergs. The water was as still as glass, mirroring the peaks. At the eastern end of the bay, tall cliffs were thronged with sea birds, their clamour muted by distance. At the western end, shining pavements of pewter rock sloped down to the sea, a stream glinted, and a tiny, ruined hut huddled among boulders. The charcoal beach was littered with silver driftwood and the giant ribs of whales. Behind it, greenish-grey slopes rose towards the harsh, white glitter of the icecap.

Despite the cries of gulls, there was a stillness about it, a great silence. And God, the light! The air was so clear I felt I could reach out and touch those peaks, snap off a chunk of that icecap. Such purity. It was like heaven. For a moment, I couldn't speak. I turned to Mr Eriksson. 'Is that . . .'

He nodded and sucked in his breath, like a gasp. '*Ja*. Gruhuken.'

Gruhuken, 7th August

Our fourth day at Gruhuken. I've been too exhausted to write.

This morning we finished unloading the ship. That meant lowering eighty tons of supplies (and dogs) into the boats and rowing them ashore; except for the fuel drums, which we floated into the shallows. I had an anxious time with my wireless crates—if anything gets wet it'll be damaged beyond repair—but, thank God, they made it OK. Then I had to protect them from the dogs who were racing about, christening things. And when a husky is loose, it eats whatever it finds: wind-proofs, rucksacks, tents. It wasn't long before Gus and Algie saw sense and tied the brutes to stakes. At first they complained with ear-shattering yowls, then they realised it was hopeless and settled down.

I've enjoyed the hard work after being cooped up on the *Isbjørn*. Every 'night'—these strange white nights that I still find magical— Mr Eriksson and the crew go back to the ship to sleep, but we're keen to take possession of Gruhuken, so we've pitched our tent on the beach, at the head of the bay. Our reindeer-hide groundsheets are supremely comfortable, and not even the sea birds keep us awake.

We've been so busy that at times I've hardly noticed our surroundings. But sometimes I'll pause and look about, and then I'm sharply aware of all the busy creatures—men, dogs, birds—and behind them the stillness. Like a vast, watching presence.

It's a pristine wilderness. Well, not quite pristine. I was a bit put out to learn that there have been others here before us. Gus found the ruins of a small mine on the slopes behind camp; he brought back a plank with what looks like a claim, roughly painted in Swedish. To make the beach safe for the dogs, we had to clear a tangle of wire and gaffs and some large rusty knives, all of which we buried under stones. And there's that hut, crouched among the boulders in a blizzard of bones.

Gus asked Mr Eriksson about it. 'So were there trappers here, too? Or was it the miners who left all the bones?'

Mr Eriksson sucked in his breath. '*Ja.*'

Gus raised his eyebrows. 'Well, which?'

The Norwegian hesitated. 'Trapper first. Miners later.'

'And after them, no one,' I said. 'Not until us.'

Mr Eriksson did not reply.

I'm glad to say that relations with him have improved, and he and his crew have worked like demons to help us set up camp; almost as if they've a deadline to meet.

And maybe they have. With every day that passes, the midnight sun dips nearer the horizon. In just over a week, on the 16th, it'll disappear for the first time, and we'll experience our first brief night. Mr Eriksson calls it 'first dark'. Algie's planning a little ceremony involving whisky to usher it in, but Mr Eriksson disapproves. He seems to think we shouldn't joke about such things.

I've told the others what he said about Gruhuken being unlucky. Gus was briskly dismissive, and Algie said I shouldn't indulge the man's penchant for superstition. Secretly, though, I think they were relieved that it wasn't worse. I feel better, too. Now it's dealt with. Out in the open.

This morning, after the last crate was brought ashore, the *Isbjørn* set off on the forty-mile trip to collect our boats, coal, and the materials for the cabin. It's good to be on our own; a sort of dress rehearsal. And it's given us a chance to explore.

Leaving the dogs tied to their stakes, Algie took his rifle and headed off to hunt, while Gus and I went for a wander to the bird cliffs at the eastern end of the bay.

The weather has been perfect since we arrived, and this was another brilliant, windless day—surprisingly warm in the sun, only just below freezing. The sea was a vivid blue, calmly mirroring the mountains and, out in the bay, I spotted three bearded seals basking on ice floes. I stopped and took deep breaths of the clean, salty air, and it went to my head like wine.

Nearer the cliffs, the smell of guano took over. We scrambled among the rocks, Gus pausing now and then to identify yellow Arctic poppies and brilliant green clumps of saxifrage. He's fascinated by nature, and likes pointing things out to me, the ignorant physicist. I don't mind. I quite enjoy it.

The cliffs echoed with the guillemots' rattling groans. Craning my neck, I saw the sky speckled black with birds, like dirty snow. Thousands more perched on ledges. In the shadow of the cliffs the dark green water was dotted with white feathers. Among them paddled guillemot chicks. Fluffy and flightless, they rode the waves uttering high, piercing cries. A lone chick was bobbing on the swell, peeping. Maybe it'd got separated from its parents, or maybe they'd been taken by the Arctic foxes which haunt the feet of the cliffs like small grey ghosts.

As we made our way round the headland, we heard the distant report of Algie's rifle. Gus found a reindeer skull, and showed me its worn-down teeth. He said it would have died of starvation as it could no longer chew its food. Sitting on the rocks, we basked in the sun, and I thought about the beauty and cruelty around me.

Without preamble, Gus said, 'The other day, I didn't express myself very well.' He paused and then continued, 'What I was trying to say is that I don't think you *have* missed your chance.'

I felt myself going red.

'What I mean,' he went on, 'is that although your family had a hard time of it, that needn't drag you down, too.'

'It already has,' I muttered.

'I don't accept that. You're here. This is a new beginning. Who knows what it'll lead to?'

'That's easy for you to say,' I retorted.

'But Jack—'

'Gus, leave it. I came out here to get away from my life, not rake it all up. OK?'

I'd spoken more sharply than I intended, and there was an uncomfortable silence. I shredded a clump of Arctic poppies. Gus counted the tines on the reindeer's antlers. Then he said, 'Fancy ending up stuck in a tent with Algie and me.' He hesitated. 'Tell me honestly. Is it a strain?'

I threw away the poppies and looked at him. Sunlight glinted in his golden hair and lit the strong, clean planes of his face. I wondered what it must be like to be so handsome. Surely it would affect the behaviour of everyone around you, always?

More powerful even than his looks, he seemed genuinely to want to know how I was getting on.

'Honestly?' I said. 'It's not as bad as I expected.'

Back at camp, we found Algie in high spirits. He'd made his way west into the next fjord, where he'd come upon a spit of land 'crammed with eider ducks'. He'd shot five, and on his return he'd bagged a seal, which he'd hacked to pieces and fed to the dogs.

For dinner we roasted the ducks on a driftwood fire, having (on advice from the ship's cook) removed the fishy-smelling skin. They are the best thing I've ever tasted. We washed up in sand and seawater, then lay about, smoking and drinking whisky. We had a long discussion about whether Amundsen was a greater explorer than Scott, and where Shackleton fitted in.

Everyone looks tousled and tanned, and our beards are becoming quite respectable. Algie's is red and fuzzy, like a hedge. Gus's is golden, of course. It suits him inordinately. He says mine makes me look like a pirate. I suppose he means because I'm dark.

I never expected to get on with them like this. OK, sometimes Algie gets on my nerves. He's obtuse and he snores, and takes up so much space. But I'm beginning to regard Gus as a friend. He's quite persuasive, is Gus. All that talk about new beginnings . . . I nearly believed him. It hurt. Like pulling off a scab.

I'm writing this in our tent. Outside it's minus five, but in here, with our eiderdown sleeping bags and Gus's fur motoring-rug on top, it's quite snug. The tent's green canvas walls are softly aglow in the white Arctic night. There's an occasional yelp from the dogs, but they're tethered a hundred yards away and full of seal, so it's not too bad. I can hear the little waves sucking at the shingle. And, now and then, there's a crack as an iceberg breaks apart in the bay.

The *Isbjørn* is due back the day after tomorrow, and then we'll start building our cabin.

I never expected this, but I feel at home here. I love Gruhuken. I love the clarity and the desolation. Yes, even the cruelty. Because it's true. It's part of life. I'm happy.

8th August

A strange day. Not altogether good.

After breakfast we decided to take a proper look at Gruhuken's ruin's, so that when the *Isbjørn* returns, we'll know what needs clearing away. To my annoyance, Algie brought the dogs. So far, I've managed to ignore them, and they've sensed my dislike and given me a wide berth.

It was another bright day, almost hot in the sun as we climbed the slopes to inspect the ruined mine—Gus and I striding ahead, Algie puffing in the rear.

I was relieved to see that there isn't much left of the mine: a rusty tram-car, a stack of tracks, a few hollows blasted from the rocks.

'No cabins,' remarked Algie.

'I asked Eriksson about that,' said Gus. 'They were buried in a rockslide.'

Algie grimaced. 'Poor chaps.'

'Oh, the miners weren't in them. But it was the last straw, and they abandoned the place.'

Gus suggested that we leave everything as it was, and we wandered down to take a look at the hut among the boulders.

A grim little place, squatting in its drifts of bones. The dogs didn't like it, either. They nosed about edgily, then raced off along the beach to investigate our tent. Which meant that Algie and Gus had to chase after them and tie them up. I went along to show willing, but they wisely didn't ask me to help.

When we got back to the hut, Gus, the inveterate biologist, paused to identify the bones. Many are scattered—the disembodied skulls of walruses and reindeer—but others are recognisable skeletons. Gus pointed out foxes, fine and brittle as porcelain, and the big, man-like frames of bears.

I tripped over a claim sign lying on the ground. A posh one, of enamelled tin with emphatic capitals punched out in English, German and Norwegian: PROPERTY OF THE SPITSBERGEN PROSPECTING COMPANY OF EDINBURGH. CLAIMED 1905.

'And now there's nothing left,' said Gus, chucking the sign away.

The hut itself was about six feet square, a lean-to, with three walls of driftwood logs built against a large boulder, presumably to save on timber. The roof was still intact, tar-paper dismally flapping, and the door was only two feet high, perhaps to keep in the heat. The side window had been smashed by a marauding bear, but the small one, facing the sea, was still shuttered. Three paces in front of it stood a driftwood post planted in a cairn of stones. Algie said it was a 'bear post', for luring bears to the trapper's gun.

Gus took out his knife and prised the shutter off the front window, loosing a cascade of splintered glass. The old hut exhaled a musty smell of seaweed. He peered in. 'I suppose we could use it for a doghouse. What do you think, Algie?'

Algie shrugged. 'Bit small. Though it's a pity to waste it.' He glanced at me. 'Want to take a look inside, Jack?'

I didn't—I've never liked confined spaces—but I couldn't think of an excuse. As I crawled in after him, my spirits sank. The cries of gulls fell away. All I could hear was the wind keening in the stovepipe. The smell was thick in my throat: rotten seaweed, and something else—as if something had crawled in here to die.

The walls were black with soot, the ceiling too low to stand without stooping. In one corner, a rusty iron stove squatted on short, bowed legs. Against the back wall, a wooden bunk had collapsed beneath a mound of storm-blown debris. Rooting around, Algie found a mildewed reindeer hide and a battered tin plate. He wrinkled his nose. 'Beastly. Hopeless for the dogs.' He crawled out. I stayed. I don't know why.

For the first time since reaching Gruhuken, I thought about the men who were here before us, who built this hut from logs dragged up from the beach, lived through the 'dark time', and then left, leaving nothing but a tin sign and a blizzard of bones. What must it have been like? No wireless, maybe not even a companion; at any rate only one, in a hut this size. To know that you're the only human being in all this wilderness . . .

Moving to the front window, I scraped the broken glass off the frame and poked out my head. No sign of Algie or Gus. The bear post dominated the view. Beyond it, the stony beach sloped down to the sea.

Suddenly, I felt desolate. The romance of trapping peeled away, and what remained was this: squalor, loneliness. It was as if the desperation of those poor men had soaked into the very timber.

I crawled out quickly, and inhaled great gulps of fresh air. I hate all this pawing over ruins. I want Gruhuken to be *ours*. I don't want to be reminded that others were here before.

11th August

The ship got back as scheduled, and we spent two days unloading. We finished today, and would've started on the cabin if it hadn't been for Mr Eriksson.

While he was away, we'd decided on where to build it—where the old hut is, at the western end of the bay, conveniently near the stream, and where the boulders give shelter from the winds off the icecap. It's far enough from the bird cliffs, too, to ensure that my radio masts get decent reception. But none of that matters to old Eriksson. As far as he's concerned, we need to be east, practically under the bloody cliffs. And we should leave the trappers' hut well alone.

'I think that's nonsense,' I said. 'That hut's no use to man nor beast: it's got to come down.'

'No,' Eriksson said flatly.

'Why?' said Gus.

Eriksson muttered something about the dogs.

'I told you,' Algie said wearily, 'it simply won't do for them.'

'It won't do for my wirelesses, either,' I said.

Eriksson ignored that. 'You're leaving the mining ruins alone; you should leave this, too.'

'The mining ruins aren't in the way,' I said. 'That hut most definitely is.'

'Not if you build the cabin further east,' he said—which brought us right back to where we'd started.

Eventually he was forced to agree that it would be better if we didn't have to trudge the length of the bay to fetch water, but he remained adamant about not touching the hut. Algie gave in, suggesting we use it as a storehouse. That's when I lost my temper. Did they want to preserve a ruin, or did they want wirelesses that actually work?

But if I'm honest, I want that hut gone because I simply can't bear the thought of it. Some places drag you down, and that's one of them. Maybe it's the poverty and the loneliness: a reminder of what I came here to escape. Maybe I just don't like it.

Anyway, I won.

12th August

It's gone, though we had the devil of a job tearing it down. For some reason, none of the crew wanted to touch it, so we had to pay them double; and Eriksson had to have a stern word with them in Norwegian.

They worked in sullen silence and we helped, dragging the timbers away and chopping them up for firewood. Nothing's left of it now, except for the bear post, which Algie told them to leave, as he wants to use it as a flagpole. I pointed out that we haven't got a flag, and he tapped the side of his nose and said, not yet. God, he can be irritating.

It's been an exhausting day, and Gus and Algie are sound asleep. Gus is frowning in his dreams. He looks young and noble, like the first officer over the top at the Somme. Algie is snoring.

An hour ago, the weather broke, and a freezing wind came howling down from the icecap. It's still blowing, sucking and smacking at the tent. The icebergs are grinding in the bay, and now and then one breaks apart with a crash. Eriksson says that if this wind keeps up, it'll clear them away, so I suppose that's something.

This evening after dinner, when it was still calm, we strolled over to admire the site of our cabin. It's perfect. We've even cleared it of most of the bones. But I wish Algie hadn't kept that bloody post. Gruhuken seems to have had a dismal past. I don't want any of it poking through.

Of course, he had to go on about how the wretched thing works. 'Apparently, it comes into its own in winter, when the pack ice gets near the coast and brings the bears. They're attracted to tall, standing things, especially with a slab of blubber dangling from the top. So all you've got to do is stay in your cabin with your rifle poking out of the window, and wait till a brute comes within range. I confess I'm rather keen to give it a shot.'

'Algie, old man,' said Gus, 'I don't think that's on. We don't want bears prowling around camp.'

He and Algie wandered off, amicably bickering, and I ambled down to the beach.

Crossing the stream, I found my way onto the rocks. It was nearly midnight, and the great sloping pavements gleamed in that deep, gold, mysterious light. From a distance, they appear to shelve gently into the shallows, but in fact they end in a nasty four-foot drop. The water's deep, and you can see right down to the bottom, to huge green boulders and undulating weeds like drowned hair.

Crouching at the edge, I watched the waves slapping, and the chunks of ice jostling and clinking. I heard that peculiar crackling as the ice talked to itself. I thought, *If I fall in, I won't be able to climb out. I'd try to swim round to where it's shallower, but the cold would get me long before then.*

As I was heading back, a shaft of sunlight struck the bear post. The wood was bleached silver, except for a few charred patches, and some darker blotches that must be blubber stains. On impulse, I drew off my glove and laid my palm against it. It felt smooth and unpleasantly cold. I didn't like it. A killing post.

And yet, I think I now understand the impulse which drives men to shoot bears. It isn't for the pelt or the meat or the sport—or not only those things. I think they need to kill that great Arctic totem to give them some sense of control over the wilderness—even if it's only an illusion.

Just now, a shadow sped over the tent, and I got such a fright I nearly cried out.

Steady on, Jack. It was only a gull.

The wind is blowing hard, and the dogs are howling long and loud. They're restless tonight.

15th August

The cabin is finished, and we've moved in!

It went up in three days, as everyone worked like Trojans, and it's beautiful. Black all over, walls covered in tar-paper, roof in felt, with the stovepipe poking a little drunkenly from the top, like the witch's hovel in *Hansel and Gretel*. There's a small, enclosed porch, above which Gus has nailed a pair of reindeer antlers: a nice baronial touch. If you turn right and go round the corner, you find the outhouse, which Algie pompously calls the lavatory. At the rear, the eastern half of the cabin is backed by a doored lean-to for the dogs, made of packing cases and wire netting, while the western half abuts the boulders. The whole cabin is surrounded (except for the doghouse and the boulders) by a boardwalk about two feet wide. When you're inside and someone treads on this, you can hear the footsteps and feel the floor vibrate—as Algie is all too fond of demonstrating.

My radio masts stand a few feet to the west; beyond them is the Stevenson screen (which is like a beehive on legs, with a louvred screen to protect the self-registering instruments inside) for the meteorological measurements. We've fenced that in to keep out the dogs, and set a line of posts with ropes slung between them all the way to the porch, as Mr Eriksson says we'll need this in bad weather. The emergency storehouse is way off near the cliffs, and we've planted the dogs' stakes in front of the cabin, so that we can keep an eye on them.

Before we were even half-unpacked, I ran a test on my wireless equipment. It works. Thank God. My heart was in my mouth as I started the petrol engine for the big transmitter. When the valves began to glow, the sweat was pouring off me. Shakily, I tapped out our first message to England. It's childish, I know, but I did enjoy impressing the others.

With headphones in place and the receiver switched on, I took down our first communication from the outside world—1,700 miles through the ether, and clear as a bell: MESSAGE RECEIVED STOP WE HAVE 5 MESSAGES FOR YOU STOP. These turned out to be from *The Times*; the Royal Geographic Society; Hugo, sportingly wishing us luck from Tromsø; Algie's girlfriend; and Gus's parents and sister.

Algie crassly asked why there was nothing for me, so I told him. Parents dead, no siblings, no friends. I think he wished he hadn't asked.

The small Gambrell transmitter also works perfectly, as does the Eddystone receiver, which I got going in time for the BBC National Programme. George Gershwin is dead, and the Japs have bombed Shanghai. It all seems very far away. Or it would have done if Algie hadn't blathered on about Mr Hitler needing a jolly good thrashing. Gus told him sharply to shut up. He's like me: he doesn't want to think about another war.

Still. All that's over now, and we've been settling into our new home.

It's thirty feet by twenty, which sounds a lot but is actually pretty cramped, as we've got so much equipment. When you enter the porch, you have to squeeze past a tangle of skis, snowshoes, shovels and brooms. Then—and I'm told this will be crucial in winter—you shut the front door before you open the one to the hall. (Mr Eriksson calls this the First Rule of the Arctic: always shut one door before opening the next. Especially in a blizzard.)

With that door shut behind you, you're in darkness, because the hall—which is narrow and extends along the frontage—has no window, only gun racks and hooks for waterproofs, and a cupboard which Gus calls his dark-room. There's also a hatch into the roof space, which is our main food store.

Having groped your way down the hall, you open the door to the bunkroom—and, *fiat lux*, a window! The bunkroom occupies the eastern end of the cabin, and is mostly bunk, with shelves made of packing cases on the opposite wall. We only needed three bunks, but it was easier to build four. I've got the bottom one at the back. (The one above me is empty; we use it as a dumping ground.) My bunk is nearest the stove in the main room, which is good; but it's got the doghouse directly behind.

From my bunk, you can see straight into the main room, as that doorway has no door. To your right as you go in, there's the stove, water barrel and shelves which make up the 'kitchen' (no sink, of course). The space is dominated by a big pine table and five chairs and, against the back wall, are shelves crammed with books, ammunition, field glasses, microscopes and provisions.

The western end of the cabin, on the site of the old trappers' hut, is my wireless area. It's packed with receivers and transmitters, the Austin engine, and the bicycle generator, which faces the west window, so that I can see my wireless masts. My work bench is at the front, under the north window, overlooking the bear post. As the wireless area is furthest from the stove, it's noticeably colder than the rest of the cabin. But that can't be helped.

After hours of unpacking, we were too exhausted to cook a proper meal, so I made a big pot of scrambled eider-duck eggs. (We bought a barrel from the crew, who gather them in their thousands and ship them back to Norway.) They're twice the size of hens' eggs, with shells of a beautiful speckled green. Delicious, although with a lingering fishy tang—I can still smell it.

It's eight o'clock, and we're safely inside for the night. I say 'night' because, although it's still light outside, it does feel like that. This evening, we saw the first faint stars.

I'm writing this at the main table, by the glow of a Tilley lamp. Outside it's light enough to read but in here we need lamps as much of the room is blind: there's only the small west window at the end, and the north one to the front.

Before we lit the stove, we could see our breath, but it's warmed up now. We've left the stove door open, and the red glow is cheering. I can hear rain hammering on the roof and the wind moaning in the stovepipe. Yesterday, the weather turned squally. When I remarked to Eriksson that it's becoming wintry, he laughed. He says that in Spitsbergen, winter doesn't begin until after Christmas.

Gus and I are at one end of the table: I'm writing this journal, and Gus is smoking and doing his notes for the expedition report. At the other end of the table, Algie has set up the Singer treadle, and is making dog harnesses. He's whistling some inane tune and, when he's not whistling, he's breathing noisily through his mouth. So, it isn't exactly quiet. Added to which, there's the noise from the dogs. They're all related to each other, which is supposed to minimise fights, but you wouldn't think so to judge by what's coming from the doghouse. Growls, snarls, yelps. Scrabblings and gnawings. Bouts of oo-oo woos. When it gets too loud, we shout and bang on the wall, and they subside into hard-done-by whines.

As usual, Mr Eriksson and the crew have gone back to the ship to sleep. It's their last night at Gruhuken, and I get the impression that they're relieved. Tomorrow we've giving a lunch in Mr Eriksson's honour, then we'll say a fond farewell to the *Isbjørn*, and be on our own.

Later

I'VE MOVED TO MY BUNK, because Algie is using his collapsible safari bath, and I'd rather not watch. Sometimes, I wonder why I'm finding it quite so hard to tolerate Algie. Maybe it's because we're so cramped in here. We're all getting hairier and dirtier, and the cabin smells of woodsmoke and unwashed clothes. You've got to duck under lines of drying socks, and pick your way between the gear. Algie's simply making it worse. He never puts anything away. And every morning he shakes out his sleeping bag and leaves it draped over the bunk 'to air'.

I never thought I'd say this, but I'm quite glad that we didn't get rid of the dogs. Of course I still don't like them, and that's not going to change, despite Gus's best efforts. Yesterday he tried to introduce me to his favourite, a russet bitch named Upik. She fawns on him, but when I approached, she growled.

I shrugged it off, but Gus was disappointed with Upik, and maybe also with me. 'I don't know why she did that,' he said. 'You're not afraid of her, I can tell.'

'No,' I said, 'but I don't particularly like her, either. I bet she senses that.'

He looked so downcast that I laughed. 'Give up, Gus! You'll never make me a dog-lover.'

Right now, I can hear them yowling and scratching at the wall behind my bunk. To my surprise, I don't mind the sound. In fact, I like it. It's reassuring to know that just behind my head, on the other side of this wall, there are living creatures. Even if they are dogs.

Midnight. First dark. 16th August.

The *Isbjørn* has finally gone, and we're on our own.

My lamp casts a little pool of yellow light, and beyond it are shadows. Just now, I went to the north window. I saw the lamp's golden reflection in the panes, which are dark blue and spangled with frost. When I cupped my hands to the glass and peered out, I saw a sprinkling of stars in an indigo sky, and the charcoal line of the bear post.

Nothing is wrong, but I want to set down what happened this afternoon. To get it straight in my mind.

Around noon, some of the crew rowed ashore, and we gave them a crate of beer as a thank-you. They've worked hard, even if it was because they're desperate to leave and get in a few weeks' sealing before the winter.

Then, we had lunch with Mr Eriksson. Guessing that he'd appreciate a change from ship food, we gave him tinned ox cheek and curried vegetables with Bengal Chutney, followed by Californian pears and Singapore pineapple, then Fry's chocolate and coffee. He enjoyed it immensely, although at first he seemed intimidated by the Royal Doulton. But then Gus opened two bottles of claret and a box of cigars, and he became quite jolly. Told us how to make the trappers' speciality, blood pancakes, and gave us advice on getting through the dark time.

'Walk every day. Keep a routine. Don't *think* too much!' He added that if we ever get into difficulty, there's a friend of his, an experienced trapper called Nils Bjørvik, overwintering on Wijdefjorden, twenty miles to the west. He made quite a point about that.

Then, he surprised us by producing three jars of pickled cloudberries, which he says are the best thing for warding off scurvy. (He scoffs at the notion of vitamin C tablets, which he considers a waste of money.) I was touched. I think the others were, too.

After lunch, the crew still had a couple of hours' work to do, assembling our German Klepper canoes. Gus went down to the beach with Eriksson to take photographs, and Algie cleaned up the lunch things, as per our rota. To clear my head of cigar fumes, I went for a walk.

I headed upstream past the mining ruins, and at first the ground was a springy carpet of dwarf willow and moss. I walked fast, and was soon sweating. That's something I'm still getting used to: having to gauge how many layers to put on. Mr Eriksson told us a Norwegian saying: *If you're warm enough when you set out, you're wearing too many clothes.*

As I climbed higher, the going got tougher. I found myself stumbling over naked scree and brittle black lichen. The wind was sharp, and I was soon chilled. Clouds obscured the icecap, but I felt its freezing breath.

Behind the hiss of the wind and the chatter of the stream, the land lay silent. I came to a standing stone by a small, cold lake. I stopped. I was aware of the noises around me—the wind, the water, my panting breath—but somehow they only deepened the stillness. I felt it as a physical presence. Immense. Overwhelming.

I suppose it's to be expected that Gruhuken should make me a little uneasy. After all, I'm town-bred, not used to the wild. But. *But*. To stand on that slope and know that there's nothing to the west until Greenland; nothing to the east except the Arctic Ocean; and nothing to the north apart from the North Pole—which is yet more nothing . . .

With a jolt, I realised that I'd forgotten my gun. I thought of bears and started back, irked that I'd made such a basic mistake. I would have to hurry, or I'd miss saying goodbye to Eriksson.

I'd come further than I'd intended and, below me, our camp looked like a child's toy, dwarfed by the prehistoric curves of the whale bones on the shore. Out in the bay, the *Isbjørn* was tiny. The sky was a strange, sickly yellow. The sun was sinking into the sea. In a few minutes, for the first time, it would disappear. An oar flashed. A rowing boat was taking a party of men back to the ship.

Twilight came on as I scrambled over the stones. The wind dropped to a whisper. I heard the creak of my anorak, my labouring breath.

I was still 500 yards above camp when I saw a man standing in front of the cabin, by the bear post. His back was turned, but I could tell it wasn't Algie or Gus. *It must be one of the crew*, I thought, *taking a last look at the cabin he'd helped to build.*

The sun was in my eyes, but I made out that he wasn't dressed like a sealer. Instead of overalls, he wore a tattered sheepskin coat and a round cap, and ragged boots.

I called out to him. 'Hulloa, there! You'd better get down to the boats, or you'll be left behind!'

He turned to face me, a dark figure against the glare. Fleetingly, I saw that his hands were at his sides, and that one shoulder was higher than the other. There was something about the tilt of his head that I didn't like.

He didn't make an agreeable impression. All right, he made a *dis*agreeable one. I wanted him away from my camp and safely heading for the ship. And, irrationally, I wished I hadn't drawn attention to myself by calling out to him.

Feeling foolish, I continued down the slope. I had to watch my footing and, when I looked again, I was relieved to see that the man had gone.

Some time later, when I reached the shore, Mr Eriksson was at the water's edge, waiting with the last of his crew to say goodbye. There was no sign of Algie or Gus, and the men seemed nervous, glancing over their shoulders at the vanishing sun.

I didn't see anyone in a sheepskin coat, so I mentioned the straggler to Mr Eriksson.

He looked at me sharply; then back to his men. Taking my arm, he drew me aside. 'You make a mistake,' he said in a low voice. 'There was no one at the cabin.'

I snorted. 'Well, there was, you know. But that's all right: he's obviously gone in the other boat.'

Scowling, Eriksson shook his head. It suddenly occurred to me that he thought I might be accusing one of his men of loitering with intent to pilfer, so I said quickly, 'It doesn't matter, I only mentioned it so he doesn't get left behind.' I gave an awkward laugh. 'After all, we'd rather not have an uninvited guest making a fourth with us in the cabin.'

Eriksson didn't seem to like that. Brusquely, he asked if I'd spoken to the man. I told him no, except to urge him to hurry up and join his fellows—which, clearly, he had.

The Norwegian opened his mouth to reply, but just then Gus and Algie came running down, bearing our parting gift of claret and cigars, so he lost his chance.

Algie and Gus made embarrassed little speeches of thanks, and Eriksson reddened and thanked them back. His manner was strained. I don't think they noticed.

When it was my turn, he took my hand and crushed it in his bear's grip. 'Good winter, Professor,' he said, his grey eyes holding mine.

At the time, I couldn't make out his expression. But now I wonder if it wasn't pity.

Then he was in the boat, and his men were pushing off. As it rocked over the waves, he glanced back—not at us, I noticed, but behind us, to the cabin. I couldn't help doing the same. All I saw were the dogs, yowling and straining at their stakes.

The three of us stood and watched the boat reach the *Isbjørn*. We watched the men climb on board. We watched them raise the boat. We heard the sputter of the engine as the ship gathered speed. By now, all that remained of the sun was a crimson slash on the horizon.

As the sun's dying glimmer turned the sea to bronze, we watched the ship disappear behind the headland.

'And then there were three,' said Algie.

Gus made no reply.

'Stay there,' Algie commanded. Running back to the cabin, he swiftly returned with his camping canteen: two crystal bottles of whisky and water, with three nested nickel tumblers in a leather carrying case. He also bore a mysterious, sacking-wrapped parcel which turned out to be a lump of ice that he'd hacked from the icecap the day before.

'For the first time in many weeks,' he panted, 'the sun is *officially* over the yardarm.'

He was right. The sun was gone. Banks of grey cloud were rolling in, obliterating its dying glow. We drank a welcome to the night.

28th August

I think I was a little on edge before, but I'm not any more. A couple of weeks' hard, routine work has set me right.

Up at six thirty to pull on your clothes before the stove. The man on dog duty lets them out; the man on kitchen duty starts the coffee. Reading duty means trudging out to the Stevenson screen. At seven o'clock, you read the charts, then check the anemometer, wind vane, snowfall and hoar frost (on a little brass sphere like an alchemist's globe).

At seven thirty I'm on the bicycle generator, wiring the readings to the Government Station on Bear Island, from where they go to the forecasting system in England. Breakfast's at eight: bread baked by 'Mrs Balfour', with bacon and eggs or porridge. At noon there's a second set of readings and transmissions, and another at five. The dogs are fed at six. In between it's hunting and collecting driftwood; Algie's off on his geological survey (to my relief), and I go in the boat with Gus and help him net plankton and little swimming snails.

Once a week I coax the Austin to life, and we contact England with messages for family and friends, and dispatches to *The Times* and our sponsors. Gus writes these: chatty pieces about the wildlife and the dogs. England feels more and more remote, and he's finding it harder to think what to say.

The weather changes so fast it's bewildering. Two weeks ago, frost turned the dwarf willows on the slopes scarlet, like splashes of blood. Ten days later, we left the bunkroom window open a crack, and woke to an invasion of fog. Last night we had our first snowfall. Like schoolboys we stood with our faces upturned to the fast-falling flakes. Now Gruhuken is clothed in white. The snow has changed the feel of the camp. It hushes everything but footfalls. That takes some getting used to.

The nights are growing longer with alarming speed: twenty minutes more each day.

What do I mean, alarming? I like it. By now I'm used to living cheek by jowl with the others, and I enjoy the long evenings in the cabin. Gus working at his microscope, calling me over to peer at some fresh marvel, then chaffing me when I pretend not to understand. Algie cleaning guns and labelling fossils. We smoke and listen to the wireless. And I catch up on the latest wild theories in physics. Before I left London, my old professor sent me a stack of periodicals. As I read them, I feel a flicker of excitement. I remember how I used to feel. How I used to dream.

I think about that when I work at my wireless bench. Sometimes I catch sight of my reflection in the window. I hardly know myself. My hair is longer, and my beard makes me look younger, more hopeful. Maybe Gus has a point. Maybe I haven't missed my chance.

It's odd, but the wireless corner is so cold that I have to put on an extra pullover. And at times there's a faint, disagreeable smell of seaweed. I've washed everything with Lysol, but it's still there. I don't think the others have noticed.

But I do still love Gruhuken. It's a million miles away from the shabby gentility of Tooting; from worrying about whether your collar can go another day. Gus loves it here too, because there aren't any servants; he says this is the first time he's ever been allowed to make his own bed. I'm not sure about Algie. He insists on having the wireless or the gramophone on all the time, and now he's taken to whistling through his teeth. Sometimes I think he can't bear a moment's silence. What's he trying to escape?

30th August

Gus was right, the dogs did get to me in the end. Well, one of them did. Until this afternoon, I'd only progressed as far as learning their names. The leaders of the pack are Upik the russet bitch, and her mate, Svarten. Eli, Kiawak, Pakomi and Jens are their progeny; and Isaak and Anadark are the youngsters, only a year old, although they look like full-grown wolves. Isaak's the one who fell in the harbour at Tromsø.

Yesterday, Gus and Algie were off hunting and I was reading in the cabin when all hell broke loose outside. Thinking instantly of bears, I pulled on my gear, grabbed my rifle and burst out of the door.

Thank God, no bears. The dogs were baying and straining at their stakes to get at the youngster, Isaak. Somehow he'd found a tin of pemmican, gnawed his way through, and got his muzzle stuck inside. He was stumbling blindly about, clunking his helmeted head against rocks.

When he heard me coming, he stopped. I didn't give myself time to think: I just ran over and clamped my knees about his middle, the way Gus and Algie do when they're putting on harnesses. Isaak squirmed, but couldn't get free, and I yanked the tin off his head.

God, he was fast. Leapt up and gave me a head butt that knocked me flat and sent the tin flying. He pounced on it—and got his head stuck again.

'Bad dog!' I shouted inanely as I struggled to my feet. Then we went through it all again—only this time, when I got the tin off his head, I jumped out of the way. I was so pleased with myself that I emptied the pemmican in the snow for him, and he downed it in one gulp, then stood lashing his tail, his ice blue eyes alight with anarchy. *Let's do it again!*

Damn. He'd torn one ear on the tin. After what he'd just put me through, I wasn't going to let him get lockjaw, so I unclipped him from his stake and started dragging him towards the cabin for treatment. Halfway there, I realised I should've fetched the disinfectant first, leaving him tied up outside. He seemed to think so too, as he gave me a doubtful look.

The trick to handling a husky is to grab it by its harness and half lift it, so that its front paws don't touch the ground and it can't run off with you. At least that's the theory; I'd never tried it till now. Half lifting Isaak in what I hoped was the approved manner, I hauled him through the front door, grabbed a bottle of disinfectant from the shelf in the hall, and hauled him out again. By the time I'd got him safely tied to his stake, I was sweating. Huskies aren't huge, but by God, they're strong.

Muttering, 'Good boy, there's a good husky,' I sloshed on the disinfectant. He didn't even growl. I think he was too surprised. When it was over, I was so relieved that I gave him another tin of pemmican as a reward.

Gus and Algie came back and I told them what had happened. Algie huffed and said I oughtn't to favour one dog in front of the others. Gus just grinned. I said there was nothing to grin about, that that was the stupidest dog I'd ever seen—imagine getting your head stuck in a tin twice.

Gus burst out laughing. 'Stupid? Jack, he got two tins of pemmican out of you!'

Since then, Isaak's been on the lookout for me. If he happens to see me, he lashes his tail and makes croaky ror-ror-ror noises. And, this afternoon, when I was smoking a cigarette outside, he came and leaned against my leg.

15th September

The birds are leaving and the nights are getting longer. It's dark when we wake up and dark when we eat supper. When I'm out on the boardwalk looking in, the windows glow a welcoming orange, and the main room is lit up like a theatre. But when I'm at the Stevenson screen, the mountains loom, and I get the sense of the dark waiting to reclaim the land. Then I'm keen to get back inside and draw the curtains and shut out the night. Only I can't, as we haven't got any.

In one of my periodicals, there's a paper by someone who's worked out that what we know of the universe is only a tiny percentage of what actually exists. He says what's left can't be seen or detected, but it's there; he calls it 'dark matter'. Of course, no one believes him; but I find the idea unsettling. Or rather, not the idea itself, for that's merely an odd notion about outer space. What I don't like is the feeling I sometimes get that other things might exist around us, of which we know nothing.

In a month, on the 16th of October, we'll see the sun for the last time. According to the books, there'll still be some light for a few weeks after that, because at noon, the sun won't be all that far below the horizon. They call it the 'midday dawn'. After that, nothing.

But my God, the colours we're seeing now! If it's clear, dawn turns the sky an amazing pinkish gold. The snow glitters like diamonds. The roof of the cabin is blanketed in white, its walls crusted with frost. After a few hours, the light turns, and the bay becomes a sheet of bronze. The day dies in a blaze of astonishing colour: crimson, magenta and violet.

So much light.

It was after supper, and I was reading and smoking at the table. Algie was playing Patience and and Gus was outside checking on the dogs. Suddenly he burst in. 'Chaps! Outside, quick!'

As it was minus ten: 'quick' meant a feverish dragging on of boots, jumpers, waterproofs, mufflers, mittens and hats.

It was worth it.

'The dogs' fur was crackling with static,' said Gus. 'That's how I knew.'

We stood craning our necks at the Northern Lights.

Photographs don't do them justice. It's the movement that impresses you most. The way those luminous pale green waves roll and break and ripple across the sky—and vanish, and appear again somewhere else—all in eerie silence. A sea of light.

I know that for some people they're a religious experience, but I found them intimidating . . . so vast, so distant. Utterly indifferent to what lies beneath. And, in a strange way, that extraordinary light seems only to emphasise the darkness beyond.

Algie broke the spell by whistling, and for once I didn't mind. Soon afterwards, he went inside.

The two of us stayed, watching the sky.

Gus said quietly, 'Hard not to be moved, isn't it?'

I grunted.

With his heel, he hacked at the snow. 'I read somewhere that the Eskimos believe they're the torches of the dead, lighting the way for the living.' He hesitated. 'They say that if you whistle, the souls of the dead will draw nearer.'

I threw him a sharp glance, but he was staring at his boots.

'D'you believe in any of that, Jack?' His face was grave. In the lamplight, frost glinted in his beard.

'Believe in what?' I said guardedly. 'Spirits brandishing torches?'

'No, no, of course not. I mean . . . unseen forces. That sort of thing.' Embarrassed, he hacked again at the snow.

I guessed what he meant by 'that sort of thing', but I didn't want to talk about it, not in the dark, so I pretended I didn't understand. 'I believe in the wind,' I said. 'That's an unseen force. And radio waves.'

For a moment he was silent. Then he laughed. 'Very well, then. Be the literal-minded scientist.'

'I'm not,' I replied. To prove it, I told him what I'd been reading in the professor's periodicals. I must have waxed enthusiastic, because he said, 'And you envy them, don't you, Jack, those physicists in their laboratories? You want to be the one thinking up the crazy theories about the universe.'

It was my turn to be embarrassed. Because he's right, I *am* jealous. That *should* be me, dreaming up mad ideas in a physics lab. And maybe I could do it, after all. Maybe when we get back, I can find some way of going in for a further degree. Gus thinks I can. That's got to count for something.

As I sit here writing, I keep breaking off to fantasise about the insights I'll gain at Gruhuken, and how I'll astonish the world on my return. How things change! When we first got here, my nerves were on edge. All that brooding about the great stillness, and getting spooked by a sealer in a sheepskin coat. Now that Gruhuken is really ours, I don't feel like that any more.

6th October

We're down to a few hours' daylight. Dawn comes, and deep down, you can't help believing that there's a full day ahead. It's a shock when you realise that the light's already on the turn, and soon it'll be night again. It's hard to get used to that sense of the dark gaining ascendancy. Waiting to take over.

At the moment there's a moon, so it isn't too bad, but I know that it won't last long. Strange. In the summer, when it was light all the time, the moon was so faint I hardly noticed it. Now I follow its every move.

I'm trying to train myself to find my way in the dark without a torch. I don't like the way the beam of light draws the eye and renders what's beyond impenetrable. I suppose it's the same as when you're inside the cabin and you light a lamp and it prevents you seeing outside. Or rather, it doesn't completely prevent it: there's a gradation. Light one lamp, and you can still make out the dogs, or the bear post. With two lamps, it's harder. With three, all you see is the lamps' reflections in the panes. A commonplace observation, of course, but here it strikes me afresh. How odd, that light should prevent one from seeing.

It's colder: minus fifteen today. Stoking the stove is becoming a preoccupation. And it takes an age to get dressed, even if it's only to fetch logs from the woodpile, right outside the door. When you come back, you've got to brush the snow off your clothes and pick frost out of your beard before entering the cabin. Last week we had to break the ice on the stream to reach the water. Now there is no water, and it's a bucket of ice that we bring back to the cabin.

The birds have gone. The cliffs are silent. But there's a sense of something waiting.

12th October

Four days before the sun goes for good. Dawn comes, then turns to dusk, with nothing in between. But for the past three days we haven't even seen that, because of the fog. Camp is an island, floating in grey—no colours. Every day you wake up and tell yourself surely the fog's lifted? But it hasn't. And by lunchtime you know that you're facing another twenty-four hours of this dead, grey stillness.

That's probably why I'm not sleeping too well. I know I have dreams, because I wake up unrested, with a sense of a struggle. But I can't remember. It's not just me: Algie gets up during the night, and Gus moans in his sleep. The dogs are unsettled, too. And when we let them off for a run, they always head for the eastern end of the bay, never the west.

Today it was my turn for the five o'clock readings. My breath crackled in my nostrils as I trudged to the Stevenson screen. I don't like the way you bring your own noise with you. I don't like it that your hood cuts off your vision, so you don't know what's behind you.

Last week I tried bringing Isaak with me, on a rope clipped to his harness. It didn't work. He was nervous, panting and setting back his ears. I think it's because the Stevenson screen is only about thirty yards from the rocks, and for some reason he doesn't like them.

It'll be better once the sun's gone for good, and we can forget about it and get on with things.

16th October

I've seen it. Writing those words makes me break out in a cold sweat, but I have to set it down. I have to make sense of it.

The sky cleared just before noon, so we got our last sight of the sun after all. It was Gus's turn to take the readings at the Stevenson screen, but I went with him. Algie stayed inside. He said it would spook him to see it go. This time, no one suggested a ceremonial whisky.

Twilight. Behind the bird cliffs, the red glow of dawn, but to the west, night and the cold glimmer of stars. The black bones of the mountains jutted through the snow. On the shore, the whale ribs glinted with frost, and the rocks sloping down to the sea were white and smooth. The water was dark purple, vivid and strange. We saw the sky turn bloody and inflamed as the sun struggled to rise. We saw a sliver of fire. An abortive dawn. The sun sank back, defeated. Gone.

I shut my eyes and it was still there, blazing behind my eyelids. I opened them. All that remained was a crimson glow.

'So that's that,' Gus said quietly.

Four months without the sun. It doesn't seem real. In the doghouse, the dogs began to howl.

'They feel it, too,' said Gus.

I forced a smile. 'Gus, I think they're just hungry.'

His mouth twisted. 'Well, they'll have to wait a few hours. Are you coming in?'

'In a bit.'

I still had time before I was due to transmit the readings, and I didn't want to lose any of that crimson glow. Listening to the diminishing crunch of Gus's boots, I watched it fade behind the cliffs, like embers growing cold. The moon wasn't yet up, but there was still enough light to see by. No wind. The dogs had stopped howling.

Out of nowhere, for no reason, I was afraid. Not merely apprehensive. This was deep, visceral, pounding dread. My skin prickled. My heart thudded in my throat. My senses were stretched taut. My body knew before I did that I was not alone.

Thirty yards away on the rocks, something moved.

I tried to cry out. My tongue stuck to the roof of my mouth.

It crouched at the edge of the rocks. It was streaming wet. It had just hauled itself from the sea. And yet the stillness was absolute. No sound of droplets pattering on snow. No creak of waterproofs as it rose. Slowly. Awkwardly.

It stood. It faced me. Dark, dark against the sea. I saw its arms hanging at its sides. I saw that one shoulder was higher than the other. I saw its wet, round head.

I knew at once that it wasn't some trapper from a nearby camp, or a polar mirage, or that hoary excuse—a 'trick of the light'. I knew what it was. I *knew*, with some ancient part of me, that it wasn't alive.

Behind me, the cabin door suddenly creaked open. Yellow light spilled onto the snow.

'Jack?' called Gus. 'It's nearly twelve thirty. The transmission . . .'

I tried to reply. I couldn't.

The rocks were empty. It was gone.

I stood breathing through my mouth. I stammered an answer to Gus; I said I was fine, told him I was coming in soon.

He shut the door and the light blinked out.

I've never felt such reluctance as I felt then, but I made myself—*willed* myself—to take my electric torch from my pocket and walk down the beach and onto those rocks.

The snow crust was brittle as glass beneath my boots. Pristine. No tracks. No marks of a man hauling himself out of the sea. I'd known that there wouldn't be. But I'd needed to see for myself.

I stood with my hands at my sides, hearing the slap of waves and the clink of ice. The dread had drained away, leaving bewilderment. My thoughts whirled. *It can't be. But I saw it. It can't be. But I* did *see it.*

And I know, although I can't say *how* I know, that what I'd seen on those rocks was the same figure I saw at the bear post two months ago, at first dark.

It's real. I saw it.

It isn't alive.

17th October

All day I've been trying to get it straight in my mind. What did I see? Should I tell the others?

When I got back to the cabin, it was 12.29, and I had to scramble to do the transmissions. But it was as if I was two people: one was a wireless operator pedalling the bicycle generator, clipboard in his left hand, tapping a key with his right; the other was a man who'd just seen a ghost rise out of the sea.

I can't remember what I did after that. But I remember looking round at the cabin: the orange glow of lamplight, the socks and dishcloths on the line above the stove, Gus and Algie tucking into Paterson's Oat Cakes and golden syrup. I didn't feel part of it. They were on one side, I was on the other. I thought, *How can all this exist in the same world as that?*

Somehow, I got through the rest of the day. And oddly enough, I slept like a log.

It was Algie's turn to do the readings today, thank God. I was on kitchen duty. I clung to it the way they say a drowning man clings to straws.

For breakfast I made what Algie calls 'boarding house kedgeree'. I told myself, *this* is reality. The smell of coffee. The buttery taste of salt cod and hard-boiled egg.

I didn't set foot outside the cabin, except to go to the outhouse. Instead, I scrubbed the kitchen and washed clothes. Made cheese scones and seal-meat hash for lunch. Tried to read one of the professor's periodicals. Saw to the transmissions.

For dinner I made my pemmican stew. Pemmican is a mix of lean and fat beef, dried and compressed into blocks with albumen. You break it into lumps and boil it with water. Too much water and you've got a slimy sludge; too little and it's disgusting. I usually get it about right. I add potatoes, dried vegetables and Oxo for a salty, filling stew.

We turned in early. I'm writing this in my bunk. Behind my head, scuffles are coming from the doghouse. Tomorrow, it's my turn to do the readings. I'm dreading it. I'm going to take Isaak.

I can't face telling the others. I wish I could believe that what I saw on the rocks was all in my mind, because then it wouldn't be real. But I know that's not true. I felt that dread. I saw what I saw.

Gruhuken is haunted. There. I've said it. That's why Eriksson didn't want to bring us here. That's why the crew always slept on the ship, and were so anxious to leave before first dark.

But what does it mean, 'haunted'? I looked it up in Gus's dictionary: 'To haunt: 1. To visit (a person or place) in the form of a ghost. 2. To recur (memory, thoughts, etc.), e.g. he was haunted by the fear of insanity. 3. To visit frequently. [From Old Norse: heimta, to bring home, Old English: hamettan, to give a home to.]'

I wish I hadn't read that. To think that something so horrible should have its roots in something so—well, homely.

But *what* is it?

It's an echo, that's what it is. An echo from the past. I've read about that; it's called 'place memory'. It's a well-known idea, been around since the Victorians. If something happens in a place—something intensely emotional or violent—it imprints itself on that place; maybe by altering the atmosphere, like radio waves, or by affecting matter, so that rocks, for example, become in some way charged with what occurred. Then if a receptive person comes along, the place plays back the event, or snatches of it. You simply need to be there to pick it up.

And who better to do that than a wireless operator? Ha ha ha.

Yes, this has to be it. I don't think I'm clutching at straws. What else could it be? It's the only explanation that makes any sense. What I saw on the rocks doesn't actually exist. It was only an echo.

18th October

A *n echo of what?* It's five in the morning and I've got to sort this out before I do the seven o'clock reading.

It has to be something that happened here. Something bad. I know it was bad, because of the dread.

I've flicked through my books on Spitsbergen, but I didn't find any mention of Gruhuken. And I've been over this journal and reread what I wrote about the men who were here before us. There isn't much, and I'm not sure how accurate it is because, at the time, I didn't think it was important. First there were trappers, then miners, that's what Eriksson said. All those bones, the mining ruins, that tangle of wire on the beach. The claim signs. The hut.

That hut. The desolation when I crawled inside. Did some trapper or miner do away with himself in there? Is that what this is about?

I need to know. It's a compulsion, a dreadful curiosity. The same curiosity, I suppose, which made me stop on the Embankment that night, and watch them pull that body from the Thames.

Time to get dressed and see to those bloody readings. And I'm definitely taking Isaak.

Should I tell the others what I saw?

19th October

Three days since I saw it and, since then, nothing. I'm feeling a little better. *Nothing in life is to be feared. It is only to be understood.* She was right, old Marie Curie. I was frightened because I didn't understand what I saw. Now that I do—or at least have a working hypothesis—I can deal with it.

I'll probably have to tell the others at some point, but not yet. Talking about it would make it real.

This afternoon, out of the blue, Algie asked if I wanted to come dog-sledging, and suddenly I did, very much. It's exactly what I need: hard physical work. To hell with everything else. I've been feeling a bit sorry for Algie. He's not a complete fool; he knows he's been getting on our nerves. Maybe asking me to go sledging was his way of building bridges.

The sledge was behind the outhouse, where it had frozen fast, so we had to hack it free. Then we had to harness the dogs and clip them to their traces. They knew at once what was up, and went wild, because they love to run. And Isaak must have told the others that I'm OK, because they were actually quite well behaved with me.

The sledge is hardwood with steel-shod runners, and virtually indestructible: it runs on snow, ice, even naked rock. Algie and I stood on the back and, as soon as he unhooked the brake, we were off: the dogs running silently and in earnest, in Eskimo fantail formation, which looks chaotic compared to the European two-by-two, but is strangely effective.

God, it was exhilarating. We jolted and shook so violently that I was nearly flung clear. Didn't bother with headlamps; you see more without them, as your eyes adjust to starlight and snow glow. We rattled west over the thick, pebbly ice of the stream, then past the rocks. No time to be scared. Not with the patter of paws and the scrape of the sledge, the dogs' tails curling to right or left. It was fast and intense; I felt vividly alive.

Algie doesn't use a whip, he just calls *ille-ille* for right, or *yuk-yuk* for left, and they turn. We ran south over snow-covered shingle, along the edge of the Wijdefjorden. Isaak, at the far right of the fantail, kept glancing round at me. Once, he decided he'd had enough and doubled back and jumped onto the sledge. I couldn't help laughing as I shoved him off. 'No hitching a lift, you lazy brute!'

Algie halted to rest the team, turning the sledge on its side so they couldn't run off with it. Upik and Svarten, the most experienced, lay down sedately and cooled their bellies, while the others rolled in the snow or stood panting, their long tongues lolling.

Algie went to help Jens and Anadark, who'd got tangled up, and I ambled over to say hello to Isaak. His back was sprinkled with snow, but his fur is so thick that it didn't melt. Nosing my thigh, he leaned against me. No jumping up—he's not that sort of dog.

To the south, the fjord thrust deep into the mountains. Somewhere on the other side was the hut of that trapper friend of Eriksson's, but I couldn't see any lights. The mountains were deep charcoal, streaked with grey snow. The sea was black.

I thought of the way home, past the rocks, and shivered.

Until then, I'd assumed that if I told anyone, it would be Gus. But now, as I watched Algie and the dogs, I had a sudden urge to blurt it out to him. *The oddest thing happened to me the other day . . .*

My next thought was, what if he thinks I'm losing my nerve? He'll tell Gus. What if they start to wonder whether they can rely on me? Or what if—what if I tell Algie and he looks at me and says, *I'm glad you saw it, Jack, because I've seen it, too.*

So I didn't tell Algie. And I didn't tell Gus when we got back to the cabin. And now, as I write this in my bunk before turning in, I regret that. I'm sick of bearing this on my own.

First thing tomorrow. Breakfast. I'll tell them at breakfast.

22nd October

Too late. You lost your chance. They're gone.

Gus didn't get up for breakfast. He lay in his bunk, looking feverish and pale. I was annoyed. I wanted—no, I needed—him to be better. I didn't believe he could be genuinely ill. Not even when the fever got worse and he lay with one knee drawn up, clutching his belly. The Red

Cross first-aid manual was no help. Nor were Andrews Liver Salts. So I wired Longyearbyen, and had a question-and-answer session with the doctor in Morse code. He said it sounded like appendicitis and he was on his way.

I don't remember much of the last two days. Algie and I did what we could for Gus with hot-water bottles and morphine. We fed ourselves and the dogs, and kept up the readings and transmissions. None of us talked much. We were all thinking, *What happens now? Is this the end?*

The doctor arrived in the *Isbjørn*—it had been at the settlement when we'd wired for help—and, after that, things happened fast.

Strange to see other people when it's been just the three of us for nearly two months. The doctor said he didn't need to operate here (thank God), but Gus had to come back to Longyearbyen and have the appendix out there. And one of us must go with him, 'in case anything happened'.

For one wild moment, I was desperate for it to be me. *Leave this place, get the hell out of here. Gus needs you.*

Gus needs you. That's what changed my mind. He cares about the expedition as deeply as I do. And if I went and Algie stayed, that would be the end. Algie would never have the discipline to go it alone. And Gus would know that I could've saved the expedition, but I funked it.

All this flashed through my mind as I hauled Algie over to the wireless corner, leaving the doctor and Mr Eriksson in the bunkroom with Gus.

'You go,' I told him.

He glanced at me and then away. 'What about you?'

'I'll have to stay, won't I?' I snapped.

'But—surely not on your own.' He swallowed. 'You could come, too. The doctor says if all goes well, it'll only be a few weeks, then we can come back and carry on.'

'The dogs, Algie! What about the dogs? No time to take them with us, is there? And we can't just leave them! We could try paying a couple of Eriksson's men to stay and look after them, but somehow I don't think they'd say yes. So where does that leave us? Eriksson would tell us to shoot the brutes and have done with it, but I couldn't do that. Could you?'

He gave me an odd look. 'You're so rational, Jack.'

'*Rational?*' I kneaded my forehead. 'Listen. Even if I came, d'you think that's what Gus wants? The whole expedition shot to hell because I can't hold the fort for a couple of weeks?'

He didn't argue. I think he'd only objected as a sop to his conscience. And he never once offered to change places.

They got Gus onto the stretcher, and Algie crammed a few things in a rucksack, then we made our way down to the shore. It was a squally night, sleet falling fast in the lamplight. As they manoeuvred the stretcher into the boat, Eriksson pulled me aside. He said I couldn't stay alone, I had to go with them. We argued it out. I won.

But then he peered into my face and said, 'This is a bad mistake. The one who walks. You have seen it. *Ja?*'

Now that shook me. Maybe, deep down, I'd been hoping all along that it was only in my mind; and here was Georg Eriksson, hard-bitten skipper of the *Isbjørn*, finally putting paid to that idea.

'It doesn't matter what I saw,' I told him. 'I can't leave the dogs, and I can't scupper the expedition because of an echo!'

He didn't understand what I meant by that and, before I could explain, they were calling him. The boat was ready to leave. And I was running over to say goodbye to Gus.

He lay bundled up on the stretcher. In the lamplight, his face looked carved in stone, disturbingly like an effigy.

'Jack,' he panted. 'Are you sure about this? You can still change your mind and come with us.'

'No, I can't,' I said as gently as I could. 'I can't let the expedition go to blazes. Besides, a couple of weeks and you'll be back, right as rain.'

'Thanks, Jack. Thanks most frightfully.' Slipping off his mitten, he moved his hand.

I gripped it hard. 'I'll miss you.'

He forced a grin. 'Me, too. Be careful. Keep the dogs with you.'

'Don't you worry, I'll look after them. Don't worry. Just get better.'

He licked his lips. 'Good show, Jack. I can't tell you . . .' He sucked in his breath. 'Good show.'

And it was a bloody good show I put on as I stood in the shallows watching the boat make its way between the icebergs, listening to the putter of the engine, seeing the lights of the *Isbjørn* heading west. Jack Miller, saviour of the expedition. Heroically holding the fort till the others returned.

The lights blinked out. Quite suddenly, I was alone, with the grey sea sucking at my boots, in this night that has no end.

But how *could* I let the whole thing founder because of a few damned echoes from the past? I can just see myself explaining that to the Royal Geographical Society: 'Frightfully sorry, chaps, couldn't carry on. Saw a ghost.' How could I do that to Gus? Besides, I'm not alone here, not really. I've got the dogs. And the wireless. And there's that trapper in Wijdefjorden if I ever need help.

The thing to remember, Jack, is that it's only an echo. It's like a footprint or a shadow. It can't hurt you. All it can do is frighten.

23rd October

Well, I got through the first day. Routine, that's the ticket. Readings at seven, noon and five o'clock; transmissions half an hour after. I've had the dogs with me and, so far, no problems—except catching them again. A handful of sweets works wonders, especially brandy balls. I save the butterscotch for Isaak.

As I bustle about, cooking, wirelessing, chopping wood, feeding and watering the dogs, I feel oddly self-conscious. 'Now then,' I say out loud, 'what's for breakfast? Fried eggs? And what about dinner? All right then, curry it is!'

And I notice that I address myself as 'we'. Not 'I', or 'you', or 'Jack'. I don't like to acknowledge my solitude out loud.

There's a novelty to spreading my things around the cabin and eating what I like. For supper last night I invented a hearty dish of onions and tinned steak pudding, fried with potatoes and cheese. I keep the stove well stoked, the lamps trimmed and the water barrel full, using the rough-and-ready system we devised: top up barrel with snow, pour on boiling water from kettle; refill kettle with more snow, place on stove to melt. Whatever I do, I do without a pause. I don't like the silence when I stop.

The worst thing about being alone is that when I go out to the Stevenson screen or for my walk with the dogs, I can't leave the stove lit or a single lamp burning in the cabin, in case of fire. That's an even more vital rule than the one about closing doors. It means I return to a cold, dark cabin. I try not to look at the blind, black windows as I approach. When I'm in the porch, my steps sound too loud, my breath like that of someone else. I hate the moment when I close the door behind me and I'm shut in the long, dark hall. In the beam of my torch, everyday things leap from the shadows. The waterproofs on the hooks look like—well, not like empty clothes.

The main room is freezing. It smells of woodsmoke and paraffin. And it's so still.

There's a sliver of moon but soon there'll be none. I'm going to hang a storm lantern from the antlers over the porch.

Last night I tried the gramophone, then the wireless, but the disembodied voices made me feel more isolated. So instead I sat and read, with the hiss of the lamps and the crackle of the stove, and the tick of Gus's travelling alarm clock. It's olive-green calfskin, smooth to the touch, and its gold-rimmed face is beautifully plain. I keep it near me.

I miss Gus more than I've ever missed anyone. Strange, that. I was ten when Father died, and although I loved him, I soon stopped missing him; perhaps because he'd been ill for years, and I'd done my grieving when he was alive. Same with Mother. She was worn out, she wanted to go. So I didn't miss either of them for long. Nothing like this. This ache that came on as soon as he left. Is this what it's like to have a brother?

Over the weeks, I've struck up an acquaintance with the operator at the meteorological station on Bear Island. His name is Ohlsen. But, since the others left, I haven't wanted to chat. I don't like being on the bicycle generator with the headphones on and my back to the room. I don't know what's happening behind me. Although, of course, nothing is.

I'm worried about Gus. They'll still be en route to Longyearbyen. What if he gets worse and they have to operate on board? I forgot to tell Algie to wire me as soon as there's news, but he'll know to do that, won't he?

The weather remains clear and cold (minus twelve) and very still. Around ten in the morning, a pallid greenish glimmer appears in the south-east, behind the cliffs: proof that somewhere, the sun still exists. To the north-west, it remains deep night. On a clear day like today, the twilight strengthens to pinkish gold, revealing every ridge of the mountains, making the icecap glow. You think that dawn is coming—but no, soon it's getting dark again, the shadows already turning violet, the twilight fading to green, then nothing.

And the worst of it is, when I'm inside, I can't see the twilight, because the cabin faces north-west, towards endless night.

24th October

I went to bed with a lamp on a chair, but I kept starting awake and checking that I hadn't knocked it over, so in the end I had to put it out. Then I had a horrible half-waking dream that there was someone in the bunk above mine. I woke with a jolt. Steeling myself, I got up and switched on my torch. Of course it revealed nothing but mounds of clothes.

I wish we'd thought to bring nightlights. I remember the exact entry in the Army & Navy pricelist: 'Clark's Pyramid Nightlights, 12s. 9d per dozen boxes, each one burns for 9 hrs.'

Surely the *Isbjørn* will have reached Longyearbyen by now? Maybe Gus has already had the operation. Maybe . . .

Stop it, Jack. Go and make breakfast. Porridge with a chunk of pemmican in it. Scones with gooseberry jam. That'll set you right.

Later

ANOTHER COLD, windless day (minus fifteen), but overcast, so no twilight. Out to sea there's a band of deepest charcoal which looks like bad weather, only I can't tell if it's advancing or receding. This stillness is getting on my nerves. Where are the blizzards we're supposed to have in the autumn?

Without daylight, terms such as 'morning', 'noon' and 'night' have no meaning. And yet I cling to them. I impose them like a grid on the formless dark. I know that 'evening' is merely the stretch between the transmission at half past five and the reading at seven in the 'morning', but still I rub my hands and say briskly, 'Now then, what shall we do this evening?'

All quiet today, nothing untoward to report. (I like the way that even in this journal, I can't bring myself to name it. I circle round it with euphemisms. 'Untoward'. What does that even mean? 'Characterised by misfortune or annoyance. Not auspicious; unfavourable. Unseemly.' *Unseemly.* That's a good one. It certainly is that.)

Funny what you come across when you're not looking for it. Again I've gone through all our books on Spitsbergen, in case I missed something about what happened here. One of them was published in 1913; it describes

Spitsbergen as a miner's paradise. Rich coal seams, easily dug. Deep anchorages. No taxes, no mining dues, no laws. Each summer, a small army of prospectors and miners arrives from Russia, America, Germany, Norway, Britain. Disputes are frequent and, with no adjudicating authority present, are summarily settled.

Settled how? Is that what this is about? A fight?

I couldn't find any mention of Gruhuken, but in another book there's a chapter on Spitsbergen folklore, which I've skipped. Damned if I'm going to let it put ideas in my head. I've got enough of those already.

In among Gus's volumes on botany and birds, I found a memorandum book bound in blue cloth. I didn't know he'd been keeping a private journal: I thought he was making notes for the expedition report. It gave me such a jolt to see his handwriting. Sounds ridiculous, but I got all choked.

I put the journal back where I found it. Unread, of course.

25th October

Amazing news! A transmission from Longyearbyen! GUS OP SUCCESS STOP ALL FINE STOP HAVE WIRED HIS PEOPLE STOP BEAR UP OLD CHAP BACK SOON STOP ALGIE

Thank Christ. I've only just realised that I've been carrying the anxiety inside me like a coiled spring. When I received the transmission, I was so relieved that I could hardly take down the words. He's OK. He's going to be OK. In a few days he'll be back and it'll be as if he's never been away.

To celebrate, I laced my breakfast porridge with golden syrup and whisky. Then I came over all dutiful, and got the Austin going for the weekly dispatches to England. (Which is easier said than done, as it's a recalcitrant beast and dislikes the chill at this end of the cabin, so I pamper it by warming the valves in the oven.) I'm quite proud of my dispatch to *The Times*. I kept it matter-of-fact, business as usual: Expedition Leader temporarily indisposed, Wireless Operator taking over in the interim. I don't want them getting all sensational about me being here on my own.

It was a clear 'day', with enough light at eleven to justify calling it that, so I took the dogs for a run on the beach.

My God, what would I do without them? They're the liveliest, most affectionate creatures. I love the sound of their paws pattering over the snow as they hurtle off to investigate things, then hurtle back to tell me about it. Upik isn't as fierce as I'd thought, but she is fearless; and her mate Svarten might be shy with me, but he certainly keeps the rest of his pack in line. Kiawak is black, like Svarten, with long soft fur and tawny eyebrows; he hates getting his paws wet. Eli is creamy white, and none too bright. Pakomi, Jens and Anadark have wolf colouring: shaggy grey-and-tan fur, tipped black at the ends. They're full of mischief, and love jumping on top of the doghouse to survey the scene; I think they have designs on the cabin roof. Isaak also has wolf colouring, but a handsomer face than the others, and arresting light blue eyes.

To think that I wanted to leave them behind. That I actually suggested shooting them.

Later

THERE'S A THIN FILM of ice on the bay.

I didn't notice when I was out with the dogs, but I saw it this evening after the five o'clock readings. It's very thin. When I threw a stone, it shattered into long, jingling slivers. The tide will disperse it. But I've got to face facts: at some stage, the sea is going to freeze over.

When? I remember Eriksson talking about the colliers at Longyearbyen and how the mines only stop running some time in November. But Gruhuken is further north than Longyearbyen. What if the sea freezes before Gus and Algie get back? What if I've got to stay here alone until spring?

26th October

Nothing happened: I just gave myself a fright. Stupid, stupid. I've got to watch that. An accident out here wouldn't be funny.

Another still day and very overcast, so no twilight. Six thirty in the 'morning', and I'm letting the dogs out, when it starts to snow. Softly, insidiously, shutting out the world. No sea, no mountains, no sky. The dogs appear and disappear in the greyness like—well, like shadows. I bless Eriksson for making us put up those guide ropes.

But that bloody Stevenson screen. The louvres are supposed to protect the instruments from the sun, but since there isn't any, all they do is become crusted with frost, which has to be removed three times a day. The only way of doing that is to scrape it off with your knife, and it's damned awkward, partly because you're wearing snowshoes, which makes it tricky crouching down, and partly because you're screwing up your eyes against flying particles and your headlamp's shooting disconcerting beams into the gloom. You long to hear Gus crunching towards you through the snow. Hell, you'd even settle for Algie, whistling 'All By Yourself in the Moonlight'.

It happened just after the five o'clock reading. The dogs were off somewhere, but I knew they wouldn't have gone far, as it was less than an hour till feeding time. It was snowing hard, with a light, persistent wind making the flakes eddy and whirl.

I'd just finished at the screen, and was plodding back towards the cabin: my headlamp off, spindrift streaming towards me like fingers, hunched into the wind with one hand on the guide rope. I could hear the rasp of my breath and the scrape of my snowshoes, and I made a point of not looking back. I don't when I'm in snowshoes, as I've learnt that they create a not very pleasant auditory illusion: you fancy you hear the scrape of other snowshoes, following right behind you.

I was wiping the snow from my eyes when I saw someone standing at the door.

I was so startled that my snowshoes crossed and I fell, bashing my hip on a rock.

And of course it wasn't anyone, it was only the bear post.

Stupid. What's the matter with you, Jack? Next you'll be scared of your own shadow! From now on, you watch your step, my lad. What if you'd broken your leg? What if you'd hit your head and knocked yourself out?

Later

IT STOPPED SNOWING around six, and we're back to the stillness. The windless calm. Except it doesn't feel calm. You can have stillness without calm. Gruhuken has taught me that.

It's hard to concentrate on anything. Often I break off to trim the lamps. I replenish them when they're still three-quarters full. I keep checking my torch batteries, and when I go out, I don't rely on my headlamp: I have a torch in either pocket and take a Tilley lamp, too. Even then, I worry. If the battery fails . . . If I drop the lamp . . .

Until now, I hadn't understood the absolute need for light. Even just an hour or so of twilight is enough to confirm normality. It allows you to say, *Yes, here is the land and the sea and the sky. The world still exists.* Without that—when all you can see out of the window is black—it's frightening how quickly you begin to doubt. The suspicion flickers at the edge of your mind: maybe there is nothing beyond those windows. Maybe there is only you in this cabin, and beyond it the dark.

Eriksson was right. One mustn't think too much. Keep busy, walk every day, that's what he said. I've got to follow that to the letter. Especially the walks.

29th October

Three days of rain. So no twilight, no moon, no stars. And this is ice rain, colder than anything I've ever experienced.

Maybe I lost my nerve a little after that incident at the Stevenson screen, because I couldn't face my usual back-and-forth along the beach. Instead I've been taking my walks by going outside and circling the cabin, with one hand on the wall, so as not to get lost. I keep my headlamp on at all times.

Round and round I go, and by now I know every nail in the planking, every loose corner of tar-paper. Each circuit has its scares and reassurances. Turn right out of the door and head past the woodpile and the drums of paraffin and petrol. Past the outhouse and the coal dump, with the dog sledge propped against it. Then I'm off the boardwalk, but I don't mind, as this is the best bit because I've reached the doghouse. I undo the latch and out comes a flurry of whiskery muzzles and flailing paws. For a circuit or two they accompany me, then they get bored and scatter—although Isaak stays close for a while longer, probably because he knows I've brought him a butterscotch. Sometimes I keep him with me on a rope, but usually I don't have the heart to deprive him of his run, so I'm left alone.

Past the doghouse it's worse, because my mittened hand must leave the cabin wall and touch naked rock. As I near the end of the boulders, I slow, fearing what I might meet round the corner. I shout to scare off—what? Foxes? Bears? I know I'm being stupid: the pack ice must still be miles out to sea, so there's not much chance of bears, and with the dogs about, they're even less likely.

Past the boulders, my hand finds the planks of the cabin again, and I'm back on the boardwalk. You'd think it'd be a relief, but I hate this end of the cabin: I can't forget that it's the site of the old trappers' hut. So, I hurry, my gaze fixed on the blessed glimmer of the storm lantern hanging from the antlers over the porch. I try not to catch sight of the bear post, three paces from the door. I hate it if the beam of my headlamp cuts across it.

I reach the door and bang on it for luck. Well done, Jack. One circuit done. Only nineteen more to go. Twenty circuits per day, that's my rule, and it must not be broken. Like the readings and transmissions, it's a peg on which my routine depends, a fixed point in my existence.

Drying out my gear has become another. I spend hours turning gloves inside out, hanging socks over the stove, checking that nothing has scorched. Every item of clothing is a trusted friend. This afternoon I had to stop myself talking to my muffler.

The stove is a friend, too, albeit a fickle one, and when it's windy, we have a love-hate relationship. I fuss over it and cajole it into doing better. I keep the door open and watch the flap of the flames, and praise the flaring hiss of a recalcitrant log. I swear at it when it refuses to burn.

I thought I was lonely back in London, but it was never like this. Lonely? I was among millions of people! Here I've got no one. I'm the only human being for . . . Shut *up*, Jack. This isn't helping.

Later

MESSAGE FROM ALGIE. GUS WELL BUT DOC SAYS CANNOT COME FOR AT LEAST TWO WEEKS STOP SORRY OLD CHAP STOP ALGIE
Two weeks?
I've been pacing the cabin, trying to take it in. I've done a week on my

own already. It feels like a month. How can I bear two more? And why did he say 'at least'? What did he mean?

Two weeks. That's mid-November! Will the sea still be clear by then? Will they be able to get through?

Whisky. Lots of it. That's the ticket.

30th October

I read that chapter on folklore. I wish I hadn't.

Most of it wasn't even about Spitsbergen, not specifically. It was just a rather dreary account of Scandinavian beliefs, some of which I recognise from old English customs: the idea that sea birds bring good luck when you're out fishing; scattering salt to ward off witches.

It says that 'some places in Spitsbergen'—unhelpfully, it doesn't say which—are haunted by *draug*s. A *draug* is the unquiet spirit of a drowned man who lurks in the shallows, waiting to drag the unwary to their doom. An extract from the book: 'When a corpse is washed up, there is always a dilemma. If you bury it, are you cheating the sea of its due? If you do not, will you be haunted by the *draug*?'

I like the 'when'. How often is a corpse washed up here, anyway?

And then there's this. Those who know the islands maintain that the beginning of the polar night is a time for particular care. Some say that seven weeks before Yule, the graves of Spitsbergen open.

Seven weeks from Christmas. That's October the 31st. Hallowe'en.

But, Jack, so *what*?

When I was a boy, Father gave me a book called *Folk Tales from the North*. Most of the stories were about witches and trolls and ghosts playing havoc on All Hallows' Eve—which, when you think about it, is completely understandable: a natural response to living in the north. Of course you'd believe in things like that when you're facing a long, dark winter, and the whole world feels dead.

What you've got to remember, Jack, is that there's nothing new in any of this. Nothing you didn't already know.

The 31st of October is tomorrow.

31st October

Did I make it happen? Was I more 'open' to perceiving it because of what I'd just read? Because of the date?

It snowed in the night. When I went to take the seven o'clock readings, it was warmer, only minus nine, and a clear 'morning'; the moon a brilliant crescent in an indigo sky prickling with stars. Fresh snow clothed the camp, and I could see the pale curves of the whale bones on the beach, the icebergs on the sea. (The sea is mercifully unfrozen; I checked.)

I felt ashamed of my cowardice over the past few days. Those dismal circuits round the cabin with me clinging to the walls—as if I'd be lost for ever if I didn't maintain contact. I can't let things affect me like this. Not with two more weeks to go. So, in a spirit of defiance, I took the dogs for a walk on the slopes behind camp.

To begin with it was beautiful. The dogs raced about, yelping, chasing each other. Isaak tugged on his rope—I'm training him to accompany me—but I was firm, and soon he was trotting along docilely, which was just as well, as I was wearing snowshoes and had a ski pole in either hand and a rifle over my shoulder.

As the twilight strengthened, we followed the frozen stream uphill, and I congratulated myself. See? All it takes is a bit of grit. And look how beautiful it is! The undulating white slopes, the glimmering peaks, the drooping heads of grasses poking through the snow. Even the mining ruins were transformed.

Isaak gave an excited wuff and, in the distance, I made out black dots moving on white. Reindeer! *See?* I told myself as I restrained an eager husky. *There is life out here. You just need the guts to go and find it.*

The dogs hurtled after the reindeer, which tilted back their heads and galloped off at surprising speed. The dogs quickly realised it was hopeless, and bounded back to me.

It was hard going uphill, and soon I was bathed in sweat. Climbing in snowshoes means digging in with your toes so that the spikes underneath can get a grip, and hauling yourself up with your ski poles till your elbows ache. And after all that rain there was ice under the snow, so each step made a glassy crunch, or an alarming scrape when I hit exposed rock, or a jolting whump in a drift.

One snowshoe came off, and I knelt to rebuckle it.

When I rose, the land had changed. The mountains floated above long drifts of fog. A gauzy curtain veiled the bay. As I watched, the fog thickened till I could only distinguish features by contrast: the inky sea against the lighter grey shore.

'Time we were getting home,' I told Isaak, and we started back. He plodded ahead, glancing back at me from time to time as if to say, why so slow? I kept my eyes down, watching my footing.

When I looked again, the mountains were gone. Sea and camp had vanished, obliterated by fog. I felt its clammy chill on my face.

Defiantly, I snapped on my headlamp. Isaak's shadow loomed: a monster dog. My light scarcely illuminated a yard ahead of me, but it showed my tracks clearly enough, leading back to camp. The best thing about snowshoes is that they make unmistakable tracks. An idiot could follow them.

I don't know how I lost the trail, but I did. In disbelief I looked about me. Gone. I took the torch from my pocket and tried that. No good. Like the headlamp, the beam scarcely lit a yard in front. And 'beam' is too strong a word. It was more of a diffuse glow, dissolving into the grey.

Downhill, I told myself. *That's the ticket.* But around me I saw only grey, and with all contrast gone, it was impossible to make out the lie of the land. I swayed. I couldn't tell up from down. I headed off again. My snowshoes slid on an icy patch. At the same moment, Isaak caught a scent and lunged forwards. I fell. The rope slipped out of my hand. He was gone.

'Isaak!' I shouted. My voice sounded muffled. He didn't come back.

Cursing, I groped for my ski poles and struggled to my feet. The fog pressed on me from all sides.

'Svarten! Upik! Anadark! Jens! Isaak!'

Nothing. I stumbled on.

No, Jack, this is the wrong way: you're going uphill.

I backtracked. But there were no recognisable features to backtrack to. By now my trail was a mess of churned snow: no use following that.

Yanking off my headlamp and throwing back my hood, I strained for some sound to guide me. The sea was too far off, and the stream was frozen. I heard nothing but my own urgent breath.

Inside my waterproofs, my sweat-soaked clothes chilled me to the bone. I willed myself to keep calm. Think logically. How do you tell up from down? Answer: you kick the snow ahead. If you can see where it goes, there's level ground in front. If not, there's a drop.

Pulling up my hood, I refixed the headlamp. Which isn't as easy as it sounds when you're wearing mittens and your hands are shaking.

My mind darted in panic. I saw myself stumbling further and further from camp, falling down some forgotten mineshaft. I thought, *When two days go by without any transmissions from me, Bear Island will raise the alarm. They'll send a search party from Longyearbyen. Two days later—ice permitting—they'll arrive to find a deserted camp and desperate dogs. Next summer, maybe someone will find my bones.* All this flashed through my mind in an instant.

Then I remembered the compass in my pocket. Idiot. All you've got to do is head north-east and you'll reach the sea.

I dropped the bloody thing in the snow. I scrabbled for it. Whipped off my mittens. Couldn't find it. Shit. Shit.

Found it. The arrow didn't move. Not broken, surely not broken? I jiggled it. The arrow swung wildly. My hand was trembling, I couldn't hold the compass steady. I set it on a rock.

The arrow—the blessed little arrow—swung round—wavered—and went still. There. That way.

Gasping, I stumbled downhill. I passed a patch of snow dotted with tufts of light-brown hair where a reindeer had rested, and this sign of life heartened me immensely. A few paces on, my headlamp caught the bright yellow spots of a dog's frozen urine. Then I heard the distant yowls of huskies.

Thirty paces more took me to the beach.

'Jesus,' I whispered.

In my wanderings I'd strayed a long way off course, and had fetched up at the eastern end of the bay, under the cliffs. Sagging with relief, I turned my back on the cliffs and started along the shore, keeping close to the water for fear of losing myself again.

The humped bulk of the emergency storehouse loomed out of the fog. Then the whale bones, glittering in the beam of my headlamp. At last I made out the bear post—and, beyond it, the miraculous glimmer of the lantern over the porch.

I shouted for the dogs. 'Upik! Pakomi! Anardark! Eli! Isaak!'

No response. But that was OK: they'd come back when they were hungry. Eagerly, I hurried on.

As I approached the tall bear post, my headlamp lit the cairn of rocks at its base. Fog had darkened the blotchy stains on its weathered grey wood to black.

The dread came from nowhere.

Without warning, my flesh began to crawl. I felt the hairs on my scalp prickle and rise. I couldn't see anything except the bear post and its cairn of stones, but my body braced itself. It knew.

Then, through the fog on the other side of the post, came an odd, muffled scraping. A sound as of metal dragged over rock.

Jerkily I turned, the beam of my headlamp sweeping the fog. I saw nothing. And yet that sound was louder, more distinct. Clink. Clink. Coming closer. Towards me.

My heart hammered in my throat. I tried to run. My legs wouldn't move. It was in front of me now, the sound only a few feet away—and still I saw nothing. *This can't be. But I hear it.*

Clink. Clink.

Silence.

It had reached the post. It was so close that if I could have moved, I might have reached out my hand and touched—what? A presence. Unseen. Unbearably close.

I stood helpless, not breathing, my arms clamped to my sides. Dread rising within me, a black tide drowning . . .

Behind me, the patter of paws.

With a moan I broke free. I staggered back. My snowshoes crossed. I fell.

Isaak ran into the beam of my headlamp and stopped, ears pricked, tail tautly raised. His eyes gleamed silver, throwing back my light.

As I got to my knees, he came towards me, lashing his tail. In his silvered eyes I saw the twin reflections of a dark, round head.

It took a moment to recognise myself.

I FOUND MY WAY to the porch. Yanked open the door and slammed it behind me. Dragged off my outer things. Stumbled down the hall. The bunkroom. The main room. My torch beam sliced the dark. My breath smoked.

I tried to light a lamp, but my hands were shaking too hard. I found a handful of birch bark and threw it in the stove with a couple of logs. At last I got them to take. I crouched, staring at the flames between my fingers. In my head I still heard that sound. Still felt that presence.

My teeth were chattering, my clothes soaked in freezing sweat. I blundered back to the bunkroom, snatched dry things, undressed and dressed in front of the stove. I found a bottle of Scotch and splashed some in a mug and gulped it down.

The whisky steadied me. I managed to light a lamp. And another and another. Suddenly I was ravenous. I made coffee and porridge. I gobbled it like a starving man. I ran to the slops pail and retched.

I longed to hear voices. Normality. I tried the wireless. The receiver needed charging. Cursing, I pedalled the bicycle generator, not looking at the windows. I tuned in to the Empire programme. A play. The clink of teacups, the brittle chatter of women.

I went to the north window and put my hands to the glass and peered out. The dogs were back: some curled up with their tails over their noses, some quietly chewing snow. All seemed oblivious of the bear post three yards from the window. I told myself it was only a stick of driftwood.

I went and sat at the table. The radio play ended. The calm, efficient voice of the BBC announced the next programme. My wristwatch told me it was ten o'clock. I'd set out on the walk at eight. Only two hours? How was that possible? It felt like years. I needed something to still the panic. Something to make the sounds go away.

Lurching to my feet, I blundered to the book shelf, found Gus's journal, and opened it. To hell with respecting his privacy. I needed him. The sight of his handwriting instantly gave me courage. It was round and schoolboyish, and he'd been so enthusiastic that at times he'd scored the paper. He'd filled pages with nature descriptions—birds, molluscs, plants—interspersed with reflections on the Arctic and on the characters of Norwegian sealers. I devoured it all, the more boring the better.

As I'd expected, he kept mostly to facts, with little emotion; presumably that's beaten out of you at Harrow. He was largely silent about Algie, although he mentioned me a few times.

I don't think Jack likes Algie very much, he'd written on the 31st of July, the day we saw Spitsbergen for the first time. *Whenever Algie says something crass, which God knows is often enough, I can see Jack's jaw tightening. I think it's a physical effort for him not to slap Algie down. It's really rather funny.* That made me smile. Gus had noticed almost before I'd realised myself.

After we'd been at Gruhuken a week, he'd written: *In one of my books it says that parts of Spitsbergen are haunted. I asked Mr Erikkson, but he wouldn't say yes or no. He said (and I translate from his less idiomatic phrasing): 'Up here a man becomes aware of things that he can't perceive further south.'*

Bafflingly, Gus made no further comment on this, but launched straight into two pages of nature notes. I've noticed that about him. He seems to have the ability to detach himself completely from anything disagreeable: to exclude it and immerse himself in something else. Maybe that's another skill he acquired at Harrow.

31st August. This place isn't right. I've felt it since the Isbjørn *left.*

What? What?

That time in the canoe when I watched the kelp moving in the water. I saw such things.

Christ, Gus, what did you see? Feverishly, I turned the pages. Nothing but bird behaviour and character studies of the dogs. I can't believe it. All that time—weeks of living together—and he knew?

16th September. Why hasn't Jack felt anything? Last night we saw our first Aurora. I started to tell him, I wanted to. But he got that severe look and changed the subject. Can he really have sensed nothing? Of the three of us he's the strongest, the most pragmatic and level-headed. And yet he's perceptive, too, and has plenty of imagination. After all, he was moved almost to tears at his first sight of Gruhuken. So it's odd that he should be the only one who has noticed nothing.

The only one? Oh, surely not Algie . . .

10th October. Poor Algie. This morning I dragged him off for a walk, and he confessed everything. He said, 'I know it sounds the most fearful rot, but this place is giving me the pips. There are times when I feel sort of— watched. And once, on those rocks, I had the most dreadful thought. Or rather, not a thought, but an image in my head. I saw knives. I don't want to say any more.'

Now that winded me.

A scrawled entry for the 14th of October. *This morning Algie told me he's started to hear things. He calls it a 'waking nightmare'. I badgered him for details, then wished I hadn't. I refuse to write them down. They're too horrific. And what unsettles me most is that they closely resemble what I experienced in the canoe. Poor Algie, he's in a frightful funk. And so ashamed. He made me swear not to tell Jack. I don't think I could even if I wanted to. Besides, I don't want Jack thinking I'm in a funk, too.*

I skimmed the remaining pages, but there was nothing more until just before Gus fell ill. *I've begun to realise,* he wrote on the 18th, *that prolonged darkness can affect the mind in ways I'd never anticipated. There's a lifeless stillness about this land that affects one shockingly. Perhaps I'm developing nerve strain or that disorder the old trappers used to get. What did Jack call it? Rar? The extraordinary thing is that what I experienced in the canoe felt so intensely real. No doubt that's in the nature of hallucinations, that they seem so real. After all, one's dreams feel real, even though they're merely artefacts of one's mind; and if my brain can create such 'pseudo-reality' while I'm asleep, surely it's capable of performing the same trick while I'm awake? And yet, how is that a comfort? To know that my own mind can create such horrors.*

That was almost the last entry. The next day, he fell ill.

I sat stunned, staring at the page. Oh, Gus. You were going through all that, and I didn't know. For your sake, I'm glad you're safe in the infirmary at Longyearbyen. If only I'd known. We could have talked of it. We could have borne it together, made sense of it.

And yet if you were here now, Gus, I'd tell you that you're wrong. Whatever you experienced, you didn't imagine it. I don't believe for a moment that what I heard at the bear post was an 'artefact of my mind'. It had objective reality. It was an auditory imprint, a lingering trace of some act of savagery that was once perpetrated here at Gruhuken.

On the kitchen shelf, Gus's alarm clock tells me that it's twenty to twelve. Time to go out for the twelve o'clock readings. I have to do it. Otherwise it's won.

But *what* has won? Steady on, Jack, you're in danger of creating a monster out of shadows. Whatever it is, what you must remember is that it's in the past. Something happened here once. Something terrible. But whatever you experienced was only an echo. Simply an echo.

Later

I DID GO OUT at noon, and again at five. Both times, the dogs gave me a rapturous welcome and came with me to the Stevenson screen. They seemed completely at ease. I found that intensely reassuring.

I haven't been near the bear post since it happened. To reach the screen I took the back way, turning right out of the porch and looping round behind the cabin. I'm going to do that from now on.

A few minutes ago I went to the window. I saw the shadowy shapes of the dogs in front of the cabin, peacefully gnawing chunks of seal meat that I'd thrown out to them. A light wind from the icecap is blowing spindrift over them, but they don't seem to mind. I haven't tied them to their stakes: I don't see the point. They're not going to run away. And like this they can warn me of bears.

It's such a normal sight. Inside, too, everything's normal. Bright lamps, crackling stove, a whisky at my elbow, one of Hugo's cigars between my teeth. When I look at myself in the shaving mirror, I see no horror, no fear. Nothing to connect me with the wild-eyed man who was retching into the slops pail a few hours ago.

What I've got to remember is that others have overwintered here and they too must have experienced things—*but they managed*. Well, so shall I. I won't let this beat me.

I have decided on a few ground rules.

First, I'll no longer kennel or tether the dogs, but will let them roam freely. I'll wedge the door of the doghouse open, so that they can come and go as they please, but still have shelter. I don't think they'll come to any harm. They were bred for the Arctic.

Second. I'll draw up a ration plan. It'd be unthinkable if Gus and Algie return to find that I'd squandered our supplies.

Third. I'll cut down on the drinking. (That one starts tomorrow.)

Fourth. No more than nine hours' sleep a night. In this endless dark, one can easily sleep twelve hours or more, but that must be resisted. I have to maintain a structure: sleeping time, eating time, work time. That's the ticket. Seeing these rules, neatly numbered on the page, is extraordinarily comforting. And it's good to know that outside there are eight watchful huskies patrolling the camp.

1st November

A good day. I slept the regulation nine hours without dreaming, and was woken by Gus's alarm clock.

My new rules are working. When I'm not busy with the usual tasks, I'm tiring myself out with new ones: cleaning, laundry, weather-proofing the doghouse with tar-paper securely tamped down and lots of straw bedding inside. I check the bay for ice (so far, thank God, it's clear). And when I'm in the cabin, I keep the wireless on. I have chats in Morse with Ohlsen on Bear Island.

And this afternoon I 'spoke' to Algie again. He told me that Gus is doing well, and I told him about my new rules. Twice he asked if I'm 'all right', and I said I'm fine. If he wants to keep things on the surface, then so will I. He knows what kind of place this is.

My rules are working, that's the point. Things would be back to normal if it wasn't for a ridiculous habit I've developed of peering out of the north window to check on the bear post. It's ludicrous, I know, but I need to reassure myself that it isn't quite as close to the cabin as I'd thought.

Of course, each time I look it's exactly where it ought to be: a good three paces from the window. But here's the irritating thing: afterwards, when I've been busy on something else, the doubt creeps back. In my mind's eye the post is nearer the door, as if it's about to gain entry. I know that's pre-posterous, but I still have to go to the window and make sure. Which means that whatever I'm doing, the wretched thing is never far from my thoughts.

Outside it's minus nine, with a south wind hissing over the snow. The barometer is falling. I wonder if we're in for a storm?

When I 'spoke' to Algie, I asked if there was any change to when they'd be coming back. He said no, but didn't go into detail. Previously, he'd said 'at least two weeks'. That was on the 29th of October. Which means they'll get here on the 12th of November—at the earliest. Eleven days from now. If I stick to my rules, I might be able to hold out till then.

Just now, I made my last check before turning in. There's a bright crescent moon. The bear post casts a long, thin shadow, reaching towards me. If only I couldn't see the bloody thing at all.

2nd November

I was finishing breakfast when it occurred to me that since waking up, I'd already checked the post at least a dozen times.

I slammed down my mug. 'Bloody hell! This has got to stop!'

Running to the bunkroom, I grabbed an armful of blankets and hurried about, tacking them over the windows. There. You've been moaning about having no curtains. Well, now you do.

It worked for about an hour. Then I drew back a corner and peered out.

And of course the post was where it's always been: a little closer than I'm comfortable with, but no more and no less than it was before.

From now on, I'm going to try an alternative strategy: acknowledge the obsession, but limit it. You're allowed ten checks a day—and no more.

I've left the 'curtains' in place, though. I can pin them back if there's anything to see but, for now, they're a distinct improvement.

Later

I'VE JUST COME IN from the five o'clock readings and I don't know what to make of it.

The readings themselves were straightforward. Decent weather, minus ten and still the wind blowing from the icecap, but the sky is clear, with a spectacular display of the Northern Lights. The camp, the shore, the icebergs in the bay—all were bathed in that wondrous pale green light. I no longer find them intimidating. They're reassuring. After all, they're merely a physical phenomenon: the result of particles from solar flares bombarding the atmosphere.

The dogs bounded up to greet me—they're taking to their new-found freedom wonderfully well—and I fed them some brandy balls. Then, whistling through my teeth (shades of Algie!), I trudged to the Stevenson screen. Isaak came with me and I gave him some butterscotch. He came back with me, too, and we followed the guide rope to the radio masts, then looped behind the cabin. We'd turned the corner past the outhouse and were heading for the porch when something brought me up short.

Surely the bear post was slightly closer than before?

Isaak nosed my thigh, wondering why I'd stopped. I ignored him and took out my torch. He looked up at me and doubtfully wagged his tail. Emboldened by his presence, I walked to the north window, then turned and paced from there to the bear post and back. Two and a half paces. Only two and a half. Before, it was three.

Unless I'd unwittingly lengthened my stride, which is perfectly possible. But I couldn't bring myself to try again.

Back in the cabin, I had a stiff drink, a couple of cigarettes, and a stern talk with myself. Logs don't move on their own. The fact that the bear post appeared closer is because it was easier to see, and that's because of the Northern Lights. My conscious mind accepts this. But the deeper part wonders if I might be wrong.

3rd November

I have been letting that bloody thing get to me. It's got to stop.

Today was awful. When I wasn't peering through the window, I was telling myself not to look; which meant that even when I was doing something else it was constantly on my mind. It was so exhausting that after lunch I had to take a nap.

I woke at three, bleary and thick-headed. The first thing I did was drag myself to the window for another check.

I was about to peel back the curtain when I realised what I was doing. *Jack, if you keep on like this, you'll lose your mind.*

'I'm not having this!' I shouted. 'I'm not having it!'

Dragging on my clothes, I grabbed a torch and an axe and flung myself out into the dark.

The dogs surged about me, sensing that something was up.

'I'm not having it,' I panted. I kept saying it over and over, like a protective charm, as I swung the axe and chopped the bloody thing down. The post was hard as granite. It didn't want to be chopped down. The dogs stood behind me in a huddle, silent for once. When at last the post groaned and crashed into the snow, they raced off with their tails between their legs.

Panting, chest heaving, I hacked the wretched thing to chunks. I left them lying in the snow. There. That's one lot of driftwood I won't be adding to the woodpile.

I've just looked out of the north window. Good. Very good. Nothing but a snowy curve down to the sea. I can't even see the pieces. And it's begun to snow, so soon they'll be obliterated. It'll be as if that post never existed. I should have done this weeks ago. I can't imagine why I didn't.

Later

THE STORM BLEW UP an hour after I chopped down the post. Thick snow whirling, wind howling and rapping at the windows.

My first thought was that I'd summoned it: I'd loosed the demon of the storm. Good old cause and effect, the human instinct to jump to conclusions. It's nice to know that my powers of reasoning aren't much better than those of a savage.

My next thought was the dogs. The storm could last a while. What do I do? I can't bring them inside: they'd wreck the place. I'd better feed them now, before it gets any worse. As for water, they'll have to make do with snow.

We keep the dog food in the roof space above the hall, where the seal meat stays frozen. Thanks to Algie, there's plenty of that, as well as crates and crates of dog pemmican. Cramming hunks of seal meat in a sack, I opened the door—and the wind hit me like a fist. Bent double, I battled along the boardwalk, the wind screaming in my ears and tearing at my clothes. Through the slit of the doghouse doorway, my torchlight revealed that the dogs seemed unfazed by the storm, and delighted at their early meal.

Fuel, I thought as I struggled back. Logs and a drum of paraffin.

It took hours to drag it all into the hall. Then I had to clear away the snow that had found its way in, too.

It's nearly midnight, and still the blizzard is battering the cabin, flinging snow at the windows like pebbles, and moaning in the stovepipe. God, I hope the roof stays on. I hope the windows hold. The shutters are in the emergency store at the other end of the bay. Might as well be in Timbuktu.

But, in a strange way, I welcome the storm. It's a known, physical force: a rush of snow-laden air, generated by pressure differentials. These are things I can understand. And it's better than the stillness.

6th November

Three days and no let-up. The din is indescribable. I'm finding it rather tiring. Even when I'm asleep. I can understand why the Vikings believed in storm giants. I keep having to remind myself that there is no intention behind this. It feels so angry. As if it wants to tear apart the cabin and carry me off into the night.

Reaching the Stevenson screen is out of the question, but I've kept up my contact with Ohlsen on Bear Island (thank God the wireless masts have held firm). In my transmissions I affect the calm of a seasoned old campaigner: IT'S A BIG ONE STOP SNOW UP TO WINDOWS STOP TIME TO CATCH UP ON MY READING

I exchange messages with Algie and, through him, with Gus. BIT OF A BLOW STOP SCREEN MUST TAKE ITS CHANCES STOP AT LEAST IS KEEPING BAY FREE OF ICE STOP DOGS FINE STOP I THINK THEY LIKE IT

Algie's replies are jaunty and Boy Scoutish: JOLLY GOOD SHOW JACK STOP WE KNOW IT TAKES MORE THAN A BIT OF A BREEZE TO SHAKE YOUR NERVE

You're right about that, Algie old chap. Unlike you, I'm not one to get in a blue funk because of a few bad dreams.

CLINGING TO MY ROUTINE, I take my walks inside the cabin, making careful circuits about the main room and berating myself if I lose count and have to start all over again. Which I often do.

I try once a day to take food to the dogs but, in reality, it's more like every other day, so I give them lots to make up for it. Each time I have to chop away the wind-packed snow blocking their doorway.

To think there was a time when I actually liked snow. It's horrible. Stinging your eyes. Blinding you, leading you astray. Each time I open the door, I let in a whirlwind and have to spend ages clearing it up (I admit that this helps keep the water barrel full). And still the snow finds its way in, sifting under doors and through hidden cracks I never knew existed.

Frost is beginning to crust the inside walls of the cabin and gather under the bunks. You wouldn't think it could get as far as the main room, but it does. I spend hours scraping it off. Mopping up damp, and drying towels over the stove.

To cheer myself up, I flouted my ration plan this evening and put our Christmas bottles of champagne to cool in the porch.

To cool? Jack, have you gone daft?

Both bottles froze within minutes, and burst with a sound like a rifle report. I picked out the broken glass and salvaged what I could: a large bowl of frozen mush. I've been eating it with a spoon. It's delicious. Bit strong, though. Whoops. Jack, you're drunk. Or 'tipsy', as Gus would say. Off to bed with you.

8th November

Six days and still blowing. Four days to go till Gus and Algie get back. Although that's only my guess and Algie did say 'at least' two weeks. weeks. And if the storm keeps up, they won't even set out.

That champagne was too much for me: I went down like a stunned ox. Bit of a sick headache this morning, but Algie's Effervescing Morning Powder put me to rights.

You're prevaricating, Jack. Out with it.

As soon as I got up, I went to the north window and peered into the swirling grey. The bear post was back. Feverishly I rubbed my breath off the glass. There it was. Straight. Tall. Not possible. You chopped it down. You hacked it to pieces with an axe. The storm must have thrown up another log from the shore. But then why does it stand so upright and still? And isn't it closer than before, and a little to the right? Nearer the porch?

A gust of extraordinary violence struck the window, and I drew back. When I looked again, the post was gone. All I saw was snow, twisting in columns in the screaming wind. There was no post. There never was a post.

That was five hours ago. Since then I've managed to get a sack of seal meat to the dogs. I've told Bear Island that I'm fine. I've eaten a tin of boiled mutton and another of pears. And I've smoked a whole packet of Player's.

I've also flicked through this journal, which was a mistake. I'm shocked at how my handwriting's degenerated from a neat copperplate into a spidery scrawl. Without reading a word, you can see the fear.

When the storm blew up, I wrote that I welcomed it. All that stuff about pressure differentials and things I can understand. But it's not true. The constant din, the screaming fury . . . It's wearing me down. Grinding away my defences.

9th November

I woke to silence. Unbroken, unbelievable silence. Not a whisper of wind disturbing the peace.

The blanket over the bunkroom window had come down, and I was lying in moonlight. The windowpanes were silver squares criss-crossed with black. Putting out my hand, I felt the light seeping into my skin. I was an underwater swimmer, floating in light. Beautiful, beautiful light. I was so grateful I wanted to cry.

At last, disentangling myself from my sleeping bag, I pulled on my clothes and padded to the window. There before me hung the full moon: huge, shining, golden. Every detail of camp lay sparklingly revealed. Where the bear post had been, I saw only a gentle curve of snow.

Like a recovering invalid, I shuffled about the cabin, tearing down blankets to let in the moon. I got the stove going. I didn't light any lamps. I didn't want anything to diminish that miraculous light.

Soon I would go out and tend to the dogs and see if the Stevenson screen was still there, but not yet. The moon drew me. I wanted to gaze and gaze. I hated to waste a moment.

At the north window, I cupped my hands to a pane and peered out.

The storm had cleared the ice from the bay. The moon cast a path of beaten silver over the sea, leading away from Gruhuken. 'Beautiful,' I murmured. 'Beautiful . . .'

I watched it rise higher, watched it gradually change from gold to silver, losing none of its brilliance. My breath misted the pane. I cleared it with my sleeve. When I looked again, a thin haze of cloud had dimmed the moon to inky blue.

At that moment, I sensed I was not alone.

With my nose pressed to the window, I felt horribly vulnerable, but I just couldn't pull away. I had to look.

Where the bear post had been, a figure was standing.

Around it the snow glimmered faintly; but no light touched what faced me. It cast no shadow.

It stood utterly still, watching me. In one appalling heartbeat I took in its wet, round head and its arms hanging at its sides, one shoulder higher than the other. I felt its will coming at me in waves. Intense, unwavering, malign. Such malevolence. No mercy. No humanity. It belonged to the dark beyond humanity. It was rage without end.

And still I pressed my hands against the pane. I couldn't pull away. A dreadful communion.

I don't know how long I stood there. At last I had to breathe, and the pane misted over. When I'd cleared it, the figure was gone.

I ran to the west window and peered out. Nothing. The radio masts mocked my terror. I ran to the bunkroom window. Again, nothing. I ran back into the main room and halted to listen. All I heard was the painful thudding of my heart.

The clouds had cleared, and once again the moon shone bright. The snow in front of the cabin was smooth. Innocent. Nothing to show that something had stood there. But it had. It had. I had felt its will. Its malevolence beating at me.

At me.

I've been wrong, wrong, wrong.

This is no echo.

I STOOD THREE FEET from the window, staring at my reflection in the pane. If only I could believe that what I'd seen had been myself. But when you see yourself in a dark window, you see your own face and build. What I'd seen had had no unkempt beard, no wild hair sticking up all over its head. It had had no face.

What is it? What does it want? Why is it angry with me? Is it because I destroyed the hut? What can I do to appease it?

Behind me, a crackle of static. The lights of the Eddystone receiver flickered to life. I must have switched it on as I hurried about taking down blankets from the windows, although I didn't remember. And yet there it was. A transmission.

My knees buckled. *A transmission*. Was that what I'd just experienced? Something forcing its way through, like blood staining a bandage?

From the doghouse came urgent yowls. *The storm's over! We're hungry!* In a cracked voice I called to them that I was coming soon.

Once again, tatters of inky cloud were drifting towards the moon, like a hand reaching to cover it.

Without taking my eyes from that bright, bruised face, I put on the headphones and grabbed my notepad. I had to keep watching the moon. If I didn't, clouds would hide it again and then . . .

GUS HERE

Gus?

Apparently against doctor's orders, he'd made Algie take him to the wireless station.

My hand shook as I tapped an inadequate reply: HOW ARE YOU

SORE BORED CROSS HOW ARE YOU

FINE

REALLY

My finger paused on the key. YES REALLY I replied. BAD DREAMS BUT BETTER NOW

The answer came in a swift staccato rattle: JACK ARE YOU ALL RIGHT STOP MR E IS HERE STOP CAN FETCH YOU IN TWO DAYS

NO AM FINE STOP STORM LONG BUT FINE NOW

Why did I say that? Why not, YES COME QUICK I CAN'T BEAR IT

Because it was Gus at the other end. Gus, the golden-haired prefect whom Jack the eager schoolboy is so desperate to impress.

JACK YOU'RE AMAZING STOP AM SO TERRIBLY GRATEFUL STOP EXPEDITION SCUPPERED WITHOUT YOU

I flushed with pleasure. Gus knew what I was braving to be here on my own; he knew what he owed me. I basked in his gratitude and admiration.

Now he was asking about the dogs.

DOGS SPLENDID, I replied. AM V GLAD HAVE THEM ESP ISAAK RIPPING HOUND

As I tapped out my message, my eyes began to sting. It was so wonderful talking to Gus, but it hurt. It made me miss him even more.

JACK YOU MUFF I KNEW YOU LIKED THEM
   YES
   IDIOT
   YES

I sat there grinning through my tears. It felt so good to have him tease me. So normal and warm and human.

On and on we talked, inconsequential chat, but everything to me. At last he said he had to go. I couldn't think of anything to delay him, so we agreed when next to speak, and said our goodbyes.

I switched off the receiver. Talking to him made me even more sharply aware of my isolation, but it also gave me strength. I was no longer the frightened obsessive who'd cowered in the storm and fought an illusory battle with a log. I was Jack Miller, the man who's keeping the 1937 Spitsbergen Expedition alive against all the odds.

I sat straighter. Looking round, I took satisfaction in the cabin's every mundane detail. The orderly tins of powdered egg and breakfast cocoa on the kitchen shelves. The clean steel lines of the bicycle generator. I felt the roughness of the table beneath my palms, I sniffed the familiar smells of paraffin, woodsmoke and unwashed clothes. This is my world. Modern. Practical. Real.

Realising I was ravenous, I tore open a bar of chocolate and wolfed it down. The sweetness burned my mouth; the rush of energy made me giddy. I brewed coffee and gulped two scalding mugs. I made a vast bowl of scrambled eggs with sausages and cheese. I lit lamps and tuned the wireless to the BBC.

Just now, I went to the bunkroom window. The sea is black and dotted with icebergs, but they're few and far between. I was right: the storm has kept the bay open. The dogs have dug their way out of the doghouse and are bounding about in the snow. Near the cabin, the drifts are almost to the window, but a few yards off it's shallower, and their paws don't sink in too far. When they saw me, they lashed their tails and yowled at me to come out. They wouldn't do that if there was anything there. Animals sense these things, don't they?

But it will be back. I know this. I carry that knowledge inside me like a stone. What does it want? What terrible thing happened here to make it haunt with such malevolence?

Later

I CAN'T BELIEVE I was so stupid. When I was 'talking' to Gus, I was so overwhelmed that I forgot to ask the all-important question: when are you coming back? Why didn't he say anything of his own accord?

The 12th of November. By my calculation, that's the soonest they'll arrive. It's three days away. But surely if they'd been about to set off, Gus would have said something. What isn't he telling me? How much longer have I got to hold on?

I have to go out again.

The sky is clear. There's no cloud to cover the moon.

10th November

Yesterday feels like a million years ago. I remember nerving myself, with a shot of whisky and a cigarette, to go outside. Then opening the door to a wall of snow.

I was relieved. Here was a physical task I could cope with.

The dogs heard me digging and set up an impatient clamour. I hacked my way though and they fell on me, lots of eager muzzles and flailing paws.

When at last I could look about me, I found Gruhuken transformed. The moon shone almost as bright as day. The snow was dazzling. Around me the camp lay radiant and serene. I felt not a trace of dread. No taint of that malign presence. The moon had banished it. Whatever had come in the dark couldn't harm me in the light.

I worked for hours. First, I fetched tin after tin of pemmican for the dogs. Then I cleared the boardwalk and shovelled a path round the back of the cabin, another to the emergency store, and one to the Stevenson screen. The luxury of working in light! And the moon stayed with me all the time. Gruhuken is so far north that when the moon is full, it doesn't set, but circles endlessly in the sky, so that you never lose sight of it. It's a miracle. A gift from the gods. Whenever you look up, there it is, watching over you.

I cleared the Stevenson screen and the other instruments, and collected my first set of data since the storm. I transmitted it to Bear Island. I got the

Austin going and sent a report to England (I'd skipped that during the storm). Then I went and stood in front of the porch and smoked a cigarette, like a settler in the old American West, surveying his homestead. I had regained possession of my camp.

The dogs had been playing on the shore but, suddenly, Upik skittered to a halt and pricked up her ears. One by one, the others did the same. Had they caught the scent of a bear? I was about to fetch my gun when Svarten gave a low bark and hurtled west. The rest of the pack raced after him.

As the patter of paws receded, I heard what they had heard: a scraping sound, echoing in the stillness. Scrape . . . scrape . . . scrape . . . Regular, long drawn out. But this was utterly different from the sound I'd heard at the bear post. This sound belonged to my world.

The dogs came rushing back, their eyes bright with excitement. Behind them, grey against the snow, I made out the figure of a man.

My heart leapt. That's a cliché, but it really did leap as I watched him approach, his arms and legs moving in a slow, sure rhythm as he skied.

Waving, I ran to meet him. 'Hulloa there! Over here!'

A stocky figure in a sheepskin coat, he wore huge fur mittens, canvas boots, a shapeless fur cap. Beneath it I saw a frost-crusted beard and a walrus moustache, bristling brows and small, bright eyes.

I was grinning like a madman, but I couldn't stop. 'Trapper Bjørvik, I presume? Welcome! You are most, most welcome!'

My visitor leaned on his ski poles in a haze of frosty breath. '*Ja,*' he said, drawing off one mitten and taking my hand in a crushing grip. 'Bjørvik.'

Later

I MADE a complete fool of myself.

I gushed, I babbled, I pawed. He was good enough not to mind, or at least not to show it. With the unpretentious formality that's so endearing in Scandinavians, he presented me with his 'visiting gift': a sack of reindeer hearts, ptarmigan livers and other choice cuts, which—with his rucksack, sleeping bag and rifle—he had carried on his back the twenty miles from his cabin.

He didn't say why he'd come, or how long he meant to stay, and I didn't ask. Eriksson once told me that in Spitsbergen you tend not to ask; you simply assume that your guest will stay for at least a week, and that his purpose is simply to visit.

'I know I'm talking too much,' I blurted out as we took off our things in the porch, 'but I've been alone for nearly three weeks.' I flushed. It occurred to me that Bjørvik must have been on his own for months.

'*Ja*,' he grunted, pulling off his boots. 'Is good to visit.'

His boots were 'trapper's boots': a double thickness of canvas with a rubber sole, worn over two pairs of socks, and stuffed with straw. He wore the blue drill overalls of a sealer, with a heavy sweater of undyed wool that smelt powerfully of sheep.

Flustered, I invited him to sit down, then bustled about lighting lamps, getting the stove going, making coffee. He planted his red hands on his knees and stared about him.

I found music on the wireless. I put together an enormous meal: tinned stewed veal and spinach, eggs, bacon, cheese, oatcakes, tinned cherries with condensed milk, peanut brittle, and everything else I could think of. To hell with my ration plan. This man had skied twenty miles to see me.

We ate in bashful silence. At least, I was abashed, as my conversational sallies had met with monosyllables. But Bjørvik told me later that he was simply absorbed in listening to Ivor Novello on the wireless. He doesn't own a radio, and it's been two years since he heard music.

After we'd eaten, I offered whisky and tobacco. Declining the whisky with grave dignity, he filled his pipe. By this time I'd stopped worrying about the monosyllables. I've never enjoyed a smoke as much as I did then.

Ivor Novello gave way to the news programme, and I lowered the volume a little.

'Is good,' said Bjørvik with his slow nod.

Resisting the temptation to nod back, in case he mistook it for mimicry, I agreed that it was very good; although I didn't know if he meant the food, music, tobacco or me.

I said, 'You know, in England, I used to prefer being on my own. Now I think the best thing in life is having a visitor.'

Beneath his brows, his eyes glinted. Slapping his knee, he barked a laugh. '*Ja*! Is good!'

I'm writing this in my bunk. Bjørvik is in Algie's, the bottom one nearest the window. He's snoring softly: a wondrous sound.

I'm not alone any more.

To see the cabin windows aglow when I come in, to feel the warmth of a well-stoked stove. And when I'm inside, to hear his tread on the boardwalk, his whistling as he chops wood and fetches ice from the stream. Yesterday feels like a million years ago.

Ja. Is good.

12th November

Two days have flown by. Yesterday I had a transmission from Algie. He said all's fine, but it'll be 'a few days' before they set off. I can cope with that now because I'm not alone. No one could have a better, kinder, easier house guest. In many ways, Bjørvik reminds me of Eriksson. The same rugged face, which at times undergoes a seismic shift as an earthquake of laughter rumbles to the surface. The same half-humorous, half-admiring respect for young English 'yentlemen' with their passion for the weather. The same avuncular protectiveness, as if I were a talented but ignorant nephew who must be watched lest he blunder. I call him 'Mister Bjørvik' and he calls me 'Mister Yack'.

We eat our main meal at two. After that we play cards or listen to the wireless—but never at the same time, as he thinks that's disrespectful to the BBC. At eight we eat a simple supper of eggs and bacon, and at half past nine he bids me good night and turns in, while I sit up, relishing the security.

He's used to plain food, mostly seal and reindeer (he calls it all 'beef'); flour bannocks, blubber, dried apricots, and gallons of coffee. It delights me to treat him to tinned mutton and pork, Australian fruit salad, tinned vegetables, Digestive biscuits and chocolate. Yesterday he shot a reindeer (he calmly ignores their protected status) and we had huge, succulent steaks and blood pancakes—which are delicious. You don't taste the blood.

My favourite time is after supper. I read and smoke, and he smokes and carves: a pair of clogs for the cold weather to come; an antler sheath for his knife. He's devouring Algie's crime novels, and is particularly fond of Edgar Wallace.

Several times an hour, I go to the window and check the sky for clouds.

I know it's silly, but I can't help myself. I resent the least haze obscuring the moon. And it happens so suddenly: one moment you're looking at that bright, pure disc; the next it's gone, swallowed by inky darkness. I thought Bjørvik would laugh at my anxiety, but he doesn't even smile. I get the sense that he understands exactly why I need the light.

I haven't mentioned the haunting, and he hasn't spoken of it, but I'm sure that he knows. He tells me he's been hunting here for years. Once, when I asked if he's ever experienced *rar*, he gave me a wary look and said he's never had any 'trouble' on his stretch of the coast. And this evening when I said that I prefer this wind we're having to 'the dead stillness', he said, '*Ja*. The stillness. When you hear yourself blink. Is terrible.'

Later he asked about the bear post, and when I told him I'd cut it down, he frowned.

That was my chance. I should have said something. Why didn't I?

Because I'm afraid that if I talk of it, I might somehow invoke it. Back in August, at 'first dark', Eriksson asked if I'd spoken to it. I understand now why he thought that was important. For the same reason, I don't want to mention it to Bjørvik; because I feel that if I did, I'd be inviting it in.

Besides, with any luck I won't need to. If all goes well and the sea stays clear, Gus and Algie will be back before Bjørvik leaves.

14th November

A storm blew up after I wrote that: a north wind from the Pole. It's over now, but this morning the sky was so overcast that I couldn't see the moon—and the bay was full of ice.

I was horrified. The sea was gone. In its place were huge chaotic slabs and tilting pinnacles, like some fantastic frozen city. I couldn't believe it. The pack ice isn't supposed to arrive until after New Year.

When I said so to Bjørvik, he barked a laugh. '*Nej, nej*, Mister Yack, this is not pack ice! That come in *Januar*, and you will know it. You will see the *islyning*, the ice blink, when it throw the light in the sky. This is just drift ice from the storm. Very dangery. You stay off it, Mister Yack. But don't worry, soon the wind change and the ice it clear.'

He was right, of course. The wind has changed, and already it's blowing the ice out to sea.

I wish I knew as much as Bjørvik. Maybe then I'd be able to cope with this place.

He leads a life of unimaginable solitude. His main cabin is on Wijdefjorden, but he's built four smaller ones a few days' walk away, with scores of fox traps and self-shooting bear traps in between. He baits his fox traps with sea bird heads, his bear traps with seal blubber, and checks them every fortnight. He wouldn't have had time to visit me if it hadn't been for the storm. It brought the deep snow, and foxes avoid that as they fear becoming trapped in drifts, and eaten by bears.

He says that over-hunting has made the catch worse than it used to be. Last winter he only caught twelve foxes and two bears; although he got a decent price for the furs, and a chemist in Tromsø gave him twenty-four krøner for the bears' gall bladders, which are a cure for rheumatism.

I find it odd that he can speak of those awe-inspiring bears and beautiful little foxes as if they were no more than animated furs; and yet he tamed an orphaned cub as a *husrev* (a 'house fox'), and grieved when it sickened and died. I suppose he's too poor to be sentimental about animals. That's a privilege only the middle classes can afford. I suspect he deplores my lavishing butterscotch on Isaak, although he's too polite to show it. He certainly disapproves of the dogs running wild. (To placate him I've reverted to staking them by 'day' and shutting them up at night, which they hate.)

I wish I knew why he always hunts alone, but he hasn't said, and I won't ask. Once, though, he let slip that when he was young, he wasn't 'God's best disciple'. And from other things, I gather that there are aspects of his past that he regrets.

The sky is clear again and the moon is back—although I'm alarmed to see how much it's waned. It changes all the time. Sometimes it's pale gold, sometimes blue-white. Sometimes it's in a greyish halo, edged faintly with red. But in fact it's not any of those colours: it's some moon colour I can't describe. Or perhaps it's no colour at all; perhaps the light isn't strong enough to allow my eyes to see in colour, so that what I'm seeing is the world in black and white, as Isaak sees it.

And why do I even try to describe the colours? Is it the human compulsion to name things, to assert control? Perhaps the same compulsion drives our meteorology: all that observing, measuring, recording. Trying to render bearable this vast, silent land.

And is that, too, why I've been writing this journal? To set down everything clearly, make sense of it? If it can be described, it can be understood. If it can be understood, it need not be feared.

If I was a different kind of man, I might be doing this to leave a record behind as a warning to others, in case something happens to me. But I'm not unselfish enough for that. I don't care what happens after I'm dead.

Later

THAT WAS A DIGRESSION, but it did help clarify my thoughts.

I know that Gruhuken is haunted. I know this. Some angry spirit walks this place. It is not an echo. It has intent. It wishes me ill. And I don't know how to appease it, because I don't know who—what—it is. Or what it wants.

Bjørvik knows something. I'm sure of it. I have to make him tell me. And I can't put it off any longer. Soon he'll leave. He's been away nearly a week; he has to check his traps. I've thought about going with him. But we couldn't take the dogs: they'd scare away the foxes and ruin his livelihood. And I can't leave them, I can't shoot them, I can't let the expedition fail. Same old arguments.

I can't put it off any longer. I have to talk to Bjørvik. He has to tell me what he knows.

16th November

Bjørvik is leaving tomorrow. He asked me to go with him. It was after supper; we were on our second mugs of coffee.

'Mister Yack. When I go, you come too, *ja*? You bring the dogs. You stay with me.'

It touched me deeply that he offered to take the dogs as well, but I also found it alarming. What danger does he think I'm in that he'd risk his livelihood to help me?

For one crazy moment, I nearly said yes. But I can't do that to him. And

I can't break faith with Gus. That's what it comes down to. I keep picturing what it'll be like when he gets back. His blue eyes shining with gratitude and admiration. *You did it, Jack. I didn't think anyone could, but you pulled it off!*

Which is why, when Bjørvik asked me to go with him, I said no.

As I was trying to explain my reasons, it suddenly occurred to me that this was the third time I've refused an offer to leave Gruhuken. First Eriksson, then Gus, now Bjørvik. There's a horrible symmetry to that. In fairy tales, don't things always come in threes? And in the Bible? *Three times before the cock crows . . .*

After I'd finished, Bjørvik said simply, 'But Mister Yack. Your friends. How long till they come?'

'Not long. Three days at the most. They're wiring me tomorrow morning to finalise things.'

He didn't reply.

I fetched the coffee pot and refilled our mugs. I sat down and met his eyes and said, 'Gruhuken is haunted.'

His gaze never left my face. '*Ja.*'

'Tell me,' I said. 'Tell me what haunts this place.'

He took a pull at his coffee and set down his mug. 'Is not good to talk of this, Mister Yack. There are things in the world we don't understand. Is best to leave it like this.'

'Mister Bjørvik. Please. I have to know.'

He was silent for a long time, staring into the stove's red heart. 'Nobody knew his name,' he said. 'A trapper. Men called him bad names. He never seemed to hear.'

I stared at him. 'You—knew him?'

'Nobody *knew* him. Once, when I was young, I saw him. In Longyearbyen, twenty-six, twenty-seven year ago.' He grimaced. 'When he was alive.'

I swallowed. 'So this was—1910, or thereabouts? Before the War.'

'*Ja.* It all happen before the War.'

What he told me then came out in fits and starts, with long silences in between. Nobody knew where the trapper had come from. The wilds of north Norway. Somewhere poor. He worked his way to Spitsbergen on a whaling ship. He was ugly, and he had that abject manner which brings out the worst in people, particularly men. They gave him the filthiest, most degrading tasks. That was all it took: nothing more than an abject manner and ill-favoured looks. Bjørvik called him something in Norwegian; I think it means 'God-forgotten'. One of life's rejects.

At Longyearbyen he tried to get a place in the mines, but he wasn't strong enough, so they wouldn't take him. He tried selling fossils to tourists, but his appearance affronted them. Somehow he got work on a sealer, and found his way to an isolated bay in the north. There he built a driftwood hut and took to fur trapping.

For a few years he lived there on his own. Every summer, he would turn up in Longyearbyen to sell his skins and pick up supplies. He couldn't read and he'd never handled money, so people cheated him. After a few days he was gone again, back to the one place where no one set the dogs on him and called him names. Gruhuken.

A mining syndicate took it from him. In this whole vast wilderness they had to have this one lonely bay. They'd found coal here. They staked their claim and threw him out.

'I don't understand,' I said. 'We found their claim sign. The Edinburgh Prospecting Company, something like that, but it was dated 1905. Wasn't that before he got here?'

'Ja, for sure. But, Mister Yack, those signs, they say what they want.'

'You mean—they backdated their claim? Wasn't that illegal?'

He snorted. 'This was no-man's-land! No law! They do what they like! He was one, they were many. They throw him out.'

'And then?'

He chewed his moustache. 'He came back . . . They say they sent him on his way again. They say they never saw him again.'

'"They say". You mean it wasn't like that?'

His gaze slid to the fire. 'I don't know. After that, nobody saw him. Alive.'

'But—you know something. Don't you?'

He shifted uncomfortably. 'When miners have money, Mister Yack, they drink. When they drink, they talk. In those days, I drink too. One night I am in the bar in Longyearbyen . . .' He broke off.

'And they were there? The miners from Gruhuken?'

'One only. By then the others were dead.'

'And this miner, he talked and you overheard?'

He glared at me. 'He was drinking himself to death. He made no sense.'

'But you guessed. What did they do to him, the trapper of Gruhuken? Tell me what you think happened.'

He rubbed a hand over his face. 'I think—I think when he came back—they were angry. I think at first they want just to beat him. Then it turn into something else.' He swallowed.

After that, there wasn't much to tell. The mine limped on for another year, he said, but it was dogged by misfortune. A cable severed a man's leg and he bled to death. A boat overturned, drowning two men within sight of the shore. Finally, a rockslide destroyed the cabins, and the surviving miners left. The following year, the prospecting company decided that the deposit wasn't rich enough after all, and abandoned the mine.

Gruhuken stood deserted. It swiftly gained a bad reputation. People who camped here met with accidents. Fire. Drowning. A Swedish trapper shot his companion and then himself. The note on the body said he'd done it to escape the *genga °nger*—'the one who walks again'.

There Bjørvik's account ended. But I know the rest of the story. For over two decades, Gruhuken remained deserted. Then, in 1935, topographers from Oxford University surveyed this stretch of coast and mentioned this bay as a likely site for future expeditions. Shortly afterwards, Gus Balfour read their report and put Gruhuken at the top of his list.

The lamp had burned out. I refilled it and replaced it on the table. The smell of paraffin made me sick.

Bjørvik sat with his hands on his knees, staring at the floor.

I'd intended to tell him what I've experienced here, but I couldn't bring myself to do it. And he didn't want to know.

I asked if he'd ever been to Gruhuken before now, and he said no, he's never hunted within ten miles of the bay. I asked if he'd experienced anything untoward while he's been here. He said his dreams have been 'bad'. Only his dreams? I envy him that.

Again I went to the window. I couldn't see the moon. A wind was blowing from the east, sending fingers of snow across the shore. I turned back to Bjørvik. 'What does it want?'

He spread his hands.

I understood. It wants Gruhuken.

And I'm in the way.

17th November

I should have gone with him. But I was so sure that Gus and Algie would be back in a day or so. Convinced that I could hold out until then.

My hands are sweating. My fingers keep slipping on the pen. Why didn't I go with him? He left nearly three hours ago, just after breakfast. Although the moon is in its last quarter, the Northern Lights were bright, and he said he'd have plenty of light for skiing. He didn't repeat his offer to take me in, and I knew that since we'd spoken of the haunting, he couldn't wait to leave. I was right about that; talking has brought it closer.

I gave him a parting gift: as much bacon as he can carry, a packet of our best Virginia tobacco, and the four Edgar Wallace's he hasn't yet read. He was pleased. So at least I got that right.

The last thing he said before he left was to be sure to keep the dogs close.

AT FIRST I didn't feel too bad about being on my own again. Then an hour later I 'spoke' to Algie.

I'd expected it to be Gus. I'd been looking forward to it. But it turns out that Gus has had some kind of setback. Algie swears he's not in danger, and I don't think he'd lie about that. But it means they can't set out yet.

SORRY JACK A WEEK TILL WE CAN LEAVE SORRY

I was in shock. I couldn't take it in. Numbly, I sent back an acknowledgement. THAT'S OK STOP TELL GUS GET BETTER SOON

OK? How is it OK? A week till they leave means maybe nine days before they get here. That's nearly December. How can I hope that the coast will be clear of ice? I could be stuck here till spring. I'll never make it.

When I got the transmission, I thought about going after Bjørvik. To hell with everything; just strap on your skis and get out of here. But by then he'd had two hours' start on me. And I don't know where his camp is. It isn't on the map. All I know is that it's somewhere on the far side of Wijdefjorden, which is vast. I even thought of tracking him. But the wind has obliterated his trail.

My wristwatch has stopped, but according to Gus's clock, it's eleven in the 'morning'. Another hour until I have to go outside and do the readings.

Yes, we're back to that again. Back to bolstering your courage with whisky and cigarettes. Back to bribing the dogs with sweets to keep them with you. Back to watching the sky for the least trace of cloud.

I keep wondering what they did to him, the trapper of Gruhuken. I think of that miner I saw at Longyearbyen. Men who are like that—when they know they won't be found out—they will do anything.

I remember the malevolence of that figure in front of the cabin. The endless, black, inhuman rage. How can I hold out for another week?

Later

I HAD A MASSIVE DRINK and a stiff talk with myself, and I feel a little steadier. What you've got to remember, Jack, is that it can't *do* anything to you. That's what I keep coming back to. That's why I still cling to the hope that I can hang on here until the others arrive.

What haunts this place is merely *spirit*. It is not *matter*. Not as I am matter, not as this pen and notebook and table are matter.

It can't hurt me. All it can do is frighten.

18th November

I knew things would change, but I didn't expect it to happen so quickly, and I never thought it would involve the dogs.

It's as if Bjørvik's visit never took place. The moon has waned. It's just a slit in the sky. The dark is back.

Yesterday, after Bjørvik left, I made a titanic effort to absorb the shock about Gus and Algie. I mustered my courage and did my work. I prepared food and forced it down. As I went about my duties, I experienced nothing untoward. No presence. No dread. Only a shrinking inside me: the apprehension of what might come.

By half-past six I had fed the dogs and was facing my first evening alone. I wasn't hungry and, although I was tired, I knew I wouldn't sleep, so I did what I've never done before and won't do again: I knocked myself out with morphine.

I slept for twelve hours and woke ten minutes before the 7 a.m. readings.

Afterwards, I was on the bicycle generator, about to start transmitting, when I remembered I hadn't let out the dogs—or rather, they reminded me with indignant complaints from the doghouse. As I was already late for Bear Island, I shouted to them to wait, and set to work. At one point I think I was aware that their howls became louder, then abruptly ceased. Or maybe that's my imagination, adding details in retrospect.

When I got outside, the doghouse door was open and they were gone.

I waved my lantern. 'Isaak! Kiawak! Upik! Jens! Eli! Svarten! Pakomi! Anadark! *Isaak*!'

Nothing.

It's not like them. They've never strayed, not even into the next bay. Huskies don't. At least, ours don't. And they always come when I call, as they know that I mean food.

That was twelve hours ago.

How did they get out? What were they trying to escape? What happened to them?

I've left food for them in front of the cabin, and wedged open the doghouse door, with more food inside. I know that risks attracting bears, but I don't care. I'll do anything to get them back.

And they will come back, won't they, when they're hungry? And since they're always hungry, they'll come back soon.

But what if they don't?

19th November

Two days since Bjørvik left. One since the dogs disappeared.

I miss the dogs. Without them, there's nothing between me and what haunts this place.

It can come at any time. It can stay away for days, as it did when Bjørvik was here. But always I sense it waiting. That's the worst of it. Not knowing when it will come. Only that it will.

A few years ago, I read a speech in the paper by the American President; he said: *The only thing we have to fear is fear itself.* He doesn't know. He doesn't know.

I've tried to pity the trapper of Gruhuken. He had a miserable life and a terrible death. But knowing who he was doesn't help me, because I can't do anything to appease him. It doesn't matter that I'm innocent. It isn't only the guilty who suffer. Besides, I am guilty. Because I'm here.

20th November

ISAAK IS BACK! I found him huddled against the door when I returned from the noon readings. He was in a terrible state, soaking wet and shaking with fright. I fell to my knees and flung my arms about him, 'Isaak, Isaak!' And still that convulsive shivering, panting with terror, his black lips drawn back, and a wildness in his eyes that I'd never seen before.

Where have you been? I wanted to ask. Tell me what you saw.

When I opened the door he was through it in a flash, scrabbling to get into the hall. Then he shot under my bunk and refused to come out.

All entreaties failed, but at last a chunk of butterscotch succeeded. I towelled him down and fed him a tin of pemmican, and gradually the shaking eased and he became more like himself. His fur fluffed up in the heat of the stove, his eyes lost their wildness. But when I rose to hang up the towel, he followed me anxiously, keeping so close to my heels that I nearly fell over.

'Don't worry, Isaak,' I told him. 'From now on you're staying in here with me. No more doghouse for you, my lad. You're safe.'

He watched my face, his ears twitching as he listened.

It's amazing how reassuring it is to have someone to soothe. It makes you so much braver and more resourceful. I suppose that's how parents feel. You've got to stay strong for the children.

'But the thing is,' I went on, 'if I left you free to roam around in here, you'd eat everything in sight. So I'm afraid I'm going to have to tie you up.'

To stop him chewing the rope, I soaked it thoroughly in paraffin. Then I tied one end to his harness and the other to the most immovable thing in the cabin: my bunk.

Of course, it didn't work. When I was out of sight in the main room, he set up a heart-rending yowl. And it turns out that he quite likes paraffin: he dispatched the rope in five minutes. So instead I dog-proofed the cabin as best I could, moving everything remotely chewable to the upper bunks and shelves. Then I scattered a few sticks of driftwood around as decoys and set him free.

Ignoring the driftwood, he burnt his nose on the stove, then rushed about, sniffing and lifting his leg whenever I couldn't stop him. Soon he began to pant alarmingly, and I realised he was hot. I gave him a bowl of water. He lapped desultorily and continued to pant. I fetched a big bowl of snow. Better. He snapped it up and the panting lessened. After that he found my reindeer hides, which I'd forgotten to move off my bunk, and settled down to eat them.

I'd been so busy that I missed the five o'clock readings and had to wire an excuse to Bear Island. I didn't care. It's wonderful having Isaak with me. To hear the click of his claws on the floor, to feel his cold nose nudging my palm. He's not house-trained—he's never been in a house—so I have to watch him constantly, and that's exactly what I need. Just now he started to squat, so I grabbed him by the harness and dragged him outside. I stood with my back to the door, like a suburban householder trying to persuade Fido to do his business. I felt no hint of the presence. Nor did Isaak show any signs of fear. The food I'd set out for the dogs was still there in the snow but, to my surprise, he ignored it. Instead, when he'd done what he needed, he trotted off a few paces and stood facing seawards, with the wind at his back. Then he lifted his muzzle and howled. I felt the hairs rise on the nape of my neck. Such loneliness. Such grief.

It didn't sound as if he was calling his pack. It sounded as if he knows they're never coming back.

21st November

He still howls for his pack, but he's becoming accustomed to being inside, and I no longer have to watch him all the time.

Nor do I need to worry about my wirelesses, because he never goes near that end of the cabin. He becomes agitated when I'm working there. Wise dog. I wish I could do as he does, and stay away.

This morning, I nearly missed my talk with Gus because of Isaak. I'd switched on the Eddystone, but Isaak was about to squat, so I'd taken him out, and when we got back inside, the lights were flickering.

I rushed to put on the headphones as I didn't want to miss a single one of those disembodied dits and dahs that are Gus's words coming through the ether.

JACK WHERE ARE YOU STOP ARE YOU OK

That he'd used an expression like 'OK' made me smile. It reminded me of one of our first conversations on board the *Isbjørn*, when I'd said 'OK' and he'd said 'grand', and I'd been so touchy. So I couldn't resist using his own word in reply. I'M GRAND STOP HOW ARE YOU

Being Gus, he got it at once. OH HA HA BUT I WAS WORRIED DOGS GONE BUT ISAAK HERE

WHAT WHAT

I told him about the dogs, and Isaak coming back. I explained that Bjørvik had left, although I didn't mention that he'd asked me to go with him and that I'd refused. Gus's anxiety crackled through the wires, and I basked in it.

JACK YOU ARE SO BRAVE STOP OUR EXPEDITION OWES ALL TO YOU

Yes, it bloody well does, I thought.

The silence after the noisy transmission was awful. The cabin looked smoke-stained and dirty. Everywhere I turned I saw Gus's possessions.

And around the table, five chairs. Five. A convocation of ghosts.

Then I spotted some scraps of reindeer hide on the floor, which Isaak had missed. I got down on hands and knees to pick them up, and he padded over to investigate, and I felt better.

I don't know what I'd do without him. I love the way he slumps down with a humph, and thumps his tail at my approach. I love it when he lies on his belly with his muzzle between his paws, and twitches his eyebrows to follow my every move. I love the leathery smell of his pads, and the croaky ror-ror-ror noises he makes when he's talking to me. His eyes are extraordinary. They're not ice blue as I used to think, but warm: the light, clear blue of a summer morning. I know that's ridiculously over the top, but it's true.

As I write, he's under the table, leaning against my calf. I reach down and sink my fingers into his fur. I feel the heat of his flank and his muscled ribs; the rapid beat of his heart.

I keep breaking off to talk to him. 'We won't be parted again, I promise.

When all this is over, you're coming home with me. To England, Isaak, that's where I live. I don't care how much it costs or how long it takes. People do keep huskies in England; Gus knows a family in Berkshire, they've got three. I'll get a job in the country. You'll like it there. And you'll love chasing rabbits. You've never seen a rabbit, but you'll know at once that it's got to be chased. You'll be good at it, too. And I'll find you a mate, and you'll father puppies. You can start your own pack.'

Isaak sits with his muzzle on my thigh, gazing up at me with his extraordinary eyes.

Later

THE SOUTH WIND is still blowing, breaking up the last of the ice. I can see the black water in the bay. I hold on to that. The bay is still open. They can still get back.

Somewhere on the outside of the cabin, a corner of tar-paper is flapping. A while ago I ventured out and tried to find it, but I couldn't. And I didn't try for very long.

Soon after I got back inside, Isaak became restless. Not playful or hungry or wanting to go out, though. He moved about, panting, but ignoring the bowl of snow in the bunkroom. His ears were back and his head was low. His eyes were glassy. He was afraid.

'Isaak?'

He ignored me.

I grabbed a lantern and a torch and stood in the middle of the room.

Isaak stopped a few feet from the north window. His hackles rose.

I held my breath, listening. My eyes darted from window to window.

Suddenly, Isaak shook himself. Then he turned to me and faintly wagged his tail.

I breathed out.

After that I couldn't face going outside, so I skipped the five o'clock readings and wired another excuse to Bear Island. I feel bad about that. I don't like to think that the rot is setting in. Tomorrow I'll get back to my routine.

My routine. I'm beginning to worry about time—that is, about being able to keep track of it. My wristwatch still won't work, and today I discovered that the Stevenson's self-timer has broken. This means that all I've got left to mark the time is Gus's alarm clock. Tomorrow, when I go outside for the readings, I'll take it with me in my pocket, wrapped in a muffler to protect it from the cold. For now, it sits on the table in the main room.

It's the only thing I've got left to tell me that the days are going by. There's no longer any twilight at midday, and the moon has dwindled to a lightless sliver. Tomorrow it will be gone.

Tomorrow it's the dark of the moon.

22nd November

Last night I learned what Bjørvik couldn't tell me. I learned what happened to the trapper of Gruhuken.

I sat up late, writing and talking to Isaak. Around eleven, I let him out, and when he came back inside I put a bowl of snow for him in the bunkroom and we settled down to sleep.

Cold outside, twenty-five below. Inside, our breath crusted the bunkroom walls with hoar frost. I couldn't get warm. I coaxed Isaak onto the bunk, but he soon jumped down. He curled up on the floor, but not for long. I couldn't tell if he'd caught the restlessness from me, or if he was sensing something.

Despite two sleeping bags and the remaining reindeer hides, I couldn't stop shivering. Eventually I went into the hall and unearthed our portable paraffin stove from beneath the dog harnesses and set it up in the bunkroom. Because of Isaak, this meant dragging the packing cases from the opposite wall and positioning the stove on top, where he couldn't knock it down.

Much better.

I dream I'm in a rowing boat with Gus. The swell rocks us gently. It's wonderfully peaceful. Together we peer over the side and watch the kelp swaying in the clear water.

The boat tilts slightly backwards, and I glance over my shoulder. A hand has risen from the sea to grasp the gunwale. I'm not frightened, merely determined. I won't let that thing haul itself out.

The dream shifts. Now I'm in the sea, deep down in blackness. Again

I'm not frightened, only disgusted. A drowned thing is clasping me in its arms. Together we roll in the slippery kelp. I feel its cheek pressed against mine, cold and soft as mouldering leather.

Now I'm tied to the bear post. Now I'm afraid. I can't see. I can't speak. I have no tongue. I smell paraffin. I hear the crackle of flames. I know that someone nearby is holding a torch.

Now I hear the clink of metal dragged over rocks. Dread squeezes my heart. It's coming closer. I can't get away. I'm bound hand and foot. Clink. Clink. Closer. The terror is overwhelming. It's coming for me. I can't move, I can't *move* . . .

With a cry I woke up.

Isaak nosed my face, his whiskers brushing my cheek. I lay gasping and shuddering, my heart pounding so hard that it hurt.

I was cold. My sleeping bag was damp. Putting out a hand, I felt the wall. Wet. It took me a moment to realise what had happened. The stove had melted the hoar frost.

The dream was still with me. I knew that the terror I had felt had not been my own. I thought of the blotchy stains on the bear post; the sound of metal dragged over rocks.

That's when I remembered the rusty relics that we found when we first came to Gruhuken. We buried them to make the place safe for the dogs: Wire. Gaffs. Knives. Big, rusty knives—the sort that you use once you've gaffed your seal and dragged it ashore.

Flensing knives.

I didn't make it to the slop pail. I vomited in the doorway till my belly ached. Then, shaky as an old man, I hobbled to the kitchen. I filled Isaak's bowl and set it down. I watched him sniff it. I scooped water into a mug and tried to drink. My teeth were chattering. I couldn't swallow.

I don't want to think about what they did to the trapper of Gruhuken. I don't want this in my head. It's two in the morning but I dread going back to sleep. If the dream came again . . .

So, instead, I'm going to deal with this hoar frost. Bjørvik told me a trick about that. You nail blankets to the walls and ceiling, and somehow that stops it collecting.

There. I've done it. I've lined the bunkroom with blankets. Having to concentrate on hammering in the nails has steadied me a bit.

Later

I THOUGHT IT wanted me gone, but now I know better.

I must have fallen asleep, because I woke huddled in my bunk. The window was a faint charcoal oblong in the dark. Isaak stood in the middle of the room. His hackles were up, his ears flat back.

Outside, by my head, a step on the boardwalk. A heavy, wet, irregular tread.

Sweat chilled my skin. I lay frozen, listening to the footsteps pass slowly down the boardwalk towards the front of the cabin. I groped in the bedclothes for my torch. Isaak came and leaned, shivering, against my bunk. I found my torch but didn't switch it on. I watched something dark move past the bunkroom window.

Clutching my torch like a talisman, I swung my legs over the side of the bunk. I stumbled into the main room. Isaak followed.

I dreaded hearing the steps halt at the porch, but they continued past as if it didn't exist. Feeling my way, I shuffled towards the north window. Nothing. I turned to the west window. There. Half seen at the edge. Something dark.

The steps on the boardwalk ceased.

I waited. Isaak stood behind me, panting with fear. My breath smoked. I began to shiver. Still I waited.

At last I couldn't stand it any longer, and went and huddled in my sleeping bag. Isaak crawled under my bunk.

I listened for an hour. It didn't come back.

For Isaak's sake, I decided to create a semblance of normality. I got up and pulled on some clothes, and lit the stove in the main room, and the lamps, and made the cabin as bright and warm as I could. I opened a tin of pemmican and emptied it onto one of the Royal Doulton plates, and watched him gulp it down, rattling the plate across the floor as he licked it clean. To my surprise, I found that I was hungry too, so I scrambled four eider-duck eggs with half a pound of cheese.

By then Isaak had stopped trembling, although he stayed close at my heels. That's how it happened. I'd washed up and was putting things on the shelves when I turned and he couldn't get out of the way and I fell over. I crashed against the table and sent the alarm clock flying.

It broke. Something inside me broke, too.

'Stupid fucking dog!' I shouted. 'Stupid! Stupid!'

I went on shouting, kicking and lashing out with my fists. He didn't try to get away; he cowered with his tail between his legs, not understanding what he'd done, only knowing that he was in the wrong because he's a dog and must take his beating.

Suddenly, I realised what I was doing. I fell to my knees, I flung my arms round him and started to cry. Big, jerky, heaving sobs. I cried till I was exhausted. By this time, Isaak had extricated himself and retreated to a safe distance. I think my crying scared him more than anything.

Drained, I got up and went to the kitchen and washed my face. I didn't recognise myself in the shaving mirror. Who is this haggard, hairy man with wild eyes and grimy furrows down his cheeks?

That's when I knew I couldn't do this any more.

'All right,' I said out loud. 'You've won. Gruhuken is yours. I've had enough. I'm beaten. I'm getting out.'

At this time in the morning, Ohlsen on Bear Island would be asleep, but there might be someone awake at the Longyearbyen wireless station. As soon as they received my Mayday, they'd wake Gus and Algie, who would wake Eriksson, and the *Isbjørn* would set off . . .

I'd forgotten about the hoar frost. It wasn't only in the bunkroom. Why should it be? And I'd done a good job of warming up the cabin. The Eddystone was beaded with moisture. So was the Gambrell and the Austin, and all my spare valves. Wet. Ruined. Useless.

That was a while ago—although of course I don't know exactly how long, because I haven't got a clock. I've mopped up as best I can, and hung the towels over the stove to dry. I don't know why I did this. Except that I'm the wireless operator, and I don't like leaving my equipment in a mess.

When Bear Island receives no transmissions for two days, they'll wire Longyearbyen to send help. Even if a ship can still get through, it'll take another two days. So that's four days at the earliest. Four days. I try to believe that I can hold out till then. Come on, Jack, you've made it this far, just a little longer.

But things are different now. There's no moon.

Four days. It'll be over by then.

My writing on the page is a deranged scrawl, but I know that I'm not mad. This is not a delusion brought on by solitude and dark. Something made Gus and Algie experience what they did. Something gave Bjørvik nightmares and opened the door of the doghouse and frightened the huskies away. Something terrified Isaak and trod the boardwalk outside.

Later

THE STILLNESS IS BACK. The dead, cold, windless dark.

Just now, I looked back to the start of this journal. I don't recognise the man who wrote it. Was he really so eager to reach Gruhuken? That strikes me as horrible.

Once, when I was a boy, I asked Father about ghosts, and he said, Jack, if they existed, don't you think Flanders would be full of them? And I said, do you mean they don't exist? And he said, maybe. Or maybe we just can't hear them.

To be conscious in eternal night. You would pray for oblivion. But there'd be no one to hear you. Is that how it is for what haunts this place? Is that what it wants for me? To be trapped here for ever in eternal night?

I'VE JUST REALISED the significance of what I wrote about the doghouse. *Something opened the doghouse door.*

It can open doors.

It can get in.

I'M NOT GOING to write this journal any more. No point. I'm finished with it. I suppose I should leave it here on the table in plain sight so that if anyone comes, they'll find it and know what happened. But I'm not going to do that. The journal is mine: I'm going to make sure that it stays with me always.

So here we are: the final page. Nothing left to write.

Jack Miller's journal. The End.

I've strapped my journal to my chest with a length of canvas webbing left over from the dogs' harnesses, and I'm wearing one of Gus's shirts on top. If by some miracle I get out of this alive, I'll tell him I mistook it for one of mine.

I'm sitting in my bunk in a mound of sleeping bags and reindeer hides. Five lamps are burning in the main room, and the stove is red hot (Isaak knows not to go near it). In here, I've got the paraffin stove on the packing

566 | MICHELLE PAVER

cases, and a lamp on a chair beside me, and two torches against my thigh. It's warmer in the main room, but I prefer it in here. I need solid walls around me.

I'm not going outside again. I've got plenty of firewood, and when I run out, I'll chop up the chairs.

The bunkroom smells of urine. I've got a bucket and I've used it a couple of times, and Isaak has lifted his leg against the doorway, although not against my bunk.

I'm rereading Gus's book on the natural history of Spitsbergen. I find its stodginess reassuring. Sometimes I break off to talk to Isaak, or read him a bit, and he sweeps the floor with his tail. Sometimes I talk inside my head, and then it's you I'm talking to, Gus. Strange, that. Even though there's only Isaak to hear, I still can't talk to you out loud, but only in my head. I tell you what's been happening. I rehearse what I'll say if I see you again. That's what keeps me going. The hope that maybe I will see you again.

I WAKE TO DARKNESS and dead cold.

In the instant of waking I know that I'm perceiving what cannot be—and yet, it is. I am awake and through the doorway I see it. It is standing in the main room looking out of the north window. It's inside.

Now it's turning towards me. Its rage crushes me to my bunk.

I fumble for my torch. Can't find it. Can't get untangled from the sleeping bag. In my panic I knock over the chair beside me. Glass shatters. A stink of paraffin.

I find the torch. The beam veers crazily off scattered shards. Isaak is huddled against my bunk. His eyes bulge as they follow something that moves out of sight behind the doorway.

Panting, I fight my way out of the sleeping bag. The torch slips from my fingers, hits the floor and blinks out. Whimpering, I fall to my knees and grope for it. I can't find it. Can't see my hand in front of my face. I feel for Isaak. He's gone. I try to call him but my throat has closed. Pain shoots through my palms, my knees. I'm crawling on broken glass. My fingers strike wood. Wall or bunk? Where am I?

Footfalls. Heavy. Wet. Uneven. Behind or in front? Which way?

I feel its rage beating at me. Sucking the air from my lungs.

Isaak is whimpering. I struggle to my feet and blunder towards the sound. I crash against something hard, burn my hands on hot metal and fall.

Wheezing, I crawl across the floor. I sense space opening up around me. I see a faint, red glimmer. The stove. Christ, I've gone the wrong way. I'm not in the bunkroom, I'm in the main room. There's no way out.

Still that heavy, wet, irregular tread.

Cornered, I spin round. The stove door is open. I see the glow within. It casts no light, only deepens the blackness. I can't see, but I feel the rage. Close. Coming for me.

Staggering to my feet, I blunder past the stove and back into the bunkroom. Darker in here. Hand over hand, I feel my way past the bunks. In my stockinged feet I slip, lurching against the packing cases. The portable stove goes down with a crash. I can't find my way past the packing cases. Can't find the hall. Dread clamps my chest. I can't move. My mind is going black. I can't bear it. The rage, the malevolence, I can't . . .

Isaak is scrabbling frantically at the door. I cannon towards the sound. I skin my knuckles on wood. The door. The door. Isaak shoots past me. I'm in the hall. Colder. Darkness presses on my eyeballs. I feel my way. Guns. Hooks. Waterproofs. Cold, stiff sleeves brush my face. My feet tangle in harnesses. Isaak has found the door. I claw at it, but can't find the handle. I'm in the porch, battling a thicket of ski sticks and shovels. I wrench open the door and burst out into the night.

The cold is a wall. I run into it, my feet crunching in snow. Cold rasps my throat, it bites my flesh. No moon. No stars. Only the faint, grey snow glow to tell up from down. Isaak streaks past me towards the shore. I run after him.

Glancing over my shoulder, I see the cabin windows flickering yellow. That's not the steady glow of lamplight. The cabin is on fire.

I lurch against a boulder. I push myself off and run. I trip over Isaak. He stands tense and still, his ears pricked. Listening. Clutching his scruff, I hear nothing but the hiss of wind.

Again, I glance over my shoulder. The fire in the windows has deepened to orange. Dark against the glare, I glimpse a wet, round head. I can't tell if it's inside the cabin or out. It's watching. It knows where I am.

Isaak squirms out of my grip and shoots off. I stumble after him. My only thought is to get away.

On the shore, the wind numbs my face. I hear the suck of water, the clink of ice. I've reached the sea. I've nowhere left to go. I've got no coat, no hat, no boots. I won't last long, but I'm past caring. Though I hate the thought of leaving Isaak on his own.

He stands alert, swivelling his ears to catch whatever it is he's hearing. His tail is high. It takes me a moment to understand. He's not afraid any more.

At last I hear what he hears. A distant splash of oars. I blink in disbelief. Now I see it: a point of light rocking on the water. A rowing boat.

A splintering crash behind us as a window blows out. Falling to my knees, I cling to Isaak. The fuel dump by the porch will be next to go.

I crouch at the edge of the black water and wait for the boat to pick us up. Eriksson is at the oars, with Algie and two burly sealers—but it's Gus I see.

Moaning, I splash into the shallows. I fall into his arms.

'Steady, old man, steady. Jack—your feet! Where are your boots? Oh, Jack!' His voice is gentle and he's stroking my back and talking all the time, as if I were a dog.

There's a whump and a rush of wind, then a deafening boom. We watch blazing debris soar skywards, then crash to earth. The cabin has become a deep red, throbbing heart.

Men are lifting me into the boat. I'm moaning insistently for Isaak. Someone throws him on top of me. Now the sealers are pushing off and Gus is wrapping my feet in Algie's muffler and flinging a blanket round my shoulders. Dimly, I make out Algie's white, shocked face. I try to speak but I can't. I can't even shiver.

There's plenty of room in the boat for six men and one dog, but I huddle in the stern, with Gus on one side, Isaak on the other. Isaak is pressed against me, forelegs splayed, claws digging in. He's scared of the sea. Numbly, I see the lights of the *Isbjørn* further out in the bay, blinking her message of sanctuary through the dark. I'm with people. I'm with Gus. I can't take it in.

The boat rocks on the swell as we head for the ship. I watch Gruhuken burn: a crimson so intense that it hurts to look. I can't drag my gaze away. I stare at the flames shooting into the sky. The fire sends flickering fingers of light towards us over the water. But we're too far out. It can't reach us now.

I begin to shudder. Gus says that's a good sign. He's still talking to me, softly, continuously.

Beside me, Isaak stiffens. I feel his hackles against my cheek. My heart stops. There are seven men in the boat. Next to Gus—a wet, round head.

Isaak goes wild. I'm shouting, clutching him, trying to drag Gus away from that thing. Men are yelling, standing up, the boat's rocking wildly. Isaak is desperate to get away, I can't hold him. He's overboard. Gus isn't there any more. I'm screaming his name, reaching for him. I can't get to him—he's too far out.

I jump in after him. The cold is a hammer to my chest. The sea is dragging me down. In the darkness, my hand touches his. I grab it. My chest is bursting. I'm trying to haul him upwards, but my fingers are numb, and he slips out of my grip. Flailing, I strike a body. It isn't Gus. My hand clutches something as soft as mouldy leather.

I struggle, I kick myself free. Up to the surface, choking, spitting out seawater. I catch a choppy glimpse of the burning camp. Against the glare, a black figure stands watching on the shore.

Epilogue

I didn't die. The boat didn't capsize, and those on board pulled the survivors from the sea and rushed us back to the ship.

For two days I lay in my old bunk, drifting in and out of consciousness.

Algie told me that he and Gus had been so concerned after our last wireless exchange that they'd persuaded Eriksson to set off at once. That's what saved me: the fact that I couldn't convince them that nothing was wrong.

It killed Gus. He was the only one who died. One of the sealers fell in too, but was pulled alive from the water, and Mr Eriksson lost the tips of three fingers to frostbite. Algie survived unscathed.

Gus's body was never found. Perhaps the current bore him out to sea. Perhaps he never escaped Gruhuken.

I swore I would never write another journal, but yesterday I bought this exercise book. Why? Maybe it's because tomorrow is the tenth anniversary of Gus's death, and I feel the need to give an account of myself.

On the journey to Longyearbyen, one afternoon, Mr Eriksson visited me. I wanted to thank him for risking his ship to rescue me; and he wanted (he later wrote) to tell me how sorry he was that he hadn't warned us that

Gruhuken is haunted. But who would have believed him? In the end, neither of us could find the words, so we smoked in silence. Then I told him what had happened in the cabin, and what I'd seen in the boat. He kept his eyes on the floor, and when I'd finished, he said, *ja*, the thing in the boat, I saw it also. That's the last time I ever spoke of it.

What I didn't tell him is that Gus saw it too. I glimpsed his face as he went overboard. I can't bear to think of it. It was for him that I stayed at Gruhuken: I wanted to impress him. I pitted myself against it, but it was Gus who died. I think of that ten times a day, every day.

A year after we returned to England, I had a letter from Mr Eriksson. He told me he'd gone back to Gruhuken to search for Gus's remains, but hadn't found them. He said he was sorry he hadn't been able to raise a cairn over the bones of our friend. And he said that he'd done what he could to warn others to stay away, by stringing coils of barbed wire along the shore.

He had no need to explain why he'd done all this. We both know that what we saw that night is still there.

I find it hard to believe that Eriksson had the courage to return to that terrible place. I can't imagine such bravery. I certainly don't have it. But I do seem to possess a rudimentary sense of honour, because I confessed to Gus's parents. I went to see them and told them that when he fell ill, it was my decision to stay at Gruhuken alone. I told them it was because of me that he came back. Because of me that he died. I thought they'd hate me. But they were grateful. Algie had told them how I'd jumped overboard to save their son, and they could see that I was shattered because I'd failed.

They've been wonderful to me. They helped us settle things about the insurance and the equipment we'd had on loan, and Gus's father had a 'quiet word' that kept the press off the story. They found a specialist for my frost-bite, and another to help me adjust after the surgeon amputated my foot. Algie told them about my nightmares and my terror of the dark, and they found a sanatorium—in Oxford, as far from the sea as one can get.

They found this position for me, too. I've been in Jamaica for nine years. I work at the research station of the Botanical Gardens in Castleton. My duties are administrative and botanical. I can no longer tolerate physics. It appals me.

The work is predictable, and I need that more than anything. I perform each task at a set time, according to the weekly plan I've written in my book. My book also prescribes times for meals, walks, reading, sleeping, gardening and seeing people. I cling to my routine because I lost it once. It reassures me.

I like Jamaica. The tropical nights are almost the same length all year round, with no lingering twilight to fray the nerves. I like the vivid colours in my garden: the scarlet ginger lilies and yellow cassia trees, the pink oleanders. I like the incessant, noisy life: the insects and the whistling frogs, the chattering birds.

My house is in the hills, in a jungle of palms and tree ferns, by a towering silk-cotton tree. The locals call it a 'dippy tree', 'dippy' being the Jamaican word for ghost. That doesn't trouble me. The local idea of ghosts strikes me as touchingly naive.

My verandah has a view of green mountains. Hummingbirds sip the flowers that hang in curtains from the eaves. There's a stephanotis, and a climbing vetch my cook calls 'the overlook' because it wards off the evil eye. The road to Castleton is a murmurous tunnel of giant bamboo, and that's good, as it means I can't see the sea. It's only a few miles away, but I never go near it, except once a year.

I still have the journal I wrote at Gruhuken. It was found on me after they hauled me from the sea. As I sit at my desk, I can see it lying on top of my bookcase, warped and salt-stained, and I picture my words inside, bleeding together. I've never opened it. I never will.

It occurs to me that I haven't mentioned Bjørvik. On our way back to Longyearbyen, Mr Eriksson put in at Wijdefjorden and asked the trapper if he wanted to leave with us, but he said no, he would overwinter as planned. He said to tell me he was sorry about my friend, and relieved that I'd survived.

Three days before Christmas that year, two of the dogs, Anadark and Upik, turned up at his camp, starving and terrified, but he nursed them back to health and, in the spring, he sent word to Algie, asking what should be done. After conferring with me, Algie sent money for their upkeep, and told Bjørvik to consider them his, with our thanks. He sold them to the mine manager in Longyearbyen for an excellent price. I'm glad. He's a poor man, and the money would have meant a lot to him. And I've no doubt that Upik and Anadark have adapted to life with a new pack.

Of the other dogs—Pakomi, Kiawak, Svarten, Eli and Jens—no trace was ever found.

Isaak is with me still. The sealers hauled him out of the sea and, during those first days on the *Isbjørn*, he never left my side. After he'd spent some months in quarantine, we were reunited, and we've scarcely been separated since. It's because of Isaak that I took this house. It catches the sea breeze in the morning and the land breeze in the evening. He's adapted surprisingly well to the heat—by which I mean he's become lazy. I've built him a shady pergola in the garden, with a wading pool, which he loves. We take our walks in the cool of the dawn, and although there are no rabbits, he's the terror of the mongoose community. He more than holds his own with the local mastiffs, and some of the puppies born to the neighbourhood bitches have a distinctly huskyish appearance.

I don't know what I would have done without him. He's my best friend, the only living creature I can really talk to, and a precious link with Gus.

In his undemonstrative way, Algie has also become a good friend, although in the beginning I blamed him. He should never have allowed Gus to come on the rescue mission. Then I realised that Algie blames himself quite enough already, without me making it worse. I value his friendship, but we never talk of Gruhuken.

Occasionally, I correspond with Hugo, but I've only seen him once. It wasn't a success. We both knew that he is on one side of the divide, and I on the other. Because he never saw Gruhuken.

My life here is a good one. It's only in October and November that I have a bad time. When I wake to darkness and I'm back in the polar night, hearing a heavy, wet, irregular tread.

Every year on the anniversary of Gus's death, I make my pilgrimage to an isolated beach on the north coast, where I can be sure of being alone. I go at midday, when the sun is at its fiercest, but I still have to nerve myself to do it. I don't sleep well for a week before. But I haven't funked it yet.

The sea here is nothing like Gruhuken. Tiny fishes dart in the turquoise water, and pelicans glide overhead. But it's the same sea. And though I stand on this white sand before the warm little waves, I know that, at Gruhuken, it's the deep of the polar night.

When I've mustered my courage, I can just bring myself to crouch at the water's edge and dip in my hand, and hold it there while I talk to Gus. But it's dangerous, for I know that I'm also communing with Gruhuken, and with what walks there in the dark.

WHEN I SAT down to write this, I didn't know who it was for, but I do now. This is for you, Gus. And maybe, tomorrow, when I go down to the sea, I'll burn these pages and scatter the ashes on the waves, and they'll reach you, wherever you are.

Recently, I've begun to wonder if perhaps your parents were right not to blame me for your death. Perhaps you didn't come back to Gruhuken to save me, but only to salvage the expedition. I'll never know.

But I can take that. It's not the worst of it. The worst is not knowing if you're still there. Are you, Gus? Are you there in the black water? Do you walk on the shore, in the dead grey stillness among the bones? Or were you snuffed out like a spark, all trace extinguished? Oh, I hope so. I can't bear to think of you still there. Because I know that I can never go back. Not even for you. Not even when I remember how it was in the beginning: the guillemots on the cliffs and the seals slipping through the green water, and the ice talking to itself in the bay.

michelle **paver**

You spent your early childhood in Malawi. Can you pick out a memory that sticks in your mind?
I've only got one strong memory. Because I left when I was three. It's of our dog, Sheba—she was an Alsatian. And she adopted me as her cub, looking after me and allowing me to crawl all over her and pull her ears.

When you were six, one of your father's gifts to you was particularly inspiring?
Yes, a book called *Once Long Ago* by Roger Lancelyn Green—a collection of fairy stories and legends from around the world. I've still got it.

You went on to study biochemistry at Oxford?
I did. I loved the natural world and I loved science and this was in the late seventies when the bio-technological revolution was happening. It was also when I began to think seriously about wanting to get published and wrote my first rejected novel.

A science career was not for you?
I did realise, towards the end of my degree, that, much as I loved biochemistry, I was hopeless in the laboratory. I'm no good at maths, so I was never any good at calculating exactly how much to put in the test tube. That was when I thought I'd have to do something else to earn my living. And rather stupidly decided to become a lawyer.

You regretted it immediately?
For the first three years it was very exciting, because I was a woman in a man's world. But it very gradually dawned on me that perhaps I wasn't as happy as I ought to be, even though I was technically successful and earning a lot of money. I took a year off, with the firm's permission, and went travelling.

And when you returned?
Pretty much as soon as I walked through the door, I thought, I can't do this any more. I handed in my notice, calculating that I had enough savings—if I sold my flat—to try writing full-time for two years. But, luckily, while I was working out my notice, I heard that a publisher wanted to publish *Without Charity*. It was the best day of my life.

And later came the best-selling *Wolf Brother* . . .
I was looking through some old manuscripts and I found one that I'd written while at university, set in 9th-century Norway, the Viking Age, which I'd always been keen on.

It was about a boy and a wolf. And that got my heart racing. I rewrote it completely, transferring the setting to the Stone Age. That was the breakthrough book. I sent an outline to my agent the next day and he phoned and said, 'Drop everything else!'

What are the recurring enthusiasms in your life?

The natural world is the big one. Animals, plants . . . And mythology. Part of the attraction of setting a book in the Stone Age was being able to create a mythology. We don't know for certain what people believed in those days . . . The supernatural has also been a long-standing interest since I was little. Animals, myth, magic . . .

How did *Dark Matter* come about?

The idea to write a ghost story came from that title. I was reading a book on the origins of the universe and the concept of dark matter. I had in my mind at that time an image of a remote observatory and an isolated scientist, on his own with a ghost. To start with it took place in a desert! That was ten years ago, and I just parked the idea.

And then you went on a voyage north . . .

Yes, a few years later, I took a journey by ship round Spitsbergen, at the time of the midnight sun. I was struck by some of the very remote bays—the isolation, the desolation, and what it must have been like if you were stranded there. Some time later, for some reason, I wrote in my notebook, which I keep beside the bed, 'a polar ghost story', and just looking at those words made me think, 'Yes!' Sometimes it's the words that do it. I wrote down impressions of Spitsbergen—all the things that I loved about it. Only later did it occur to me how perfect months and months of darkness would be for a ghost story! This is how stories come to me: not in a blinding flash, but in bits and pieces.

Did you go back to Spitsbergen during the winter?

Yes, and I timed my next visit to coincide with the full moon. I'd read about it not setting that far north. When you actually witness it, it's incredibly eerie. When the full moon is shining, it's very beautiful and you can see quite clearly but, in the Arctic, the weather changes very, very quickly and then you see these big, inky clouds covering it. I could sense very strongly that, for Jack, it's when the ghosts come.

Did you get to know any huskies?

My guide on that trip had his favourite husky with him on a lead as a sort of canine early-warning system, to smell out the polar bears. He was a lovely dog and he gave me the inspiration for Isaak. I spent some hours with a team of sledding dogs, too, helping to feed and care for them and getting to know their individual characters. Isaak, in *Dark Matter*, is based on two of them.

Where in the world would you like to visit, given the chance?

Japan. New Zealand . . . I also need to go back North at some point. Just talking about it has made me realise I have to go back.